**STEPHEN JONES** lives in London, Eng[...] World Fantasy Awards, four Horror W[...] Awards and three International Horror Guild Awards as well as being a twenty-time recipient of the British Fantasy Award and a Hugo Award nominee. A former television producer/director and genre movie publicist and consultant (the first three *Hellraiser* movies, *Night Life, Nightbreed, Split Second, Mind Ripper, Last Gasp* etc.), he is the co-editor of *Horror: 100 Best Books, Horror: Another 100 Best Books, The Best Horror from Fantasy Tales, Gaslight & Ghosts, Now We Are Sick, H.P. Lovecraft's Book of Horror, The Anthology of Fantasy & the Supernatural, Secret City: Strange Tales of London, Great Ghost Stories, Tales to Freeze the Blood: More Great Ghost Stories* and the *Dark Terrors, Dark Voices* and *Fantasy Tales* series. He has written *Coraline: A Visual Companion, Stardust: The Visual Companion, Creepshows: The Illustrated Stephen King Movie Guide, The Essential Monster Movie Guide, The Illustrated Vampire Movie Guide, The Illustrated Dinosaur Movie Guide, The Illustrated Frankenstein Movie Guide* and *The Illustrated Werewolf Movie Guide,* and compiled *The Mammoth Book of Best New Horror* series, *The Mammoth Book of Terror, The Mammoth Book of Vampires, The Mammoth Book of Zombies, The Mammoth Book of Werewolves, The Mammoth Book of Frankenstein, The Mammoth Book of Dracula, The Mammoth Book of Vampire Stories by Women, The Mammoth Book of New Terror, The Mammoth Book of Monsters, Shadows Over Innsmouth, Weird Shadows Over Innsmouth, Dark Detectives, Dancing with the Dark, Dark of the Night, White of the Moon, Keep Out the Night, By Moonlight Only, Don't Turn Out the Light, H.P. Lovecraft's Book of the Supernatural, Travellers in Darkness, Summer Chills, Brighton Shock!, Exorcisms and Ecstasies* by Karl Edward Wagner, *The Vampire Stories of R. Chetwynd-Hayes, Phantoms and Fiends* and *Frights and Fancies* by R. Chetwynd-Hayes, *James Herbert: By Horror Haunted, Basil Copper: A Life in Books, Necronomicon: The Best Weird Tales of H.P. Lovecraft, The Complete Chronicles of Conan* and *Conan's Brethren* by Robert E. Howard, *The Emperor of Dreams: The Lost Worlds of Clark Ashton Smith, Sea-Kings of Mars and Otherworldly Stories* by Leigh Brackett, *The Mark of the Beast and Other Fantastical Tales* by Rudyard Kipling, *Darkness Mist & Shadow: The Collected Macabre Tales of Basil Copper, Pelican Cay & Other Disquieting Tales* by David Case, *Clive Barker's A–Z of Horror, Clive Barker's Shadows in Eden, Clive Barker's The Nightbreed Chronicles, The Hellraiser Chronicles* and volumes of poetry by H.P. Lovecraft, Robert E. Howard and Clark Ashton Smith. A Guest of Honour at the 2002 World Fantasy Convention in Minneapolis, Minnesota, and the 2004 World Horror Convention in Phoenix, Arizona, he has been a guest lecturer at UCLA in California and London's Kingston University and St Mary's University College. You can visit his website at *www.stephenjoneseditor.com*

*Also available in the Mammoth series*

# THE MAMMOTH BOOK OF

# BEST NEW HORROR

## VOLUME 21

Edited with an Introduction by

## STEPHEN JONES

ROBINSON

RUNNING·PRESS
PHILADELPHIA · LONDON

Constable & Robinson Ltd
3 The Lanchesters
162 Fulham Palace Road
London W6 9ER
www.constablerobinson.com

First published in the UK by Robinson,
an imprint of Constable & Robinson, 2010

A copy of the British Library Cataloguing in Publication
Data is available from the British Library

UK ISBN 978-1-84901-372-7

1 3 5 7 9 10 8 6 4 2

First published in the United States in 2010 by Running Press Book Publishers
All rights reserved under the Pan-American and
International Copyright Conventions

9   8   7   6   5   4   3   2   1
Digit on the right indicates the number of this printing

US Library of Congress number: 2009943390
US ISBN 978-0-76243-997-3

Running Press Book Publishers
2300 Chestnut Street
Philadelphia, PA 19103-4371

Visit us on the web!

www.runningpress.com

Printed and bound in the EU

# CONTENTS

# ACKNOWLEDGMENTS

I would like to thank David Barraclough, Kim Newman, Mandy Slater, Amanda Foubister, Sara and Randy Broecker, Andrew I. Porter, Rodger Turner and Wayne MacLaurin (*www.sfsite.com*), Peter Crowther, Gordon Van Gelder, Ray Russell, Bill Schafer, Andy Cox, Johnny Mains, Steve Holland and, especially, Duncan Proudfoot and Dorothy Lumley for all their help and support. Special thanks are also due to *Locus*, *Variety*, *Ansible* and all the other sources that were used for reference in the Introduction and the Necrology.

*This edition of* Best New Horror *is dedicated
to the memory of my other "brother" in Chicago
– JAY BROECKER –
(1946–2010)
whose support of my career and many kindnesses
to me over the years will never be forgotten.*

# INTRODUCTION

## Horror in 2009

ALTHOUGH THE HORROR GENRE has been going from strength to strength in recent years, the global recession hit the publishing industry and booksellers very hard in 2009.

In the UK, Penguin laid off around 100 people from its London office, while Games Workshop sold its Solaris Books imprint to fellow game company Rebellion, also the publisher of Abaddon Books.

In America, Barnes & Noble closed the final fifty of its B. Dalton bookstores, which were primarily located in shopping malls, and Borders Group Inc. announced plans to close 200 Waldenbooks stores.

After the sale of all its fifty-one UK stores earlier in the year in a management buy-out, the Borders high street bookshop chain, which also included the Books Etc. brand, went into administration at the end of November. The chain had been on the brink of collapse since a rescue deal to sell some of its forty-five stores to WH Smith fell through, and such major publishers as Hachette UK and Random House cut off book supplies, leading to the suspension of the Borders website online orders. The collapse of Borders was blamed on declining sales as a result of competition from online retailers such as Amazon and cut-price offers on best-sellers from supermarkets.

London specialty bookstores Murder One and Fantasy Centre both closed their doors in 2009, and the last branch of

Woolworth's ceased operations in January, 100 years after the retailer began trading. During the 1930s, Woolworth's used to sell American pulp magazines which were brought over as ballast on returning ships, and the chain is credited as launching the Penguin paperback imprint when it purchased 63,000 copies of the first title in 1936.

Reportedly adding to the decline in secondhand booksellers was the rise in the number of Oxfam charity bookstores in the UK, which number around 130, making it the largest used book dealer in Europe. With Oxfam earning an estimated $32 million from just its book operation, it is perhaps no wonder that Britain's secondhand booksellers have declined from around 3,000 thirty years ago to about half that number now.

Still, it wasn't all doom and gloom: in July HarperCollins launched its new SF and fantasy imprint, Angry Robot, in the UK, and in the rest of the world two months later.

Meanwhile, as a result of ongoing restructuring at the Random House Publishing Group, the Bantam Spectra imprint changed its name to Ballantine Spectra.

On June 10, a Texas-based web-monitoring firm declared the millionth word in the English language to be "Web 2.0", which stands for the next generation of web products or services. The word beat out such other terms as "Jai ho", "slumdog" and "N00b".

However, many linguists rejected the claim as being unscientific, pointing out that it was impossible to count the number of English words currently in use or even agree on what constitutes a legitimate English word.

RDR Books finally withdrew its appeal against a New York court's decision blocking publication of *The Harry Potter Lexicon*. As a result of the judgment, the book was re-edited and expanded, and it appeared as *The Lexicon: An Unauthorized Guide to Harry Potter Fiction* in January.

The chair on which J.K. Rowling wrote the first two books in the "Harry Potter" series went up on eBay in July and sold for £19,555. Before the sale the author personalized the chair with a message, and a fifth of the proceeds went to the Books Abroad charity.

In September, former George W. Bush speechwriter Matt Latimer claimed in a book that Rowling was denied the Presidential Medal of Freedom because the Bush administration feared that her "Harry Potter" volumes "encouraged witchcraft". However, the author was made a knight in the French Legion of Honour in February, in a ceremony hosted by President Nicolas Sarkozy.

Stephenie Meyer's fourth "Twilight" novel, *Breaking Dawn*, was reissued in America in a hardcover special edition that included a poster on the reverse of the dustjacket, a *Breaking Dawn* concert DVD and a twenty-seven page supplement containing lyrics and an interview.

In a *USA Weekend* interview, Stephen King claimed that the real difference between the "Harry Potter" and "Twilight" series was that "Jo Rowling is a terrific writer and Stephenie Meyer can't write worth a darn . . . She's not very good."

Despite King's pertinent observation, a depressing statistic in *USA Today* claimed that Meyer's novels accounted for 16 per cent of *all* book sales in the first quarter of 2009.

At least one good thing to come out of the "Twilight" phenomenon was a massive boost in sales of Emily Brontë's *Wuthering Heights* and William Shakespeare's *Romeo and Juliet*, after both classics were repeatedly referenced by the main characters in Meyer's series.

In August, Meyer was sued for plagiarism by Jordan Scott, who claimed that *Breaking Dawn*, the fourth in the best-selling author's "Twilight" series, was influenced by her own 2006 novel *The Nocturne*. The US District Court judge subsequently dismissed the lawsuit, stating that the two books were "vastly different".

As he did earlier with *The Tommyknockers*, Stephen King revisited some old memories (in this case, John Wyndham's *The Midwich Cuckoos* or more likely the film version, *Children of the Damned*) for his blockbuster SF novel *Under the Dome*. When the inhabitants of the small Maine town of Chester's Mill found themselves imprisoned beneath an invisible barrier, they fractioned into opposing groups, each attempting to seize control for very different reasons.

Echoing similar themes found in King's *The Stand*, the novel originally began life in the 1980s under the title *The Cannibals*, and film rights were quickly snapped up by executive producer Steven Spielberg for television.

In a one-man attempt to stem the decline in bookselling, King delayed the release of the e-book version of *Under the Dome* for more than a month "to give bookstores a chance to make some money".

To promote *Under the Dome*, King and film director David Cronenberg engaged in an on-stage discussion on November 19 at the Canon Theatre in Toronto, Canada.

Meanwhile, Dean Koontz's latest thriller, *Relentless*, was apparently a thinly veiled attack on crazed book reviewers, and the author's *Breathless* involved the discovery of two exotic creatures in the Colorado mountains. *Dead and Alive* was the third volume in *Dean Koontz's Frankenstein* series. It topped the mass-market book charts and Koontz had his co-authors' names taken off reissues of the previous two books in the series.

Known for her international best-seller *The Time Traveler's Wife*, former graphic novelist Audrey Niffenegger's follow-up, *Her Fearful Symmetry*, was a ghost story set in and around North London's Highgate Cemetery (where the author was once a tour guide). It revolved around the ghost of a woman who died of cancer and the two identical "mirror" twins she bequeathed her flat to. The author reportedly received a $4.8 million advance for the book from her US publisher, Scribner.

Terry Pratchett OBE was made a knight for his services to literature in the Queen's New Year's Honours list. "I am pleased that this has gone to a fantasy author," said Sir Terry, "it's not a genre that is usually in the frame for these kinds of things."

Virgin Books' nascent line of horror trade paperbacks continued with Conrad Williams' new post-apocalyptic novel *One*, along with reprints of *Thieving Fear* by Ramsey Campbell and Thomas Ligotti's linked collection *My Work is Not Yet Done*, before the publisher abruptly announced that it was closing down the list.

When a man received an e-mail from a stranger claiming to know what happened to his missing son, it led to a terrifying sequence of events in the aptly-titled *Bad Things*, the latest dark thriller from Michael Marshall (Smith).

Brian Lumley's *Necroscope: The Lost Years: Harry and the Pirates* collected six stories (three original) featuring Harry Keogh, who had the ability to converse with the dead. In America, the book was published as *Necroscope: Harry and the Pirates and Other Tales from the Lost Years* and contained just the three new stories. Both editions featured (different) covers by artist Bob Eggleton.

A police officer investigated sightings of mysterious lights above a remote Texas town in David Morrell's *The Shimmer*, and Charles de Lint's *The Mystery of Grace* was a hot-rod romance set on Halloween night, when the barrier between worlds was thin and the dead could touch the living.

A murder investigation led Aloysius Pendergast to a zombie cult in *Cemetery Dance* by Douglas Preston and Lincoln Child, while the dead were returning to life during a heatwave in Stockholm in *Handling the Undead*, a zombie novel from *Let the Right One In* author John Ajvide Lindqvist.

A teenager became involved in a mystery surrounding an old mansion that was once connected to a prison for the insane in *House of Reckoning* by John Saul, and *Ground Zero* was the twelfth volume in the "Repairman Jack" series by F. Paul Wilson and concerned a secret cosmic war that led to the events of 9/11.

*Jaclyn the Ripper*, Karl Alexander's belated sequel to *Time After Time*, featured H.G. Wells and his time machine pursuing a sex-changed Jack the Ripper to Los Angeles in 2010.

*Delia's Gift* and *Delia's Heart* were the latest Gothic novels published under the long-dead V.C. Andrews® byline.

Meanwhile, Japanese horror writer Koji Suzuki teamed up with a paper manufacturer to have his latest novella published on . . . toilet paper. *Drop* was the tale of an evil spirit that inhabited a toilet bowl.

A psychic found herself being tracked through the wilderness by something inhuman in Alice Henderson's *Voracious*, and young boys mysteriously disappeared in contaminated woods in John Burnside's *The Glister*.

*The Map of Moments* by Christopher Golden and Tim Lebbon was the second volume in the "Hidden Cities" series and a sequel to *Mind the Gap*.

An archaeologist inadvertently released the spirits of a band of sadistic thugs in *Ghost Monster* by Simon Clark, and Conrad Williams added the middle initial "A." to his byline for *Decay Inevitable*, which boasted a cover by Dave McKean.

A female writer was haunted by dreams of an ancient oak tree associated with local legends of supernatural magic in *The Red Tree*, a complex new novel by Caitlín R. Kiernan.

*Speak of the Devil* was the fourth volume by Jenna Black about exorcist Morgan Kingsley, and freelance exorcist Felix Castor explored his bleak childhood in *Thicker Than Water*, the fourth in the series by Mike Carey. It was followed by *The Naming of the Beasts*.

A year after they went missing on an uninhabited Pacific island, the survivors attempted to get their story straight in *Primal* by Robin Baker.

Quincey Morris and his white witch partner Libby Chastain attempted to avert a magical apocalypse in *Evil Ways*, the second book in the "Quincy Morris Supernatural Investigator" series by Justin Gustainis.

John Shirley's *Bleak History* was a Lovecraftian-inspired novel about a former army ranger who had a connection with the "Hidden" world of the supernatural.

Released from a military prison, Jake Hatcher found himself confronting a race of supernatural women and a New York serial killer in *Damnable* by Hank Schwaeble.

A sequel to *The Secret War*, *The Hoard of Mhorrer* by M.F.W. Curren involved a group of nineteenth-century soldier-monks dispatched to Egypt to find and destroy a great evil before it could fall into the hands of agents of Hell.

*The Book of Illumination: A Novel from the Ghost Files* by Mary Ann Winkowski and Maureen Foley was the first in a new series about a woman who could see ghosts.

Phantom cop Kevin Fahey had to correct his own mistakes in *Desolate Angel*, the first in a new mystery series by Chaz McGee.

*Ghouls Just Want to Have Fun* was the third book in Victoria Laurie's "Ghost Hunter" mystery series about psychic sleuth M.J. Holiday who, this time, was participating in a new reality TV show.

The restoration of an old Victorian house led to a century-old mystery involving two ghosts in P.J. Alderman's *Haunting Jordan*.

A woman renovating a cursed Florida mansion discovered dozens of walled-up bodies, a ghost and a killer with the ability to transcend time in *Unhallowed Ground* by the prolific Heather Graham [Pozzessere]. From the same author, *The Death Dealer* was a sequel to *The Dead Room*, about ghosts helping a detective and a social worker track a Poe-inspired serial killer.

When a woman moved into a too-good-to-be-true Manhattan apartment in Sarah Langan's near-future haunted house novel, *Audrey's Door*, she uncovered the horrific history of the place she now called home.

Sarah Waters' *The Little Stranger* was a 1940s ghost story with an unreliable narrator set in a crumbling English country pile that echoed with the sound of pattering footsteps. A psychic psychology professor investigated a haunted house in *The Unseen* by Alexandra Sokoloff.

Joe Schreiber's *No Doors, No Windows* involved a forgotten manuscript and an old house with a secret history, while in *His Father's Son* by Bentley Little a son investigated his father's sudden madness.

As if just books themselves were no longer worth the cover price, J.C. Hutchins and Jordan Weisman's *Personal Effects: Dark Arts* – a novel about a suspected murderer who claimed to be possessed by a Russian demon – came with all sorts of paraphernalia, which included notes and business cards containing real phone numbers and Internet addresses.

When a video game producer escaped a werewolf attack, he learned about the eponymous group of supernatural hunters in *Skinners Book 1: Blood Blade* by Marcus Pelegrimas. It was followed by *Book 2: Howling Legion*.

*Monster Hunter International* was the first in a new series by Larry Correia about an accountant-turned-hunter of supernatural creatures.

James Morrow's *Shambling Towards Hiroshima* was set during World War II and involved a plot to scare the Japanese into surrender by putting a "B" movie actor into a rubber giant monster suit before a breed of real fire-breathing mutant lizards were unleashed as the ultimate weapon.

History seemed to be repeating itself on the site of a historic massacre in Jeff Mariotte's *Black Hearts*.

J. Robert King's *Angel of Death* was about the hunt for a serial killer in Chicago. The book also included an interview with the author.

Following on from *Dark Rain*, Tony Richards' *Night of Demons* was the second novel set in the magical village of Raine's Landing, where a psychotic serial killer breached the magical safeguards and preyed upon the descendants of the Salem witches.

Michael McBride's *Spectral Crossings* was about a new housing development being built on land surrounding a cursed marsh.

When her father, who just happened to be Death himself, was kidnapped, Calliope Reaper-Jones had to save the family business in *Death's Daughter* by *Buffy the Vampire Slayer* actress Amber Benson.

Kate Mosse's "illustrated novella" *The Winter Ghosts* was set in a mysterious French village in the late 1920s, and a group of Scottish teenagers undergoing grief counselling was more than a match for monsters that had escaped from Hell in Christopher Brookmyre's *Pandaemonium*.

As usual, the Leisure paperback imprint kept the flag flying for midlist horror: a Scottish manor house was haunted by an ancient evil in *Black Cathedral*, the latest volume in the "Department 18" series by L.H. Maynard and M.P.N. Sims, and spider-like creatures invaded London in Sarah Pinborough's *Feeding Ground*, the sequel to *Breeding Ground*.

*Blind Panic* was the conclusion of Graham Masterton's "Manitou" saga, as people across America were struck suddenly and totally blind.

The cast and crew of a desert island reality TV show were being killed off in Brian Keene's *Castaways*, while a group of teenagers took refuge in a house of horrors in *Urban Gothic* from the same author.

When a small-town evangelist climbed out of his coffin, he brought a demon horde with him in *Jake's Wake* by John Skipp and Cody Goodfellow, based on Skipp's as-yet-unproduced directorial debut.

A survivor of a mass murder returned to the town of Cedar

Hill in Gary A. Braunbeck's *Far Dark Fields*, and the inhabitants of an isolated rural town tortured and sacrificed anyone unlucky enough to stumble into their traps in *Depraved* by Bryan Smith.

When a family moved to a small town in Quebec, the young daughter soon started having premonitions of blood and death in Nate Kenyon's *The Bone Factory*, and a small Tennessee town was taken over by a soul-sucking Lamia in Bryan Smith's *Soultaker*.

While Ray Garton's werewolf novel *Bestial* was a sequel to the author's *Ravenous*, W.D. Gagliani's werewolf novel *Wolf's Gambit* was a sequel to *Wolf's Trap*.

Edward Lee's *The Golem* featured an army of creatures formed from riverbed clay that brought terror to the Maryland coast.

The late Richard Laymon's 1987 novel *Tread Softly* was reissued by Leisure under the title *Dark Mountain*, while Graham Masterton's *The Painted Man* was reprinted as *Death Mask* and Edward Lee's *Gast* appeared as *The Black Train*.

Other reprints included John Everson's *Sacrifice* and *The 13th*, *Cover* by Jack Ketchum (Dallas Mayr), *Pressure* by Jeff Strand, *Crimson* by Gord Rollo, and *Ghost Monster* by Simon Clark.

In conjunction with Canada's *Rue Morgue* magazine and the *Chiaroscuro* website, Leisure Books launched a "Fresh Blood" contest to find a previously unpublished horror author to add to the list in 2011.

Prodigious paranormal romance publisher Harlequin Books caused controversy in America after it announced that it was creating a new imprint, DellArte Press, that would publish books rejected from the company's other imprints in return for a fee.

The vanity press was immediately condemned by writers' groups, including the Romance Writers of America, the Mystery Writers of America and the Science Fiction and Fantasy Writers of America, who responded by banning *any* of Harlequin's books from award eligibility and its authors using their credits for the company to qualify for membership.

A man was haunted by the ghost of his first love in Lisa Child's paranormal romance *Immortal Bride*, and a woman who could see dead people was a suspect in her ex-husband's death in Cara Lockwood's *Every Demon Has His Day*.

Satan opened a music store across the street from clairvoyant Nicki Styx's vintage clothing store in *You're the One That I Haunt*, the third book in the series by Terri Garey. In the next volume, *Silent Night Haunted Night*, three demons decided to teach Nicki a lesson at Christmas.

While continuing to deal with the usual vampires, werewolves and ghosts, the fourth volume in Patricia Briggs' "Mercy Thompson" series, *Bone Crossed*, featured the usually tough heroine dealing with the emotional trauma of being drugged and raped before killing her attacker. From the same author, *Hunting Ground* was the second volume in the spin-off werewolf series, in which a meeting of the werewolf clans was attacked by vampires using magic.

Plagued by ghosts and nightmares, psychic PI Harper Blaine was sent by the Seattle vampires to London in *Vanished*, the fourth in Kat Richardson's "Greywalker" series.

Meanwhile, Seattle cop Joanne Walker had to use her shamanic powers to deal with ghosts, zombies and even the Wild Hunt at Halloween in *Walking Dead*, the fourth in the "Walker Papers" series by C.E. Murphy.

While on a business trip to Chicago, Pepper Martin encountered more ghosts in the paranormal mystery *Night of the Loving Dead*, the fifth in the series by Casey Daniels (Connie Laux).

In the seventh volume of Kim Harrison's series, *White Witch, Black Curse*, investigator Rachel Morgan and her vampire and pixie partners faced a rogue banshee along with some personal problems.

*Dracula the Un-Dead* was billed as "The Official Sequel" because its co-author, Canadian-born Dacre Stoker, was the great grandnephew of Bram Stoker and the novel was "endorsed by the Stoker family".

Co-written by American scriptwriter Ian Holt (*Dr Chopper*) and reportedly based on characters and plot threads deleted from the original book, the sequel was set twenty-five years after the events of that story and revolved around a troubled theatrical production of *Dracula* at the Lyceum and the murder of Jonathan Harker.

The first in a proposed trilogy, *Dracula the Un-Dead* was sold in thirty-seven countries for more than $2 million before publication, and a movie adaptation was in pre-production.

Mexican film director Guillermo Del Toro teamed up with thriller novelist Chuck Hogan to write *The Strain*, the first volume in a trilogy about a vampire plague that was unleashed on New York. Apparently, Del Toro originally conceived the idea as a TV series for the Fox Network, who turned it down.

In David Wellington's *23 Hours: A Vengeful Vampire Tale*, police investigator Laura Caxton found herself locked in a Pennsylvania correctional facility and being hunted by the oldest living vampire.

Russian investigator Anton Gorodetsky travelled to Scotland to investigate an apparent vampire murder in *Last Watch*, the fourth in Sergei Lukyanenko's series that began with *Night Watch*.

A tabloid reporter discovered that a playboy tycoon was secretly a vampire hunter in *The Vampire Affair* by Livia Reasoner, and a doctor was forced to help a wounded vampire in *Love Without Blood* by Raz Steel.

Amnesiac Lilith escaped from a clandestine CIA project to breed vampires in Maggie Shayne's *Bloodline*, while *Thirsty* was a Christian vampire novel by Tracey Bateman, about an alcoholic woman stalked by a vampire.

An Iraq War veteran found himself battling a plague of drug-created vampires in contemporary London in Thomas Emson's *Skarlet*, the first volume in the "Vampire Babylon" series.

The first volume in Alex Bledsoe's "Rudolfo Zginski" series, *Blood Groove*, was set in the American South of the 1970s, where the teenage vampires of Memphis found themselves forming an uneasy alliance with a centuries-old Nosferatu to track down a street drug that could destroy them all.

A couple in the middle of a bad break-up discovered a vampire baby in *Bite Marks*, the first in the "Vampire Testament" series by new author Terence Taylor.

Set during World War II, powerful ancient vampires battled Nazis in *The Midnight Guardian*, the first in the "Millennial" series by new author Sarah Jane Stratford.

The first book in "The Supernatural Battle for WWII" trilogy,

*Bloody Good* by Georgia Evans (Rosemary Laurey), involved vampire Nazi invaders and heroic Devonshire pixies. It was followed by *Bloody Awful* and *Bloody Right*.

Covering all the bases, Nina Bangs' *Eternal Craving* was the first in the "Gods of the Night" series and managed to combine vampires with the Mayan prediction of the end of the world in 2012. From the same author, *My Wicked Vampire* was the fourth in the "Castle of Dark Dreams" series, set in an erotic theme park.

Psychometric investigator Simon Canderous from the Department of Extraordinary Affairs discovered that something had sucked a boat full of lawyers dry in Anton Strout's *Deader Still*, a sequel to *Dead to Me*.

*Undead and Unwelcome* was the eighth volume in MaryJanice Davidson's humorous "Betsy the Vampire Queen" series, also involving the Wyndham werewolves.

With almost 600,000 copies in print, Charlaine Harris' *Dead and Gone*, the ninth Southern Vampire mystery about telepathic barmaid Sookie Stackhouse, went straight to the top of the *New York Times* and *Publishers Weekly* best-seller charts in May. When her shape-changing sister-in-law was found crucified, Sookie discovered that someone was out to eliminate creatures of mixed blood.

The twelfth book in P.N. Elrod's series, *The Vampire Files: Dark Road Rising*, saw Jack Fleming teaming up with a vampire mobster to save his own life.

*The Thirteenth* was the twelfth and reportedly final volume in L.A. Banks' "Vampire Huntress Legends" series. The book included a reading group guide and an eight-page colour comics section.

Laurell K. Hamilton's Anita Blake, vampire hunter, was still going strong in *Skin Trade*, the seventeenth book in the ludicrously best-selling series. This time the sex-obsessed heroine was on the trail of a serial-killer vampire in Las Vegas.

*Burning Shadows* was the twenty-second volume in Chelsea Quinn Yarbros' long-running series about the vampire Saint-Germain, who this time helped defend an isolated Roman monastery against invading Huns.

*Vampire A Go-Go* by Victor Gischler was a comedic romp narrated by a ghost chained to a mysterious castle in Prague.

Credited to the Harvard Lampoon, *Nightlight: A Parody* was a spoof of Stephenie Meyer's *Twilight*, complete with romance, danger, insufficient parental guardianship, creepy stalker-like behaviour and a vampire prom.

At a July meeting of the British Society for the History of Science, Brian Regal of Kean University in Union, New Jersey, explained how Charles Darwin's *Origin of the Species* (1859) killed off the folklore of the werewolf. By spreading the idea of evolution, Regal hypothesized, the idea of a half-man, half-wolf no longer made any sense and, instead, reports of ape-men – such as the Yeti, Sasquatch and Bigfoot – began to spread in popular tales.

A new law-enforcement agency attempted to control a were-wolf epidemic in Los Angeles in John Farris' *High Bloods*.

An adolescent werewolf, trained to kill by the Church, was protected by a family unaware of her true nature in the historical novel *Wolfbreed* by S.A. Swann (S. Andrew Swann, aka "S.A. Swiniarski").

Jacqueline Carey's *Santa Olivia* was set in the near-future and involved a genetically engineered half-werewolf vigilante trapped between the US-Mexican border.

*Undead on Arrival* was the third book in L.A. Banks' "Crimson Moon" series, about a werewolf Special Ops team. It was followed by *Cursed to Death*.

Werewolf radio talk show host Kitty Norville and her boyfriend Ben eloped to Las Vegas in *Kitty and the Dead Man's Hand*, the fifth in the series by Carrie Vaughn. It was quickly followed by *Kitty Raises Hell*, in which a team of paranormal TV investigators helped Kitty with an invisible attacker, and *Kitty's House of Horrors*, in which Kitty took part in a deadly reality TV show about the supernatural.

Kelley Armstrong's *Frostbitten* was the tenth book in the "Women of the Otherworld" series, while the same author's collection *Men of the Otherworld* contained four stories (one original and three first published online) about men from the werewolf Pack.

*Bad Moon Rising* was the twenty-sixth volume in the "Dark-Hunter" series by Sherrilyn Kenyon (aka "Kinley MacGregor").

Were-Hunter Fang Kattalakis (yes, that really is his name!) was forced to defend the woman he loved. The book was also released on a nine-CD audio set read by Holter Graham.

In July, Permuted Press, an independent print-on-demand publisher of apocalyptic zombie fiction, entered into a co-publishing deal with Pocket Books to reissue five of the imprint's most popular titles, along with two new books. Permuted titles released in trade paperback under the deal included *Day by Day Armageddon* and *Day by Day Armageddon: Beyond Exile*, both by J.L. Bourne; *Plague of the Dead* by Z.A. Recht; *Dying to Live: Life Sentence* by Kim Paffenroth; *Empire* by David Dunwoody; *Down the Road* by Bowie Ibarra and *Escape* by James Melzer.

Meanwhile, excavation work on a new shopping mall uncovered a Nazi weapon that turned people into flesh-eating zombies in *The Estuary* by Derek Gunn, and *The World is Dead* was a new zombie anthology from Permuted Press, edited by Kim Paffenroth.

Abaddon Books' "Tomes of the Dead" series of zombie novels continued with *Way of the Barefoot Zombie* by Jasper Bark, *Tide of Souls* by Simon Bestwick and *Hungry Hearts* by Gary McMahon.

Zombie PI Matt Richter confronted a city's evil vampire lords in the revised and expanded version of Tim Waggoner's 2004 horror spoof *Nekropolis*.

An American black-ops team hunted for a seven-year-old girl infected with a mysterious plague in Scott Sigler's *Contagious*, a follow-up to the podcast author's *Infected*, and a terrorist bioweapon turned people into blood-seeking zombies in Jonathan Maberry's *Patient Zero*.

*Death Troopers* by Joe Schreiber was the first horror novel in the *Star Wars* franchise and involved the survivors on an Imperial prison barge battling the reanimated dead. The hardcover included a colour poster on the reverse of the dustjacket.

A resurrected party girl and her two friends took a drive across country in Mark Henry's *Road Trip of the Living Dead*, the second in the "Amanda Feral" series.

Guillermo del Toro bought the film rights to David Moody's novel *Hater*, in which normally rational, self-controlled people suddenly changed into maddened killers. Originally published in 2006, it was reissued by Gollancz.

Credited to Jane Austen and Seth Grahame-Smith, *Pride and Prejudice and Zombies* was a high-concept literary mash-up that caught the imagination of publishers and the media.

Despite not being very good, the book was still a surprise hit for independent non-fiction publisher Quirk Books, quickly going through eight printings in the US in only a few months. It was even reissued in a *faux* leather-bound "deluxe heirloom edition" with colour illustrations by Robert Parada and added material.

Its success, predictably, led to other publishers jumping on the bandwagon of literary/horror pastiches such as *Sense and Sensibility and Sea Monsters* by Ben H. Winters and the inevitable *Mr Darcy, Vampyre* by Amanda Grange and *Vampire Darcy's Desire* by Regina Jeffers.

*Mr Darcy's Diary* by Amanda Grange was yet another "sequel" to *Pride and Prejudice*, in which Elizabeth discovered that her new husband was from a family of vampires. Jane Austen herself was a 200-year-old vampire working in a bookstore in upstate New York in Michael Thomas Ford's *Jane Bites Back*.

Adam Roberts' *I Am Scrooge: A Zombie Story for Christmas* was a pastiche of Charles Dickens' seasonal classic, with nods to Richard Matheson's *I Am Legend*, George Romero's *Night of the Living Dead* and even H.G. Wells' *The Time Machine*.

Scraping the bottom of the coffin, Michael P. Spradin's *It's Beginning to Look a Lot Like Zombies: A Book of Zombie Christmas Carols* was illustrated by Jeff Weigel and came with an Introduction by Christopher Moore.

After vampires and zombies, it looked like fallen angels were set to become the next big publishing phenomenon: *Covet* by J.R. Ward (Jessica Bird) was the first in the "Fallen Angels" series and featured a carpenter-turned-angel attempting to avert the Apocalypse.

Lauren Kate's *Fallen* stuck strictly to the "Twilight" formula, as its alienated reform school girl was torn between the love of two angels, while the heroine of Becca Fitzpatrick's *Hush, Hush* unwittingly gave her heart to a classmate, another fallen angel.

In Nalini Singh's *Angels' Blood*, vampire hunter Elena

Deveraux was hired by the Archangel Raphael to hunt down a renegade angel.

Laurie Sheck's debut novel *A Monster's Notes* purported to be notes and correspondence written by the Monster and others connected with Mary Shelley's *Frankenstein*.

Jasper Kent's ambitious debut *Twelve* was a historical vampire novel set during Napoleon's 1812 invasion of Russia.

A couple moved into an apparently haunted house that was once a home for unwed mothers in Christopher Ransom's first novel, *The Birthing House*. To publicize the book in the UK, publisher Little, Brown launched a short horror story competition through Borders bookstores.

A police detective used her powers to summon a demon to catch a serial killer in Diana Rowland's debut novel *Mark of the Demon*, and a New Orleans psychologist uncovered her own family's secret past in Rhodi Haek's first novel, *A Twisted Ladder*.

A failed playwright used a diminutive version of himself to carry out his suppressed desires in Jerry Stubblefield's debut *Homunculus*, and although its genius creator was dead, an autonomous computer program lived on and began to take control of people's lives in software designer Daniel Suarez's first novel *Daemon*.

Nicole Peeler's debut, *Tempest Rising*, involved a girl and her new vampire friend, and a female murderer discovered what lay beyond death in Australian writer Kaaron Warren's supernatural serial killer novel, *Slights*.

*Breathers: A Zombie's Lament* was a humorous first novel by S.G. Browne, about a reanimated corpse having trouble adjusting to its new existence.

A mad scientist journeyed to Hell and did a deal with Satan to reclaim his soul in computer games designer Jonathan L. Howard's comic debut, *Johannes Cabal the Necromancer*.

*Soulless* was the first in a new series of supernatural Victorian comedies by Gail Carriger. When a woman was rudely attacked by a vampire that she was forced to kill, it brought her to the attention of the Bureau of Unnatural Registry and its werewolf leader.

During a long hot summer in Louisiana, a young girl encountered the ghost of a young local boy who disappeared in *Shadowed Summer*, a first novel by screenwriter Saundra Mitchell.

When her brother was stolen by Skerridge the Bogeyman on the orders of the mysterious Mr Strood, a young girl named Nin escaped to a fantasy world called the Drift in Caro King's debut novel *Seven Sorcerers*.

A girl discovered that her late grandfather had pledged her soul to the Devil in return for a car in David Macinnis Gill's YA debut, *Soul Enchilada*, while in Sarwat Chadda's first book, *Devil's Kiss*, a young girl was raised by her father to become the first demon-fighting Knights Templar.

Carrie Ryan's YA zombie novel *The Forest of Hands and Teeth* was set in a future where a zombie plague had decimated civilization and the survivors lived in a fenced village surrounded by the "Unconsecrated".

In Stacey Jay's debut novel, *You Are So Undead to Me*, high school student Megan discovered that she was a zombie settler, destined to help the reanimated "unsettled" find their final rest.

Heather Davis' first book, *Never Cry Werewolf*, was a YA romance in which a girl sent off to brat camp met a bad boy with a secret.

Published in Greece by Jemma Press, Abraham Kawa's inventive debut novel *Screaming Silver: A Tale from Pandora's Box* involved paranormal investigator Pandora Ormond investigating a zombie uprising and a collection of macabre films that were not supposed to exist. The author gave each of the book's thirty-one chapters the title of a horror movie.

From Dover, *The Vampyre, the Werewolf and Other Gothic Tales of Horror*, edited with an Introduction by Rochelle Kronzek, contained seven classic nineteenth-century stories by John Polidori, Edward Bulwer-Lytton and others.

*The Strange Adventures of Mr Andrew Hawthorn & Other Stories* collected eighteen often supernatural tales by John Buchan with an Introduction by Giles Foden.

Published as part of the Penguin Modern Classics series, *Heroes in the Wind: From Kull to Conan: The Best of Robert*

*E. Howard* was selected by John Clute, who also supplied the Introduction.

As part of its new "The Further Adventures of Sherlock Holmes" series, Titan Books reprinted Manly Wade Wellman and Wade Wellman's 1975 pastiche *The War of the Worlds*, marking the book's first publication in the UK.

Some of Britain's top children's authors – including Philip Pullman, Anthony Horowitz, Quentin Blake and Anne Fine – protested in July at the government's "preposterous" plan to make them pay a fee and register on a database designed to protect children from paedophiles before they could visit schools.

The Vetting and Barring Scheme, which also applied to clowns and other children's entertainers, was set to go online in October and would list those adults approved to work with youngsters and those who were prohibited.

*His Dark Materials* author Pullman described the policy as "Corrosive and poisonous to every kind of healthy social interaction", while former Children's Laureate Fine declared, "I shall only continue to work in foreign schools, where sanity prevails."

In January it was announced that Neil Gaiman's *The Graveyard Book*, which spent more than fifty-two consecutive weeks on the *New York Times* best-seller list, had won the 2009 John Newbery Medal. Presented by the Association for Library Service to Children (a division of the American Library Association), the award is the highest honour a children's book can receive in America. Other awards were announced for Terry Pratchett and Margo Lanagan.

Anyone over fourteen who survived a sickness became a flesh-eating killers in *The Enemy*, the first book in a new post-apocalyptic series for children by scriptwriter/actor Charlie Higson.

An eleven-year-old boy decided to stop Satan from using the Large Hadron Collider to escape from Hell on Halloween in John Connolly's *The Gates*.

Two children had the ability to see ghosts in *The Devil's Ladder* by Graham Joyce, and a girl preferred her phantom friends to the living in Megan Crewe's debut *Give Up the Ghost*.

A group of friends discovered their childhood offerings to a woodland myth had been rejected in *The Pricker Boy* by Reade Scott Whinnem.

A girl made friends with a ghost in *Ruined* by Paula Morris, while a young girl who could speak with the dead spent the night in a graveyard in *Tombstone Tea* by Joanne Dahme.

A girl suspected that her sister was possessed in *Bad Girls Don't Die* by Katie Alender, while a teenager was possessed by a demon in Dale Peck's *Body Surfing*.

*The Well* was a YA horror novel inspired by Shakespeare's *Hamlet*, written by A.J. Whitten (Shirley and Amanda Jump).

Nancy Holder's *Possessions* was the first in a new series set in a haunted boarding school, while *Wicked: Resurrection* was the fifth and final volume in the popular teen witches series by Holder and Debbie Vigulé.

The Disciples were being manipulated by beings older than time in *Dark Calling*, the ninth volume in the "Demonata" series by the "number one master of horror" Darren Shan (Darren O'Shaughnessy).

An apprentice to a monster-hunting doctor revealed his secrets in *The Monstrumologist* (aka *The Monstrumologist: The Terror Beneath*), the first in a new series by Rick Yancey, and a girl discovered that her missing best friend had secrets of her own in *The Hollow*, the first in a new series by Jessica Verday set in Sleepy Hollow.

A girl was forced to scream whenever somebody nearby was about to die in *My Soul to Take*, the first book in Rachel Vencent's "Soul Screamers" series.

An American teen moved to a new school in Japan where a girl was recently murdered in *The Waking: Dreams of the Dead*, the first in a new trilogy by Thomas Randall (Christopher Golden).

A young boy plotted to escape from a Hellish underground prison in Alexander Gordon Smith's *Furnace: Lockdown*, the first in a new YA series.

A love spell accidentally turned a high school class into zombies in *The Zombie Queen of Newbury High* by Amanda Ashby, and when most of their schoolmates were turned into the walking dead, pupils were told to pretend that nothing had happened in the humorous *Never Slow Dance with a Zombie* by E. Van Lowe.

A teenage girl was romantically involved with two zombie boyfriends in Daniel Walters' *Kiss of Life*, the second volume in the humorous "Generation Dead" series.

When a fifth-grader was accidentally doused with an experimental serum he became one of the walking dead in David Lubar's comedic *My Rotten Life: Nathan Abercrombie Accidental Zombie*.

Teenage vampire Cassandra Gray fed on tears in Patrick Jones' *The Tear Collector,* a teen vampire had problems adjusting to her human boyfriend becoming her stepbrother in *Bite Me!* by Melissa Francis and another teen vampire started turning human again in Francesca Lia Block's novella *Pretty Dead*.

A vampire had to prove she did not kill her high school's football star in *Never Bite a Boy on the First Date* by Tamara Summers. A member of a vampire support group, which fed on guinea pigs, was murdered in Catherine Jinks' comedy *The Reformed Vampire Support Group*.

*Night Life* and *After Dark* were the second and third volumes in Nancy A. Collins' "Vamps" series about the privileged teen vampires who studied at Bathory Academy.

*The Vampire is Just Not That Into You* was a humorous guide to dating the undead, supposedly written by bloodsucker "Vlad Mezrich".

*The Spook's Sacrifice* (aka *The Last Apprentice: Clash of the Demons*) was the sixth book in Joseph Delaney's series about an apprentice ghost hunter, illustrated by Patrick Arrasmith, while *The Spook's Tale* (aka *The Last Apprentice: The Spook's Tale and Other Horrors*) contained three stories about other characters in the series, plus a gallery of villains illustrated by Arrasmith.

*The Battle of the Red Hot Pepper Weenies and Other Warped and Creepy Tales* collected thirty-five YA horror stories (all but four original) by David Lubar.

*The Silver Kiss* by Annette Curtis Klause included the 1990 vampire novel of the title plus two connected stories (one original), along with a new Introduction by the author.

*Half-Minute Horrors* edited by Susan Rich contained fifty-four short-short horror stories (one reprint) and five poems by, amongst others, Lemony Snicket, Margaret Atwood, R.L. Stine, Holly Black and Neil Gaiman.

Edited by Trisha Telep, *The Eternal Kiss* was an anthology of thirteen young adult vampire stories by Kelly Armstrong, Holly Black, Cassandra Clare and others.

*Stephen King Goes to the Movies* collected five stories adapted into movies (with varying results). The author contributed new introductions to each.

*We'll Always Have Paris* was an original collection of twenty-one stories and a poem by Ray Bradbury. *A Touch of Dead: Sookie Stackhouse: The Complete Stories* collected five reprint stories by Charlaine Harris with an Introduction by the author.

As part of the University of Texas Press' "Southwest Writers Collection" series, *Sanctified and Chicken-Fried: The Portable Lansdale* collected nine stories (one original) and two novel extracts by Joe R. Lansdale, with a Foreword by Bill Crider.

*Aftershock & Others* collected sixteen stories by F. Paul Wilson in the order they were written, along with notes and an Afterword by the author.

Available from Big Finish Productions in both trade paperback and a 150-copy leather-bound hardcover edition, Robert Shearman's *Love Songs for the Shy and Cynical* collected eighteen often surreal and quirky stories about different types of love by the World Fantasy Award-winning author and playwright, plus a hidden story. Steven Hall supplied the Introduction.

Celebrating the double century since his birth, *Poe: 19 New Tales of Suspense, Dark Fantasy and Horror Inspired by Edgar Allan Poe* edited by Ellen Datlow contained an eclectic selection of nineteen original stories loosely inspired by the works of Poe. The impressive line-up of contributors, including Kim Newman, Laird Barron, Glen Hirshberg, Barbara Roden, M. Rickert, Pat Cadigan, Nicholas Royle, David Prill, Lucius Shepard and Suzy McKee Charnas, also provided Afterwords to their contributions discussing how they were inspired by Poe's original works.

*Lovecraft Unbound: Twenty Stories*, also edited and introduced by Datlow, suffered from the same problems as the Poe volume, insofar as most of its contributors appeared to do all they could to distance their work from the anthology's inspiration – in this case, H.P. Lovecraft. Although there is nothing wrong with redefining the boundaries of the genre, these twenty stories (four reprints) by Joel Lane, Holly Phillips, William Browning Spencer, Marc Laidlaw, Simon Kurt Unsworth, Michael Shea, Gemma Files, Laird Barron and Nick Mamatas, amongst others, were rarely satisfying as Lovecraftian fiction.

Published as a two-volume boxed set by the prestigious Library of America, *American Fantastic Tales: Terror and the Uncanny from Poe to the Pulps* and *American Fantastic Tales: Terror and the Uncanny from the 1940s to Now* were two hefty volumes edited with introductions by Peter Straub. They featured eighty-five seminal stories; amongst the authors represented were Henry James, Charles Brockden Brown, Fitz-James O'Brien, Robert W. Chambers, H.P. Lovecraft, David H. Keller, Robert E. Howard, Robert Bloch, Fritz Leiber, Harlan Ellison, John Crowley, Joyce Carol Oates, Stephen King, T.E.D. Klein, Thomas Tessier, Thomas Ligotti, Poppy Z. Brite, M. Rickert, Kelly Link, Tim Powers, Gene Wolfe, Joe Hill and the editor himself.

Stephen King and Lawrence Block were among those who contributed twenty essays to editor Michael Connelly's *Mystery Writers of America Presents: In the Shadow of the Master: Classic Tales by Edgar Allan Poe*, which contained sixteen stories and poems by Poe, illustrated by Harry Clarke. A companion volume was *Mystery Writers of America Presents: On a Raven's Wing: New Tales in Honor of Edgar Allan Poe*, edited by Stuart M. Kaminsky and featuring twenty stories by Mary Higgins Clark and others.

Edited with an Introduction by John Skipp, *Zombies: Encounters with the Hungry Dead* contained thirty-two stories split into two sections, "Zombies of the Old School" and "Emancipation". The book also included two Appendices exploring zombies in a historical perspective and in popular culture, and among those authors represented were Stephen King, Joe R. Lansdale, David J. Schow and Lisa Morton.

Coincidentally, all those authors were also featured – but with different stories – in *The Dead That Walk: Zombie Stories* edited with an Introduction by Stephen Jones. The book contained twenty-four tales of the walking dead (eleven original).

Based on Clive Barker's novella "The Hellbound Heart" (the inspiration for the *Hellraiser* films), *Hellbound Hearts* edited by Paul Kane and Marie O'Regan was an original anthology of twenty-one stories set in the same universe. Contributors included Peter Atkins, Sarah Pinborough, Mick Garris, Tim Lebbon, Kelley Armstrong, Richard Christian Matheson, Nancy Holder, Nancy Kilpatrick and others, including a comic strip by Neil Gaiman and Dave McKean, and an illustrated story from Christopher Golden and Mike Mignola. There was a Foreword by Barker, an Introduction by Stephen Jones, and "Pinhead" actor Doug Bradley provided the Afterword.

Editor Otto Penzler raided a lot of other anthologies for the seventy-eight stories, four poems and three non-fiction pieces found in *The Vampire Archives*, which came with a Foreword by Kim Newman, a Preface by Neil Gaiman and an extensive bibliography of vampire stories and novels compiled by Daniel Seitler.

*Dark Delicacies III: Haunted*, edited by Del Howison and Jeff Gelb, featured nineteen original stories by David Morrell, Chuck Palahniuk, Mick Garris, Victor Salva, Richard Christian Matheson, John Connolly, Heather Graham, Simon Clark and others, along with a Foreword by actor Steven Weber.

Edited with an Introduction by Rod Serling's widow Carol, *Twilight Zone: 19 Original Stories on the 50th Anniversary* featured an eclectic line-up of contributors that included Whitley Strieber, Kelley Armstrong, R.L. Stine, Carole Nelson Douglas and Tad Williams.

*The Darker Sex: Tales of the Supernatural and Macabre by Victorian Women Writers* contained eleven stories selected by always reliable editor Mike Ashley, including work from E. Nesbit, Emily Brontë and Elizabeth Gaskell.

Edited by Trisha Telep, *The Mammoth Book of Paranormal Romance* contained twenty-four stories (one reprint) by Kelley Armstrong, Carrie Vaughn, Holly Lisle and others. From the same editor, *Love Bites* (aka *The Mammoth Book of Vampire Romance 2*) contained twenty-five vampire romance stories (two reprints) by Dawn Cook, Carole Nelson Douglas, Caitlin Kittredge and others.

*Mean Streets* collected four urban dark fantasy novellas by Jim Butcher ("Dresden Files"), Simon R. Green ("Nightshade"),

Kat Richardson ("Greywalker") and Thomas Sniegoski ("Remy Chandler").

Edited by P.N. Elrod, *Strange Brew* contained nine original stories by some of the biggest names in "urban fantasy". The theme was potions, and plenty of witches, werewolves, zombies and vampires turned up in the stories by Charlaine Harris, Jim Butcher, Caitlin Kittredge, Patricia Briggs and others, including the editor.

*Strip Mauled,* edited by Esther Friesner, brought together twenty urban werewolf stories by Jody Lynn Nye, K.D. Wentworth and others.

Edited by Martin H. Greenberg and Kerrie Hughes, *Zombie Raccoons & Killer Bunnies* was one of DAW Books' monthly paperback anthologies, containing sixteen new stories about killer critters by Jody Lynn Nye, Tim Waggoner, Carrie Vaughn, Richard Lee Byers, Nina Kiriki Hoffman and less well-known names.

*Bitten* was an anthology of fifteen erotic ghost stories (five reprints) edited by Susie Bright, while *Holiday with a Vampire III* collected three vampire romance novellas set at Christmas by Linda Winstead Jones, Lisa Childs and Bonnie Vanak.

After St Martin's Press ceased publication of the annual *The Year's Best Fantasy and Horror* after twenty-one years, Ellen Datlow's re-boot of her half of the long-running series, *The Best Horror of the Year Volume One*, appeared from Night Shade Books. It featured twenty-one stories, the editor's summation of the year and the usual list of so-called "Honorable Mentions".

*The Mammoth Book of Best New Horror* celebrated its twentieth anniversary with the same number of stories and novellas, along with a summary of the preceding year and in-depth Necrology. For the first time in a long while, the UK and US editions had very different covers. There were no stories that appeared in both volumes, and Steve Duffy was the only author represented in each.

Throughout 2009, Google continued to make revisions to its highly controversial Books Settlement, following concerns from the US Department of Justice and foreign governments over the company's apparent attempts to create a digital monopoly of copyrighted works.

In December, a Paris court found Google guilty of copyright violation and ordered the company to pay £300,000 in interest and damages and cease reproducing any copyrighted material from French publishers unless it had made an individual deal to do so.

That same month Ursula K. Le Guin resigned from the Authors Guild after thirty-seven years, in protest against the organization's acceptance of the Google Books Settlement.

In July, Barnes & Noble launched its online e-book store with 700,000 titles, including more than half-a-million out-of-copyright works available free from Google. The e-books were accessible via a number of formats for every type of electronic reader.

In August, Wikipedia announced that it would finally introduce editorial controls to prevent people maliciously changing entries provided by the online encyclopaedia. In future, experienced editors would check revisions to improve accuracy.

Stephen King's original novella, "UR", was only available on Amazon's Kindle, and the e-book reading device was itself an integral part of the story. Just three weeks after it was released, downloads had reached five figures.

In an attempt to compete with the Kindle, Sony launched its own electronic reader, the Reader Daily Edition. Using a seven-inch touch screen, users could store up to 1,000 books chosen from a digital bookstore containing more than a million titles.

Meanwhile, Google launched the Google Book Reader, a free service allowing people to read 1.5 million out-of-copyright novels on their smart phones.

In September, it was announced that the Kindle version of Dan Brown's latest blockbuster, *The Lost Symbol*, was outselling the hardcover edition on Amazon and selling more than ten times the number of any other e-book.

The Texas-based online magazine *Lone Star Stories*, which had published six issues a year since 2004, ceased publication.

*Sci Fi Wire*, the Syfy channel's online news division, abruptly cancelled all its columns as a result of research showing that "the medium had evolved". Among those affected were John Clute, Michael Cassutt and Will McCarthy.

Actor Jon Heder imagined that he might have turned into a zombie in the Sony Crackle web series *Woke Up Dead*, which also featured comedian Wayne Knight.

Virgin's first web TV series, *Dr Hoo*, starred Ian Hart as a mentally ill man who lived in a shed and might have been the saviour of the galaxy. It ran for ten two-minute webisodes.

For fans of the Showtime Network's favourite serial killer, *Dexter: Early Cuts* was a twelve-part animated prequel to the TV series available on the Internet. The webisodes filled in the gaps in the characters, early years and were narrated by star Michael C. Hall. New *Dexter* games and e-cards could also be found online.

Computer effects artist George Taylor's short live-action musical film, *Fishmen*, was based on H.P. Lovecraft's "The Shadow Over Innsmouth" and featured the song "It's Beginning to Look a Lot Like Fish-Men", originally recorded for the H.P. Lovecraft Historical Society's Christmas album, *A Very Scary Solstice*.

Advances in new printing technology meant that more print-on-demand (PoD) titles were being published than regular books. It appeared that the inmates had finally taken over the asylum.

From editor Charles Black's PoD imprint, Mortbury Press, *The Fourth Black Book of Horror* and *The Fifth Black Book of Horror* were an improvement over earlier volumes. These unashamed pastiches of *The Pan Book of Horror Stories* featured some old-fashioned grue from Craig Herbertson, Paul Finch, Joel Lane, David A. Sutton, Gary McMahon, Reggie Oliver, Ian C. Strachan, Gary Fry, Rosalie Parker, David A. Riley and others, with one story by John Llewellyn Probert even referencing specific stories from the Pan series.

Published by Hippocampus Press and inspired by Frank Belknap Long's *The Hounds of Tindalos*, *The Hound Hunters: A Southwestern Supernatural Thriller* was the third novel in Adam Niswander's "The Shaman Cycle", which mixed Lovecraftian mythology with Native American culture. The book was originally announced in 1995 as coming from Integra Press and it was followed by *The War of the Whisperers*, the fourth in the series.

*Seven Deadly Pleasures* contained seven stories (four original) by schoolteacher Michael Aronovitz, while *Blood Will Have Its*

*Season* collected forty-one – frankly, incomprehensible – stories and poems by Joseph S. Pulver, Sr (thirty original). Both books included slightly hyperbolic Forewords by S.T. Joshi.

*Classics & Contemporaries* collected thirty-six essays about the horror genre by Joshi.

*The Outer Gate: The Collected Poems of Nora May French* gathered together the verse of the Californian poet, a friend of George Sterling, who committed suicide in 1907 at the age of twenty-six. Edited by Donald Sidney-Fryer and Alan Gullette, it featured an impressive biographical Introduction by Sidney-Fryer and copious notes and tributes.

Also from Hippocampus, Dan Clore's *Weird Words: A Lovecraftian Lexicon* was exactly what the title said it was, and extremely useful if you wanted to look up the meaning of "eldritch". *The Unknown Lovecraft* collected thirteen essays by Kenneth W. Faig, Jr, while the third paperback edition of *The Lovecraft Annual*, edited by S.T. Joshi, included a number of articles about the author by Will Murray, Leigh Blackmore and others, along with some minor Lovecraft verse not included in *The Ancient Track* (2001).

Fred Chappell's 1968 Lovecraftian novel *Dagon* was reissued in a PoD edition by Boson Books, while *Weird Inhabitants of Sesqua Valley* from Terradan Works collected ten Lovecraftian stories (five original) by W.H. Pugmire with an Introduction by Jeffrey Thomas.

From Gray Friar Press with an Introduction by Gary McMahon, *Pictures of the Dark* was an overview collection of Simon Bestwick's more disturbing tales, the earliest dating back to 1997. Of the twenty-three stories included in the on-demand trade paperback, eleven were original.

John L. Probert's third collection, *The Catacombs of Fear*, once again owed its inspiration to the anthology films of Amicus and featured five original stories linked by a framework narrative involving a new priest.

*Groaning Shadows* from Gray Friar Press contained four long novellas by Paul Finch, while Stephen Volk's novella *Vardøger* from the same publisher was inspired by Norwegian mythology and involved a man suspected of a murder committed by his doppelgänger.

*Visions* from Mythos Books was a hardcover collection of twelve fantasy and horror stories (four original, featuring psychic detective Abraham ben Zaccheus) by Richard A. Lupoff, with an Introduction by Peter S. Beagle.

From Apex Publications, Gene O'Neill's *Taste of Tenderloin* was a collection of eight stories (three original) set in a run-down area of San Francisco, with an Afterword by the author and an Introduction by his son, Gavin.

Zombies demanded their own political representation in B.J. Burrow's humorous novel *The Changed*, also available from Apex.

Edited with an Introduction by Mike Allen, *Clockwork Phoenix 2: More Tales of Beauty and Strangeness* from Norilana Books contained fifteen new stories by Tanith Lee, Steve Rasnic Tem, Forrest Aguirre and others.

*Hopeful Monsters* was a self-published debut collection under the Bleed Red Books imprint that contained seventeen stories (one reprint) by graphic artist Jenny Ashford that definitely deserved a wider audience than the PoD market.

Produced by Star Publishing in conjunction with three Canadian university bookstores, *Campus Chills,* edited by Mark Leslie, was a welcome attempt to produce an original on-demand anthology for students at Halloween. It contained thirteen stories by Kelley Armstrong, Sèphera Girón, Michael Kelly, Nancy Kilpatrick, Douglas Smith, Edo van Belkom, Steve Vernon and others, along with an Introduction by Robert J. Sawyer and notes on the authors.

From Shroud Publishing, *Mama Fish* by Rio Youers was a novella set in the 1980s, about an oddball kid at school.

*The Terror of Fu Manchu* from Black Coat Press was an authorized first novel by William Patrick Maynard, based on the series created by Sax Rohmer.

From New Jersey's Newmedia Publishing, *Predatoress* by "Emma Gábor" was a first-person PoD novel in which the author/narrator claimed to be a reluctant member of the undead who vampirized her three best friends so she would have some-body to hunt with. There was no explanation as to why the book was laid out in chunks of text, but at least it was promoted with its own "Blood" red wine.

Subtitled *A Vampire Satire*, and with chapters titled after different vampire movies, *Liquid Diet* was the first solo novel from Michael McCarty. Available in trade paperback from DemonicClown Books/KHP Industries, it featured an Introduction by Michael Romkey and an Afterword by C. Dean Anderson.

Editor and author Jeffrey Thomas' Necropolitan Press resumed publication after eight years with Paul G. Tremblay's slipstream novella *The Harlequin & the Train*, which was published as a 400-copy trade paperback. Readers were encouraged to use a yellow highlighter to colour certain text.

Something from the black depths stalked eight survivors drifting on a life raft in the middle of the ocean in Scottish author Carole Johnstone's debut novella *Frenzy*, from Canadian PoD and e-book imprint Eternal Press.

*Malpractice: An Anthology of Bedside Terror,* edited with an Introduction by Nathaniel Lambert, was the first print anthology from Necrotic Tissue/Stygian Publications. The thirty-one original stories (almost half just 100 words in length) were set in and around the mysterious Bloom Memorial Hospital.

*Robin Hood & Friar Tuck Zombie Killers: A Canterbury Tale* was written in rhyming couplets and iambic pentameters by Paul A. Freeman. Involving the legendary outlaws' battle against a zombie plague brought back from the Great Crusade in the Holy Land, the epic narrative poem was published by Canada's Coscom Entertainment as a PoD chapbook.

The two attractive PoD issues of *Talebones: Science Fiction & Dark Fantasy* featured fiction and verse from Scott Edelman, Carrie Vaughn, Cat Rambo, Don D'Ammassa, Darrell Schwitzer and others, along with a reprint interview with Roger Zelazny by the late Ken Rand. Patrick Swenson announced in his editorial that #39 was the final issue, as he wanted to concentrate on his own writing and Fairwood Press.

Originally published online as a PDF magazine for its first six issues, R. Scott McCoy's *Necrotic Tissue: The Horror Writers' Magazine* from Stygian Publications moved to a print-on-demand format in 2009. Although the design still left much to be desired, the first three perfect-bound issues included plenty of fiction from new authors, along with an interview with Joe R. Lansdale.

PS Publishing was possibly the busiest independent publisher of the year, releasing a raft of books covering the entire spectrum of fantastic literature.

Edited by Angus Mackenzie with an Introduction by *Hellraiser* actor Doug Bradley, *Spook City* collected four stories by Peter Atkins (one original), three by Clive Barker and five by Ramsey Campbell (plus a harrowing new memoir about his mother). All the contributors were sons of Liverpool, which is where the stories were set. The 200-copy slipcased edition was signed by all the contributors and featured alternative cover artwork by Barker.

Containing thirty-two marvellous stories, *The Very Best of Gene Wolfe: A Definitive Retrospective of his Finest Short Fiction* was limited to 100 slipcased hardcovers signed by the author and Kim Stanley Robinson, who contributed the Introduction, and 300 unjacketed hardcovers just signed by Wolfe. The book also boasted a superb wraparound cover design by J.K. Potter.

*Vaitor Plus* was a new collection of eight recently published pieces of fiction by Lucius Shepard, including the full text of the title novel for the first time, and *The Black Heart* collected fourteen stories (two original) by Patrick O'Leary, along with Introductions by James Morrow and the author.

*Harsh Oases* collected seventeen career-spanning stories (two original) by Paul Di Filippo, including a collaboration with Rudy Rucker, along with an Introduction by Cory Doctorow, while twelve of Paul Witcover's superb short stories (five original) were collected in *Everland and Other Stories* with an Introduction by Elizabeth Hand.

T.M. Wright's surreal novel *Blue Canoe: A Memoir of the Newly Non-corporeal* was issued in the same format with cover art by the author and an Introduction by Tom Piccirilli.

An obsession with a painting seen in a friend's apartment led sculptor Jacob Lerner to search for a long-dead artist in Robert Freeman Wexler's *The Painting and the City*.

Later in the year, PS changed its 100-copy slipcased format to an even more deluxe traycased limited edition.

Ramsey Campbell's latest novel, *Creatures of the Pool*, about an ancient evil that resided below a Lovecraftian version of Liverpool, was issued in this new format and 500 unsigned hardcovers. Bryan Talbot supplied the entertaining Introduction. *Just Behind You* was a new collection of Campbell's short fiction, containing eighteen mostly recent stories and a new Afterword by the author. The limited hardcover also included a very strange extra story.

*Grazing the Long Acre* was the first collection of Gwyneth Jones' fiction in the UK, containing thirteen reprint stories, while both *Impossible Stories II* and *The Bridge* collected some of Zoran Zivkovic's newer stories, translated from the Serbian.

*Passing for Human* was an excellent reprint anthology edited by Michael Bishop and Steven Utley that included sixteen stories about creatures in human guise by Theodore Sturgeon, Donald A. Wollheim, Ray Bradbury, Robert Silverberg, Barry N. Malzberg, Howard Waldrop, Tom Reamy, Lisa Tuttle, Carol Emshwiller and others.

PS' ambitious series of novellas were limited to 100 signed and numbered jacketed hardcovers and 500 trade copies: a fifteen-year-old orphan with special powers and an itinerant spirit-photographer confronted restless spirits in 1920s rural Nebraska in *Cast a Cold Eye* by Derryl Murphy and William Shunn, which came with an Introduction by Charles de Lint.

Alex Irvine's *Mystery Hill* was an expanded version of his 2008 story from *The Magazine of Fantasy & Science Fiction*, and Rio Youers' *Old Man Scratch* was about the ultimate neighbour from Hell.

Inspired by the medieval French tale *Valentine and Orson*, Marly Youmans' *Val/Orson* came with an Introduction by Catherynne M. Valente, while; Terry Bisson's *Billy's Book* was for old people of all ages.

A middle-aged writer travelled to a provincial town in Japan in Quentin S. Crisp's spectral novella *Shrike*, which came with an Introduction by Lisa Tuttle.

Intrepid necromancers Bauchelain and Korbal Broach returned in *Crack'd Pot Trail*, the fourth in the humorous fantasy series by Steve Erikson, and a time traveller returned to eleventh-century Britain to try to change the course of history in John Gribbin's return to SF, *Timeswitch*.

Uncle River's satirical *Camp Desolation and an Eschatology of Salt* was introduced by Don Webb.

Writer G.K. Chesterton met Edgar Rice Burroughs in Eric Brown's *Gilbert and Edgar on Mars*, while Beth Bernobich's *Ars Memoriae* was a novella of political intrigue set in an alternate Ireland called Éireann.

Sarah Pinborough's ambitious and moving novella *The Language of Dying* was about having to face up to the inevitable death of a loved one. It came with an Introduction by Graham Joyce.

An updating of the Orpheus myth, Joel Lane's novella *The Witnesses Are Gone* involved a newspaper editor's journey into darkness while searching for the work of a little-known French film director. Conrad Williams supplied the Introduction.

*Glass Coffin Girls* was *PS Showcase* #6. It collected eight stories by Paul Jessup with an Introduction by Jeff VanderMeer.

Edited by Peter Crowther and Nick Gevers, PS Publishing's hardcover fiction magazine, *Postscripts*, went through some major changes of its own in 2009. The eighteenth number, *This is the Summer of Love: A Postscripts New Writers Special*, was a transitory hardcover volume that contained ten stories by Norman Prentiss, Chris Bell, Monica J. O'Rourke, R.B. Russell and Rio Youers, amongst others.

After the release of the hardcover anthology *Enemy of the Good: Postscripts 19*, the title reduced its frequency from four times a year to twice-yearly, but more than doubled in size. Volume 20/21, *Edison's Frankenstein*, included twenty-six stories by, amongst others, Chris Roberson, Kit Reed, Simon Strantzas, Darrell Schweitzer, Lisa Tuttle and Stephen Baxter.

For subscribers, the *PS Holiday Chapbook* #5 was *The Night Cache* by Andy Duncan.

Meanwhile, new imprint Drugstore Indian Press reissued Peter Crowther's 2002 SF-horror novel *Darkness, Darkness: Forever Twilight Book 1* as an attractive hardcover with cover art by Vincent Chong. The follow-up volume, *Forever Twilight 2: Windows to the Soul*, appeared in a signed limited edition from Subterranean Press and involved a small band of survivors making their way across an apocalyptic Earth where "new" people had the power to kill with just a touch.

Despite the continuing success of PS and other independent UK publishers, two British small press imprints disappeared in 2009: Andrew Hook announced that he was discontinuing Elastic Press to concentrate on his own writing, while Chris Teague put Pendragon Press on hold for the year, saying it would return in 2010.

It was also announced that Deborah Layne's US imprint Wheatland Press was going on hiatus in 2009 due to "current financial uncertainties".

Edited by Christopher Conlon, *He Is Legend: An Anthology Celebrating Richard Matheson* from Gauntlet Press was a tribute volume containing fifteen original stories by F. Paul Wilson, Mick Garris, William F. Nolan, Richard Christian Matheson, Joe R. Lansdale, Whitley Strieber, and the father and son team of Stephen King and Joe Hill, amongst others, with an Introduction by Ramsey Campbell and illustrations by Harry O. Morris. The book also included the original screenplay by Matheson and Charles Beaumont for the film *Conjure Wife*, which eventually became *Night of the Eagle* (aka *Burn, Witch, Burn*).

*Visions Deferred: Three Unfilmed Screenplays* contained Richard Matheson's unproduced scripts for *I Am Legend*, *The Distributor* and *Sweethearts and Horrors*, with associated material by Matheson, his son Richard Christian Matheson, Mark Dawidziak and Matthew R. Bradley.

Also from Gauntlet, *Bullet Trick* contained seven teleplays by Ray Bradbury (two for *The Twilight Zone* that were never produced) along with correspondence and other associated items. The book was available in an edition of 500 signed copies and a lettered traycased edition that added the teleplay for *I Sing the Body Electric*.

*As Fate Would Have It (A Prolonged Love Letter)* by Michael Louis Calvillo was published by California's Bad Moon Books in a special signed edition of 150 numbered copies and twenty-six lettered. The novel was about the love between a cannibal chef and a heroine addict and came with an Introduction by John R. Little and an Afterword by Lisa Morton.

The jacket blurb for Gene O'Neill's *Shadow of the Dark Angel*, published under Bad Moon's Eclipse imprint, compared the novel to Thomas Harris' Hannibal Lector tales as a pair of homicide detectives pursued a vicious serial killer. The book was available in a special signed hardcover edition with colour plates by John Pierro, limited to just 100 copies.

Perhaps the imprint's biggest coup of the year was publishing *The Adventures of Mr Maximillian Bacchus and His Travelling Circus*, a collection of four magically inventive stories written by Clive Barker forty years ago, but never previously published. Richard A. Kirk supplied the illustrations and David Niall Wilson the Afterword. Not surprisingly, Bad Moon issued the collection in multiple signed editions, including 1,500 trade, 300 numbered and slipcased, twenty-six lettered and traycased, and ten ultra-traycased copies.

From the Donald M. Grant imprint, *The Little Sisters of Eluria* contained the title novella by Stephen King, along with the 2003 revised and expanded version of *The Dark Tower: The Gunslinger*. The 4,000-copy slipcased edition was signed by illustrator Michael Whelan, and there was also a boxed "gift edition" of 1,250 copies signed by both King and Whelan.

The third volume in the series edited and introduced by Danel Olson, *Exotic Gothic 3: Strange Visitations*, was one of the more satisfying anthologies of the year. Although never quite sure what it meant by "Gothic", this latest volume from Ash-Tree Press was certainly *exotic*, featuring stories split over such locations as Oceania and Australia, Asia, Europe and North America by Robert Hood, Lucy Taylor, Terry Dowling, Steve Duffy, Tina Rath, Stephen Volk, Simon Clark, Simon Kurt Unsworth, Paul Finch, Adam L.G. Nevill, Reggie Oliver, Zoran Zivkovic, Barbara Roden, Steve Rasnic Tem and others.

From Subterranean Press, Brian Lumley's *The Nonesuch and Others* was a thin volume containing the original title story plus reprints of "The Thin People" and "Stilts", all featuring the unnamed protagonist's unexpected encounters with the supernatural. With an Introduction by the author and a cover and interior sketches by Bob Eggleton, the deluxe hardcover was limited to 1,500 signed copies.

Subterranean also produced a 500-copy slipcased edition of Neil Gaiman's *The Graveyard Book* signed by both the author and illustrator Dave McKean ($250), and a twenty-nine copy lettered edition in a hand-made traycase that included an original sketch by the artist ($900).

Subterranean's edition of *Stephen King Goes to the Movies* was limited to 2,000 copies, printed in two colours throughout and featuring five full-colour plates by Vincent Chong.

Dan Simmons' *Drood* and *The Terror* were both published in signed editions limited to 500 copies plus $500 lettered and traycased editions of twenty-six copies apiece.

*Seven for a Secret* was an alternate world vampire novella by Elizabeth Bear, available in a trade edition and also as a signed edition limited to 250 copies with a bonus chapbook.

*Unchained and Unhinged* was a collection of ten short stories and six previously published essays by Joe R. Lansdale, who also supplied an Introduction.

Edited by Stefan R. Dziemianowicz, the second volume of *The Reader's Bloch: Skeleton in the Closet and Other Stories* contained sixteen previously uncollected stories by the late Robert Bloch with a cover by Gahan Wilson. The hardcover was limited to 750 copies signed by the editor.

*Crimson Shadows: The Best of Robert E. Howard Volume One* from Subterranean Press included a Foreword and the usual disappointing interior illustrations by Jim and Ruth Keegan. It was available in a limited edition of 750 numbered copies, signed by the artists.

It perhaps didn't help that the delayed anthology *British Invasion* from Cemetery Dance Publications was, in fact, co-edited by two Americans (Christopher Golden and James A. Moore) and just one Brit (Tim Lebbon). As a result, the twenty-one original stories were a decidedly mixed bag that failed to reflect accurately the current state of British horror fiction (not helped by the inclusion of a number of expatriates). That said, there were still some fine stories from the always-reliable Ramsey Campbell, Sarah Pinborough, Paul Finch, Peter Crowther and others, along with an Introduction by Stephen Volk and an Afterword by Kim Newman. However, it's hard to imagine that any American readers understood the many in-jokes to be found in the anonymous contribution "British Horror Weekend".

*Mind the Gap: A Novel of the Hidden Cities* by Golden and Lebbon was also set in the UK, as a young girl was pursued through the forgotten tunnels of London's Underground network by a cabal of mysterious black-clad strangers. The novel was published by Cemetery Dance in a signed limited edition of 1,000 hardcover copies.

A man was pursued by an unstoppable assassin in Brian Keene's *Kill Whitey*, which was limited to 360 signed copies and fifty-two traycased copies.

Edited by Bob Booth, *The Big Book of Necon* was a thirtieth anniversary tribute to the Northeast Horror and Fantasy Convention, with memoirs and reprint fiction by the late Charles L. Grant, Stephen King, Peter Straub, Neil Gaiman, F. Paul Wilson, Elizabeth Hand, Thomas Monteleone and others, mostly taken from the event's programme books. It was published as a trade hardcover and three signed, limited editions, only the two most expensive of which were signed by King.

*Midnight Grinding & Other Twilight Terrors* contained thirty-two Southern Horror stories (two original) by Ronald Kelly, who also supplied the story notes. It was issued in an edition of 1,250 copies and a twenty-six copy traycased edition.

Cemetery Dance also issued Al Sarrantonio's "Orangefield" novel *Halloweenland* in a special signed hardcover edition of 1,250 copies. It was originally published in different form, under another title, in 2006. The publisher also reissued Sarrantonio's 1989 werewolf novel *Moonbane* in a special signed edition of 1,500 copies with a new Preface by the author and nice interior artwork by Keith Minnion.

From the same imprint, *Halloween and Other Seasons* contained eighteen stories by Sarrantonio in a signed edition limited to 1,250 copies, while *Got to Kill Them All and Other Stories* collected eighteen "unflinching" reprint tales by Dennis Etchison with an Introduction by George Clayton Johnson. It was limited to 750 copies signed by the author and a traycased, leather-bound edition of twenty-six copies.

Richard Laymon's novel *The Woods Are Dark* was published in a restored edition that added almost fifty pages to the original 1981 version. A fifty-two copy traycased edition included colour artwork.

Cemetery Dance also reissued William Peter Blatty's 1999 haunted house novella *Elsewhere* with new interior illustrations by Alex McVey in a 350-copy signed edition and fifty-two tray-cased, leatherbound and lettered copies ($250).

*Shivers V* was the latest volume in the original trade paper-back anthology series edited by Richard Chizmar for Cemetery Dance. It contained twenty-four stories by Sarah Langan, Robert Morrish, Mick Garris, Scott Nicholson, John Skipp and Cody Goodfellow, Sarah Pinborough, Graham Masterton, Nicholas Kaufmann, Simon Clark, Al Sarrantonio, Nick Mamatas, Steve Rasnic Tem, Rick Hautala, Chet Williams and others, including two by Robin Furth.

Joe Morey's Dark Regions Press continued to promote new and upcoming authors with illustrated and often signed trade paperback collections and novels.

*Thought Forms* was a new novel by Jeffrey Thomas which the author had originally written back in the late 1980s, while Jeff Strand's aptly titled *Gleefully Macabre Tales* not only contained thirty-two stories (two original), but also the novella *Disposal*.

Apparently inspired by Charles L. Grant's "Oxrun Station" stories, the twelve tales (one reprint) in David B. Silva's *The Shadows of Kingston Mills* were set in the eponymous horror-haunted town. Paul F. Olson supplied the Introduction. *The Darkly Splendid Realm* collected thirteen stories (eleven origi-nal) by Canadian writer Richard Gavin, with an Introduction by Laird Barron and an Afterword by the author.

*Voices from the Dark* was a slim volume containing the blank verse of Gary William Crawford with an Introduction by Bruce Boston. Boston's own *Double Visions* contained twenty-one poems, all collaborations, with an Introduction by J.L. Comeau.

As if all that wasn't enough, Dark Regions also launched a "New Voices in Horror" series that showcased the work of emerg-ing talents. The first four volumes in the series were #1: *Dark Entities* by David Dunwoody with a Foreword by James Roy Daley; #2: *Shades of Blood and Shadow* by Angeline Hawkes; #3: *Resurrection House* by James Chambers with a Foreword by C.J. Henderson, and #4: *Undertow and Other Laments* by Michael Kelly with an Introduction by Gary Braunbeck.

For fans of the fiction of M.R. James, from Dark Regions' companion imprint Ghost House, came the slightly ungrammati-cally titled *They That Dwell in Dark Places and Other Ghost*

*Stories* by Scottish author Daniel McGachey. The trade paperback collection contained thirteen very impressive Jamesian pastiches (five original), along with story notes by the author and an Introduction by Charles Black.

The latest anthology from DarkArts Books, edited with an Introduction by Bill Breedlove, was *Mighty Unclean*, which featured sixteen original and reprint "unwholesome tales" by Cody Goodfellow, Gemma Files, Mort Castle and Gary A. Braunbeck.

Launched by Sandra Kasturi and Brett Alexander Savory, ChiZine Publications (CZP) was an ambitious new Canadian small press imprint devoted to dark fiction. The list launched with David Nickle's impressive short-story collection *Monstrous Affections*, which contained fourteen stories (three original) and an Introduction by Michael Rowe.

*Horror Story and Other Horror Stories* collected nineteen tales (five original) by Robert Boyczuk, while *Objects of Worship* contained twelve stories (two original) by Claude Lalumière with an Introduction by James Morrow and an Afterword by the author.

Also from ChiZine, Daniel A. Rabuzzi's *The Choir Boats* was the first volume of "Longing for Yount", set on a bizarre world where a nineteenth-century London merchant held the key to self-redemption. Brent Hayward's novel *Filaria* was set on a crumbling world, while a young boy disappeared into the forest behind his house in Robert J. Wiersema's novella *The World More Full of Weeping*.

*The Tel Aviv Dossier* was a biblical mystery with Lovecraftian overtones by Lavie Tidhar and Nir Yaniv, also from ChiZine, who entered into a distribution deal with Diamond Book Distributors to supply their titles to bookstores in both the US and UK.

Edited by D.M. Mitchell, *Starry Wisdom Vol. 2: Songs of the Black Würm Gism* was an anthology of twenty-one Lovecraftian stories from Creation Oneiros, with an Introduction by John Coulthart.

From Cycatrix Press/Dark Discoveries Publications, *The Bleeding Edge: Dark Barriers, Dark Frontiers* was a mess of an anthology apparently thrown together by editors William F. Nolan and Jason V. Brock. Despite featuring minor contributions from such heavy-hitters as Ray Bradbury (a brief "Martian" tale), James Robert Smith, Earl Hammer Jr and John Tomerlin, there were new stories from John Shirley, Nancy Kilpatrick, Gary A. Braunbeck, Joe R. Lansdale, Christopher Conlon, Kurt Newton, Lisa Morton, Steve Rasnic Tem, Cody Goodfellow and both editors, along with scripts and teleplays by Richard Matheson and Richard Christian Matheson, George Clayton Johnson, Dan O'Bannon and Norman Corwin, and a biographical essay about collecting pulps by Frank M. Robinson. The book was limited to 400 trade copies signed by the editors and seventy-five deluxe numbered hardcovers signed by all contributors with additional artwork by Kris Kuksi.

A junior FBI agent and a geeky barista teamed up to prevent a group of Cthulhu cultists from awakening the Great Old Ones in Seamus Cooper's irreverent novel *Mall of Cthulhu*, from San Francisco's Night Shade Books, which expanded its staff and publication schedule in 2009.

Tim Lebbon's novel *Bar None* was subtitled *A Novel of Chilling Suspense, Apocalyptic Beauty, and Fine Ales* and was set six months after the end of the world, when a group of Welsh survivors set out to find quite possibly the last pub on Earth.

Mark Teppo's *Lightbreaker* was the first volume in the "Codex of Souls" series and featured an antiquities dealer with psychic powers pursuing a body-hopping spirit while trying to stay out of the clutches of various secret socities and cults. Meanwhile, John Langan's *House of Windows* wove a number of phantasmal stories around a beautiful widow living in an old mansion.

*The Dream of X and Other Fantastic Visions* was the fifth and final volume in Night Shade's admirable compilations of the fiction of William Hope Hodgson. Edited by Douglas A. Anderson with an Introduction by Ross E. Lockhart, this volume contained a number of alternate versions of the author's work.

*The Maze of the Enchanter* was the fourth volume in *The Collected Fantasies of Clark Ashton Smith* series edited by Scott Connors and Ron Hilger. Gahan Wilson supplied an Introduction to the nineteen stories and extraneous material.

*The Improbable Adventures of Sherlock Holmes* and *By Blood We Live* were two more (mostly reprint) anthologies plundered from other anthologies by editor John Joseph Adams for Night Shade.

*Strange Tales Volume III* was another handsome-looking original anthology from Tartarus Press. Along with a Preface by uncredited editor Rosalie Parker, the hardcover featured seventeen slightly old-fashioned supernatural stories by Mark Valentine, Gary McMahon, Reggie Oliver, Tina Rath, John Gaskin, Gerard Houarner, Simon Strantzas and others.

Also from Tartarus, Simon Strantzas' second short-story collection, *Cold to the Touch*, was just as good as his first, *Beneath the Surface*. It contained thirteen stories (six original) and an Afterword by the author.

Published in Bucharest, Romania, in editions of just 400 jacketless hardcover copies, Dan Ghetu's Ex Occidente Press issued new limited edition collections by a number of British authors: R.B. Russell's *Putting the Pieces in Place* contained five genteel ghost stories with an Afterword by Elizabeth Brown.

Reggie Oliver's *Madder Mysteries* contained eight stories (five original, including a posthumous collaboration with M.R. James), along with five articles about such authors as Stella Gibbons, Montague Summers, Henry James and M.R. James, and ten short "Curiosities", all illustrated by the author.

Joel Lane's *The Terrible Changes* contained fourteen previously uncollected "quiet" stories (two original) and was limited to 300 copies, while *The Nightfarers*, Mark Valentine's collection of fourteen literary ghost stories (eight original), was published by Ex Occidente in a much classier format with a print run of just 350 copies.

Charnel House returned to the small press collector's market with a numbered and signed 250-copy edition of Dean Koontz's *Your Heart Belongs to Me*, and a twenty-six lettered copy priced at $1,500!

The same imprint also issued Koontz's *Relentless*, while Tim Powers' novella *A Time to Cast Away Stones* purported to be the waterlogged notebook of Percy Bysshe Shelley. A celebration of the imprint's twentieth anniversary with an Introduction by publisher Joe Stefko, it was also limited to 250 signed and numbered editions and a leather-bound lettered edition of twenty-six copies ($1,250).

According to editor Lisa Morton, her anthology *Midnight Walk*, the premiere release from the Darkhouse Publishing collective, did not include any of "the same old crap" to be found elsewhere in the horror genre. It did contain fourteen original stories by mostly Californian or mid-western writers, including John Palisano, Mike McCarty, Vince Churchill, Del Howison, Kelly Dunn and the editor herself.

From New York's Dark Scribe Press, *Unspeakable Horror: From the Shadows of the Closet* was a gay-themed horror anthology edited by Vince A. Liaguno and Chad Helder. It featured twenty-four original stories by Gary McMahon, Lisa Morton, Scott Nicholson, Kealan Patrick Burke and Sarah Langan, amongst others.

*In the Closet, Under the Bed* from the same imprint collected fifteen stories (nine original) by Lee Thomas, with a Foreword by David Thomas Lord and an Afterword by Michael Rowe.

*Different Skins* from Screaming Dreams contained two new novellas by Gary McMahon with an Introduction by Tim Lebbon and an Afterword by the author.

Sponsored by Boston's Interstital Arts Foundation, *Interfictions 2: An Anthology of Interstital Writing* edited by Delia Sherman and Christopher Barzak contained twenty-one original stories by Jeffrey Ford, M. Rickert, Ray Vukcevich, Lavie Tidhar and others, along with an interview with the editors.

Published by California's Counterpoint Press, *A Robe of Feathers and Other Stories* was the first collection from Japan-based author Thersa Matsuura. The seventeen original stories were all based on Japanese folk myths and legends.

*Cern Zoo* was the ninth volume in the *Nemonymous* series of anthologies from Megazanthus Press. Not only did the book provide a list of the authors in the previous volume, but it also revealed the contributors to the current volume, just not in the same order as the twenty-five stories found on the Contents.

From Immediate Direction Publications, *The Edge of the Country and Other Stories* contained fourteen tales (three original) and a poem by Trevor Denyer, the editor and publisher of *Midnight Street* magazine. The thin paperback came with an Introduction by Allen Ashley and all the reprint stories had been fully revised.

Limited to just 200 copies, *Horror Reanimated 1: Echoes* was a softcover collection of three original stories by Joseph D'Lacey, Bill Hussey and Mathew F. Riley that was designed to promote the authors' blogging website.

Meanwhile, Hussey's *The Absence* from Bloody Books was a ghost story set in a Fenland millhouse, while D'Lacey's novel *Garbage Man* from the same imprint came with a cover quote by Stephen King.

*Shards: Short Sharp Tales* from Australia's Brimstone Press was a collection of thirty-one stories (eight original) by Shane Jiraiya Cummings, with an Introduction by Richard Harland and illustrations and an Afterword by Andrew J. McKiernan.

*Festive Fear: A Collection of Dark Tales* was an anthology of fourteen seasonal stories from Australian imprint Tasmaniac Publications. From the same publisher, Matt Venne's 1980s coming-of-age serial killer novel *Cruel Summer* came with an Introduction by Joe R. Lansdale and illustrations by Daniele Serra.

Published by Golden Gryphon Press and inspired by Fritz Leiber's *Conjure Wife*, George Zebrowski's *Empties* was about a third-rate detective investigating a series of murders where the victims' brains had been removed.

Andrew Hook's *And God Created Zombies* was a novella from NewCon Press.

S.T. Joshi edited and supplied the Foreword to *Copping Squid and Other Mythos Tales* from Perilous Press, a collection of eight Lovecraftian stories (half original) set in or around San Francisco by Michael Shea. The signed limited hardcover edition of 250 copies was illustrated by Steven Gilberts.

From Elder Signs Press, *The Anthology of Dark Wisdom: The Best of Dark Fiction*, edited with an Introduction by William Jones, collected twenty-five award-winning reprints and previously unpublished works by Peter Straub, John Shirley, Richard A. Lupoff, Alan Dean Foster, Tom Piccirilli, Gerard Houarner and others.

Side Real Press began reprinting the works of German author Hanns Heinz Ewers (1871–1943). *Nachtmahr: Strange Tales* collected eleven stories (many newly translated) and an essay on Edgar Allan Poe, with an Introduction by J.N. Hirschhorn-Smith. It was limited to just 350 numbered hardcover copies.

From Canada's Edge Science Fiction and Fantasy Publishing, *Tesseracts Thirteen: Chilling Tales from the Great White North* edited by Nancy Kilpatrick and David Morrell was the latest volume in the acclaimed Canadian anthology series. After separate introductions by the two editors, the book was split into four themed sections and featured twenty-three original stories by Edo van Belkom, Suzanne Church, Bev Vincent, Kelley Armstrong, David Nickle, Michael Kelly, Gord Rollo and Alison Baird, amongst others. However, the best part of the book was the fourth section, which consisted solely of an extensive and fascinating article by the incredibly knowledgeable Robert Knowlton, chronicling two centuries of Canadian dark fantasy and horror.

From the same imprint, *Gaslight Grotesque: Nightmare Tales of Sherlock Holmes* was edited by J.R. Campbell and Charles Prepolec and contained thirteen new stories by Lawrence C. Connolly, James A. Moore, Mark Morris, Barbara Roden, Simon Kurt Unsworth, Stephen Volk and others.

Edited by Martin H. Greenberg and Robert Eighteen-Bisang, *Vampire Stories* from Skyhorse Publishing collected nine stories by Arthur Conan Doyle along with a story by Bill Crider in which Sherlock Holmes met up with Bram Stoker and Van Helsing.

With an Introduction by Simon Clark and an Afterword by publisher Terry Grimwood, *Mostly Monochrome Stories* from The Exaggerated Press contained twenty-four stories (seven original) by British writer John Travis.

Swedish publisher Morrigan Books issued *Dead Souls*, a non-themed anthology of twenty-five stories edited by Mark S. Deniz. Contributors included Ramsey Campbell, Robert Hood and Gary McMahon.

Edited by Jennifer Brozek and Amanda Pillar, *Grants Pass* was a post-apocalyptic anthology of nineteen connected stories by Jay Lake, Cherie Priest and others from the same imprint.

*Apparitions* was an original anthology of thirteen stories about ghosts and revenants from Canadian imprint Undertow Publications. Despite being edited by Michael Kelly and featuring an impressive line-up of contributors that included Christopher Conlon, Joel Lane, Paul Finch, Gemma Files, Iain

Rowan, Barbara Roden, Simon Bestwick, Gary A. Braunbeck, Gary McMahon and Steve Duffy, amongst others, the most chilling thing about the book was Erin Wells' superbly spooky cover illustration.

A large corporation created the undead in John G. Rees' *Anoxic Zone* from Black Water Books.

Published as a horribly designed trade paperback by TotalRecall Publications, *Chicago Warriors: Midnight Battles in the Windy City* was a Christian police procedural about the confrontation between the forces of Good and Evil by former Chicago cop and FBI Special Agent John M. Wills. The book featured 67(!) chapters, along with a Prologue and Epilogue.

From New Jersey's Lethe Press, *The Haunted Heart and Other Tales* was a collection of twelve ghost stories (six original) by Jameson Currier about gay men and the memories that haunt them. The trade paperback also included an Introduction and story notes by the author.

Editor Sean Wallace acquired Prime Books from John Gregory Betancourt's Wildside Press and relaunched the imprint in May as an independent publisher, while Paula Guran's Juno romantic fantasy line moved from Wildside to become an imprint of Pocket Books. Wildside retained the Cosmos Books imprint and Betancourt continued to publish *Weird Tales* magazine.

However, original owner Philip Harbottle soon terminated his licence with Wildside to publish the Cosmos line, which had been edited by Wallace since 1997.

Published under the Prime imprint, *Northwest Passages* was an attractive hardcover collection of Barbara Roden's work. Two of the ten stories were original to the book, which also included an Introduction by Michael Dirda and detailed story notes by the author.

*Phantom* was an original horror anthology from Prime edited by Paul Tremblay and Sean Wallace. It contained fourteen stories by Steve Rasnic Tem, Lavie Tidhar and others.

Roy Robbins' Bad Moon Books issued a handsome series of signed and numbered chapbooks, most of them illustrated in full colour. Titles included *The Hunger of Empty Vessels* by Scott Edelman, *This Ghosting Tide* by Simon Clark, *The Gray*

*Zone* by John R. Little, *The Lucid Dreaming* by Lisa Morton, *Doc Good's Traveling Show* by Gene O'Neill, *The Better Year* by Bridget Morrow, *Necropolis* by John Urbanick and *The Watching* by Paul Melniczek.

Nicholas Royle launched his new Nightjar Press with two attractive short story chapbooks: *What Happens When You Wake Up in the Night* by Michael Marshall Smith and *The Safe Children* by Tom Fletcher.

The annual Rolling Darkness Revue chapbook from Earthling Publications was titled *Bartlett: A Centenary Symposium*. Not only did it include two fine ghost stories by Peter Atkins and Glen Hirshberg, but also the first printing of the complete version of "The Memory Pool", a 1917 story by obscure British weird fiction author Thomas St John Bartlett (1875–1909). In addition, the attractive booklet featured three author biographies of Bartlett from various respected reference books and a historical Introduction by Barbara Roden.

The Rolling Darkness Revue 2009 was performed by Atkins and Hirshberg at the Alliance Repertory Theatre, Burbank, California, on October 22 and 29, with Kevin Gregg playing Thomas Bartlett.

Ray Bradbury's *The Shop of the Mechanical Insects* was illustrated in full colour by Dave McKean and was limited to 500 deluxe copies from Subterranean Press.

*Brief Encounters* was a self-published booklet of four stories (two original) about Captain Luís da Silva by Chico Kidd, who also supplied a new Introduction.

From Canada's Burning Effigy Press, *Primeval Wood* was a new story by Richard Gavin, while *Fresh Blood* from the same imprint collected three original tales by Dave Alexander, Kelli Dunlap and Bob Freeman.

Baltimore's Old Earth Books reissued Howard Waldrop's 1980 story *The Ugly Chickens* with a new Afterword by the author as a special 250-copy edition chapbook distributed free to members of the 2009 World Fantasy Convention. Convention members also received the first issue of *The Fabulist* from California's Pharos Publications/Illuminated Media, featuring five stories originally published online.

A dying country singer made a deal with a vampire in Derek

McCormack's *The Show That Smells*, published by Akashic Books/Little House on the Bowery.

*The Sour Aftertaste of Olive Lemon* by British writer Catherine J. Gardner was the first chapbook from Bucket 'O' Guts Press, and *Marley's Ghost* and *Button*, both by Simon Kurt Unsworth, were published as somewhat basic chapbooks by Dorset's Ghostwriter Publications.

From Gothic Press, *The Sound of Dead Hands Clapping* contained six stories by Mark Rich.

Gordon Van Gelder's *The Magazine of Fantasy & Science Fiction* (*F&SF*) switched from eleven issues a year to a bi-monthly schedule with the April/May issue. The publisher cited rising postage costs and the state of the economy for the cutback on frequency, although the page count was substantially increased and subscribers received all the issues they had paid for.

Among the authors contributing to *F&SF* were Charles Coleman Finlay, Carol Emshwiller, Fred Chappell, Marc Laidlaw, Ellen Kushner, Mike O'Driscoll, Terry Bisson, Melinda M. Snodgrass, Lawrence C. Connolly, Bruce Sterling, Nancy Springer, Tim Sullivan and Kit Reed, although no serious new horror stories were published in the magazine in 2009.

Both William Tenn and Ted White provided wonderful historical Introductions to Robert Bloch's "That Hell-Bound Train" and Edward Jesby's "Sea Wrack", respectively, and there were other classic reprints by Patricia Ferrara, Jack Cady, Thomas M. Disch, John Varley, Gary Jennings, Tina Kuzminski and Jessie Thompson (with a typically exuberant Introduction by Harlan Ellison).

Charles de Lint, Elizabeth Hand, Michelle West, James Sallis, Chris Moriarty, Lucius Shepard and Kathi Maio supplied the usual book and movie review columns, and F. Gwynplaine MacIntyre, Lawrence Person, David Langford, Roberto de Sousa Causo, Graham Andrews and Patricia A. Martinelli all contributed to the "Curiosities" column.

*F&SF*'s 60th Anniversary Issue ran to more than 320 pages and contained fiction and reminiscences by Lucius Shepard, Elizabeth Hand, Albert E. Cowdrey, Robert Silverberg, Ron Goulart, Carol Emshwiller, Geoff Ryman, Joe Haldeman, M.

Rickert and Kate Wilhelm, amongst others. The magazine also launched an online writing workshop run by Gardner Dozois, provoking some bloggers to accuse the publication of an ethical conflict.

*The Very Best of Fantasy & Science Fiction: 60th Anniversary Anthology* was edited by Van Gelder for Tachyon Publications. It contained twenty-three stories by Stephen King, Ray Bradbury, Shirley Jackson, Philip K. Dick, Neil Gaiman and others.

Now billing itself as "The UK's Premier Horror and Dark Fantasy Fiction Magazine", Andy Cox's *Black Static: Transmissions from Beyond* published its usual six issues.

Nina Allan, Maurice Broaddus, Gary Couzens, Paul Finch, Christopher Fowler, Joel Lane, Gary McMahon, Steve Rasnic Tem and Stephen Volk were amongst those who contributed fiction to the bi-monthly title. There were interviews with Tony Richards, Thomas Ligotti, Ellen Datlow, Steve Mosby, Gary A. Braunbeck, Joel Lane and Gary McMahon, along with the usual columns and reviews by Fowler, Volk, Mike O'Driscoll, Peter Tennant and Tony Lee.

*Black Static*'s companion title, *Interzone*, also produced six issues and, with #223, became the UK's longest-running SF magazine, overtaking *New Worlds*. *Interzone* featured interviews with Jeffrey Ford, Bruce Sterling, Paul Di Filippo and artist Jim Woodring, Joe Abercrombie and Robert Holdstock.

Richard Chizmar's *Cemetery Dance* managed three issues in 2009, with co-editor Robert Morrish bowing out with #60 and being replaced by Brian Freeman. Issue #61 also saw a welcome redesign of the logo and the interior layouts, along with the addition of a new subtitle: "The Magazine of Horror and Suspense".

Don D'Auria, Ellen Datlow and Ed Gorman joined regular columnists Bev Vincent, Thomas F. Monteleone, Robert Morrish, John Pelan, Michael Marano and Mark Sieber, and there was new fiction from Thomas Tessier, Lisa Morton, Simon R. Green (a "Nightside" story), Tim Waggoner, Douglas Clegg (a new serial), Gary Raisor, David Morrell, Cody Goodfellow and others.

Among those interviewed were Ray Garton, Jeff Strand, Tananarive Due, Jeff Long, Glenn Chadbourne and Larry and Debra Roberts of Bloodletting Press, along with Peter Straub and William Peter Blatty, who both had special issues devoted to their work.

Stephen H. Segal's *Weird Tales* from Wildside Press managed to squeeze out three issues featuring fiction and poetry by Kathe Koja, Tim Pratt, Michael Bishop, Jeffrey Ford and film-making Eric Red, amongst others. Along with the obligatory interview with Neil Gaiman, the magazine also talked with Thomas Ligotti, Richard Corben and Simon Thalmann, and there were articles on J.G. Ballard, Edgar Allan Poe and a M.R. James stage show, along with the usual book reviews. The magazine won the Hugo Award for Best Semiprozine in 2009.

The sixth issue of *New Genre* edited by Adam Golaski included four original stories by Michael Filimowicz, Stephen Graham Jones, Eric Schaller and Matthew Pendleton, along with an essay by the editor.

From Piaizo Publishing, the attractively revived *Planet Stories* pulp featured special issues devoted to Henry Kuttner, A. Merritt, Piers Anthony and Manly Wade Wellman ("Who Fears the Devil?"), with new introductions from F. Paul Wilson, Tim Powers, Chris Roberson and Mike Resnick, respectively.

After fifteen years and almost 100 issues, *Realms of Fantasy*, edited by Shawna McCarthy, was axed by Sovereign Media after the April issue due to drastically falling newsstand sales. However, the title was quickly acquired by Warren Lapine's new publishing company, Tir Na Nog Press, which assumed all the magazine's liabilities and contracts.

Following the collapse of his DNA Publications in 2007, Lapine announced the launch of Tir Na Nog Press and a new SF imprint, Fantastic Books. However, a planned revival of the quarterly magazine *Fantastic Stories* was cancelled due to the acquisition of *Realms of Fantasy*, which returned with its August issue.

*Paradox: The Magazine of Historical and Speculative Fiction* was not so lucky, and the twice-yearly title ceased publication with its May issue. Patrick Swenson also announced that he would be ceasing publication of *Talebones* with issue #38, planning to move the magazine to an annual anthology format from 2011.

The eleventh and final copy of Kevin L. Donihe's *Bare Bones* from Raw Dog Screaming Press included eighteen new stories and ten poems by Michael Kelly, Kurt Newton, Cody Goodfellow, Gary Fry, Steve Rasnic Tem, Gary McMahon, Paul Finch, Michael Arnzen and others. Editor Donihe announced that he was moving on to other editing projects as well as concentrating on his own writing.

The delayed fourth edition of *Allen K's Inhuman* was a bumper issue featuring sixteen pulp-inspired stories (three reprints) and two poems, plus an article about Stephen King's monsters by Bev Vincent and an interview with obscure author H.B. Gregory (*Dark Sanctuary*) by John Pelan. Contributors included Joseph Nassise, Bruce Boston, Steven Vernon, Joe R. Lansdale, Darren Speegle, Chet Williamson, Darrell Schweitzer, Robert Silverberg and Stephen Mark Rainey, while editor-in-chief Allen Koszowski contributed all the illustrations.

The summer issue of the excellent *Illustration* magazine contained an article about the career of pulp illustrator Rudolph Belarski.

After thirty-three years, *Fangoria*'s sister SF publication *Starlog* announced that is was going to online publication after issue #374, while the UK's *Starburst* suspended publication "for the foreseeable future" after its frequency began to slip.

Also facing an uncertain future was *The Dark Side*, with Allan Bryce's horror magazine forced to cease publication temporarily due to "the current financial climate" after more than twenty years. A relaunch was planned in 2010.

Tim and Donna Lucas' *Video Watchdog: The Perfectionist's Guide to Fantastic Video* passed its 150th issue, while the Canadian *Rue Morgue: Horror in Culture & Entertainment* passed its ninetieth. The latter's special Halloween issue celebrated Edgar Allan Poe's 200th anniversary with commentary by Roger Corman, Clive Barker and others.

Stephen King's "The Pop of King" column in *Entertainment Weekly* included the author's wishlist for 2009, his favourite villains (Dracula was #1), his memories of Michael Jackson, how it was to work in front of a computer, and the poor distribution of a horror movie called *Carriers*.

The magazine's August 7 issue included a special vampire

section with an article by Charlaine Harris and short interviews with fellow authors Anne Rice, Laurell K. Hamilton, Melissa De La Cruz and P.C. Cast, while the first week of November edition contained an excerpt from King's latest novel, *Under the Dome*.

The August issue of *Book and Magazine Collector* published "August Derleth: A Centenary Tribute", a fine overview of the author's career (not just SF and horror) by David Whitehead with special emphasis on the individual value of different editions.

In January, England's *Guardian* newspaper issued a special supplement listing the *100 Science Fiction & Fantasy Novels Everyone Must Read*. M. John Harrison was one of the members of the review panel which apparently could not bring itself to utter the word "horror", although among the alphabetically-listed authors were Clive Barker (*Weaveworld*), Poppy Z. Brite (*Lost Souls*), Ramsey Campbell (*The Influence*), Shirley Jackson (*The Haunting of Hill House*), Henry James (*The Turn of the Screw*), Stephen King (*The Shining*), Michael Marshall Smith (*Only Forward*), Richard Matheson (*I Am Legend*), Mary Shelley (*Frankenstein*), Robert Louis Stevenson (*The Strange Case of Doctor Jekyll and Mr Hyde*) and Bram Stoker (*Dracula*).

In 2009, *Locus* celebrated its forty-first anniversary and included a personal career overview by Frederik Pohl, along with interviews with Jonathan Lethem, Michael Swanwick, Graham Joyce, Kim Harrison, Patricia Briggs, John Clute, Cory Doctorow, Michael Dirda and Nina Kiriki Hoffman.

The May edition was a special devoted to the new "Urban Fantasy", with contributions from Ginjer Buchanan, Charlaine Harris, Kelley Armstrong, Mike Carey, T.A. Pratt and Diana Gill, amongst others.

The sudden death of *Locus* publisher, editor and founder Charles N. Brown in early July resulted in executive editor Liza Groen Trombi assuming the mantle of editor-in-chief with the September issue, which also featured numerous tributes to Brown.

The thirteenth issue of James R. Beach's greatly improved *Dark Discoveries* was a tribute to Forrest J Ackerman. It also included fiction by Steve Rasnic Tem and interviews with Tem and Ray Bradbury. The following edition was devoted to *The*

*Twilight Zone*, with fiction by William F. Nolan (based on a story by Charles Beaumont), Richard Matheson and others, an interview with George Clayton Johnson, plus numerous articles about the original series and its various spin-offs.

Keeping to its theme of special issues, *Dark Discoveries* #15 was all about H.P. Lovecraft and featured fiction from Brian Lumley, W.H. Pugmire, Cody Goodfellow and David A. Riley, interviews with Lumley and S.T. Joshi, and various related articles.

New editor Hildy Silverman got *Space and Time: The Magazine of Fantasy, Horror, and Science Fiction* back on a regular schedule with four issues featuring stories and poems by Norman Spinrad, Kurt Newton, John B. Rosenman, Mary A. Turzillo, Scott Edelman (a new zombie story), Scott E. Green, Mark McLaughlin, Dennis Danvers and C.J. Henderson, amongst others, and a two-part interview with Peter S. Beagle. As always, the magazine featured some fine black-and-white illustrations by David Grilla, Russell Morgan and Brad W. Foster. In an effort to maintain production costs, Silverman announced that the magazine had forged an alliance with Dark Quest Games.

David Longhorn's much-improved *Supernatural Tales* put out two perfect-bound issues featuring original fiction by Joel Lane, Rosalie Parker, Gary Fry, Ray Russell, Tina Rath, William I.I. Read and Michael Chislett, amongst others, along with reviews by the editor.

The two issues of British magazine *Midnight Street: Journeys Into Darkness* featured fiction and poetry by Tony Richards, Joel Lane, Allen Ashley, Ian Hunter, Gary Couzens and others, along with interviews with Guy N. Smith and Gord Rollo, and the usual book reviews. Because of publishing delays, editor Trevor Denyer announced that #13 was the final print edition, and the title would in future be available as PDF downloads from the website and as an annual paperback anthology.

The two issues of the perfect-bound Irish magazine *Albedo* included fiction by Mike O'Driscoll and Robert Reed, interviews with Paul Di Filippo and Greg Egan, and various book reviews.

The four issues of David Lee Summer's perfect-bound *Tales of the Talisman* contained bumper helpings of stories and poems, while the thirteenth issue of John O'Neill's pulp-inspired periodical *Black Gate: Adventures in Fantasy Literature* featured the usual mixture of fiction and articles wrapped up in a stunning cover painting by Malcolm McClinton.

The seventh and only issue of Chris Roberts' *One Eye Grey* published in 2009, *The Last of the Chelsea Smilers*, was a bumper edition containing thirteen original stories about London.

Issue #24 of *Lady Churchill's Rosebud Wristlet* from Gavin J. Grant and Kelly Link's Small Beer Press featured the expected slipstream fiction and poetry.

The three full-colour issues of *Morpheus Tales* included stories by Michael Laimo, Joe R. Lansdale (a reprint), Ian Hunter and many others, plus interviews with Christopher Golden, Gareth L. Powell, Ray Garton and Elastic Press' Andrew Hook. The magazine also issued an *Undead Special* and a *Fantasy Femmes Special* in the same format.

The ninth issue of South Africa's *Something Wicked: Science Fiction & Horror Magazine* edited by Joe Vaz featured the usual mixture of short fiction, reviews and columns, along with an interview with actress Eva Mendes. After this edition, the magazine shifted to online publication.

The ninth and tenth issues of Justin Marriott's fascinating *The Paperback Fanatic* contained interviews with Peter Berresford Ellis (aka Peter Tremayne), Chris Lowder (aka Jack Hamilton Tweed) and Lovecraft cover artist John Holmes, plus articles on artist Richard Clifton-Dey, authors Gerald Suster and Barry Sadler (the "Casca" series), the Ballantine Adult Fantasy series, Don Glut's German *Frankenstein* series, and a lively and informative letters column.

The April issue of *The New York Review of Science Fiction* included an essay on the short fiction and poetry of Elizabeth Counselman, while Mike Barrett looked at Mary E. Wilkins Freeman's ghost stories in the June edition.

The British Fantasy Society (BFS) had a somewhat patchy year, with Lee Harris turning out three scrappy-looking issues of the society's newsletter, *Prism*. Other than the occasional article and entertaining columns by Ramsey Campbell, Mark Morris and Eric Brown, they mostly consisted of randomly assembled reviews, and the magazine was marred by sloppy design.

At least editor Stephen Theaker packed as much as he could into the two issues of the BFS' *Dark Horizons*, including articles and poetry by Ian Hunter, Mike Chinn, Shaun Jeffrey and others, along with an appreciation of Charles L. Grant, an interview with Robert Holdstock and a fascinating article by Mike Barrett about forgotten *Weird Tales* contributors C. Hall Thompson and Clifford Ball.

With the second and third issues of the BFS' *New Horizons*, editor Andrew Hook published original fiction by Allyson Bird, Ian Whates, Adam Nevill, Cyril Simsa and others, plus interviews with Ekaterina Sedia and artist Vincent Chong.

Commissioned by Guy Adams and published in hardcover format, *The British Fantasy Society Yearbook 2009* was an impressive "sampler" of (mostly dark) original fiction by twenty-one authors connected with the society, including Mark Morris, Stephen Volk, Christopher Fowler, Tim Lebbon, Conrad Williams, Sarah Pinborough, Gary McMahon, Adam L.G. Nevill, Garry Kilworth, Nicholas Royle and Rob Shearman, along with an Introduction by Gail Z. Martin.

Produced by the Friends of Arthur Machen, the *Machenalia* newsletter edited by Gwilym Games featured numerous Machen-related articles and reviews, including further historical sightings of the "Angels" (and hound!) of Mons.

*Stephen King: The Non-Fiction* by Rocky Wood and Justin Brooks was the first significant look at the author's non-fiction, reviewing more than 560 columns, articles, book reviews, criticism and even unpublished pieces. The huge volume also reprinted a difficult-to-find article by King. Cemetery Dance published the book as a special signed and slipcased hardcover limited to 2,000 numbered copies and in a fifty-two copy tray-cased edition ($500).

Published by Barnes & Noble/Fall River as an instant remainder edition, *The Stephen King Illustrated Companion: Manuscripts, Correspondence, Drawings, and Memorabilia from the Master of Modern Horror* contained numerous facsimile manuscripts, letters, illustrations and pull-out items compiled by Bev Vincent.

Not that we probably needed one, but *Haunted Heart: The Life and Times of Stephen King* by Lisa Rogak was yet another biography of the best-selling author. From McFarland & Company, *Inside the Dark Tower Series: Art, Evil and Intertextuality in the Stephen King Novels* was a critical examination by Patrick McAleer of the writer's dark fantasy series.

*From Wollstonecraft to Stoker: Essays on Gothic and Victorian Sensation Fiction* edited by Marilyn Brock was also published by McFarland. It contained thirteen critical essays on such authors as Bram Stoker, J. Sheridan Le Fanu and Charles Dickens.

*Bram Stoker's Dracula* was a reader's guide to the novel by William Hughes, while *The Devil is a Gentleman: The Life and Times of Dennis Wheatley* was a biography of the once-best-selling British writer by Phil Baker.

Edited by John Pelan and Jerad Walters, and weighing in at an impressive 753 pages, *Conversations with the Weird Tales Circle* from Centipede Press was an illustrated hardcover collection of interviews and articles by and about the contributors to "The Unique Magazine", including H.P. Lovecraft, Clark Ashton Smith, Robert E. Howard, Frank Belknap Long, E. Hoffman Price, Ray Bradbury, Robert Bloch, Fritz Leiber, Manly Wade Wellman, August Derleth, Donald Wandrei, Jack Williamson, Hugh B. Cave, Seabury Quinn and many others. The volume also included an informative essay about *Weird Tales* cover artists by Robert Weinberg, illustrated with numerous colour reproductions.

*Les nombreuses vies de Cthulhu* (*The Many Incarnations of Cthulhu*) by Patrick Marcel was a highly illustrated French paperback that looked at the history of H.P. Lovecraft's cosmic mythology. The book also included two short Lovecraftian pastiches by Peter Canon and Kim Newman, plus a bibliography of Lovecraft's work.

Edited by Benjamin Szumskyj, *The Man Who Collected Psychos: Critical Essays on Robert Bloch* from McFarland & Company contained twelve articles by S.T. Joshi, Darrell Schweitzer, Leigh Blackmore, John Howard, Randall D. Larson, Joel Lane and others, along with a Foreword by Robert Hood.

Harlan Ellison, Dean Koontz, William F. Nolan and Gahan Wilson were among those who contributed essays and appreciations to *The Twilight and Other Zones: The Dark Worlds of Richard Matheson* edited by Stanley Wiater, Matthew R. Bradley and Paul Stuve. The book also included a bibliography/filmography of Matheson's work.

Limited to just 250 hardcover copies and profusely illustrated (often in colour), *Memory, Prophecy and Fantasy: The Works and Worlds of Clive Barker Volume One: Liverpool Lives* was a meticulously researched biography of the author's early years by Phil and Sarah Stokes.

*Paperboy* by Christopher Fowler was by turns a hilarious and also moving autobiography about growing up in Britain in the 1950s and 1960s.

Practically pole-jumping on the bandwagon, George Beahm's *Twilight Tours: A Guide to the Real Forks* from Underwood Books was a travel guide to the town and locations used in Stephenie Meyer's "Twilight" series.

Published by the British Fantasy Society but sold only outside the membership, the clumsily-titled *In Conversation: A Writer's Perspective: Volume One: Horror* was a hardcover containing original interviews with sixteen of "today's leading practitioners of horror fiction", including Ramsey Campbell, Joe R. Lansdale, Stephen Gallagher, Peter Crowther, Tim Lebbon, Ray Garton, Mark Morris, Graham Joyce and others.

However, editor James Cooper soon found himself in hot water when several blogs and websites accused him and the society of sexism, pointing out that the book did not contain a single interview with a female horror writer. Even the online versions of *Guardian* and *Publishers Weekly* picked up the story.

As a result, BFS Chairperson Guy Adams, who commissioned the volume, issued a grovelling apology to just about everyone, apparently speaking on behalf of every male working in the genre when he said that it was "disgustingly simple for a man not to notice these things, a blindness to the importance of correct gender representation that I feel embarrassed to have fallen into ... I can only apologise and hope that the discussion has made other editors and publishers realize that this kind of lazy sexism is unacceptable and to watch their own lists in future."

Adams' response appeased his vociferous group of detractors and Cooper's proposed series of interview books was quickly cancelled.

Edited by Michael Knost, *Writers Workshop of Horror*

from Woodland Press included twenty-four articles on writing horror fiction by Joe R. Lansdale, Elizabeth Hand, Thomas F. Monteleone and others, along with interviews with Clive Barker, Ramsey Campbell, F. Paul Wilson and Tom Piccirilli.

*Esoteria-Land: The Authentic, Eclectic, & Eccentric Nonfiction of Michael McCarty* from BearManor Media collected twenty-six interviews, sixteen articles and various reviews, along with an Introduction by actress Linnea Quigley and an Afterword by The Amazing Kreskin (who also turned up in McCarty's vampire novel *Liquid Diet* as a character).

From McFarland & Company, *Metamorphoses of the Werewolf: A Literary Study from Antiquity Through the Renaissance* by university professor Leslie A. Sconduto explored the context that created the traditional image of the werewolf as a savage beast.

For those who needed it, Jay Stevenson's *The Complete Idiot's Guide to Vampires* supplied all the answers, while *Zombies for Zombies* was a humorous guide to being one of the walking dead by David P. Murphy.

M. Keith Booker's *Red, White, and Spooked: The Supernatural in American Culture* was published by Greenwood Press/Praeger.

Available from Beccon Publications in both hardcover and trade paperback formats, *Canary Fever* was the fourth volume of John Clute's collected literary reviews, the majority of them dating from between 2003 and 2008.

In November, Frank Frazetta's original cover painting for the 1967 Lancer paperback edition of *Conan the Conqueror* by Robert E. Howard sold to a private collector for a reported $1 million, which was four times the previous record for a Frazetta painting.

However, the following month, Alfonso Frank Frazetta, the fifty-two-year-old son of the artist, was arrested for allegedly trying to steal millions of dollars' worth of paintings from the Frank Frazetta Museum in East Stroudsburg, Pennsylvania. Frank Jr, as he is known, claimed his father had given him permission to remove the paintings, but it appeared that the theft was the result of a family feud between the four Frazetta children.

As usual edited by Cathy Fenner and Arnie Fenner, *Spectrum 16: The Best in Contemporary Fantastic Art* from Underwood Books covered the year 2008 and featured more than 400 pieces of art by over 300 artists, along with a profile of Grand Master Award winner Richard V. Corben.

Also edited by the Fenners, *Strange Days: Aliens, Adventurers, Devils, and Dames* from the same publisher featured some beautifully reproduced plates of original pulp covers by Virgil Finlay, Edd Cartier, Margaret Brundage, Hannes Bok, Harold W. McCauley, George Rozen, J. Allen St John and other artists, but suffered from lazy research.

With essays by George Beahm, *Knowing Darkness: Artists Inspired by Stephen King* from Centipede Press was a massive volume featuring more than 500 images by numerous artists, including Michael Whelan, J.K. Potter, Les Edwards and Dave McKean. Frank Darabont supplied the Introduction and publisher Jerad Walters contributed an Afterword. As with the imprint's previous Lovecraft art book, it was available in a bewildering variety of expensive editions, including a "regular" slipcased edition of 1,500 copies ($295); a 300-copy traycased edition with extra prints signed by thirty-three artists ($995), and a traycased edition of fifty copies containing an original drawing by Michael Whelan ($1,295).

From Fantagraphics Books, *Gahan Wilson: 50 Years of Playboy Cartoons* was a collection of all the artist's macabre cartoons for *Playboy* (many in full colour), along with five short stories and an interview with Wilson about working for the magazine. The three-volume slipcased set was edited by Gary Groth, with Introductions by Hugh Heffner and Neil Gaiman.

Published by McFarland & Company, Jane Frank's *Science Fiction and Fantasy Artists of the Twentieth Century: A Biographical Dictionary* contained information on 400 artists, including biographical data and a bibliographical listing of each artist's published work in the genre. The hardcover also included an historical overview of the last quarter of a century written by the author and Robert Weinberg, along with Appendices listing the artist recipients of all the major genre awards.

The legendary (and sometimes controversial) Shasta imprint

from the 1950s returned to publishing with *From the Pen of Paul: The Fantastic Images of Frank R. Paul* edited with an Introduction and commentary by Stephen D. Korshak. The large-size retrospective included articles by Forrest J Ackerman, Gerry de la Ree and Sam Moskowitz, amongst others.

It was available from Shasta/Phoenix in a hardcover trade edition, a 184-copy slipcased deluxe edition, and a $395.95 "ultra deluxe" edition limited to 100 numbered and twenty-six lettered copies that included additional art and the last signature of the late Arthur C. Clarke, who supplied the Preface. A revised deluxe edition subsequently added a bibliographical index of Paul's artwork by Jerry Weist and Robert Weinberg.

From Illustrated Press, *Norman Saunders* was a handsome hardcover art book about the eponymous pulp and magazine artist (1907–89) with biographical text by his son, David.

Daniel Zimmer and David J. Hornung's *Reynold Brown: A Life in Pictures* from the same imprint was a sumptuous hardcover showcasing the work of the artist best known for his iconic horror and SF movie posters for American International Pictures during the late 1950s and '60s.

*The Child Thief,* written and illustrated by Brom, was a dark retelling of *Peter Pan*, while *Tim Burton's The Nightmare Before Christmas: The Thirteen Days of Christmas* by Steve Davis and Carolyn Gardner was an illustrated book based on characters from the 1993 movie.

Written and illustrated by Bryan Talbot, *Grandview* was a full-colour steampunk adventure inspired by the nineteenth-century French caricaturist J.J. Grandville, and *Crazy Hair* was a children's picture book written by Neil Gaiman and illustrated by Dave McKean.

*The Black Doll* contained the art and screenplay for an unproduced silent film by Edward Gorey, along with an interview with the late artist.

Andrzej Klimowski and Danusia Schejbal illustrated a sadly abridged version of Robert Louis Stevenson's *Dr Jekyll and Mr Hyde*, while *Tales of Death and Dementia* was a young adult collection featuring four tales by Edgar Allan Poe, with illustrations by Gris Grimly.

From Titan Books, *The Best of Simon and Kirby* was a hefty

hardcover compilation devoted to the eighteen-year partnership between legendary comics veterans Joe Simon and Jack Kirby, the team that created *Captain America*. With informative essays by Mark Evanier and an Introduction by the ninety-six-year-old Simon himself, the oversized hardcover reprinted twenty-six full-colour strips and various covers covering the superhero, science fiction, war, romance, crime, Western, horror and comedy genres, along with a useful checklist.

*Illusions* was a slim print-on-demand paperback from Black Coat Press showcasing the colour and black-and-white artwork of Daniele Serra.

At the beginning of September, the Walt Disney Company announced a $4 billion (£2.5 billion) shares and cash deal to buy Marvel Entertainment, which gave the Disney organization control of more than 5,000 Marvel characters.

From Marvel, *Laurel K. Hamilton's Anita Blake, Vampire Hunter: The First Death* was a graphic novel prequel to the book series written by Hamilton and Jonathon Green and illustrated by Wellington Alves. *Anita Blake, Vampire Hunter: Guilty Pleasures: The Complete Collection* reprinted the first twelve issues of the 2007–08 comic book series with a new Introduction by Hamilton.

Marvel's *The Stand: Captain Trips* collected the five-issue mini-series based on the first part of Stephen King's novel in hardcover format.

The first release from Del Rey Comics was *The Talisman: The Road of Trials*, a new collaboration by Stephen King and Peter Straub, illustrated by Tony Shasteen. The mini-series began with an "Issue 0", with the first edition published in November.

Dean Koontz's *Frankenstein: Prodigal Son Volume One* was a graphic adaptation by writer Chuck Dixon and illustrator Brett Booth of the novel by Koontz and Kevin J. Anderson, based on Koontz's original concept for a TV series.

*Mercy Thompson: Homecoming* was a graphic origin story of the shapeshifter heroine by Patricia Briggs and David Lawrence, illustrated by Francis Tsai and Amelia Woo. The hardcover also included an interview with Briggs.

*The Dark-Hunters Volume 1* was a manga adaptation of

the second novel in Sherrilyn Kenyon's series by Joshua Hale Fialkov, illustrated by Claudia Campos.

Based on the YA vampire novel by Darren Shan (Darren O'Shaughnessy), *Cirque du Freak Volume 1* was another manga comics adaptation, illustrated by Takahiro Arai.

P. Craig Russell adapted and illustrated Neil Gaiman's *Coraline* into graphic novel format.

In DC Comics' limited mini-series *Blackest Night* and related titles, Earth's Green Lanterns discovered that a dark power could bring recently killed superheroes back to life.

*House of Mystery 2: Love Stories for Dead People* from DC/Vertigo was a graphic anthology of creepy stories written by Matthew Sturges with superb art by Luca Rossi and several guest artists (including Bernie Wrightson), along with a special sketchbook by Rossi.

In May, Dark Horse Comics launched the first volume of *Boris Karloff Tales of Mystery Archives*, a hardcover collection of the Gold Key comic series of the 1960s and 1970s, with a new Introduction by Sara Karloff. Two months later, the publisher also revived the old Warren title *Creepy* with new material from Bernie Wrightson, Angelo Torres and others.

From Top Shelf Productions, the third volume of *The League of Extraordinary Gentlemen: Century*, written by Alan Moore and illustrated by Kevin O'Neill, contained three stories that spanned almost a century as the Antichrist Project spawned the apocalyptic Moonchild. One scene set in a gentleman's club involved a number of classic occult detectives.

Ray Bradbury contributed a new Introduction to Tim Hamilton's "Authorized" graphic adaptation of his novel *Fahrenheit 451*, issued as a full colour trade paperback by Harper/Voyager.

Bradbury also supplied the Introduction to Garry Gianni's exquisite graphic version of Jules Verne's *Twenty-Thousand Leagues Under the Sea*, published in oversized hardcover format by California's Flesk Publications. As a bonus, the book also included H.G. Wells' 1896 short story "Sea Raiders", also illustrated by Gianni. It was available as a 600-copy signed and numbered edition, and a fifty-copy deluxe edition that included original preliminary artwork.

Also from Flesk, *Major Thrill's Adventure Book* was an inexpensive showcase of Gary Gianni's distinctive, pulp-inspired black-and-white artwork.

Robert M. Heske's independent Heske Horror imprint published *Cold Blooded Chillers: Tales of Suburban Murder & Malice: Bone Chiller* featuring nine black-and-white illustrated stories and a short script all written by Heske. From the same publisher came *2012: Final Prayer: An End of Times Anthology*.

Series star John Barrowman collaborated with his sister Carole on the script for "Captain Jack and the Selkie", a comic strip in the first 100-page issue of the *Torchwood* magazine, published in February.

Greg Cox wrote the film novelization of *Underworld: Rise of the Lycans*, while the very busy Alan Dean Foster churned out the tie-ins to the new *Star Trek* movie and *Transformers: Revenge of the Fallen*.

*Transformers: The Veiled Threat* was an official prequel to the two film series by Foster, while Max Allan Collins wrote the film tie-in *G.I. Joe: The Rise of Cobra* along with *G.I. Joe: Above & Beyond*, which was an official prequel to that proposed movie franchise based on the Hasbro toys and cartoons.

*Terminator: Salvation: From the Ashes* was a prequel by Timothy Zahn, and Steve Perry's *Indiana Jones and the Army of the Dead* was set in the world of the movie series.

Based on a screenplay by Diablo Cody, Audrey Nixon's YA novelization *Jennifer's Body* only featured Cody's name on the cover.

Screenwriter Dave Eggers' *The Wild Things*, a loose novelization of the film version of *Where the Wild Things Are*, came in both a regular hardcover and a *faux* fur-covered edition.

*The Box* was a movie tie-in reissue of the collection *Button, Button*, which contained eleven stories and a poem by Richard Matheson, and the tie-in edition of Stephenie Meyer's *New Moon* contained a bound-in colour poster.

"The Movie Collector's Edition" of Neil Gaiman's *Coraline* not only included the original novel illustrated by Dave McKean, but also eight pages of colour stills, extensive notes by the author and screenwriter/director Henry Selick, and an excerpt from the script.

The tenth Doctor found himself on a haunted planet trying to destroy a powerful weapon in *Doctor Who: The Eyeless* by Lance Parkin, while the Time Lord encountered an old foe in *Doctor Who: Prisoner of the Daleks* by Trevor Baxendale and teamed up again with companion Donna Noble in *Doctor Who: Beautiful Chaos* by Gary Russell.

In Jacqueline Rayner's "Quick Reads" chapbook *Doctor Who: The Sontaran Games*, the Doctor investigated a series of murders at an academy for top athletes.

Based on the ITV series, *Primeval: Fire and Water* by Simon Guerrier involved Professor Cutter and his team investigating anomalies at a South African safari park and in a rain-swept East London.

Paranormal romance writer Doranna Durgin's *Ghost Whisperer: Ghost Trap* was the latest tie-in to the TV series, while James Swallow's *SG-U: Stargate Universe: Air* was another TV tie-in.

Meanwhile, David Mack's *The 4400: Promises Broken* was a belated tie-in to the CBS TV show that was cancelled in 2007.

Tim Lebbon's *Hellboy: The Fire Wolves* was a tie-in to the comic book series created by Mike Mignola, while *30 Days of Night: Light of Day* by Jeff Mariotte was set in the graphic novel world created by Steve Niles and Ben Templesmith.

*Doom 3: Maelstrom* by Matthew Costello was based on the video game.

Despite showcasing some superb stills and posters, Michael Mallory's *Universal Studios Monsters: A Legacy of Horror* was a disappointing trip through the studio's history, from the silent era to the early 1960s. *The Mummy* director Stephen Sommers' perfunctory Foreword pretty much exemplified the cash-in nature of Universe Publishing's overpriced hardcover.

Apparently aimed at Dirty Old Horror Fans, Marcus Hearn's sumptuous *Hammer Glamour* from Titan Books was a tribute to the studio's female stars, including Valerie Leon, Caroline Munro, Kate O'Mara, Ingrid Pitt, Barbara Shelley and many others, with new interviews and previously unseen photographs from the Hammer archives. A special 600-copy was also available, signed by a number of the featured actresses.

From Telos Publishing, *It Lives Again! Horror Movies in the New Millennium* was a year-by-year look by actress Axelle Carolyn at horror films released in the first decade of the twenty-first century. The oversized, full-colour volume included a Foreword by the author's husband, director Neil Marshall, and an Introduction by Mick Garris.

The inevitable *Twilight: The Complete Illustrated Movie Companion* and *New Moon: The Complete Illustrated Movie Companion*, both by Mark Cotta Vaz, were guides to the awful film series based on the books by Stephenie Meyer.

*Coraline: A Visual Companion* by Stephen Jones was a full-colour coffee-table book looking at the creation of the stop-motion movie, the original novel and other related items, with an Introduction by Neil Gaiman.

Polish author Bartłomiej Paszylk's *The Pleasure and Pain of Cult Horror Films* from McFarland & Company covered eighty-eight so-called "cult" movies, dating from 1921 through to 2005.

Rick Atkins' *Among the Rugged Peaks . . . An Intimate Biography of Carla Laemmle* was published by Midnight Marquee Press. Unfortunately, the ninety-nine-year-old niece of Universal Pictures founder Carl Laemmle, who appeared in the original *Phantom of the Opera* (1925) and *Dracula* (1931), deserved something better than this poorly written and scrappily written tome.

At the 81st Academy Awards on February 23, the late Heath Ledger was predictably announced as the winner of the Supporting Actor Oscar for his portrayal of a maniacal Joker in the otherwise overrated *The Dark Knight*. The film also picked up the award for Sound Editing, while other Oscars went to the equally inflated *Wall•E* for Animated Feature and *The Curious Case of Benjamin Button* for Art Direction, Make-up and Visual Effects.

In November, the once-powerful Hollywood studio Metro-Goldwyn-Mayer announced that it was considering a "potential sale" to raise the $4 billion (£2.4 million) it needed to get the company out of debt.

Meanwhile, independent UK distributor Redemption Films, set up by Nigel Wingrove in 1992 to release horror and soft-porn movies, went into administration.

After a failed attempt in June by New Line Cinema to have a judge rule on a compensation claim by the estate of J.R.R. Tolkien for more than $270 million (£180 million), a settlement was agreed in September, just a month before the case was set to go to trial. The agreement meant that two films based on *The Hobbit* could finally move ahead.

The seventy-six-year-old *Rosemary's Baby* director Roman Polanski was arrested by Swiss police in September on an international warrant related to a 1977 charge of having unlawful sex with a thirteen-year-old girl. Polanksi admitted the crime, but fled the US in 1978 before he could be sentenced.

The Oscar-winning film director, who had been fighting extradition back to America for thirty years, was held after arriving in Switzerland to receive an honorary award at the Zurich Film Festival. Salman Rushdie and Neil Jordan were among those who signed a petition urging Polanski's release from prison, before the director was granted bail at the end of November after his fourth attempt.

In June, the US box-office fell behind the previous summer's results for the third straight week in a row as the expected blockbusters failed to materialize. However, in the UK cinema, box-office takings in 2009 reached a record £1 billion as admissions were at their highest since 2002. Although British films only accounted for a 16.5 per cent share of the market, according to the UK Film Council overseas investment more than doubled, making it the second best year for production on record.

David Yates' *Harry Potter and the Half-Blood Prince* had the most successful opening of any film in the series so far, taking $79.5 million in its first three days at the US box-office. An adaptation of the penultimate book in the series, it featured the death of a major character.

Six years after Pope Benedict XVI (then Cardinal Ratzinger) denounced the "Harry Potter" books for "distorting Christianity", in July the Vatican's newspaper *L'Osservatore Romano* proclaimed its approval of the latest film in the series for depicting good triumphing over evil. However, the same publication slated *Avatar*, describing the SF epic as "technology without emotion".

James Cameron's film was sneak-previewed in August at IMAX theatres with an unprecedented sixteen-minute trailer. Reportedly costing more than $300 million, it took 3-D computer animation to a new level. Unfortunately, the story – about a disabled marine (Sam Worthington) travelling to the mineral-rich planet of Pandora and taking the form of one of the native life-forms – was surprisingly simplistic for the most expensive movie ever made.

Despite its narrative shortcomings, *Avatar* recouped its budget in just fifteen days and went on to become the fastest film ever to earn $1 billion (£625.6 million) at the worldwide box-office, passing that milestone just two days later.

Michael Bay's noisy sequel *Transformers: Revenge of the Fallen* once again teamed Shia LaBeouf's nerdish hero and his unlikely girlfriend played by Megan Fox with the heroic Autobots in a race against time to prevent the Decepticons from raising the ultimate evil. Depressingly, after just five weeks it became the tenth highest-grossing film of all time.

Another sequel, *The Twilight Saga: New Moon*, had one of the biggest openings in 2009, doubling the gross of the first film. It broke opening day records with a $72.7 million take, and went on to earn $140.7 million over its first weekend.

Unfortunately, admissions collapsed by the second weekend, plunging a massive 70 per cent. However, *New Moon* became the most successful vampire film on record as, spurred on by its opening numbers, the film passed the $200 million mark in just eight days.

In November, a spokesman for the Vatican condemned the film as "nothing more than a moral vacuum with a deviant message". This came three weeks after the Catholic Church condemned Halloween as "anti-Christian and dangerous", urging parents not to allow their children to dress up for the festivities.

Meanwhile visiting "Twi-hards" – fans of the book and movie series – resulted in a 600 per cent increase in tourism to the Pacific Northwest town of Tiny Forks, Washington State, where much of the first two movies were filmed. Even the small Tuscan city of Volterra, Italy, became a cult destination after it was featured as the backdrop to scenes in *New Moon*.

If nothing else, 2009 will be remembered as another year of sequels and remakes. Despite Hugh Jackman recreating his role as the clawed Logan for the prequel, Gavin Hood's *X-Men Origins: Wolverine* was perhaps one spin-off too far, as the $150 million film dropped a massive 69 per cent in its second week in the US. However, the movie did much better worldwide. It probably didn't help that an unfinished version of the film was leaked on to the Internet a month before it opened.

Having just failed to beat the opening numbers for *Terminator 3: Rise of the Machines* (2003), the fourth entry in the series, *Terminator: Salvation*, was most memorable for star Christian Bale's much-publicized on-set rant at the director of photography. Directed by McG, the film barely managed to cover its $200 million budget at the US box-office.

Once again starring Malcolm McDowell as Dr Loomis, Rob Zombie's disappointing sequel *Halloween II* opened at #3 at the end of August.

Given how over-hyped the original was, Jon Harris' *The Descent Part 2* was another sequel we didn't need.

Scripted by Luc Besson, the French-made *District 13: Ultimatum* was set in a near-future Paris and was a sequel to the original 2004 film.

With a new lead (Rhona Mitra) and a new director (Patrick Tatopoulos), the prequel *Underworld: Rise of the Lycans* was the third film in the diminishing vampires vs. werewolves series.

Ray Stevenson took over the eponymous role in *The Punisher: War Zone*, the third film based on the Marvel Comics character.

Following a speedway accident, a group of bland teens met their gory fates in digital 3-D in *The Final Destination*, the fourth instalment in the series. It opened at #1 at the US box-office, taking $27.4 million in its first weekend. The film also topped the UK box-office, grossing more than £3.6 million.

Although his character was killed off in an earlier entry, Tobin Bell was back for the inevitable *Saw VI*, which had the lowest opening weekend gross ($14.1 million) for any film in the series to date.

After playing the Winchester brothers on TV's *Supernatural*,

Jared Padalecki and Jensen Ackles both turned up in horror remakes. Based on the 1981 superior slasher film, *My Bloody Valentine 3-D* starred Ackles and was about a serial killer dressed as a miner.

Produced by Michael Bay, Marcus Nispel's *Friday the 13th* starred Padalecki and opened at the top of the American box-office with a record-breaking $43.6 million for a horror film before dropping 82 per cent the following week. The 1980 original was also released on video in an uncut version that reinstated around ten seconds of extra gore initially cut to earn an "R" rating.

Dennis Iliadis' *The Last House on the Left* was a remake of Wes Craven's equally unpleasant 1972 debut, while Dylan Walsh took over the role of the psychotic patriarch looking for his "perfect" family in an unnecessary remake of the 1987 chiller *The Stepfather*.

*Sorority Row* was another slasher remake, based on the 1983 movie *The House on Sorority Row*, and starred Rumer Willis (the daughter of Bruce Willis and Demi Moore) and a bunch of screaming girls in lingerie.

A teenager suspected that her father's new fiancée (Elizabeth Banks) was more than she seemed in the supernatural thriller *The Uninvited*, which was a remake of the superior Korean film *A Tale of Two Sisters*.

It is doubtful that we needed yet another version of Oscar Wilde's *Dorian Gray*. Ben Barnes was the handsome Victorian rake who remained forever young as his portrait aged, while Colin Firth turned up as Lord Henry Wotton, who instructed his young protégé in debauchery.

J.J. Abrams' entertaining reboot of the *Star Trek* franchise opened at #1 in the US with a $79.2 million gross in May and four weeks later became the first film of 2009 to break the $200 million barrier.

Costing $100 million, with a hefty advertising budget and Will Ferrell as its star, *Land of the Lost* was a comedy reworking of the 1960s TV series that still failed at the box-office. An appearance by original child stars Kathy Coleman and Wesley Eure never made it into the final cut.

The Disney SF adventure *Race to Witch Mountain*, based on the two 1970s films, did feature original stars Kim Richards and

Ike Eisenmann in cameos, as Dwayne Johnson's Las Vegas cab driver befriended two stranded teen aliens.

Suburban dad Matthew Perry magically transformed into Zac Efron in the teen comedy remake *17 Again*.

Starring Woody Harrelson as a redneck zombie hunter, Ruben Fleischer's horror-comedy *Zombieland* was set in a post-apocalyptic future overrun by cannibal corpses. Bill Murray had an amusing cameo as himself. The film opened as the #1 film in the US with a strong $24.7 million gross.

Ben Foster and Dennis Quaid discovered that their interstellar spaceship had been overrun by mutant zombies in the German-made *Pandorum*, co-produced by Paul W.S. Anderson.

A Canadian radio shock jock (Stephen McHattie) was at the centre of a zombie virus spread by language in Bruce McDonald's low-budget *Pontypool*, adapted by Tony Burgess from his own novel.

Reportedly made for £45 (mostly spent on tea and biscuits) after first-time British director Marc Price called in favours from anybody he could find, *Colin* was a zom-com about the eponymous hero (Alastair Kirton), who returned to only a slightly altered existence after being bitten by the walking dead. Shot on a camcorder in Wales and London, the film was well received at the Cannes Film Festival and even received a brief theatrical release in the UK.

Set in a village filled with female cannibal zombies, *Doghouse* was another cheap horror-comedy from British director Jake West.

Only slightly better was *Lesbian Vampire Killers*, a one-joke homage to Hammer Films starring unfunny TV comedians James Corden and Matthew Horne.

Based on the popular series of YA books by Darren Shan, *Cirque du Freak: The Vampire's Assistant* was a dull entry in the teen vampire stakes despite support from John C. Reilly, Willem Dafoe and Salma Hayek (as a bearded lady).

A Korean priest was turned into a vampire in Park Chan-wook's stylish *Thirst*, apparently inspired by Émile Zola's nineteenth-century novel *Thérèse Raquin*, while *Blood: The Last Vampire* was a live-action version of the popular manga/anime series about a half-vampire female samurai (Gianna Jun).

Made for just $11,000 in seven days, Oren Peli's disturbing haunted house movie *Paranormal Activity* grossed $7.9 million during its initial limited release in 160 US cinemas, averaging a remarkable $49,379 per screen (the highest all-time gross for a movie playing in less than 200 theatres). DreamWorks originally bought the film in 2008 for remake rights, but eventually decided to distribute it theatrically over Halloween. As a result, it grossed more than $100 million.

Co-scripted by Adam Simon and supposedly "based on true events", *The Haunting in Connecticut* involved Virginia Madsen and her family moving into a haunted home that turned out to be a former mortuary.

Also supposedly based on true stories were *The Spell*, a micro-budget UK horror film about witchcraft shot in Leeds, and *Summer Scars*, in which a deranged drifter tortured a group of teenage truants.

*Tormented* was another low-budget British horror film given a theatrical release in 2009. It involved a group of selfish schoolfriends getting their come-uppance from the classmate they bullied to death.

A couple found themselves locked in a recording studio haunted by a dead 1970s rock star in *Reverb*, and a cocktail of drugs turned a coma patient into a body-hopping psycho in Paddy Breathnach's derivitive *Red Mist* (aka *Freakdog*). Mark Tonderai's low-budget feature debut *Hush* was no British *Duel*.

A group of friends out sailing found themselves trapped in a time loop in Christopher Smith's UK/Australian co-production *Triangle*, and a voyeur (Karra Elejaide) found himself trapped in a time loop in the Spanish-made *Timecrimes* (*Los cronocrímenes*).

Based on the best-seller by Audrey Niffenegger, *The Time Traveler's Wife* starred Eric Bana as the husband who moved backwards and forwards in time. Unfortunately, the film version failed to match the huge success of its source novel.

Brad Pitt aged backwards in David Fincher's *The Curious Case of Benjamin Button*, loosely based on a story by F. Scott Fitzgerald.

*Spider-Man* director Sam Raimi returned to his low-budget horror roots with the inventive *Drag Me to Hell*, in which a bank clerk (Alison Lohman) was cursed by an old gypsy woman (Lorna Raver) whose mortgage extension she had turned down.

Ti West's *The House of the Devil* was the twenty-nine-year-old editor/writer/director's low-budget tribute to the horror films of the late 1970s and early 1980s as college student Samantha (Jocelin Donahue) found herself babysitting in a spooky house of horrors. Genre veterans Mary Woronov, Tom Noonan and Dee Wallace all had supporting roles.

Newlywed couples were being stalked and killed in a tropical paradise in David Twohy's accomplished slasher film *A Perfect Getaway*, featuring Steve Zahn, Milla Jovovich and Timothy Olyphant. Jovovich also starred in *The Fourth Kind*, an alien-abduction thriller that told its story by juxtaposing the "movie" version with "actual" events.

Based on a story by Richard Matheson, Richard Kelly's *The Box* featured Cameron Diaz and James Marsden as a couple given an impossible choice by a mysterious stranger (Frank Langella).

Despite being scripted by Oscar-winner Diablo Cody (*Juno*) and starring Megan Fox as a man-eating cheerleader, *Jennifer's Body* took a pathetic $6.8 million on its opening weekend.

Gary Oldman was obviously slumming as a rabbi exorcist in David S. Goyer's *The Unborn*, in which a teenage babysitter (Odette Justman) was possessed by the lost soul of a "dybbuk". James Remar, Carla Gugino and Jane Alexander must also have wondered where their careers were heading as well.

An adopted nine-year-old (Isabelle Fuhrman) was hiding a dark secret in Spanish director Jaume Collet-Sarra's *Orphan*.

Executive produced by her father, David, Jennifer Lynch's *Surveillance* involved FBI agents Julia Ormond and Bill Pullman investigating a series of gruesome murders in a small town.

After Twentieth Century Fox and Warner Bros. reached a resolution in their copyright infringement dispute in early January, Zack Snyder's impressive *Watchmen* opened in March at the top of both the US and UK box-office charts. Based on Alan Moore's "unfilmable" 1986 graphic novel, it revolved around a series of murders amongst a group of retired superheroes.

Based on the Hasbro toy line, *G.I. Joe: The Rise of Cobra* was made by the same people behind the *Transformers* franchise and sported numerous scenes of equally mindless violence.

James Wong's hyperactive *Dragonball Evolution* was based on the cult manga series and involved a quest to find seven Dragon Balls to save the world. Chow Yun-Fat, Emmy Rossum and James Marsters were all somehow involved.

Ignoring the 1994 film starring Jean-Claude Van Damme, *Street Fighter: The Legend of Chun-Li* featured Kristin Kreuk and Michael Clarke Duncan and was also based on the popular video game.

Robert Downey Jr's dynamic detective and Jude Law's dapper Dr Watson pitted their wits against Mark Strong's Victorian Satanist, Lord Blackwood, in Guy Ritchie's troubled but surprisingly entertaining re-imagining of *Sherlock Holmes*.

German director Roland Emmerich once again destroyed the world spectacularly in *2012*, when an ancient Mayan prophecy came true as the Earth's crust exploded and John Cusack's science fiction writer tried to save his family. It opened with a $65 million box-office in the US and had the fifth-biggest international opening ever.

Meanwhile, MIT astrophysics professor Nicolas Cage investigated a series of fifty-year-old numbers that appeared to predict past and future disasters, including the end of the world, in Alex Proyas' apocalyptic *Knowing*.

When Heath Ledger died while filming Terry Gilliam's *The Imaginarium of Dr Parnassus*, Colin Farrell, Johnny Depp and Jude Law stepped in to play the same character in various fantasy incarnations, while Christopher Plummer's titular carnival owner pitted his wits against the Devil (Tom Waits).

Four strangers co-existed between two parallel cities in Gerald McMorrow's ambitious, if incomprehensible, debut *Franklyn*, and Paul Giamatti's actor found a place to store his soul in Sophie Barthes' equally oddball *Cold Souls*.

Based on his own Oscar-nominated short film, Shane Acker's computer-generated SF tale *9* was co-produced by Tim Burton and featured the voices of Elijah Wood, John C. Reilly, Jennifer Connelly, Christopher Plummer and Martin Landau.

Set in an alien shanty town outside Johannesburg (does nobody remember *Alien Nation*?), Neill Blomkamp's *District 9* topped the US box-office charts in early August and went on to take more than $100 million. Made for just over $30 million, it was produced by Peter Jackson and also based on a short film.

Crashed alien Jim Caviezel teamed up with John Hurt's tribe of Vikings to battle a fire-breathing monster in *Outlander*, while Gerard Butler played an Iraq special ops veteran in a near-future prison forced to participate in violent scenarios in *Gamer*.

Based on a graphic novel, Jonathan Mostow's *Surrogates* starred Bruce Willis as a futuristic detective investigating the killings of synthetic avatars and their operators.

Following a car accident, Lena Headey's radiologist believed that everyone around her had been replaced by deadly doppelgängers in Sean Ellis' *The Brøken*, and Lunar miner Sam Rockwell apparently encountered his own doppelgänger in *Moon*, written and directed by David Bowie's son Duncan Jones (aka Zowie Bowie).

*Ghosts of Girlfriends Past* was a chick flick re-imagining of Charles Dickens' *A Christmas Carol* starring an unsympathetic Matthew McConaughey, Jennifer Garner and Michael Douglas.

Meanwhile, Jim Carrey voiced Ebenezer Scrooge and all three ghosts in Robert Zemeckis' more traditional adaptation of *A Christmas Carol*, filmed in his 3-D performance-capture technique.

Jennifer Garner also featured in *The Invention of Lying*, co-directed, co-written and co-produced by Ricky Gervais, who starred as a screenwriter in an alternate world who discovered that he was the only person who could lie.

A neglectful father (Eddie Murphy, back on a downward career path) started getting financial advice from his daughter's imaginary friends in the dire *Imagine That*.

Literary characters swapped places with people in the real world in *Inkheart*, based on the 2003 YA novel by Cornelia Funke. Brendan Fraser found himself trapped amongst a cast of British character actors that included Helen Mirren, Jim Broadbent and Andy Serkis.

A young girl (Dakota Blue Richards) was sent to live in a magical mansion in *The Secret of Moonacre*, based on Elizabeth Goudge's *The Little White Horse* (said to be J.K. Rowling's favourite childhood book).

Featuring Jon Cryer, James Spader and William H. Macey, Robert Rodriguez's *Shorts* was a children's fantasy film about a colourful magic rock that could grant wishes.

Reuniting most of the original cast against Hank Azaria's Karloff-like pharaoh, the family-friendly sequel *Night at the Museum: Battle of the Smithsonian* (aka *Night at the Museum 2*) opened at #1 over the Memorial Day weekend with a take of just over $70 million.

Dakota Fanning was a teen with telekinetic powers in Hong Kong in the convoluted *Push*, and the young actress also voiced the titular animated character in Henry Selick's *Coraline*. The impressive 3-D stop-motion movie was based on the popular children's novel by Neil Gaiman and also featured the voices of Teri Hatcher, John Hodgman, Ian McShane, Dawn French and Jennifer Saunders.

Wes Anderson's stop-motion fable *Fantastic Mr Fox* was based on a 1970 children's book by Roald Dahl, while Spike Jonze's long-awaited *Where the Wild Things Are* was an adaptation of Maurice Sendak's illustrated children's classic that was shot in Australia.

Reese Witherspoon, Seth Rogen and Hugh Laurie were among those who provided voices for DreamWorks' fun 3-D cartoon *Monsters vs. Aliens*. Amongst the other animated films presented in 3-D were Disney/Pixar's *Up*, *Cloudy with a Chance of Meatballs*, *Ice Age 3: Age of the Dinosaurs* and *Battle for Terra*. Meanwhile, *Astro Boy*, *Aliens in the Attic* and *Planet 51* were all released "flat".

Thorold Dickinson's marvellously creepy *The Queen of Spades* (1940), based on Alexander Pushkin's classic short story, was given a welcome UK cinema reissue at the end of the year.

In America, the year's most successful film was *Transformers: Revenge of the Fallen*, followed at some distance by *Harry Potter and the Half-Blood Prince* (which topped both the UK film and DVD charts). Then came *Up* (#3), *The Twilight Saga: New Moon* (#5), *Star Trek* (#6), *Monsters vs. Aliens* (#7), *Ice Age: Dawn of the Dinosaurs* (#8), *X-Men Origins: Wolverine* (#9) and *Night at the Museum 2* (#10). In fact, the only non-genre title in the US Top 10 for 2009 was the comedy *The Hangover* at #4.

The *Ice Age* sequel (#2), *Up* (#3), the *Transformers* sequel

(#5), *Star Trek* (#7), *Monsters vs. Aliens* (#8) and the *Night at the Museum* sequel (#9) all featured in the UK Top 10, which also included *Slumdog Millionaire* (#4), *The Hangover* (#6) and *Angels and Demons* creeping in at #10.

It may be too late now, but it was revealed in 2009 that the UK's infamous Video Recordings Act 1984 was never actually referred to the European Commission. As a result, the ill-conceived "video nasties" law brought in by Margaret Thatcher's Conservative government was never officially enacted and should never have been enforced.

Doug ("Pinhead") Bradley had a cameo role in *Clive Barker's Book of Blood*, a impressive direct-to-DVD release, shot in Scotland by John Harrison and based on the author's haunted house story "On Jerusalem Street" and the wraparound tale "The Book of Blood".

Based on a story within the graphic novel, *Watchmen: Tales of the Black Freighter* was an animated adventure about a ship-wrecked sailor (voiced by Gerard Butler) haunted by phantom buccaneers. Extras on the DVD release included *Under the Hood*, a *faux* documentary about 1940s masked crime-fighters.

Eric Red's haunted house chiller *100 Feet*, starring Famke Janssen as a woman who murdered her husband (Michael Paré), premiered on DVD in the UK and on the Sci Fi Channel in the US.

The once-mighty Steven Seagal used his martial arts skills to lead a band of survivors against a world overrun with vampire zombies in *Against the Dark*.

A group of medical students on a skiing holiday encountered cannibal Nazi zombies in Norwegian writer/director Tommy Wirkola's entertaining *Dead Snow* ("Ein! Zwei! Die!").

A young couple and a car-jacker found themselves trapped in a rural gas station by thorny parasites in Toby Wilkins' fun *Splinter*.

The studios' tradition of issuing redundant direct-to-DVD sequels to much better films continued with Chris Fisher's disappointing time-travel fantasy *S. Darko: A Donnie Darko Tale* (aka *S. Darko: Donnie Darko 2*).

Who even knew there was a sequel, let alone *The Butterfly*

*Effect 3: Revelations*, in which Chris Carmack's character jumped back through time to try to identify the serial killer who murdered his girlfriend and ended up changing his own reality.

Marina Sirtis was the best-known name in Toby Wilkins' *The Grudge 3: The Curse Continues*, which moved the evil spirits to a run-down building in Chicago.

Featuring nobody you'd ever heard of and filmed in Bulgaria, Ghost House Pictures' *Messengers 2: The Scarecrow* was a prequel to the 2007 film which starred *Twilight*'s Kristen Stewart.

Now a personified monster in the Freddy Krueger mould, Gary Jones' *Boogeyman 3* was a Bulgarian-shot, no-star entry in the direct-to-DVD franchise in which the titular menace stalked a psychology student (Erin Cahill) who witnessed him killing her best friend.

Lance Henriksen, Bill Moseley, Danny Trejo, Jason Connery, Michael Paré and P.J. Soles all added their names to the sequel *Alone in the Dark II*, once again based on the video game. The director of the original, Uwe Boll, was back with another video game adaptation, *Far Cry*, in which Emanuelle Vaugier, Udo Kier, Craig Fairbrass, Michael Paré (yet again!) and the late Don S. Davis were involved with the creation of an army of super-soldiers.

Directed by George Romero's less-talented son Cameron, *Staunton Hill* was set in the late 1960s and featured a group of hitchhikers menaced by backwoods crazies.

Left sitting on a shelf at Warner Bros. for nearly two years, Bryan Singer "presented" Michael Dougherty's *Trick 'r Treat*, an anthology of five Halloween tales featuring Brian Cox and Anna Paquin.

Glenn McQuaid's blackly humorous *I Sell the Dead*, an expanded version of his own 2005 short film, was about a pair of luckless grave-robbers played by Dominic Monaghan and Larry Fessenden. Genre veterans Ron Perlman and Angus Scrimm added welcome support.

Comedy troupe Flight of the Conchords had cameo roles in the New Zealand horror-comedy *Diagnosis: Death*, about a haunted hospital, and an unlikely Faye Dunaway played a one-armed American cop in the Welsh rockabilly zombie comedy *Flick*.

Hollywood "B" movie actor Bruce Campbell found himself kidnapped by the residents of a small backwoods community in Oregon to help them rid the local graveyard of a nineteenth-century Chinese demon in the low-budget comedy *My Name is Bruce*, directed by Campbell himself.

Jeremy London starred as a human resistance fighter battling cyborgs in The Asylum's *The Terminators* which, as with most titles released by that company, had absolutely nothing in common with any other successful film with a similar concept.

Brian Krause's scientist had to save the Earth from cosmic disaster in *2012: Supernova*, and former 1980s singer Deborah (Debbie) Gibson and Lorenzo Lamas were as unconvincing as their two rubber co-stars in The Asylum's humourless *Mega Shark versus Giant Octopus*. Incredibly, the film received a brief theatrical release in the UK.

At least their two Edgar Rice Burroughs adaptations, *The Land That Time Forgot* with C. Thomas Howell and Timothy Bottoms, and *Princess of Mars* with Antonio Sabato, Jr and Traci Lords(!), were something of a step-up for the company, which isn't saying much.

From veteran director Harry Bromley Davenport (*Xtro*), the low-budget ghost story *Haunted Echoes* featured an impressive cast that included Sean Young, M. Emmett Walsh, Barbara Bain and her real-life daughter Juliet Landau.

After forty years, Brazil's own horror star José Mojica Marins returned as his most famous character, Zé do Caixão (Coffin Joe), in *Embodiment of Evil*. Co-written and directed by Marins (now in his seventies), the crazed gravedigger continued his search to find the perfect woman to give him a son.

Adapted from H.P. Lovecraft's "Haunter of the Dark", Robert Carrelletto's contemporary low-budget film *Pickman's Muse* starred Barret Walz and Maurice McNicholas.

Eric McCormack and Robert Patrick starred in the "lost" 1950s sci-fi spoof *Alien Trespass*, in which a crashed extra-terrestrial hunted for an escaped cyclopian monster amongst a small desert community.

*The William Castle Film Collection* was a boxed set of eight fun chillers, including *The Tingler*, *Mr Sardonicus*, *Strait-Jacket*, *Homicidal* and the obscure *13 Frightened Girls*, plus a feature-length documentary about the legendary director/showman.

Synergy Entertainment's three-disc *Sherlock Holmes: The Archive Collection* contained a fascinating selection of material dating from 1912–55, including the TV play "Sting of Death" starring Boris Karloff as a mysterious beekeeper named Mycroft.

The two-disc *An American Werewolf in London: Full Moon Edition* included a feature-length documentary about John Landis' cult favourite.

Boasting a Sid and Marty Krofft commentary, *Land of the Lost: The Complete Series* was available in both a boxed set and a cool retro-style lunch box.

Keri Russell, Rosario Dawson, Alfred Molina, Virginia Madsen and Nathan Fillion all supplied voices for the impressive animated *Wonder Woman* movie, which told the origin of the Amazon heroine and included her battling reanimated zombie warriors.

John E. Hudgens' *American Scary* was billed as "a nostalgic homage to the glory days of the late night horror shows". The DVD documentary included interviews and archive footage of such horror hosts as Zacherley (John Zacherle), Ghoulardi (Ernie Anderson) and Vampira (Maila Nurmi), along with celebrity fans Forrest J Ackerman, Bob Burns, Tim Conway, Neil Gaiman, John Kassir, Leonard Maltin, Tom Savini and John Stanley.

On July 7 the American Sci Fi channel rebranded itself Syfy in a ludicrous attempt to "grow into a global lifestyle brand", while in September Canada's Scream TV changed its name to Dusk for pretty much the same reason.

Despite trying to reach a wider audience, that did not stop Syfy from pumping out the same old type of TV movies and mini-series: Kandyse McClure and David Anders starred in a remake of Stephen King's *Children of the Corn*, co-scripted by the author and director Donald P. Borchers.

A slacker (Christopher Marquette) discovered that the world had been taken over by giant alien insects in the Bulgarian-filmed horror comedy *Infestation*, which also featured Ray Wise.

*Razortooth* involved a giant genetically-modified swamp eel terrorizing the Florida Everglades, while Crystal Allen and John Rhys-Davies battled big snakes in *Anacondas: Trail of Blood*.

*Thor: Hammer of the Gods* was the best Vikings vs. were-wolves movie ever shown on the Syfy channel, which isn't saying much. It was filmed in Bulgaria and starred *Home Improvement*'s Zachery Ty Bryan as a miscast warrior with a destiny.

An earthquake released prehistoric sharks to menace a group of Californian lifeguards in *Malibu Shark Attack*, and Mark Moses' scientist-turned-SF author had to save the world from a weather experiment gone wrong in *Ice Twisters*.

Meanwhile, Robin Dunne's Robin Hood and Erica Durance's Maid Marian were confronted by the Sheriff of Nottingham's supernatural monster in Peter DeLuise's *Beyond Sherwood Forest*.

Following the network's "re-imagining" of *The Wizard of Oz*, Syfy's four-hour mini-series *Alice* was an updating of the Lewis Carroll classic, with Caterina Scorsone as a heroine with some very modern problems. The supporting cast included Kathy Bates' Queen of Hearts and Harry Dean Stanton's Caterpillar.

Natasha Henstridge, James Cromwell and Steven Culp starred in ABC-TV's two-part mini-series *Impact*, about the Moon being on a collision course with Earth. Meanwhile, NBC's two-part *Meteor* featured Bill Campbell, Christopher Lloyd, Michael Rooker, Stacy Keach and Jason Alexander amongst those trying to survive another direct hit from space.

The BBC's new two-part adaptation of John Wyndham's classic dystopian novel *The Day of the Triffids* may have featured the best-looking (CGI) man-eating plants ever seen on the small screen, but Patrick Harbinson's risible script did no favours for a cast that included Dougray Scott, Joely Richardson, her mum Vanessa (as a crazed nun), Brian Cox, a surprisingly good Jason Priestley, and Eddie Izzard as a hammy villain.

Even worse was the BBC's feature-length version of Henry James' much-filmed *The Turn of the Screw*. Although Sandy Welch's script interestingly updated the story to the 1920s, it borrowed heavily from previous versions (notably the best, *The Innocents*) and totally misunderstood the nature of the ghosts apparently glimpsed by Michelle Dockery's unstable and naive governess.

Based on David Almond's Whitbread Children's Award-winning novel, Sky's feature-length production of *Skellig* was about a young boy (Bill Milner) who discovered the eponymous winged being (Tim Roth) living in a dilapidated shed at the bottom of the garden.

The live-action prequel *Scooby Doo! The Mystery Begins* revealed the origins of the four teenage investigators and their always-hungry dog on the Cartoon Network.

On June 12, America switched over to digital television from the old analogue system. Surprisingly, the world did not come to an end.

Taking a "break" from the regular series format, the BBC's *Doctor Who* instead presented four one-hour specials as David Tennant's role as the Doctor headed towards its much-hyped conclusion.

In the silly Easter special, "Planet of the Dead", Michelle Ryan guest-starred as a sexy jewel thief who, along with the other passengers on a London double-decker bus, found themselves transported to a desert-like planet inhabited by a deadly flying Swarm.

Later in the year, Lindsay Duncan brought some much-needed class to the equally derivative "The Waters of Mars", which was set in a biosphere on the Red Planet, where an alien entity was using the water supply to turn crew members into liquefied zombies.

David Tennant also voiced the Doctor in a computer-animated special, *Dreamland*, which was not only screened on TV but was also converted into a comic book format for smartphones.

Before Tennant's final fling as the Doctor, he also made a maniacal guest appearance in the two-part "The Wedding of Sarah Jane" during the third season of *The Sarah Jane Adventures*.

The busy actor even starred in the BBC's on-screen Christmas idents leading up to the two-part "The End of Time", which saw the Doctor teaming up with Bernard Cribbins' Wilfred before finally meeting his fate at the hands of John Simms' crazed Master and regenerating into the body of twenty-seven-year-old actor Matt Smith. Despite a totally self-indulgent wrap-up that included guest appearances from many old companions, 10.4 million viewers tuned into the BBC to watch the Doctor's demise, which accounted for an impressive 35.5 per cent share of the total UK audience.

In another two-part episode of *The Sarah Jane Adventures*, "The Eternity Trap", the Doctor's former assistant (Elisabeth Sladen) and her young friends Clyde (Daniel Anthony) and Rani (Anjli Mohindra) investigated an apparently haunted mansion. To celebrate Comic Relief Red Nose Day, the BBC broadcast a special episode of the juvenile show with appearances by robot dog K-9 and veteran comedian Ronnie Corbett as an alien ambassador who turned out to be one of the Slitheen.

Another *Doctor Who* spin-off experienced a change to the regular series format when *Torchwood: Children of Earth* was shown in five one-hour episodes over consecutive nights in early July. The gripping story involved a monstrous alien race desig-nated "the 456" arriving on Earth and demanding 10 per cent of the planet's children.

Scripted by Russell T. Davies, John Fay and James Moran, the mini-series was a terrific example of British dystopian SF in the grand tradition of the *Quatermass* serials and the works of John Wyndham. Stylishly directed by Euros Lyn, the entire cast stepped up to the adult material, especially Peter Capaldi as a career politician betrayed by a duplicitous British govern-ment, and Lucy Cohu as the estranged daughter of a guilt-ridden Captain Jack Harkness (John Barrowman).

Following the deaths of two major cast members at the end of the previous series, another popular member of the dwindling Torchwood team was surprisingly killed off as the third season moved towards its grim conclusion. Fans of the show expressed their anger and outrage at this development by contacting James Moran through his blog and Twitter account. Unfortunately, he did not write that particular episode.

Viewing figures for the *Torchwood* mini-series held up well over the five nights, with almost six million people tuning in to the first and final episodes.

HBO premiered the second season of its sex 'n' vampire show *True Blood* in June. Inspired by Charlaine Harris' best-selling books, psychic waitress Sookie Stackhouse (Anna Paquin) and her undead boyfriend Bill Compton (Stephen Moyer) travelled to Dallas to investigate the disappearance of a powerful vampire. Meanwhile, Sookie's wayward brother Jason (Ryan Kwanten) joined the vampire-hating church group, the Fellowship of the Sun, and Bill's teenage protégé Jessica (Deborah Ann Woll) flexed her newfound powers as shape-changing bar owner Sam (Sam Trammell) tried to protect the inhabitants of Bon Temps from the lascivious pleasures of the mysterious Maryann (Michelle Forbes).

The premiere attracted 3.7 million viewers in the US, a rise of 51 per cent from the previous Season One episode, making it the most-watched cable programme since the season finale of *The Sopranos* in 2007.

The CW television network jumped on the vampire bandwagon with Kevin Smith's tediously predictable *The Vampire Diaries*, which was basically an undead reworking of Smith's *Dawson's Creek*. Based on the young adult books by L.J. Smith, good vampire Stefan Salvatore (Paul Wesley) and his bad-boy brother Damon (a scenery-chewing Ian Somerhalder) returned to the aptly named town of Mystic Falls to fall out over angst-ridden high school heroine Elena (Nina Dobrev), who resembled their lost love from the nineteenth century. The opening episode achieved the biggest audience ever for a CW premiere, with 4.8 million tuning in.

Although having started out as a BBC3 pilot for a supernatural sitcom, the six-part spin-off series of Toby Whithouse's *Being Human* took a much darker turn as ghost Annie (Lenora Crichlow) had to literally escape death's door, werewolf George (Russell Tovey) finally found himself a girlfriend, and reformed vampire Mitchell (Aidan Turner) was forced to take a stand against his undead brethren. The first episode attracted the channel's second-highest audience for an original drama.

The third series of ITV's enjoyable dino-drama *Primeval* featured a creepy "haunted house" episode that introduced Jason Flemyng's policeman Danny Quinn, who went on to replace series hero Nick Cutter (Douglas Henshaw) when the latter was apparently "killed" by his time-travelling wife Helen (the wonderful Juliet Aubrey). After confronting a giganotosaurus, a flesh-eating fungus, a medieval knight and giant ants, the cliffhanger ending ranged from the birth of mankind to an apocalyptic future.

Despite a healthy average audience of five million in the UK (down from six million for the first two series), the show was cancelled in June because the excellent CGI effects were deemed too expensive. However, four months later it was announced that BBC Worldwide (who successfully distribute the programme overseas) had come to the rescue and would become the largest investor in a fourth series, scheduled to air in 2011.

A candidate for worst genre show of the year was ITV's *Demons*, which starred Philip Glenister (with a dodgy American accent) as the unreliable mentor of teenage monster-slayer Luke Van Helsing (a charmless Christian Cooke). A blatant inversion of *Buffy the Vampire Slayer*, the British series also featured Zoë Tapper as a blind, psychic Mina Harker contaminated by vampire blood, and Holliday Grainger as Luke's annoying girlfriend. Thankfully it only lasted for six episodes.

A sequence of grainy pictures transmitted from an unknown point in space revealed near-future catastrophes to maverick astrophysicist Dr Christian King (Emun Elliott) and DI Rebecca Flint (a miscast Tamzin Outhwaite) in the five-part *Paradox*. The BBC's most bonkers show of 2009 shared its "multiple worlds" concept with *FlashForward*, *Fringe*, *Primeval*, *Merlin* and even *Family Guy*.

At the end of the disappointing second season of the BBC's *Life on Mars* sequel, *Ashes to Ashes*, Alex Drake (Keeley Hawes) apparently returned to 2008 after being accidently shot by DCI Gene Hunt (Philip Glenister) in 1982.

ABC-TV's inferior American remake of *Life on Mars* lasted just seventeen episodes. When the network informed the producers early that the show would not be renewed, they came up with a ludicrously literal interpretation of the title, as out-of-time cop Sam Tyler (Jason O'Mara) discovered that he wasn't in 1973 but, um . . . actually on Mars!

Inspired by a 1999 novel by Robert J. Sawyer, *FlashForward* began impressively with everyone on Earth blacking out for exactly two minutes and seventeen seconds. When it was realized that all the survivors had a vision of what they would be doing on April 29, 2010 – some six months into the future – glum FBI agent Mark Benford (Joseph Fiennes) headed up a task force to discover who was responsible.

Unfortunately, the series soon descended into soap opera scripting, *Lost*-like flashbacks and multi-character arcs until ABC temporarily shut down production after ten episodes as a result of plummeting ratings and the departure of co-showrunner Marc Guggenheim.

NBC's still pointless *Heroes* ended its fourth volume ("Fugitives") with the evil Sylar (Zachary Quinto) believing he was the dead Nathan Petrelli (Adrian Pasdar) after finding out that his *real* father was John Glover's chain-smoking taxidermist. The equally rambling new season ("Redemption") owed much to HBO's cancelled *Carnivàle*, as the creepy Samuel (Robert Knepper) and his travelling freak show started recruiting people with superpowers.

After bringing John Locke (Terry O'Quinn) back from the dead, and apparently killing off Juliet (Elizabeth Mitchell) and everybody else in a hydrogen bomb explosion, ABC's exasperating *Lost* ended its chaotic fifth and penultimate season with another two-hour special that introduced two warring super-beings, Jacob (Mark Pellegrino) and the sinister Mr Loophole (Titus Weaver), and left its intriguing time-travel premise hanging. Earlier in the year, the show passed its 100th episode.

Co-creator J.J. Abrams' *Fringe* ended its premiere season on the Fox Network with FBI agent Olivia Dunham (Anna Torv) being transported to a parallel dimension, where she finally met the mysterious industrialist Dr William Bell (genre icon Leonard Nimoy). For the second season, Olivia, Peter Bishop (Joshua Jackson) and his eccentric scientist father Walter (the delightful John Noble) continued to investigate *X Files*-like cases while trying to uncover more details about the Pattern, the enigmatic Observers, and the alternate universe and its possible threat to their own reality.

Joss Whedon's *Dollhouse*, which premiered from Fox in February with just 4.7 million viewers, was about a secret underground organization that wiped people's personalities and then imprinted them with new ones, basically turning them into high-priced hookers. Eliza Dushku played one of these "actives", Echo, who began to remember her past.

Like Whedon's *Buffy the Vampire Slayer*, the show took some time to settle down. Despite an intriguing stand-alone final episode set in a post-apocalyptic 2019 (only available on the DVD set in America but shown on UK TV), against the odds the show got renewed for a second series. Summer Glau joined the cast in the recurring role of programmer Bennett, and Ray Wise guest-starred as the head of Washington's Dollhouse.

Despite a basic concept resembling the 1980s TV show *Friday the 13th: The Series*, the Syfy channel's enjoyable twelve-episode *Warehouse 13* starred the likeable Eddie McClintock and Joanne Kelly as two bickering secret service agents reassigned to recover supernatural "artefacts" for a mysterious government storage facility run by Saul Rubinek's Artie Nelson.

The second season of Syfy's *Sanctuary* featured an episode set in a dystopian future world ravaged by zombie-like mutations of humans and "Abnormals", before the series returned to normal as 157-year-old Dr Helen Magnus (Amanda Tapping) and her team continued to protect their supernatural charges. Following the apparent death of Magnus' brainwashed daughter Ashley (Emilie Ullerup) by the evil Cabal, Agam Darshi joined the cast as petty criminal Kate Freelander.

Sam (Jared Padalecki) and Dean (Jensen Ackles) found they could not trust each other, let alone the angels, as the End of Days approached in the CW's *Supernatural*, which enjoyed one of its best seasons yet, averaging three million viewers per show.

After Sam killed the demon Lilith and inadvertently released Lucifer (the busy Mark Pellegrino) from Hell, the fifth season found the brothers teaming up with former angel Castiel (Misha Collins) to save the world from the impending Apocalypse. Sam and Dean found themselves transported to an alternate dystopian future where a virus had turned people into zombies and, in a couple of unusually fun episodes, the brothers were trapped in retro-TV hell and attended a fan convention based on their "fictional" exploits. The show even found a guest spot for Paris Hilton as a homicidal Pagan god.

Scripted by *The League of Gentleman*'s Reece Shearsmith and Steve Pemberton, the BBC's *Psychoville* was a twisted comedy that lasted seven episodes and featured Dawn French, Eileen Atkins and Christopher Biggins as himself. Pemberton also turned up ITV's *Whitechapel*, a three-part serial in which a contemporary murderer recreated Jack the Ripper's killings in the East End of London.

Based on the novel by John Updike, *Eastwick* should have been retitled *Desperate Witches* as three women (Lindsay Price, Jaime Ray Newman and Rebecca Romjin) were given magical powers by the devilishly charming Darryl Van Horne (Paul Gross). Guest stars included Martin Mull, Cybill Shepherd, Jerry O'Connell, Rosanna Arquette and Veronica Cartwright (who was also in the 1987 movie version).

Two previous attempts to adapt the material never progressed beyond the pilot stage, and ABC wisely put the feather-light show on hiatus after just thirteen episodes.

A cross between *Dawson's Creek* and *Friday the 13th*, *Harper's Island* was an enjoyable thirteen-episode series set on an island with an unsavoury reputation where a wedding guest was gruesomely murdered each week. CBS was accused of burying the show in an unpopular time slot on Saturday nights, despite supporting it with an interactive website.

Veteran John Lithgow played the nondescript church deacon and family man turned "Trinity Killer" for the knockout fourth season of Showtime's *Dexter*, which also included appearances by Keith Carradine and Adrienne Barbeau. Fans of the show could also buy a Dexter action figure with interchangeable arms.

In the second and final season of the CW's *Reaper*, Sam (Bret Harrison) began to question if he really was the son of the Devil (Ray Wise), while his human father returned from the dead as a zombie. Also complicating things was the scheming Morgan (Arnie Hammer), the Devil's jealous *other* son.

Just days after NBC cancelled *Medium*, CBS picked the successful psychic show up for a sixth season. In the first-ever Halloween episode, Allison Dubois (Patricia Arquette) and her family battled black and white zombies as the actors were digitally inserted into scenes of George Romero's 1968 classic *Night of the Living Dead*.

After the fifth series jumped forward five years, Melinda (Jennifer Love Hewitt) discovered that her son Aiden (Connor Gibbs) had his own special powers and she also encountered Sleepy Hollow's real headless horseman in CBS' faltering *Ghost Whisperer*.

Both Arquette and Hewitt made their directorial debuts on their shows in 2009.

In ITV's four-part *Boy Meets Girl*, a DIY store employee (Martin Freeman) and a female fashion journalist (Rachael Sterling) swapped bodies due to a freak electrical storm.

A shallow, dead fashion model (Brooke D'Orsay) found her soul sharing the "plus-size" body of smart but insecure lawyer Jane Bingum (Brooke Elliott) in Lifetime's feel-good fantasy series *Drop Dead Diva*. Guest stars included Rosie O'Donnell, Paula Abdul, Jorja Fox, Liza Minnelli and Delta Burke.

Meanwhile, the self-obsessed Erica Strange (Erin Karpluk) was magically transported back in time by her mysterious therapist (Michael Riley) so that she could change the mistakes she made at pivotal moments in her life in CBC's own feel-good series *Being Erica*, which ran for two seasons in 2009.

Filmed in South Africa and shown over three nights in the US, AMC's six-episode "reinterpretation" of *The Prisoner* featured Jim Caviezel as the nonconformist Number Six, who found himself in the surreal Village run by Ian McKellen's dapper Number Two. Caviezel admitted that he had never even heard of Patrick McGoohan's cult 1960s original.

ABC's remake of the 1980s mini-series *V* featured Morena Baccarin as the leader of an invasion by reptilian aliens hidden beneath cloned human skin. FBI special agent Erica Evans (Elizabeth Mitchell) suspected that the visitors were not quite as friendly as they first appeared. In the US, the show ran for just four episodes in November before being put on hiatus until the following March.

After five seasons, the penultimate episode of the Sci Fi Channel's *Stargate Atlantis* was set in an alternate reality and featured loner detective John Sheppard (Joe Flanigan) pursuing a serial-killing Wraith through Las Vegas. The 100th and final episode aired in early January.

It was quickly replaced by *SG-U: Stargate Universe*, a grim blending of *Battlestar Galactica* and *Lost in Space* with Robert Carlyle slumming in the Dr Zachary Scott role.

Nothing was as dreary as the thirteen-part international co-production *Defying Gravity*, about eight astronauts on a mysterious space mission to Venus that was designed to last six years. Despite the introduction of a sinister sub-plot, the ABC show failed to take off.

The strike-delayed final ten episodes of Sci Fi's *Battlestar Galactica* finally revealed the identity of the final Cylon (it wasn't as big a revelation as some might have hoped) and the crew of humans and Cylons finally found Eden (literally) in the disappointing series finale.

Meanwhile, the revisionist movie *Battlestar Galactica: The Plan* was directed by series star Edward James Olmos and looked at the show's first two seasons from the perspective of the Cylons, while *Caprica* was a pilot movie prequel to the show that premiered on DVD.

Picking up its eighteen-episode run in July, the third season of Syfy's amiable *Eureka* (aka *A Town Called Eureka*) moved to Friday nights and ended with Sheriff Jack Carter (Colin Ferguson) and his new girlfriend Tess Fontana (Jaime Ray Newman) having to deal with not only a dark energy leak but also how their lives were changing.

After Rufus Sewell's dull Dr Hood investigated a mercury poisoning epidemic and a perfume that caused violence, CBS' *Eleventh Hour* was cancelled, despite regularly being in the top twenty rated shows of the week. At least series creator Stephen Gallagher got to script a couple of episodes before it ended.

The final three episodes of *Pushing Daisies* guest-starred David Arquette, Richard Benjamin, George Segal, Robert Picardo, Gina Torres, Fred Williamson and George Hamilton before ABC pulled the plug on the second season in March.

The Connor family continued their battle against the evil SkyNet before the Fox Network finally cancelled *Terminator: The Sarah Connor Chronicles* at the end of the second season, and NBC's misguided *Knight Rider* revival killed off three major characters and reintroduced the evil transforming KARR before getting a creative reboot in January that still could not prevent the show from being cancelled after just one season.

Inspired by the 1998–99 series of the same name, ABC's reboot of *Cupid* starred Bobby Cannavale as the Mt Olympus exile. It ran for just seven episodes – eight fewer than the original series.

When the CW's *Smallville* returned in January, Clark (Tom

Welling) was helped by a scruffy Legion of Super-Heroes –
Cosmic Boy, Black Canary and Impulse – to find Chloe (Allison
Mack), who had been abducted from her own wedding by the
Doomsday monster that ended up killing Jimmy Olsen (Aaron
Ashmore).

Although the producers backed away from earlier claims that
the ninth season would be the darkest to date, it still involved
Clark (Tom Welling) and Lois (Erica Durance) fighting virus-
created zombies in Metropolis. Meanwhile, Julian Sands turned
up as Superboy's father, Jor-El (previously voiced by Terence
Stamp in the series) and Callum Blue played the crazed Major
Zod (the character played by Stamp in the movies).

The third and final season of ABC Family's *Kyle XY* saw the
test-tube teen (Matt Dallas) using his powers to search for his
girlfriend (Kirsten Prout), who was kidnapped by the mysterious
Latnok Society.

On the Season Three premiere of the Disney's Channel's
sitcom *Wizards of Waverly Place*, budding sorcerer Justin Russo
(David Henrie) created a Franken-girl to protect his stuff from
his inquisitive sister Alex. In another episode, he had to capture
his own vampire girlfriend.

A resurrected sorcerer (Mackenzie Crook) commanded
an army of living gargoyles to destroy Camelot in the second
season opener of the BBC's much-improved *Merlin*. Meanwhile,
Morgana (Katie McGrath) discovered her own magical
powers, Charles Dance turned up as a distinctly non-Arthurian
Witchfinder and the evil Mordred (a creepy Asa Butterfield)
became the show's chief villain.

In the series finale, the Great Dragon (voiced by John Hurt)
was finally freed, with tragic consequences. Unfortunately, the
first series of *Merlin* failed to find an audience when shown by
NBC in America over the summer.

Based on the series of fantasy books by Terry Goodkind, the syndicated *Legend of the Seeker* supplied plenty of magic, sword-fights
and romance for those who like that kind of thing. In the second
season, Richard Cypher (Craig Horner), Kahlan (Bridget Regan) and
the wizard Zedd (Bruce Spence) battled the dead after discovering
that they had inadvertently opened a doorway into the underworld.

At least a cameo by John Rhys-Davies brought some

much-needed class to the BBC's six-part fantasy spoof *Kröd Mändoon and the Flaming Sword of Fire*, which starred Matt Lucas as an evil chancellor.

The better than usual twentieth anniversary episode of Fox's *The Simpsons* "Treehouse of Horror" not only featured the classic creatures – Dracula, Frankenstein's Monster, the Mummy and the Wolf Man – participating in Springfield's Halloween celebrations, but also amusing pastiches of Alfred Hitchcock's *Dial M for Murder*, *28 Days Later* and the musical stage version of *Sweeney Todd*.

Based on the DreamWorks movie, *Monsters vs. Aliens: Mutant Pumpkins from Outer Space* was a half-hour animated Halloween special on NBC featuring the voices of Reese Witherspoon, Seth Rogan and Hugh Laurie.

*Star Trek*'s George Takei supplied the voice of power-crazed general Lok Durd in a two-part episode of the Cartoon Network's *Star Wars: The Clone Wars*, while Seth Green contributed to the show's second season as the voice of a butler droid working for ruthless bounty hunter Cad Bane.

Stewie built a transporter and beamed the cast of *Star Trek: The Next Generation* to Quahog in Fox's *Family Guy*, which also presented an episode that parodied the Stephen King movies *Stand By Me*, *Misery* and *The Shawshank Redemption* with the voices of Richard Dreyfuss, the late Roy Scheider, George Wendt and Adam West.

In the Season Eight opener, Stewie and Brian explored a series of alternative universes, including one based on Disney cartoons; there was a *King Kong* spoof involving a Miley Cyrus Terminator (don't ask!), and the season closed with "Something, Something, Something, Dark Side", the show's second full-length *Star Wars* homage based, this time, on *The Empire Strikes Back*.

The Caped Crusader teamed up with Green Arrow, Wildcat, the original Blue Beetle and Atom in the Cartoon Network's *Batman: The Brave and the Bold*. Neil Patrick Harris sang his way through the role of the villainous Music Meister.

With Professor X and Jean Grey missing, Logan found himself leading the mutant fight in the aptly-titled cartoon series *Wolverine and the X-Men*, on the Nicktoons Network, and fledgling hero Tony Stark battled a group of evil scientists, amongst other foes, in the same channel's *Iron Man: Armored Adventures*. Over on Disney XD, *The Spectacular Spider-Man* chronicled the early exploits of Peter Parker's webslinger.

Based on Julia Donaldson and Axel Scheffler's children's picture book (which has sold four million copies worldwide), *The Gruffalo* was a half-hour animated film featuring the voices of Robbie Coltrane, John Hurt and Tom Wilkinson.

*Statuesque* was written and directed by Neil Gaiman for Sky's *10 Minute Tales* series of short films. Bill Nighy and Amanda Palmer starred in a tale of love involving living statues.

At The Big Chill music festival in early August, more than 4,000 revellers set the world record for the largest zombie gathering while also being featured in a scene for a Film4/Warp Films mockumentary entitled *I Spit on Your Rave*.

In February, the busy Dominic Monaghan guest-starred in a 3-D episode of NBC's sci-spy series, *Chuck*. Unfortunately, getting hold of the special glasses proved to be a bit of a problem on both sides of the Atlantic, not that the process actually worked anyway. Meanwhile, the Subway sandwich chain became a major sponsor of the struggling show's third season.

When a serial killer started recreating murders from his books, a successful mystery novelist (Nathan Fillion) teamed up with a female NYPD detective (Stana Katic) in the first two seasons of ABC's entertaining *Castle*. The pair investigated a series of ritualistic voodoo murders, Cyndi Lauper as a psychic suspected of murder and, in the Halloween episode, the staking of a vampire fetishist in a cemetery.

Brennan (Emily Deschanel) and Booth (David Boreanaz) were called in to investigate a mystery involving a missing ancient Egyptian mummy in an October episode of Fox's *Bones*, and an episode of *CSI: Crime Scene Investigation* involved a murder at a science fiction convention.

Following a spoof episode based on the *Friday the 13th* movies, Shawn (James Roday) and Gus (Dulé Hill) investigated a suicide apparently caused by the Devil and were hired to protect a man who thought he was a werewolf in the USA Network's *Psych*. In the season finale of Fox's *Mental*, a man claiming to be a werewolf took the psych ward hostage.

Having started out as a religious-themed radio show in the

late 1930s, CBS-TV's daytime soap opera *Guiding Light* finally ended after seventy-two years in September. The longest-running drama series ever moved to TV in 1952, and its 15,700 episodes included *Wizard of Oz* fantasies, time-travel, cloning and characters returning from the dead.

Meanwhile, on the same network's *The Young and the Restless*, an entire episode was narrated by an exhumed corpse (eighty-year-old Jeanne Cooper), and Marcia Wallace played a crazed knife-wielding psycho nurse named 'Annie' – a homage to Stephen King's *Misery*.

Sam Raimi was one of the producers on the CW's horror-themed game show, *Fear is Real*, in which contestants competed for a $66,666 prize.

Shown on BBC4 for Halloween, *Ghosts in the Machine*, narrated by Robert Hardy, was a fascinating look back at the supernatural – both imagined and "real" – on British television. It included clips from *Quatermass and the Pit*, *Whistle and I'll Come to You*, *Randall and Hopkirk (Deceased)*, *The Stone Tape*, *Ghostwatch*, *Sea of Souls*, *Crooked House* and other shows, along with interviews with Kim Newman, Mark Gattiss, Stephen Volk, Sir Jonathan Miller, Jane Asher, Kenneth Cope, Louise Jameson and Bill Paterson, amongst others.

The BBC's go-to man for horror, Mark Gatiss, hosted a new five-part series of *The Man in Black* on Radio 7, which debuted in October with "Phish Phood", a half-hour drama scripted by Kim Newman. The show's original concept dated back to the 1940s.

*Weird Tales* was an original series of four half-hour plays broadcast on Radio 4 in late January and February narrated by a character named "Lovecraft".

As a curtain-raiser to its week-long *Torchwood* event, the BBC broadcast three new forty-five-minute radio plays at the end of June on Radio 4's *Afternoon Play* slot. "Asylum", "Golden Age" and "The Dead Line" reunited John Barrowman as Captain Jack Harkness, Eve Myles as Gwen Cooper and Gareth David-Lloyd as Ianto Jones in stories about an unusual teenage runaway, a mystery surrounding Torchwood India and the cause of a coma-like plague in Cardiff.

For fans of classic radio SF, the same week Radio 4 revived the Charles Chilton's series *Journey Into Space* with a new half-hour story ("The Host") in which stiff space captain Jet Morgan (Toby Stephens) and his crew searched for life on one of Saturn's moons. The voice of the alien "Host" was performed by David Jacobs – the original voice of Jet Morgan in the 1950s.

Broadcast on Radio 4 in November, Nick Perry's first radio play, *The Loop*, was about a writer named Nick Perry struggling to write his first radio play who found himself talking on the phone with a stranger in New York in 1959 who was trying to write the first episode of a new TV series called *The Twilight Zone*.

Broadcast that same month, *It Was a Dark and Stormy Night* was a half-hour look at the life of Victorian author Edward Bulwer-Lytton, who coined the classic phrase in his now-forgotten novel *Paul Clifford*.

In December, Radio 4's *Book at Bedtime* featured a ten-part adaptation of *The Ingoldsby Legends*, a collection of myths, legends and ghost stories written by "Thomas Ingoldsby of Tappington Manor" (the Reverend Richard Harris Barham) and published in *Bentley's Miscellany* in 1837.

Derek Jacobi introduced five fifteen-minute adaptations *M.R. James at Christmas* on BBC Radio 7, featuring "Oh, Whistle, and I'll Come to You, My Lad", "The Tractate Middoth", "Lost Hearts", "The Rose Garden" and "Number 13".

*Dark Adventure Theatre Presents H.P. Lovecraft's Shadow Over Innsmouth* was the latest audio CD from the H.P. Lovecraft Historical Society. Along with the radio play adaptation, the package included a fishy scratch and sniff map, matchbook, postcard and newspaper clippings.

The recession and a strong dollar badly affected New York's theatre district with more than fourteen shows closing in the first two months of 2009. However, that didn't stop numerous new shows trying to attract an audience: *Shrek the Musical* opened on Broadway with Brian D'Arcy James playing the green-faced ogre and Sutton Foster as Princess Fiona, the object of his affections.

*The Toxic Avenger Musical*, based on the cult 1980s film series, opened in New York in April and ran for more than 300 performances. The show then moved on to Toronto, where it opened on Halloween.

Angela Lansbury and Rupert Everett starred in a hit Broadway revival of Noël Coward's 1941 play *Blithe Spirit*. The show ran for four months and Lansbury won a Tony Award for her performance as the eccentric medium, Madame Arcati.

Ahead of its Broadway premiere, *The Addams Family* musical opened in Chicago in November with Nathan Lane playing Gomez and Bebe Neuwirth as Morticia.

*Creature from the Black Lagoon* was a twenty-five-minute Broadway-style musical that opened in July as an attraction at Universal Studios theme park in California. The production's climax featured a twenty-three-foot-tall puppet version of the Gill Man. However, the comedy show, staged by Tony Award-nominated director and choreographer Lynne Taylor-Corbett, was not really suitable for younger children, and it apparently closed early following unfavourable reviews.

*Thriller – Live*, a three-hour stage musical based around twenty-eight songs by Michael Jackson, opened at London's Lyric Theatre in January.

For fifteen days in May, Kevin Spacey's Old Vic theatre and the Punchdrunk company turned the disused British Rail tunnels under London's Waterloo Station into a free performance-installation entitled *Tunnel 228*, inspired by Fritz Lang's classic 1927 movie *Metropolis*. All 15,000 tickets, sponsored by Bloomberg, were claimed within hours of the venture being announced.

Mike Oldfield's 1973 album *Tubular Bells*, which provided the theme music for *The Exorcist*, was performed in cities across the world at 6.00 p.m. on June 6. The time and date – 666 – was a reference to the number of the Devil. The global event was held in London, Paris, Berlin, Milan, Sydney and elsewhere to promote a digitally remastered version of the popular album.

*The Woman in Black*, Stephen Mallatratt's stage adaptation of the 1983 novel by Susan Hill, celebrated its twentieth anniversary in London's West End with a gala performance in June.

In October, the city's Southwark Playhouse presented *Terror 2009*, a quartet of half-hour horror plays by Lucy Kirkwood, Mark Ravenhill, Anthony Neilsen and Neil LaBute. Under eighteen-year-olds were banned from the show, which featured two world premieres.

Terry Pratchett's YA historical desert island adventure *Nation* opened in November at London's Olivier National Theatre as a musical, while a stage version of Stephen King's *The Shawshank Redemption* closed the same month at Wyndham's Theatre amid allegations that a quote used to publicize the play was "misleading" because it referred to the 1994 film version.

In the improved multiplayer sequel game *Left 4 Dead 2*, four survivors of a zombie apocalypse worked together to overcome hordes of neck-biting and fire-retardant walking dead in the American South.

Creepy child Alma was back to spread terror in *Fear 2: Project Origin*, and Agent Chris Redfield was slaying zombies in Africa in Capcom's *Resident Evil 5*. To promote the latter game, severed body parts were scattered across a London bridge in March.

The following week, a publicity stunt to promote Sega's *Madworld* videogame also backfired when fake severed limbs left around London provoked outrage from MPs and decency campaigners.

*Wolfenstein* was an updated version of the old shooter game featuring evil Nazi monsters, while *Deep Space: Extraction* was a prequel to the hit SF game.

*Aliens: Colonial Marines* was based on the James Cameron movie, as was *Avatar: The Game*, a third-person shooter you could play in 3-D that was actually a prequel to the movie that inspired it.

*Harry Potter and the Half-Blood Prince* continued one of the most successful film tie-in franchises, and it was especially well suited for playing on the Wii system.

Also designed to tie in to the movie, *G.I. Joe: The Rise of Cobra* was an old-fashioned shooter game, and Dan Aykroyd, Bill Murray and Harold Ramis recreated their original roles for a new game version of *Ghostbusters*.

The Joker and his gang of crazies were running the madhouse in *Batman: Arkham Asylum*, and only the Dark Knight could stop them.

\*     \*     \*

Toy manufacturer Hasbro posted returns above expectations in the second quarter of 2009. The company made a £24 million profit, mostly as a result of the movie *Transformers: Revenge of the Fallen* sending children out to buy action figures.

For those with some spare cash in their pockets (£165 to be precise), *The Creature from the Black Lagoon Diorama* was a hand-painted polystone figure of the Gill Man holding his unconscious victim in a classic pose. There was also *The Creature from the Black Lagoon Super-Size Creepy Collector's Figure*, which stood 22 inches high.

Robert Pattinson and Kristen Stewart may have got their own *Twilight* dolls in November, but far more exciting was the 12-inch collector's action figure of William Marshall as Blacula, which came with three interchangeable heads.

The second in a series of deluxe action figures from George A. Romero's *Day of the Dead* was Dr Tongue, which featured the zombie's shotgun-blasted face and a rubbery tongue.

From Sideshow Collectibles, the 12-inch Vincent Price *Masque of the Red Death* figure from the 1964 movie came with a removable mask.

Available from St Martin's Press in a boxed set, *The Vampire Tarot* written and illustrated by Robert M. Place featured a four-colour, fully illustrated seventy-eight-card deck and booklet that explored the history of the undead from Bram Stoker's *Dracula* onwards.

Issued each month for fifteen months by Black Phoenix Alchemy Lab, Neil Gaiman's *Fifteen Painted Cards from a Vampire Tarot* featured a small bottle of perfume inspired by the story and a corresponding tarot card created by Madame Talbot. T-shirts were also available through the company's website, and all proceeds went to the Comic Book Legal Defense Fund.

A 22-inch metal animation skeleton of the 1933 King Kong, which was used in the climactic scenes where the giant ape scaled the Empire State Building, was sold at the London Christie's in November for £121,250 ($200,000) to an anonymous bidder.

Following the announcement in the Queen's Birthday Honours list, eighty-seven-year-old Christopher Lee was knighted by Prince Charles for services to drama and charity the day before Halloween. Meanwhile, the woollen cape the actor wore in

Hammer's 1958 *Dracula* (aka *Horror of Dracula*) was sold at auction in London for £26,400 ($43,290).

In January, the United States Postal Service issued a stamp to celebrate the 200th anniversary of the birth of Edgar Allan Poe. Later in the year there was a good chance that the USPS' stamp of *The Twilight Zone*, one of a set of twenty commemorating "Early TV Memories", might have diverted your letter to the fifth dimension. *Alfred Hitchcock Presents* and *The Lone Ranger* were among the other shows featured.

In June, the UK's Royal Mail issued a series of six "Mythical Creatures" postage stamps illustrated by Dave McKean. The presentation pack included a very short short story for each of them by Neil Gaiman.

The World Horror Convention 2009 was a complete disaster. Held in Winnipeg, Canada, April 30 – May 3, almost nobody showed up, despite a Guest of Honour list that included Conrad Williams, Edo van Belkom and F. Paul Wilson, artist Tommy Castillo and editor Joshua Gee. Tanith Lee was announced as the winner of the Grand Master Award.

The winners of the 2008 Bram Stoker Awards for Superior Achievement were announced at a banquet on June 13, held as part of the Horror Writers Association's excellent Stoker Awards Weekend in Burbank, California.

Stephen King's *Duma Key* was the recipient of the Novel award, and First Novel went to *The Gentling Box* by Lisa Mannetti. John R. Little's *Miranda* received the award for Long Fiction, and Sarah Langan's *The Lost* picked up Short Fiction. King's *Just After Sunset* was announced for Collection, *Unspeakable Horrors* edited by Vince A. Liaguano and Chad Helder collected Anthology, *A Hallowe'en Anthology* edited by Lisa Morton received Non-Fiction, and Bruce Boston's *The Nightmare Collection* topped the votes for Poetry Collection.

F. Paul Wilson and Chelsea Quinn Yarbro received Life Achievement Awards, the Specialty Press Award went to Larry and Debra Roberts for Bloodletting Press, Sèphera Girón received the Silver Hammer Award for outstanding service to the Horror Writers Association, and the President's Richard Laymon Service Award went to John R. Little.

Jasper Fforde, Gail Z. Martin and legendary scriptwriter Brian Clemens were the Guests of Honour, and Ian Watson was Master of Ceremonies at FantasyCon 2009, held on September 18–20 in Nottingham.

The winners of the British Fantasy Awards were announced at a banquet on the Saturday night. *The Dark Knight* and *Doctor Who* won two new awards for Best Film and Best Television, while *Locke & Key* by Joe Hill and Gabriel Rodriguez won Best Comic/Graphic Novel.

The Best Non-Fiction Award went to *Basil Copper: A Life in Books* edited by Stephen Jones, Vincent Chong won for Best Artist, and Andrew Hook's Elastic Press picked up the Best Small Press Award sponsored by PS Publishing.

Best Anthology was *The Mammoth Book of Best New Horror 19* and Best Collection was *Bull Running for Girls* by Allyson Bird (Screaming Dreams). Sarah Pinborough collected the Best Short Fiction Award for her story "Do You See" in *Myth-Understandings*, Tim Lebbon won the Best Novella Award for *The Reach of Children* (Humdrumming), and Graham Joyce was presented with the August Derleth Fantasy Award for Best Novel for *Memoirs of a Master Forger* (Gollancz).

The Karl Edward Wagner Award for Special Achievement went to Hayao Miyazaki and the Sydney J. Bounds Best Newcomer Award was presented to Joseph D'Lacey for his novel *Meat* (Bloody Books).

The World Fantasy Convention in San Jose, California, at least had nice weather to recommend it. Held on October 29–November 1, the Guests of Honour were Garth Nix, Lisa Snellings, Michael Swanwick, Ann and Jeff VanderMeer and Zoran Zivkovic, with Jay Lake as Toastmaster and Donald Sidney-Fryer and Richard A. Lupoff as Special Guests.

The World Fantasy Awards were announced on the Sunday at the banquet. Michael Walsh's Old Earth Books won the Special Award, Non-Professional for its Howard Waldrop collections, while the Special Award, Professional went to Kelly Link and Gavin J. Grant for their . . . er, small press imprints Small Beer Press and Big Mouth House.

Australian Shaun Tan won the Artist award; the Collection award went to *The Drowned Life* by Jeffrey Ford

(HarperPerennial) and *Paper Cities: An Anthology of Urban Fantasy* edited by Ekaterina Sedia (Senses Five Press) collected the Anthology.

Short Fiction was awarded to "26 Monkeys, Also the Abyss" by Kij Johnson (*Asimov's*) and Richard Bowes' "If Angels Fight" (*The Magazine of Fantasy & Science Fiction*) picked up the award for Novella.

The Novel award was a tie between *The Shadow Year* by Jeffrey Ford (Morrow) and *Tender Morsels* by Margo Lanagan (Allen & Unwin and Knopf).

At least the Life Achievement Awards for Ellen Asher and Jane Yolen made a bit more sense.

So when, exactly, did it become wrong to be honest about your views?

The reason I ask is that I have had a couple of recent experiences where people who I consider to be close friends took great offence to my unbiased opinion of their work.

I began in the genre by working my way up as a reviewer back in the 1970s and 1980s for a number of small press and later professional magazines, and I have always held the belief that I would rather get a negative review from a critic whose views I respect than a rave review from someone whose judgment I didn't.

It surely goes without saying that when you produce a piece of creative work – either as a writer, editor, artist, performer, musician or whatever – you leave yourself open to being reviewed. People either will or will not like your work. That's the nature of the business.

However, these days, it seems that anybody can be a critic. What people have to realize is that just because you can post a "review" on Amazon (anonymously!) or on your own blog telling the world why you like or dislike a certain thing, that does not necessarily make you a critic. It just makes you opinionated.

Any critic worth the title needs to support their comments with knowledge, experience and, perhaps most importantly of all, *critical acumen*. Otherwise, it's *just an opinion*.

I feel I have worked in this genre for enough years and read and seen enough material over the decades to have a pretty good idea of what works and what does not in the horror field (obviously still within the context of my own personal likes and dislikes).

So when an actor friend asked me what I thought of his new DVD project, I told him that although I considered his performance remarkable, I was disappointed by the packaging and felt that the supporting graphics let him and the production down. That apparently was not what he wanted to hear.

More recently, a Californian specialist bookstore cancelled its entire order of the previous edition of this anthology because I had happened to mention that, in my opinion, a book one of the owners was involved with putting together was not worthy of a major award nomination.

What I was perhaps not aware of at the time was that my actor friend wasn't actually interested in my opinion but probably just wanted to be told how good his product was, and, in the second instance, some people just can't take criticism – no matter how honestly and sincerely it is given.

I have to admit that this is apparently a cultural thing. Whereas the British will invariably tell you straight about what they think of something, many Americans would rather not say anything negative (presumably under the cultural delusion that "everybody's a winner").

Well, everybody's not. Just because you've written a story, published a book or produced a piece of art, it does not automatically mean that you have achieved anything special (no matter how many self-help manuals and reality TV talent shows tell you differently).

Once you put your work into the public arena, then you are leaving yourself open to criticism. Whether you ultimately agree with that criticism or not is entirely up to you, but I know I would prefer someone to tell me honestly what they liked or didn't like about my work rather than hide their true opinion behind false – or even worse, bland – platitudes.

But maybe that's because I've always tried to be honest in my opinions. If I think something is special, then I am more than happy to share my enthusiasm with the world. And if I don't care for it, then I will also express my convictions in a manner that I hope is at least a constructive and informed.

As a reviewer, if you are going to assert your opinions, then you have to do it honestly and without bias. And any creative person should be aware that they will sometimes have to accept the bad along with the good. Otherwise, how is that individual going to develop and hopefully mature in their chosen field?

Criticism can be both important and beneficial – but only when it is given knowledgeably and without prejudice. Which is useful because, as far as I am concerned, I simply do not believe anybody who tells me that they don't read, or don't care about, reviews of their own work.

I, for one, shall be look forward to seeing the comments about this volume . . .

The Editor
June, 2010

# MICHAEL KELLY

## The Woods

MICHAEL KELLY WAS BORN in Charlottetown, Prince Edward Island, Canada. He currently resides near Toronto.

A rising star of Canadian horror, he is the author of two short story collections, *Scratching the Surface*, and *Undertow and Other Laments*; and co-author of a novel, *Ouroboros*. *Apparitions*, an anthology he edited and published under his own literary imprint, Undertow Publications, was nominated for a Shirley Jackson Award.

About the first of two stories he has in this volume, the author reveals: "'The Woods' was written for an anthology seeking regional horror and ghost stories. I'd just read Hemingway's 'Hills Like White Elephant's'. Now, in no way am I comparing myself to Hemingway but I wanted to write a similarly brief tale, with only two main characters, and where the horror was off-stage. As well, the setting had to be distinctly Canadian. What, I thought, could be more Canadian than the frozen north and allusions to mythical beasts?"

IT HAD BEEN SNOWING FOR DAYS. Icy needles of teeth tumbled from the ash-flecked sky, clotted the woods.

The thick shroud of snow shifted, moved with the weeping wind, pushed against a cabin. A bug-bright snowmobile rested near a leaning woodshed like some alien invader, its engine cooling, ticking, though the two men inside the cabin could not hear this. They could hear nothing of the outside world but the wind and its ceaseless winter lament.

Inside, logs crackled and smouldered in a fireplace. A black cast-iron pot hung above the small fire, suspended from a metal rod attached to stanchions. A spicy tang permeated the cabin.

The old man in the old rocking-chair, who had a face like tree bark, blinked crusty eyes, looked up at the younger man (who nonetheless was near retirement himself but was still much younger than the old man in the chair) and gestured to the only other chair in the cabin. "Have a seat, Officer Creed."

The younger man grinned weakly. "How many times I have to tell you, Jack, you don't have to call me that. It's just the two of us. We go back a long way."

The old man blinked again, nodded, stared at the younger man's uniform; the gold badge on the parka, the gun holstered at his side. "Well, Ned," croaked the old man, "it looks like you're out here on business, so it's only proper."

Ned clutched a small, furry, dead animal, fingers digging deep. He sat on the proffered chair, laid the dead thing on the floor, where it resembled a hat. "We go back a long way," he repeated, wistful.

They were silent for a time. The old man rocked slowly and the pine floor creaked. Ned stared at his wet boots, glanced out the window at the swirling sheets of grey-white.

Jack stopped rocking. "Get you some coffee, Ned?"

"No, thanks. Can't stay long. Have to get back before the storm comes full on."

A sad chuckle came from the old man. "You may be too late."

"I fear I am, Jack."

Another brief silence ensued. Jack rocked slowly and Ned brushed wet snow from his pants.

"You still trapping?" Ned asked. "Still getting out?"

Jack paused, as if carefully considering his words. "Course I am. I'm old, not dead." Another brief pause, then, "Man's got to eat."

"That's why I'm here."

"I see."

"We go back a long way, don't we, Jack?"

The old man blinked, nodded.

"I mean, you'd tell me if you needed anything, wouldn't you? You'd tell me if anything was wrong?"

The old man leaned forward. "Checking up on me, Ned?"

"You might be snowbound awhile, is all. Just doing my job. You're like a ghost out here."

Jack eased back into the rocker. "Pantry is stocked. Plenty of rabbit in the woodshed."

Ned grimaced. "You were always a good trapper."

"Been here a long, long time, Ned. You do something often enough you get good at it."

"True enough."

"You learn about things," Jack said. "By necessity. You learn how the world works. The good. The bad. All of it."

"Hmm, yes."

"I know things," Jack said. He was staring hard at Ned. "But . . . tell me, what do you know, Ned?"

Ned fidgeted, returned Jack's look. "Not as much as you, Jack. That's the gospel. I know certain things, that's all. And other stuff I'm not so certain about. Trying to figure things out, is all."

"Oh, you're a sly one, aren't you, Ned?"

Ned turned away, sighed, gazed at the window. "Not so much. No."

"What do you see?" Jack asked.

"I can just make out a few trees. Nothing else. The woods and nothing."

"I know these woods like the back of my hand."

"I bet you do," Ned said.

Gusts of blowing snow swept past the window, a curtain of ice. The cabin door groaned. Each man sat, staring at the other, stealing glances at the window, then the door, expectant, as if waiting for a visitor.

Ned broke the silence. "Tom Brightman's got a spot of trouble."

Jack's face creased into a sneer. "You don't say."

"Wendigo," Ned whispered, as if afraid to say it aloud.

Jack sniggered. "That old saw again?"

"I'm afraid so." Ned scratched his head. "Every year. The same old superstitions. We've heard them all, me and you. We go back some ways."

"Stop saying that."

"It's true, though. There's not much between us. Is there, Jack? There are no secrets in these parts."

"Yes," Jack said.

Ned stretched his legs out, crossed them, uncrossed them. A log in the fireplace popped, split. The room smelled of spice and meat and wet fur. He turned toward the fire.

Jack followed Ned's gaze. "Get you something to eat? To tide you over?"

"No." Ned squirmed. "You hungry, Jack?"

"All the time. Seems the older I get, the hungrier I get." Jack stared off into a far corner. "It's not something I can explain. Not something you'd understand."

Ned gestured to the pot. "Don't mind me. Help yourself."

Jack smirked, swung his gaze around to Ned. "It's okay, I'll wait. I've some manners still."

"You've got a nice little set up out here, Jack. All by yourself. No one around for miles. Must get mighty lonely at times, I'd imagine."

The old man shrugged. "Not really. A man can find plenty of things to occupy his time. Idle hands and all that."

"That's what worries me, Jack. This place, this solitude, this . . . *nothingness*. It does things to people." Ned leaned forward, nodded toward the window. "You ever spot anything out there, in the woods? Anything . . . *strange*?"

"Ha." Jack's tree-bark face glowed orange from the fire, a winter pumpkin. "Stealthy man-eating beasts, Ned? Slavering cannibals? Wendigo?"

Ned blinked, watched Jack, said nothing.

"Tom Brightman is a damn fool," Jack said. "Every year it's the same damn thing. Can't control his dogs so he blames everyone else. Myths. Legends. Old wives' tales. Easier for some men to cast blame than take responsibility."

"What do you know about such things, Jack?"

"How many, Ned? How many of his sled dogs have gone missing this year?"

"None." Ned straightened and leaned forward. Rigid and intent. "It's the youngest boy. Johnny. Been gone a week now."

Jack was quiet. He began to rock slowly. Then, "He's a damn fool."

"May very well be." Ned scratched his chin. "You positive there's nothing I can get you, Jack? Nothing you need?"

"Nothing."

"Don't suppose," Ned asked, "at this point it'd make a lick of difference if I peeked into the woodshed on my way out? To make sure?"

"Not a lick, Ned. Not at this point."

Ned picked up his hat, stood, let out a heavy breath. "That's what I thought." He pulled the hat over his head, went to the door, opened it a crack and peered into the gathering white nothingness. "I'll try and swing by later in the week, Jack. Watch yourself." He shoved through the gap, into the outside, pulled the door shut.

The old man rose from the rocking chair and scuttled across the worn pine floor. He went to the window, pressed his face against the frost-veined pane and spied the younger man, a blurry black smudge, trudging through the blizzard. The younger man stopped at the woodshed, pulled open the door and slipped inside.

Jack watched. Waited. It had been snowing forever. Glassy shards struck the ground, formed an icy shell. He thought surely that the world would crack, that *something* would crack.

Ned exited the shed, paused, gazed back at the cabin, shambled over to his snowmobile. Soon, the white swallowed him.

Jack turned, walked to the cupboards, grabbed a chipped bowl and a spoon, and went over to the fireplace and the pot. Stew bubbled and simmered in the pot. His stomach grumbled, empty, always empty. It wasn't something he could explain. Wasn't something that he understood. A vast emptiness inside him. Nothingness.

He ladled stew into the bowl, spooned the hot meal into his mouth. Chewed. Swallowed. His thoughts turned to Tom Brightman, his dogs, his son . . . and his daughters.

Jack ate. The emptiness abated. Then he didn't think about anything except the woods.

The woods and nothing.

# JOE HILL and STEPHEN KING

## Throttle

JOSEPH HILLSTRÖM KING WAS born in Bangor, Maine, in 1972. He is the second child of authors Stephen and Tabitha King. Under the pseudonym "Joe Hill" he burst upon the literary scene with his acclaimed first collection of short stories, *20th Century Ghosts*, and quickly followed it up with the best-selling novels *Heart-Shaped Box* and *Horns*.

As a comic-book writer, IDW has issued the second volume of his series *Locke & Key: Head Games* in hardcover, and *Locke & Key: Keys to the Kingdom*, the fourth arc in the series, was recently published by the same imprint. He is currently working on a new novel.

Hill is a winner of the World Fantasy Award, the Bram Stoker Award, two British Fantasy awards, the Ray Bradbury Fellowship, the William L. Crawford Award for Best New Fantasy Writer and the Sydney J. Bounds Award for Best Newcomer.

Stephen King is the world's most famous and successful horror writer. His first novel, *Carrie*, appeared in 1974, and since then he has published a phenomenal string of best-sellers, including *Salem's Lot*, *The Shining*, *The Stand*, *Dead Zone*, *Firestarter*, *Cujo*, *Pet Sematary*, *Christine*, *It*, *Misery*, *The Dark Half*, *Needful Things*, *Rose Madder*, *The Green Mile*, *Bag of Bones*, *The Colorado Kid*, *Lisey's Story* and *Duma Key*, to name only a few.

The author's short fiction and novellas have been collected in *Night Shift, Different Seasons, Skeleton Crew, Four Past Midnight, Nightmares and Dreamscapes, Hearts in Atlantis, Everything's Eventual, The Secretary of Dreams* (two volumes), *Just After Sunset: Stories* and *Stephen King Goes to the Movies. Full Dark, No Stars* is a new collection of four novellas.

The winner of numerous awards – including both the Horror Writers Association and World Fantasy Convention Lifetime Achievement Awards, and a Medal for Distinguished Contribution to American Letters from the National Book Foundation – he lives with his wife in Bangor, Maine.

"Throttle" was written for an anthology celebrating the work of genre giant Richard Matheson. Inspired by Matheson's 1971 story, "Duel", which was filmed that same year by a young Steven Spielberg, it marks the first-ever collaboration between father and son.

"My dad showed me *Duel* when I was about eight years old," recalls Hill. "He had it on video disc, the format that preceded DVD – it was exactly like DVD, except the movies came on these enormous record-sized silver platters, with twenty minutes of video on each side. A single movie was usually spread across about six discs and you had to keep getting up to flip 'em over, or to put a new one in.

"I know we watched *Duel* at least four times one summer, and that we would talk about it when we went on drives, imagining what we would do if *we* had The Truck after us. My dad also led me to the novels and stories of Richard Matheson – stories marked by a lack of adornment, Freudian subtexts, and a relentless commitment to cranking up the suspense.

"Matheson's novella 'Duel' is no exception. When the chance came up to do a story for *He Is Legend*, an anthology of original stories inspired by and honouring the fiction of Richard Matheson, it seemed natural for the two of us to jump in together. And we had a blast."

"Joe called me and explained that someone was doing a book of Richard Matheson tribute stories, and proposed that we do a riff on 'Duel'," adds King. "I was thrilled, because it gave me a chance to work with two writers I admire . . . at the same time!"

THEY RODE WEST FROM THE SLAUGHTER, through the painted desert, and did not stop until they were a hundred miles away. Finally, in the early afternoon, they turned in at a diner with a white stucco exterior and pumps on concrete islands out front. The overlapping thunder of their engines shook the plate glass windows as they rolled by. They drew up together among parked long-haul trucks, on the west side of the building, and there they put down their kickstands and turned off their bikes.

Race Adamson had led them the whole way, his Harley running sometimes as much as a quarter-mile ahead of anyone else's. It had been Race's habit to ride out in front ever since he had returned to them, after two years in the sand. He ran so far in front it often seemed he was daring the rest of them to try and keep up, or maybe had a mind to simply leave them behind. He hadn't wanted to stop here but Vince had forced him to. As the diner came into sight, Vince had throttled after Race, blown past him, and then shot his hand left in a gesture The Tribe knew well: *follow me off the highway*. The Tribe let Vince's hand-gesture call it, as they always did. Another thing for Race to dislike about him, probably. The kid had a pocketful of them.

Race was one of the first to park, but the last to dismount. He stood astride his bike, slowly stripping off his leather riding gloves, glaring at the others from behind his mirrored sunglasses.

"You ought to have a talk with your boy," Lemmy Chapman said to Vince. Lemmy nodded in Race's direction.

"Not here," Vince said. It could wait until they were back in Vegas. He wanted to put the road behind him. He wanted to lie down in the dark for a while, wanted some time to allow the sick knot in his stomach to abate. Maybe most of all, he wanted to shower. He hadn't got any blood on him, but felt contaminated all the same, and wouldn't be at ease in his own skin until he had washed the morning's stink off.

He took a step in the direction of the diner, but Lemmy caught his arm before he could go any further. "Yes. Here."

Vince looked at the hand on his arm – Lemmy didn't let go, Lemmy of all the men had no fear of him – then glanced toward the kid, who wasn't really a kid at all any more and hadn't been for years. Race was opening the hardcase over his back tyre, fishing through his gear for something.

"What's to talk about? Clarke's gone. So's the money. There's nothing left to do. Not this morning."

"You ought find out if Race feels the same way. You been assuming the two of you are on the same page even though these days he spends forty minutes of every hour pissed off at you. Tell you something else, boss. Race brought some of these guys in, and he got a lot of them fired up, talking about how rich they were all going to get on his deal with Clarke. He might not be the only one who needs to hear what's next." He glanced meaningfully at the other men. Vince noticed for the first time that they weren't drifting on into the diner, but hanging around by their bikes, casting looks towards him and Race both. Waiting for something to come to pass.

Vince didn't want to talk. The thought of talk drained him. Lately, conversation with Race was like throwing a medicine ball back and forth, a lot of wearying effort, and he didn't feel up to it, not with what they were driving away from.

He went anyway, because Lemmy was almost always right when it came to Tribe preservation. Lemmy had been riding six to Vince's twelve going back to when they had met in the Mekong Delta and the whole world was *dinky dau*. They had been on the look-out for tripwires and buried mines then. Nothing much had changed in the almost forty years since.

Vince left his bike and crossed to Race, who stood between his Harley and a parked truck, an oil hauler. Race had found what he was looking for in the hardcase on the back of his bike, a flask sloshing with what looked like tea and wasn't. He drank earlier and earlier, something else Vince didn't like. Race had a pull, wiped his mouth, held it out to Vince. Vince shook his head.

"Tell me," Vince said.

"If we pick up Route 6," Race said, "we could be down in Show Low in three hours. Assuming that pussy rice-burner of yours can keep up."

"What's in Show Low?"

"Clarke's sister."

"Why would we want to see her?"

"For the money. Case you hadn't noticed, we just got fucked out of sixty grand."

"And you think his sister will have it."

"Place to start."

"Let's talk about it back in Vegas. Look at our options there."

"How about we look at 'em now? You see Clarke hanging up the phone when we walked in? I heard a snatch of what he was saying through the door. I think he tried to get his sister, and when he didn't, he left a message with someone who knows her. Now why do you think he felt a pressing need to reach out and touch that toerag as soon as he saw all of us in the driveway?"

To say his goodbyes was Vince's theory, but he didn't tell Race that. "She doesn't have anything to do with this, does she? What's she do? She make crank too?"

"No. She's a whore."

"Jesus. What a family."

"Look who's talking," Race said.

"What's that mean?" Vince asked. It wasn't the line that bothered him, with its implied insult, so much as Race's mirrored sunglasses, which showed a reflection of Vince himself, sunburnt and a beard full grey, looking puckered, lined, and old.

Race stared down the shimmering road again and when he spoke he didn't answer the question. "Sixty grand, up in smoke, and you can just shrug it off."

"I didn't shrug anything off. That's what happened. Up in smoke."

Race and Dean Clarke had met in Fallujah – or maybe it had been Tikrit. Clarke a medic specializing in pain management, his treatment of choice being primo dope accompanied by generous helpings of Wyclef Jean. Race's specialties had been driving Humvees and not getting shot. The two of them had remained friends back in The World, and Clarke had come to Race half a year ago, with the idea of setting up a meth lab in Smith Lake. He figured sixty grand would get him started, and that he'd be making more than that per month in no time.

"True glass," that had been Clarke's pitch. "None of that cheap green shit, just true glass." Then he'd raised his hand above his head, indicating a monster stack of cash. "Sky's the limit, yo?"

*Yo.* Vince thought now he should have pulled out the minute he heard that come out of Clarke's mouth. The very second.

But he hadn't. He'd even helped Race out with twenty grand of his own money, in spite of his doubts. Clarke was a slacker-looking guy who bore a passing resemblance to Kurt Cobain: long blond hair and layered shirts. He said *yo*, he called everyone *man*, he talked about how drugs broke through the oppressive power of the overmind. Whatever that meant. He surprised and charmed Race with intellectual gifts: plays by Sartre, mix tapes featuring spoken word poetry and reggae dub.

Vince didn't resent Clarke for being an egghead full of spiritual-revolution talk that came out in some bullshit half-breed language, part Pansy and part Ebonics. What disconcerted Vince was that when they met, Clarke already had a stinking case of meth mouth, his teeth falling out and his gums spotted. Vince didn't mind making money off the shit, but had a knee-jerk distrust of anyone gamy enough to use it.

And still he put up money, had wanted something to work out for Race, especially after the way he had been run out of the army. And for a while, when Race and Clarke were hammering out the details, Vince had even half-talked himself into believing it might pay off. Race seemed, briefly, to have an air of almost cocky self-assurance, had even bought a car for his girlfriend, a used Mustang, anticipating the big return on his investment.

Only the meth lab caught fire, yo? And the whole thing burned to a shell in the space of ten minutes, the very first day of operation. The wetbacks who worked inside escaped out the windows, and were standing around, burnt and sooty, when the fire trucks arrived. Now most of them were in the county lock-up.

Race had learned about the fire, not from Clarke, but from Bobby Stone, another friend of his from Iraq, who had driven out to Smith Lake to buy ten grand worth of the mythical true glass, but who turned around when he saw the smoke and the flashing lights. Race had tried to raise Clarke on the phone, but couldn't get him, not that afternoon, not in the evening. By eleven, The Tribe was on the highway, headed east to find him.

They had caught Dean Clarke at his cabin in the hills, packing to go. He told them he had been just about to leave to come see Race, tell him what happened, work out a new plan. He said he was going to pay them all back. He said the money was gone now, but there were possibilities, there were contingency plans. He said he was so goddamn fucking sorry. Some of it was lies, and some of it was true, especially the part about being so goddamn fucking sorry, but none of it surprised Vince, not even when Clarke began to cry.

What surprised him – what surprised all of them – was Clarke's girlfriend hiding in the bathroom, dressed in daisy print panties and a sweatshirt that said CORMAN HIGH VARSITY. All of seventeen and soaring on meth and clutching a little .22 in one hand. She was listening in when Roy Klowes asked Clarke if she was around, said that if Clarke's bitch blew all of them, they could cross two hundred bucks off the debt right there. Roy Klowes had walked in the bathroom, taking his cock out of his pants to have a leak, but the girl had thought he was unzipping for other reasons and opened fire. Her first shot went wide and her second shot went into the ceiling, because by then Roy was whacking her with his machete, and it was all sliding down the red hole, away from reality and into the territory of bad dream.

"I'm sure he lost some of the money," Race said. "Could be he lost as much as half what we set him up. But if you think Dean Clarke put the entire sixty grand into that one trailer, I can't help you."

"Maybe he did have some of it tucked away. I'm not saying you're wrong. But I don't see why it would wind up with the sister. Could just as easily be in a Mason jar, buried somewhere in his backyard. I'm not going to pick on some pathetic hooker for fun. If we find out she's suddenly come into money, that's a different story."

"I was six months setting this deal up. And I'm not the only one with a lot riding on it."

"Okay. Let's talk about how to make it right in Vegas."

"Talk isn't going to make anything right. Riding is. His sister is in Show Low today, but when she finds out her brother and his little honey got painted all over their ranch—"

"You want to keep your voice down," Vince said.

Lemmy watched them with his arms folded across his chest, a few feet to Vince's left, but ready to move if he had to get between them. The others stood in groups of two and three, bristly and road dirty, wearing leather jackets or denim vests with the gang's patch on them: a skull in an Indian head-dress, above the legend THE TRIBE • LIVE ON THE ROAD, DIE ON THE ROAD. They had always been The Tribe, although none of them was Indian, except for Peaches, who claimed to be half-Cherokee, except when he felt like saying he was half-Spaniard or half-Inca. Doc said he could be half-Eskimo and half-Viking if he wanted, it still added up to all retard.

"The money is gone," Vince said to his son. "The six months too. *See it.*"

His son stood there, the muscles bunched in his jaw, not speaking. His knuckles white on the flask in his right hand. Looking at him now, Vince was struck with a sudden image of Race at the age of six, face just as dusty as it was now, tooling around the gravel driveway on his green Big Wheels, making revving noises down in his throat. Vince and Mary had laughed and laughed, mostly at the screwed-up look of intensity on their son's face, the Kindergarten road warrior. He couldn't find the humour in it now, not two hours after Race had split a man's head open with a shovel. Race had always been fast, and had been the first to catch up to Clarke when he tried to run, in the confusion after the girl started shooting. Maybe he had not meant to kill him. Race had only hit him the once.

Vince opened his mouth to say something more, but there was nothing more. He turned away, started towards the diner. He had not gone three steps, though, when he heard a bottle explode behind him. He turned and saw Race had thrown the flask into the side of the oil rig, had thrown it exactly in the place Vince had been standing only five seconds before. Throwing it at Vince's shadow maybe.

Whisky and chunks of glass dribbled down the battered oil tank. Vince glanced up at the side of the tanker and twitched involuntarily at what he saw there. There was a word stencilled on the side and for an instant Vince thought it said SLAUGHTERIN. But no. It was LAUGHLIN. What Vince knew about Freud could be summed up in less than twenty words – dainty little white beard, cigar, thought kids wanted to fuck their parents – but you didn't need to know much psychology to recognize a guilty subconscious at work. Vince would've laughed if not for what he saw next.

The trucker was sitting in the cab. His hand hung out the driver's-side window, a cigarette smouldering between two fingers. Midway up his forearm was a faded tattoo, DEATH

BEFORE DISHONOR, which made him a vet, something Vince noted, in a distracted sort of way, and immediately filed away, perhaps for later consideration, perhaps not. He tried to think what the guy might've heard, measure the danger, figure out if there was a pressing need to haul Laughlin out of his truck and straighten him out about a thing or two.

Vince was still considering it when the semi rumbled to noisy, stinking life. Laughlin pitched his ciggie into the parking lot and released his air brakes. The stacks belched black diesel smoke and the truck began to roll, tyres crushing gravel. As the tanker moved away, Vince let out a slow breath, and felt the tension begin to drain away. He doubted if the guy had heard anything, and what did it matter if he had? No one with any sense would want to get involved in their shitpull. Laughlin must've realized he had been caught listening in and decided to get while the getting was good.

By the time the eighteen-wheeler eased out on to the two-lane highway, Vince had already turned away, brushing through his crew and making for the diner. It was almost an hour before he saw the truck again.

Vince went to piss – his bladder had been killing him for going on thirty miles – and on his return he passed by the others, sitting in two booths. They were quiet, almost no sound from them at all, aside from the scrape of forks on plates, and the clink of glasses being set down. Only Peaches was talking, and that was to himself. Peaches spoke in a whisper, and occasionally seemed to flinch, as if surrounded by a cloud of imaginary midges . . . a dismal, unsettling habit of his. The rest of them occupied their own interior spaces, not seeing each other, staring inwardly at who-knew-what instead. Some of them were probably seeing the bathroom after Roy Klowes finished chopping up the girl. Others might be remembering Clarke face down in the dirt beyond the back door, his ass in the air and his pants full of shit and the steel-bladed shovel planted in his skull, the handle sticking in the air. And then there were probably a few wondering if they would be home in time for *American Gladiators*, and whether the lottery tickets they had bought yesterday were winners.

It had been different on the way down to see Clarke. Better. The Tribe had stopped just after sunup at a diner much like this, and while the mood had not been festive, there had been plenty of bullshit, and a certain amount of predictable yuks to go with the coffee and the donuts. Doc had sat in one booth doing the crossword puzzle, others seated around him, looking over his shoulder, and ribbing each other about what an honour it was to sit with a man of such education. Doc had done time, like most of the rest of them, and had a gold tooth in his mouth in place of one that had been whacked out by a cop's nightstick a few years before. But he wore bifocals, and had lean, almost patrician features, and read the paper, and knew things, like the capital of Kenya and the players in the Wars of the Roses. Roy Klowes took a sidelong look at Doc's puzzle and said, "What I need is a crossword with questions about fixing bikes or cruising pussy. Like what's a four-letter word for what I do to your momma, Doc? I could answer that one."

Doc frowned. "I'd say 'repulse', but that's seven letters. So I guess my answer would have to be 'gall'."

"Gall?" Roy asked, scratching his head.

"That's right. You gall her. Means you show up and she wants to spit."

"Yeah and that's what pisses me off about her. 'Cause I been trying to train her to swaller while I gall her."

And the men just about fell off their stools laughing. They had been laughing just as hard the next booth over, where Peaches was trying to tell them about why he got his nuts clipped: "What sold me on it was when I saw that I'd only ever have to pay for one vasectomy . . . which is not something you can say about abortion. There's theoretically no limit there. *None.* Every jizzwad is a potential budget buster. You don't recognize that until you've had to pay for a couple of scrapes and begin to think there might be a better use for your money. Also, relationships aren't ever the same after you've had to flush Junior down the toilet. They just aren't. Voice of experience right here." Peaches didn't need jokes, he was funny enough just saying what was on his mind.

Now Vince moved past the cored out, red-eyed bunch, and took a stool at the counter beside Lemmy.

"What do you think we ought to do about this shit when we get to Vegas?" Vince asked.

"Run away," Lemmy said. "Tell no one we're going. Never look back."

Vince laughed. Lemmy didn't. He lifted his coffee halfway to his lips but didn't drink, only looked at it for a few seconds and then put it down.

"Somethin' wrong with that?" Vince asked.

"It ain't the coffee that's wrong."

"You aren't going to tell me you're serious about taking off, are you?"

"We wouldn't be the only ones, buddy," Lemmy said. "What Roy did to that girl in the bathroom?"

"She almost shot him," Vince said, voice low so no one else could hear.

"She wasn't but seventeen."

Vince did not reply and anyway no reply was expected.

"Most of these guys have never seen anything that heavy and I think a bunch – the smart ones – are going to scatter to the four corners of the earth, as soon as they can. Find a new purpose for being." Vince laughed again, but Lemmy only glanced at him sidelong. "Listen now, Cap. I killed my brother driving blind drunk when I was eighteen. And when I woke up I could smell his blood all over me. I tried to kill myself in the Corps to make up for it, but the boys in the black pyjamas wouldn't help me. And what I remember mostly about the war is the way my own feet smelled when they got jungle rot. Like carrying a toilet around in my boots. I been in jail, like you, and what was worst wasn't the things I did or saw done. What was worst was the smell on everyone. Armpits and assholes. And that was all bad. But none of it has anything on the Charlie Manson shit we're driving away from. Thing I can't get away from is how it stank in the place. After it was over. Like being stuck in a closet where someone took a shit. Not enough air, and what there was wasn't any good." He paused, turned on his stool to look sidelong at Vince. "You know what I been thinking about ever since we drove away? Lon Refus moved out to Denver and opened a garage. He sent me a postcard of the Flatirons. I been wondering if he could use an old guy to twist a wrench for him. I been thinking I could get used to the smell of pines."

He was quiet again, then shifted his gaze to look at the other men in their booths. "The half that doesn't take a walk will be looking to get back what they lost, one way or another, and you don't want any part of how they're going to do it. 'Cause there's going to be more of this crazy meth shit. This is just beginning; the tollbooth where you get on the turnpike. There's too much money in it to quit, and everyone who sells it does it too, and the ones who do it make big fucking messes. The girl who tried to shoot Roy was on it, which is why she tried to kill him, and Roy is on it himself, which is why he had to whack her forty fucking times with his asshole machete. Who the fuck besides a meth-head carries a machete, anyhow?"

"Don't get me started on Roy. I'd like to stick Little Boy up his ass and watch the light shoot out his eyes," Vince told him, and it was Lemmy's turn to laugh then. Coming up with deranged uses for Little Boy was one of the running jokes between them. Vince said, "Go on. Say your say. You been thinkin' about it the last hour."

"How would you know that?"

"You think I don't know what it means when I see you sittin' straight up on your sled?"

Lemmy grunted and said, "Sooner or later the cops are going to land on Roy or one of these other crankies and they'll take everyone around them down with them. Because Roy and the guys like him aren't smart enough to get rid of the shit they stole from crime scenes. None of them is smart enough not to brag to their girlfriends about what they been up to. Hell. Half of them are carrying rock right now. All I'm saying."

Vince scrubbed a hand along the side of his beard. "You keep talking about the two halves, the half that's going to take off and the half that isn't. You want to tell me which half Race is in?"

Lemmy turned his head and grinned unhappily, showing the chip in his tooth again. "You need to ask?"

The truck with LAUGHLIN on the side was labouring uphill when they caught up to it around three in the afternoon.

The highway wound its lazy way up a long grade, through a series of switchbacks. With all the curves there was no obvious place to pass. Race was out front again. After they departed from the diner, he had sped off, increasing his lead on the rest of The Tribe by so much that sometimes Vince lost sight of him altogether. But when they reached the truck, his son was riding the guy's bumper.

The ten of them rode up the hill in the rig's boiling wake. Vince's eyes began to tear and run.

"*Fucking truck*," Vince screamed, and Lemmy nodded. Vince's lungs were tight and his chest hurt from breathing its exhaust and it was hard to see. "*Get your miserable fat ass truck out of the way!*" Vince hollered.

It was a surprise, catching up to the truck here. They weren't that far from the diner . . . twenty miles, no more. LAUGHLIN must've pulled over somewhere else for a while – but there was nowhere else. Possibly he had parked his rig in the shade of a billboard for a siesta. Or threw a tyre and needed to stop and put on a new one. Did it matter? It didn't. Vince wasn't even sure why it was on his mind, but it nagged.

Just past the next bend in the road, Race leaned his Softail Deuce into the lane for oncoming traffic, lowered his head, and accelerated from thirty to seventy. The bike squatted, then *leaped*. He cut in front of the truck as soon as he was ahead of it – slipping back into the right-hand lane just as a pale yellow Lexus blew past, going the other way. The driver of the Lexus pounded her horn, but the *meep-meep* sound of it was almost immediately lost in the overpowering wail of the truck's air horn.

Vince had spotted the Lexus coming and for a moment had been sure he was about to see his son go head on into it, Race one second, roadmeat the next. It took a few moments for his heart to come back down out of his throat.

"*Fucking psycho*," Vince yelled at Lemmy.

"*You mean the guy in the truck?*" Lemmy hollered back, as the blast of the air horn finally died away. "*Or Race?*"

"*Both!*"

By the time the truck swung through the next curve, though, Laughlin seemed to have come to his senses, or had finally looked in the mirror and noticed the rest of The Tribe roaring along behind him. He put his hand out the window – that sun-darkened and veiny hand, big-knuckled and blunt-fingered – and waved them by.

Immediately, Roy and two others swung out and thundered past. The rest went in twos. It was nothing to pass once the go-to was clear, the truck labouring along at barely thirty. Vince and Lemmy swept out last, passing just before the next switchback. Vince cast a look up toward the driver on their way by, but could see nothing except that dark hand hanging out against the door. Five minutes later they had left the truck so far behind them they couldn't hear it any more.

There followed a stretch of high open desert, sage and saguaro, cliffs off to the right, striped in chalky shades of yellow and red. They were riding into the sun now, pursued by their own lengthening shadows. Houses and a few trailers whipped by as they blew through a sorry excuse for a township. The bikes were strung out across almost half a mile, with Vince and Lemmy riding close to the back. But not far beyond the town, Vince saw the rest of The Tribe bunched up at the side of the road, just before a four-way intersection – the crossing for Route 6.

Beyond the intersection, to the west, the highway they had been following was torn down to dirt. A diamond shaped orange sign read CONSTRUCTION NEXT 20 MILES BE PREPARED TO STOP. In the distance, Vince could see dump trucks and a grader. Men worked in clouds of red smoke, the clay stirred up and drifting across the tableland.

He hadn't known there would be roadwork here, because they hadn't come this way. It had been Race's suggestion to return by the backroads, which had suited Vince fine. Driving away from a double homicide, it seemed like a good idea to keep a low profile. Of course that wasn't why Race had suggested it.

"What?" Vince said, slowing and putting his foot down. As if he didn't already know.

Race pointed away from the construction, down Route 6. "We go south on 6, we can pick up I-40."

"In Show Low," Vince said. "Why does this not surprise me?"

It was Roy Klowes spoke next. He jerked a thumb towards the dump trucks. "Bitch of a lot better than doing five an hour through that shit for twenty miles. No thank you. I'd rather ride easy and maybe pick up sixty grand along the way. That's my think on it."

"Did it hurt?" Lemmy asked Roy. "Having a thought? I hear it hurts the first time. Like when a chick gets her cherry popped."

"Fuck you, Lemmy," Roy said.

"When I want your think," Vince said, "I'll be sure to ask for it, Roy. But I wouldn't hold your breath."

Race spoke, his voice calm, reasonable. "We get to Show Low, you don't have to stick around. Neither of you. No one's going to hold it against you if you just want to ride on."

So there it was.

Vince looked from face to face. The young men met his gaze. The older ones, the ones who had been riding with him for decades, did not.

"I'm glad to hear no one will hold it against me," Vince said. "I was worried."

A memory struck him then: riding with his son in a car at night, in the GTO, back in the days he was trying to go straight, be a family man for Mary. The details of the journey were lost now; he couldn't recall where they were coming from or where they had been going. What he remembered was looking into the rear-view mirror at his ten-year-old's dusty, sullen face. They had stopped at a hamburger stand, but the kid didn't want dinner, said he wasn't hungry. The kid would only settle for a Popsicle, then bitched when Vince came back with lime instead of grape. He wouldn't eat it, let the Popsicle melt on the leather. Finally, when they were twenty miles away from the hamburger stand, Race announced that his belly was growling.

Vince had looked into the rear-view mirror and said, "You know just because I'm your father doesn't mean I got to like you." And the boy had stared back, his chin dimpling, struggling not to cry, but unwilling to look away. Returning Vince's look with bright, hating eyes. Why had Vince said that? The notion crossed his mind that if he had known some other way to talk to Race, there would've been no Fallujah and no dishonourable discharge for ditching his squad, taking off in a Humvee while mortars fell; there would've been no Dean Clarke and no meth lab and the boy would not feel the need to be out front all the time, blasting along at seventy on his hotshit jackpuppy when the rest of them were doing sixty. It was him the kid was trying to leave behind. He had been trying all his life.

Vince squinted back the way they had come ... and there was that goddamn truck again. Vince could see it through the trembling waves of heat on the road, so it seemed half-mirage, with its towering stacks and silver grill: LAUGHLIN. Or SLAUGHTERIN, if you were feeling Freudian. Vince frowned, distracted for a moment, wondering again how they had been able to catch up and pass a guy who'd had almost an hour lead on them.

When Doc spoke, his voice was almost shy with apology. "Might be the thing to do, boss. Sure would beat twenty miles of dirt bath."

"Well. I wouldn't want any of you to get dirty," Vince said.

And he pushed away from the side of the road, throttled up, and turned left on to 6, leading them away towards Show Low.

Behind him, in the distance, he could hear the truck changing gears, the roar of the engine climbing in volume and force, whining faintly as it thundered across the plain.

The country was red and yellow stone, and they saw no one on the narrow, two-lane road. There was no breakdown lane. They crested a rise, then began to descend into a canyon's slot, following the road as it wound steadily down. To the left was a battered guardrail, and to the right was an almost sheer face of rock.

For a while Vince rode out front beside Lemmy, but then Lemmy fell back and it was Race partnered beside him, the father and the son riding side by side, the wind rippling Race's movie star black hair back from his brow. The sun, now on the western side of the sky, burned in the lenses of the kid's shades.

Vince watched him from the corners of his eyes for a moment. Race was sinewy and lean, and even the way he sat on his bike seemed an act of aggression, the way he slung it around the curves, tilting to a forty-five degree angle over the blacktop. Vince envied him his natural athletic grace, and yet at the same time, somehow Race managed to make riding a motorcycle look like work. Whereas Vince himself had taken to it because it was the furthest thing from work. He wondered idly if Race was ever really at ease with himself and what he was doing.

Vince heard the grinding thunder of a big engine behind him and took a long lazy look back over his shoulder just in time to see the truck come bearing down on them. Like a lion breaking cover at a watering hole where a bunch of gazelles were loafing. The Tribe was rolling in bunches, as always, doing maybe forty-five down the switchbacks, and the truck was rushing along at closer to sixty. Vince had time to think *He's not slowing down* and then LAUGHLIN slammed through the three running at the back of the pack with an eardrum-stunning crash of steel on steel.

Bikes flew. One Harley was thrown into the rock wall, the rider – John Kidder, sometimes known as Baby John – catapulting off it, tossed into the stone, then rebounding and disappearing under the steel-belted tyres of Laughlin's truck. Another rider (*Doc, no not Doc*) was driven into the left lane. Vince had the briefest glance of Doc's pale and astonished face, mouth opening in an "O", the twinkle of the gold tooth he was so proud of. Wobbling out of control, Doc struck the guardrail and went over his handlebars, flung into space. His Harley flipped over after him, the hardcase breaking open and spilling laundry. The truck chewed up the fallen bikes. The big grill seemed to snarl.

Then Vince and Race swung around another hard curve side by side, leaving it all behind.

The blood surged to Vince's heart, and for a moment there was a dangerous pinching in his chest. He had to fight for his next breath. The instant the carnage was out of sight, it was hard to believe it had really happened. Hard to believe the spinning bikes hadn't taken out the speeding truck, too. Yet he had just finished coming around the bend when Doc crashed into the road ahead of them. His bike landed on top of his body with an echoing clang. His clothes came floating after. Doc's sleeveless denim jacket came drifting down last, ballooning open, caught for a moment on an updraft. Over a silhouette of Vietnam in gold thread was the legend: WHEN I GET TO HEAVEN THEY'LL LET ME IN BECAUSE I'VE ALREADY BEEN TO HELL IRON TRIANGLE 1968. The clothes, the owner of the clothes, and the owner's ride had dropped from the terrace above, falling seventy feet to the highway below.

Vince jerked the handlebars, swerving around the wreck with one boot-heel skimming the patched asphalt. His friend of thirty years, Doc Regis, was now a six-letter word for lubricant: *grease*. He was face down, but his teeth were glistening in a slick of blood next to his left ear, the goldie among them. His shins had come out through the backs of his legs, poles of shining red bone poking through his jeans. All this Vince saw in an instant, then wished he could *un-see*. The gag muscles fluttered in his throat and when he swallowed, there was a burning taste of bile.

Race swung around the other side of the ruin that had been Doc and Doc's bike. He looked sideways at Vince, and while Vince could not see his eyes behind his shades, his face was a rigid, stricken thing ... the expression of a small kid up past his bedtime, who has walked in on his parents watching a grisly horror movie on DVD.

Vince looked back again and saw the remnants of The Tribe coming around the bend. Just seven now. The truck howled after, swinging around the curve so fast that the long tank it was hauling lurched hard to one side, coming perilously close to tipping, its tyres smoking on the blacktop. Then it steadied and bore on, striking Ellis Harbison. Ellis was launched straight up into the air, as if bounced off a diving board. He almost looked funny, pin-wheeling his arms against the blue sky – at least until he came down and went under the truck. His ride turned end over end before being swatted entirely aside by the eighteen-wheeler.

Vince caught a jittery glimpse of Dean Carew as the truck caught up to him. The truck butted the rear tyre of his bike. Dean highsided and came down hard, rolling at fifty miles an hour along the highway, the asphalt peeling his skin away, his head bashing the road again and again, leaving a series of red punctuation marks on the chalkboard of the pavement.

An instant later the tanker ate Dean's bike, bang, thump, *crunch*, and the lowrider Dean had still been making payments on exploded, a parachute of flame bursting open beneath the truck. Vince felt a wave of pressure and heat against his back, shoving him forward, threatening to lift him off the seat of his bike. He thought the truck itself would go up, slammed right off the road as the oil tanker detonated in a column of fire. But it didn't. The rig came thundering through the flames, its sides streaked with soot and black smoke belching from its undercarriage, but otherwise undamaged and going faster than ever. Vince knew Macks were fast – the new ones had a 485 powerplant under the hood – but *this* thing ...

Supercharged? Could you supercharge a goddamn *semi*?

Vince was moving too fast, felt his front tyre beginning to slurve about. They were close to the bottom of the slope now, where the road levelled out. Race was a little ahead. In his rearview he could see the only other survivors: Lemmy, Peaches, Roy. And the truck was closing in again.

They could beat it on a rise – in a heartbeat – but now there were no rises. Not for the next twenty miles, if his memory was right. It was going to get Peaches next, Peaches who was funniest when he was trying to be serious. Peaches threw a terrified glance back over his shoulder, and Vince knew what he was seeing: a chrome cliff. One that was moving in.

*Fucking think of something. Lead them out of this.*

It had to be him. Race was still riding okay but he was on autopilot, face frozen, fixed forward as if he had a sprained neck and was wearing a brace. A thought struck Vince then – terrible but curiously certain – that this was how Race had looked the day in Fallujah that he drove away from the men in his squad, while the mortar rounds dropped around them.

Peaches put on a burst of speed and gained a little on the truck. It blasted its air horn, as if in frustration. Or laughter. Either way, the old Georgia Peach had only gained a stay of execution. Vince could hear the trucker – maybe named Laughlin, maybe a devil from Hell – changing gears. Christ, how many forward did he have? A hundred? He started to close the distance. Vince didn't think Peaches would be able to squirt ahead again. That old flathead Beezer of his had given all it had to give. Either the truck would take him or the Beez would blow a head-gasket and *then* the truck would take him.

*BRONK! BRONK! BRONK-BRONK-BRONK!*

Shattering a day that was already shattered beyond repair . . . but it gave Vince an idea. It depended where they were. He knew this road. He knew them all, out here, but he had not been this way in years, and could not be sure now, on the fly, if they were where he thought they were.

Roy threw something back over his shoulder, something that twinkled in the sun. It struck LAUGHLIN's dirty windshield and flew off. The fucking machete. The truck bellowed on, blowing double streams of black smoke, the driver laying on that horn again—

*BRONK-BRONK! BRONK! BRONK-BRONK-BRONK!*
—in blasts that sounded weirdly like Morse.

*If only . . . Lord, if only . . .*

And yes. Up ahead was a sign so filthy it was only barely possible to read it: CUMBA 2.

Cumba. Goddamn Cumba. A played-out little mining town on the side of a hill, a place where there were maybe five slots and one old geezer selling Navajo blankets made in Laos.

Two miles wasn't much time when you were already doing eighty. This would have to be quick, and there would only be one chance.

The others made fun of Vince's sled, but only Race's ridicule had a keen edge to it. The bike was a rebuilt Kawasaki Vulcan 800 with Cobra pipes and a custom seat. Leather as red as a fire alarm. "The old man's La-Z-Boy," Dean Carew had once called the seat.

"Fuck that," Vince had replied indignantly, and when Peaches, solemn as a preacher, had said, "I'm sure you have," they all broke up.

The Tribe called the Vulcan a rice-burner, of course. Also Vince's Tojo Mojo El Rojo. Doc – Doc who was now spread all over the road behind them – liked to call it Miss Fujiyama. Vince only smiled as though he knew something they didn't. Maybe he even did. He'd had the Vulcan up to one-twenty and had stopped there. Pussied out. Race wouldn't have, but Race was a young man and young men had to know where things ended. One-twenty had been enough for Vince, but he'd known there was more. Now he would find out how much.

He grasped the throttle and twisted it all the way to the stop.

The Vulcan responded not with a snarl but a cry and almost tore out from under him. He had a blurred glimpse of his son's white face and then he was past, in the lead, riding the rocket, desert smells packing his nose. Up ahead was a dirty string of asphalt angling off to the left, the road to Cumba. Route 6 went past in a long lazy curve to the right. Towards Show Low.

Vince looked in his right-hand rear-view and saw the others had bunched, and that Peaches still had the shiny side up. Vince thought the truck could have taken Peaches – maybe all the others – but he was laying back a little, knowing as well as

Vince did that for the next twenty miles there were no upgrades. Beyond the turn-off to Cumba, the highway was elevated, and a guardrail ran along either side of it; Vince thought miserably of cattle in the chute. For the next twenty miles, the road belonged to LAUGHLIN.

*Please let this work.*

He let off the throttle and began squeezing the handbrake rhythmically. What the four behind him saw (if they were looking) was a long flash . . . a short flash . . . another long flash. Then a pause. Then a repeat. Long . . . short . . . long. It was the truck's air horn that had given him the idea. It only *sounded* like Morse, but what Vince was flashing with his brake-light *was* Morse.

It was the letter R.

Roy and Peaches might pick it up, Lemmy for sure. And Race? Did they still teach Morse? Had the kid learned it in his war, where squad-leaders carried GPS units and bombs were guided around the curve of the world by satellite?

The left turn to Cumba was coming up. Vince had just time enough to flash R one more time. Now he was almost back with the others. He shot his hand left in a gesture The Tribe knew well: *follow me off the highway.* Laughlin saw it – as Vince had expected – and surged forward. At the same time he did, Vince twisted his throttle again. The Vulcan screamed and leaped forward. He banked right, along the main road. The others followed. But not the truck. LAUGHLIN had already started its turn on to the Cumba spur. If the driver had tried to correct for the main road, he would have rolled his rig.

Vince felt a white throb of elation and reflexively closed his left hand into a triumphant fist. *We did it! We fucking did it! By the time he gets that fat-ass truck turned around, we'll be nine miles from h—*

The thought broke off like a branch as he looked again into his rear-view. There were three bikes behind him, not four: Lemmy, Peaches and Roy.

Vince swivelled to the left, hearing the old bones crackle in his back, knowing what he would see. He saw it. The truck, dragging a huge rooster-tail of red dust, its tanker too dirty to shine. But there was shine fifty or so yards in front of it; the gleam of the chromed pipes and engine belonging to a Softail Deuce. Race either did not understand Morse, didn't believe what he was seeing, or hadn't seen at all. Vince remembered the waxy, fixed expression on his son's face, and thought this last possibility was most likely. Race had stopped paying attention to the rest of them – had stopped *seeing* them – the moment he understood LAUGHLIN was not just a truck out of control, but one bent on tribal slaughter. He had been just aware enough to spot Vince's hand gesture, but had lost all the rest to a kind of tunnel vision. What was that? Panic? Or a kind of animal selfishness? Or were they the same, when you came down to it?

Race's Harley slipped behind a low swell of hill. The truck disappeared after it and then there was only blowing dust. Vince tried to catch his flying thoughts and put them in some coherent order. If his memory was right again – he knew it was asking a lot of it; he hadn't been this way in a couple of years – then the spur-road ran through Cumba before veering back to rejoin Highway 6 about nine miles ahead. If Race could stay in front—

Except.

Except, unless things had changed, the road went to hardpan dirt beyond Cumba, and was apt to drift across sandy at this time of year. The truck would do okay, but a motorcycle . . .

The chances of Race surviving the last four miles of that nine-mile run weren't good. The chances of him dumping the Deuce and being run over were, on the other hand, excellent.

Images of Race tried to crowd his mind. Race on his Big Wheels: the Kindergarten warrior. Race staring at him from the back seat of the GTO, the Popsicle melting, his eyes bright with hate, the lower lip quivering. Race at eighteen, wearing a uniform and a fuck-you smile, both present and accounted for and all squared away.

Last of all came the image of Race dead on the hardpan, a smashed doll with only his leathers holding him together.

Vince swept the pictures away. They were no help. The cops wouldn't be, either. There *were* no cops, not in Cumba. If someone saw the semi chasing the bike, he might call the State Police, but the closest one was apt to be in Show Low, drinking java and eating pie and flirting with the waitress while Travis Tritt played on the Rock-Ola.

There was only them. But that was nothing new.

He thrust his hand to the right, then made a fist and patted the air with it. The other three swung over to the side behind him, engines clobbering, the air over their straight-pipes shimmering.

Lemmy pulled up beside him, his face haggard and cheesy-yellow. "*He didn't see the tail-light signal!*" he shouted.

"*Didn't see or didn't understand!*" Vince yelled back. He was trembling. Maybe it was just the bike throbbing under him. "*Comes to the same! Time for Little Boy!*"

For a moment Lemmy didn't understand. Then he twisted around, and yanked the straps on his right-hand saddlebag. No fancy plastic hardcase for Lemmy. Lemmy was old school all the way.

While he was rooting, there was a sudden, gunning roar. That was Roy. Roy had had enough. He wheeled around and shot back east, his shadow now running before him, a scrawny black gantry-man. On the back of his leather vest was a hideous joke: NO RETREAT NO SURRENDER.

"*Come back, Klowes, you dickwad!*" Peaches bellowed. His hand slipped from his clutch. The Beezer, still in gear, lurched forward almost over Vince's foot, passed high-octane gas, and stalled. Peaches was almost hurled off, but didn't seem to notice. He was still looking back. He shook his fist; his scant grey hair whirled around his long, narrow skull. "*Come back you chicken-shit DICKWAAAAD!*"

Roy didn't come back. Roy didn't even *look* back.

Peaches turned to Vince. Tears streamed down cheeks sun-flayed by a million rides and ten million beers. In that moment he looked older than the desert he stood on.

"*You're stronger'n me, Vince, but I got me a bigger asshole. You rip his head off; I'll be in charge of shittin' down his neck.*"

"*Hurry up!*" Vince shouted at Lemmy. "*Hurry up, goddamn you!*"

Just when he thought Lemmy was going to come up empty, his old running buddy straightened with Little Boy in his gloved hand.

The Tribe did not ride with guns. Outlaw motorheads like them never did. They all had records, and any cop in Nevada would be delighted to put one of them away for thirty years on a gun charge. One, or all of them. They carried knives, but knives were no good in this situation; witness what had happened to Roy's machete, which had turned out as useless as the man himself. Except when it came to killing stoned little girls in high school sweaters, that was.

Little Boy, however, while not strictly legal, was not a gun. And the one cop who'd looked at it ("while searching for drugs" – the pigs were always doing that, it was what they lived for) had given Lemmy a skate when Lemmy explained it was more reliable than a road-flare if you broke down at night. Maybe the cop knew what he was looking at, maybe not, but he knew that Lemmy was a veteran. Not just from Lemmy's veteran's licence plate, which could have been stolen, but because the cop had been a vet himself. "Au Shau Valley, where the shit smells sweeter," he'd said, and they had both laughed and even ended up bumping fists.

Little Boy was an M84 stun grenade, more popularly known as a flash-bang. Lemmy had been carrying it in his saddlebag for maybe five years, always saying it would come in handy some day when the other guys – Vince included – ribbed him about it.

Some day had turned out to be today.

"*Will this old sonofabitch still work?*" Vince shouted as he hung Little Boy over his handlebars by the strap. It didn't look like a grenade. It looked like a combination Thermos bottle and aerosol can. The only grenade-y thing about it was the pull-ring duct-taped to the side.

"*I don't know! I don't even know how you can—*"

Vince had no time to discuss logistics. He only had a vague idea of what the logistics might be, anyway. "*I have to ride! That fuck's gonna come out on the other end of the Cumba road! I mean to be there when he does!*"

"And if Race ain't in front of him?" Lemmy asked. They had been shouting until now, all jacked up on adrenaline. It was almost a surprise to hear a nearly normal tone of voice.

"One way or the other," Vince said. "You don't have to come. Either of you. I'll understand if you want to turn back. He's my boy."

"Maybe so," Peaches said, "but it's our Tribe. Was, anyway."

He jumped down on the Beezer's kick, and the hot engine rumbled to life. "I'll ride witcha, Cap."

Lemmy just nodded and pointed at the road.

Vince took off.

It wasn't as far as he'd thought: seven miles instead of nine. They met no cars or trucks. The road was deserted, traffic maybe avoiding it because of the construction back the way they had come. Vince snapped constant glances to his left. For a while he saw red dust rising, the truck dragging half the desert along in its slipstream. Then he lost sight even of its dust, the Cumba spur dropping well out of sight behind hills with eroded, chalky sides.

Little Boy swung back and forth on its strap. Army surplus. *Will this old sonofabitch still work?* he'd asked Lemmy, and now realized he could have asked the same question of himself. How long since he had been tested this way, running dead out, throttle to the max? How long since the whole world came down to only two choices, live pretty or die laughing? And how had his own son, who looked so cool in his new leathers and his mirrored sunglasses, missed such an elementary equation?

Live pretty or die laughing, but don't you run. Don't you fucking run.

Maybe Little Boy would work, maybe it wouldn't, but Vince knew he was going to take his shot, and it made him giddy. If the guy was buttoned up in his cab, it was a lost cause in any case. But he hadn't been buttoned up back at the diner. Back there, his hand had been lolling out against the side of the truck. And later, hadn't he waved them ahead from that same open window? Sure. Sure he had.

Seven miles. Five minutes, give or take. Long enough for a lot of memories of his son, whose father had taught him to change oil but never to bait a hook; to gap plugs but never how you told a coin from the Denver mint from one that had been struck in San Francisco. Time to think how Race had pushed for this stupid meth deal, and how Vince had gone along even though he knew it was stupid, because it seemed he had something to make up for. Only the time for make-up calls was past. As Vince tore along at eighty-five, bending as low as he could get to cut the wind resistance, a terrible thought crossed his mind, one he inwardly recoiled from but could not blot out – that maybe it would be better for all concerned if LAUGHLIN *did* succeed in running his son down. It wasn't the image of Race lifting a shovel into the air and then bringing it down on a helpless man's head, in a spoiled rage over lost money, although that was bad enough. It was something more. It was the fixed, empty look on the kid's face right before he steered his bike the wrong way, on to the Cumba road. For himself, Vince had not been able to stop looking back at the Tribe, the whole way down the canyon, as some were run down and the others struggled to stay ahead of the big machine. Whereas Race had seemed incapable of turning that stiff neck of his. There was nothing behind him that he needed to see. Maybe never had been.

There came a loud *ka-pow* at Vince's back, and a yell he heard even over the wind and the steady blat of the Vulcan's engine: "*Mutha-FUCK!*" He looked in the rear-view mirror and saw Peaches falling back. Smoke was boiling from between his pipe-stem legs, and oil slicked the road behind him in a fan shape that widened as his ride slowed. The Beez had finally blown its head-gasket. A wonder it hadn't happened sooner.

Peaches waved them on ... not that Vince would have stopped. Because in a way, the question of whether Race was redeemable was moot. Vince himself was not redeemable; none of them was. He remembered an Arizona cop who'd once pulled them over and said, "Well, look what the road puked up." And that was what they were: road-puke. But those bodies back there had, until this afternoon, been his running buddies, the only thing he had of any value in the world. They had been Vince's brothers in a way, and Race was his son, and you couldn't drive a man's family to earth and expect to live. You couldn't leave them butchered and expect to ride away. If LAUGHLIN didn't know that, he would.

Soon.

Lemmy couldn't keep up with the Tojo Mojo El Rojo. He fell further and further behind. That was all right. Vince was just glad Lemmy still had his six.

Up ahead, a sign: WATCH FOR LEFT-ENTERING TRAFFIC. The road coming out of Cumba. It was hardpan dirt, as he had feared. Vince slowed, then stopped, turned off the Vulcan's engine.

Lemmy pulled up beside. There was no guardrail here. Here in this one place, where 6 rejoined the Cumba road, the highway was level with the desert, although not far ahead it began to climb away from the floodplain once more, turning into the cattle chute again.

"Now we wait," Lemmy said, switching his engine off as well.

Vince nodded. He wished he still smoked. He told himself that either Race was still shiny-side-up and in front of the truck, or he wasn't. It was beyond his control. It was true, but it didn't help.

"Maybe he'll find a place to turn off in Cumba," Lemmy said. "An alley or somethin' where the truck can't go."

"I don't think so. Cumba is nothing. A gas station and I think a couple houses, all stuck right on the side of a fucking hill. That's bad road. At least for Race. No easy way off it." He didn't even try to tell Lemmy about Race's blank, locked-down expression, a look that said he wasn't seeing anything except the road right in front of his bike. Cumba would be a blur and flash that he only registered after it was well behind him.

"Maybe—" Lemmy began, but Vince held up his hand, silencing him. They cocked their heads to the left.

They heard the truck first, and Vince felt his heart sink. Then, buried in its roar, the bellow of another motor. There was no mistaking the distinctive blast of a Harley running full out.

"He made it!" Lemmy yelled, and raised his hand for a high-five. Vince wouldn't give it. Bad luck. And besides, the kid still had to make the turn back on to 6. If he was going to dump, it would be there.

A minute ticked by. The sound of the engines grew louder. A second minute, and now they could see dust rising over the nearest hills. Then, in a notch between the two closest hills, they saw a flash of sun on chrome. There was just time to glimpse Race, bent almost flat over his handlebars, long hair streaming out behind, and then he was gone again. A second after he disappeared – surely no more – the truck flashed through the notch, stacks shooting smoke. LAUGHLIN on the side was no longer visible; it had been buried beneath a layer of dust.

Vince hit the Vulcan's starter and the engine bammed to life. He gunned the throttle and the frame vibrated.

"Luck, Cap," Lemmy said.

Vince opened his mouth to reply, but in that moment, emotion, intense and unexpected, choked off his wind. So instead of speaking, he gave Lemmy a brief, grateful nod, before taking off. Lemmy followed. As always, Lemmy had his six.

Vince's mind turned into a computer, trying to figure speed versus distance. It had to be timed just right. He rolled towards the intersection at fifty, dropped it to forty, then twisted the throttle again as Race appeared, the bike swerving around a tumbleweed, actually going airborne on a couple of bumps. The truck was no more than thirty feet behind. When Race neared the "Y" where the Cumba bypass once more joined the main road, he slowed. He had to slow. The instant he did, LAUGHLIN vaulted forwards, eating up the distance between them.

"*Jam that motherfuck!*" Vince screamed, knowing Race couldn't hear over the bellow of the truck. He screamed it again anyway: "*JAM that motherfuck! Don't slow down!*"

The trucker planned to slam the Harley in the rear wheel, spinning it out. Race's bike hit the crotch of the intersection and surged, Race leaning far to the left, holding the handlebars only with the tips of his fingers. He looked like a trick rider on a trained mustang. The truck missed the rear fender, its blunt nose lunging into thin air that had held a Harley's back wheel only a tenth of a second before . . . but at first Vince thought Race was going to lose it anyway, just spin out.

He didn't. His high-speed arc took him all the way to the far side of Route 6, close enough to the bike-killing shoulder to spume up dust, and then he was scat-gone, gunning down Route 6 towards Show Low.

The truck went out into the desert to make its own turn, rumbling and bouncing, the driver down-shifting through the gears fast enough to make the whole rig shudder, the tyres churning up a fog of dust that turned the blue sky white. It left a trail of deep tracks and crushed sagebrush before regaining the road and once more setting out after Vince's son.

Vince twisted the left handgrip and the Vulcan took off. Little Boy swung frantically back and forth on the handlebars. Now came the easy part. It might get him killed, but it would be easy compared to the endless minutes he and Lemmy had waited before hearing Race's motor mixed in with LAUGHLIN's.

*His window won't be open, you know. Not after he just got done running through all that dust.*

That was also out of his control. If the trucker was buttoned up, he'd deal with that when the moment came.

It wouldn't be long.

The truck was doing around sixty. It could go a lot faster, but Vince didn't mean to let him get all the way through those who-knew-how-many gears of his until the Mack hit warp-speed. He was going to end this now for one of them. Probably for himself, an idea he did not shy from. He would at the least buy Race more time; given a lead, Race could beat the truck to Show Low easily. More than just protecting Race, though, there had to be balance to the scales. Vince had never lost so much so fast, six of The Tribe dead on a stretch of road less than half a mile long. You didn't do that to a man's family, he thought again, and drive away.

Which was, Vince saw at last, maybe LAUGHLIN's own point, his own primary operating principal . . . the reason he had taken them on, in spite of the ten-to-one odds. He had come at them, not knowing or caring if they were armed, picking them off two and three at a time, even though any one of the bikes he had run down could've sent the truck out of control and rolling, first a Mack, and then an oil-stoked fireball. It was madness, but not *incomprehensible* madness. As Vince swung into the left-hand lane and began to close the final distance, the truck's ass-end just ahead on his right, he saw something that seemed not only to sum up this terrible day, but to explain it, in simple, perfectly lucid terms. It was a bumper sticker. It was even filthier than the Cumba sign, but still readable.

PROUD PARENT OF A CORMAN HIGH HONOR ROLL STUDENT!

Vince pulled even with the dust-streaked tanker. In the cab's long driver's-side rear-view, he saw something shift. The driver had seen him. In the same second, Vince saw that the window was shut, just as he'd feared.

The truck began to slide left, crossing the white line with its outside wheels.

For a moment Vince had a choice: back off or keep going. Then the computer in his head told him the choice was already past; even if he hit the brakes hard enough to risk dumping his ride, the final five feet of the filthy tank would swat him into the guardrail on his left like a fly.

Instead of backing off he increased speed even as the left lane shrank, the truck forcing him toward that knee-high ribbon of gleaming steel. He yanked the flash-bang from the handlebars, breaking the strap. He tore the duct-tape away from the pull-ring with his teeth, the strap's shredded end spanking his cheek as he did so. The ring began to clatter against Little Boy's perforated barrel. The sun was gone. Vince was flying in the truck's shadow now. The guardrail was less than three feet to his left; the side of the truck three feet to his right and still closing. Vince had reached the plate-hitch between the tanker and the cab. Now he could only see the top of Race's head; the rest of him was blocked by the truck's dirty maroon hood. Race was not looking back.

He didn't think about the next thing. There was no plan, no strategy. It was just his road-puke self saying *fuck you* to the world, as he always had. It was, when you came right down to it, The Tribe's only *raison d'être*.

As the truck closed in for the killing side-stroke, and with absolutely nowhere to go, Vince raised his right hand and shot the truck driver the bird.

He was pulling even with the cab now, the truck bulking to his right like a filthy mesa. It was the cab that would take him out.

There was movement from inside: that deeply tanned arm with its Marine Corps tattoo. The muscle in the arm bunched as the window slid down into its slot, and Vince realized the cab, which should have swatted him already, was staying where it was. The trucker meant to do it, of course he did, but not until he had replied in kind. *Maybe we even served in different units together*, Vince thought. *In the Au Shau Valley, say, where the shit smells sweeter.*

The window was down. The hand came out. It started to hatch its own bird, then stopped. The driver had just realized the hand that had given him the finger wasn't empty. It was curled around something. Vince didn't give him time to think about it, and he never saw the trucker's face. All he saw was the tattoo, DEATH BEFORE DISHONOR. A good thought, and how often did you get a chance to give someone exactly what they wanted?

Vince caught the ring in his teeth, pulled it, heard the fizz of some chemical reaction starting, and tossed Little Boy in through the window. It didn't have to be a fancy half-court shot, not even a lousy pull-up jumper. Just a lob. He was a magician, opening his hands to set free a dove where a moment before there had been a wadded-up handkerchief.

*Now you take me out,* Vince thought. *Let's finish this thing right.*

But the truck swerved away from him. Vince was sure it would have come swerving back, if there had been time. That swerve was only reflex, Laughlin trying to get away from a thrown object. But it was enough to save his life, because Little Boy did its thing before the driver could course-correct and drive Vince Adamson off the road.

The cab lit up in a vast white flash, as if God himself had bent down to take a snapshot. Instead of swerving back to the left, LAUGHLIN veered away to the right, first back into the lane of Route 6 bound for Show Low, then beyond. The tractor flayed the guardrail on the right-hand side of the road, striking up a sheet of copper sparks, a shower of fire, a thousand Catherine wheels going off at once. Vince thought madly of July 4th, Race a child again and sitting in his lap to watch the rockets' red glare, the bombs bursting in air; sky-flares shining in his child's delighted, inky eyes.

Then the truck crunched through the guardrail, shredding it as if it were tinfoil. LAUGHLIN nosed over a twenty-foot embankment, into a ravine filled with sand and tumbleweeds. The wheels caught. The truck slued. The big tanker rammed forwards into the back of the cab. Vince had shot beyond that point before he could brake to a stop, but Lemmy saw it all: saw the cab and the tanker form a "V" and then split apart; saw the tanker roll first and the cab a second or two after; saw the tanker burst open and then blow. It went up in a fireball and a greasy pillar of black smoke. The cab rolled past it, over and over, the cube shape turning into a senseless crumple of maroon that sparked hot shards of sun where bare metal had split out in prongs and hooks.

It landed with the driver's window up to the sky, about eighty feet away from the pillar of fire that had been its cargo. By then Vince was running back along his own skid-mark. He saw the figure that tried to pull itself through the misshapen window. The face turned towards him, except there was no face, only a mask of blood. The driver emerged to the waist before collapsing back inside. One tanned arm – the one with the tattoo – stuck up like a submarine's periscope. The hand dangled limp on the wrist.

Vince stopped at Lemmy's bike, gasping for breath. For a moment he thought he was going to pass out, but he leaned over, put his hands on his knees, and presently felt a little better.

"You got him, Cap." Lemmy's voice was hoarse with emotion.

"We better make sure," Vince said. Although the stiff periscope arm and the hand dangling limp at the end of it suggested that would just be a formality.

"Why not?" Lemmy said. "I gotta take a piss, anyway."

"You're not pissing on him, dead or alive," Vince said.

There was an approaching roar: Race's Harley. He pulled up in a showy skid stop, killed the engine, and got off. His face, although dusty, glowed with delight and triumph. Vince hadn't seen Race look that way since the kid was twelve. He had won a dirt-track race in a quarter-midget Vince had built for him, a yellow torpedo with a souped-up Briggs & Stratton engine. Race had come leaping from the cockpit with that exact same expression on his face, right after taking the chequered flag.

He threw his arms around Vince and hugged him. "You did it! You *did* it, Dad! You cooked his fucking ass!"

For a moment Vince allowed the hug. Because it had been so long. And because this was his spoiled son's better angel. Everybody had one; even at his age, and after all he had seen, Vince believed that. So for a moment he allowed the hug, and relished the warmth of his son's body, and promised himself he would remember it.

Then he put his hands against Race's chest and pushed him away. Hard. Race stumbled backwards on his custom snakeskin boots, the expression of love and triumph fading—

No, not fading. *Merging.* Becoming the look Vince had come to know so well: distrust and dislike. *Quit, why don't you? That's not dislike and never was.*

No, not dislike. Hate, bright and glowing.

*All squared away, sir, and fuck you.*

"What was her name?" Vince asked.

"What?"

"Her name, John." He hadn't called Race by his actual name in years, and there was no one to hear it now but them. Lemmy was sliding down the soft earth of the embankment, towards the crushed metal ball that had been LAUGHLIN's cab, letting them have this tender father–son moment in privacy.

"What's wrong with you?" Pure scorn. But when Vince reached out and tore off those fucking mirror shades, he saw the truth in John "Race" Adamson's eyes. He knew what this was about. Vince was coming in five-by, as they used to say in Nam. Did they still say that in Iraq, he wondered, or had it gone the way of Morse Code?

"What do you want to do now, John? Go on to Show Low? Roust Clarke's sister for money that isn't there?"

"It could be there." Sulking now. He gathered himself. "It is there. I know Clarke. He trusted that whore."

"And The Tribe? Just . . . what? Forget them? Dean and Ellis and all the others? Doc?"

"They're dead." He eyed his father. "Too slow. And most of them too old." *You too*, the cool eyes said.

Lemmy was on his way back, his boots puffing up dust. He had something in his hand.

"What was her name?" Vince repeated. "Clarke's girlfriend. What was her name?"

"Fuck's it matter?" He paused then, struggling to win Vince back, his expression coming as close as it ever did to pleading. "Jesus. Leave it, why don't you? We *won*. We *showed* him."

"You knew Clarke. Knew him in Fallujah, knew him back here in The World. You were tight. If you knew him, you knew her. What was her name?"

"Janey. Joanie. Something like that."

Vince slapped him. Race blinked, startled. Dropped for a moment back to ten years old. But just for a moment. In another instant the hating look was back; a sick, curdled glare.

"He heard us talking back there in that diner parking lot. The trucker," Vince said. Patiently. As if speaking to the child this young man had once been. The young man he had risked his life to save. Ah, but that had been instinct, and he wouldn't have changed it. It was the one good thing in all this horror. This filth. Not that he had been the only one operating on filial instinct. "He knew he couldn't take us there, but he couldn't let us go, either. So he waited. Bided his time. Let us get ahead of him."

"I have no clue what you're talking about!" Very forceful. Only he was lying, and they both knew it.

"He knew the road and went after us where the terrain favoured him. Like any good soldier."

Yes. And then had pursued them with a single-minded purpose, regardless of the almost certain cost to himself. Laughlin had settled on death before dishonour. Vince knew nothing about him, but felt suddenly that he liked him better than his own son. Such a thing should not have been possible, but there it was.

"You're fucked in the head," Race said.

"I don't think so. For all we know, he was going to see her when we crossed his path at the diner. It's what a father might do for a kid he loved. Arrange things so he could look in, every now and then. See if she might even want a ride out. Take a chance on something besides the pipe and the rock."

Lemmy rejoined them. "Dead," he said.

Vince nodded.

"This was on the visor." He handed it to Vince. Vince didn't want to look at it, but he did. It was a snapshot of a smiling girl with her hair in a ponytail. She wore a CORMAN HIGH VARSITY sweatshirt, the same one she had died in. She was sitting on the front bumper of LAUGHLIN, her back resting against the silver grill. She was wearing her daddy's camo cap turned around backwards and mock-saluting and struggling not to grin. Saluting who? Laughlin himself, of course. Laughlin had been holding the camera.

"Her name was Jackie Laughlin," Race said. "And she's dead, too, so fuck her."

Lemmy started forwards, ready to pull Race off his bike and feed him his teeth, but Vince held him back with a look. Then he shifted his gaze back to his boy.

"Ride on, son," he said. "Keep the shiny side up."

Race looked at him, not understanding.

"But don't stop in Show Low, because I intend to let the cops know a certain little whore might need protection. I'll tell them some nut killed her brother, and she might be next."

"And what are you going to tell them when they ask how you happened to come by that information?"

"Everything," Vince said, his voice calm. Serene even. "Better get moving. Ride on. It's what you do best. Keeping ahead of that truck on the Cumba road . . . that was something. I'll give you that. You got a gift for hightailing it. Not much else, but you got that. So hightail your ass out of here."

Race looked at him, unsure and suddenly frightened. But that wouldn't last. He'd get his fuck-you back. It was all he had: some fuck-you attitude, a pair of mirrored sunglasses, and a fast bike.

"Dad—"

"Better go on, son," Lemmy said. "Someone will have seen that smoke by now. There'll be Staties here soon."

Race smiled. When he did, a single tear spilled from his left eye and cut a track through the dust on his face. "Just a couple of old chickenshits," he said.

He went back to his bike. The chains across the insteps of his snakeskin boots jingled . . . a little foolishly, Vince thought.

Race swung his leg over the seat, started his Harley, and drove away west, toward Show Low. Vince did not expect him to look back and was not disappointed.

They watched him. After a while, Lemmy said: "You want to go, Cap?"

"No place to go, man. I think I might just sit here for a bit, side of the road."

"Well," Lemmy said. "If you want. I guess I could sit some myself."

They went to the side of the road and sat down cross-legged like old Indians with no blankets to sell and watched the tanker burn in the desert, piling black oil-smoke into the blue, unforgiving sky. Some of it drifted back their way, reeking and greasy.

"We can move," Vince said. "If you don't like the smell."

Lemmy tipped his head back and inhaled deeply, like a man considering the bouquet of a pricey wine.

"No, I don't mind it. Smells like Vietnam."

Vince nodded.

"Makes me think of them old days," Lemmy said. "When we were almost as fast as we believed we were."

Vince nodded again. "Live pretty—"

"Yep. Or die laughin'."

They said nothing more after that, just sat there, waiting, Vince with the girl's picture in his hand. Every once in a while, he glanced at it, turning it in the sun, considering how young she looked, and how happy.

But mostly he watched the fire.

# BARBARA RODEN

## Out and Back

BARBARA RODEN IS A World Fantasy Award-winning editor and publisher (for Ash-Tree Press), whose short stories have appeared in numerous publications, including *Year's Best Fantasy and Horror: Nineteenth Annual Collection*, *Horror: Best of the Year 2005*, *Bound for Evil*, *Strange Tales 2*, *Gaslight Grimoire* and *Gaslight Grotesque*, and *Poe*. Her first collection, *Northwest Passages*, was published by Prime Books in October 2009.

"My cousin-by-marriage Sean Lavery, knowing my love for weird and outré websites, sent me a link to the Dark Roasted Blend site (*www.darkroastedblend.com*)," reveals the author, "where I found several pages featuring photographs of abandoned places.

"My imagination was fired by pictures taken at Chippewa Lake Park in Medina, Ohio, which opened in 1878 and was abandoned in 1978, with the buildings and rides left to rot where they stood, and I began looking around for some information about the park.

"I've always had a fondness for amusement parks, ever since I was a child visiting Vancouver's Pacific National Exhibition with my father and my brother: an annual trip which was one of the red-letter days on my childhood calendar. The photographs of Chippewa Lake Park were equal parts eerie and sad, for anyone who has ever thrilled to the sights and sounds of a midway, and the story sprang, almost fully-formed, into my head; one of the few times that's happened."

To see some of the pictures that inspired the following story, visit: *www.defunctparks.com/parks/OH/ChippewaLake/chippewa-lake.htm.*

"KEEP YOUR EYES OPEN. I don't want to miss it."

"How hard can it be to miss?" Linda asked, pushing a strand of hair behind her ear. "It's not the sort of thing you're going to drive past and not see."

"It's been abandoned for a long time," said Allan patiently. "It's not like there are going to be signs. Besides," – he waved one hand at the dispirited housing development they were driving through – "the place has grown up a lot. Back when it was built it was a long way from anywhere; nothing but scrub and fields."

"So why'd anyone build an amusement park miles from where people lived?" Linda wasn't particularly interested in the answer, but it had been a long drive, and she was tired of the silence; tired, full stop.

Allan shrugged. "I dunno. Guess land was cheap. And there's a lake; that's what it was named after. Must've been a popular spot for people to come with their families."

"What are you expecting to see?"

"I'm not sure. I haven't been able to find out much. It's kind of off the beaten track" – Linda gave a hollow laugh, as if to say *You're kidding me* – "and not too many people seem to have been here. I'm hoping to get some good pictures; put them up on my website."

"Great." Linda stared out the window. "We take a day out of our vacation just so you can maybe get some pictures of you're not sure what – *if* it's still there, and *if* we find it – and then you'll spend hours putting them up on a website for three people to see. Hooray."

Allan glanced sideways at her. "Hey, it's just one day. I didn't think you'd mind."

"Well, you got it wrong then. It's one day out of the vacation I've been looking forward to for months, thinking – stupid me – that we'd have a nice relaxing time, no chasing around like we do every weekend, me being dragged off to some abandoned place or weird site that you just *have* to see. All I want is a *rest*, Allan."

"You didn't have to come, you know. You could have stayed back at the hotel."

"Yeah, I guess I could. While you took the car, I could've stayed in the hotel room, and then when I got bored I could've gone down to the pool, and then I could've gone back to the room. Thrilling. Holidays are supposed to be about doing things together."

Allan shook his head. There was no point arguing with her when she got like this. When he'd realized their trip would take them so close – well, within a hundred miles or so – to White Lake Park he'd planned to visit it; he just hadn't mentioned it to Linda until that morning. He'd honestly thought that the idea of visiting another abandoned amusement park would appeal to her as much as it did to him. It wasn't every day you got a chance to see something like this. He was trying to figure out a way to say that without provoking her further when he glanced to his left and saw something that made him start, so that the car swerved and Linda uttered a startled "Hey!"

"Look! Over there! Do you see it?" Allan slowed the car to a crawl. "There!"

Linda craned her neck and peered through the driver's window. Behind the tired, sagging houses that lined the road she could see the tops of trees, an unbroken line stretching in both directions and apparently away from the houses as well. For a few moments that was all she could see, and she was about to ask what he was looking at when she saw it too.

It came into focus so suddenly that she almost jerked her head back in surprise. One moment she was looking at an innocuous treescape, leafy green boughs of maples and oaks and buckeyes fluttering in the breeze, and the next she could see, twisting its way through the branches, the unmistakable silhouette of a roller coaster track, wooden supports criss-crossing beneath. Her eye followed the track and she saw it dip out of sight behind the houses; then, further ahead, it rose again, and she had an impression as of some huge beast crouched behind the houses, watching, waiting. She shook her head and blinked, and despite the heat of the day she shivered.

Allan had pulled onto the shoulder and stopped the car. "There must be a way in," he muttered. "Some sort of entrance . . ."

"Long gone, I'll bet," said Linda. "Place is probably locked up tighter than a drum. Can you imagine the lawsuits?"

Allan didn't hear; or at least pretended not to. "There's got to be access from behind these houses. They back right on to it."

"What are you going to do? Walk through someone's back yard, climb their fence? Honestly, Allan . . ."

"There." He pointed to a house that stood slightly apart from its neighbours. It was a good deal older than most of the other houses in the area, sitting in the middle of an unkempt lawn choked with dandelions, a battered wooden fence which had once been white standing guard in front like a mouthful of broken teeth. To one side was a dusty laneway with a half-dozen cars parked in it, and Allan looked at them with suspicion.

"Typical," he muttered. "Bet all these people are here to look at the park. Won't be able to move for tripping over them, gawking, taking pictures."

"And that makes them different to you – how, exactly?"

Allan said nothing as he pulled in beside the last one in the row, a dirty Ford Focus with a baby seat in the back. He reached into the back of their own car and fished around for the bag containing his camera and notebook. When he got out, he slammed the door with more force than Linda thought was strictly necessary, although she refrained from commenting.

The late morning heat was oppressive, like a wet woollen blanket. Linda pushed a limp strand of brown hair behind one ear, then smoothed out her skirt, which felt damp and clammy. Allan glanced at her.

"Don't know why you wore that," he muttered. "Not very practical."

"Yeah, well, maybe if you'd told me we'd be climbing over fences and forcing our way through undergrowth I'd've worn something more suitable, like Army fatigues and steel-toed boots. Silly me, I thought when you said 'amusement park' it meant some place civilized, with a midway and something to eat. My own stupid fault. After all this time I should've known better."

Allan said nothing. They were here now, and he was

determined to make the most of it. Nothing Linda said would get him down. He'd deal with it later, like he always did, try to smooth things over. The main thing at the moment was to figure out a way into the park.

"Looks as if there might be a door in that fence." He glanced at the house. "Wouldn't be surprised if this was built when the park was."

"Maybe." Linda shrugged. She had been looking at the row of cars. "Don't think you have to worry too much about anyone else beating you to your scoop." When Allan looked puzzled, she pointed. "Most of these are pretty old. They don't look like they've gone anywhere in years. Someone probably has a spare parts business on the side."

Allan looked more closely at the cars, and had to admit that Linda was probably right. They all looked old and battered; at least two of them had flat tyres, and the oldest one – a mid-1970s station wagon at the far end of the row – was so rusted that the car would likely fall to pieces if anyone tried to move it. *No competition*, he thought with satisfaction.

Linda's voice broke in on his thoughts. "So, what're we going to do? Stand here all day? C'mon, Allan, let's get this over with."

"All right, all right." He slung the bag over his shoulder. Part of him wanted to head straight to the fence and go in, not bother with anything like permission in case someone tried to stop him, but another part of him knew from experience that it was best to get acknowledgment from someone – anyone – of what he was doing, to save awkwardness later on. Not that something like lack of permission would stop him; he'd just find another way in. He always did. He jerked his head in the direction of the house. "I'm just going to go and make sure it's okay," he said, and began walking towards what looked like the main door, at the back of the house facing the park. After a moment Linda followed him.

There was no doorbell, so Allan rapped on the wooden door, the sound harsh in the still morning air. After a few moments there was a noise from inside, as of footsteps hurrying. A woman's voice called out anxiously "Bill?", and the door opened so suddenly that both of them stepped back a pace.

The woman who stood framed in the peeling paint of the door

frame was probably in her early thirties, but looked considerably older: her hair had obviously not been cut for some time, and was streaked with grey, and she wore no make-up on her pale face. She was dressed in a faded T-shirt and skirt, the latter with its hem trailing down at one side and two or three rips, inexpertly mended, threatening to unravel further. A small child – a boy, no more than three or so – was peering from behind her legs, looking half-fearfully, half-hopefully at Allan and Linda. There was a suggestion of more people further down the hallway – a muffled murmur, as of voices whispering – but no one else appeared.

Allan cleared his throat. "Uh, hi. We were – we were hoping to be able to get into the park, have a look around. Do you think that would be a problem?"

The woman looked them both up and down. A look almost of disappointment had appeared on her face when she had opened the door and seen them. It was now replaced by one of resignation, and Allan had a sinking feeling that she was going to tell them they couldn't go in. *Some sort of caretaker*, he thought, *there's bound to be one*. He was taken aback when she said, in a flat voice, "There's nothing to stop you going in, if you want to."

"Really? Wow, that's – that's great. Thanks."

"Don't thank me. It's got nothing to do with me. Anyone who wants to go in there is free to do so."

"Ah. Well, that's good to know. Are you the caretaker or something?"

"No. This used to be the caretaker's house, a long time ago. You can get into the park through there." She pointed to the door in the fence at the bottom of the yard.

"I see." Allan nodded towards the parked cars. "Guess you get a lot of people coming here, wanting to have a look."

The woman followed his gaze. "A few. Not many. Those cars are all ours."

"'Ours'?" Allan queried.

"Yes. The people in this house."

"Have you lived here long?"

"I've been here for . . ." The woman paused and her brow furrowed, as if the effort of calculating were a difficult one. "Two years. Maybe. Not as long as some."

"I see." There was a pause, and when it looked set to continue indefinitely Allan said, "So it's okay if we go in, then? We won't disturb anything, cause any damage. We'll let you know when we're done, if you want, tell you when we're leaving."

"Oh, that's fine. We'll know when you're done."

"Ah. Well, that's – that's great, then. We'll see you later."

The woman said nothing as they turned and headed towards the door in the fence. They were both conscious of her gaze on them as they made their way through the long grass, although when Linda turned and looked while Allan wrestled with the door in the fence she saw that the woman had gone and the house door was shut. She thought she saw a curtain twitch at one of the lower windows, and there was a suggestion of a figure standing at one of the upstairs windows, but she could not be sure.

Allan grunted and swore as he struggled with the door, which was jammed shut. "One good thing, it means no one else has been this way for a while," he said, giving the door a shove. With a creak and a groan it swung open, and Allan almost fell through, recovering his balance at the last moment. He peered through the opening and took a deep breath. She couldn't see his face, but Linda knew that his eyes were shining and that he had a goofy smile on his face, like a kid getting his first look at the tree on Christmas morning. *How can I compete with that?* she thought. Before she could block it, out came the answer: *You can't.*

She watched as Allan disappeared through the door, and for a moment thought about not following him, of heading back to the car – she had a spare set of keys in her bag, after all, she could just get in and drive away, leave him here to his precious park, go do something interesting, something *she* wanted to do, instead of trailing after him as she had so many times, pretending to be interested. He probably wouldn't even notice she wasn't there. Then, as she saw him receding into the undergrowth that choked the other side of the fence, Linda took a deep breath of her own and followed him in.

If she hadn't known she was in a former amusement park, she would never have guessed. Trees crowded round on all sides and weeds ran rampant. There was the suggestion of a trail, but nothing to indicate what the site had once been, until she was brought up short by Allan stopping suddenly in front of her and muttering "Holy shit, that's brilliant." A moment later he was fumbling inside his bag for his camera, and Linda moved around him so that she could see.

A white shape loomed out of a thicket of buckeyes ahead and to their right. It looked as though the vegetation were trying to seize the building and pull it back in amongst the trees, and it took Linda a moment to realize what it was: a small booth with an overhanging roof and windows on three of the four sides, one of them half-covered with a wooden shutter. The building had once been painted in gay shades of red and yellow, but the paint had faded and peeled, and one side showed signs of scorching. Linda was trying to figure out what it was when Allan spoke.

"Ticket booth," he flung over his shoulder. "Great, isn't it?"

"Brilliant." Linda took a step closer. "Why's it burned?"

"I dunno. I think there's a lot of fire damage in the park. People get in, start fires just for the fun of it."

"Whatever turns you on, I guess." Linda tried to picture what the booth would have looked like with children lined up in front, jostling each other as they waited impatiently to buy tickets, coins and crumpled dollar bills clutched in sticky hands, the sounds and smells of the midway assailing and enticing them from all sides, but failed utterly. Nothing of that past remained. Instead of the music and clatter of the rides there was the soft, sad sound of wind through branches; instead of the smell of corn dogs and fried onions and cotton candy there was the scent of grass and dirt and dead leaves. She shivered and moved closer to Allan.

"Can we go now?" she asked, and he turned to her, startled.

"What do you mean, go? We only just got here. There's tons more to see."

"I just meant can we move on? How many pictures of a ticket booth do you really need?"

"Yeah, okay, I see what you mean." He dug around inside his bag for a moment and pulled out a crumpled piece of paper. He studied it, twisting it and glancing round him as if trying to orientate himself. "Okay, we came in about here," he muttered, looking at the paper, "which means that if we head in that direction" – he pointed – "we should hit the midway. C'mon, let's go."

They skirted round the empty booth, Linda casting a backward glance at it as they moved away. The one shutter still in place moved slightly, as if waving at her, and she quickly turned and headed after Allan, who was following a rough path which led deeper into the trees.

"So, are we headed anywhere in particular, or are we just wandering aimlessly?" Linda's voice sounded harsh in the silence.

"Well, I really want to see some of the midway rides. What's left of them, anyway. That's where the real interest is."

"Interest? You're kidding me." Linda waved one hand at the desolation around them. "If there was any interest in this place it wouldn't be left here to rot. What happened to it, anyway?"

Allan shrugged. "I don't know. There're different stories. There was a big fire in the grand ballroom, when the park was still going, and they had to shut it down for a while, and I think people started drifting away, forgot it was here. And there's supposed to have been someone who died on one of the rides."

Linda stopped in her tracks. "Tell me you're joking."

"No, of course not." Allan stared at her. "What's wrong?"

"Are we here on another one of your ghost hunts?"

"No, we're not here on a 'ghost hunt'. Honestly, what do you take me for?"

"It wouldn't be the first time. Remember that house you just *had* to go to on a certain date, and that place – where was it – where that ghost ship was supposed to appear? Took me two days to get warm again, all so you could think that maybe you saw something. That I *didn't* see, in case you forgot."

Allan shook his head. "Jeez, Linda, would you stop twisting things? All I said was there's a story about someone dying here on one of the rides. I don't even know if it's true. It's hard to pin down that kind of thing, 'cause these places always try to hush it up if they can. If it did happen, it was a long time ago."

Linda looked around. Trees whispered in the faint breeze, and somewhere far off a bird chirped. "Everything here happened a long time ago," she said flatly. "I've never been anywhere so empty."

"Yeah, well, it's not that empty." Allan pointed to their left, and Linda saw a faint glimmer of white. "Lots to see, for those who are interested. Who *care*."

"I care," Linda muttered. "I care about getting the hell out of here and getting on with our holiday."

"I know. You've made that clear. Only – well, we're here now. Let's just look around a bit more, okay? Please."

"Fine. But you owe me, big time."

Allan, having gained his point, said nothing, but hurried off in the direction of the blur of white they had seen. Linda, after a moment's hesitation, followed.

As they got closer the shape revealed itself as a large building that had once, no doubt, been impressive, but was now in danger of collapsing in on itself. Two blank windows, like eyes, stared out from under a high roof, and what had once been an overhang running the length of the building's front had had its supports give way and was now hanging limp against the wall. Beside it was another building in even more desperate shape, a tangle of trees and vines choking collapsed timbers, threatening to drag the whole structure into the ground. Allan whistled.

"This is great." The camera was out again and he was snapping away. "I'm going to get some brilliant pictures."

"Of what?"

Allan spared her a quick glance. "What d'you mean?"

"I mean what is it we're looking at, exactly?"

"Oh. I see." Allan considered the buildings, then looked at his plan of the park. "I *think* this one" – he pointed to the more intact of the two buildings – "was the Bumper Car ride, and the other one was the Fun House."

"Some fun." Linda looked at the battered building and shivered. "Looks like a good stiff breeze would knock it over."

"Yeah, I'm lucky I got here before that happened." Allan headed towards the Bumper Car ride. "I'm gonna take a look inside."

"Are you sure that's safe?" Linda didn't really want to get any closer to it, but she followed anyway, picking her way through the weeds pushing their way up through the cracked ground.

"Only one way to find out," said Allan, his voice muffled as he pushed his way through an opening where several boards had fallen, in to a section that was leaning – dangerously, Linda thought – to one side. "Oh, man, look at this!"

It took a few moments before Linda's eyes adjusted to the gloom of the building, which was in stark contrast to the brassy brightness outside. The openings along the sides, which would once have been thronged with onlookers watching the happy mayhem within, were boarded up in places, and in others choked with trees, which stifled the sunlight trying to filter in from without. The floor was covered in dirt and leaves and splintered pieces of wood, and in one corner lay a heap of what looked like broken chairs. Running along the back, across from where they stood, was what had obviously once been a covered gallery: a few shafts of sunlight punched their way through holes in the roof, and cables dangled limp from overhead, the lights they had once supported long gone.

Allan was picking his way carefully across the floor, pausing every now and then to take a picture. "Jeez, I'd love to find some of the cars," Linda heard him say. "Wonder what happened to them. Oh, hey, look at this!"

"What?" Linda had only moved a couple of feet away from where they had entered, and was reluctant to advance any further. The building looked anything but stable.

"There's a hole in the floor here. Looks like someone cut through with a chainsaw. I can't really see much . . . hang on a sec." He fished around inside his bag and pulled out a flashlight, then shone it through the hole. "Nothing but a load of junk," he said, disappointed. "Hey, what the . . ." He moved suddenly to his left, trying to angle the flashlight as if to see better, and there was a cracking sound from beneath his feet. He scrambled backward as Linda retreated to the side of the building.

"Allan, for heaven's sake, come away from there. That floor's probably rotted through. If it gives way you could kill yourself."

"No, it's okay, just something shifting. All right, all right," – as Linda opened her mouth to protest – "I'm coming back. Nothing much more to see in here anyway."

"What was down there?"

"I told you. A load of junk, dead leaves, that sort of thing."

"I thought you saw something else."

"No, just shadows, that's all." They were back outside, and Linda breathed a bit more freely now that they were on safe ground. "C'mon, I want to check out the Fun House."

"You've got to be kidding." Linda glanced at the dilapidated building beside them. "It makes that last one look like a prize home exhibit."

Allan said nothing, but walked away around the front of the Fun House, past a rusting, peeling iron rail that led up a concrete slope to where the entrance had apparently been. There was a wire cage beside it half-obscured by trees, and Allan pointed to it.

"That would have been where the ticket guy sat, probably. Look, you can see the exit sign on the other side of it. Looks like they had another fire here." Out came the camera. "I'm just going to walk round, see if I can get a better shot." Before Linda could say anything, Allan disappeared around the corner.

Linda ran her eyes over the front of the building. The entrance looked almost passable, but the exit was covered with boards clumsily stacked against it. One was slightly askew, as if someone had tried to get in that way, and all showed signs of scorching.

*Too bad the whole thing didn't go up*, thought Linda. *Would've been an improvement.*

There was a sound behind her, off in the trees, as of a branch snapping. She whirled round, peering into the undergrowth. Nothing moved. "Allan?" she called, rather faintly; then, more loudly, "Allan? Where are you?"

No answer. Damn, she hoped he hadn't found a way in. The place was ready to collapse. "Allan!" she called, anger giving an edge to her voice. "Allan, come back here!"

Still nothing. She turned and looked again at the undergrowth, and, as she did so, caught out of the corner of her eye movement inside the wire cage by the Fun House entrance. She swung her head back towards it and could see, between the trees, a figure inside it, half-crouched down as if looking for something. *Or trying to hide.*

"Allan! Allan, this isn't funny. It may have been a Fun House once, but that's no reason to . . ."

"Who're you talking to?"

Linda spun round. Allan had come up behind her, from the

passage between the Fun House and the Bumper Car building. "Is there someone here?"

"No, I . . ." Linda looked back at the wire cage. The trees shifted in the wind, almost as if obliging her, and she could see that it was empty. "I thought there was someone in there, that you were playing a joke."

"Not me. The only way to get in there is from inside the building, and I can't find any way in that looks safe." He sounded regretful. "Got some good pictures, though."

"Oh, well, as long as you've got some good pictures then everything's okay, isn't it?"

"What's wrong?" Allan sounded genuinely puzzled.

"Nothing. Nothing at all. I'm just getting tired of poking around old buildings that should've been pulled down years ago, that's all. Like that abandoned factory two months ago, where I got that gash on my knee. Thought I was going to need stitches."

"Well, you didn't, did you?" pointed out Allan, in a reasonable tone that set Linda's teeth on edge. "Okay, c'mon, let's see what else we can find."

"More abandoned buildings, probably. Thrilling. Let's face it: you've seen one, you've pretty much seen them all."

"I guess." Allan didn't sound convinced. "But there's more here than just empty buildings; lots of rides still on the site. One site I found said that there's a Tumble Bug ride somewhere. There are only four in existence still."

Linda stared at him. "You know, I've been trailing after you to places like this for three years now, but you never cease to amaze me. You're thirty-two, for God's sake, Allan. Shouldn't you have grown out of this sort of thing? Going around looking at all this shit that no one except you and a handful of other people care about? Children's rides! Why?"

"Because – well, because I like it, that's why!" He shook his head. "What's not to like? It's all a part of our past, and it's disappearing, and unless people like me find it, see it, photograph it, it'll be as if it never existed. It'll just be pictures in books that no one looks at." He gestured at the expanse of greenery around them, the forlorn buildings behind them. "This used to be an amusement park. Not just that, it was the midway, the heart of the whole place. Can't you picture it the way it would have been fifty years ago, with kids, families, music playing, the smell of fried onions, the sound of the rides? All those children, almost sick with excitement at the thought of a day at White Lake Park? All the happiness that was here once? *Someone* has to remember it, otherwise it might as well never have been."

Linda started to say something, but was stopped by the look on Allan's face. He looked like a big kid himself; in the car, on the drive out to the park, his face had worn the expression of a child anticipating a major treat. She sighed instead, and made a *You win* gesture with her hands. "I don't want to be here all day, Allan, okay? It's too hot, and this place gives me the creeps."

"Yeah, what was it that spooked you so much back there?" Allan gestured at the Fun House.

"I told you. I thought I saw someone in that wire cage thing." She recalled something else. "And before that I thought I heard someone in the bushes over there." She pointed.

"Really?" Glad to be back on neutral territory, Allan took a few steps in that direction. "Over here?"

"Yeah. Look, it was probably just the wind or a squirrel or something. Forget it."

"No, hang on a minute . . ." Allan moved away through the trees, and it did not take many steps before he appeared to be swallowed up by the foliage. Linda waited for a moment, staring intently at where he had vanished. Suddenly she heard a choked cry, followed by a short laugh. "Hey, Linda, come here. I found your intruder."

"What? Allan, this isn't funny."

"No, honest." He reappeared between the trees. "Come look."

She followed him into the undergrowth, peering nervously around her. Allan motioned to a dense clump of maple saplings. "Come and see." Gingerly she stepped forward, and parted the lower branches; then jumped backward with a screech.

A face was leering at her: livid and fierce, vivid reds and too-pale whites. It took a moment for her to register what it was, and when she did she turned on Allan in anger.

"You bastard! You knew I'd jump, that it'd scare me half to death. Jerk."

It was a wooden sign, in the shape of a clown. Out of the garish red mouth came a speech balloon, inside which were the words YOU MUST BE THIS TALL TO RIDE THIS RIDE. One of the clown's arms had obviously indicated the height requirement, but it had vanished, and only a jagged stump bleeding splinters remained.

Allan raised his arms in a would-be placating gesture. "Hey, I'm sorry, I didn't realize it would make you jump like that. Startled me, too, but look." He pointed further into the trees, and Linda unwillingly looked in that direction, her heart still pounding. She could vaguely make out, in the undergrowth, metal shapes, trees growing through and around them.

"What is it?"

Allan had set off in the direction of the shapes. "I think it's the – yeah, it's the Flying Cages!" he called over his shoulder. "Man, I've never seen one of these rides. Read about them, though. Used to be in the touring carnivals that went round the county fairs and things, but you don't see them anymore."

When she got closer, Linda wondered why anyone had bothered in the first place. The ride seemed to consist of four large metal cages, each one originally a different colour, although the paint had faded and chipped away, leaving only a few traces on the metalwork. One of the cars still had remnants of pale blue cloth trailing from the sides, and Allan nodded.

"That would have been where the cages were padded," he said. He went up to the nearest one and gave it a push. There was a harsh squealing noise and the cage began to move slightly, and Allan gave it another, harder push. It rocked back and forth for a few moments, the framework which supported it groaning in protest at the unexpected movement. After a few moments its movements stilled and it came to rest once more, and there was silence.

"Wow, it still works. This one, anyway."

"Is that all it did? Swung back and forth?"

"I think so. Like I said, I've never actually seen one before."

"Guess those really were simpler times."

"Oh, c'mon, Linda. A lot of rides look pretty tame from the ground, but when you're in 'em they're terrifying. That whole loss-of-control thing. I mean, imagine being in one of these, it's swinging back and forth, higher and higher, faster and faster, and there's music playing, and you're bouncing from side to side, trying not to lose your balance, watching the ground come at you, people screaming, yelling . . . it's a real rush."

"I'll take your word for it. That kind of thing never appealed much to me. I like to keep my feet on the ground. Even when I was a kid I didn't like to . . . hey, are you listening?"

Allan had turned his head suddenly, and was gazing back the way they had come. When Linda repeated her question he turned back to her with a start, as if only just remembering she were there.

"Did you hear that?" he asked, puzzled.

"What? I didn't hear anything."

"I heard – well, I thought I heard music."

"Music?" Linda stared at him. "No, I didn't hear any music. Maybe someone's car stereo turned up, or music from a nearby house."

"No." Allan shook his head. "It almost sounded like . . . I don't know, like old-fashioned calliope music." When Linda looked puzzled, he said impatiently, "You know, like on a carousel. A merry-go-round."

"Nope. Didn't hear anything like that." She gave a short laugh. "What a pair. I see things, you hear things. Maybe it's time to leave."

"No. Not yet. There's too much more I want to see."

Linda glanced at her watch, then at the sun overhead. "Okay, Allan. But not too much longer. And no more scares, right?"

"Right."

They headed back the way they'd come, Linda carefully not looking at where she knew the clown stood. Once back in front of the Fun House they stopped, and Allan looked at his plan.

"This way, I think," he said.

"You *think*? Where're we going now?"

"Further along the midway."

"Looking for your Stumble Bugs?"

"Tumble Bugs," he said impatiently. "No, well, yes. I mean, I want to see them, obviously—"

"Obviously."

"But there's lots of stuff here I want to see. I just want to wander down the midway, see what we find." And he set off, once more leaving Linda to trail behind.

They walked for thirty yards or so, Linda looking over her shoulder now and then to see where they'd come from. She wanted to be sure they knew how to get out again when Allan finally got tired and called it a day. She also couldn't quite shake the feeling that they were being followed, and she wondered if the woman at the house had tipped someone off that they were in there. She was glancing over her shoulder again – was that someone moving back behind a tree, just out of sight? – when Allan stopped dead and she stumbled against him. She was about to say something when he shushed her and pointed to their right.

"What is it?" she asked, any urge she might have had to say "Sorry" gone, but he merely made a shushing noise and pointed again. She looked in that direction, but even then it was a few moments before she realized what she was looking at.

"Ferris Wheel," Allan whispered. "Wonderful!" And he was off, camera raised, leaving Linda to stand and stare.

It had been a Ferris Wheel, once, but now it was a shell of its former self. They were sideways on to it and she could see the outer rings which had once supported the cars, which were gone. Trees grew up and through the Wheel's structure, and it looked like a giant child's toy suspended in the branches, ready to break free and roll away in a heavy wind. She would not even have seen it had Allan not pointed it out, and Linda shivered, wondering what else was in the trees, then hurried to catch up to Allan, who was at the base of the Wheel, staring at it in admiration.

"This is incredible," he said, turning to her, eyes aglow. "I had no idea there was so much of it left. Amazing."

"Wonderful." She gazed up through the branches to where the Wheel sat silently above them. "This place is like a graveyard. No, it's like a morgue, full of dead bodies. Couldn't someone have given them a decent burial, at least?"

Allan shrugged. "Probably cost too much. Cheaper to leave it here than break it up and haul it out." He raised the camera again. "Just a few more shots."

"I've heard that song before," Linda muttered, but stood while he took a few more pictures, stopping every now and then to throw out some comment that she only half-heard. She glanced back the way they had come, and there it was again; that faint trace of movement at the corner of her eye, as of someone ducking out of sight. She shook her head. If someone had tipped off the police then the cops wouldn't be hiding behind trees.

"Okay, let's go." Allan was beside her, his eyes sparkling, his face happier than she had seen it in some time. "I've got a real treat for you now. No" – he raised a finger to his lips – "I'm not going to tell you. You'll see for yourself. We're almost there. It wasn't too far from the Ferris Wheel."

They walked back to the cracked surface of what Linda supposed had been the main course of the midway, and had not gone far before Allan stopped. "There," he said proudly, as if he had conjured it up out of mid-air in a spectacular piece of magic, and Linda saw the Coaster.

It had looked impressive and faintly menacing from the road, but now, close to, it was even more startling. They were standing near one end – the turnaround, Linda knew it was called – and could just make out the rest of the structure stretching out through the trees, dipping and twisting. Allan, of course, had his camera up, and Linda gazed at him for a moment, wondering how a person could be so enthusiastic about something like this. She had been wondering for three years now, and was beginning to think the question would never be answered; at least not in a way she would ever understand.

Her gaze fell to the uneven surface in front of them. The sun was at their back and she could see her own shadow, clear and sharp, on the ground in front of her. Her eyes flicked to the ground in front of Allan, and she noted that his own shadow was much less distinct. *Some trick of the light, or the ground* she thought, and was about to say something when she caught her breath with a hiss.

There was a third shadow stretched out in front of them.

It was clearly the head and shoulders of someone – a man, she thought – who appeared to be standing roughly equidistant between her and Allan, and slightly behind them. She turned her head so suddenly that she felt something pop between her shoulders.

There was no one there.

When she looked forward again, the shadow was gone.

She blinked and shook her head, her eyes darting from side to side. She had seen it, as clearly as she had seen their own shadows but it couldn't have been there. She told herself that, firmly, as she followed Allan towards the Coaster, which seemed to emerge from the trees the closer they got to it, as if shaking itself off like a dog coming out of water. Allan was in such a fever of excitement that Linda was surprised he could keep the camera steady as he darted about, taking pictures from every angle.

"Oh, man, this is incredible. I had no idea it was in this good a state!" He looked up at the wooden struts which now rose above them, criss-crossing, supporting the track, which looked to be intact. "Amazing. Almost looks operational. Wouldn't be surprised to see a car coming along the tracks."

Linda knew that he was seeing a different Coaster to the one she was looking at; one without maples choking the tracks, or dead trees leaning drunkenly against the supports of the first turnaround, one where guard rails weren't missing and footings weren't rotting and sinking into the muddy earth. To Allan, she knew, it looked as it had in its heyday, a place of happiness and excitement and laughter, and for a moment she wished she could see it through his eyes. Before she could say anything, however, he was off again, heading towards a long, low building with an arched roof at the far end of the track, calling "Loading station!" over his shoulder as he went.

Linda picked her way through the trees, cursing as something caught at her skirt. It took her a few moments to work it free, and when she looked up Allan was gone. On the archway over the entrance she could make out the word COASTER, or at least what remained of it. Some of the letters had fallen off, and what was left was the word COST, with only shadows of the other letters marking where they had once stood.

She dropped her eyes, trying to see into the station, but all she could make out was a suggestion of railings, with a bench at one side. It was full of shadows, and she wished again that she could see it as Allan did.

She was suddenly aware of how exposed she must look, alone and vulnerable, and her eyes automatically raked the under-growth around her, which seemed full of movement, although when her eyes fell directly on a spot there was nothing to be seen. She thought she saw someone move quickly behind a small outbuilding on the far side of the track, by the dips, and remembered her earlier impression of being followed. If there was someone else in the park, she definitely didn't want to be there by herself, so even though she had no desire to go inside the station she trudged towards it and climbed the cracked ramp leading up from ground level.

Within it was cooler, and she could smell rotted leaves and damp earth and something else, something more pungent, less wholesome. She did not want to think about what it was. From outside came the sound of a voice, and her immediate thought was Allan, calling her; but after a moment she realized that it didn't sound like Allan at all, certainly not him calling her, more like someone having a conversation. The contrast between the dimness inside and the sunshine outside meant she could see little beyond the station, and she made her way down the platform towards the sound of the voice, noting the rails still standing primly alongside the track, the faded yellow line on the concrete indicating where those waiting had had to stand, the brake levers standing at odd angles like thin tombstones.

Something skittered under one of the benches. *A leaf, or maybe a mouse*, she told herself, and hurried forward.

There was movement from outside the station, but when she emerged there was no one in sight. She stared, wondering where Allan could have got to. She looked down what she knew was the brake run, and could see more maples and buckeyes poking between the rails, but there was no sign of Allan. She was about to call out when she heard his voice behind her, down at the other end of the platform.

"What're you doing down there? Come here! You've got to see this – it's great!"

Linda had turned in the direction of his voice, and now whipped her head back round, gazing down the brake run once more. No one was there, of course, and yet . . . She shook her head, surprised to find herself on the verge of tears. She didn't understand what was going on, and she wanted to run, bolt like an animal, back to the car, get the hell out of Dodge . . .

Allan called again. "You coming? I want to show you something. Hurry!"

She was on the verge of asking why she had to hurry. It wasn't as if anything in the park was going anywhere. Instead she took a deep breath, set her shoulders, and marched determinedly down the centre of the platform, looking neither to left nor right, ignoring the whispers which started up outside the station as soon as she turned her back. *Only trees, Linda; it's only the trees.*

Allan was standing on the stretch of track that left the station heading towards the lift hill. She had obviously missed seeing him on her initial walk past. The track curved sharply to the right and she could see, beyond Allan, what looked like a shed built across the track, curving with it. The open entranceway was choked with undergrowth and blocked by a fallen tree, and she could make out blackness beyond, but nothing more.

"Look at that!" Allan gestured to the shed. "This is really something special. The track is pretty basic – your ordinary out-and-back layout – but you don't often see this."

"What's 'this'?" asked Linda. "Why did someone build a shed over the track?"

"It's not a shed, it's a tunnel. Look," – Allan pointed back towards the station – "the train would have left the station, started into the curve towards the lift hill, and then – wham! into a tunnel." He peered at the opening. "Hard to tell what sort of doors there would have been. Probably crash doors, like in a dark ride." He shook his head. "Can't tell from here. Maybe the other side is better." And without another word he was off, heading around the inside of the curve, leaving Linda trailing in his wake.

She caught up to him at the other end of the tunnel. To her right the lift hill ascended, a dead tree suspended across it, and to her left she could see the tunnel exit. A corrugated iron door stood across one side; the other gaped open, and for a moment Linda thought that something darted back into the shadows. *This is crazy*, she thought, *you're seeing things.* Yet when Allan moved towards the opening she heard an edge of panic in her voice as she called out "Where are you going?"

"I want to look inside the tunnel, see how clear it is." Linda cast her eyes along the structure, which looked more or less intact at either end but appeared badly damaged in the middle, where a tree had come down on the roof.

"I don't think that's a very good idea, Allan." She didn't move, couldn't, from where she stood. "C'mon," – this as he approached the entrance, shining his flashlight through the open side – "let's go. We still have to find your Tumble Bugs, or whatever they're called."

"I don't care about those." Allan pushed through the open door, and she saw his figure swallowed up by the tunnel. She wanted to scream, but bit her lip and called out again "Allan! Please!"

"Oh, Linda, you've got to see this," she heard him say. His voice sounded as if it was coming from far away. "Man, this is better than I could have imagined. There's an old coaster car in here, in pretty good shape. This is just amaz—"

His voice stopped suddenly, like a needle jerked off a record. Linda waited for a moment, then called "Allan?" in a voice she barely recognized as her own. When there was no reply she called again, louder, but there was nothing except the sound of branches clattering against each other and, somewhere, a faint snatch of music that was snuffed out almost instantly.

She knew she had to go look, knew that she had to go up to the tunnel entrance and see what had happened – he'd fallen, something had hit him, he'd collapsed – but the mouth of the tunnel seemed . . . *busy*, somehow, as if there were too many shadows there. She gave a thin scream, like an animal in a trap. Then, as the shadows seemed to thicken and grow darker she turned, turned and ran, like a frightened child, heedless, uncaring, back the way they had come, her bag banging against her side with each step, her breath coming in ragged gasps, her ears filled with sounds she did not want to identify, shadows running alongside her, thin shapes clutching at her legs, until she was somehow – miraculously – back at the door in the fence, shouldering her way through, careless of how she might look to anyone watching, running up to the house, pounding on the door, and only then, it seemed, pausing for a moment to think about what had happened, what had to be done . . .

The door swung inward and the woman they had spoken with earlier stood framed inside the opening. She looked at Linda; then her eyes travelled past her, and Linda, even in her confusion, saw a look of pain mixed with sadness settle in her face. She looked back at Linda.

"My boyfriend," Linda gasped, trying to form her thoughts into something coherent, something that would make sense. "My boyfriend – he's in there, in the park, something's happened to him . . ."

"I know." The voice was quiet, but there was sorrow contained within it.

"What do you mean, you know? How can you know?"

"I do. We all do."

Linda took a deep breath, tried to calm herself. "I need to use your phone, call the police, the ambulance, someone. I think he might be hurt."

"No, he's not hurt."

"How do you *know*?" Linda almost screamed. "You weren't there. He was inside that tunnel, by the Coaster; some of it had collapsed, he might be lying there injured, I need to get *help*."

"No one can help." The woman's eyes flicked over Linda's shoulder again, towards the park. "There's nothing anyone can do. Believe me."

"But you don't *understand*," begged Linda, her voice harsh. "He's in there, he could be hurt, I need to *do* something."

"There's nothing you can do. He'll come out if he wants to. Some of them do. You can wait here with us, if you like."

Linda tried to make sense of what she was hearing. "What do you mean, some of them do? Some of who? And who do you mean by 'us'?"

The woman half-turned her head, towards the hallway behind her. "Us," she said simply.

Linda looked over the woman's shoulder, and saw that there were others behind her; women, all, half-a-dozen or so. One or two looked to be the same age as the woman in the doorway, but the others were older, middle-aged at least, or perhaps they only looked so. It was difficult to tell. All were plainly dressed, in clothing that ranged from threadbare to out-of-date. Apart from that, their only commonality was a look that Linda could only think of as resigned sadness. She turned back to the woman in the doorway.

"Who are you?" she asked, in a voice that sounded as if it came from many miles away. "Why are you here?"

"We're waiting," the woman said simply. "Some of us have been waiting a long time." She nodded towards the cars parked in the lane beside the house. "Some of us can't leave. So we wait. What else can we do?"

Linda shivered. Her mind seemed to be retreating from her body, but she heard herself say, "So they come back – sometimes?"

"Yes. But it can be a long time, if it happens." The woman looked at Linda, her gaze steady. "You have to be prepared to wait. Are you prepared?"

Linda took a deep breath and drew herself upright. As she did so her bag shifted against her hip, and she heard the rattle of the car keys from deep inside it. An image of Allan's face as she had seen it at the Coaster flashed before her: excited, eager, happy, in a way that she had seldom seen it.

"I don't know," she replied finally. "Can I think about it for a minute?"

"Yes, of course. We have all the time in the world."

There was nothing more to be said. The door closed.

*All the time in the world.*

But it would not take her that long to decide.

# RAMSEY CAMPBELL

## Respects

RAMSEY CAMPBELL'S MOST RECENT books are the novel *Creatures of the Pool* and the collection *Just Behind You*, both from PS Publishing, and from Titan Books, *Solomon Kane*, "based on the movie and various drafts of the screenplay, it attempts both to capture the film and include deleted elements that director Michael J. Bassett would have liked to include," explains the author. Forthcoming is another novel, *The Seven Days of Cain*, and *Ghosts Know* is in progress.

"'Respects' was suggested by a local incident in which a car thief in his early teens killed himself while fleeing the police," recalls Campbell. "A lamp standard at the site of his demise is still decorated with flowers years after the incident, and the tributes on the obituaries page of one Wallasey newspaper were at least as grotesque as the ones I've invented – the romanticisation of a petty criminal.

"How much has this to do with the public hunger for a moment in the media? The tendency has produced its own clichés. There almost seems to be a standard script (created by the demand for sound bites) for grieving parents to deliver at press conferences. A lost daughter inevitably becomes 'my little princess', and it isn't uncommon to hear very young children described as 'my best friend'.

"Does this cheapen the grief? People may need to express their feelings (although not doing so, at least in public, can be useful too), but how much does banality and inaccuracy express?"

B Y THE TIME DOROTHY finished hobbling downstairs, somebody had rung three times and knocked several more.
Charmaine Bullough and some of her children were blocking the
short garden path under a nondescript November sky. "What
did you see?" Charmaine demanded at once.

"Why, nothing to bother about." Dorothy had glimpsed six-
year-old Brad kicking the door, but tried to believe he'd simply
wanted to help his mother. "Shouldn't you be at school?" she
asked him.

Brad jerked a thumb at eight-year-old J-Bu. "She's not," he
shouted.

Perhaps his absent siblings were, but not barely teenage
Angelina, who was brandishing a bunch of flowers. "Are those for
me?" Dorothy suggested out of pleasantness rather than because
it seemed remotely likely, then saw the extent of her mistake.
"Sorry," she murmured.

Half a dozen bouquets and as many wreaths were tied to the
lamp-standard on the corner of the main road, beyond her gate.
Charmaine's scowl seemed to tug the roots of her black hair
paler. "What do you mean, it's not worth bothering about?"

"I didn't realise you meant last week," Dorothy said with the
kind of patience she'd had to use on children and parents too
when she was teaching.

"You saw the police drive our Keanu off the road, didn't
you?"

"I'm afraid I can't say I did."

At once, despite their assortment of fathers, the children resembled their mother more than ever. Their aggressive defensiveness
turned resentful in a moment, accentuating their features, which
were already as sharp as smashed glass. "Can't or won't?"
Charmaine said.

"I only heard the crash."

Dorothy had heard the cause as well – the wild screech of
tyres as the fifteen-year-old had attempted to swerve the stolen
Punto into her road apparently at eighty miles an hour, only
to ram a van parked opposite her house – but she didn't want
to upset the children, although Brad's attention seemed to have
lapsed. "Wanna wee," he announced and made to push past her,
the soles of his trainers lighting up at every step.

As Dorothy raised a hand to detain him, J-Bu shook a fist that set bracelets clacking on her thin arm. "Don't you touch my brother. We can get you put in prison."

"You shouldn't just walk into someone else's house," Dorothy said and did her best to smile. "You don't want to end up—"

"Like who?" Angelina interrupted, her eyes and the studs in her nose glinting. "Like Keanu? You saying he was in your house?"

Dorothy might have. The day before the crash she'd come home to find him gazing out of her front room. He hadn't moved until she managed to fumble her key into the lock, at which point he'd let himself out of the back door. Apart from her peace of mind he'd stolen only an old handbag that contained an empty purse, and so she hadn't hurried to report him to the overworked police. If she had, might they have given him no chance to steal the car? As Dorothy refrained from saying any of this, Charmaine dragged Brad back. "Come out of there. We don't want anyone else making trouble for us."

"I'm sorry not to be more help," Dorothy felt bound to say. "I do know how you feel."

Angelina peered so closely at her that Dorothy smelled some kind of smoke on the girl's breath. "How?"

"I lost my husband just about a year ago."

"Was he as old as you?" J-Bu said.

"Even older," said Dorothy, managing to laugh.

"Then it's not the same," Angelina objected. "It was time he went."

"Old people take the money we could have," said J-Bu.

"It's ours for all the things we need," Brad said.

"Never mind that now," said Charmaine and fixed Dorothy with her scowl. "So you're not going to be a witness."

"To what, forgive me?"

"To how they killed my son. I'll be taking them to court. The social worker says I'm entitled."

"They'll have to pay for Keanu," said Brad.

Dorothy took time over drawing a breath. "I don't think I've anything to offer except sympathy."

"That won't put shoes on their feet. Come on, all of you. Let's see Keanu has some fresh flowers. He deserves the best," Charmaine added louder still.

Brad ran to the streetlamp and snatched off a bouquet. About to throw them over Dorothy's wall, he saw her watching and flung them in the road. As Angelina substituted her flowers, Dorothy seemed to hear a noise closer to the house. She might have thought a rose was scratching at the window, but the flower was inches distant. In any case, the noise had sounded muffled by the glass. She picked up a beer can and a hamburger's polystyrene shell from her garden and carried them into the house.

When she and Harry had moved in she'd been able to run through it without pausing for breath. She could easily outdistance him to the bedroom, which had been part of their fun. Now she tried not to breathe, since the flimsy shell harboured the chewed remains of its contents. She hadn't reached the kitchen when she had to gasp, but any unwelcome smell was blotted out by the scents of flowers in vases in every downstairs room.

She dumped the rubbish in the backyard bin and locked the back door. The putty was still soft around the pane Mr Thorpe had replaced. Though he'd assured her it was safe, she was testing the glass with her knuckles when something sprawled into the hall. It was the free weekly newspaper, and Keanu's death occupied the front page. LOCAL TEENAGER DIES IN POLICE CHASE.

She still had to decide whether to remember Harry in the paper. She took it into the dining-room, where a vase full of chrysanthemums held up their dense yellow heads towards the false sun of a Chinese paper globe, and spread the obituary pages across the table. Keanu was in them too. Which of the remembrances were meant to be witty or even intended as a joke? "Kee brought excitement into everyone's life"? "He was a rogue like children are supposed to be"? "There wasn't a day he didn't come up with some new trick"? "He raced through life like he knew he had to take it while he could"? "Even us that was his family couldn't keep up with his speed"? Quite a few of them took it, Dorothy suspected, along with other drugs. "When he was little his feet lit up when he walked, now they do because he's God's new angel." She dabbed at her eyes, which had grown so blurred that the shadows of stalks drooping out of the vase appeared to grope at the newsprint. She could do with a walk herself.

She buttoned up her winter overcoat, which felt heavier than last year, and collected her library books from the front room. Trying to read herself to sleep only reminded her that she was alone in bed, but even downstairs she hadn't finished any of them – the deaths in the detective stories seemed insultingly trivial, and the comic novels left her cold now that she couldn't share the jokes. She lingered for a sniff at the multicoloured polyanthuses in the vase on her mother's old sideboard before loading her scruffiest handbag with the books. The sadder a bag looked, the less likely it was to be snatched.

The street was relatively quiet beneath the vague grey sky, with just a few houses pounding like nightclubs. The riots in Keanu's memory – children smashing shop windows and pelting police cars with bricks – had petered out, and in any case they hadn't started until nightfall. Most of the children weren't home from school or wherever else they were. Stringy teenagers were loitering near the house with the reinforced front door, presumably waiting for the owner of the silver Jaguar to deal with them. At the far end of the street from Dorothy's house the library was a long low blotchy concrete building, easily mistaken for a new church.

She was greeted by the clacking of computer keyboards. Some of the users had piled books on the tables, but only to hide the screens from the library staff. As she headed for the shelves Dorothy glimpsed instructions for making a bomb and caught sight of a film that might have shown an equestrian busy with the tackle of her horse if it had been wearing any. On an impulse Dorothy selected guides to various Mediterranean holiday resorts. Perhaps one or more of her widowed friends might like to join her next year. She couldn't imagine travelling by herself.

She had to slow before she reached her gate. A low glare of sunlight cast the shadow of a rosebush on the front window before being extinguished by clouds, leaving her the impression that a thin silhouette had reared up and then crouched out of sight beyond the glass. She rummaged nervously in her handbag and unlocked the door. It had moved just a few inches when it encountered an obstruction that scraped across the carpet. Someone had strewn Michaelmas daisies along the hall.

Were they from her garden? So far the vandals had left her flowers alone, no doubt from indifference. As her eyes adjusted to the dimness she saw that the plants were scattered the length of the hall, beyond which she could hear a succession of dull impacts as sluggish as a faltering heart. Water was dripping off the kitchen table from the overturned vase, where the trail of flowers ended. She flustered to the back door, but it was locked and intact, and there was no other sign of intrusion. She had to conclude that she'd knocked the vase over and, still without noticing unless she'd forgotten, tracked the flowers through the house.

The idea made her feel more alone and, in a new way, more nervous. She was also disconcerted by how dead the flowers were, though she'd picked them yesterday; the stalks were close to crumbling in her hands, and she had to sweep the withered petals into a dustpan. She binned it all and replenished the vase with Harry's cyclamen before sitting on the worn stairs while she rang Helena to confirm Wednesday lunch. They always met midweek, but she wanted to talk to someone. Once she realised that Helena's grandchildren were visiting she brought the call to an end.

The house was big enough for children, except that she and Harry couldn't have any, and now it kept feeling too big. Perhaps they should have moved, but she couldn't face doing so on her own. She cooked vegetables to accompany the rest of yesterday's casserole, and ate in the dining-room to the sound of superannuated pop songs on the radio, and leafed through her library books in the front room before watching a musical that would have made Harry restless. She could hear gangs roving the streets, and was afraid her lit window might attract them. Once she'd checked the doors and downstairs windows she plodded up to bed.

Girls were awaiting customers on the main road. As Dorothy left the curtains open a finger's width she saw Winona Bullough negotiate with a driver and climb into his car. Was the girl even sixteen? Dorothy was close to asking Harry, but it felt too much like talking to herself, not a habit she was anxious to acquire. She climbed into her side of the bed and hugged Harry's pillow as she reached with her free hand for the light-cord.

The night was a medley of shouts, some of which were merely conversations, and smashed glass. Eventually she slept, to be wakened by light in the room. As she blinked, the thin shaft coasted along the bedroom wall. She heard the taxi turn out of the road, leaving her unsure whether she had glimpsed a silhouette that reminded her of stalks. Perhaps the headlamps had sent a shadow from her garden, though wasn't the angle wrong? She stared at the dark and tried not to imagine that it was staring back at her. "There's nobody," she whispered, hugging the pillow.

She needed to be more active, that was all. She had to occupy her mind and tire her body out to woo a night's unbroken sleep. She spent as much of Saturday in weeding the front garden as the pangs of her spine would allow. By late afternoon she wasn't even half finished, and almost forgot to buy a wreath. She might have taken Harry some of his own flowers, but she liked to support the florist's on the main road, especially since it had been damaged by the riots. At least the window had been replaced. Though the florist was about to close, he offered Dorothy a cup of tea while his assistant plaited flowers in a ring. Some good folk hadn't been driven out yet, Dorothy told them both, sounding her age.

She draped the wreath over the phone in her hall and felt as if she were saying goodbye to any calls, an idea too silly to consider. After dinner she read about far places that might have changed since she and Harry had visited them, and watched a love story in tears that would have embarrassed him. She was in bed by the time the Saturday-night uproar began. Once she was wakened by a metallic clack that sounded closer than outside, but when she stumbled to the landing the hall was empty. Perhaps a wind had snapped the letterbox. As she huddled under the quilt she wondered if she ought to have noticed something about the hall, but the impression was too faint to keep her awake. It was on her mind when church bells roused her, and as soon as she reached the stairs she saw what was troubling her. There was no sign of the wreath.

She grabbed the banister so as not to fall. She was hastening to reassure herself that the flowers were under the hall table, but they weren't. Had she forgotten taking them somewhere? They were in none of the ground-floor rooms, nor the bathroom, her bedroom, the other one that could have been a nursery but had all too seldom even done duty as a guest room. She was returning downstairs when she saw a single flower on the carpet inches from the front door.

Could a thief have dragged the wreath through the letter-box? She'd heard that criminals used rods to fish property from inside houses. She heaved the bolts out of their sockets and flung the door open, but there was no evidence on the path. It didn't seem worth reporting the theft to the police. She would have to take Harry flowers from the garden. She dressed in her oldest clothes and brought tools from the shed, and was stooping to uproot a weed that appeared to have sprouted overnight when she happened to glance over the wall. She straightened up and gasped, not only with the twinge in her back. One of the tributes to Keanu looked far too familiar.

She clutched at her back as she hobbled to the streetlamp. There was the wreath she'd seen made up at the florist's. It was the only item to lack a written tag. "Earned yourself some wings, Kee" and "Give them hell up there" and "Get the angels singing along with your iPod" were among the messages. The wreath was hung on the corner of a bouquet's wrapping. Dorothy glared about as she retrieved it, daring anyone to object. As she slammed the front door she thought she heard small feet running away.

She had no reason to feel guilty, and was furious to find she did. She locked away the tools and changed into the dark suit that Harry used to like her to wear whenever they dined out. A bus from the shattered shelter on the main road took her to the churchyard, past houses twice the size of hers. All the trees in their gardens were bare now. She and Harry had been fond of telling each other that they would see them blossom next year. The trees in the graveyard were monotonously evergreen, but she never knew what that was meant to imply. She cleared last week's flowers away from Harry's stone and replaced them with the wreath, murmuring a few sentences that were starting to feel formulaic. She dropped the stale flowers in the wire bin outside the concrete wedge of a church on her way to the bus.

As it passed her road she saw the Bulloughs on her path. Charmaine and her offspring strode to meet her at the lamp. "Brad says you lifted our Keanu's flowers."

"Then I'm afraid he's mistaken. I'm afraid—"

"You should be," said Arnie, the biggest and presumably the eldest of the brood. "Don't talk to my mam like that, you old twat."

Dorothy had begun to shake – not visibly, she hoped – but stood her ground. "I don't think I'm being offensive."

"You're doing it now," Arnie said, and his face twisted with loathing. "Talking like a teacher."

"Leave it, Arn," his mother said more indulgently than reprovingly, and stared harder at Dorothy. "What were you doing touching Keanu's things?"

"As I was trying to explain, they weren't his. I'm not accusing anybody, but someone took a wreath I'd bought and put it here."

"Why didn't you?" demanded Angelina.

"Because they were for my husband."

"When are you going to get Kee some?" J-Bu said at once.

"She's not," Charmaine said, saving Dorothy the task of being more polite. "Where were these ones you took supposed to be?"

"They were in my house."

"Someone broke in, did they? Show us where."

"There's no sign of how they did it, but—"

"Know what I think? You're mad."

"Should be locked up," said Angelina.

"And never mind expecting us to pay for it," Arnie said.

"I'm warning you in front of witnesses," said their mother. "Don't you ever touch anything that belongs to this family again."

"You keep your dirty hands off," J-Bu translated.

"Mad old bitch," added Brad.

Dorothy still had her dignity, which she bore into the house without responding further. Once the door was closed she gave in to shivering. She stood in the hall until the bout was over, then peeked around the doorway of the front room. She didn't know how long she had to loiter before an angry glance showed that the pavement was deserted. "Go on, say I'm a coward," she murmured. "Maybe it isn't wise to be too brave when you're on your own."

Who was she talking to? She'd always found the notion that Harry might have stayed with her too delicate to put to any test. Perhaps she felt a little less alone for having spoken; certainly while weeding the garden she felt watched. She had an intermittent sense of it during her meal, not that she had much appetite, and as she tried to read and to quell her thoughts with television. It followed her to bed, where she wakened in the middle of the night to see a gliding strip of light display part of a skinny silhouette. Or had the crouching shape as thin as twigs scuttled across the band of light? Blinking showed her only the light on the wall, and she let the scent of flowers lull her to sleep.

It took daylight to remind her there were no flowers in the room. There seemed to be more of a scent around her bed than the flowers in the house accounted for. Were her senses letting her down? She was glad of an excuse to go out. Now that they'd closed the post office around the corner the nearest was over a mile away, and she meant to enjoy the walk.

She had to step into the road to avoid vehicles parked on the pavement, which was also perilous with cyclists taking time off school. Before she reached the post office her aching skull felt brittle with the sirens of police cars and ambulances in a hurry to be elsewhere, not to mention the battering clatter of road drills. As she shuffled to the counter she was disconcerted by how much pleasure she took in complaining about all this to her fellow pensioners. Was she turning into just another old curmudgeon weighed down by weary grievances? Once she'd thanked the postmaster several times for her pension she headed for the bus stop. One walk was enough after all.

Although nobody was waiting outside her house, something was amiss. She stepped gingerly down from the bus and limped through gaps in the traffic. What had changed about her garden? She was at the corner of the road when she realised she couldn't see a single flower.

Every one had been trampled flat. Most of the stalks were snapped and the blossoms trodden into the earth, which displayed the prints of small trainers. Dorothy held onto the gatepost while she told herself that the flowers would grow again and she would live to see them, and then she walked stiff as a puppet into the house to call the police.

While it wasn't an emergency, she didn't expect to wait nearly four unsettled hours for a constable less than half her age to show up. By this time a downpour had practically erased the footprints, which he regarded as too common to be traceable. "Have you any idea who's responsible?" he hoped if not the opposite, and pushed his cap higher on his prematurely furrowed forehead.

"The family of the boy you were trying to catch last week."

"Did you see them?"

"I'm certain someone must have. Mrs Thorpe opposite hardly ever leaves the house. Too worried that clan or someone like them will break in."

"I'll make enquiries." As Dorothy started to follow him he said "I'll let you know the outcome."

He was gone long enough to have visited several of her neighbours. She hurried to admit him when the doorbell rang, but he looked embarrassed, perhaps by her eagerness. "Unfortunately I haven't been able to take any statements."

"You mean nobody will say what they saw," Dorothy protested in disbelief.

"I'm not at liberty to report their comments."

As soon as he drove away she crossed the road. Mrs Thorpe saw her coming and made to retreat from the window, then adopted a sympathetic wistful smile and spread her arms in a generalised embrace while shaking her head. Dorothy tried the next house, where the less elderly but equally frail of the unmarried sisters answered the door. "I'm sorry," she said, and Dorothy saw that she shouldn't expect any witness to risk more on her behalf. She was trudging home when she caught sight of an intruder in her front room.

Or was it a distorted reflection of Keanu's memorial, thinned by the glare of sunlight on the window? At first she thought she was seeing worse than unkempt hair above an erased face, and then she realised it was a tangle of flowers perched like a make-shift crown or halo on the head, even if they looked as though they were sprouting from a dismayingly misshapen cranium. As she ventured a faltering step the silhouette crouched before sidling out of view. She didn't think a reflection could do that, and she shook her keys at the house on her way to the door.

A scent of flowers greeted her in the hall. Perhaps her senses were on edge, but the smell was overpowering – sickly and thick. It reminded her how much perfume someone significantly older might wear to disguise the staleness of their flesh. Shadows hunched behind the furniture as she searched the rooms, clothes stirred in her wardrobe when she flung it open, hangers jangled at her pounce in the guest room, but she had already established that the back door and windows were locked. She halted on the stairs, waving her hands to waft away the relentless scent. "I saw you," she panted.

But had she? Dorothy kept having to glance around while she cooked her dinner and did her best to eat it, though the taste seemed to have been invaded by a floral scent, and later as she tried to read and then to watch television. She was distracted by fancying there was an extra shadow in the room, impossible to locate unless it was behind her. She almost said "Stay out of here" as she took refuge in bed. She mouthed the words at the dark and immediately regretted advertising her nervousness.

She had to imagine Harry would protect her before she was able to sleep. She dreamed he was stroking her face, and in the depths of the night she thought he was. Certainly something like a caress was tracing her upturned face. As she groped for the cord, the sensation slipped down her cheek. The light gave her time to glimpse the insect that had crawled off her face, waving its mocking antennae. It might have been a centipede or milli-pede – she had no chance to count its many legs as it scurried under the bed.

She spent the rest of the interminable night sitting against the headboard, the bedclothes wrapped tight around her drawn-up legs. She felt surrounded, not only by an oppressive blend of perfume that suggested somebody had brought her flowers – on what occasion, she preferred not to think. As soon as daylight paled Keanu's streetlamp she grabbed clothes and shook them above the stairs on her way to the bathroom.

She found a can of insect spray in the kitchen. When she made herself kneel, stiff with apprehension as much as with rheuma-tism, she saw dozens of flowers under her bed. They were from the garden – trampled, every one of them. Which was worse: that an intruder had hidden them in her room or that she'd unknowingly done so? She fetched a brush and dustpan and shuddered as she swept the debris up, but no insects were lurking. Once she'd emptied the dustpan and vacuumed the carpet she dressed for gardening. She wanted to clear up the mess out there, and not to think.

She was loading a second bin-liner with crushed muddy flowers when she heard Charmaine Bullough and her youngest children outdoing the traffic for noise on the main road. Dorothy managed not to speak while they lingered by the memorial, but Brad came to her gate to smirk at her labours. "I wonder who could have done this," she said.

"Don't you go saying it was them," Charmaine shouted. "That's defamation. We'll have you in court."

"I was simply wondering who would have had a motive."

"Never mind sounding like the police either. Why'd anybody need one?"

"Shouldn't have touched our Kee's flowers," J-Bu said.

Her mother aimed a vicious backhand swipe at her head, but a sojourn in the pub had diminished her skills. As Charmaine regained her balance Dorothy blurted "I don't think he would mind."

"Who says?" demanded Brad.

"Maybe he would if he could." Dorothy almost left it at that, but she'd been alone with the idea long enough. "I think he was in my house."

"You say one more word about him and you won't like what you get," Charmaine deafened her by promising. "He never went anywhere he wasn't wanted."

Then that should be Charmaine's house, Dorothy reflected, and at once she saw how to be rid of him. She didn't speak while the Bulloughs stared at her, although it looked as if she was heeding Charmaine's warning. When they straggled towards their house she packed away her tools and headed for the florist's. "Visiting again?" the assistant said, and it was easiest to tell her yes, though Dorothy had learned to stay clear of the churchyard during the week, when it tended to be occupied by drunks and other addicts. She wouldn't be sending a remembrance to the paper either. She didn't want to put Harry in the same place as Keanu, even if she wished she'd had the boy to teach.

Waiting for nightfall made her feel uncomfortably like a criminal. Of course that was silly, and tomorrow she could discuss next year's holiday with Helena over lunch. She could have imagined that her unjustified guilt was raising the scents of the wreath. It must be the smell of the house, though she had the notion that it masked some less welcome odour. At last the dwindling day released her, but witnesses were loitering on both sides of the road.

She would be committing no crime – more like the opposite. As she tried to believe they were too preoccupied with their needs to notice or at least to identify her, a police car cruised into the road. In seconds the pavements were deserted, and Dorothy followed the car, hoping for once that it wouldn't stop at the Bullough house.

It didn't, but she did. She limped up the garden path as swiftly as her legs would work, past a motor bicycle that the younger Bulloughs had tired of riding up and down the street, and posted the wreath through the massively brass-hinged mahogany door of the pebbledashed terrace house. She heard Charmaine and an indeterminate number of her children screaming at one another, and wondered whether they would sound any different if they had a more than unexpected visitor. "Go home to your mother," she murmured.

The police were out of sight. Customers were reappearing from the alleys between the houses. She did her best not to hurry, though she wasn't anxious to be nearby when any of the Bulloughs found the wreath. She was several houses distant from her own when she glimpsed movement outside her gate.

The flowers tied to the lamp-standard were soaked in orange light. Most of them were blackened by it, looking rotten. Though the concrete post was no wider than her hand, a shape was using it for cover. As she took a not entirely willing step a bunch of flowers nodded around the post and dodged back. She thought the skulker was using them to hide whatever was left of its face. She wouldn't be scared away from her own house. She stamped towards it, making all the noise she could, and the remnant of a body sidled around the post, keeping it between them. She avoided it as much as she was able on the way to her gate. As she unlocked the door she heard a scuttling of less than feet behind her. It was receding, and she managed not to look while it grew inaudible somewhere across the road.

The house still smelled rather too intensely floral. In the morning she could tone that down before she went for lunch. She made up for the dinner she'd found unappetising last night, and bookmarked pages in the travel guide to show Helena, and even found reasons to giggle at a comedy on television. After all that and the rest of the day she felt ready for bed.

She stooped to peer under it, but the carpet was bare, though a faint scent lingered in the room. It seemed unthreatening as she lay in bed. Could the flowers have been intended as some kind of peace offering? In a way she'd been the last person to speak to Keanu. The idea fell short of keeping her awake, but the smell of flowers roused her. It was stronger and more suggestive of rot, and most of all it was closer. The flowers were in bed with her. There were insects as well, which didn't entirely explain the jerky movements of the mass of stalks that nestled against her. She was able to believe they were only stalks until their head, decorated or masked or overgrown with shrivelled flowers, lolled against her face.

# SIMON STRANTZAS

## Cold to the Touch

SIMON STRANTZAS' MOST RECENT short-story collection, *Cold to the Touch*, was published by Tartarus Press in 2009. Meanwhile, his first collection, *Beneath the Surface*, has recently been reprinted by Dark Regions Press. The author's work has also appeared in the previous two volumes of *The Mammoth Book of Best New Horror*, as well as *Cemetery Dance*, *PostScripts* and elsewhere.

"Stories often find their origins in unexpected ways," Strantzas reveals. "I was inspired in this case by a photograph of a Zen garden I once used as my computer's desktop background. After staring at it day-in and day-out while I worked, I began to wonder about that dark circle of rocks and just what its true purpose might be.

"There was something there in the coldness of the photograph, something that brought to mind the barren vistas of the Canadian Arctic, which ended up being the perfect setting for my tale of tested faith."

Along with its appearance here, "Cold to the Touch" will appear in *Holy Horrors*, a two-volume anthology of religious horror edited by T.M. Wright and Matt Cardin, from Ash-Tree Press.

ANDREW LAUZON STOOD surrounded by his equipment on the
tarmac of a small airport just beyond Iqaluit. He had gone
as far north as aeroplanes could take him, but he still needed to
go further, deep into the Nunavut Territory, to the edge of the
Arctic itself.

He shivered uncontrollably as he waited for Luis to arrive.
The cold October wind scratched his face like sandpaper and,
beneath his crossed arms, he felt the shape of the small book
pressed into his ribs.

God, at least, had a plan for him.

Andrew spotted the truck moving towards him through the
greyish landscape of the northern brush, and when it arrived it
was mottled with a haze of salt and snow. Behind the wheel the
thick dark-skinned Inuk was barely older than Andrew himself,
yet his face was broad and wrinkled, as though a lifetime of icy
wind had dug grooves into his features. Those deep crags did not
move when he spoke.

"You weren't waiting long," Luis said. It wasn't a question.
He glared at the young scientist, while behind him blue fumes of
sweet poison filled the air.

Andrew introduced himself. Luis said nothing, and scratched
the coarse stubble along his chin.

"Should we ... um ... where should the bags go?" Andrew
said. Luis sighed and got out of the dirty truck to unchain the
tailgate.

"Right here. All you had to do was open your eyes."

The inside of the truck smelled of old vinyl and stale cigarettes
and beer. The two travelled along a solitary road northward,
with nothing on the horizon before them but flat brush. Even
that slowly thinned, and the ground gradually became whiter.
Luis smoked cigarettes one after the other, and tossed each
finished butt through a cracked window, while Andrew read
quietly from his Bible. He could feel Luis' periodic scowl, but
the man said nothing. Andrew eventually put away the book,
and only then did Luis return his full attention to the road. After
an hour, Andrew struggled for something to say.

"Have you seen it?"

"Seen what?" Luis took the cigarette from his mouth and spat
carelessly until a small piece of tobacco landed on the dashboard.

"The anomaly I was sent to study. The satellite photos were very unclear about what I'd see."

"No. What the hell do you do, anyway?"

"I specialize in abnormal weather patterns, in climate fluctuations."

Luis tossed another cigarette through the window. "You can remove your hood; the climate in here doesn't fluctuate." Andrew smiled uncertainly and removed the fur-lined hood.

Luis pointed a thumb over his shoulder. "Is that what all the equipment's for?"

"Yes. It's primarily thermometers and temperature sensors. Some seismic monitors, too."

"Sounds fascinating," Luis said, feigning interest poorly.

Andrew looked out the window at the shifting landscape. He could see how perfect it all was, even when the Arctic weather was coldest, when the sun hung just on the precipice of the horizon yet refused to fall off for months, and time itself seemed to stand still.

"Everywhere I look, I can see the hand of God."

Luis scoffed. "There's nothing out there but nothing."

"How can you say that? I thought the Inuit saw the North as sacred?"

"Yeah, and we all ride dog-sleds. Don't worry, the igloo's well heated."

Andrew touched his Bible through his coat.

It took two more hours to reach their destination, though Andrew didn't realize at first they had arrived. He expected something bigger, more settled, than a single cabin. There was no one around to greet them, but he thought he saw a shadow move behind the murky window. Smoke rose from the tiny chimney, trying desperately to keep the cold at bay.

Luis pulled the truck off the road and parked it beside a pair of snowmobiles at the rear of the building.

Andrew unlocked the door to the small cabin. The place was little more than a room with a large iron stove and two cots, and whoever had lit the fire for them was no longer there.

The two men unloaded the equipment from the truck bed, and carried it into the cabin. When they stepped back outside another Inuk, shorter and wider than Luis, waited by the snowmobiles for them. Andrew said hello, and the man nodded, then let loose a stream of grunts like nothing Andrew had ever heard.

"His name's Akiak," Luis said, and kicked his steel-toed boot against the doorframe. "Nobody speaks English up here, and they don't do much talking, especially to a *qallunaat* like you. They're all outcasts; they don't fit in anyplace else, and they don't like being disturbed."

"Is that what you are? An outcast?"

"No," Luis said, and paused to light another of his cigarettes. "I'm a heathen. And I'm too poor to live anywhere else."

Andrew cleaned his hands in the small washroom at the opposite end of the cabin, happy to be rid of the dirt he had managed to accumulate over the past day of travelling. He already felt exhaustion creeping into his mind, and he found it difficult to focus. The buckled laminate that covered the walls and floor made the whole place seem unreal, as though part of some dream. Behind everything a generator droned, powering ineffectual lights that were unable to prevent the dim shadows from crowding at the window. Andrew felt claustrophobic, and he closed his eyes and prayed until he felt safe again.

The cots faced each other from opposite sides of the room: one caught in the yellow light from the window, the other beside the old iron stove. Luis settled on the warmer cot and stretched out until his dripping feet hung over the edge. His cigarette pointed straight into the air, and a thin column of smoke twisted upward. He coughed then snorted, and wondered aloud, "When do we start?"

Andrew put down his bag to consult his watch. He had been travelling for almost twenty hours straight. "I think we ought to get some sleep. We can start work in the morning."

"Morning isn't coming," Luis said. He sat up, and plucked the cigarette out from between his lips. He looked straight at Andrew, then flicked the butt at the iron stove. It slipped through the grate and into the fire. "Don't forget to shut the blinds when you're done praying," he said. "That sun isn't going anywhere soon, and I don't like God watching me sleep."

If Andrew slept, he did not remember doing so. Even if light hadn't continued to slip past the closed blinds and into his eyes, the odour would have been enough to keep him awake. It was like wet leather and old sweat, like a dampness that would never dry no matter how hot the stove burned. Luis remained unaffected; instead, he was splayed across the bed, and the creak from his throat filled Andrew's mind.

Andrew prayed for silence, but it was in those moments, alone and in the dark, that he feared no one was listening, that if he didn't do all he could to hold his faith together, everything would fall apart.

He put the thought out of his mind and sat up. His eyes felt thick, and he rubbed his lower back where the cot's metal frame had pressed into it. He sighed heavily and checked his watch in the light from around the edges of the wooden blinds.

Upon the wall by the door hung a painting Andrew hadn't registered the day before. It was about two feet square and depicted a sea of white scratched with greys and blues. Within this blizzard sat a large rounded figure, curled and grey, featureless but for the large hands that it held cupped. They were one above the other, and between them swirled clouds of red and yellow. The figure was painted with thick black lines and rounded joints, very much like the native art he had seen before, but the painting held no Inuit totems. There was nothing but the curled figure, and the light between its hands that danced like millions of glowing red men.

Andrew first sensed, rather than heard, the sound emanating from the wall before him. It was a slight vibration, a hum, which progressively increased in volume. The timbre, the rhythm, sounded like a voice echoing from the painting, more than one in fact, as if the painting spoke to him, but he couldn't understand what it was saying. He leaned closer, his breath on the canvas, and he jumped when, behind him, Luis spoke.

"What the hell are you doing?"

"I thought – I heard *voices*!"

"What? Are you Joan of Arc, now?" Luis sat still a moment, then shook his head. "I don't hear squat."

A sharp knock made them both jump.

At the door, stood Akiak, his fur-lined jacket embroidered with the pattern of sprinting animals. He said something, and Luis grunted back and got out of bed.

"Grab your 'Good Book'," he said. "It's time to go."

The two snowmobiles idled outside the cabin, though only one
had a small sled attached. After they loaded the equipment on to
it, Luis pointed a gloved finger at Andrew's face. "You'll go with
Akiak. Try not to fall off."

There was a moment of hesitation, and Akiak beckoned
Andrew impatiently. Andrew sat on the back of the vehicle
and put his hands around the Inuk's chest, closed his eyes, and
nodded. Akiak put the snowmobile in gear and Andrew was
yanked back. Then they were moving across the snow.

The snowmobile vibration rattled Andrew's teeth, and he
ducked his head to keep his face from freezing. After a while,
he opened his eyes to nothing but white. Snow lay everywhere,
great plains of it, and it would have been impossible to tell where
it met with the grey sky if not for the giant yellow orb that sat on
the horizon, halfway between night and day.

When the snowmobile finally began to slow down, it came
to a stop in the middle of nowhere. Andrew's legs vibrated as
though he were still moving, and for a moment he didn't trust
them. Akiak stepped off without pause, and was already unloading the sled when Luis pulled up beside them.

"This is as far as we can go. We're walking the rest of the way.
Unless you don't think you can make it."

Andrew furrowed his brow. "Why here?"

Luis pointed ahead, and then Andrew understood.

The white surface of snow before them dipped into the ground
and formed a crater at least five miles wide. In the distance,
Andrew could see a darkness at its centre: some blackened rocks
that stood out from the ground, in relief against the white of the
crater walls. Akiak swung the equipment cases on to his back,
then carefully stepped to the edge of the crater. He hesitated,
then hiked his load further and started down. Luis followed,
then Andrew.

The walk was harder than Andrew had expected; the muscles
in his legs burned after only a few minutes. Luis and Akiak had
already left him behind as they effortlessly moved through the
snow. Andrew tried to remain unconcerned – they couldn't do
much without him, after all – but he couldn't shake his sense of

dread. Even the prayer he said under breath didn't help; the cold of the snow was sneaking through the soles of his boots, and he wondered how long it would take to die if he were left out there alone.

As if on cue, Luis and Akiak stopped and looked back at him. "We're almost there," Luis shouted, then said something to the guide that Andrew couldn't hear over his own heavy breathing.

As they came nearer, Akiak grunted something that slowed Luis. He stopped and looked around, then he stuck out his arm to prevent Andrew from going further. "Watch out," he said.

Andrew looked down and found himself one creaking step from a deep fissure in the ice. It stretched about ten feet long, and the snow from Andrew's halted footsteps was swallowed by the darkness.

"There's about three miles between us and the actual Earth," Luis said. "The rest is ice, and sometimes it cracks. Nothing to worry about. Unless you step in one."

"What happens then?"

"You go straight down to hell."

Luis and Akiak laughed. Andrew looked out across the ice and snow and saw more cracks, dark marks like fingerprints upon the empty whiteness.

Andrew was careful to watch the ground as they proceeded, and planted his feet on firm snow. He didn't see the dark rock formation until he was almost upon it.

In the snow towered five black stone monuments of various heights arranged roughly in a circle almost twenty feet across. The tallest measured at least ten feet, and each was about three feet wide. Their surfaces were rough and uneven, yet covered in a swirling pattern of shallow grooves.

And all five stood incongruous in the icy tundra.

Andrew's eyes widened. "It can't be," he muttered. "Those rocks are completely dry."

Akiak spoke, and Luis translated. "He says these rocks have always been here, but he avoids this place. It's bad luck." The Inuk didn't seem comfortable in the ring of stones. He kept glancing at them, though, and ran his hands across the leg of his pants.

"Why?"

"This place is called *Okralruserk*, and no one is allowed to come here, not even *Torngasak*, the spirit of Good. It's just a superstition," he said, and began to reorganize the empty equipment cases.

Andrew placed sensors and instruments around the stones. It felt no warmer within the circle than elsewhere, but the thermal satellite photos indicated otherwise. He was determined to discover the cause. While Andrew worked, Akiak appeared mesmerized by the five monuments. He stared for some time, then approached one cautiously, and stopped inches from its rocky surface. With a sense of wonder on his face, he let his eyes follow the swirling grooves. Akiak rubbed his mouth with the back of his hand, then removed his glove. Whispering something, he slowly raised his arm, fingers spread wide, and laid his palm upon the rock. Andrew thought he heard the man sigh.

When Luis yelled, Akiak snatched his hand back and Andrew dropped the thermosensor he'd been holding; it smashed to pieces on the frozen ground. Luis said something in a stern voice and Akiak simply nodded, then went to help Luis with the cases, doing his best to ignore the five monoliths.

When Andrew finished setting up the equipment, and they were preparing to leave, Andrew asked Luis what the yelling was about.

"I was trying to scare the love of God into him."

There was only the sound of wind and ice creaking underfoot during the long walk back to the snowmobiles. Andrew was tired, lost in contemplation, and he felt the effects of the twilight sun upon his body. Akiak suffered the burden of the equipment wordlessly while Luis, cigarette hanging from an exposed lip, ignored them both. As snow fell from the dark amber sky, Andrew wondered what kind of a man would willingly spend his life so far from everyone and everything.

Perhaps all Luis needed was a little salvation.

Andrew had trouble with his dinner. He had never tasted deer meat before, and the caribou was sweeter than he expected. He paused after the first bite, unsure what to do, and Luis laughed.

"I guess you'd rather have a hamburger and some fries," he said, and took a large piece of steak from Andrew's plate.

"It's just new to me, that's all."

Luis chewed on this a moment, then said, "I don't see any reason why you think you're wanted up here; the weather's fine."

"It's not, not really. We're sitting on one of the largest stores of methane and carbon dioxide on the planet, and it's trapped in the ice. The temperature here over the last forty years has gone up almost six degrees! That means it's only a matter of time before the gases are released back into the atmosphere. Once that happens, the chain-reaction will make the hole in the ozone layer look like a pinprick. Something's happening, and everyone's in a panic. Global warming makes people jittery; they all think Armageddon's coming."

"Do you?"

"It's coming, the Bible says so," he said, and placed his copy on the table; "But not today."

"Right. I forgot. So if you don't believe it, why did you come?"

"It's not that I don't believe – I've seen the projections – but I suppose I just wanted some time to see things myself."

Luis snorted, and pushed his plate away. "Well, all you get up here is time. Time and space."

"You make it sound lonely."

"All of us are alone. All of the time."

"You know," Andrew said, laying his hand on the book, "You aren't alone now."

Luis shook his head. "Open your eyes and look around. God is dead. Don't be a chump."

"I used to feel the same, but just because *Science* doesn't believe in *Faith* doesn't mean *Faith* doesn't believe in *Science*. God is there for you if you'll listen."

"Why don't *you* listen," Luis said, then stopped himself. He stood. "Suddenly I feel a bit crowded up here by all your saints. I'm going out. Don't wait up."

"Just because you don't feel His love, doesn't mean you've been abandoned . . ." Andrew said, but it was too late. Luis had gone.

Andrew lay in bed and read his Bible. He scoured every page – ran his fingers along the text, feeling the grooves of the printed letters. He read until his eyes itched and the words began to swirl in strange patterns, then he stood and pushed the bed until it was out of the sunlight. If he were lucky, he would manage to sleep through the night.

Andrew sat up, wakened by a sound that nearly stopped his heart. His ears still rang, and he looked around the room but saw nothing wrong. Luis lay unmoving, dead to the world, and the smell of liquor and cigarettes hovered in the air. Nothing moved.

Then, the air was disturbed by a low creak. It grew with each passing second and filled his head. He covered his ears, but it was useless; the sound broke through. It became louder, then louder, and just when Andrew feared his skull would burst, there was a crack as if the world had split open, and Andrew leapt from his bed, terrified, and fell to his knees. He prayed for the noise to end.

The air fell quiet, and though he waited, the sound did not return; yet when Andrew got back into bed, he could not sleep. Across from him, above the motionless Luis, rays of light slipped through the covered window.

The next morning Luis laughed while rubbing the sleep from his bloodshot eyes.

"I saw the show last night. You city people are all the same – can't take the isolation."

Andrew made an effort to smile, and touched the book in his pocket. "What *was* that?"

"The ice. It cracks like that all the time. Usually, though, it's not that loud unless you're closer to the water."

When they met with Akiak at the snowmobiles, he was bundled up against a cold that surprised even Luis. Andrew could still hear the ice cracking, though the fresh snow seemed to dampen the noise of the changing landscape.

Akiak was unnerved by the sound, and he jumped at each crack, disquieting Andrew. The wind had gone for the moment, yet it seemed colder somehow. Andrew wrapped his scarf higher on his face as Akiak started the snowmobile's engine. When they took off, the small rectangle of the Bible pushed into Andrew's ribs.

The new snow lay over everything and instantly obliterated any landmark Andrew might recognize. Within minutes he was lost in the Arctic tundra.

On the edge of the giant crater, the snowmobiles came to a stop and Andrew hastily dismounted. He stumbled as he did so, and the Bible slipped out of his pocket and disappeared beneath the surface of the snow. Andrew reached into the collapsing hole until his arm sank to his shoulder, but he felt nothing. He thrashed his hand in panic, while Luis and Akiak stood idle. It wasn't until Andrew's fingers grazed a solid corner that he relaxed, and he pulled out the snow-covered book as he stood.

"Is it okay?" Luis asked, his eyebrow cocked in amusement.

"I think so," Andrew said as he inspected the book. Snow had slipped into the binding beneath the *faux* leather covers, and he brushed off as much as he could.

"If not, there might be a hotel ahead where you can grab another." Luis laughed and started walking again, while Andrew carefully unzipped his coat and placed the book inside. He shivered as the cold of the wet volume pressed up against his chest. It took a few minutes for the book to warm, and even then he could feel the dampness seep into his clothes.

The snow was deepest at the crater's bottom; Andrew sank to mid-thigh, and his progress slowed. Luis and Akiak moved more easily, though they too were panting.

Andrew continued to hear the muffled creaking, and saw more fissures in the ground. The snow was deep, but not deep enough to fill them, only to better hide them. More than once, he found himself a step away from falling inside one. Though the cracks were not large enough to consume him, they were wider than any he had seen the day before, and he worried that he might be pulled beneath the snow before anyone noticed that he was gone.

Ahead, Luis had stopped. He was panting and staring at Okralruserk when Andrew reached him.

"I feel drawn to this place," Luis said, almost to himself. Akiak grunted. It did not sound like a word, but it caught Luis' attention. He was himself again. He removed the pack of cigarettes from his front pocket and lit one. "There it is," he said, and started walking.

The rocks looked bigger than Andrew had remembered, taller, even with the extra foot of snow on the ground, but he couldn't be sure. Okralruserk was still a few hundred yards away, with only a background of white for reference.

They finally reached the circle of rocks, and Luis stopped again. "What is it?" Andrew asked.

"Look," Luis said. "Don't you see?"

But Andrew couldn't see anything. Okralruserk looked just as they had left it the day before. Luis pointed.

"Why aren't they covered in snow?"

He was right. The snow that had caused them so much trouble had not touched the tall dark rocks. Luis walked around the stones and inspected them. "They don't have *ice* on them," he said. "They're completely dry."

"The darker the surface, the more light it absorbs," Andrew said as he checked the readings on the instruments. "This constant sunlight, even half-light – maybe it's warmed the rocks enough that the snow and ice have simply melted away."

Luis made a strange noise, then removed his glove and laid his bare hand on the stone. "This one's cold."

"Well, the electric thermometers haven't recorded anything significant. Wait—" Andrew said, and bent closer to the plastic box he had previously installed. It was crushed; the sensors inside had been rendered useless, and it was the same for the boxes at the other stones. "My equipment's been damaged. I can't accurately determine if there were changes to temperature delta."

Luis continued to touch the five rocks, looking unsuccessfully for one that might still be warm. He ran his fingers over them, along the swirling grooves, and suddenly he stopped and looked closer.

"Hey, these are symbols, like something's written in the stone."

"What?" Andrew put the broken equipment down and went over.

Akiak stood rubbing his hands together at the edge of Okralruserk, keeping as far away as he could from the rocks. Luis beckoned him closer, but the older Inuk would not come.

Andrew inspected the writing. "Do you recognize it? It looks old."

"It's not Inuit. We didn't have a written language until around the twenties, and this looks . . . older."

Luis bent on his knee and inspected the foot of one of the stones. "These grooves go all the way down, *under* the snow and ice."

"I wonder how big these rocks are."

"Let's find out." From one of the equipment cases, Luis removed a large hammer with a thin, sharp head. "Let's see if we can dig far enough to get below the writing."

Luis swung the pick down with all his strength, aiming at the ground from where the monument emerged, but the thick ice proved stronger than he'd expected, and the hammer kicked up in his hand, then smashed into the stone. A large chunk of black rock broke free and hit Luis square in the temple. Unconscious, he crumpled to the frozen ground and twitched as blood coursed from his head.

Akiak was at Luis' side a moment later. He pulled a rag from his pocket and held it to the wound, then pointed urgently at the scientist's waist.

"My belt?" Andrew said, his head swimming in mounting panic. Akiak pointed again and nodded.

Andrew had to remove his gloves first, and his fingers quickly became numb in the chill. He fumbled the buckle open as quickly as he could and handed the belt over.

Akiak wrapped the belt around the unconscious man's head and pulled it tight to keep the makeshift bandage in place.

The two men carried Luis across the deep snow, narrowly avoiding the fissures that multiplied with every creaking sound, back to the crater's edge. They pulled Luis up and over the ridge, then strapped him to the sled and covered him with a blanket. Andrew prayed aloud as he climbed on the back of the vehicle behind Akiak. They drove faster than Andrew thought possible, and he pressed his head against the driver's back to avoid the stinging snow.

Luis moaned as the two men carried him inside the cabin and placed him on his bed. Blood had seeped through the makeshift bandage, and Akiak loosened the belt to check the wound. He turned and grabbed Andrew by the wrist, then pulled him closer and pressed his hand to Luis' wound. Akiak stood and said something else then ran out the door. Andrew remained, quiet and unmoving, and prayed that God might help the unconscious Luis.

The heat of the cabin did not warm him.

After twenty minutes, Akiak returned with another Inuit behind him. This second man pushed Andrew aside and started checking Luis, then opened the small bag he was carrying and removed a stethoscope. Andrew stood, then he ran to the washroom and vomited in the sink. He wiped his mouth, but stayed in the small room for a few moments and tried to steady his breathing. In the other room, there was very little talking. Then, he heard the loud rap of something heavy being dropped, and no further sound followed. When Andrew emerged, though, both the doctor and Akiak were still there.

Andrew paced the room for a few minutes, then stopped at the window and ran his fingers through his thin hair. Outside, clouds had managed to dampen the setting sun.

Akiak spoke and Andrew shook his head. "What? I don't understand."

The Inuk looked at him a moment, then put his wool hat on and walked out.

On the table beside Luis' head sat a chunk of dark rock, about the size of a fist. Even from that distance, Andrew could see swirls of writing upon it.

He checked his watch. It had been hours since the doctor left, yet Akiak had still not returned. Luis slid in and out of consciousness, mumbling incoherently. Half his words were not words, instead just noises pretending to be words. Andrew had no idea how long he might be incapacitated, or what kind of care to provide. There seemed to be no one nearby other than Luis who spoke English. The doctor had tried to communicate with him before leaving, eventually settling in frustration on a pantomime of sleep, though Andrew was unsure to which of the three it referred. He wasn't sure if the doctor planned on returning.

Andrew knelt beside the bed, Bible in hand, to pray for Luis. The book had still not dried, had become warped by the moisture of the snow, and as he opened it to find the verse he wanted pages began to fall out. The entire book then crumbled in his hands, and he struggled unsuccessfully to keep the leaves in order as they spilled onto the ground.

He scooped up the pages and carried them to his bed. He felt uneasy at the sight of Luis, as though the air were being sucked from his lungs. He faced away from the window, closed his eyes and breathed deeply, in and out, willing himself to relax.

He no longer felt safe. He felt trapped.

Andrew checked his watch and wondered what was keeping Akiak. At the door, he looked out and saw everything bathed in late afternoon sunlight, but Andrew knew that it was far later. He felt out of sync with the world and was unsure what to do.

On the table beside Luis, the stone fragment from Okralruserk watched over him. Andrew remembered it being larger, and picked it up to feel its weight.

And almost dropped it.

The rock was covered in something dark and wet and sticky, and it had turned Andrew's hand almost black in the shaded cabin. There was blood everywhere, more than Andrew imagined there should be, and it filled the symbols carved into the rock's surface.

Andrew felt sick and quickly went to wash his hands. The porcelain of the small basin turned red as he rinsed the blood from between his fingers, and he stared, lost in worry, as the tainted water circled the drain.

He dried his hands and sat down on his bed again. Across from him, Luis lay with half his head swathed in white gauze. He had not stopped muttering anxiously, though about what Andrew couldn't understand.

The day had been a long one, and Andrew was starting to feel its effects. He yawned, then laid his head down only a moment to still his troubled mind. He closed his eyes, and was awoken hours later by the sound of a deafening crack. Across from him, Luis' bed was empty.

The door stood wide open and Luis' coat and boots were gone. Cold filled the room, a dull light fell upon the unoccupied bed. Andrew ran to the door, but the sudden white was too much for his eyes. When they adjusted, he saw a set of tracks across the snowy tundra, and a small dark spot disappearing into nothingness.

Andrew stood in the doorway feeling utterly alone.

He had no idea where Akiak had gone, no idea where he might find help. Behind the cabin sat Luis' snowmobile, but even if Andrew could drive it he didn't have the key. The tiny figure grew smaller by the second, and he feared at any moment it would be gone forever. His heart beat faster in his ears, and he tried to control the breath that moved too quickly through him. The ends of his fingers tingled in the cold, and he clutched them together and prayed for direction. He closed his eyelids tight until he saw stars, and then opened them slowly. All breath left his body for a moment.

Then, he put on his own gear and went after Luis.

He hoped he might catch up quickly, but the depth of snow fought against him, and he had no choice but to follow at a slower pace.

Periodically, the dark figure would stop, wait for Andrew to gain ground, and then start moving again. It did this for the better part of an hour, each time leaving Andrew further behind.

Then, without warning, Andrew was following only footprints.

The air howled with cold wind and shifting ice. It had become deafening, and Andrew held his gloved hands against the hood of his parka to stamp it out.

He was exhausted, and felt more uneasy the further he travelled from the cabin. If Luis didn't tire soon, Andrew would never catch him.

The trail brought Andrew to the edge of the crater. He stopped and called out as loudly as he could, but the wind and cracking ice swallowed the sound. He strained his eyes, looking for movement in the white, but there was nothing between him and the silhouette of Okralruserk at the depression's dark centre.

Andrew prepared to descend the crater's edge when he looked down and felt a chill run through him. The snowmobile Akiak had been driving was at the bottom of the sharp decline, about twenty feet away and wedged into the ground. A giant fissure stretched from it; the entire floor of the crater was full of them, long gaping cracks that had churned up large slabs of ice. He tried to get to the snowmobile and see if Akiak lay there wounded, but the upheaval prevented his approach. He reached instinctively to touch the Bible in his coat, and felt nothing in its place. Andrew's heart started racing, yet he was powerless to slow it. He tried to calm down, but the blood moved faster and faster until his head began to throb. Sparks of light filled his eyes, and he closed them, terrified he would faint. He crouched and held his breath. After a moment he forced it, as slowly as he could, through his pursed lips, and told himself over and over that things were okay, that God was with him, that nothing would go wrong. When he finally believed it, he opened his eyes.

And saw that it was snowing. Large flakes filled the air, and where they landed they erased the footprints and landmarks that were Andrew's last tether to the world behind him.

If not for Okralruserk's dark blemish, visible through the swirling white, Andrew would have dropped to his knees and abandoned himself to the cold. Even so, the image only flickered in the brewing storm, as though it was insubstantial. The monument beckoned him, and Andrew had no choice but to go forward, tripping over the upturned ice, before Okralruserk vanished completely into the blinding snow.

The wind howled as it cut through his thick clothes, but he kept moving straight towards the darkness. He had to find Luis before it was too late, or else neither of them might survive what was coming.

The weight of snow against Andrew took its toll, and he almost collapsed when he reached Okralruserk. He needed a moment to catch his breath, and when he looked up he was astounded. The giant black rocks were completely untouched by the storm, though the ground beneath them was a maze of extensive fissures that radiated from the foot of each stone like ripples in the ice.

The remains of his thermal equipment were scattered around the site, some half-buried in the snow within the circle, others blown into the periphery. Andrew picked up a piece, unsure of what it once had been, then dropped it to the ground. Everything he had was destroyed.

The wind pushed hard against him, and it threw the snow up into eddies around Okralruserk. He twisted his body to escape the brunt of it and caught from the corner of his eye a shadow move behind one of the five monoliths.

Luis knelt at the base of the stone, his hands tangled in his thick hair. He giggled and whispered in delirium at the dark rocks.

"Are you okay?" Andrew asked, his voice drowning in the wind.

Luis looked up and his frozen red cheeks cracked as he spit out more laughter.

"I knew it! Even when I didn't know I knew it was here!"

He turned back to the rock and eyed it up and down, then mumbled something more to it. He ran his hands along its deep grooves as though he could read every word of the chiselled writing. The left side of Luis' face was stained with dark red blood from his wound.

"We have to go," Andrew said.

Luis only laughed, and the wind howled in unison. Andrew had to yell to be heard.

"Have you seen Akiak?"

Luis stopped laughing, and looked straight into Andrew's eyes.

"He's here! He's come back for us."

"Where?" Andrew said, and spun around, but the swirling snow beyond Okralruserk blurred everything, and Andrew couldn't tell which shadows within the storm were real. He stumbled, as though something had moved beneath his feet.

"He's here," Luis said, and he was crying. "He's here to save us all." Andrew realized then that Luis' mind had gone, lost in the miles of white empty snow.

And worse, Andrew felt another sudden and cold understanding deep within him.

He had been abandoned.

"He's here," Luis screamed with a manic joy into the wind, and he wept as he clutched at the tall black stone.

The ground beneath Andrew then shifted, revealing something in the snow beyond the circle of Okralruserk.

Snow drained into the newly-formed crevasse, filling a hole thousands of feet deep. Andrew approached it, his mind struggling to understand what he saw within the snow that remained, but the shape seemed beyond comprehension.

Then, just as he was upon it, it reformed itself in his mind, and he gasped.

It was a glove, and beneath it, trapped in the fissure, was Akiak.

Andrew stood back, thoughts in his head crashing into one another. Then the ground began to shake, and all around him the dull cracking sound grew sharper, louder.

"You see?" said Luis as he stared into the half-lit sky. "He's back for us now. God is back for us now."

Andrew fell over, but his eyes would not leave the sight of the dead man's hand as it slid further down into the ice.

"Look!" Luis said, and pointed at the giant black rocks that circled them both. "They just moved again!"

And Andrew did look. He looked at those five dark fingers sticking up from the snow, and then at the five black rocks that rose from the frozen ground, and, for a moment, they looked the same. Like a hand trying to break free of its frozen prison.

But, as he watched the monoliths in the harsh arctic light, his eyes open wide, he did not see what Luis saw. He saw the land around them quake and open wide to swallow great pieces of ice and rock. He saw the arctic wind throw frozen chunks of snow into the air, and saw them swirl in a frenzy. But, as hard as he tried, Andrew did not see the five towering black stones move. They were as cold and as lifeless as the icy tundra that surrounded them.

"See?" Luis said. "I told you we weren't alone."

And Andrew cried, his unblinking eyes burning from the cold.

# M.R. JAMES and REGGIE OLIVER

## The Game of Bear

THOUGH ROUGHLY A CENTURY divides them, both Montague Rhodes James and Reggie Oliver were educated at Eton and were Newcastle Scholars at that institution. Thereafter, their careers diverged slightly. James went on to Cambridge and an academic career; Oliver went to Oxford and then into the theatre.

Both have published four acclaimed collections of "ghost stories". James' classic tales can be found in *Ghost Stories of an Antiquary*, *More Ghost Stories of an Antiquary*, *A Thin Ghost and Others* and *A Warning to the Curious*. For Oliver, recent publications include his novel *Virtue in Danger*, and a vast collected edition of his stories entitled *Dramas from the Depths*, published by Centipede Press, as part of its *Masters of the Weird Tale* series.

About the posthumously published collaboration that follows, Oliver explains: "James left 'The Game of Bear' in manuscript unfinished at his death in 1936, stopping at the words: 'No, she mayn't.' In completing this story, I have tried as far as possible to enter into James' mind and style and provide the ending James himself might have produced had not death intervened.

"Permission to do this was kindly granted by James' great nephew, Mr Nicholas Rhodes James, whom I had the pleasure of meeting while attending one of Robert Lloyd-Parry's famous theatrical renditions of James' work."

Two ELDERLY PERSONS sat reading and smoking in the library of a country house after tea on an afternoon in the Christmas holidays, and outside a number of the children of the house were playing about. They had turned out all the lights and were engaged in the dreadful game of "Bear" which entails stealthy creepings up and down staircases and along passages, and being leapt upon from doorways with loud and hideous cries. Such a cry and an answering scream of great poignancy were heard just outside the library door. One of the two readers – an uncle of the young things who were disporting themselves there – leapt from his chair and dashed the door open. "I will *not* have you doing that!" he shouted (and his voice was vibrant with real anger); "Do you hear? Stop it at once. I can't stand it. You – you – why can't you find something else? What? ... Well, I don't care, I can't put up with it ...Yes, very well, go and do it somewhere where I can't hear it." He subsided into a growl and came back to his chair but his friend saw that his nerves were really on edge, and ventured something sympathetic. "It's all very well," said the uncle, "but I cannot bear that jumping out and screaming. Stupid of me to fly out like that, but I couldn't help it. It reminded me of all that business – *you* know."

"Well," said the friend after a short pause, "I'm really not sure that I do. Oh!" he added, in a more concerned tone, "unless you mean Purdue."

"That's it," said the uncle.

There was another silence, and then the friend said, "Really, I'm not sorry that happened just now, for I never did hear the rights of the Purdue business. Will you tell me exactly what happened?"

"I don't know," said the uncle. "I *really* don't know if I ought. But I think I will. Not just now, though. I'll tell you what: if it's fine tomorrow we'll take a walk in the morning and tonight I'll think over the whole affair and get it straight in my mind. I *have* often felt somebody besides me ought to know about it, and all his people are out of the way now."

The next day *was* fine, and the two men walked out to a hill at no real distance, which was known as Windmill Hill. The mill that had topped it was gone but a bit of the brick foundation remained and afforded a seat from which a good stretch of pleasant wild country could be seen. Here then Mr A and Mr B sat down on the short, dry grass with their backs against the warm brick wall, and Mr A produced a little bundle of folded paper and a pocket-book which he held up before Mr B as an indication that he was prepared not only to tell the story to which he stood pledged, but to back it with documentary evidence.

"I brought you here," he said, "partly because you can see Purdue's place. There!" He pointed with his stick to a wooded slope, which might be three or four miles off. In the wood was a large clearing and in the clearing stood a mansion of yellow stone with a portico, upon which, as it chanced, the sun was shining very brilliantly, so that the house stood out brightly against the background of dark trees.

"Where shall I begin?" said Mr A.

"Why," said Mr B, "I'll tell you exactly how little I know, and then you can judge. You and Purdue, you remember, were senior to me at school and at Cambridge. He went down after his three years; you stayed up for part of a fourth, and then I began to see more of you. Before that, I was more with people of my own year, and, beyond a fair number of meetings with Purdue at breakfast and lunch and so on, I never saw much of him – not nearly as much as I should have liked, in fact. Then I remember your going to stay with him – there, I suppose" (pointing with his stick) – "in the Easter Vac, and – well, that was the last of it."

"Just so," said Mr A. "I didn't come up again, and you and I practically didn't meet till a year or two back, did we? Though you were a better correspondent than any of my other Cambridge friends. Very well, then, there it is. I was never inclined to write the story down in a letter, and the long and short of it is that you have never heard it: but you do know what sort of man Purdue was, and how fond I was of him.

"When I stayed with him over there, the place was his only home, and yet it wasn't his. He was an orphan and practically adopted by his uncle and aunt who were quite old childless people. There had been another uncle who had married a village woman, and had one daughter. That couple were very odd squalid creatures, and died, I think from drink, but the daughter survived and went on living in a cottage in the next parish. She wasn't left destitute by any means in the way of money but she lived all by herself, and I think always with a sense of injury upon her that she wasn't noticed by the county families and such. The remaining uncle and aunt had been kind enough to her and at one time used to invite her over to their place, but she had a very difficult temper and was always on the look-out for slights and injuries, and at last they gave up the effort to be cordial, and saw no more of her. It wasn't to be expected after that that they would pass on the property to her (it was entirely at their disposition, to do what they liked with it) and no more they did. When they died it went to Purdue, about a year before his own death, that was.

"So there he was, settled, you would say, into a happy life. He'd been brought up in the country and knew all the neighbourhood, places and people, very well; and was interested in farming and forestry and prepared to make himself useful. That last visit I paid him was particularly delightful. He was on such excellent terms with everybody in the village, 'Master Henry' to all of them, and just as well liked by the neighbours in the larger houses. I think the only fly in the ointment was that woman Caroline Purdue. She took to attending our parish church and we used to find her in our pew every Sunday morning. She didn't say much to Henry, but all the service time she sat and looked at him through her veil. A short stout red-faced woman she was, with black hair and snappy black eyes. She used to wait in the churchyard till we had gone out and then set off on her three-mile walk home. She gave me the creeps, I couldn't say why; I suppose there was a flavour of concentrated hostility about her.

"Henry was anxious of something of the same kind. His lawyer told me after his death that he had tried through them to get her to accept a handsome addition to her income and the gift of a suitable house wherever she liked in some other part of the county. They said she was as impracticable a woman as they had ever come across: she just sat and smiled broadly at them and said she was quite comfortable where she was, and didn't want to move out of reach of her cousin Henry. 'But wouldn't it be more lively and amusing for you to be in some place where there's more to be seen – theatres, and that sort of thing?' No, oh no, she had plenty of things to occupy herself with, and – again – she didn't want to move out of reach of her cousin Henry.

"'But, but – your cousin Henry, you know; he's likely to be a busy man – travelling about a good deal, and occupied with his men friends; it isn't probable that he'll be able to see much of you.' Oh, she was quite content to take her chance of that: they would often be meeting when he was riding about, and no doubt there would be times when he was alone at the Court, and she could look in on him. 'Ah well, that's just the point. Are you sure that Mr Purdue will welcome that?' 'Yes, to be sure, why not?' 'Well, we have reason to think that he doesn't wish it.' Oh indeed! and pray had he commissioned these gentlemen to tell his own cousin that he had cast her off? A nice thing for a relative to hear, that her own flesh and blood preferred not to have anything to do with her. What had she done, she should like to know, to be treated in that way?

"There was more to the same effect, and the storm rose quickly, culminating in a short burst of tears, and a rapid stumping out of the room. The gentlemen who had been conducting the interview were left looking at each other and feeling they had not done much to advance their client's wishes. But at least Miss Purdue left off her attendance at our church and, we gathered, did not favour any other place of worship in its stead.

"She was not more popular with the rest of the community than with Henry.

"How is the rest of this to be told? I have here some papers which bear on it, but they are fragmentary, of course. When Henry Purdue was alone in that big house he did what at other times was rather foreign to his habits – confided his feelings to paper. Here are some entries.

"'Letter from CP' (Caroline Purdue, of course). 'Infernal woman. May she come and see me and talk over this painful matter. No, she mayn't.'

"That one is dated fifth December 1883, a year to the day before his death, as it happens. You can see he wrote on loose sheets of paper, sometimes putting in the date in full, sometimes merely the day of the week. I had the devil of a job arranging them in some sort of order, but I felt, as his sole executor, under an obligation to do so. There is a pocket diary for the year of his death that contains a few terse jottings. That helped me to establish a chronology of events. Here is the next relevant entry.'

'*18th December*. Letter from Hardacre (Lawyers) today saying CP quite impossible, and actually suggesting *I* talk to her! Am I not paying them handsomely to do this for me? I have no intention of conversing with the woman on any subject and intend to keep her at arm's length. A figure of speech, of course, for I wish her to be at considerably more than an arm's length from me. I have instructed my gamekeeper that if she is seen on my land she is to be turned off. (Politely of course.)

'Wednesday. Yesterday evening I was in the library. Until recently I have not been at leisure to study my uncle's collection of books, which turns out to contain some unexpected treasures. I have spent several delicious evenings of late slowly examining them, but that is by the by.

'It was four o'clock; evening was already drawing in, and the light was clear, cloudless and wintry. The windows of my library face West. From them one sees a lawn, then the wooded slopes which surround – I might almost say *hem in* – my property. There is a gap in the trees on the library side through which I can see the sun descend below the brow of the hill. On this evening I noticed that upon this slope a solitary figure was standing in silhouette against the pallid evening sky.

'Instinct told me at once who it was before reason confirmed that the squat, black-bombazined and bonneted figure must be my cousin CP. She was, of course, too far off for me to be certain of it, but I was nonetheless convinced that she was watching me. After trying in vain for some minutes to ignore her presence I rang for Marston.

'I indicated the figure on the skyline and told him to go and send her about her business. Marston seemed reluctant to comply with my instructions and I am afraid I spoke to him rather sharply. He obeyed, but by the time he was walking across the lawn towards her, CP had turned tail and disappeared over the brow of the hill.'

"The very first note in Henry's pocket diary for 1884 are the words 'CP again' against the date of the 3rd January. By this time, evidently, his cousin's visitations had become a regular irritant. Then comes this paper which is headed '20th January'.

'My guests had left not half an hour since, when there comes a banging on my front door. I peep out of the little window that looks onto the porch and there is CP, looking more than ever like Mrs Gamp, complete with umbrella with which she is hammering on my door. I instruct Marston to go to see what she wants but on no account to let her in.

'Marston returns to tell me – as I had expected – that my cousin wishes to see me. I instruct him to inform her that I am indisposed and cannot. He conveys the message but she continues to hammer. It comes on to rain heavily, so I send out Marston to drive her home in the dogcart, but she will have none of it. She puts up her gamp and stumps off home by herself through the wet. Impossible woman!

'Friday. I hear from the Rector's wife that CP has caught a chill from her adventure in the rain. Feeling some small responsibility for her condition I sent Mrs Burns [his housekeeper] round to CP's cottage with a bowl of broth and some calves' foot jelly. Needless to say the offering is indignantly refused. I now wash my hands of her completely.

'25th January. The chill, no doubt exacerbated by CP's stubborn refusal of any assistance from myself and others, has finally done for her. A pulmonary infection had set in and the Rector found her dead in her bed when he paid a call on her this morning. Naturally I will see to all the proper funerary arrangements. God forgive me if I feel more than a little relieved that this dreadful incubus has now departed for good.'

'In Purdue's diary against the date 4th February are the words 'CP Funeral, St Jude's'. These words have been underlined three times in black ink. We now return again to the papers.

'3rd March. Most unexpectedly and very much to my annoyance Hardacre informs me that my wretched cousin, CP has left me something in her will. It is only a parcel of books, but still, it is a nuisance. Perhaps she had heard tell of my bookish tastes, for I made no secret of them. Doubtless they are all so much valueless trash and barely worth sending to the church jumble sale.

'Friday. The parcel of books that CP left me has arrived and, as I expected, there is little of value or interest. There are some religious tracts, a large old family Bible, which I suppose I must keep, and several volumes of eighteenth-century sermons of the dullest possible kind. Not even a Sherlock, let alone a Sterne, among them!

'There is perhaps one item of interest. It is a small volume, quarter octavo, entitled: *The Child's Keepsake. Improving Rhymes Composed Expressly for Young Persons by A Lady.* There is no date, but from the style of printing and the crude woodcuts which adorn the text I would guess it to be very late eighteenth- or early nineteenth-century, and I have no doubt that the 'Lady' in question was some member of an Evangelical sect, an Enthusiast at any rate, perhaps one of Hannah More's circle. My bibliophilic tastes do not extend to early literature for children, but I can recognize a rarity when I see one. The condition is excellent too, with the original boards, bound no doubt by a provincial bookseller, but a competent one.

'The text is addressed to the young and consists of tales told in verse of an improving and moral character. At the head of each poem is a rectangular woodcut depicting an incident from the story. Here is a fair example. Its title is, "Reverence For the Aged Advised", and it begins:

> Mock not the old in youth, young friend
> Lest you should meet a bitter end . . .

'It then goes on to tell the biblical story from Kings [II Kings ii, verses 23–24] about the children who derided Elisha for his baldness. He put a curse on his tormentors whereupon two she-bears came out of the wood to destroy them. The cut which accompanies this rhyme depicts the offending children being torn to pieces in a most savage manner. One of the she-bears has a small child's head clamped between its merciless jaws.

'I was not very favourably struck. That biblical tale has always exemplified for me the savagery – dare I say it, the *inhumanity*? – of the Old Testament, and it seems to me a cruel legend to tell to a child. Perhaps I am something of a sentimentalist in these matters, not having any children of my own.

'Most of the verses are of the same punitive character, dwelling more on sin and retribution than virtue and reward. One in particular impresses me with its horrid severity. It is entitled: "The Dreadful Fate of Young Master Henry Who Stole an Apple From An Old Woman".' (My name happens to be Henry!) In it a young boy steals an apple from a poor old woman and runs away home. Once there he secretes himself in a cupboard under the stairs in order to devour the purloined fruit in peace. He hears his mother calling for him but does not dare come out until he has finished eating. When he does, he encounters a woman whom he takes to be his mother, but she has a veil over her face.

> . . . And when he drew aside the veil
> The wicked child let out a wail,
> Transported by a sudden fear
> For it was not his mother dear.
> The face he met was quite unknown,
> A pale and hollow mask of bone
> For Death Itself had found him there
> In cupboard dark beneath the stair.

'I cannot say much for the Lady's versifying abilities, but I must reluctantly admit that that I found the tale rather hard to put out of my mind. Added to which, the accompanying woodcut is quite dreadful. If I were not so absurdly reverential of all books I would have torn it out on the spot lest some young friend of mine accidentally encountered it. It depicts, crudely of course, but with considerable vividness, a dark corridor with a staircase going up on the right hand side. You can just see the door of the cupboard under the stairs lying open and a slice of blackness within.

'In the corridor stands a strikingly disagreeable female figure. She is thin and wears the high-waisted gown of a woman of Jane Austen's period. The head is covered by what appears to be a dark muslin veil through which the engraver's cunning has allowed the more horrible features of her face to be seen. There is a hollow-eyed skull with just a few rags of skin clinging to the cheeks, and a gaping mouth full of horridly sharp teeth. Although common sense dictates that the eye-sockets must be empty the viewer forms the distinct impression that he is being watched by the ghastly figure on the page.

'After that, I must say I leafed through the book rather rapidly, but encountered nothing so terrible. However there is something of interest at the very end of the book.

'On the flyleaf, after the last printed page, another verse has been copied out by hand in a fair but childish copperplate. (Could it have been CP's handwriting? Possibly, but the orthography looks older, around 1800, perhaps contemporaneous with the book's publication.) It has no title and is in the same moralizing vein as the printed verses; yet it is different, more enigmatic. I note it down simply as a curiosity because it may represent quite an early reference to a particular children's game, now popular. It runs as follows.

> Let us play the Game of Bear
> Let us find out who is there.
> Let us find out where you are:
> Be you near, or be you far?
> Are you in a state of Grace,
> Pure of soul, and clean of face?
> Are you in the mire of Sin,
> Sinking deeper, deeper in?
> Do not be in any doubt
> That your sins will find you out.
> Let the wicked child beware
> When he plays the Game of Bear

'Having now sorted through my Uncle's books I have extracted a good few which, though of some antiquarian value, are of no interest to me. I intend to send them up to London to be sold or exchanged for more congenial volumes. I shall add *The Child's Keepsake* to this pile. Or perhaps family *pietas* will forbid me.

'*10th April*. Lovely spring day. Rode over to Aylsham to see M. In the evening after dinner I was just crossing the hall to go to the library and was by the main staircase when I heard a voice, so close to me it was almost in my ear. It said:

> Let us play the Game of Bear
> Let us find out who is there.

'The voice was elderly, but whose it was, or even whether it was male or female, I could not tell. It had a breathy sort of tone, *sotto voce*, as the Italians say. There was no one in the hall. I rang for Marston and he came eventually, but I am sure it was not him. The verse reminded me of that book *The Child's Keepsake* which my cousin left me and which I still have somewhere, but I could not find the thing when I searched for it just now in the library.

'The voice must have been some kind of auditory hallucination. I think I should get away from this place and travel for a while. If it were not for the progress I am making with M, I would go at once.'

"Incidentally," said Mr A, "M was a Miss Mary Mills, daughter of a local landowner over at Aylsham. I will spare you the various eulogies he composes about her in these papers. Suffice it to say that it was a thoroughly suitable match for a young man of Henry Purdue's station in life. Well, over the months of April and May there are a number of random jottings concerning the house: he mentions rats, odd whisperings and other inexplicable sounds such as those of heavy footsteps where none should have been, various minor domestic mishaps, that kind of thing. They all seem to weigh on him rather more than perhaps they should have done, and several times he writes 'I must get away' with the word 'must' underscored. Then under the heading '5th June' comes the following:

'When I went for my walk in the grounds after dinner it was rather close and oppressive. Must create more avenues in the trees that surround me. A curious thing: usually at this time of day the park is full of bird song and a nightingale often starts up in a nearby brake, but this evening there was not a sound to be heard. The air was thick and silent as if stuffed with cotton wool. I went indoors and just as I was about to mount the stairs in the hall I heard that voice again. It said:

> Let the wicked child beware
> When he plays the Game of Bear.

'What the deuce does it mean? I think the words come from that book I can't find. I *must* get away.'

"Well," said Mr A, "in July he *did* get away. The diary records his journeyings through France and Italy with nothing more enterprising than the name of a place written against a date. By September he was back in England and in October I met him in London. It was, as it happens, the last time I was to see my friend Henry Purdue. By this time Miss Mills had consented to be his bride and he seemed excessively pleased with life. It may be hindsight, but I do think that I detected a touch of feverishness in his high spirits. He was unusually excitable. I remember how he started violently in the smoking room of my club when an old member on a nearby sofa suddenly began to snore. He begged me to come to stay with him in the country which I agreed to do, but somehow, and to my everlasting regret, I never got round to it.

"What happened next I have from various witnesses, including his old butler Marston who was dreadfully cut up about it all.

"As winter approached Purdue went in for a round of gaiety and socializing. Doubtless his approaching nuptials – it was to be a spring wedding – added to his circle of friends and the goodwill everyone felt towards him. He opened up his own house to parties and festivities of various kinds, and it was at one of these that the tragedy occurred.

"It was early in December and Purdue had a house full of guests, several of them being husbands and wives with children. As it was late in the year it got dark several hours before it was time to put the young people to bed and so indoor games were proposed. Among those suggested was the Game of Bear. Marston told me that Purdue had at first objected strenuously to the idea, until he was overborne by the importunings of adults and children alike.

"The Game of Bear, as you know is like a conventional game of hide-and-seek except that if the hider can spring out and surprise the finder, he then 'captures' the finder and can draw the victim into the hiding place with him. Thus the game becomes a kind of battle between the hiders and the finders, but generally it descends into good-humoured chaos long before any clear result is discernible.

"Well, on this occasion the game was unusually prolonged and boisterous, especially as Purdue's house, as you may guess, being a rambling structure, was well stocked with places of concealment. When the game was over and the children had been dispatched exhausted to their beds it was suddenly realized that the host was still missing. What could have happened to him? Had he perhaps hidden himself too well and then fallen asleep in his fastness? A search of the house was instituted in which all the adult guests and the servants took part.

"It was Marston who eventually found him in a cupboard under the stairs. Henry Purdue was huddled into a corner with his knees up to his chin, 'like a whipped child' as Marston put it. Of course poor Purdue was dead but the surprise was that he was cold and stiff. Fortunately, there were no children present but two of the ladies fainted when they caught a glimpse of him. The corpse had a dreadful look of fear on its face, and the eyes were open, fixed and staring. Marston also told me – although I rather I wish he hadn't – that in his death throes my friend had bitten his thumb clean through to the bone."

"Did you find that book among poor Purdue's things?" said Mr B who was by way of being a bibliophile. "*The Child's Keepsake*, wasn't it? I should rather like to see it."

"*I* shouldn't, and I'm very glad to say I found no such thing," said Mr A severely.

# CHRIS BELL

## Shem-el-Nessim:
## An Inspiration in Perfume

CHRIS BELL WAS BORN in Holyhead, Wales. He moved to Hamburg, via London, before arriving in New Zealand, where he worked as a magazine editor and writer. His short stories have appeared in *The Third Alternative*, *Grotesque*, *The Heidelberg Review* and *Not One of Us*, while his story "The Cruel Countess" was anthologized in *The Year's Best Fantasy & Horror: 10th Annual Edition*.

The author's short stories have been collected in *The Bumper Book of Lies*, while his first novel, *Liquidambar*, won the UKAuthors/PADB "Search For a Great Read" competition. In 2005 he was a contributing editor to a commemorative booklet marking Russell Hoban's eightieth birthday, published by Bloomsbury Books.

"'Shem-el-Nessim' (subtitled 'An Inspiration in Perfume') was inspired by a real perfume of that name," reveals Bell, "or at least by a framed advertisement for it that once hung in my girlfriend's parents' house. Now that we live together, it hangs above our bed.

"The story took a year to write. I began making notes in England in 2005. When I discovered more advertisements and packaging by J. Grossmith & Son, Distillers of Perfumes (the firm fictionalized in the story) on the Internet, Stan Tooprig, the mystery woman and the *Cairo Gazette* journalist narrator came alive.

"In a piece of synchronicity in the real world, Grossmith Ltd was recently resurrected and its managing director contacted me to ask how I came to write 'Shem-el-Nessim'. 'It was partly because of your description of Stan Tooprig in the story that I thought you had some special insight into the Grossmith family,' said Simon Brooke, a Grossmith descendant himself."

T HE MU'EZZIN OF THE Sultan al-Zahir Barquq mosque in the City of the Dead was calling for morning prayers when in one last rattling exhalation the Englishman opposite me expired. As his head fell forward, jangling our coffee cups and startling the clientele, his skin appeared translucent in the dust-dappled light. "*Shem-el-Nessim*!" were his final words. While the proprietor sent for a doctor from the Coptic Hospital on Ramses Street, I slipped the gold ring from the third finger of Stan Tooprig's left hand on to my own.

The Cairo of 1926 was the city of Moslem legend, seat of Saracen art, home of the Arabian Nights. The coffeehouse in the Khan el-Khalili bazaar on Gawhar el-Kaid Street was so far below the domes and minarets that it didn't even merit a name. Five times a day the Mu'ezzin would summon the faithful, halting the hammerings from the silver smithy next door. But at all other times it was too noisy for us to sit outside with the pipe smokers if we wished to converse, so we were confined to the shadows within.

Most of the coffee drinkers were fantasists. In their daydreams, they would be smuggling whisky, writing novels and returning home wealthy and triumphant. I had met plenty who had never left Cairo and would not – at least not alive. These star-crossed fools drifted here on inauspicious currents and were marooned by ancient history. Stan Tooprig was something else altogether, and I am still not sure what. He had come here from London in search of something, or merely to escape himself. As I had done with all the rest, I struck up a conversation with him over coffee.

The unlikely surname resulted from an unusual ancestry: a Dutch trader who had made his fortune in London around the time of the Great Fire and whose descendants had been there ever since. Tooprig claimed he had always wanted to visit Egypt because his father had once produced a ring of yellow gold engraved with strange foreign symbols, and which he claimed had once belonged to a Pharaoh. He had won it in payment of a debt while on a trip to Venice, he assured the young Stan. After his father died, Stan inherited the ring, along with a considerable fortune. It was many years before he learned that what was engraved on the ring was a cartouche of Egyptian hieroglyphs.

The Stan Tooprig I met in Cairo was no longer the well-to-do English gentleman he had once been. Behind everyday reality, there is a deeper reality so cruel that it condemns to death those whose crime is no greater than the pursuit of their own curiosity. I know this to be true because it happened to Stan Tooprig. And, as strange as it may sound, it was piqued by a woman's perfume.

Tooprig required something of women that was not physical but sensory. Although he claimed to be as partial to blondes as he was to brunettes, he had always favoured the civet cat-like scent of redheads; there was a certain astringency about them he said he found entirely libidinous. Unless she could tantalize his nose, her other charms would be of no consequence, and a fragrant woman invigorated all of his senses, not merely the olfactory.

He lived just off Baker Street, on two floors, with modest living quarters for his valet. One might have described him as a gentleman of leisure; on most days, he took long walks through the city and sometimes, on a whim, would follow a particularly fragrant woman in the hope of a closer encounter. He had cultivated a succession of these, but he was fastidious and discarded his subject if she did not smell "right". He even classified them by type and aroma: Thyme and Basil (blondes); Sandalwood and Vetivert (brunettes); and Lemon and Petit Grain (redheads). But then came Shem-el-Nessim, the perfume worn by the raven-haired mystery woman. And it was in a London winter that he first crossed paths with the creature that was to be his downfall.

Klinge & Schneider, the barbershop on Jermyn Street renowned for the closest shave in London, was a haven of sandalwood and Turkish soap; a darkly timbered respite from the rumble and clatter of the city. Tooprig particularly enjoyed cold mornings when there was a touch of frost; stepping out across the threshold, lightly powdered, with the *frisson* of cologne vibrant on cheeks met by the first chilled fingers of fresh air.

On this morning, his barber had left him to strop the razor when a spicy, oriental perfume wafted deliciously between the hot towel and Tooprig's nose. He didn't recognize the scent, but by the time his barber had turned back to him with a keenly glinting cut-throat, Tooprig had cast off his towel and was at the door, which was still closing against its jamb as though someone had left the shop but a moment before.

"Who was that just now?" Tooprig asked.

The barber professed to have seen no one. "Perhaps, sir, a customer too impatient to wait," he said. "It happens."

"No, this was a woman. I can still smell her." Although Tooprig had no idea what fragrance the young woman had been wearing, it was on his nose nonetheless. Tipping the barber for his trouble, Tooprig resolved to follow her; the bouquet was so heady and distinctive. His eye soon settled on the only woman within a plausible distance of the barbershop door. She was waiting to cross at the next junction: a tall, even willowy creature, with her raven hair very straight and short for the fashion.

He followed her at a distance as far as the eastern reaches of the city, north of Paternoster Row, even more fascinated by her scent than by the woman wearing it. His pursuit continued towards St Paul's Cathedral, across the junction of Newgate Street, beyond the Alpine Club. She did not look back, was untroubled by the traffic and moved swiftly. Her hair had a sable quality like a broad brush. She had limbs like the legs of a racehorse, though they were barely visible beneath her long coat. Her walk was a study in poise. She paused only at side roads to ensure she would not collide with turning traffic and, in profile, her skin seemed so pale that it was almost luminous. She had slightly plump cheeks and widely set eyes. Her face was a harmony of curves and palenesses. There was a middle-eastern turn to her features, as though her forebears might have hailed from the Orient, but then she also had something of the film star Louise Brooks as *Lulu* about her, Tooprig claimed.

It was on Newgate Street, at the corner of Ivy Lane, that the woman disappeared into a doorway. By the time Tooprig had reached it, the door had closed behind her. Tooprig had to step into the street in order to read the sign, J. Grossmith & Son, but there was no mention of the business being conducted within.

The door opened with a chime when he pushed against it. Inside, a display advertised what were apparently J. Grossmith & Son's products: Phul-Nana Bouquet of Indian Flowers; Old Lavender Cottage and White Fire fragrances, along with a range of sixpenny sachets, soap, face powders and dentifrice.

Behind the counter, a man with a balding head and a waxed moustache eyed Tooprig who, feeling discomfited that he had entered the store with no plan in mind, was at a loss for words. "That woman, the one who just entered . . . I, er, she . . ."

"You are mistaken, sir," said the man, with a hint of a foreign accent. "You are our first customer. We have just this minute opened, at nine o'clock." The man nodded politely towards a clock set above the window, which indeed showed the time to be just after the hour.

Tooprig tried to buy time as he considered what his next move might be. His gaze settled on the perfume displays. It seemed an odd but perfect coincidence. "If I were looking for a particular scent, for a lady, do you think you might carry it?" Tooprig asked.

The man smiled. "It's highly likely that we would be able to obtain it for you, sir. Or, if you can describe it to me, I would be happy to assist you in blending a scent that matches your requirements. We distil our own perfumes, and also sell a range of proprietary scents from other manufacturers."

"Well, I wouldn't really know how to describe it to you," Tooprig confessed. "It's not a scent I have ever encountered before."

The Grossmith assistant regarded Tooprig calmly and introduced himself as Monsieur Duat. "Is the scent fresh and of a citrus nature, or something deeper and more musky?"

"I can only say it had a kind of oriental quality."

"Well sir, that certainly narrows the field. I shall be back in a moment." He disappeared into a back room, returning with a wooden box into which were set a number of vials capped by rubber bulbs. He siphoned one drop of perfume from each of the three vials on to a strip of blotting paper. The scent Tooprig was looking for drew its richness – or so Duat surmised – from musk and vanilla. It was exotic and spicy rather than floral, but there was some other substance, perhaps a precious wood, that remained elusive even to the expert. Duat experimented by adding lighter, woodier notes to his existing blends.

As odd as it might seem, Tooprig had almost forgotten about the woman and was now more eager to solve the mystery of her perfume. After some deliberation, Duat produced an elaborate cylindrical carton and offered it to Tooprig. Floral designs in pink intertwined with curlicues; abstract urn shapes repeated around the base, and large, blue stylized lettering with drop shadows spelled out the transverse words SHEM-EL-NESSIM. "I don't know why I didn't think of this before. I feel certain that this is the scent you have been looking for, Mister Tooprig." Duat dabbed a tiny quantity of the Shem-el-Nessim on to one of his blotting paper strips.

Tooprig soon ascertained that it was indeed the perfume that the woman had been wearing. It was her very essence. Duat was evidently a master *parfumier*, a veritable alchemist in fragrances, to be able to identify a perfume from the clues provided by a neophyte.

Tooprig was eager to discover Shem-el-Nessim's formula, but Duat would say only that its recipe was protected and registered "in all the leading countries of the world". He purchased as much of it as seemed judicious in a single transaction, wary that Duat might consider him unhinged, which indeed he may already have been.

In the following weeks, Tooprig haunted the British Museum's reading rooms, looking for information on Shem-el-Nessim. After a painstaking search, he found but one solitary reference, in the works of an eccentric occultist. In *The Confessions of Aleister Crowley*, Tooprig read that Oscar Eckenstein, an acquaintance, had suffered from an aversion to artificial scent. "One day my wife and a friend came home from shopping. They had called at the chemist's who had sprayed them with Shem-el-Nessim. We saw them coming and went to the door to receive them. Eckenstein made one rush – like a bull – for the window of the sitting room, flung it open and spent the next quarter of an hour leaning out and gasping for breath."

Tooprig's desire to be with the mystery woman, now that he had identified her perfume, grew like a strange addiction; he craved her closeness although he could not explain why. The days came and went and often it was only his valet who roused him from a trance as he came into the study with his cocktail, whereupon it became apparent to him that he hadn't moved from his wing-chair since retiring there after breakfast. All the while, the scent of Shem-el-Nessim filled his senses and his mind. What did these reveries expect of him, he wondered; had its mysterious wearer been but a figment of his imagination?

It wasn't until much later that I discovered why, soon after, Tooprig booked himself a cabin on a steamer at the Port of London. And it was only my own research that led me to discover it had been on a French-registered vessel named *Cachous* that sailed to Alexandria, where he boarded a felucca up the Mahmoudieh Canal and the Nile, to Cairo.

I had been in Cairo for five years, ever since we declared Egypt a sovereign country, working mainly as a reporter for the English language *Cairo Gazette*. To my mind, we were treating the Egyptians rather more as enemies than as friends, but I was well treated by the locals and found life in the city most pleasant. I had airy rooms off Al Geish Square and the pace of life was slower than in Europe; one achieved in a week in Cairo what one might in a day in London. The boys were alluring if not always compliant, and there was an abundance of *kif* and *majoun* with which to help stave off the boredom.

But Cairo brought Stan Tooprig no luck whatsoever. When I first set eyes on him he looked emaciated. His skin had the leathery appearance of the mummified corpse of Sethos I in the Cairo Museum. He toadied up to me in the coffeehouse and, from behind the semi-transparent skin of his face, a refined English accent said, "I say, nobody else will buy me a drink. Would you?"

I acceded to his request and he rewarded me with his story. "It's quite the most remarkable thing," Tooprig claimed and, by the time I had heard the foregoing, I must say I had to agree with him.

Although he had elected to live in the most luxurious hotel in all of Cairo, the hideously expensive Hotel Savoy, there was no trace whatsoever of the mysterious Shem-el-Nessim woman on either side of its daunting white façade. Although its employees were open to all manner of bribes, none even dared to feign an encounter with this woman. Tooprig hadn't yet apprised me of the reason he believed she was in Egypt – or why, apart from its magnificence, he had chosen this hotel for his accommodation.

He enjoyed no special knowledge of Cairo's geography, its businesses or its people to help him in his quest. Since arriving, he had carried out reconnaissance missions at all of the other fine hotels to no avail. He made a mischief of himself with the officials at the British Embassy on Ahmed Raghab Street and became a regular of the expatriate cocktail circuit, but there wasn't a solitary sighting. He realized his journey had been in vain: if the woman had ever been in Cairo, she was no longer.

When he tired from the exertion of his account, we ordered more coffee and sized one another up. "There's an Egyptian chap I've heard about from my contacts on the Gazette who entered the grave of a Pharaoh and his Queen. He claims to have been possessed by her perfume," I told him.

Tooprig pleaded with me to take him to this man.

I knew of Ahmed Rezk quite by chance. One evening he had told me an implausible tale about his exploits as an erstwhile grave-robber. Since Rezk's adventure also involved the supposed supernatural effects of a perfume, I agreed to arrange a meeting between them, feeling sorry for Tooprig and foolishly thinking it might comfort him. He was eating practically nothing and virtually subsisting on coffee, in the hope that if he remained awake long enough he would eventually see the Shem-el-Nessim woman again. "Rezk broke into the undiscovered tomb in the western branch of the Valley of the Kings in Thebes," I explained as I walked Tooprig back in the direction of the Savoy. "They sold most of their spoils to foreigners around town, but Rezk retrieved a canopic jar he claims reeks of the perfume from the tomb."

Each year, in early spring, the Egyptians celebrate "smelling the breezes", an anniversary dating back to the time of the Pharaohs, over 4,000 years ago. Tooprig was so frail he could barely manage the short journey to Rezk's apartment in the old city but, with the aid of my interpreter from the Cairo

*Gazette*, we eventually conquered the staircase and arrived at his door.

His wife led us to Rezk, who was on the balcony, eating *fisikh*: salted, almost rotting fish. The sulphurous stink of it was noticeable two floors below. There are many cases of food poisoning each year in Cairo, suffered by those who purchase improperly preserved *fisikh* from unlicensed salting factories. Rezk looked terrible. His skin was sallow and his breath came in wheezing gasps. His wife was clearly distraught, beseeching him to eat fruit and to drink water, but Rezk brushed her aside as she attempted to dab at his brows with a damp cloth.

Rezk and an accomplice, he purported, had tunnelled through rock to the tomb's burial chamber and eventually found the king and queen in their sarcophagi. "We opened their coffins, where we found the mummy of this king," our interpreter translated as Rezk guzzled down mouthfuls of the stinking *fisikh* in the pauses in his confession. "There were amulets and golden ornaments at its throat; its head had a mask of gold upon it. The mummy was overlaid with gold, its coverings all wrought with silver and inlaid with lapis lazuli. We stripped off the gold and all the amulets and ornaments, then found the king's wife and stripped off all that we found on her, too. We stole their furniture and vases of gold, silver and bronze. We divided the gold from the mummies, and the amulets, ornaments and coverings between us."

Both Tooprig and I found Rezk's explanation for consuming so much of the rotting *fisikh* extraordinary, and it was linked to his confession: "It's the only way I can think of to be rid of this smell," he told my interpreter with a defeated expression on his face. Rezk went on to explain how, once the queen's mask had been removed, the chamber had filled with a beguiling perfume. The thieves narrowed down its source to an alabaster canopic urn in one corner of the tomb. They packed it into one of their swag bags and took it with them.

However, upon their return to Cairo they discovered that the urn contained but the foul, stinking viscera of the embalmed mummies, and no longer exuded the pungent perfume that had so intoxicated them. Nevertheless, it had somehow pursued the grave-robbers ever since, and they couldn't shake it; even rotting *fisikh* succeeded only in masking it slightly.

"Show me the urn!" Tooprig pleaded, but Rezk explained that his wife had forced him to abandon it in the desert, so foul had its smell become. I began to doubt Rezk's story; in particular that such a large and elaborate tomb could have existed undiscovered for so long in the Valley of the Kings, which was famously crawling with archaeologists. Rezk stubbornly refused to return to the tomb and also proved incapable of describing its location, so we had him draw a map of the site.

Tooprig was so infirm by this stage that I offered him my services and those of my interpreter to accompany him on an expedition to Thebes. It took us several days to get to the Valley of the Kings by train, by camel and finally on foot. The place Rezk had marked for us was close to a cliff-face about nine feet high. But there was no sign of an entrance, concealed or otherwise. The wind was whipping up the dust and so, in spite of Tooprig's pleas, after several hours of searching, we were forced to admit defeat as the sun began to rise.

When, at Tooprig's insistence, we returned to Cairo and to Rezk's dwellings, we found his wife in mourning. Her beloved Ahmed, she said, had stopped eating altogether – even the stinking *fisikh* – and had wasted away. The identity of his accomplice thus went with him to his grave.

Tooprig and I would meet once a week for coffee at the Khan el-Khalili coffeehouse and each week he would appear thinner and to have lost a little more of his feeble grip on life. Occasionally, he would be roused from a reverie to ask me the time or the date; annoyingly, often several times in the same morning. Then once, quite out of nowhere, as though there had merely been a brief pause in a long stream of conversation, Tooprig lit his final cigarette and wheezed, "I say, do you know what happened to me at The Savoy in London? It was quite the damnedest thing. Buy me a coffee and I shall tell you all about it."

About a week after his first encounter with the woman, it seemed, on a quite separate errand off Bond Street, Tooprig fancied he saw her again. She had emerged like an apparition between behatted heads and traffic, bobbing on her long limbs as if to gyroscopically navigate herself through the crosshatching of obstacles.

As he drew closer to her, the woman's scent became unmistakable. He followed her to Trafalgar Square, around which she walked before stopping in her tracks and turning to face him. She didn't speak, just looked at him and smiled. "There was something terrifyingly lascivious about her lips," Tooprig claimed, trembling as he recalled her. She held up a key to Room 941 at The Savoy Hotel, proffered it, then turned and continued on her way along the Strand and into the hotel lobby. When the elevator door opened, the woman entered it and turned to look at Tooprig with a sphinx-like smile. He followed her only after an interval and discovered her waiting outside the door to Room 941.

When he unlocked the door with the key she had given him, the room was dark and all the air had gone from it. In the twilight, she took off her coat and threw it on to the bed. Her clinging black dress was the next to go, and soon she was naked, skin shimmering and pearlescent with the sheen of shot silk.

They lay together into the failing light of a late afternoon, all the while the indescribable oriental fragrance of her skin buffering the room's airlessness. Hardly a word was spoken by either of them, but there was a prevailing tenderness, a lightness of touch, and from what Tooprig told me, it was not spoiled by the directness of their passions; at least not at first.

"Her body was warm, and yet she seemed to be draining me of heat," he said. "I felt the life being sapped out of me. Her ministrations were tender, and yet it was as though she were embalming and not making love to me. Her kisses tasted salty and bitter."

Tooprig said he felt an obstruction in his airways, as if something viscous and too large for the passages was being pulled out of him. "I had my eyes closed and yet, when I attempted to open them to see what was happening, it was as though I was asleep – I simply didn't have the energy to lift my eyelids. A vinegary odour filled the room, as though of some unctuous preservative."

All at once, there were not merely two but a manyness of hands upon him; not soft and womanly, but large, coarse and oiled. "They sought and prodded, poked and peeled to such an extent that I could no longer keep track of their location on my body. I felt a sharp stroke below my left ribs and a sensation of something being quickly removed. I grew even weaker. My heart was suddenly heavy, as though it were about to fall through both me and the bed and on to the floor. And yet, *her* hands were soft, like clean linen. I felt as though I was being wrapped in her arms. But I could not defend myself against the other violations – whatever they were – and I began to feel afraid. All the while, my eyelids were as though sewn shut. I tried to call out, but I couldn't; my senses were paralysed. And although my heart was beating hard, my blood felt sluggish in my veins."

The darkness throbbed and, out of it, he seemed to hear male voices chanting. Tooprig claimed he felt something peppery with the texture of grit being inserted into his nostrils, but he found it impossible to provide resistance to the sensations assailing him, and soon fell into unconsciousness.

"Afterwards, I was numb. In a dream of red velvet drapes, I smelt her perfume again, sweeter than any bloom, warmer and more satisfying than any musk, fresher than any exotic fruit. And, like a dream, it dissipated as I woke, until I was left with nothing, for when I awoke she had gone."

It was only when Tooprig left The Savoy that he fully became aware of Shem-el-Nessim again, because traces of it had been left on his clothing and skin. It was the perfume from his dream, and it had been with him permanently ever since – night and day, no matter where he went.

Some time later, he returned to The Savoy and approached the concierge's desk, where he engaged him in conversation about his liaison with the woman. "She was staying in Room 941," he said. "We met for tea. It was a Tuesday – I distinctly remember that, and the date must have been late in January, perhaps the last day of the month."

"Sir, no such rendezvous can have taken place in this hotel," said the concierge.

Tooprig was infuriated by such impertinence. "Dash it all, man, are you calling me a liar?"

"Not at all, sir, but no such liaison can have taken place in that room, as there is no Room 941 in The Savoy Hotel."

Tooprig turned from the counter, quite sure that he had not misremembered the room number. He decided to try a different approach and bribed a bellboy who claimed to remember such a woman from Tooprig's description. Although the boy didn't recall the woman's name, Tooprig asked where she had gone after she had checked out. He slowly spelled out a word he had memorized from the label on her cabin trunks: K-A-I-R-O.

Stan Tooprig had spoken to me often of returning to London, but he never did. He spent his final days in the coffeehouse in Khan el-Khalili, and a man more out-of-sorts with himself you couldn't hope to meet. It was soon after recounting his tale that he died. He was buried here in Cairo at the Beb el-Wezir cemetery with a view of the Citadel and the Mohammed Ali Mosque, beyond.

In everything there is an element of the mysterious, and yet we know the world can only be this way. For, as the biologist J.B.S. Haldane observed, "The Universe is not only queerer than we suppose; it is queerer than we *can* suppose." It is with a heavy heart that I acknowledge the mystery of Shem-el-Nessim might never be solved. Whether that woman existed only in the mind of Stan Tooprig has never been entirely relevant to me since, once imagined, she existed for him as did everything else in his world.

I am old now. I have memories, and that is all I have. They are like the loose leaves of a book that has lost its binding, the pages are in the wrong order, are torn and discoloured. Each year, on the anniversary of Tooprig's death, his haunted, bony face comes back to me, and each year I doubt the veracity of his story more – he had woven a tale as one might a ghost story, seemingly omitting anything that did not assist his narrative.

But recently I have reproached myself for questioning Tooprig's honesty. In recording the foregoing events, I was forced to refer to some back issues of the *Cairo Gazette*. And so, one evening, I found myself in the reading rooms of the Al-Azhar University library in the shadow of the Fatima az-Zahraa mosque. In an issue from the spring of 1926, I turned the page from an account of the Palestinian labour camps to a full-page advertisement for the company J. Grossmith & Son. It featured a drawing of a turbaned woman on a night-time camel ride in front of the Great Pyramids. She had some of the allure of Louise Brooks. Two oversized bottles of Shem-el-Nessim hung like water vessels from either side of her camel as she smiled gaily at me from the newsprint. The advertising copy read:

## SHEM-EL-NESSIM, SCENT OF ARABY
## AN INSPIRATION IN PERFUME

While gazing at the woman's face I was struck by an intense fragrance; something oriental laced with spice and perhaps a suggestion of sandalwood. It filled my nostrils, lungs and my imagination, and I almost swooned. I tried to ascertain its source but, apart from me, the room was unoccupied and quite still, save for an odd shadow that paused fleetingly against the open door and a curtain that billowed over a window left ajar.

The Shem-el-Nessim woman may have been an inspiration to Monsieur Duat and the *parfumiers* of Grossmith & Son, but her "scent of Araby" was tainted by the miasma of early death. I myself fell ill soon after that visit to the library. My vitality has been sapped and I doubt I shall live to see my seventieth birthday. She, though, will never grow old and I fear the lifelong curse of her fragrance, which seduced me like a memory of London long ago, will be on the air long after we are all gone.

# MICHAEL MARSHALL SMITH

## What Happens When You Wake Up in the Night

MICHAEL MARSHALL SMITH IS a novelist and screenwriter. Under this name he has published seventy short stories and three novels – *Only Forward*, *Spares* and *One of Us* – winning the Philip K. Dick, International Horror Guild, August Derleth and British Fantasy Awards, as well as the Prix Morane.

Writing as "Michael Marshall", he has published five internationally best-selling thrillers, including *The Straw Men*, *The Intruders* and *Bad Things*, while 2009 saw the publication of the supernatural novel *The Servants* under the name "M.M. Smith". His most recent Michael Marshall novel, *The Breakers*, is forthcoming.

"'What Happens When You Wake Up in the Night' was one of those stories which come along once in a while," reveals Smith, "the kind that drops straight into your head, fully-formed, as if fulfilling a forgotten order you made from the great Ideas shop in the sky.

"The only problem was that, once this one had dropped on my mental doormat, I didn't want it. It wasn't an idea I liked. It was clearly some part of my brain serving up a notion simply because it could, and because it knew it could frighten me with it.

"It *did* frighten me, and so I did what I always do when that happens – which is write it down, in the hope it will go away."

The first thing I was unhappy about was the dark. I do not like the dark very much. It is not the worst thing in the world, but it is also not the best thing in the world, either. When I was very small I used to wake up sometimes in the middle of the night and be scared when I woke up, because it was so dark. I went to bed with my light on, the light that turns round and round, on the drawers by the side of my bed. It has animals on it and it turns around and it makes shapes and patterns on the ceiling and it is pretty and my mummy's friend Jeanette gave it to me. It is not too bright but it is bright enough and you can see what is what.

But then it started that when I woke up in the middle of the night, the light would not be on any more and it would be completely dark instead and it would make me sad. I didn't understand this, but one night when I'd woken up and cried a lot my mummy told me that she came in every night and turned off the light after I was asleep, so it didn't wake me up. But I said that wasn't any good, because if I *did* wake up in the night and the light wasn't on, then I might be scared, and cry.

She said it seemed that I was waking every night, and she and daddy had worked out that it might be the light that woke me, and after I was awake I'd get up and go into their room and see what was up with them, which meant she got no sleep any night ever and it was driving her completely nuts.

So we made a deal, and the deal said I could have the light on all night, *but* I promised that I would not go into their room in the night unless it was *really* important, and it is a good deal and so I'm allowed to have my light on again now, which is why the first thing I noticed when I woke up was that it was dark.

Mummy had broken the deal. I was cross about this, but I was also very sleepy and so wasn't sure if I was going to shout about it or not.

Then I noticed it was cold.

Before I go to bed, mummy puts a heater on while I am having my bath, and also I have two blankets on top of my duvet, and so I am a warm little bunny and it is fine. Sometimes if I wake in the middle of the night it feels a bit cold but if I snuggle down again it's okay.

But this felt *really* cold. My light was not on and I was cold.

I put my hand out to put my light on, which was the first thing to do. There is a switch on a white wire that comes from the light and I can turn it on myself – I can even find it in the dark when there is no light.

I tried to do that, but I could not find the wire with my hand.

So I sat up and tried again, but still I could not find it, and I wondered if mummy had moved it, and I thought I might go and ask her. But I could not see the door. It had been so long since I had been in my room in the night without my light being on that I had forgotten how dark it gets. It's *really* dark. I knew it would be hard to find the door if I could not see it, so I did it a clever way.

I used my imagination.

I sat still for a moment and remembered what my bedroom is like. It is like a rectangle and has some drawers by the top of my bed where my head goes. My light is on the drawers, usually. My room also has a table where my colouring books go and some small toys, and two more sets of drawers, and windows down the other end. They have curtains so the street lights do not keep me awake, and because in summer it gets bright too early in the morning and so I wake everybody up when they should still be asleep because they have work to do and they need some sleep. And there is a big chair but it is always covered in toys and it is not important.

I turned to the side so my legs hung off the bed and down on to the floor. In my imagination I could see that if I stood up and walked straight in front of me, I would nearly be at my door, but that I would have to go a little way . . . left, too.

So I stood up and did this walking.

It was funny doing it in the dark. I stepped on something soft with one of my feet, I think it was a toy that had fallen off the chair. Then I touched one of the other drawers with my hand, and I knew I was close to the door, so I turned left and walked that way a bit.

I reached out with my hands then and tried to find my dressing gown. I was trying to find it because I was cold, but also because it hangs off the back of my bedroom door on a little hook and so when I found the dressing gown I would know I had got to the right place to open the door.

But I could not find the dressing gown. Sometimes my mummy takes things downstairs and washes them in the washing machine in the kitchen and then dries them in another machine that makes them hot, so maybe that was where it was. I was quite awake now and very cold, so I decided not to keep trying to find the gown and just go wake mummy and daddy and say to them that I was awake.

But I couldn't find my doorknob. I knew I must be where the door is, because it is in the corner where the two walls of my room come together. I reached out with my hands and could feel the two sides of the corner, but I could not find the doorknob, even though I moved my hands all over where it should be. When I was smaller the doorknob came off once, and mummy was very scared because she thought if it happened again I would be trapped in my bedroom and I wouldn't be able to get out, so she shouted at daddy until he fixed it with a different screw. But it had never come off again, so I did not know where it could be now. I wondered if I had got off my bed in the wrong way because it was dark and I had got it mixed up in my imagination, and maybe I should go back to my bed and start again.

Then a voice said: "Maddy, what are you *doing*?"

I was so surprised I made a scared sound, and jumped.

I trod on something, and the same voice said "Ow!" I heard someone moving and sitting up. Even though it was in the dark I knew it was my mummy.

"Mummy?" I said. "Where are you?"

"Maddy, I've *told* you about coming into our room."

"I'm not."

"It's just not *fair*. Mummy has to go to work and daddy has to go to work and you have to go to school and we *all* need our sleep. We made a *deal*, remember?"

"But *you* broke the deal. You took away my light."

"I haven't touched your light."

"You did!"

"Maddy, don't lie. We've talked about lying."

"You took my light!"

"I haven't taken your light and I didn't turn it off."

"But it's not turned on."

She made a sighing sound. "Maybe the bulb went."

"Went to where?"

"I mean, got broken."

"No, my whole *light* is not there."

"Maddy . . ."

"It's not! I put my hand out and I couldn't find it!"

My mummy made a sound like she was very cross or very tired, I don't know which. Sometimes they sound the same. She didn't say anything for a little minute.

"Look," she said then, and she did not sound very cross now, just sleepy and as if she loved me but wished I was still asleep. "It's the middle of the night and everyone should be in bed. Their *own* bed."

"I'm sorry, mummy."

"That's okay." I heard her standing up. "Come on. Let's go back to your room."

"What do you mean?" I said.

"Back to your room. Now. I'll tuck you in, and then we can all go back to sleep."

"I *am* in my room."

"Maddy – don't start."

"I *am* in my room!"

"Maddy, this is just silly. Why would you . . . Why is it so dark in here?"

"Because my light is off. I told you."

"Maddy, your light is in *your* room. Don't—"

She stopped talking suddenly. I heard her fingers moving against something, the wall, maybe. "What the hell?"

Her voice sounded different.

"'Hell' is a naughty word." I told her.

"Shush."

I heard her fingers swishing over the wall again. She had been asleep on the floor, right next to the wall. I heard her feet moving on the carpet and then there was a banging sound and she said a naughty word again, but she did not sound angry but like she did not understand something. It was like a question-mark sound.

"For the love of *Christ*."

This was not my mummy talking.

"Dan?"

"Who the hell else? Any chance you'll just take her back to

bed? Or I can do it. I don't mind. But let's one of us do it. It's the middle of the fucking night."

"Dan!"

" 'Fucking' is a *very* naughty—"

"Yes, yes, I'm terribly sorry," my daddy said. He sounded as if he was only half not in a dream. "But we have *talked* about you coming into our room in the middle of the night, Maddy. Talked about it endlessly. And—"

"Dan," my mummy said, starting to talk when he was still talking, which is not good and can be rude. "Where *are* you?"

"I'm right *here*," he said. "For God's *sake*. I'm . . . Did you put up new curtains or something?"

"No," mummy said.

"It's not normally this dark in here, is it?"

"My light has gone," I said. "That's why it is so dark."

"Your light is in *your* room," daddy said.

I could hear him sitting up. I could hear his hands, too. They were not right next to mummy, but at the other end of my room. I could hear them moving around on the carpet.

"Am I on the floor?" he asked. "What the hell am I doing *on the floor?*"

I heard him stand up. I did not tell him "hell" is a naughty word. I did not think that he would like it.

I heard him move around a little more, his hands knocking into things.

"Maddy," mummy said, "where do you think you are?"

"I'm in my *room*," I said.

"Dan?" she said, to daddy. My daddy's other name is "Dan" It is like "dad" but has a nuh-sound at the end instead of a duh-sound. "*Is* this Maddy's room?"

I heard him moving around again, as if he was checking things with his hands.

"What are we doing in here?" he said, sounding as if was not certain. "Is this her room?"

"Yes, it's *my room*," I said.

I was beginning to think daddy or mummy could not hear properly, because I kept saying things over and over but they did not listen. I told them again. "I woke up, and my light was off, and this is my room."

"Have you tried the switch by the door?" Daddy asked mummy.

I heard mummy moving, and her fingers swishing on the wall, swishing and patting. "It's not there."

"What do you mean it's not there?"

"What do you think I mean?"

"For Christ's sake."

I heard daddy walking carefully across the room to where mummy was.

Mummy said: "Satisfied?"

"How *can* it not be there? Maddy – can you turn the light by your bed on, please?" Daddy sounded cross now.

"She says it isn't there."

"What do you mean, not there?"

"It's not *there*," I said. "I already told mummy, fourteen times. I was coming into your room to tell you, and then mummy woke up and she was on the floor."

"Are the street lamps out?"

This was mummy asking. I heard daddy go away from the door and go back to the other end of the room, where he had woken up from. He knocked into the table as he was moving and made a cross sound but kept on moving again.

"Dan? Is that why it's so dark? Is it a power cut?"

"I don't know," he said. "I . . . can't find the curtains."

"Can't find the gap, you mean?"

"No. Can't find the *curtains*. They're not here."

"You're sure you're in the right—"

"Of course I'm in the right place. They're not here. I can't feel them. It's just wall."

"It is just wall where my door is too," I said. I was happy that daddy had found the same thing as me, because if he had found it too then it could not be wrong.

I heard mummy check the wall near us with her hands. She was breathing a little quickly.

"She's right. It's just wall," she said, so we all knew the same thing. "It's just wall, everywhere."

But mummy's voice sounded quiet and a bit scared and so it did not make me so happy when she said it.

"Okay, this is ridiculous," daddy said. "Stay where you are. Don't move."

I could hear what he was doing. He was going along the sides of the room, with his fingers on the walls. He went around the drawers near the window, then past where my calendar hangs, where I put what day it is in the mornings, then along my bed.

"She's right," he said. "The lamp isn't here."

"I'm really cold," mummy said.

Daddy went past me and into the corner where mummy had been sleeping, where I had trod on her when I was trying to find the door.

But he couldn't find the door either.

He said the door had gone, and the windows, and all the walls felt like they were made of stone. Mummy tried to find the curtains, but she couldn't. They tried to find the door and the window for a long time but they still couldn't find them and then my mummy started crying.

Daddy said crying would not help, which he says to me sometimes, and he kept on looking in the dark for some more time, trying to find the door.

But in the end he stopped, and he came and sat down with us. I don't know how long ago that was. It's hard to remember in the dark. But I think it was quite long ago.

Sometimes we sleep, but later we wake up and everything is still the same. I do not get hungry but it is always dark and it is always very cold.

Mummy and daddy had ideas and used their imaginations. Mummy thought there was a fire, and it burned all our house down. Daddy says we think we are in my room because I woke up first, but he says really we are in a small place made of stone, near a church somewhere. I don't know, but we have been here a very long time now and still it is not morning yet.

It is quiet and I do not like it. Mummy and daddy do not talk much any more, and this is why, if you wake up in the night, you should never ever get up out of bed.

# NICHOLAS ROYLE

## The Reunion

NICHOLAS ROYLE IS THE author of five novels and two novellas, and the editor of thirteen anthologies, including *Darklands* and *The Time Out Book of New York Short Stories*. His own collection, *Mortality*, was shortlisted for the inaugural Edge Hill Prize, and he has won three British Fantasy Awards.

Born in Manchester in 1963, Royle teaches creative writing at Manchester Metropolitan University and reviews fiction for *The Independent* newspaper. He also runs Nightjar Press, publishing original short fiction in signed, limited-edition chapbooks. Currently he is editing a new anthology of uncanny bird stories for Two Ravens Press.

"'The Reunion' is based on actual events," reveals the author, "but the story only really came into focus for me when I was invited to contribute to Ellen Datlow's *Poe* anthology.

"Poe is brilliant. I was at a conference recently where a teacher revealed that she had read Poe's 'The Black Cat' to a lecture theatre full of schoolchildren. She switched off all the lights and used a torch to read by. A number of parents lodged complaints, which she took as a measure of the event's success. My tale is inspired by a different Poe story."

O N ARRIVAL, we'd had to wait behind a man in jumbo cords and a pastel polo shirt who was giving the receptionist a hard time about some problem in his room, a missing towel or a faulty light, and we formed an immediate impression of him that was somewhat negative. It wasn't long, however, before we realized he had a point.

They didn't have any record of our booking, despite having sent us an email of confirmation, which happily Maggie had printed out and brought along. So we had to fill in a form, holding up those who had arrived after us, and finally the girl behind the desk gave us a key card and a map.

Yes, a map. It was a big hotel. A huge hotel. One of those places you get apparently in the middle of nowhere but actually no more than twenty miles from one or other dreary Midlands town. A former RAF training camp or stately home or converted mental asylum. This appeared to be all three, with not only west wings and east wings, but whole houses and vast halls tacked on to the main building. The room belatedly assigned to us was in one of the modern blocks.

We walked along one edge of a grand, colonnaded reception hall, past a tuxedoed piano player, through a little ante-room dominated by two stags' heads mounted on adjacent walls. We passed a bar with its shutter down, then turned right into a wide corridor.

The further we got from the main part of the hotel with its marble columns and wide, red-carpeted staircases, the shoddier and tattier everything became. There was an armchair in a corner that was missing a castor, a cabinet of drawers covered in scuff marks.

I said to Maggie that it was like that scene in *Jacob's Ladder* where Tim Robbins is wheeled down into the bowels of a hospital that turns into a vision of hell with crazy people banging their heads against the wall and gobbets of bloody flesh lying around on the floor.

Maggie gave me her standard nod of impartial assent, the one kept for observations beyond her frame of reference. I realized, though, that if I was overly critical of the hotel, and therefore, by extension, of the evening itself, it could provoke a reaction. This was Maggie's evening – a medical school reunion – and the fact that I had readily agreed to come along meant that if at any point I regretted my decision, it would not be fair to allow it to show.

As we trailed past a rather tired series of framed prints of the hotel in its heyday, I felt the raised glands in my neck. The prints on the wall were undated and there were no outward signs that would enable you to assign them to a particular period. They were like idealizations or artists' impressions. One hung askew and I wanted to straighten it, but I sensed Maggie's impatience to get to the room and so left it.

We pushed through a set of glass doors and found ourselves in a lobby area. There was a lift to our right, a corridor behind wood-panelled doors beyond that, and another corridor heading off from the far side of the lobby. An old-fashioned three-piece suite occupied the middle of the space. Facing the lift doors was a walnut table that had seen better days. On it was a folded copy of *The Independent*.

It appeared that we had to go up two floors; I'm not very good at waiting around for lifts. Or buses. Or anything that you suspect might never come.

"I'll take the stairs," I said, "and I'll still get there before you."

I took Maggie's bag in my spare hand and shouldered open the door to the stairs. I ran up one flight, barged through the equivalent door on the next floor and found myself in an identical lobby space. I pressed the call button and while wondering if the lift would ever arrive tried on a number of expressions. It was certainly taking its time, the lift. On a walnut table that was indistinguishable from the one on the floor below was another copy of *The Independent* folded in the same manner. I thought to myself it had been a waste of money my buying one that morning.

When the lift arrived, the doors trundled open to reveal Maggie and a middle-aged couple, who looked as though they wanted to get out. She introduced them to me as Henrik and Caroline. I thought I could see a slightly guarded look in Henrik's eyes as we swapped places; Caroline looked as if, like Maggie, she just wanted to get to their room. Henrik had been a contemporary, Maggie told me as the lift doors closed behind me and I turned to press the button. He'd seemed a lot older than me, but then Maggie is four years my senior and some men age worse than others.

The interior of the lift was mirrored on three sides, which

created a theoretically endless series of reflections in both side walls. I checked myself out. I wasn't ageing too badly. My problems were *inside* my head. I knew that. Maybe physiologically, certainly mentally.

"You look beautiful," Maggie said in a way that managed to be affectionate and mocking at the same time.

When we finally got to our room, the third on the left beyond the wood-panelled doors, and managed to get the keycard to flash green rather than red on the fifth attempt, we found we had one small towel between the two of us, no complimentary toiletries, and the shower produced either a trickle of boiling water or an icy torrent. I thought about helping Maggie out of her travelling clothes and suggesting we test out the mattress, but I sensed she wanted to get back downstairs for pre-dinner drinks as soon as possible.

So while Maggie plugged in her hair-straighteners I stood to one side of the hot trickle in the shower cubicle pressing at my neck and trying to work out if the gland was bigger or smaller than the day before. I had mentioned it to Maggie and she had dismissed it. Ideally, this would have sufficed. Whereas the average person might think they had a cold coming on and the raised gland was their body's natural way of fighting it, my thoughts turn to leukaemia, lymphoma, Hodgkin's disease.

I leaned over the washbasin and wiped a swathe of condensation from the mirror so that I could see my reflection. I fancied that it was studying me rather than I it. If so, perhaps it felt sorry for me with my imaginary ailments and constant nagging anxiety. Or perhaps it just thought I was ridiculous. It wasn't bothered by anything like that. It was free.

Towelling myself dry, I returned to the bedroom, where Maggie was just stepping into her specially bought ballgown with its flatteringly high waist and gratifyingly plunging neckline. I slipped into my oversize dead man's DJ and a pair of highly polished shoes that were coming away from their soles.

We left the room and headed back to the lifts. I suggested we walk down and Maggie acquiesced. She looked good in the ballgown and I thought she would prefer to watch the movement of the dress over her long legs than stand around waiting for the lift that might never arrive. I knew that was my preference.

I pushed open the door to the stairwell and ushered Maggie through.

As we walked down, a small party in tuxedos and ballgowns was coming up. They passed us and turned left. They were going in the right direction, but they were on the wrong level.

"They're going the wrong way," I whispered to Maggie.

But as I made the remark, I lost confidence in its content.

"Are you going to the reunion?" I asked the disappearing party while they were still within earshot.

"Yes," they said.

"It's this way," I said. "Down two flights. Unless you can get down at the other end?"

"No, this is the way," said a tall man with thinning hair and a perfectly fitting suit.

"How *can* it be?" I said to Maggie.

I pictured the two identical lobbies with their walnut tables and copies of *The Independent*. How had we gone wrong?

Maggie had stopped. We exchanged puzzled looks. The people who knew where they were going headed off while we dithered on the stairs. Eventually, I thought we might as well follow them. When we got as far as we could go and hadn't reached the main part of the hotel, and couldn't find another stairwell, *then* we could come back.

So Maggie and I walked down the corridor, which was as similar to the one down which we had walked to get to our room as it is possible to be without actually being the same corridor. There would be no way out at the far end, and even if there was it would only be a stairway and we'd have to descend two flights to get to where we wanted to be.

Even the series of prints on the wall looked the same, one hanging askew. We passed a facsimile of the scuffed cabinet. I looked at the armchair in the corner. It sat unevenly due to a missing castor.

We entered a wide corridor and turned left at the end of it, past a bar that still had its shutters down. Then there was the room with the stags' heads, the piano player on the edge of the main reception hall (which was now heaving with well-dressed bodies) and we were back where we'd started, without having had to go down two floors.

Maggie and I looked at each other in puzzlement and I just had time to start asking, "What the fuck—?" when a tall woman in a taffeta ballgown swept past and dragged Maggie off to meet someone else she hadn't seen for twenty years.

They were giving out drinks. The choice was champagne or orange juice. I wandered off to a bar in an adjoining room where I waited behind a fat man who was ordering two turkey sandwiches.

Back on the fringes of the main room where the welcome drinks were still being served, I stood with a pint of Guinness – the nearest I could get to something drinkable – and looked on. At the far side of the room I could see Maggie laughing generously at somebody's joke, her head dropping forward so that her straightened hair fell in front of her face.

I became aware of a tall, slim man with silver hair standing near to me. A picture of understated elegance, in his own tailored suit and carefully polished shoes, he sipped at a glass of champagne.

"It's strange being an outsider at one of these events," he said with an almost imperceptible turn of the head.

"Very strange," I agreed. "Will," I added, offering him my hand.

"Gordon," he said with a warm smile.

We raised our glasses to our lips and watched the increasingly animated crowd in the centre of the room.

"Do you know?" he began, "I was reading in the paper today – just now, upstairs, in fact – that during the Cold War the East Germans used to pay Bulgarian border guards for every East German they shot trying to cross the frontier into the West. It's almost unbelievable, isn't it?" He tipped the last of his champagne into his mouth and swallowed. "I don't know what made me think of that."

"Extraordinary," I agreed.

"I'm not sure I could kill anybody, even if ordered to do so."

"Not even for money?" I joked.

"Especially not for money," he said, turning to me. "Nice to meet you, Will. Excuse me."

As he walked away to look for his wife, I ticked myself off for my banal and unfunny joke.

I became aware of my fingers probing inside the collar of my dress shirt. I wondered if this latest fixation on head and neck cancers would end up with another referral to a specialist. I remembered with a jolt the not-so-smooth progress of the endoscope up my nose and down past my ear.

One of the organizers appeared up in the gallery with a photographer. Cupping her hands, the organizer announced a complicated sequence of group photographs.

I took this as my cue to wander back to the bar and secure a second pint of Guinness. When I returned to the reception hall the photographer had finished. I looked for Maggie and saw her talking to a man with a paisley-patterned bow tie but when she lifted her head up to the light I saw it wasn't Maggie at all. The direct light revealed deeper lines, a less youthful skin texture.

I felt a hand on my shoulder and turned around. *This* was Maggie, looking several years younger than the woman I'd thought was her. She introduced me to a well-meaning gastroenterologist from Peterborough and we had a conversation about five-a-side football. Despite both being regular players of the game, neither one of us was at all interested in what the other had to say.

Fortunately dinner was announced, so I was able to escape and find Maggie again and together we joined the throng heading towards the ballroom.

"I can't remember," I said to her, "is Jonathan coming to this?"

Maggie and Jonathan had met in their first year and started going out. They'd stayed together for a number of years, until a mutual acquaintance had lured Jonathan away from Maggie for a one-night stand that had turned into marriage, kids, the lot.

"No," Maggie answered, looking all around as she spoke, "this is not Jonathan's scene at all."

I wanted to say that it wasn't mine. It wasn't mine possibly even more than it wasn't Jonathan's. But I kept quiet. My hand crept up to my neck as we shuffled towards the seating plan resting on an easel by the entrance to the ballroom.

"No doubt we'll be on a table at the back," Maggie said, "with all the other people who booked at the last minute."

As we duly made our way towards the back of the ballroom, I had a look around. Two large video projection screens were each showing a series of stills, mugshots taken on enrolment. They were monochrome and the images had either become degraded or had been drenched with a sepia hue.

There were probably 200, maybe 300 people at the event; less than half of those would be partners, and possibly a not insignificant proportion of the partners would have been fellow students.

I was trying to work out how long I might have to watch the parade of faces before Maggie's might appear. I had seen photographs of Maggie – and Jonathan – from back then. I was confident I'd recognize her. It's not as if the passage of twenty-five years actually makes you a different person. You just look a little older. Or a lot older.

I saw a picture of the organizer, the woman who had appeared on the balcony to orchestrate group photographs. She'd been slimmer, but you could already see the confidence in her eyes. For her it seemed a short step from enrolling to sending out invitations for a twenty-five-year reunion. She already knew she was going to do it. Maybe not explicitly, but she knew herself very well, she knew what she was capable of.

On the other screen I saw an early mugshot of the guy from the lift, Henrik, and he did indeed look a lot younger, but, again, the eyes were the same. That reticence, suspicion even.

I looked away from the mugshots in order to be introduced to the people at our table. Through a combination of first impressions, whispered intel from Maggie and the fruits of my own efforts at conversation, I gathered that they were a mixture of old friends of Maggie's and former fellow students: a likeable psychologist whose husband had left her for another man; a guy in his early fifties who had given up medicine for web design, but whose ideas seemed mired in the 1990s; a woman who had trained as a GP, before taking time out to have kids and finally going back to do a day a week; another part-time GP and editor of medical journals and his wife, a teacher who called herself a freelance journalist on the strength of writing a column for her husband's magazine about being married to a doctor.

When I next looked towards the front of the ballroom, there was Maggie's mugshot just fading from the screen on the left.

I'd gathered now that the two screens were showing the same photographs, but out of synch. I saw the psychologist from our table. She was smiling at the camera, her eyes full of hope and expectation.

I turned back to the table, where three Polish waitresses in black and white costumes had converged. Drinks were being ordered, but the choice appeared to be limited to red or white, as far as I could tell from my attempts at dialogue with the three Poles, who, in terms of their mental and practical preparedness, were still on the plane from Warsaw.

"I'm going to the bar," I told Maggie.

I watched the faces fade in and fade out on the screens as I crossed the room. The last face I saw before the angle became too narrow to see anything at all made me come to an abrupt halt with a silly expression on my face.

Because it was mine.

I backtracked. The face that had looked a lot like mine twenty years earlier had gone and been replaced by that of Gordon, the man I had met in the reception hall. I looked at the other screen, but it would be a while before the shot came around again and I'd be able to see it and realize that the guy who looked like me didn't look that much like me after all.

I stood waiting for the bartender to pour me a pint of Guinness. He tried to make conversation. He was Greek, very friendly, and he didn't have many customers, but I wasn't up for it. I felt strange, dissociated from my surroundings. I palpated my neck.

"Hello Will," said a voice.

I turned around to see Henrik leaning on the bar. He asked the bartender for a Scotch. From the glassy look in his eyes I guessed he'd already had a couple.

"It's weird, isn't it?" he said.

"What?"

"This. This place. This whole evening. The mugshots. I didn't know they were going to do that. With that picture constantly flashing up on screen, it's like there's two of you. You now and you then. Do you know what I mean?"

"I saw yours," I said. "You've not changed a bit."

He gave a little laugh and knocked back his Scotch.

"I'm going to head back," I said.

"Cheers."

Seated at the table with the starters arriving, I waited for a gap in the conversation and turned to Maggie.

"What was going on with that whole lift thing?" I asked her.

"I can't explain it," she said, her eyes shining. "We went up but then didn't need to come down again. It's this place. The rules are different here."

I could tell Maggie was having a good time; she wouldn't normally come out with something like that. She's a very rational person. Either being a doctor made her like that or she became a doctor because that was the kind of person she was. Bit of both probably.

"Do you think it's possible," I said, "that we actually went down when we thought we were going up? After I got in?"

"But then we'd have just got back where we started and that wasn't the right floor. It's just—" She stopped and her eyes widened and she sang the theme tune to *The Twilight Zone*. I couldn't remember the last time she'd done that – perhaps ten years ago. I smiled and she leaned forward and I kissed her, then immediately she turned away and put her hand on the psychologist's arm to impart some fascinating piece of gossip she'd just remembered.

Thinking that it would be a while before the main course arrived, I got up from the table. On one of the big screens I recognized the sequence of mugshots that had preceded that of the guy who looked a bit like the younger me. When the face came up again, I studied it. Was he here, in the room? He would be four years older than me if he was Maggie's contemporary. Would he have aged better?

I thought of him as a version of me four years on, just as the second lobby I'd visited with the identical walnut table was a version of the one on the floor below. It was simply a floor higher. Separated in space rather than time.

I wondered if I should get another pint, but remembered I hadn't finished the last one.

On a table next to the easel just outside the ballroom was a laptop. It was playing a slideshow of the pictures taken in the hotel's reception hall. I picked out Maggie, smiling broadly and looking up at the camera just like everybody else. I saw the web designer and the boring gastroenterologist and even, standing on the edge of the group, Gordon, the man I had talked to briefly. I spotted Henrik and his wife, Caroline. There was the divorced psychologist, the tall man with the thinning hair who had known where he was going, there was the woman in taffeta and the man from the reception desk who had changed out of his jumbo cords and pastel polo shirt.

And there, just to the left of centre, was I, my neck tendons straining with the effort of holding my head up to smile for the camera. Maybe I looked a little tired around the eyes, perhaps I appeared a tad heavier in the jowls, even slightly paunchier.

I turned around and headed back into the ballroom. I checked out the nearest tables, but there was no sign of anyone who looked a bit like me. I reached our table, but remained standing, scanning the room, running my eyes over every table in there. He wasn't to be seen. I sat down, thanked the waitress for my main course and smiled at Maggie, who still looked like she was having a good time.

"This is *so* weird," she said quietly but emphatically.

She didn't know how weird.

I pushed back my chair.

"Where are you going?" she asked.

"I won't be long."

"How's your neck?"

I looked at her.

"Are your glands still up?"

"I've just got to . . ."

My legs took me away from the table. I didn't like it when she didn't show concern, and I didn't like it when she did. She couldn't win, and neither could I. I prodded my neck as I crossed to the exit. I glanced at the group photo on the laptop, wondering, as I sometimes did, what was the point of a life like this, a life lived in constant fear of its ending. Wouldn't it just be easier to cut short the wait?

I fingered the keycard in my pocket with one hand and the raised gland in my neck with the other as I walked slowly and softly past the wonky chair and the scuffed cabinet. I stopped to straighten the print that was hanging askew. The glass doors gave on to the lift lobby. The walnut table looked bare. Sitting on the shiny velveteen sofa reading *The Independent* was Gordon.

"Hello Will," he said, turning the page.

I had no doubt that if I were to go up a floor, there he would be again, sitting on the sofa reading the same newspaper. And whichever floor I was on, our room would be three doors down on the left beyond the wood-panelled doors.

I reached the door and slid the keycard into the slot. It flashed red. I tried again. Still red. I tried sliding it in very slowly and extracting it just as slowly. Still the red light flashed. I stood for a moment and listened to my breathing, which was fast and shallow.

And then I heard a man's voice. It was very close. I looked behind me to see if someone had left their door open. They'd left the ballroom to make a phone call and decided to do it in the privacy of their room. But the doors on the other side of the corridor were all shut and the corridor was empty.

Sometimes, when I play five-a-side football and we're warming up while waiting to begin, I count the players to see if we're all there. I count four and wonder who's missing, and it takes me a few moments to realize I've failed to count myself.

The frightening thing was that the corridor did genuinely feel empty, as if even I wasn't there. I would try the card in the door one more time before going to report the fault. I shoved it into the slot, which pushed the door open half an inch with an audible click of the mechanism.

I wondered if we'd left the door unlocked and what valuables might have been at risk. Then I heard the voice again, louder this time. It was coming from inside the room.

# SIMON KURT UNSWORTH

## Mami Wata

SIMON KURT UNSWORTH'S STORIES have appeared in the Ash-Tree Press anthologies *At Ease with the Dead*, *Exotic Gothic 3* and *Shades of Darkness*, as well as *Lovecraft Unbound*, *Gaslight Grotesque*, *The Black Book of Horror 6*, *Creature Feature*, *Where the Heart Is* and *Black Static* magazine.

His story "The Church on the Island" was nominated for a World Fantasy Award and was reprinted in *The Mammoth Book of Best New Horror 19* and *The Mammoth Book of the Best of Best New Horror*. His first collection, *Lost Places,* was recently issued by Ash-Tree, to be followed by *Strange Gateways* from PS Publishing.

"When I was first asked to contribute to *Exotic Gothic 3* (which was to feature Gothic-influenced stories in non-Gothic environments), I agreed without really thinking about it," Unsworth explains, "and then spent a long time struggling, trying to work out how, precisely, I was going to manage it or quite how to make a start.

"I knew what I wanted to do, sort of, but not exactly how to do it, so one day alarmingly close to the deadline I did a fun thing: I freewheeled through Google. Using a small document about Zambian myths and cultures I found online (I set the story in Zambia for no reason other than an old family friend lives there and it seemed exotic in Gothic terms), I used one Zambian word from it as a search term and read what came up, took one intriguing Zambian term from the search results and searched for that, etc, and disappeared into Google's merry depths.

"I ended up with an academic paper about a particular myth, a travel blog about a sort of beer made from corn and a weird little 'my God's better than your God' blog by a kid in Africa, and somewhere in the middle of that, the story appeared."

THE HEAT WAS like a brick.

Thorley had never seen shadows like it; they seemed edged in gold and darker at their centre than pitch. Even indoors, they pooled at his feet like glorious ink, gathering around his ankles and under the tables in the *chibuku* tavern. They even reflected themselves in the sweat that gathered on the brow of Chilongo, Thorley's companion seated on the other side of the table.

"This is a good place," Chilongo was saying. "An honest place. Sure, we have our problems, like anywhere, but we've always worked hard. I don't know why they had to send you."

"They sent me," said Thorley, "because the mine's production has fallen by over half and they want to know why." Behind Chilongo, bottles glittered on the shelves lining the bar, throwing their own shadows across the mural painted on to the wall. A mermaid, golden haired and naked, had her back to the bar's interior but looked over her shoulder into the room. Her tail was splayed out in front of her, half hidden by her body. Beyond, painted smaller so that they looked insignificant and weak, were rows of men. They looked awe-struck, frightened.

Actually, Thorley hadn't been sent, he had chosen to come, even though he didn't need to. The loss of production was a financial concern but it could have been sorted out by phone and email with the onsite managers. It was Chilongo's voice that had done it in the end, its rich musicality dancing down the telephone line and making the already grey British day greyer. Thorley had heard the sun in Chilongo's voice, heard the rhythms of African speech, heard something brighter than the drear that faced him through the window, and it had called to him, irresistible and powerful.

"Every mine has runs of luck, good and bad," said Chilongo. "We've just hit a bad period."

"Indeed?" said Thorley. "And yet the last report said shaft four had hit a new seam, was promising great dividends."

"It didn't play out," insisted Chilongo. "It looked good, but then it turned out to be nothing. We've had some flooding in the deepest shaft, some machinery problems. Nothing to worry about. You know how it goes."

"No," said Thorley, "I don't," and as he said it he thought to himself, *but I know when someone's lying to me. What I don't know is why.*

Thorley had decided not to stay in one of the large hotels. Travelling in from Kitwe, the town nearest to the mine, would have been a waste and besides, he wanted to see what industrial Zambia was really like. He had seen the brochures that sometimes came across his desk, glossy things filled with pictures of wild animals and wide, sweeping plains, telling prospective investors about the landscape and the abundant workforce and the stable government, and about mines that produced yield after impressive yearly yield of copper or nickel or cobalt, but he had never visited. He had never needed to; previously, things had run smoothly and the local managers had dealt with things.

He also didn't want to stay with the expats, although several of them had offered him accommodation when they discovered he was coming. He had never liked expat communities, which seemed to him to fall too easily into patterns of casual racism redolent of colonialism. They were a necessary evil as Thorley saw it, useful for the skills pool they provided but claustrophobic with nostalgia and boredom, and he certainly didn't need to expose himself to it any more than was strictly necessary. Instead, he had chosen to stay in a workers' motel on the outskirts of Kitwe, not far from the mine.

Thorley could have been in a room anywhere; the bed with nondescript covers and sagging mattress, the cheap sideboard that doubled as a television stand, the shower room created by partitioning off one corner and installing a plastic cubicle and shower, the chair on which he hung his clothes.

He placed his underwear and shirts in the sideboard drawers, seeing as he did so a Gideon's bible. It was old, bleached by the heat, and its spine cracked painfully when he lifted and opened it, the imitation leather dry and brittle. The drawers were lined with newspaper, he saw, aged to the colour of sand and as brittle as the Gideon's spine. He lifted out a sheet and tried to read it, but the print had faded so that he could only make out some of the words. The headline on the page read FOUR DEAD MEN and below was a date in July, three months previously. He put the sheet back in the drawer and decided to work.

Even after sundown, the heat was oppressive. The motel had no air conditioning, and Thorley soon found that the only way to stay even close to comfortable was to strip to his pants and fan himself with the papers he was supposed to be reading. It was impossible to concentrate anyway; he knew most of the facts already, about how the mine's production had fallen off dramatically in the previous five months, down from around 450 tonnes to less than 300, how there was no official explanation (apart from Chilongo's "bad luck") for this drop in output. Much of the explanation, Thorley saw, would lie in the significant drop in workforce numbers that had occurred over the previous months. The mine still operated, of course; they had not lost that many men, just more than was normal or usual, for reasons that weren't clear.

Thorley could hear the mine workings as he lay on his bed, a distant throatless rumble peaking occasionally into dull booms or percussive echoes. Closer to, someone was playing a radio loud, the signal fading in and out so that the music and voices seemed to sway about Thorley. He was exhausted and hot, his eyes gritty from tiredness and the dry air, his sweat loosed across him like a second skin. The tap water was only lukewarm and did not quench his thirst, no matter how much he drank. He was wondering about dressing and going in search of ice when he must have, finally, drifted into slumber.

When Thorley awoke it was still dark, and not much cooler. He sat up, realizing as he did so that some of his papers had stuck to his body. They peeled off with a sound like kissing, leaving the ghosts of letters on his flesh that rubbed away under his fingers. In the distance, he heard sirens, or one siren echoing, it was hard to tell, and men shouting. He went to the window of his room, picking up his glass of tepid water as he went, and pulled aside the curtains.

His rented car was a grey shape in the darkness, and the flat apron of the car park beyond a smooth shadow segmented by painted lines. Despite the noises, which seemed to be getting closer, he could see no movement except the distant shimmer of thorn bushes moving in the slight breeze.

Actually, that wasn't quite true. The far edge of the car park bordered the road to the mine, and now he could see someone walking along it, heading away from the motel. Shadows from the buildings on the far side of the road swept across the figure as it walked, an alternating, dappling pattern. It was a woman, Thorley saw, tall and thin and white with straggly blonde hair that fell down her naked back.

Naked? No, that couldn't be right. She must surely have some backless top or dress on, something cool for this stifling heat. He couldn't see her lower half, so shrouded in shadow was she, but he thought he could hear the *swish* of material as she walked.

Just before she walked out of view, an ambulance went past heading away from the mine, its swirling light illuminating her fully for a moment, showing Thorley her long arms and splayed hands with dark nails. In the moment of her disappearance, she turned her face to him and smiled, her teeth white as alabaster against the surrounding night. She was young, and very pretty.

The next morning, Thorley ate breakfast and waited for Chilongo. The motel had no dining room, so he had walked over the road to a tavern that had a sign outside advertising GOOD FOOD FROM EARLY TIL LATE and ordered himself a coffee and the fruit plate. Although it was before eight, the sun had already cast itself hard across the ground, creating more of those shadows that seemed so dark.

It was worse inside the tavern, where the large glass windows, cataracted with dust and dirt though they were, magnified the heat of the morning far beyond anything the slowly turning ceiling fan could cope with. Flies buzzed across the trays of wild mango, plum and sand apple, the owner flicking a red cloth at them half-heartedly, making the insects rise and fall.

Thorley sat at the table farthest from the windows, hoping to find some respite from the light. At a nearby table, two men stared with undisguised interest at him. He smiled, nodded, broke eye contact by looking down at the papers he had brought with him.

The coffee was poor, weak and gruel-like, but the fruit was excellent, fleshy and juicy and, to his palate, exotic, and he enjoyed the sensation and taste of it in his mouth. As he ate, he looked around the tavern. The other diners were mostly men, workers from the mine, he assumed, some coming off nightshift, others going on. The men going on shift, cleaner and fresher, ate fruit and spoke to each other; the men coming off shift ate plates of vegetables and meat in silence. Most of the men looked over at him during their meals, eyes sullen and wary.

Behind the counter and counterman, painted on the rear wall, was a mural. This one showed a dark-skinned woman with long hair confidently facing into the room, with a comb in one hand. She was naked apart from a snake, draped around her shoulders, its tail and head covering her breasts. The artist had painted her well, and she glowed with large, expressive eyes and a ripe, full mouth. The landscape behind her, however, was cruder, showing only the barest of detail. Hills and a vast plain stretched out, the plain full of what Thorley first thought were apes or horses but then realized were men. There were hundreds of them, mostly barely more than stick figures, all facing the woman. Some appeared to be kneeling, others had their arms raised. It was an odd mix of primitive and modern art styles, although an impressive one.

Chilongo appeared late, stressed but apologetic, and with some of the dancing cadences gone from his voice. He was tired, Thorley saw, the bruised flesh under his eyes sagging and dark. The man was rumpled, his clothes creased. Rings of sweat, dried and fresh, gathered under his shirtsleeves. He smelled anxious and sour.

"I am so sorry," he said. "It has been a difficult morning and I was unavoidably delayed."

"Problem?" Thorley asked.

"No. Well, yes," said Chilongo. "There was an incident last night, and one of the men died. One of the miners, I mean. He was in another motel, like yours, and he was found dead."

"Not an incident at the mine? An accident, I mean, onsite?"

"No."

"Then why should that be a problem for you?" asked Thorley.

"Because," said Chilongo, "I am the man in charge of the miners and of the visitors to the mine. I am responsible for them." He sounded angry, indignant, and Thorley raised a placatory hand, motioning Chilongo to sit.

"Sorry," he said, "I meant no offence. Now, we have a long few days ahead of us. Please, take me to the mine and you can tell me what's been happening on the way."

"We like to keep visitors away," said Chilongo, noticing Thorley wince as they bounced across yet another rut over the deteriorated track that led to the small mine, a smaller site, specializing in the deepest seams. "Originally, it was to keep ourselves insignificant in the eyes of others, so that they would not bother us. The larger companies are not above having their trucks deliberately break down to block access, or staging the accidental shedding of loads of trash in awkward places, if they perceive you as a threat. Now, however, it stops the inquisitive attempting to get onsite. Reporters and the like."

"Reporters? Why reporters?"

"Because of the deaths."

The mine, even though small by comparison with some of the others scattered across the copperbelt, was still huge. As they juddered along the road, and through two security checkpoints, Thorley waited to see the investment he was here to protect.

He wasn't sure what he expected, exactly; a series of sheds around a caged lift-head, possibly, or a carved expanse of parched earth hollowed out from the ground, but in reality it was neither. It was a complicated, layered series of huts and prefab buildings, of varying heights, built in the centre of a vast, dusty plain. The separate structures were clustered together, creating the impression of a huge, ever-expanding castle, sprawling its way across the earth like some creeping, cancerous thing.

As they drew close, Thorley saw the individual huts were huge, boxy structures painted green and brown and coated in sand and dirt, their fronts open to allow trucks to drive in and out. More trucks and dirty buildings lined the perimeter, these stranger shapes with sloped roofs or walls that were missing entirely, all of them linked by rumbling, moving multi-layered conveyor belts like arteries. All over the site, chimneys pierced the air, stretching up from the ground and loosing spiralling coils of dirty grey smoke at the sky.

Thorley enjoyed the size of it, could feel the vibration of the machinery even in the car. Even with the windows closed, he smelled the sharp stench of acid and machinery and burning, could hear the lupine growl of the conveyor belts and smelting units. He turned to Chilongo, wanting to say something about the sheer immensity of what he was seeing and hearing, but saw that the other man was looking at the approaching mine works with a strange expression on his face; he looked scared.

Thorley spent the day going through the mine's records, interviewing the managers and supervisors. He soon realized that there was a distinct split in attitude between those staff who worked solely overground, mainly the expat managers, and those who went underground, mostly locals or supervisors brought in from other areas. The managers put the fall in production down to worker greed, blaming miners who had slowed down or left in the hope of getting higher pay, shorter hours or more benefits. They showed him lengthy technical reports, most written by the same expat managers that were showing them to him, full of technical dialogue and graphs and phrases like *unexpected seam depletion* and *shaft misalignment*, none of which told him anything. In one he came across the phrase *enviro-cultural factors having an impact upon workforce cohesion and permanence*, but it was not clear what this meant. The workers who went underground all reported variations on a theme; that the mine was simply "unlucky".

That night, Chilongo took Thorley to a different tavern to eat, this one closer to Kitwe. It looked to have been built out of an old barn, although the inside was nicely decorated and the tables were large and spaced far enough apart that Thorley didn't feel overlooked or overheard.

The meal was pleasant, and although he had little inclination to talk to Chilongo, the other man seemed to have recovered some of his energy since the morning and spoke enough for both of them. Thorley listened only partially, chewing his food and glancing around. This was a place couples came, and although it was only early evening, there were several pairs dining around the room. Most looked at him, some fleetingly, some with longer, more intense stares. The couple nearest to him held a fierce, whispered conversation, clearly about him. Thorley caught the word *muzungu* once or twice. He had heard it this morning at breakfast as well, and the previous day, never spoken to his face.

"It means 'Westerner'," said Chilongo. "That word you keep hearing. We are used to foreigners here, of course, but you are clearly not a mine operator and you have arrived at a bad time. It makes people nervous."

"How can you tell I'm not a mine operator?" asked Thorley, intrigued.

"Ha! You are soft-looking, as though you have spent your life behind a desk. Mine operators, underground or overground, tend to look like the thing they mine eventually. Hard, in the case of copper. Even when a miner is clean, he looks crusted with dirt, no?"

Thorley nodded; it was true. He had met miners ten years into their retirement and they still appeared as though their skin was grainy with cinders and grit.

"You aren't dirty. To miners and the people that know them, you don't look as if you've ever been dirty in your life."

"Why is this a difficult time? Because of the deaths?"

Chilongo didn't answer straight away, but took a sip of his pulpy elephant orange drink, what he called *muhuluhulu*, crunching on an ice cube. "The deaths are part of it," he said eventually. "A small part. It's not easy to explain. This isn't a happy place now, or at least, not as happy as it was. But working towns are never that happy, are they? Always worried about production or closures or being undersold, or accidents, or death. There's no one here who isn't related to a miner, or to a trucker or a boss or a guard for the mine. The expats tell us to get on with the work, but they don't understand either."

"Understand what?"

"Are you still planning to come underground tomorrow, to see the mine in operation?"

Thorley nodded.

"Then maybe you'll see then."

\*     \*     \*

His motel room was no cooler that evening, although Thorley had managed to get a bucket of ice from reception and had dropped two bottles of water into it in the hope that they would stay chilled for the night. He had also bought himself Scotch whisky and drunk several shots after returning from his meal.

He thought about Chilongo; the man was hiding something, that was for sure, and the mine managers had no idea of what was happening. Despite all the reports and conversations today, he was no clearer about why this mine was losing staff, had falling production figures.

They paid well and were generous employers, the conditions were no worse than any of the other companies working in the area and better than some, and yet people were walking away from their jobs. Six per cent of the workforce last month, four per cent the month before, seven the month before that, and few were being replaced. The positions were being advertised, but there were few if any applicants. It made no sense. None.

The car park was fuller tonight, Thorley saw. As well as his own rental Toyota, already picking up a thin layer of sand and dust after only a day's disuse, there were two jeeps with mine company logos and three or four other cars.

The radio was playing again, its indistinct tones tonight accompanied by singing, although whether by a man or woman Thorley could not tell. People were drinking in another of the rooms, he knew; there had already been one shouted argument, the voices slurred, and a bout of raucous laughter that ended in the sound of a bottle breaking. Thorley sipped his whisky and waited for the world to cool.

At just before midnight, the woman appeared again. She walked into Thorley's view on the far side of the car park, this time coming from the mine rather than walking towards it. In the sodium orange of the streetlights, her skin seemed the colour of mocha and her auburn hair gleamed like the copper he had spent the day investigating. She walked across the road to the edge of the concrete apron and then stopped, appearing to stare at him even though she was surely too far away to see him. There was something enticing in her gaze, even at this distance, something feral and erotic.

Thorley became uncomfortably aware that he was standing at the window wearing only boxers and with a growing erection.

Stepping back into the shadows of the room, he continued watching. The woman began to walk across the car park, and although he couldn't see her lower half because of the cars and jeep between her and him, he suddenly became convinced she was naked. He could see the sweep of her clavicles and neck, her hair framing a rounded, attractive face and dropping away down a chest he was suddenly sure was bare. He could see no T-shirt neckline or blouse collar, no thin vest straps or bandeau top.

When the man came into view and saw the woman, he was as surprised as Thorley was. Drunk, he swayed as he walked, was scrabbling in his pockets for something, head down and oblivious. The woman turned towards the new man, with his skin dark and sweating in the humid night, and smiled broadly. He, seeing her, took two stumbling steps back and then turned and staggered back the way he had come. With a last look towards Thorley, she shifted direction, following the other man.

Thorley watched her go, somewhere between disappointed and glad; his visit here was complicated enough without adding a woman into the scenario. Finishing his whisky, he went to bed. It was only later, as he drifted towards sleep, that Thorley realized that the woman had been blonde the night before.

She could easily have dyed her hair, he thought the next morning. People did, after all. It wasn't unusual. Looking around the tavern, he saw that of the two of the women in there, one had plaits woven into her hair, making it a tangle of straw blonde, red and black that framed her dark face like a halo. Thorley lifted another piece of papaya into his mouth, gazing again at the mural.

"She is beautiful, yes?" said a voice. Thorley looked around to find Chilongo standing at his side. "*Mami Wata*. Water mother. You will find her in most of the bars and taverns in the copper-belt. Across large parts of Africa, really."

"Are they all pictures of her? All the different women in the murals?"

"They are all versions of her. She lives in our bars because she attracts men, and where men come, they want to drink. She likes the noise and the attention."

Thorley raised his eyes to Chilongo; he was staring at the woman on the wall with a look on his face that Thorley could not completely recognize, a mix of fascination and anger and something else. Lust, maybe. Looking again at the mural, he realized that the mermaid reminded him of the woman from the midnight street.

Outside, the dusty pavement glowed a heated yellow in the glare of the early morning sun. The road, a strip of darker tarmac, glinted as Thorley and Chilongo walked across it. It was already hot enough to create ripples in the air that Thorley could *feel*, warm pulsations that tickled his ankles. Crossing towards Chilongo's car, Thorley saw a crowd gathering in a loose, mutating cluster a couple of hundred yards away.

"What's happening?" asked Thorley.

"Nothing," said Chilongo. He kept his eyes fixed on the car, and it seemed to Thorley that his companion was deliberately not looking at the crowd.

"Nothing?" he asked.

"Nothing. Come, we have to get you underground."

The lift cage was empty, but it smelled of men, muscular, sweaty, exhausted. Chilongo and one of the mine engineers, a dark-bearded expat named Rowe, checked each other's equipment one last time and then closed the doors for descent.

"We're going to almost the deepest point in the mine, to one of the newer shafts, so that you can observe the operation and maybe talk to some of the men," said Rowe as though this was news to Thorley, as though he hadn't been the one who requested this excursion. *Take me deep*, he had said, *and let me talk to the miners. I need to know what the problem is.*

It was clear Rowe didn't like him, or didn't trust him. Thorley could see it in the looks that were even now surreptitiously coming his way. He had the impression that Rowe and Chilongo didn't like each other, but now Rowe was talking to Chilongo as though they were friends, pointedly excluding Thorley. Thorley didn't really mind; it gave him a chance to look around.

It was several years since he had been underground, but he found he still enjoyed it. The temperature drop as they descended was satisfying, an escape from the raw heat of the day above, diving into some cooling swathe that refreshed rather than chilled. He liked the sound of the lift, the metallic clatter dancing above the rumble of the motor and the fainter sound of the mine's working belly. He even liked the feel of the clothes he had changed into and the weight of the helmet on his head.

When the descent was over, the lift opened out into a wide shaft that went in both directions, sloping down and echoing with voices and the clank of machinery. Lights were strung out in cabled lines along the tunnel, the air around them haloed in dust and hanging moisture. Two conveyor belts, one above the other, ran along the centre of the tunnel. Both were currently motionless, the heavy rubber belts empty apart from streaks of crushed earth and dry, friable rock fragments.

Down here, the change in air pressure made Thorley's ears ache slightly. The smell had changed, from the strong male odour of the lift to one of burning rock and the heavy, tarry scent of oil and exhaust fumes. The three walked down the tunnel, passing under ribs of wood and tight cabling. The noise grew louder as they walked until talking to each became almost impossible. At one point, Chilongo stopped Thorley and pointed down an unlit side tunnel.

"It is the flooded one, the deep one," he shouted. "It did not play out, and we had water problems. It is why our production fell so far."

*No,* thought Thorley, *it's not.* One failed excursion should not have affected output that dramatically, despite what Chilongo said. The mine was always sending out exploratory shoots, some of which played out and some of which did not. It was normal behaviour. But something else was going on here.

They came upon the man about ten minutes after passing the abandoned deep shaft. He was positioned under one of the lights, peering intently back up along the tunnel. Under his covering of dirt and sweat, it was near-impossible to tell if he was black or white. Only his eyes, gleaming white against the grime on his face, showed clearly. When he saw them, the man started, stepping back away from the light and into one of the shadowed areas between the bulbs.

"You! Come here! What are you doing?" Rowe demanded.

"Watching," said the man.

"Watching? For what?" Rowe shouted and Thorley could feel the anger coming from him, fury that showed itself in his bared teeth and reddening face.

"Watching," repeated the man. Chilongo nodded at him and drew Rowe aside, leaning into his ear and speaking too fast and low for Thorley to hear. Feeling his own anger build, he stepped after them, trying to discern what the Zambian was saying.

Chilongo, seeing him, broke off and shouted, with forced cheerfulness, "Let us go. We are almost there."

The large gang of men was working on a new shaft, operating a huge excavator. Water sprayed against the rock-face, massive blades chewing into it and spitting the savaged chunks out behind where they were taken by smaller belts to be sorted and disposed of. The noise, nearly unbearable even through Thorley's ear protectors, was a constant roar of tortured stone and the grind of machinery and the gearshift crunch of an engine labouring under huge pressure merging with the reptile hiss of the water and men calling to each other. The sound was a physical thing, the air vibrating and beating against Thorley's clothes and exposed skin in a tattoo of industrial rhythms.

Dust was hanging in the air, reducing the light to a murky yellow gleam punctuated by bright spotlights on the excavator and the paler eyes of the helmet lamps. Rowe, leaving Chilongo and Thorley, went to find the supervisor, going from man to anonymous man to locate him. He was on his way back towards them, pulling a smaller man with him, when the man from the main tunnel reappeared. He was running, banging into Thorley as he dashed past, leaping up onto the running board of the excavator and screaming at the operator. In a moment, the machine fell silent and still, the men shouting and rushing around. Lights clicked off, the sudden darkness shocking in its intensity.

Thorley heard Rowe shout something and then Chilongo was at Thorley's side and reaching up to turn his helmet lamp off. Thorley went to speak, to reach up and switch the lamp back on, but Chilongo gripped his hand tightly and said, "Leave it. Stay silent. Please." Rowe shouted again and as the last of the lights went off, Thorley saw one of the miners wrap a hand around his mouth and drag him to the floor. "You will be safe if you stay silent and still," said Chilongo. "Please, trust me."

The darkness, now complete, brought with it silence. Thorley tried to move but Chilongo pulled him back against the rough wall, tightening his grip on Thorley's hand as he did so. Thorley, recognizing that he was powerless, submitted and remained still.

The first sound was a frictional rustle. It was initially very faint but grew rapidly louder, a constantly shifting, moving sound that made Thorley think of heavy drapes in a breeze or a taffeta ballgown wrapped around a dancing woman's thighs. Under it there was something else, a clink like stones being tapped together or teeth clicking. Surrounded by the blackness of the absolute, Thorley could not help but populate the darkness with shapes, although what shapes he did not know.

Something was even now slipping around the corner, heading towards them, he was sure. The noise was growing louder, sounding less like material, becoming more like paws stepping delicately over uneven ground or scales rasping against stone. A new scent came to Thorley's nostrils, foetid and sour like water that cannot flow.

Something moved in the darkness before Thorley's face. He felt the air shift as it went past, and his face prickled with fevered heat.

Towards the excavator, one of the men whimpered and the thing in the darkness darted away, snapping like a whipping canvas sail in the feverish air. Something skittered away from him, the chitinous clatter not quite covering a noise like some subtle beast scenting the air.

Another man whispered something before being shushed, and the air shifted once more as the thing moved, swift and invisible, among the group. A third man let out a stifled cry and then a fourth (*Rowe*, Thorley thought) moaned. Another movement, another displacement of air and a hollow, terrible sucking. Rowe groaned again and one of the other men shouted. Someone screamed, the panic echoing as the sucking came again, and Rowe let out a rattled breath. Thorley realized that Chilongo was pulling at him, that he had stepped forward without knowing why, and then the air moved again and the burning heat caressed his cheek once more. Chilongo yanked him once and he was falling, banging, careening into the darkness as a something wheeled back towards the main tunnel.

*        *        *

"What was it?"

Chilongo did not answer, but merely shook his head.

"An animal? *A lion in the tunnels*?" asked Thorley, insistent. The sun caught in the sweat on Chilongo's face, birthing shadows around his eyes.

They were in the workers' canteen, above ground and alone. The rest of the shift had gone, and Rowe had been taken home. Their exit from the tunnel had been frantic and confused, all shouts and pushes and pulls, carrying the half-conscious Rowe and looking around as they ran, stumbling across uneven floors and past side tunnels that yawned like expectant mouths.

They had not turned on the main lights before fleeing, using only the lamps of their helmets, the hazy beams crossing and criss-crossing in the wide tunnel, illuminating men running gracelessly on all sides of him, heading back up the slope. Even in the lift, claustrophobic and full, Thorley couldn't relax, but stared through the lattice of the closed door as it began to rise, half-expecting to see something appearing from the darkness to snatch them back into the gloom.

Nothing came.

Rowe was not injured that Thorley could see, although he seemed exhausted and dopey, as though he had heat-stroke. One of the other managers had agreed to drive him home and Thorley had watched as the supervisor was taken to the car, walking like an old man. He seemed thinner, somehow, as though being underground had wasted him in some way. Even his shadow looked old, grey and brittle and shrunken and not the depthless and expansive black of the shadows of the man who escorted him or the surrounding cars and buildings.

"It is not an animal," the African said finally. "It is something else. A tourist, really. She has come like a snake from one of the lakes, Kashiba or Namulolobwe perhaps, is merely enjoying a change of scenery. It has happened before. She never stays long. It is nearly over and she will move on soon, find somewhere new to be. It's said Mobutu kept her, or one like her, in the Congo, and she gave him strength and jewels for thirty years."

"She? It's a woman?" asked Thorley.

"Not a woman, no," said Chilongo. From over his shoulder, another painted mermaid stared at Thorley. *Even here,* he thought, although this picture was like cave art. In it, the mermaid, with a fat serpent wound around her body, was grinning widely and holding up a hand upon which a stick figure danced. The figure was male, had swollen genitalia but no facial features. The mermaid's breasts were exposed, full and rounded and with dark, prominent nipples. She was pale, almost white, with red hair.

"If not a woman, then what?" asked Thorley.

"*Mami Wata,*" said Chilongo. "A water demon."

Thorley finished his whisky while making the call. Yes, the mine had suffered some local staffing problems, he said, but they were on their way to being sorted. Production would rise again soon. Chilongo and Rowe had been the very essence of helpfulness, showing him what he needed to see. All was well in Zambia . . .

He didn't believe it.

He wasn't sure what was happening here, but he knew he would never get to the bottom of it. He saw it in the suspicion on the faces of the mineworkers, heard it in the voices of the others eating in the taverns, felt it in the heat and in Chilongo's deferential touch to his shoulder as he got out of the car. "Go back," Chilongo had said. "Go back and leave us to finish this. It is nearly over, she has almost all she wants. Things will be well again soon."

Thorley could see no other course of action; demon or animal, imagination or reality, he had no way to understand what was happening here and no strategy for dealing with it. His own places were calling him now, where the shadows weren't so dark, and the streets were slick and definable and dull. He wanted to go home.

It was late on Thorley's last night in Zambia. A frantic scratching was beckoning him from a heated sleep, as he lay on top of cheap blankets that stuck to his skin. Clad only in his shorts, he went to the window and drew back the curtains.

The woman was on the other side of the glass.

She smiled. Thorley's original suspicions were right; she was naked, her breasts pressed flat against the pane. One hand was also flattened against the glass, the fingers scratching at it slowly.

In the darkness, her skin seemed to shift from a rich, lustred brown to a pale pink, and her hair to shimmer from black to blonde. Her smile showed teeth as white as milk, her eyes dark and feral and inviting.

Thorley stepped away from the window, uncomfortably aware of his stiffening erection. Her incisors were long, gleaming against pomegranate-red lips, the nails on the end of her fingers curved into wicked hooks. Her areolae were perfect circles and he knew that if he stepped close enough and looked down, he would see that her legs were long and shapely, meeting in a delta of musky hair. He stepped towards the door, pulling off his shorts as he went.

Outside, a slight breeze blew air that was warmer and dry against Thorley's naked flesh. The woman came to him, holding her arms out, naked as he'd expected and hoped, her tongue poking out slightly from between enticing lips.

Thorley stepped into the cage of her arms, feeling himself tremble. She made a noise like a hissing snake and her smile widened so that it seemed to crawl around her entire face and her mouth opened and that tongue came out, long and red and black and curling and tasting the air, tasting *him* and then Chilongo rasped, "Leave him be."

He was standing just out of the woman's reach, holding a shotgun and pointing it at her. "He is *muzungu*. Taking him will mean trouble. Find another."

The woman hissed again and Thorley suddenly wondered how he had seen her as attractive. She smelled wild, of earth and urine and spoiled meat and her tongue was longer than any had a right to be, her only sound a hiss, instinctive and vicious. He stepped back but she moved with him, stepping to follow him, staring at him.

Chilongo moved forwards, pushing the gun barrel into her belly and saying, "No. *Fingi!* Go into the town, there are men there who will only be missed by us, not by anyone else."

Her tongue was on his skin, wet and warm, slipping against his neck.

Chilongo pushed with the barrel and she moved, opening her arms and releasing Thorley. She glared at Chilongo, who gestured briefly with the shotgun towards the road.

Away from her, the smell of her dissipating, Thorley was aroused again as he looked at her breasts, at the way her lips were parted and her breath came in tiny gasps.

Chilongo looked across at him and said, "Go. She is not for you, nor you her."

As if in reply, the woman sibilated, low and venomous, and her tongue appeared again, lapping at the air. Revulsion washed across him and he backed away.

Thorley managed to stumble to his room as the woman, the *thing*, remained motionless, staring at Chilongo. He met her gaze without moving, the gun barrel's black maw hovering at the height of her belly. On the far side of the car park a car sped past, horn braying. Chilongo, distracted, glanced away and in the briefest moment that his eyes were averted, the woman moved.

She covered the distance to Chilongo incredibly fast, dropping low as she went and shrieking like wind across glass bottles. As the car moved along the road, Chilongo's shadow shifted around him, dancing with the moving headlights, and the woman went with it. Her face brushed the ground, the scraped-porcelain noise of her teeth grinding across the pavement making Thorley's own teeth ache in sympathy. Her tongue lashed at the ground ahead of her face, writhing and lapping at Chilongo's shade, sucking violently. Chilongo let out a scream, high and thin, and took two steps forwards, wobbling. The woman darted away from the African, rising as she did so, licking tendrils of blackness that dangled from her mouth and dripped across her breasts.

Chilongo fell to his knees and gave a last, weak exhalation. He looked across at Thorley, and Thorley saw tears glittering in his eyes as he fell forwards, his head cracking against the floor. Thorley slammed his room door shut, backed away further until his knees hit the bed and he fell across it. Ignoring the terrible, liquid sucking sounds coming from outside, he pulled the blanket around him so that it covered his head and thought about home.

The sounds carried on for a long time, impossible to avoid, too audible, slithering into his ears like old grease. Thorley curled up, pulling his knees into a foetal position and wrapping his arms around his legs. The rough grey blanket prickled against this skin as he prayed for the noises to stop.

In the morning, Chilongo was still there. Thorley hadn't slept; dressing quickly, packing and leaving the motel room early before anyone in the rooms around him stirred, he saw the man's body was in the same place, legs on the road and head towards Thorley's door.

Kneeling beside Chilongo, he looked into his glassy, dead eyes and said a silent *thank you*. The low rising sun glared into his face as he rose, and he saw that Chilongo was the only thing in the car park not casting a shadow. He went to his car, throwing his bag in the rear seat, and drove away quickly.

He did not look back, but he did drive to the mine. The smelting works and storage units and the spiderweb connections of conveyor belts and ramps twisted around him as he wound to the front of the main building and parked.

Thorley got out of his car, sensing the difference in this place. He walked out to the centre of the open space, looking around him. The air burned hot with the acidic scour of industry. All was busier than it had been on his previous visits despite the early hour. Two men, crossing the dusty apron to the lorries parked on the far side, laughed. Machinery roared, its volume shivering the dust hanging in the air. The mine pulsed with energy and movement and life.

Whatever she was, whatever darkness had been deep in the belly of the mine, had gone. Suddenly exhausted, Thorley turned and moved back towards the car. It was time to go.

As the rental limped down the road, he saw in the rear-view mirror the towering battlements and turrets of the mine, the chimneys spewing ropes of smoke into the morning air, curled like snakes against the sun.

# RICHARD CHRISTIAN MATHESON

## Venturi

RICHARD CHRISTIAN MATHESON IS a film and television writer/producer/director. He has worked with Bryan Singer, Steven Spielberg and Roger Corman, among others, and has written/produced three mini-series, eight feature films, thirty pilots and hundreds of comedic/dramatic television series episodes for HBO, TNT, NBC, CBS, ABC, Showtime Networks, Fox Network and Syfy. He has also published two short-story collections and a novel.

Matheson is a studio musician who studied with Ginger Baker of Cream and has played drums with The Smithereens and Rock Bottom Remainders. He has worked as a paranormal investigator for UCLA, and is considered an expert in parapsychology. He runs his own production company in Los Angeles and the Matheson Company with his father.

"Nineteenth-century physicist G.B. Venturi discovered a compressive phenomenon which effects fire, moving through a canyon, causing the flames to be intensified, feeding upon themselves," Matheson explains. "This acceleration, called the 'Venturi Effect', is as apt a metaphor for paranoia as I have encountered.

"When my own house in Malibu burned down, some years back, my senses altered. As fires ate hillsides and smoke drowned sun, I was forced to evacuate in twenty minutes and ultimately lost everything. I even watched my house go up in flames, on the TV news – a surreal pain.

"The loss awakened me to signs of oncoming fire – rising wind, distant scents of smoke, angry glows on mountains that rim the bay. To this day, even a burning cigarette, anywhere nearby, triggers a vigilant circuit within me.

"I still live in Malibu, aside its dreamy spell, but am never as completely at ease here as I once was. When winds convulse and fire engines wail, my heart races and I know everything could change."

### 3:34 P.M.

"When did you first notice this?"

"Week ago," said David. "Three days after the fire."

"Any pain?"

"No."

The doctor's gloved fingers probed shoulder blade. It was soft, egg-sized; under skin.

". . . saw the fire on TV. Did you have to evacuate?"

David watched smoke swarm the medical building, tall flames lash, wanting in.

He looked at the doctor.

"You still up in that canyon in Malibu? I hear they don't give you much time to get out."

Banshee winds hammered the glass, black plumes muting sun. The room darkened, the doctor's face a feral shadow.

"I had fifteen minutes. You take what you can." His mouth was dry. Body numb. "My house didn't burn. But the neighbourhood's gone." He felt ill. "Thirty-eight houses."

The doctor stopped. Tried to picture it. "My God."

Dense smoke suddenly filled the examination room; gushing through vents; seeping under doors. Grimy ash swirled; sick snow.

"Fire creates its own wind," said David, ". . . it's called the Venturi Effect."

The doctor's breathing deepened.

"The flames feed on themselves. Like a frightened animal."

"*Venturi* . . ." the doctor repeated.

David could see his next door neighbour's house clawed by apricot blades, cooked black. "Got to ninety-six miles an hour on my hill."

The doctor fell silent. "Awful. Gotta be exhausted. Getting any sleep?"

"Not really."

He nodded, re-washed hands. Voice apothecary calm. "Far as I can tell, this thing feels like a muscle spasm. Tension."

Smoke snaked around the doctor, luscious pleats of it fingering his neck, sliding between lips and teeth.

"I want you to take hot showers. I'll give you some muscle relaxant. It'll ease up."

David heard winds outside moan louder.

"Let's just watch it. Call me if anything changes."

"Like what?"

The doctor scrawled on prescription pad. "You look exhausted, David. You gotta get some sleep. These'll help."

"I can't sleep. It's fire season." His eyes were red with exhaustion. "Anything could happen."

The doctor looked outside. Smiled, told David it was a nice day. "Weather guy says it may even rain."

David heard axes smashing through doors and quietly left the office.

**4:47 P.M.**

The freeway couldn't breathe.

Drivers hunched. Eyes eating; devouring. Watching mirrors; lips sewn in disgust. Exhaust pipes fuming; vile, chrome mouths.

David felt his shoulder blade. Wanted whatever was in there to die.

**2:17 A.M.**

The folded chair was in a carpet of soot.

David sat on his deck, surrounded by charred mountains that smelled like wet, dead cigarettes. Their burnt flesh rose from shore; soft, black cameos, looming and silent.

He sipped coffee. Scanned his dead neighbourhood; grey casket streets. It had been days since he'd slept and his bones felt wrong; aching, drilled with holes. He yawned, eyes bloodshot. Watched insomniac sea. Surf broke far below; pale blades on ink.

"*. . . the meridian where conscious and unconscious meet,*" the Swedish widow up the street had told him, days before she died in the '97 firestorm, trapped in her house, chased by red infuriations.

He stopped, mid-swallow. Smelled smoke.

Somewhere; maybe close; the first sign death neared. It was *everywhere*; the warm, charcoal breath. Those who hadn't survived fires didn't notice the hateful, uninvited scent of it. Billowing, citric welts, rushing closer, making birds shriek in terror, trees bend.

He heard groaning red trucks curving up his narrow road, tires crunching, blinded by smoke. Seventy-foot flames swaying in the ravine like burning kelp.

Then, nothing.

He searched with binoculars, found distant Los Angeles skyline, scanned surrounding hills. Nothing unusual. He breathed in, deeply, as leaves began to rattle in his sycamore. Closed fatigued eyes. He'd taken the shower and muscle relaxant but no sleeping pill; closing eyes would be a fatal mistake.

He breathed in, again. Maybe he'd imagined the smoke. He needed to be careful; after a fire, everything smelled of it. He tried to distinguish, isolating nuance, turning his head to find it.

*Smoke.*

The world was filling up with it; choking, flesh sweating, slick with fear. Flames crawling horizon, gobbling. Raving gusts of it, moving in for the kill. To sleep was to die. Awaken to sirens, evacuations. Screams in the night.

There was no stopping it.

It just got worse.

Boxes filled with personal belongings thrown into frantically idling cars. Children panicked, crying. He could see his collie, Jack. Ears flat, as the crackle of burning hillsides drew him, and he ran, whining, scared, into fevered skirts of smoke. David had heard his cries, pleading for a way out.

Then, nothing. Just houses and creatures and trees burning as flames took them like fast cancer.

He felt sick to his stomach. Remembered when he'd first seen the house, nestled atop mountain, overlooking a trance of water and land. Despite its helpless perfection, perched calmly in the middle of a fire path, he'd bought it. It had nearly burned in a '94 firestorm that took 200 hillside homes; a hot, windy afternoon, when the sky bloodied to third-degree burn. The owner had decided to stay, as her world went red and black; listening to flames getting closer; starved for helpless things. She'd slit both wrists and, as they slowly drained, applied make-up and taken a cool bath.

At this elevation, the death winds found everyone.

He stared into the night.

Listening for sirens; desperate calls for help. Santa Ana winds began moving across the hills like rabid gangs and he saw himself on fire; insides blazing, smoke filling his throat like a chimney; drifting from his dying mouth. Ash silently fell and he thought he saw smoke spiralling just over one hill; furious crows of it moving closer.

He could hear ghouls in cars, racing up his narrow road, hungry to see the decimation. Cigarettes in idiot mouths. Teenagers on the beach, burning driftwood, paying no attention as embers twinkled fatally away. Hikers making campfires.

Arsonists. All of them.

He grabbed for his binoculars, again, and gasped as the rise on his shoulder blade moved. He instantly shed jacket and T-shirt to check and, to his shock, found more rises, on upper arm, forearm and chest; sheeted by flesh.

He rushed into the dark house, turned on the light and stood before bedroom mirror.

There were *more*.

He hesitated, afraid of what they might be and, after a moment, carefully poked at one on his chest. The rise responded, pushing outward, slowly straining against skin until finally splitting it open; a wound in reverse. David gasped at sharp pain as, one after another, the rises pushed, tearing through his flesh, each now visible in its own raw, puckered socket, slowly orbiting.

Lids lifted and the eyes stared intensely at him; brown like his own, unblinking, whites shining. They seemed neither trapped nor accusatory and each began to stare, alertly, in different directions, searching for something.

He felt them covering his back, blood trickling where they'd erupted, and frantically sifted through his hair to find more. When he touched them, the lids tightly shut, gradually re-opened; watching, pupils dilating. The ones on his forearms and palms studied the room, taking everything in with a detailed scan.

*It was exhaustion; the trick of a traumatized mind.* He knew it; thought about calling his doctor.

But it was pointless.

He'd recommend sleep, a hospital. There was no leaving the house now; death was everywhere. Hot winds howling, fire galloping closer.

Coming for him.

He moved out onto the deck, stared at pewter sky, heard sirens in the distance; bleak arias. Tree branches shuddered and he was sure he saw vicious orange coming over the hill, mowing towards sea.

He stripped off the rest of his clothes, saw more eyes covered him; vigilant, unblinking stares that swept the hills and ravines for danger. His arms slowly outstretched at his sides to allow them unimpeded view and, as they surveyed horizon with restless detection, he began to calm.

He stood, naked in warm, ominous winds, fears gradually easing, as the scores of eyes kept watch and his own slowly closed.

# JOHN GASKIN

## Party Talk

JOHN GASKIN WAS EDUCATED at the City of Oxford High School and Oxford University. In his early years, Gaskin worked for British Railways and as a banker before taking a lectureship at Trinity College, Dublin, where he became a Fellow and held a professional chair in philosophy.

Since 1997 he has mainly written fiction: his most recent publications include a volume of poems and two collections of short stories, *Tales of Twilight and Borderlands: The Dark Companion* (2001) and *The Long Retreating Day* (2006). Forthcoming is the non-fiction *A Traveller's Guide to Classical Philosophy* and a full-length tale of murder and haunting, *A Doubt of Death*. The author lives in a remote part of Northumberland, and doubts that he will ever be connected to the Internet.

"A year or two ago I was planting roses against the wall of a village church, and found strange things," recalls the author. "A little later I was at a lunch in one of the larger houses overlooking a deserted railway, and a river . . ."

> The guests are met, the feast is set:
> May'st hear the merry din.
> – Coleridge

S HE HAD THE SWEET SMELL of faded roses that I associate with polite mortality in decay. I would have preferred talking to someone else at the Selwoods' lunch party – after all, buffets are designed to shuffle sheep and goats – but she held me with deep-set eyes that might almost have been blind, or perhaps they were focused upon something beyond me or the house. I could not politely escape.

"You write ghost stories," she stated in a gravelly whisper that seemed to require no movement in the mask-like tightness of her face.

"I have published a few – not real ghost stories – mere tales of the uncanny – the boundaries between chance and significance, agency and accident, eidetic imagery and actual perceptions."

"But you do not believe in ghosts, 'real' or otherwise."

"No. I have to confess I don't. At least not as the intention of dead persons bringing about new events in the world. But I believe in the power of the living brain to influence directly other physical things in the world with results it does not expect or always understand – like the poltergeist effect."

My analysis elicited no comment.

She was sitting at the high-backed end of an expensive Victorian chaise longue, somewhat over-clothed (as I thought) for a well-heated house, even if it was January in the Cheviots. I was aware of a large and vague wrap of material round her shoulders, a grey headscarf of dusty silk drawn tightly over her head, a garment that might have been a jacket or a coat, and a long dark skirt. I could not see her feet, but there were smears of mud on the carpet near her that appeared to have been carried in from the garden, not from the gravelled forecourt of the house where I had entered. There were black gloves over her evidently thin fingers. She gestured towards the far end of the chaise longue.

"Sit down."

For a moment I had sight of her open mouth. "I have a tale you must hear," she said.

I mumbled something about not wishing to keep her from the rest of the company. But the rest of the company was receding from us, intent upon itself or upon food in the adjacent dining room, and there was no one at hand to offer rescue. I settled at the far end of our chair in a position that made it easy not to look at her too intently. I must have grimaced.

"Yes, you'll find it as hard as stone – horsehair and leather under silk tapestry. They always preferred show to comfort, even in Gosforth. It wouldn't have been tolerated in my day. Everything was for comfort then – except for the bedrooms and the plumbing. I remember the chill of the bedrooms. I was eighteen. I'm accustomed to it now."

She paused, as if looking back into a place to which I was not admitted. Then to my embarrassment I heard her say:

"You do not wish to hear me, Dr Smyth. But you have no choice now your glass is all but empty. Be still and I shall take you deeper than its emptiness."

It was a ridiculous style of speaking, and I should have braced myself for a period of the sleepy half-attention in which one hopes to be able to say "yes", "no", "how nice" and "what a pity" in the right places – except that I was uncomfortable, it was cold near the window, and for some reason I was acutely wide awake. She was speaking again.

"I left school that spring and was supposed to be filling in time learning German before wintering at a finishing school in Switzerland where they only spoke French. I believe my father thought German might encourage me to listen to more Bach cantatas. German was not in fashion at the time and cantatas are some of the drearier manifestations of religion. I rebelled. The rebellion took the form of Thomas, the gardener's boy who, unlike German irregular verbs, was beautiful and tempting. It was beyond my mother's ability to come to terms with what she found us doing uncomfortably behind a hedge one afternoon.

"Tom was mercifully called up almost immediately afterwards. I was banished to the care of my mother's aunt, a robust-minded woman of considerable experience of the world who had never married and lived in a lonely house several hundred miles away. My love was warm and strong. Home, as I discovered too late, was comfortable and safe.

"Todburn Hall, as it was called before they rediscovered the old religious connection, was large and untenanted by youth or laughter. It seemed to me that my great aunt lived in a plush cocoon of velvet and chilly comfort. She tried to receive me well and be kind in the practical ways she understood, but I was vexed with life and gave her little help."

The voice ceased, and I glanced sideways against the pale light of the window. The sun had disappeared behind winter clouds and the ribbon of river lay grey and cold a field or two away below the house. I could see only her vague silhouette against the blank glass. The spreading web of her clothes filled the end of our chair like a shadow.

But the voice had resumed – a penetrating whisper that was both clear and quiet, like listening inside the private world of some exquisitely engineered earphones.

"I was lonely, but it was not loneliness for people or company in general. It was the raw, torn-off space beside me that had been the fresh animal smell of Tom, the soft bloom of his skin, his talk, his touch, his strength. I walked by the river. I painted pictures in dark and fervent colours. I cried out in my heart. I was morose and withdrawn when my aunt tried to draw me out of myself. She knew more of life than I could then recognize or would ever know, but there were no words she could find to bridge the gap between us. Every generation thinks its own pain is unique. That is the glory and the pity of life.

"Her solution was to divert my attention with hearty activity. Having already drawn the garden and made a catalogue of its contents for her, checked the silver inventory, painted the view of the river in several unsuitable versions, and read to her a number of Oscar Wilde's stories – the longest was missing from her collection. She later told me it was lost when she was in charge of the British Expeditionary Force's hospital in Alexandria.

"As I was saying, having completed all these tasks, I found myself one afternoon – about a month after my banishment – tidying a strip of garden against the south wall of the village church.

"A number of disused grave stones had been set close against the wall of the transept. They were old stones, much defaced, but they were close and I felt watched as I worked on my knees below them. A foolish fancy! It is the keeper of the gate that watches, not the gate.

"I was to prepare the ground and plant a dozen roses donated by my aunt – Rosa Mundi they were called. Yes, Rose of the

Earth. Beauty from the dust. None survive now. Some did not survive my planting, particularly at the eastern end of the wall where the soil was mostly sand and fragments, like the ground at Xanthos. You do not know it . . ." Her voice faded away as if in exhaustion, and for a moment I hoped to see her fall asleep, but she resumed more strongly.

"Roses have deep roots, and I did not at first recognize what I was finding. The earth was dry, and in one area seamed with brown fibrous material like peat. It was in this that I dug up part of a bone. I was at the corner of the transept, where the wall turned back to join the chancel a few yards away. At the corner and just past it, one of the old headstones had been positioned leaving a few inches of dark space between its back and the church wall.

"I threw the thing down there out of sight – and other bits that left no doubt at all concerning my finds. It was as I was disposing – with some distaste – of part of a broken bone with discoloured teeth still in place that a shadow moved on the wall in front of me. My back was to the path through the graveyard, and I turned sharply. I had heard no one approaching, and was feeling uneasy about concealing my finds behind someone else's memorial. It was only a young clergyman who was watching me – probably the curate I thought. Those were the days when country livings were properly staffed.

"'What are you doing with those?' he asked.

'Planting them. My aunt, Miss Addison, is a member of the Select Vestry, and she has given them to the church. I'm doing it for her.'

"'No, I mean with the bones.'

"'I . . . well they're only bits and pieces. I suppose they have been brought to the surface as other graves have been dug. I presumed that behind a gravestone would be a suitable place.'

"'Yes indeed,' he said, before bending down to look, closer to me than appeared to be necessary. 'You've finished planting?'

"'Yes. I'm tidying up.'

"'And this . . . brown stuff – it's not like the rest of the earth.'

"'No. It's a layer, about eighteen inches down. I hope the roots will reach it and gain some nourishment. Do you think I've gone too deep?'

"'I don't know. Earth like that should not be near the surface. But your roses will certainly draw life from it.'

"He stood up and looked at the gravestone where I had concealed the bones. I had not been able to see the name earlier. The lettering was much eroded and it was the angle of the sun, now flush with the face of the stone, that showed up the antique lettering as shadows. The name was Elenor Ward. There was no mention of family or husband, merely the year of her birth and that she had died at the age of sixteen. She was commended to the mercy of God. I sensed before I was told the mercy she might have needed from men, and almost certainly did not get.

"'An old parishioner learnt her story when she was a child, and told me about her one day when I was standing here,' he said. 'She was . . .' he hesitated, 'to have a child by one of the village labourers, an unrepentant sinner. She wasn't the first he'd got into trouble, but she was the last – at least in this place. He went away before the child was born. That's her grave, not just a moved stone like the rest. She's under there. But I'm sorry. This is morbid talk and I haven't even introduced myself. My name is Thornton, Peter Thornton. I'm assisting here for the summer.'

"I told him my name and that I was staying at Todburn Hall.

"'Good gracious!' he exclaimed with what seemed to me contrived and certainly unnecessary concern. 'That's almost three miles away. Have you transport?'

"I explained that I had not. I preferred walking along the south side of the river and crossing at Pauperhaugh.

"'May I have the pleasure of walking with you a part of the way?' he enquired. I could find no reason to refuse his company, and we strolled along pleasantly enough in the August sunshine. He showed me a short cut over the railway. It was probably forbidden, but trains were few and could be heard long before they came round the bend and could see anyone on the rails. As we walked, some dark worm of curiosity made me return to the story of Elenor Ward.

"'Did her child survive?' I asked as if it were the most natural question in the world.

"'I was told not. None of the creature's offspring survived. There was something wrong about him. They were stillborn. I suppose there are tales like that in most old parishes if one listens, tales embellished by time and the desire for justice in this world.'

"'And the father – what happened to him?'

"'As I said, time does not relate. My informed source was not that well-informed.'

"Then we spoke of other things. He was interested in hearing about Todburn Hall, having visited my aunt there on parochial business.

"'It's a lovely reuse of Hanoverian ideas,' he said. 'Perhaps a little heavy in details, but so much better than that damp museum of a place the original family had down by the river. But it's a pity, if I may say so without offence, that the main front faces north, and is so near to the road. It can gain very little light and only a lot of dust on that side.'

"'Yes,' I agreed, 'but upstairs, like the ground floor, it's almost entirely corridors and landings on the north – apart from maids' bedrooms. I have a delightful room at the head of the stairs looking south. I can get the sun there all day if I want, and see it setting up the river every evening, and the morning train puffs away quite prettily in the distance round Pike Hill. It tells me the time if I'm not already up.'

"'Are you staying long?' he asked as we reached the bridge.

"I said I did not know.

"'I hope I'll see you again – at church on Sunday I mean.' But that was not what he meant.

"The remainder of my walk along the gritty road to the house was not agreeable. For one thing I tired and feeling the lack of Tom. Mr Thornton had reminded me of the need, not supplanted it. For another, there was something small down the side of my boot that irritated without being uncomfortable enough to justify undoing all the lacing.

"At the side door of the house I found what it was – a thin tooth, brown and stained. It was careless of me to have let it lodge there, and I should have thrown it away into the garden without a thought. But I didn't. To do so felt somehow sacrilegious, at least a disrespect to the dead whom I had disturbed – as if they could care!

"Rather than leaving it on the window-sill of the porch where my aunt or a maid could see it and would ask questions, I took it to my bedroom and placed it on the chimney-piece intending to drop it back in the churchyard again on Sunday.

"That evening after supper I was sitting pretending to read. We were still enjoying the long sunsets of the north, and I did not think it cold, but Aunt May suddenly got up and closed the French windows.

"'There's a chill in the place,' she announced. 'It's the river air. I hope you didn't catch cold walking home? The Rector much approves of the roses. Thank you for planting them. I phoned him about the Sunday School outing and he mentioned that his curate had met you. Such a nice young man. Pity about his father. I hope you didn't find the planting too hard?'

"'Not at all. It was most interesting digging up all the bits of bone. If I'd gone on I could almost have made a man of him again.' I don't know if my levity was inadvertently or intentionally sarcastic, but my aunt bridled.

"'Oh dear! I'm so sorry. They will have been fragments from old graves that have been re-used. You left them alone? One isn't supposed to touch things like that, although I don't know why. We smashed up living men easily enough in the last war.'

"'I put them behind Elenor Ward's headstone, and Mr Thornton said that would not be wrong.'

"'Elenor . . . ?'

"'Round the corner at the end of the rose bed. Mr Thornton said—'

"'Oh yes, of course. That unfortunate girl! They say she killed her lover you know.'

"'Mr Thornton didn't tell me that.'

"'He wouldn't. It was never proved and he's too charitable to repeat old gossip. I should be, but I'm not. It's more interesting than modern parish chit-chat. She and the others – there were others – had reason enough. He took his pleasure where he could get it without asking – a brutal, ugly creature by all accounts, more like a Cairo street dog than a man. He disappeared, God knows how or where, but she was blamed.

"'Will you take a cup of cocoa with me before we go to bed? I'm still cold, and cocoa always reminds me of nights in the desert with the wounded. I never saw a man die that really wanted to live you know, but I remember one that really wanted to die, and did, merely because his school friend had been killed beside him in the trenches near Gaza. Silly boy! Life is more than love.'

"I said I would take cocoa, partly to humour her, partly because I was becoming concerned about myself for a reason I need not mention, and I knew she normally put some mild sleeping draught in the cocoa for herself and, since it was the same making, I would gain the same benefit.

"My great-aunt was right about the chill. My bedroom had not retained the heat of the afternoon sun, and I didn't know whether to open the window to let the summer air in, or keep it closed against the dampness of the river.

"I slipped out of my clothes and into a night-dress as quickly as possible. The tester bed was large and needed to be warmed by the heat of one's own body. I lay on my back, looking up at the ceiling through the space where the canopy ought to have been. The four posts were there, and the top rails joining them, but there was nothing more than a box-pleated frill of tapestry round the outside to look at, and a spider out of reach in the middle of the ceiling, motionless and waiting for a victim. I hoped it would not drop on to the bed.

"The room *was* cold, and I ought to have opened the window to freshen it, but I couldn't summon up the will to get out of bed again. I thought about Tom. I worried about the future. I tossed about. I told myself I was tired. I insisted that I should sleep. But sleep would not come. Perhaps my aunt had been too sparing with whatever she used.

"The air felt oppressive, and there was no clarity in breathing: a cold stuffiness permeated everything. Eventually I sank into a state of semi-inertia, motionless in body and lethargic in mind. The last gleam of summer light faded away into the north leaving the walls dark, and my uncurtained windows visible only as pale oblongs hanging in space. There was no wind, and the sound of the river where it hurried over shallows was not strong enough to penetrate the room. I might have heard the harsh screech of an owl, or a curlew trilling down on the water meadows below the house, or far away on the moor, but there was nothing, and I lay in isolation from the world.

"I was not aware of falling asleep, but I must have done so, for I experienced again the walk from the churchyard with Mr

Thornton. He was by my side talking foolishly. I walked with the helpless acceptance of a sleeper, except that I knew that if I could turn there would be something at my side I would not wish to see. But it was a dream. At the bridge, Mr Thornton turned away, but the other remained with me like a footstep scarcely heard in an empty street at night. The road wavered, bent upwards, and divided itself again into the windows of my room.

"I hear nothing now, but then I could sense even the smallest of creatures walking or scratching on wood or among leaves. Perhaps the spider wrought his business. But he had moved to a new place. Something was feeling along the woodwork beyond the foot of the bed – little pushings and scrapings which were not the living silence of one's inner ear that never departs except with death.

"I was now thoroughly awake, but subject to the strangest delusion. Normally one moves without thought. I found myself thinking very intently about moving, but unable to put the matter to the test for fear of finding that I could not. The scraping had stopped, but I could detect behind the swishing of the blood in my ears some other disturbance. The blankets were becoming heavier. I do not understand how I failed to notice the beginning of that dreadful experience, but something was covering the bed. My feet were held down by a weight that was moving up my legs like a carpet of lead being slowly unrolled. I was on my back. The weight was on my belly, trapping my arms, creeping over my breasts, suffocating and sick. I wanted to shrink into the bed, to be lifted away, to die – anything to escape the horror of what was being done to me. But two things held me in being for later. One was an agonizing thrust of pain as if something had broken within me under the pressure. The other was a protracted flickering of lightening somewhere to the south, beyond the river, that lit up the whole room and let me see everything in it with the clarity and certainty of full light.

"My aunt could not have been asleep, for within seconds, even before the long undulations of thunder had caught up with its lightening, she was knocking urgently at the door. She came in before I could speak. I had fallen out of bed and knocked over a chair and small table in my struggles, but my first reaction was to look down to see if I was bleeding. Of course I was not, but embarrassment in my generation was almost as strong a motive as fear.

"She was a wise and practical woman behind the formal exterior, and must at once have seen that something far beyond thunder and bad dreams had moved me. She put her arm round me, and sat with me on the side of the bed. I was shivering uncontrollably and couldn't tell her. To her everlasting credit she did not ask.

"'You'd better come back to my room for the night,' she said after a few moments. 'It's got the biggest bed between Weldon and Windyhaugh, so you'll be perfectly comfortable and safe. I'll make tea, and you'll take sugar in it whether you like it or not.'

"I went with her thankfully. She had an electric kettle and tea things in the room, and a little nursery light that burned in a corner. I lay close to her but did not sleep.

"With the return of light she took me back to the room to collect my clothes. It was cold, and she flung open the windows. The rain-washed freshness of grass and the honeyed smell of the earliest heather wafted in with all the sweetness of the world. Then she examined the room. It was as I had left it – bedclothes flung about and the table on its side.

"'What's that disgusting object?'

"She was pointing at the chimney-piece. A funnel of dirty grey, like rotting lace, was woven into the angle between shelf and wall. Shrunk into it, but still moving, was the tip of an obscene pink worm. I thought I was about to faint; instead I was violently and horribly sick.

"'What's the matter, child? You must tell me. Something happened here.'

"I told her what I could, what I had felt. But I could never bring myself to tell any other living person what I had seen. I do not know how much she believed to be real, but it was enough. Some things cannot be spoken. She found the tooth beside the pillow. I explained how I had brought it into the room, and where I had left it.

"'I'll take it away,' she said. 'It will go back where it belongs.'

"On the Sunday she pushed it into the ground where, as she said, Elenor or another, must have hidden the body. 'Quite clever,' she observed judiciously, 'like hiding a book on a bookshelf.'

"Before Daniel, my aunt's gardener, could be summoned to remove the web, its tenant had disappeared. The maids took my things to a small room next to Aunt May's where later my worst fears became manifest. She was very matter-of-fact and invented an acceptable story. My father was already away in France and died in an accident without ever being told. My mother did not wish to know. I never went to Switzerland. I heard Tom was one of the few killed in the big German push across the Ardennes. His baby was stillborn a month late – or so they insisted. I did not see him. The pain was like being torn apart by stones. I never wanted to recover. I took my departure by the railway as soon as I was well enough to move. It was easy enough in the end. The darkness was deep and cold. Sometimes I see the man who must hear my story. When his time is near he has no choice."

"My dear Harry, what *are* you doing? You look quite stunned! They've all been at the food, and you haven't had anything yet."

Vivienne Selwood almost rushed at me, and I stood up in some confusion with my back to the window.

"I'm sorry. I haven't been attending. I've been listening to . . . to . . ." I made a helpless gesture, and turned to indicate my companion in the hope of a belated introduction, but she had slipped away. "To the old lady who was sitting here. I didn't get her name."

"Old lady? What old lady? Really, you men do exaggerate! What was she like?"

"Well . . . very old. A dry, grey face, shrunken mouth and deep-set eyes, dark clothes and black gloves. She seemed to have no—"

I broke off, aware that what I was saying might give offence if I was describing a relative or old friend of the Selwoods'.

Vivienne laughed. She was very beautiful, and when she laughed her fair Nordic features had a power that negated argument. "I don't think any of my guests would like to hear themselves described like that!"

She paused.

"But there may be someone living up near the old railway who fits your description. Dad told me he'd spoken to someone like that. It was last year; but he died in November, so we can't really ask him now can we?" She laughed again. "Tony and I don't know all the locals yet, but if she came here she was certainly an uninvited guest. You didn't get her name?"

"No. She mentioned a clergyman – Thornton – and I think she said her aunt or grand aunt's name was Addison."

"There are dozens of *Harrisons* in this area. I believe one lived here before the Malings and there was some sort of tragedy. But do come and have some food before the farming contingent demolishes everything. Tony has some rare whisky he wants you to try, and the other Scots are *dying* to sound you out about the bank's share price."

Before following her I looked across the valley at the still perceptible line of the abandoned railway. It curved into an oblivion of hills to the south. There was no one to be seen, and the mud on the carpet had already turned to dust.

# TERRY DOWLING

## Two Steps Along the Road

TERRY DOWLING HAS BEEN called "Australia's finest writer of horror" by *Locus* magazine, and "Australia's premier writer of dark fantasy" by *All Hallows*. His collection *Basic Black: Tales of Appropriate Fear* won the 2007 International Horror Guild Award for Best Collection, earned a starred review in *Publishers Weekly* and was hailed as "one of the best recent collections of contemporary horror" by the American Library Association.

Other award-winning horror collections by Dowling are *An Intimate Knowledge of the Night* and *Blackwater Days*, while the *The Year's Best Fantasy and Horror* series featured more horror stories by the author during its twenty-one-year run than by any other writer. His latest titles include *Amberjack: Tales of Fear & Wonder* and his debut novel, *Clowns at Midnight*.

"'Two Steps Along the Road' came out of a conversation with US editor Danel Olson," Dowling explains, "where we discussed me doing a ghost story set in Vietnam for *Exotic Gothic 3*, and the interesting possibilities it might provide for delivering atmosphere and an interesting perspective on familiar things.

"Before I knew it, I was blending two separate elements that were demanding attention: the notion of a root-form behind all hauntings, regardless of what form they took, and the unnerving realization that the eyes of a quite attractive teaching colleague would be truly terrifying to behold if they were set just a tad closer together.

"The ideas were intended for very different stories but, as so often happens, *they* decided they were meant for each other."

W HEN THOMAS NEVILLE climbed from the white runabout at the ramshackle jetty and saw the Hotel Dis 300 yards off in the clearing, he felt he'd been thrown back not just in time but into other identities as well.

He went back forty years to his father's tours of duty at Da Nang and Long Tan, of course, and the stories that damaged, often unsettling man had been persuaded to tell in Sydney before he died, making those stories, those events Thomas' own after a fashion. But it went beyond old Deek's experiences, much further beyond, back to when the dream of a French Indo-China had still seemed possible.

Thomas couldn't explain it. It was as if he were seeing the sprawling two-storey structure through Deek's eyes as well as his own, and through those of Gerard Larier who had built the place in 1924.

Then he was back in an instant, as if a switch had been thrown, and he was remembering to call "*Cảm ơn!*" to the boatman. The young Vietnamese waved, worked the throttle of the outboard with easy skill. The narrow craft made a long slow arc on the brown surface and began the four-mile journey back to the great waterway of the Mekong. Only when it had vanished from sight and there was a blazing insect-laden silence all around, did Thomas heft his bag again and carry it the eight or so yards to where the jetty met the road. The path more like. There was a good chance it was decades since it had last seen a wheeled vehicle.

*Wait till someone comes for you,* Yosen's final letter had said. *It is most important that you do this.*

And since Stefan Yosen was the client, and the advance suitably impressive, Thomas did just that. He set his bag down again and stood in what shade he could find, watching the weathered wooden structure off in the clearing for any signs of life.

Maybe it was the absence of rice paddies and farmed terraces, any signs of the usual wetland farming, but the Hotel Dis was unnervingly familiar, that was the problem, the sort of run-down mansion you saw in too many old movies featuring antebellum plantation estates in forgotten Louisiana bayous, or those decaying colonial hotels you still found in the backwaters of the various Congo republics or in the Cameroon. More so when Thomas took off his sunglasses to wipe the sweat from his eyes. In the blur of heat and humidity, the Hotel Dis truly was too much like something out of time. It brought the borrowed memories, the other identities, crowding in again: Deek's R&R stint at the Market Hotel on Cranbow Road, Larier's journal entries for the Unitat and his meetings with Sainteny and others from the Deuxième Bureau.

"You're wondering why it's never been renovated," the words came, not from the road leading to the decrepit hotel but from the jungle to the side. Stefan Yosen appeared from a track concealed there, pushing low fronds aside as he stepped into view. He was a tall, long-faced man in his late sixties, twenty years Thomas' senior, and wore modern enough clothes – white trousers and shirt, wide-brimmed hat, synthetic fibre sandals, sunglasses – but in the broad strokes he looked as much of some other time as the building itself.

They shook hands, exchanged the right pleasantries for two people who did but most certainly did not know each other, both aware of an edginess between them, possibly to remain. It had been in the initial letters, the few phone calls, the careful e-mails. It came with the nature of the project too, the reason for this visit now.

"Tourism's booming everywhere but here," Yosen said, gesturing to include the deserted tributary and the cleared stretch of the estate. "It's as if they don't see. That boatman just now knew where he was bringing you. Thang's been here hundreds of times. He'll be out to get you Tuesday. But he doesn't see it, will have put it out of his mind already. This is a short-term memory place. The way it sits in the mind. It doesn't exist."

"And why is that, Stefan?" Thomas had come a long way from Saigon (they still called it that in the South); these details had been promised.

His host's answer was almost a question. "But you see it. The hotel. That's what matters."

As if there could be any doubt. "You knew I would."

"I certainly expected it. Some people don't. But let's get you settled. Then we can talk."

They started along the road and soon reached a tall wooden post beside the trail, with a modern-enough solar-cell lantern fitted to the top. As soon as they passed it five Vietnamese appeared on the wide veranda: three trim women, two lean men. One of the men came running to meet them, arrived breathless but smiling – he was clearly older than he had first looked – bowed and took Thomas' bag.

"Thank you, Long. Please tell Miss Elizabeth that Thomas Neville is here."

"She knows, Mister Stefan."

As they drew closer, Thomas could hear a piano playing somewhere in the house.

"She plays the piano."

"*It* plays the piano."

"You're still insistent. Not your daughter?"

"Not even human, I suspect."

Thomas barely hesitated. "What does she say to that these days?"

"Shakes her head. Continues to insist that it's my problem. I've been out here too long and she should have come sooner. Recalls details from her life, *our* lives, no one else could possibly know." Stefan Yosen hesitated, sighed. He'd been through this before. "As my initial proposal explained, I only require your co-operation and acceptance, Thomas, not your absolute belief. Though from what you've said, I am hoping for much more."

"You're what, may I ask? Sixty-five? Sixty-six?"

"Sixty-six. My daughter would be thirty-eight."

"But she's dead."

"Precisely. The plane crash six years ago, as I explained in my letters. Her body and her mother's were among those recovered and conclusively identified."

"I'm very sorry, Stefan. But you say she knows things."

"More than an impostor should unless well schooled. And schooled by me, I must add. Plus the other things."

"The other things?"

"Please. Let's get you settled first."

The Hotel Dis showed its age. The ale-dark timbers were old, the imported carpeting worn, many of the windows grimy behind repaired grey shutters and rattan blinds, all the signs of too much heat and humidity, too many years of monsoonal rains, too much time.

But with its impressive façade, its two storeys and fourteen guest rooms, there was an old-world charm about it as well, touches of a France that could never have been, that had been sea-changed into something other, just as the French themselves had been by the elusive, reality-crazing *ennui*, *cafard*, *accidie* that had descended upon them well before Dien Bien Phu, the same quiet desperation that had gripped the Americans and their allies twenty years later in Deek's day.

After being introduced to the staff on the veranda – the old housekeeper, Trang, the maids, Lan and Hoa, an older house-boy, Hùng, who all bowed respectfully in greeting – Thomas expected to be introduced to the so-called impostor in the hotel's shadowy interior. But Stefan Yosen wanted it otherwise. Rather than taking him into the conservatory, he led the way upstairs and down a long hallway to a surprisingly spacious and well-appointed end room overlooking the main approach to the hotel. His bag was already on the bed where Long had left it.

When Thomas raised the rattan blinds, he could see the trail leading across to the jetty, found the patch of shade where he had just now waited. The tributary was still deserted, he noticed, such an unlikely thing this close to the upper delta, an unmoving brown line against the rich green line of mangroves and rainfor-est, all of it set against the hazy overlit sky of a pre-delta noon.

The sound of the piano came from below – Chopin? Schubert? – distant but comforting somehow and fittingly old world.

"Suitable?"

"It's fine. Thank you."

"My room is across the hall. Hers is at the far end. The other rooms up here are used for storage or are empty and locked."

"Stefan, nothing has changed? You're still convinced she's Jeune Petite? I have to ask."

"More than ever. Lizzie *is* Jeune Petite, pretty much as described in the earliest notes my father kept for Larier. He only saw her a few times during his own initial visits, many times more once he took over the place. But even from the beginning he felt the melancholy and the dread she brought pretty well daily. And Jeune Petite continued to be seen frequently enough until Lizzie's plane crashed. Then, no more. A week or so later Lizzie arrived."

"So, no further sightings in the past six years?"

Stefan shook his head. "Not as Jeune Petite, no. Just the *cafard* as we call it – and Lizzie. After that week-long gap."

"And Larier's phantom didn't look anything like your daughter? I have to be sure."

"Different features and colouring, but same slight build, and with some important signature mannerisms in common. I'll confirm those after you've met her. Mainly it's the atmosphere, the attendant dread. It's as bad as ever."

Which was a quality as much of a place as a particular person, neither of them needed to add.

The piano played on, filling the old rooms.

"The staff continue to feel it?"

Stefan nodded. "They stay on only because they're like family. And I'm sure you'll feel it too, Thomas. It will surprise you when you do. There will be mood swings. A slow despair. Halitosis will come on, a flat brassy taste. There will be irritations. If you have a minor infection, it will sting; a recent cut will bleed. You will stumble as you walk, get a splinter from a banister, drop a glass you are carrying. Your shoes will be too tight. You will be convinced the weather is wrong, find that you smell wrong things."

"Synaesthesia?"

"Of a kind. The senses misfire. The way you attach to the world. You will see why I approached you, why I need to apply *your* tactics. Your requests to Luc Clarie at the Sorbonne for anything conforming to multi-phase manifestations came just before I made my own enquiries about day-ghosts in July. You cast your net so much wider: allow zombie manifestations, demon possession, everything. I only allowed the ghost and poltergeist elements, the synaesthesia confusion, all very localized, as I tried to get across in my letters. At first I took Lizzie for a remarkable look-alike, then realized she was Jeune Petite tailored to my own circumstances rather than Larier's. We never learned who Jeune Petite was in Larier's own life. He refused to say. Someone from his youth perhaps. But my first thought was a fake, an impostor, then our ghost returned to us. I never considered the other possibilities you've hinted at. I still wonder why you play this so close to your chest."

"You said in your first letters that she may be able to read your thoughts. I wanted to take no chances. But what have you found for me?"

"I did as you said, looked for everything on your list. At one extreme, the expected things, the tourist things, major regional hauntings: the hospital at DàLat, the prison at Khám Chí Hoà. At the other, village tales closer to here. Werewolf and vampire equivalents. More than I expected. Under local names, of course, sometimes much older names. Even French namings."

"Like what?"

"Oh, *sangmangeur*, for instance."

"Blood eater?"

Stefan nodded. "A French coining for a Vietnamese spirit from centuries ago, well before the days of Cochin China. Why would the French have had such a regional word for it unless there was something?"

"And werewolves?"

"Not as conventional *loups-garous*, of course, but stories of people changing into local animals. Pigs. Monkeys. Animanthropy at its most diverse. Thomas, look, before I introduce you—"

"Stefan, let me go down alone right now. First impressions. She knows why I'm here. She's waiting."

"As you wish. But one thing. Her appearance—"

"First impressions, please. Give me fifteen minutes alone. Then come in."

Stefan nodded and went off to his room. Thomas splashed water on his face, then set off to meet the phantom of the Hotel Dis.

Elizabeth Yosen stopped playing the moment Thomas entered the old conservatory, stood, closed the piano and came forward to shake his hand. She was slender, of middle height and striking to look at, though not in any comfortable way. She had the sort of features that with a few degrees less of everything might have been attractive. But her eyes, green as the darkest water lilies on the Mekong, were far too close together (Thomas tried to recall the medical term for it), her nose too sharp in a pale heart-shaped face framed by shoulder-length hair that was dark but matte, flat as kohl.

It was her smile that completed the effect. It was too full, too generous, more a manic grin below that narrow, intense gaze, like someone barely able to contain a secret, knowing something hilarious and about to burst into laughter.

Thomas found himself fascinated, found it hard to look away when he wanted more than anything to do just that.

"I know, Mr Neville," she said, relaxing the grin, thank goodness, speaking in a full, well-modulated voice as she released his hand, but astonishing and embarrassing him all the same. "What was exotic and piquant in my mother became rather alarming in me, I'm afraid."

It was intensely unsettling to have her catch his thoughts so exactly, no doubt the result of a lifetime enduring such scrutiny.

"Miss Yosen—"

"Lizzie, please. And I'm used to it. You are here to out me as an impostor, I understand. This old French ghost, Jeune Petite."

"Possibly something even older. Are you?"

"Of course not." At least when she spoke the smile went away.

"But you're supposed to have died."

The grin was there again, sweeping up to become a grimace, changing only when she spoke. "Evidently not. Papa will have told you. I took a later flight. I had a last-minute opportunity to meet up with an old friend from New York and so swapped flights with a young woman my mother was having a conversation with in the airport. Such a small thing. This woman looked enough like me. My mother had borrowed my jacket, then must have lent it to this new friend. Maybe the cabin aircon was too cold. A comedy of errors."

"A tragedy."

"Truly that. But a comedy now. No DNA testing was done. Our flight swap wasn't properly registered in the airline database. No next of kin came forward to claim the young woman's body. It all seemed conclusive at the time. But I survived."

"Or didn't."

The eyes glittered, the darkest malachite green. The smile hooked up once more, locked for a moment, fell away. "As you say."

"And returned here."

"Where else? Despite his concerns and later misgivings, Papa needed me." The dark gaze, the alarming smile were there in every pause. Thomas actually wondered if he spoke to fend them off.

"Autopsy records?"

"Missing, yes? Misfiled, whatever, if one was ever done. Like the flight change. Very convenient, I know, but how does one begin to arrange something like that?"

The usual way, Thomas was tempted to say. By lying. How many people actually checked such things? "Jeune Petite might have no trouble removing autopsy records, replicating finger-prints and DNA results."

"My, but we modern-day phantoms are resourceful, aren't we?"

Thomas refused to be baited. "You know why I'm here."

"I do. You believe I'm Jeune Petite in her latest incarnation. The household phantom re-vamped as a day-ghost for modern times. Any DNA testing you care to arrange will conclusively show I am Elizabeth Jane Yosen, though I'm sure that will no longer be enough given your theories."

"Stefan told you about those? My theories?" Another stab of dismay. She knows things, Stefan had said.

"Hardly. Just that you are a man with things to prove. They have to concern me or why else would you be here, n'est-ce pas?"

"You don't mind me being here? Investigating?"

"I welcome it. Anything that helps Papa through this. My returning was quite a shock as it turned out." Her tone shifted. All traces of the grimace fell away. "Look, Thomas, I hope you can see that I'm the one who needs your help here. It's been six years, for heaven's sake! The local phantom stops appearing, so suddenly it has to be me. What sort of logic is that? Please, you must do what you can." The narrow, too narrow eyes held him. The smile was on hold, a change almost as striking as the smile itself.

It lasted all of ten seconds. Then, like a spaniel shaking itself dry, Lizzie shook her head and her former wry manner was back in place, complete with the intense gaze, the startling smile. "And you are doing remarkably well. Do you know how many people – mostly men and mostly Westerners for some reason – cannot maintain conversation for this long? They find they need to be elsewhere: off to use the toilet, to check on something they meant to pack. But you seem resolute. Perhaps seeing me as a specimen makes all the difference."

"Miss Yosen, I mean no offence with any of this."

"Lizzie or Elizabeth, please. And none is taken, Thomas. I simply accept how it is. So, what it this to be? Exorcism by nego-tiation? You will try to persuade me away, convince me to be gone."

"Just build up a case profile of the situation this time. Interview the staff, some of the locals, yourself if you'll allow it. And please excuse the indelicacies of self-interest. As Jeune Petite you could very well be the classic case of something I've been investigating for a long time. Something important."

"And as Lizzie, the maligned and put-upon, cruelly trauma-tized daughter of a coldly sceptical father? Is it to be quid pro quo for everyone but me? You and Stefan gain. What is in this for me? Apart from entertainment, that is?"

The smile was merciless.

"If what I suspect is true, then what is happening here may well be the fulfilment of vital imperatives, deep-seated tropisms—"

"Dark designs." The smile. The smile. The green eyes flashed. "Since you put it that way. Precisely what you would live for."

"Live for! If that's the term." He actually expected her to burst out laughing, the rictus truly promised it.

"If that's the term." He tried to sound conciliatory.

Stefan entered then, and with him the old housekeeper, Trang, who announced in her distinctive patois of French and Vietnamese that lunch was served at the long table on the side veranda.

Thomas had never felt such a sense of reprieve in his life. As they moved towards the double-doors, amid Stefan's polite smalltalk about the day-to-day trivialities of hotel life, Thomas caught a single glance from Lizzie.

Saved, it might have said, but with such a face there could be no way of knowing.

There was *Phō Bo* and elephant ear fish with rice, plenty of fresh fruit, even a flask of the local rice wine, and the act of eating gave Stefan a chance to tell more about how the hotel came to be, how it had fared during the decades of conflict and dramatic change. Again, the idea became clear that something – either the special nature of the place, its short-term memory quality, possibly the presence of Jeune Petite – had led to the Hotel Dis being spared most of the depredations and turmoil, most of the later Communist interference too. Not once did he address Lizzie by name.

Towards the end of the meal the staff withdrew and, as if by pre-arrangement, Lizzie rose and excused herself as well, leaving the two men alone.

Stefan waited, then raised a cautionary hand. "Remember. Possibly never truly alone."

Thomas looked around at the empty veranda, then off across the clearing to the river. "Understood. So tell me, Stefan. That light on the post over there."

"Our ghost-light, we call it. Something to show where we are to visitors after dark. Saves on kerosene. We have the generator but tend to use kerosene lamps, with very few showing after we retire for the evening."

"Despite the ghost?"

"Despite our ghost. We'll leave more on during your stay."

"It meant something reaching that post earlier. Your houseboy Long waited until we were past it before he came for my bag."

"He did. The *cafard* often hits less frequently, less severely, when we respect it as a boundary. Lizzie won't comment, of course."

"Then you will suffer because you came to meet me at the dock?"

"Only a little. And I'm used to it."

"You said before that Lizzie and Jeune Petite shared important signature mannerisms. They include the eyes and the smile, yes?"

"More how they are used. Especially when she first greets you."

"As if she's about to burst out laughing."

"Exactly. On the edge of losing control. It's disconcerting, I know. You always feel like asking what's wrong."

"She wasn't like that before?"

"Given her features, yes, but with nowhere near the manic intensity. Much less severe."

"She says you are wrong about everything."

"I know. So your visit deals with it either way. How do you wish to play this, Thomas?"

"As we agreed initially. She knows your feelings on the matter. You're open about it. All she doesn't know is how we intend to proceed. Unless, as you say, she can *know* things. Reads your thoughts. Mine, for that matter."

"That part's inconclusive. Only my own family background till now. Not all of it, but surprisingly personal things."

*The things any real daughter would and wouldn't know.* Thomas realized he didn't need to say it. "Then I'll be open about everything but my theories. I'll speak to her alone, of course, but will interview the house staff and the appropriate villagers first. Since I'm recording it all, we'll start with a general meeting tomorrow with everyone present so I can set parameters."

Stefan gave a wintry smile. "Like a trial."

"An official hearing at least. Get it all out, build up a formal profile at the very least. She says she's willing to assist, wants this settled as much as you do."

"That's just it. She's always willing."

"The body in the crash?"

"She will have told you misidentification, yes? That Marie flew on to Denver without her. The flight change wasn't logged, the autopsy wasn't filed properly. No one enquired about the dead girl."

"I'll be confirming everything you've told me. That you think she's an apparition? How it comes up openly in daily conversation, openly in front of staff. I'll want it all."

"Of course, but reassure me, please. She's more than just a day-ghost, you say?"

"Given how events match existing profiles, yes. You must trust me."

"And the procedure includes an exit strategy? I want this ended."

"I'm here three days this first visit. I'll compile and confirm data as discreetly as I can. At the right time, we present her with the evidence. See her reaction. Try exorcism by negotiation, as she so aptly put it."

"Again, she may already know what you intend."

"Immaterial if what I suspect is true."

"And what if there's no conclusive outcome? Your time—"

"I won't fake data or force conclusions, Stefan. I'm used to disappointment. I'm happy just to have the profile. It's what we said back in July. Everyone is fascinated by tales of ghosts and spirits, hauntings and possession. But only as tales. They don't go far enough. They only ever go one step along the road. Starting tomorrow, we try to go further."

In the night there was rain that wasn't.

Exhausted from the flight down from Tokyo and the long river journey from Saigon in the heat and humidity, wearied by the sheer intensity of his first meetings with the occupants of the Hotel Dis, Thomas excused himself at eight o'clock and went to his room.

He slept well at first, but woke a little after midnight, to lie watching the streaks of shifting lesser darkness between the slats of the blinds, certain that there was the steady fall of rain on the roof, running off the eaves. There was the fresh smell of it too, flooding in through the insect screens: wet leaves, night orchids, rich loam, a spicy almost pungent fragrance he couldn't quite name, even more elusive scents.

It was only when he went to use the water-closet off the bathroom and was on his way back to bed that he thought to look out and be sure. He lifted the blind and pressed close to the insect screen. The smells of the humid jungle night were stronger than ever, but there was no rain, just stillness, complete darkness but for the glow of the solitary ghost-light on its post, the tiny lantern haloed with insects.

The sensory dislocation brought a quiet panic, but then Thomas remembered Stefan's words about the *cafard*.

*You will be convinced the weather is wrong.*

It was enough to make him light his lamp, check his room, the reasonably familiar surroundings he now depended on more than ever to anchor him in time and place. The hotel was so quiet. There were just the jungle sounds and an occasional dull bump-bumping somewhere outside that Thomas thought might be the generator or a water pump working.

And suddenly the thought was there.

*Lizzie is outside the door!*

He was sure of it. It was like the old childhood fear of something under the bed or in the closet. You had to look to be free of it.

Lizzie was out there!

But to open the door! To actually go over, turn the key and the handle, pull it back. To look out and find her grinning her grin, having the dark, too narrow eyes locked on his. He couldn't do it, couldn't bear to do it. Not at this hour. Not at any hour.

But how could he leave it unresolved? He could almost hear her breathing on the other side, pressing close to the wood. He could. He could. She's right there. Face against the timber, breathing against it. He could feel the pressure of her presence.

Thomas stumbled back to the bed and checked the time: 12:34. It was the lamp! She'd seen its light under the door. He extinguished it at once, then sat quietly in the close darkness watching the door.

There was a knocking then, definite, unmistakable, several firm raps, over so quickly, followed by a long silence. Half a minute? A minute? Then the pattern again, the short quick raps. But no words, no voice, no one calling his name.

Could it be Stefan? Was it Long or Trang or one of the other house staff paying a late call to share secrets, things they dared not reveal in daylight?

The imaginary rain was falling again. Thomas heard the steady patter through the blinds and window screens, heard the impossible drip, drip, drip from the eaves, smelled the wet leaves, the rich earth.

But no more knocking came, no other sound but the false rain, possibly more of the odd bumping, he couldn't be sure.

Lizzie was out in the hall, grinning in the dark, just waiting. More than a day-ghost, a night-ghost now, the classic haunt-form. Jeune Petite.

*If* she were out there. Only if.

And what if not Lizzie at all?

Thomas sat barely breathing, staring at the door.

Then remembered the obvious. What were locked doors to a phantom? Lizzie, Jeune Petite, could be *inside* the room already if she chose to be! Pressed up against the door on *this* side, utterly still. Thomas was sure he could see her there, darkness in darkness, the first crimplings and twinklings of her smile giving her away.

*She has me!* It was all he could think of.

But then a far-off door closed, the door at the other end of the hall. Her door.

And the ghost rain stopped, just like that. The night was still, filled with insects and night-birds calling, the occasional faint thumping sound from above.

A second reprieve.

Thomas settled back, tried to sleep again, telling himself that it didn't matter. Whether Lizzie or just this old, well-known, re-vamped Jeune Petite playing her tricks, she was something known and knowable.

But he had felt the dread, the *cafard*.

And it was the longest night of his life.


The morning sunlight changed everything, of course, brought the fierce pre-delta sun, the empty river, the line of mangroves in the early haze, the rainforest burgeoning with life.

He neither mentioned nor asked about his experiences of the night before. According to Stefan, everyone present would allow that *la maladie du cafard* would have left its calling card. It was a given here; of course he would have felt something. You got on with things in spite of it. The fact that *they* didn't ask even became strangely comforting.

The first session was at ten with everyone in the conservatory, sitting in the old-fashioned armchairs and sofas close by the piano. Thomas was given the place of honour in Stefan's big armchair, with Stefan to his right and Lizzie to his left around the small circle they made. He switched on his digital recorder, opened the type-written history Stefan had provided and scanned the highlighted points, needing to anchor himself in the reality of the Hotel Dis as much as anything, then began.

"Larier built this place in 1924, originally as a plantation residence but with an eye to catering for select tourists from Europe. In 1941 he returned to Paris, ostensibly for professional reasons, but the political situation had changed. There was the Japanese occupation, an impotent and token French government desperate that the French retain their business holdings, not to mention their fading dreams of a colonial empire. Everything was uncertain. Stefan, you say Larier left because the ghost sightings were becoming more frequent, increasingly disturbing. He couldn't stand it. This Jeune Petite, as he called her—"

Elizabeth raised a hand schoolgirl fashion.

"Yes?" Thomas said.

"Present." She giggled. "That's me apparently."

Stefan sighed, rolled his eyes. "Please."

Not "Please, Lizzie", Thomas noticed. *He avoids naming her to her face.*

"So your father says. For the record, are you or have you ever been Jeune Petite?"

"No." She turned to Stefan. "You hear me, Papa? No!"

Thomas left no time for an answer, continued reading from his notes. "Stefan, within the immediate area, fifty square miles or so, you've logged twenty-four spirit sightings in living memory where more than one supposedly reliable witness was present; eighteen alleged shapeshifter manifestations; five cases of what can be identified as possession as much as an any kind of allowable mental illness. If we extend that area to 300 square miles then we now have five times that number."

"Though hardly reliable scientifically," Stefan said. "Folk tales, rumours, hearsay. What you'd expect."

"Of course. Impossible to substantiate clinically. But it's just the range we're after at this point, a sampling of manifestations to match my samplings from elsewhere so that we have a range of forms."

And so it went, the start of what ended up being a long day. Many of the surrounding villagers couldn't come in to tell their stories until after sundown, so the actual interviews confirming local accounts of shapeshifters and demon possession went on well after ten o'clock.

It ended with Long and Hoa translating for an old man named Venny, who told a surprisingly consistent and detailed story of two villagers bitten in the night, showing puncture marks on their necks, some exsanguination but with no fatalities involved. No, not the bites of bats, snakes or monkeys, Long translated, nor any known night creature. The wounds were too large, too far apart, too distinctive. Venny knew of others who had suffered similarly; they often talked about such things at the markets and festivals.

Thomas retired around eleven, exhausted but pleased. However it went with trying to determine Lizzie's role in everything, he had made a good start on a valuable regional profile.

There was no "visit" from Jeune Petite that night, no knocking, no phantom Lizzie, thank goodness. No trace of the *cafard* either that Thomas was aware of, just the occasional odd bumping sound he had heard the previous night. He slept through, which had the effect of softening the former night's terrors, of making the false rain and the late-night caller at his door seem the result of travel fatigue, the rigours of being in a new place, primed by Stefan Yosen's stories and his own vivid imaginings.

The following day went much like the first, with Long translating for the old housekeeper, Trang, so Thomas could learn all he could about Gerard Larier and how life had been in the hotel before Anton and Marguerite Yosen, Stefan's parents, had assumed permanent residence, then outright ownership at Larier's departure.

Trang had been born at the Hotel Dis ten years after it was first built. Her tales of Jeune Petite's appearances spanned an entire lifetime and were not only thorough, earnest and respectful, but often chilling in their unadorned frankness and simplicity.

That afternoon there was an hour with Lizzie, which went much better than Thomas had feared it might. For a start, much of the time he was either making notes or reading prepared questions, with Lizzie in the big armchair and turned slightly away from him.

She seemed resolved to make it easier too. For most of that hour she presented as a loving, concerned and helpful daughter. She held back the smile, breaking form only near the end when she leant around the wing of the high-backed chair and snared him with her gaze. Instantly it was the other Lizzie.

"I think we've been very good with this, don't you? Played very nicely together?"

It may well have negated everything, Thomas wasn't sure. If a ploy rather than a natural lapse, then it had the same effect: it was like a psychotic episode, something pathological, as if she were suddenly possessed by Jeune Petite, some other here-again, gone-again presence.

"I was just about to say thank you," Thomas managed, and kept his voice steady considering how he felt. "You've been very helpful."

"But I've ruined it?"

"I don't know yet. You've been through a great deal. A wry detachment is entirely appropriate. My intrusion into your lives warrants all sorts of reasonable reactions: indignation, resentment, some form of serious emotional response."

"You're unfailingly gracious. Thank you for not saying 'schizoid event'. I think I like you."

"Did you knock on my door the other night?" Thomas couldn't help himself.

Lizzie stood, her smile merciless. "Even if you *are* a bit too full of yourself, Mr Neville. Papa's room is opposite yours. Maybe I wasn't outside *your* door at all! Now please excuse me."

And she left the conservatory.

That evening some of Trang's old friends arrived: two villagers who had travelled all the way up from the delta to tell their stories. Lâm Doan and his brother Bảo were motorcycle repairmen from one of the more industrialized delta towns. They confirmed one another's accounts of a series of shapeshifter incidents involving a local who had turned into a wild pig, then, on a second occasion, a crazed dog that had to be shot. They insisted that the dog had changed back into human form after death, but that fellow villagers had burned the remains before any kind of official investigation could be arranged.

Lâm and Bảo were invited to stay the night in the downstairs staff quarters, but they politely refused, preferring the long journey downriver to the prospect of facing the *cafard* and possibly Jeune Petite. While Trang, Lan and Hoa saw them as far as the ghost-light, Thomas asked Stefan about the odd thumping sound he'd heard in his room.

"That. It's just the eels in the water tank on the roof."

"Eels! Stefan, how on earth—?"

"Who knows?" Stefan shrugged. "A bird catches an eel, drops it on its way to the forest. The eel is pregnant, finds its way into the tank. Is it a problem?"

"Not at all."

"Not like the *tristesse*, eh? I can tell you feel it. The eels are real. The true real."

Thomas could only smile. Two days under Stefan's roof and a term like the "true real" made perfect sense, the *cafard* just one more commonplace of hotel life.

That third night was as humid and still beyond the windows as the previous two, with just the sound of insects and nightbirds calling from the forest and the occasional bump, bump of the eels on the roof (though how, how, how, Thomas wondered on the edge of sleep, *did* the eels really get up there in the first place and what did they eat apart from each other?). The thought of them blindly circling remained strange rather than alarming, just another odd fact in a world of amazing facts, and Thomas managed to sleep with little trouble.

On Monday there were some last-minute interviews, one with a boatman bringing in supplies who had a story of walking dead in the upper Mekong. Two fresh corpses, he insisted, a Laotian man and a Vietnamese woman, both pronounced dead from eating poisoned fish, had left their death-beds the next morning, rose up one after the other and walked the half-mile to the river then plunged into the water. Both had started making an eerie droning on their way to the river's edge, a dismal sound that could still be heard as the corpses were swept away.

After lunch, Thomas spent the afternoon transcribing the fifteen most useful interviews into his laptop, wanting to have hard-copy back-ups and to leave Stefan with a preliminary version of what would be edited down, possibly expanded, back in Tokyo before he flew home to Sydney.

For a special final dinner that evening, Trang served *Bun Cha Gio*, *Banh Hoi* and *Bun thit nuong* prepared according to recipes learned from her mother and grandmother back in Larier's day. Afterwards, Thomas suggested to Stefan that the two of them adjourn to the long sofa on the veranda inside the insect screen. When they were settled with whisky sours brought by Lan, Thomas announced that it was time to explain his line of research; at least to bring it all together in a quick thumbnail sketch.

"For nearly ten years I've been gathering evidence to support a case for there being a single haunt-form for *all* paranormal sightings. All the multi-phase manifestations: ghost, vampire, werewolf, zombie, demon possession, poltergeist events, the lot, are the results of this basic form being present."

"You're saying it's all one thing?"

"The basic haunt-form is an entity called a *stoyen*." He spelled it out. "Whatever it actually is, it is at the root of all the classic paranormal manifestations. If you are a traditional Navajo, then you get *chindi* and skinwalker sightings. If you're among the tribes of West Africa, you'll have shapeshifters like those in the Anansi mythos. Here in Vietnam we go back before the Hung native rulers to the first manifestations of the dragon lord Lac Long Quan. It's such a rich data-pool, both global and regional, general and specific."

"A *stoyen*?"

"One of the oldest Indo-European names for it. But the basic haunt-form, giving back what's expected, whatever is sought or feared, even what is needed in a given culture, to look at it that way. For Venny it was a vampire experience, but very much a regional one manifested in local terms. Here at the hotel you've had a *stoyen* projecting for Larier as Jeune Petite, possibly even the same one Venny told us of. Now it's projecting for you, exactly what you told me when you first showed me to my room: that it's Larier's phantom tailored to your own circumstances."

"This *stoyen*?"

"You *expect* her to be Lizzie *as* Jeune Petite, do you see? So that is what you get! Not just Jeune Petite, not just Lizzie. But Lizzie as Jeune Petite. A very precise haunting."

"This is extraordinary. But what is next? What will you do now?"

"Before I leave tomorrow, I will confront Lizzie with what I've just told you. Give her an ultimatum."

"An ultimatum? And what is that?"

"Something obvious really. I know she may read both our thoughts, but since she's Lizzie, customized to you, there's a chance she won't read mine yet. If you can bear with me a little longer, I'd prefer to leave it till I confront her with it."

\* \* \*

As if in reprisal for secrets kept, games played, the *cafard* returned that night.

Thomas woke around 2:00 a.m., lay listening to the night, wondering about Lizzie. Would she know? Did she know? Lizzie with her mantis-green gaze and dark designs.

No rain flagged it this time, no wrong weather. All the safe signatures were there: the insects, the bird-calls, the eels blindly turning, striking the walls of the tank now and then in their restless sweeps.

Then the certainty was there like before.

*She's outside. She's come calling again.*

All part of the world, Thomas told himself. Just another part of the world. Nothing less, nothing more.

This time he would brave it. Endure it. Go out into the hall. Talk to this *stoyen* of the Hotel Dis as to any thing of the world with sense enough to understand.

He left his bed, dressed quickly and went to the door.

She could just as easily have been inside the room. *She wants me to go to her. Wants the fear, the control. Her dark designs.*

Thomas opened the door, but there was no one, nothing.

He stepped into the hall, made himself do it.

Lizzie was at the far end outside her room, just standing, watching, staring with her dark, too narrow eyes, her swept-up, I-know-something-you-don't grin.

He actually took four, five steps towards her, needing to be sure of what he was seeing.

"Lizzie?"

The smile curved up. He shouldn't have been able to see it, not the eyes or the grimace, not at this distance, not for a moment. There was just the one lamp giving light behind her on the stand near the top of the stairs. But he did, he could. There was light on her face, impossible light. She was bending light to show her eyes, the dreadful, overdone smile.

*Here for you this time!*

"Lizzie?" he said again, and fought not to blink. She'd be gone if he did and this mattered: Lizzie as Jeune Petite. Jeune Petite as Lizzie.

*Why didn't Stefan hear him calling? Were they in collusion? Let's serve up the stranger!*

Perspiration beaded his forehead, beaded and ran, fell, stinging his eyes, blurring his vision. He had to blink. Had to.

Resisted but couldn't help it, did so quickly.

And she hadn't gone.

She was closer, much closer, halfway down the hall now, arms at her sides, grin slashed and curving, just standing there.

He hadn't seen her move.

"Lizzie?"

He began retreating, step by backward step, not daring to turn or look away, reached his room, found the door shut – shut! – fumbled for a knob that wasn't there, glanced to find it.

It had been moved, was half a yard higher on the door!

He reached up and turned it, glanced back as the door swung in.

She was right there, four yards away now in the dark hallway, the light on her face all wrong.

Then – third reprieve! – he was through and had it shut and locked, stood giggling and shaking, sobbing, triumphant.

He'd left his bedside lamp lit, thank God. But when he looked, he saw Lizzie sitting on the end of his bed.

*Got you!*

He wished she'd say it, say something, anything. It was too quiet, just the jungle sounds, the night insects, the bump-bump of the eels on the roof.

And she raised her arms.

*Come to me!*

Her eyes held him. The smile cut, slashed, struck out, drew him forward. The eels kept circling, turning, thumping in the dark.

And it happened. Whatever it was. Everything it was. The cool mouth, the thrusting tongue. The slim body against his, atop his when the clothes were gone, the arms clamping, legs locking him hard, the mouth fixed, open, thrusting, breathing into his, giving, taking.

And, all the while, the eels kept turning.

Again there was the blazing day, the river bright with sunlight, the night terrors over and done with.

He told Stefan about it all over breakfast, owed him that, recorded everything this time too, trying to stay impartial:

how confused he was, how uncertain about what had actually happened, just that it had, seemed to have.

Stefan nodded, accepted, then matched stories one for one, helping Thomas to feel better knowing that such similar, intimate encounters had been part of it for him too.

"But *not* Lizzie, you understand," he kept saying. "She's not."

It was easy for Thomas to allow it. "Of course," he said, then realized how that sounded. "Of course not."

At 10:30, he went looking for Lizzie to say goodbye, found her in the conservatory, quietly reading in the big armchair.

"Back to normal soon," he said, not mentioning the previous night.

"But you'll be back."

"I still have some things to do here."

"I notice you don't say my name now, Thomas."

"You know what I told Stefan?"

"Enough. How does it concern me?"

"We require you to move on. Give Stefan and the others some peace."

"Of course you do. But if I choose otherwise?"

"We bring in the research groups. Turn you into an on-site case study. I've made preliminary arrangements."

"I can damage them. Bring their worst fears."

"They'll sign waivers. There'll be constant observation. Welcome to the twenty-first century."

"I can maim and kill. Do such lasting harm."

"They'll still come. We'll choose carefully. A chance to survive Jeune Petite will be like a chance to pull the Sword from the Stone. Only the bravest, the most committed will come."

"Probably the most ignorant, the most gullible."

"Not this time. You *will* be known. Quantified like any other phenomenon in the world. Something with a process, a methodology. Re-natured."

"Now there's a word."

"It fits." He wouldn't name her. "Nothing supernatural. Not really. If anything happens to Stefan, the hotel is bequeathed to a local university in Ho Chi Minh City for research projects. That or burnt to the ground. You can haunt the jungle again."

"I must think about this."

"Thang gets here around eleven."

"Is that a farewell or an invitation?" Her dark eyes flashed.

Without another word, Thomas turned and left the room.

Forty minutes later the white runabout pulled in at the dock. Stefan and Long came as far as the ghost-light post, observing old proprieties just in case. They shook hands and waved Thomas on his way.

"Don't forget us," Stefan called after him, which Thomas suddenly realized was a more pointed request than it first seemed. *This is a short-term memory place. The way it sits in the mind.*

"I won't!" Thomas called back and tried to keep his thoughts straight. The Hotel Dis *would* stay in long-term memory. It would, though again he wondered if Jeune Petite would ever really leave, or even if there would be some final trick, a legacy, something. He had just stepped past the boundary post after all.

But he reached the jetty without incident. The glare on the river was terrible at this hour, leaching the sky of colour, filling the world. It made Thomas squint even through his sunglasses, made him look down at the boards through half-closed eyes as he carried his bag to the runabout, passed it down to the young boatman.

But it wasn't Thang who took it. It wasn't the young Vietnamese at all.

It was Deek grinning up at him, Deek beckoning, urging, the flashing, dazzling water at his back.

"Thought I'd get you myself," his father said. Enough of his father. "Get you back to Saigon in no time. We might even drop by the Market Hotel on Cranbow Road and consider our options."

And the old man smiled. And in all that light, his eyes were uncommonly fixed, as green as the darkest water lilies on the Mekong, and the smile, the inescapable smile, swept up to become one with the blazing heart of the river.

# MARK VALENTINE

## The Axholme Toll

MARK VALENTINE IS THE author of the acclaimed 1995 biography *Arthur Machen*. His short fiction has been collected in *14 Bellchamber Tower*, *In Violet Veils*, *Masques and Citadels*, *The Nightfarers*, *The Rite of Trebizond and Other Tales* and *The Collected Connoisseur* (the latter two both with John Howard).

He has also edited the anthologies *The Werewolf Pack* and *The Black Veil and Other Tales of Supernatural Sleuths* for Wordsworth Edition's budget "Tales of Mystery and the Supernatural" series, and is the editor of *Wormwood*, the journal of the literature of the fantastic, supernatural and decadent.

"In the following story, the book called *The MS. in a Red Box* really exists," the author reveals. "All of the legends about the Isle, and about Beckett's assassins, are also genuine, except (so far) that of the Toll, and their final place of rest – or unrest."

IT WAS STEVENSON, I think, who most notably observed that there are some places that simply demand a story should be told of them.

Such was the case with the Isle of Erraid, a tidal islet off Mull, where he stayed as a young man while assisting his father with his profession as a lighthouse engineer. It led to his story, "The Merry Men", full of the wild lore of the sea. There are many such tales told of islands, which seem always to draw the imagination of the mainlander, and to nourish their own myths too. Yet I wonder if there are not also enclaves within the solid land of the country, which are islands in a different sense. They are somehow set apart from the rest of the everyday world. We enter them, and a sense steals over us of being in a different domain. Some subtle change in the terrain tells us that we are not quite wholly in a reliable realm.

For me, the Isle of Axholme, in the far north-western marge of Lincolnshire, will always figure as exactly such a place, for it was indeed once an island, and it is still remote and peculiar.

It was, as I say, until the seventeenth century, a real inland island, surrounded by three rivers at their widest span, traversable only by ferry. Even within the bounds these formed, much of the terrain was inhospitable marshland, whose narrow tracks only natives knew thoroughly. It was the practice for the isle folk to stalk these murky wastes on nimble stilts, and there was competition to be deftest at this unusual skill. Drainage by Dutch engineers under charter from Charles I ended its isolation a little, but it retained a distinctive character for quite a while afterwards.

Islonians, as they call themselves, are proud of their particular family names and still refer to "the Isle", even though it is strictly not that any longer. In fact, it was always a series of islands: one long ridge in the middle, bearing four villages upon it, some outlying outcrops, and a cluster of ferry settlements by the riverbanks.

I found that its mysteries begin in the Dark Ages, when some astral catastrophe or other – a fireball, or so it is inferred – spread flame even through its wateriness, burning trees down to their roots deep underground, and denuding it for a while of vegetation. Modern conspiracists regard this as one sign among many of the cogency of the prophecies of Ezekiel. It has also been claimed as the true locality of Avalon – the fact of it being an island only accessible with difficulty, and the deceptive similarity of its name, being in its favour. Against that, however, is the sad absence of any other Arthurian links, or of orchards, for Avalon is generally held to mean "Isle of Apples".

It has also had, through the ages, other reputations. Not surprisingly, its remoteness bred talk of magic, and it is said to have had a hermit-wizard in occupation for a century or so, on one of its lonelier knolls. The Templars, too, are naturally said to have had a priory here: although, in fact, it seems to have been Carthusian. There are astrological links, suggesting a lost zodiac, known now only by an old local saying, "'Tis Scorpio in Crowle" (the latter being the northernmost village on its spine), meaning a time of ill omen.

Then, it has its own literary mystery too. In April 1903, the publisher John Lane received a parcel through the post at his London offices in Vigo Street, under the sign of The Bodley Head. It contained the manuscript of a novel. There was nothing uncommon about that, of course, except that the manuscript had no sign of the author, and no title, and there was no accompanying letter. Nor was there any indication where it had come from. It arrived in a red box, and that was just about all that could be known about it.

The work was sent to the publisher's reader in the usual way, and he reported favourably. As was his habit with anything out of the ordinary, John Lane then read it himself. He had made his name in the 1890s as the publisher of "daring" and "modern" books that came to epitomize the period as the "Naughty Nineties", especially in his Keynotes series of novels.

He also issued his flagship periodical, *The Yellow Book*, which gave its name to the decade: the Yellow Nineties. It was, at first anyway, embellished with some of the audacious black-and-white drawings of Aubrey Beardsley. Their boldness, and the bright gold covers, soon made sure it was seen and hotly discussed.

But by 1903, John Lane had mellowed more into the role of a mainstream publisher. He was a shrewd businessman, who liked to be on good terms with his authors and to socialize with them: but still had a keen-eyed understanding of the exact commercial value of their work. The previous year, he had scored a success with Kenneth Grahame's gentle pastoral pieces, *Dream Days*, with a verse play, *Ulysses* by Stephen Phillips (compared in his day to Shakespeare, Milton and Tennyson), and (rather more in the vein of the book before him), a rip-roaring historical study, *King Monmouth* by Allan Fea. Still, a strong seller in fiction had really eluded him. He was ready to find one.

When he looked at the untitled book, he agreed with his reader's assessment. The mystery manuscript was a great historical romance in the tradition of Stevenson and Scott, about the seventeenth-century struggle between the proud and independent people of the Isle of Axholme in Lincolnshire and the Dutch drainage lords who had come to change their world forever, and drive them from their lands. It was a gripping, twisting and turning, swashbuckling, yet also thoughtful and sometimes eerie book, with the isolated marshlands of Axholme so strongly evoked that the reader almost felt they had lived there themselves.

Accordingly, Lane decided to publish the book. But how to do so, without even a title, and no author? No doubt with an eye to the publicity value, he placed an advertisement in the press:

## TO AUTHORS

NOTICE – If the Writer of an Historical Novel without Title, Author's Name or Address, sent some weeks ago to The Bodley Head in a Red Box, will communicate with the Publisher, he will hear something to his advantage.

—John Lane, Vigo Street, London, W.2

"Hear something to his advantage"! It was the very phrase used by solicitors in mystery novels when a large or unusual legacy awaits the hero. The notice had the desired effect. It created what one newspaper called a "hullabaloo of excitement". Yet no author came forward. The publisher tried again, with a further notice, saying he would publish the book at a certain date unless he heard from the author. This, of course, was very cleverly stoking up the interest in the book, and some acid commentators thought it was all just a stunt. But it was not.

John Lane went ahead and published the book as *The MS. in a Red Box*, and it has been known by this title ever since. After all the discussion leading up to its appearance, it was not surprising that it sold well. So much might be expected. But, gratifyingly for Lane's and his reader's judgment, critics and the public agreed about its qualities. It had an enthralling, well-devised plot, the right blend of adventure and love interest, the historical setting was just familiar enough but also original and unusual; the island scenes were strange and appealing to the reader. Indeed, the Axholme dimension may have had much to do with the book's success: it was seen as a curious and inaccessible region still.

After the book came out, it is said Lane received many letters claiming authorship, but none of them were at all convincing. Two things, however, were tolerably clear about the author. He was a proficient, very capable prose writer and storyteller, and he knew the Isle of Axholme and its people and history intimately well.

Much of the book is a vivid, pretty brisk adventure story: the tale of Frank Vavasour, son of a local squire, who leads the revolt against the Dutch clearances, aided by loyal friends, betrayed by squinting villains, and never near enough to the arms of the vivacious woman he loves, who is inconveniently the daughter of a Dutch doctor – though a fair-minded and moderate man.

But there is also a strangeness about the book, caused by its Axholme setting: there are weird visions and curses, and the sense of an inexorable working-out of fate. In one episode, young Vavasour, hotly pursued by the King's men, takes to the green alleys of the marshes, where their horses cannot go because of the treacherous terrain. And yet, it still seems to him that he is pursued, for over the wastes there comes to him the drumming of hooves where no horses could possibly be; he wonders what riders these beasts must bear. No more is said of the matter; Vavasour evades his predators, but the reader is left to think that the phantom author is hinting here at more than he can tell.

A strong candidate for the authorship has been put forward in recent years, to the extent that some editions now definitely attribute it to him, and so does the catalogue of the British Library. This is the Reverend John Arthur Hamilton (1854–1924), who was a minister of the Congregational Church at Crowle, in Axholme, from 1870 to 1878: only eight years, but perhaps important ones, for he was very young and it was his first pastorate. He later went on to hold office at Saltaire, Yorkshire from 1878 to 1896, and finally in Penzance from 1897 until his death. He gave his house in Cornwall the name "Axholme". This suggests the Isle remained steadfast in his memory.

This John Hamilton was an author. He pioneered the idea of sermons written as stories for children. His books included *A Mountain Path and Forty Three Other Talks for Young Children* (Low & Co, 1894), *The Life of John Milton, Partly In His Own Words* (Congregational Union, 1908), *The Giant and the Caterpillar and Other Addresses to Young People* (Allenson, 1912) and *The Wonderful River and Other Addresses to Young People* (Allenson, 1913). Somewhat more to the point, he also wrote at least one historical romance – *Captain John Lister: A Tale of Axholme* (Hutchinson, 1906) – set in the time of the English Civil War. But to that he put his name.

Yet all – bar one – of these worthy titles are not in the least like *The MS. in a Red Box*. That book is full-blooded, vigorous, and very rarely pious. This could, of course, be the reason why the author wanted it only issued anonymously. But could a man who had already put his name to these other books resist claiming authorship in some way for a work that must have cost him many hours of work, hours diverted from his more sacred duties? And could a cleric who was so concerned to mix storytelling with an improving message completely resist the opportunity to do so in this work too? Certainly, he could have sent the book to Lane anonymously, in the red box, just as Lane recounted – or collaborated with him on an elaborate hoax.

It was in the hope of throwing more light upon this literary mystery that I made my way to the Isle one day in late summer. I may as well confess now that I learnt very little new as to the book, or its author, but what I encountered instead gave me ample cause to remember the Isle well.

Axholme does not attract many visitors. There is a lot of ugliness within or in sight of it. Pylons, power stations, motorways, dredging operations and more obscure industrial plant are all too blatant upon it, and only escaped in its most hidden parts. Rashes of new houses make no attempt to emulate the local style – which at its quirkiest has hints of the Dutch influence – instead, they are often big, porticoed and made of a pale brick, all starved of colour, as if no one cared who builds what here. I even saw one with gateposts topped by lions whose heads were painted bronze and bodies gold. Yet its real architectural riches are not to be seen: all but one church was padlocked, perhaps due to vandalism.

Still, there were hints of the Isle's inner richness, of what it might have been. The road from the most remote village, Wroot, following dead-straight dikes for four or five miles north to Sandtoft, is little-used, since there is a major road to the east following a similar alignment. But as I drove, I passed fields where there hovered drifts of blue flax, ethereal as clear, still, sky-filled pools. And these were bordered on the roadside edge by blazons of bright red poppies and the white mist of daisies, so the experience was at moments like riding through a phantas-magoric parade. It was as if, I thought then, the Isle was trying to put forth at least one show of beauty in defiance of all that was around.

The Isle supports a weekly newspaper – actually about eight pages of local news wrapped around standardized media features from its parent press. It must be one of the few papers to bear a quotation from Tennyson upon its masthead: "Ring out the old, Ring in the new, Ring out the false, Ring in the true." The *Epworth Bells (& Crowle Advertiser)* has been published for 130 years. Among its fascinating pages, with the usual reports on fêtes, council meetings, juvenile delinquency, court appear-ances, there is a notice of high-water times on the Trent, which forms the isle's eastern boundary.

To this column is added the cryptic comment, seemingly straight out of some ancient almanac: "The Aegir usually appears during high spring and midwinter tides and arrives about two hours before high waters in Gainsborough, about three hours before in Owston Ferry . . .". Who or what, I natu-rally wondered, is the Aegir whose coming is so watched for? Some wrathful river-guardian?

Well, almost. It is a visible, lunging tidal current, rather like the Severn Bore, which broils the slow, broad waters of the Trent into foaming energy as it passes. The name, with its legendary ring, is of unknown origin. It would seem people do still gather to watch it pass, and talk about it as if it were a living thing: "Aegir's on its way" or "Aegir's strong today."

I was left with the clear impression that, despite the intru-sion of industry, the diminishing of its island status by drainage and dual carriageways, and the rash of incomers commuting to Scunthorpe or Doncaster, it still does have a deep-buried differentness about it. And I felt there was some thread linking all the legends together, which had somehow been lost, but which might be rediscerned. If it was not Avalon, was it the last refuge of some other legendary figure? If the Templars were not here, was there some other order of knights or priests? If the place was somehow blasted, always to be barren and with ugliness thrust upon it, was there some reason for this? And was it only the Aegir that was watched for here?

Well, I had my answer to all those questions.

That winter I went back to Axholme, and took a cottage there at Christmas. I dislike that time of year, for I am by nature solitary and prefer nothing better than quietness and my own company, with a good fire and a good book. So it is a habit of mine to go away then, somewhere quite remote and unexpected, where I shall not be disturbed and the rites of the season can pass me by, unobserved. I confess, too, that the Isle had taken a hold of me, for all its hardness and harshness, and I wanted to reflect more upon its mysteries.

The place I took I had found in a notice in the *Epworth Bells*. It was an old ferry cottage, a simple, tall, redbrick building, with few rooms, standing by a narrow track, which had once led down to the crossing; since that had closed many years ago, there was now little use for the track at all, and people seldom took it. Grass and moss grew down its middle and the hedges either side were thick and high.

When I walked down the lane from the little station, bearing my modest luggage, there was still the skeleton of a hard white frost lingering from the morning, crusting the dark wood of the hedge and the rank green of the road with a lichen of white.

The house still belonged, through some long process of bureaucratic accretion, to a semi-somnolent drainage board, and they largely left it to itself, getting what meagre income they could from rentals. And since Axholme is hardly a prime place for visitors, it was often empty. A caretaker, from off-isle (as they say there) had charge of it, and apologized when I spoke to him that it would be rather cold, for there had been few winter lets and he said it was very seldom wanted at this time of year. However, kindling and logs had been left for the fire, and he hoped I should soon be fairly comfortable.

When I retrieved the keys from under a brick, and let myself in, the chill enveloped me at once, and it almost seemed warmer outside in the frost-charged day. Exploring the house did not take very long. It was functional, and its only characteristic touch was a pair of opposing high-arched windows, one on the wall facing the road, the other facing the river. They had, I supposed, enabled the ferryman to watch for passengers. They let a great light into the main room of the place, even from the drawn winter sky, giving it a curious church-like quality, a sense of sanctuary, of radiance. I felt at once that it would do very well to dwell in during the day, as I pursued my studies.

There were other relics of the place's past as a ferry-keeper's cottage – four rotting stumps on the bank, old mooring posts, and a pitted, scabbed brass bell by the side of the house, once used, I surmised, to summon the boatman's attention if he had not seen his passengers approach. A raggedy strand of hoar-encrusted rope hung down from the clapper.

Over the succeeding days I soon established the unvarying routine I prefer and which conduces, I claim, to the most concentration in pursuing obscure studies. In the morning, I would make myself a pan of porridge, sufficiently staunch to see me through until evening. Then I would take a brisk walk as far as I could across the Isle, becoming accustomed to its byways and channels, its rusting iron manufactories and machines, its hideous haciendas and pompous-porticoed new halls. Returning in the early noon, I would get a fire going, surly at first, later more eager, in the blackened grate, and settle down with my notebooks. By four o'clock it was quite dark and I felt myself snugger and securer still, a dweller in a far redoubt that none had need to disturb.

Though I thought I knew the Isle well from my previous visit and from the study of both ancient and modern maps, I found my morning walks often took me to curious corners or tracks that I had not encountered before, and which were unknown to the cartographers. Since the three great rivers and all their tributaries continue to shift their course when in spate, and since the people here seem pretty free to do what they want with the land, this did not surprise me too much.

Yet there was one dismal plot which did puzzle me somewhat. It was some three days after Christmas, and I had gone far into the hinterland of the Isle, perhaps as remote from any settlement as it was possible to get there, for I always seek the furthest solitude possible.

Mostly the terrain is unvarying, and my way took me along straight dull tracks between flat fields holding only the dry husks of sapless stalks, or great turned clods of earth. Hungry crows wheeled in the dim white sky. At last, I came to a crossroads, of a kind: my thin, purposeless track carried on and further on, but it was intersected by an even more doubtful byway, merely an alley between great, clawing, overgrown bare hedges. No sign indicated where any of the four ways went. I was casting about to see if I could descry any landmark which might hint where I had got to, or where I might get to, when I noticed beyond the nameless track an unexpected hollow in the land.

Nowhere in the Isle has the pleasant undulations of some of our downland or shire country, and this sudden descent surprised me somewhat. I went nearer, and found it looked for all the world like a pit caused by quarrying – except that there is no quarrying here, and there was no sign of the loose rubble usually left behind at such sites.

Further, this was no great excavation, but an open maw in the ground which could probably be descended, in a loping run, in a dozen or so strides. It would not be easy to accomplish, for there was barely any vegetation to offer a foothold. It was all ash-coated earth as if there had once, long ago, been some great fire here, and the dead cold embers had never yielded to the wind but clung instead to the sides of the pit.

Here, too, the crust of frost which had dissipated elsewhere in dank trickles of moisture as the weak sun rose, had retained its crystalline grip. I saw that once inside this sullen depression, it would be no easy matter to climb back up through the treacherous dust.

I was about to resume my walk, when, taking a final look at the pit to see if there was any clue to its purpose, my attention was snagged by a stump at the very depth of the hollow. It was all but indistinguishable from the dreary bleached soil, except that it stuck out slightly like a dotard's back tooth from bony gums, ground down by the years. It put me in mind of the decaying mooring posts outside the ferry cottage and I involuntarily, for no intelligent reason whatever, looked to see if there were any more. And indeed I did soon see a second, even more sunken into the hard defile, and then, with a mounting sense of unease, a third and a fourth; and no more.

Well, it was a coincidence, and that was all – so I reassured myself. Old rotting wooden posts are to be found often enough in the country – the remains of a stockade, rubbing posts for cattle, gallows for crows, or simply marking out a plot of land. I chided myself for letting the place get the better of me, and, to shake off my subdued feeling, I picked up a nearby pebble, like an ossified egg, and sent it clattering down into the hollow where it bounced and jerked and – turned by some unseen obstruction – suddenly swerved and struck against one of the stumps. It was no art of mine that had achieved that, and I shrugged.

Yet as I resumed my former road I could not shake off the disquiet that had stolen upon me as I stared down into the pit at those four whittled stakes, driven down hard into the grim earth and weathered, perhaps by centuries, into gnarled relics.

That evening I stirred up the fire higher still than usual, and sat for a while meditating as the flames threw their benison upon my body and the shadows flickered over my face. My books and my notes lay to one side and I reflected again upon the curious history and mythology of the Isle, mulling over my growing conviction that some greater legend lay behind it all.

I knew that lore may reach backwards as well as forwards, and take upon itself, in a new guise, all the potency of the past. Arthur, a Dark Age warrior, becomes also a Roman Emperor and a medieval king. Robin Hood, a peasant outlaw, is transformed in retrospect as a pagan demi-god, and reinterpreted as a freedom fighter. That monkish chronicle of a great meteor's descent in the Dark Ages, for example, might be perfectly veridical in the essentials – embroidered a little, given a pious gloss, certainly, but the record of a true event. Looked upon later, though, it might be seen as the harbinger of some even greater doom or *wyrd* which was to befall the Isle.

As I crouched upon the flagstones before the hearth, dreamily turning over these things in my mind, I heard in the distance the sound of a furious drumming. I got up and tilted my head to one side, the way a creature does when it wants to listen more intently. The rapid pounding noise did not relent. I went to the great window that gave out on to the ferry road. I saw myself and the room reflected in the blackness beyond, and a glassy fire leaping.

I turned off the electric light, and these images dimmed, letting through a vista of the road. There was a fine three-quarters moon, but it was harried by dark clouds, and threw only a pale, veiled light. I craned my gaze and made out a haze of dimness moving in the direction of the house, which my mind at once connected with the onset of the monotonous thudding. Despite the glow of the fire, I felt as if I was back in the room when I had first entered it, confronted by a slab of cold.

I could not draw away from the window. The sound became harder, heavier, faster, fiercer until I thought it was rising to a pitch I could not endure. And then there emerged, as the moon shrugged itself free of its sable assailants, a great burst of sudden light, which, however, only served to heighten and accentuate the aureole of darkness which massed around its edges.

Then there fell upon me a deep, harrowing, rivening surge, like pain or grief or shame. I had no understanding of its cause, nor of how it began or when it passed, but only that it bore in upon me and ran through all my thoughts and senses like fire or ice. And I felt overborn, as if by a measureless force that would fling aside any feeble attempts to resist.

That force, that cloud of darkness seemed to encompass the ferry house and all the terrain around, and I imagined it stalking across the whole Isle. For how long I stood transfixed by its presence, I could not say. But I know that it was followed by two simple, stark sounds, which struck me then as even more dreadful than the thundering clamour that had been raised before. One was the cracked clanging of a single bell; the other was of laughter, deep, full-throated and careless.

Both sounds echoed shrilly, and then receded in the brittle silence. Yet I seemed to listen to those echoes throughout most of the rest of the night, until dawn trickled into the sky with thin scarlet rivulets amid a great pallor of cloud.

As soon as the daybreak grew, I packed up my papers and my cases, placed the key back under the brick, and went to the station to wait for the earliest train. There was a chill wind and as I looked back, the bell was creaking and swaying, causing a dull tolling.

There were still a few days left of my time away, but I had not the will to go very far and so I made my way to the village of Allborough, perhaps a dozen miles beyond the river from Axholme. It looks out from its green bluff over the estuaries of the Don and the Trent and towards the broad waters of the Humber, and I gazed upon their slow silver waters for several hours, allowing the gentle, secluded atmosphere to restore me somewhat.

Allborough is known for its great round medieval labyrinth, carved upon the turf, and carefully preserved by the village. After threading this quietly by myself, meditating as calmly as I could upon what I had heard and felt, a new heartening came upon me.

From the green maze, I went to the church, where a replica is laid out in tiles on the floor. It was growing dusk by now, and the door had just been locked for the night, but the church-warden, whose house was opposite, saw me, and came out to let me in. He was an amiable and pottering sort of man, just the sort of harmless company I needed, and, peering from his thick glasses, he soon told me somewhat about himself and the village.

He was not from these parts, but knew all about the local history, more so – he lightly implied – than those who had lived here much longer. He showed me the church's treasures, which included a Thompson admiralty clock with its vast pendulum, an eighteenth-century bier, looking only like a hand-cart, and a Roman foundation stone concealed beneath a small trap door.

By a plain side altar, too, four shields were displayed. But instead of showing arms, they were all utterly black. "Those are Victorian," he said, "but we always put them out at this time of year." And then he asked if I knew that the nave had been restored by Becket's murderers, for the shields represented the suppressed emblems of the four assassins, and they were placed there on the eve before each December 29, the anniversary of the saint's martyrdom in 1170.

For penance, he said, these knights had been ordered by the Pope to go to Jerusalem, then in Saracen hands, and expend their wealth upon the preservation of a church there. This they all took an oath to do. But, legend said, the assassins were more cynical, and more cunning, than that. For they had a ruse in mind. One of them knew that a part of the village of Allborough had always been called Jerusalem, and so they came here. Until around 1690, the verger said, when it was stolen, a stone recorded their part in preserving the church. There was still today in the village, he averred, a house called Jerusalem Cottage: though it was quite modern, it was on the site of earlier buildings of that name.

If you look for them, you will find many legends of the Canterbury assassins, Reginald Fitzurse, Hugh de Moreville, William de Tracy and Richard le Breton. The four cursed knights seem to have roamed throughout England, and left some sort of holy legacy wherever they went, in a vain attempt to atone for their infamous deed.

Yet one thing you will not find: their graves. They have no known tombs. By some it is said they did in the end journey to the real Jerusalem, and finish their days in vigil, fasting and penance. They were buried, by this account, in some obscure monastery of the Crusader kingdom, or by the Templars in one of their citadels. Other traditions say that this was not so and only later piety, clerical inventions, credit them with such great expiation; in truth they never strayed far from England. No hallowed place would have their bones, nor did their families wish to have the taint of their relics upon them, so that when they each died, their bodies were taken to a remote place for secret, shameful burial. And several places now lay claim to that dishonour. But I think I would believe more in the truth of a place that does *not* claim them.

After all, perhaps Stevenson had only half of the matter. It is true there *are* places which stir the mind to think that a story must be told about them. But there are also, I believe, places which have their story stored already, and want to tell this to us, through whatever powers they can; through our legends and lore, through our rumours, and our rites. By its whispering fields and its murmuring waters, by the wailing of its winds and the groaning of its stones, by what it chants in darkness and the songs it sings in light, each place must reach out to us, to tell us, tell us what it holds.

# ROBERT SHEARMAN

## Granny's Grinning

ROBERT SHEARMAN IS AN award-winning writer for stage, television and radio. He was resident playwright at the Northcott Theatre in Exeter, and regular writer for Alan Ayckbourn at the Stephen Joseph Theatre in Scarborough. *Easy Laughter* won the *Sunday Times* Playwriting Award, *Fool to Yourself* the Sophie Winter Memorial Trust Award, and *Binary Dreamers* the Guinness Award for Ingenuity in association with the Royal National Theatre.

For BBC Radio he is a regular contributor to the afternoon play slot, produced by Martin Jarvis, and his series *The Chain Gang* has won two Sony Awards. However, he is probably best known for his work on TV's *Doctor Who*, bringing the Daleks back to the screen in the BAFTA-winning first series of the revival in an episode nominated for a Hugo Award.

Shearman's first collection of short fiction, *Tiny Deaths*, was published in 2007 and won the World Fantasy Award for Best Collection. It was also shortlisted for the Edge Hill Short Story Prize and nominated for the Frank O'Connor International Short Story Prize. One of the stories from the book was selected by the National Library Board of Singapore as part of the annual Read! Singapore campaign.

His second collection, *Love Songs for the Shy and Cynical*, won both the Shirley Jackson Award and the Edge Hill Short Story Reader's Prize, and is currently nominated for the British Fantasy Award.

A collection of his stage plays, *Caustic Comedies,* was recently published, and his third short-story collection, *Everyone's Just So So Special,* is forthcoming.

"I love Christmas," says Shearman. "Always have done, and always a bit too passionately. The intensity with which I loved Christmas was delightful when I was eight years old, slightly unusual by the time I was eighteen, and increasingly disturbing thereafter.

"Into my thirties I was still wanting my family to celebrate the big day with all the same rituals of yesteryear. Giving out presents in a certain order. Listening to the same gramophone record of carols that we had when I was a kid. (Knock your heart out, Andy Williams.) Pulling crackers at the very same break of courses in the very same turkey meal served at the very same time of day – all of us sitting around the table, wearing colourful paper hats as I read out the jokes and mottoes, and threatened everyone with Trivial Pursuit.

"I was the last one to grow up. It suddenly dawned on me one year, looking into the faces of my parents, and of my sister, that they were all older, and fatter, and less and less festive. And that they were trying so hard to keep me happy each Christmas, pretending they wanted all those presents I'd bought, all those sausage rolls and Quality Street chocs. That what I was trying to do, each December, was somehow reach back into the past and resurrect a time that was dead, that was long dead.

"I still love Christmas. But now I recognize – as I still make them perform party games, as I still make them open their gifts and smile and say thank you – that they're zombies now. All of them, zombies. I'll never get my childhood back again, not really, or the innocence of that family get-together. So I'll make do with the dead, and pretend.

"This is a story all about that."

SARAH DIDN'T WANT the zombie, and she didn't know anyone else who did. Apart from Graham, of course, but he was only four, he wanted *everything*; his Christmas list to Santa had run to so many sheets of paper that Daddy had said that Santa would need to take out a second mortgage on his igloo to get that lot, and everyone had laughed, even though Graham didn't know what an igloo was, and Sarah was pretty sure that Santa didn't live in an igloo anyway. Sarah had tried to point out to her little brother why the zombies were rubbish. "Look," she said, showing him the picture in the catalogue, "there's nothing to a zombie. They're just the same as us. Except the skin is a bit greener, maybe. And the eyes have whitened a bit." But Graham said that zombies were cool because zombies ate people when they were hungry, and when Sarah scoffed Graham burst into tears like always, and Mummy told Sarah to leave Graham alone, he was allowed to like zombies if he wanted to. Sarah thought that if it was all about eating people, she'd rather have a vampire: they sucked your blood for a start, which was so much neater somehow than just chomping down on someone's flesh – and Sharon Weekes said that she'd tried out a friend's vampire, and it was great, it wasn't just the obvious stuff like the teeth growing, but your lips swelled up, they got redder and richer and plump, and if you closed your eyes and rubbed them together it felt just the same as if a boy were kissing you. As if Sharon Weekes would know: Sharon Weekes was covered in spots, and no boy had ever kissed her, if you even so much as touched Sharon her face would explode – but you know, whatever, the rubbing lips thing still sounded great. Sarah hadn't written down her Christmas list like Graham had done, she'd simply told Santa that she'd like the vampire, please. Just the vampire, not the mummy, or the werewolf, or the demon. And definitely not the zombie.

Even before Granny had decided to stay, Sarah knew that this Christmas was going to be different. Mummy and Daddy said that if she and Graham wanted such expensive toys, then they'd have to put up with just one present this year. Once upon a time they'd have had tons of presents, and the carpet beneath the Christmas tree would have been strewn with brightly wrapped parcels of different shapes and sizes; it'd have taken hours to open the lot. But that was before Daddy left his job because he wanted to "go it alone", before the credit crunch, before those late-night arguments in the kitchen that Sarah wasn't supposed to hear. Graham groused a little about only getting one present, but Daddy said something about a second mortgage, and this time he didn't mention igloos, and this time nobody laughed. Usually the kitchen arguments were about money, but one night they were about Granny, and Sarah actually bothered to listen. "I thought she was staying with Sonia!" said Mummy. Sonia was Daddy's sister, and she had a sad smile, and ever since Uncle Jim had left her for someone less ugly she had lived alone. "She says she's fallen out with Sonia," said Daddy, "she's coming to spend Christmas with us instead." "Oh, for Christ's sake, *for Christ's sake*," said Mummy, and there was a banging of drawers. "Come on," said Daddy, "she's my Mummy, what was I supposed to say?" And then he added, "It might even work in our favour," and Mummy had said it better bloody well should, and then Sarah couldn't hear any more, perhaps because they'd shut the kitchen door, perhaps because Mummy was crying again.

Most Christmases they'd spend on their own, just Sarah with Mummy and Daddy and Graham. And on Boxing Day they'd get into the car and drive down the motorway to see Granny and Granddad. Granny looked a little like Daddy, but older and slightly more feminine. And Granddad smelled of cigarettes even though he'd given up before Sarah was born. Granny and Granddad would give out presents, and Sarah and Graham would say thank you no matter what they got. And they'd have another Christmas meal, just like the day before, except this time the turkey would be drier, and there'd be brussels sprouts rather than sausages. There wouldn't be a Boxing Day like that again. Partly because on the way home last year Mummy had said she could never spend another Christmas like that, and it had taken all of Daddy's best efforts to calm her down in the Little Chef – but mostly, Sarah supposed, because Granddad was dead. That was bound to make a difference. They'd all been to the funeral, Sarah hadn't even missed school because it was during the summer holidays, and Graham had made a nuisance of himself during the service asking if Granddad was a ghost now and going to come back from the grave. And during the whole thing Granny had sat there on the pew, all by herself, she didn't want anyone sitting next to her, not even Aunt Sonia, and Aunt Sonia was her favourite. And she'd cried, tears were streaming down her face, and Sarah had never seen Granny like that before, her face was always set fast like granite, and now with all the tears it had become soft and fat and pulpy and just a little frightening.

Four days before Christmas Daddy brought home a tree. "One of Santa's elves coming through!" he laughed, as he lugged it into the sitting room. It was enormous, and Graham and Sarah loved it, its upper branches scraped against the ceiling: they couldn't have put the fairy on the top like usual, she'd have broken her spine. Graham and Sarah began to cover it with balls and tinsel and electric lights, and Mummy said, "How much did that cost? I thought the point was to be a bit more economical this year," and Daddy said he knew what he was doing, he knew how to play the situation. They were going to give Granny the best Christmas she'd ever had! And he asked everyone to listen carefully, and then told them that this was a very important Christmas, it was the first Granny would have without Granddad. And she was likely to be a bit sad, and maybe a bit grumpy, but they'd all have to make allowances. It was to be *her* Christmas this year, whatever she wanted, it was all about making Granny happy, Granny would get the biggest slice of turkey, Granny got to choose which James Bond film to watch in the afternoon, the one on BBC1 or the one on ITV. Could he count on Graham and Sarah for that? Could he count on them to play along? And they both said yes, and Daddy was so pleased, they were so good he'd put their presents under the tree right away. He fetched two parcels, the same size, the same shape, flat boxes, one wrapped in blue paper and the other in pink. "Now, no peeking until the big day!" he laughed, but Graham couldn't help it, he kept turning his present over and over, and shaking it, and wondering what was inside, was it a demon, was it a zombie? And Sarah had to get on with decorating the tree all by herself, but that was all right, Graham hadn't been much use, she did a better job with him out of the way.

And that was just the start of the work! The next few days were frantic! Mummy insisted that Granny come into a house as spotless and tidy as could be, that this time she wouldn't be able to find a thing wrong with it. And she made Sarah and Graham clean even the rooms that Granny wouldn't be seeing in the first place! It was all for Granny, that's what they were told, all for Granny – and if Graham sulked about that (and he did a little), Daddy said that one day someone close to *him* would die, and then *he* could have a special Christmas where everyone would run around after *him*, and Graham cheered up at that. On Christmas Eve Daddy said he was very proud of his children, and that he had a treat for them both. Early the next morning he'd be picking Granny up from her home in the country – it was a four-and-a-half hour journey there and back, and that they'd been *so* good they were allowed to come along for the trip! Graham got very excited, and shouted a lot. And Mummy said that it was okay to take Graham, but she needed Sarah at home, there was still work for Sarah to do. And Sarah wasn't stupid, the idea of a long drive to Granny's didn't sound much like fun to her, but it had been offered as a treat, and it hurt her to be denied a treat. Daddy glared at Mummy, and Mummy glared right back, and for a thrilling moment Sarah thought they might have an argument – but they only *ever* did that in the kitchen, they still believed the kids didn't know – and then Daddy relaxed, and then laughed, and ruffled Graham's hair, and said it'd be a treat for the boys then, just the boys, and laughed once more. So that was all right.

First thing Christmas morning, still hours before sunrise, Daddy and Graham set off to fetch Granny. Graham was so sleepy he forgot to be excited. "Goodbye then!" said Daddy cheerily; "Goodbye," said Mummy, and then suddenly pulled him into a tight hug. "It'll all be all right," said Daddy. "Of course it will," said Mummy, "off you go!" She waved them off, and then turned to Sarah, who was waving along beside her. Mummy said, "We've only got a few hours to make everything perfect," and Sarah nodded, and went to the cupboard for the vacuum cleaner. "No, no," said Mummy, "to make *you* perfect. My perfect little girl." And Mummy took Sarah by the hand, and smiled at her kindly, and led her to her own bedroom. "We're going to make you such a pretty girl," said Mummy, "they'll all see how pretty you can be. You'll like that, won't you? You can wear your nice dress. You'd like your new dress. Won't you?" Sarah didn't like her new dress, it was hard to romp about playing a vampire in it, it was hard to play at *anything* in it, but Mummy was insistent. "And we'll give you some nice jewellery," she said. "This is a necklace of mine. It's pretty. It's gold. Do you like it? My Mummy gave it to me. Just as I'm now giving it to you. Do you remember my Mummy? Do you remember the Other Granny?" Sarah didn't, but said that she did, and Mummy smiled. "She had some earrings too, shall we try you out with those? Shall we see what that's like?" And the earrings were much heavier than the plain studs Sarah was used to, they stretched her lobes out like chewing gum, they seemed to Sarah to stretch out her entire face. "Isn't that pretty?" said Mummy, and when Sarah said they hurt a bit, Mummy said she'd get used to it. Then Mummy took Sarah by the chin, and gave her a dab of lipstick – and Sarah never wore make-up, not like the girls who sat on the back row of the school bus, not even like Sharon Weekes, Mummy had always said it made them look cheap. Sarah reminded her of this, and Mummy didn't reply, and so Sarah then asked if this was all for Granny, and Mummy said, "Yes, it's all for Granny," and then corrected herself, "it's for *all* of them, let's remind them what a pretty girl you are, what a pretty woman you could grow up to be. Always remember that you could have been a pretty woman." And then she wanted to give Sarah some nail varnish, nothing too much, nothing too red, just something clear and sparkling. But Sarah had had enough, she looked in the mirror and she didn't recognize the person looking back at her, she looked so much older, and greasy and plastic, she looked just like Mummy. And tears were in her eyes, and she looked behind her reflection at Mummy's reflection, and there were tears in Mummy's eyes too – and Mummy said she was sorry, and took off the earrings, and wiped away the lipstick with a tissue. "I'm sorry," she said again, and said that Sarah needn't dress up if she didn't want to, it was her Christmas too, not just Granny's. And Sarah felt bad, and although she didn't much like the necklace she asked if she could keep it on, she lied and said it made her look pretty – and Mummy beamed a smile so wide, and gave her a hug, and said of course she could wear the necklace, anything for her darling, anything she wanted.

The first thing Granny said was, "I haven't brought you any presents, so don't expect any." "Come on in," said Daddy, laughing, "and make yourself at home!", and Granny sniffed as if she found that prospect particularly unappealing. "Hello, Mrs

Forbes," said Mummy. "Hello, Granny," said Sarah, and she felt the most extraordinary urge to curtsey. Graham trailed behind, unusually quiet, obviously quelled by a greater force than his own. "Can I get you some tea, Mrs Forbes?" said Mummy. "We've got you all sorts, Earl Grey, Lapsang Souchong, Ceylon ..." "I'd like some tea, not an interrogation," said Granny. She went into the lounge, and when she sat down in Daddy's armchair she sent all the scatter cushions tumbling, she didn't notice how carefully they'd been arranged and plumped. "Do you like the tree, Mummy?" Daddy asked, and Granny studied it briefly, and said it was too big, and she hoped he'd bought it on discount. Daddy started to say something about how the tree was just to keep the children happy, as if it were really their fault, but then Mummy arrived with the tea; Granny took her cup, sipped at it, and winced. "Would you like your presents, Mummy? We've got you presents." And at the mention of presents, Graham perked up: "Presents!" he said, "presents!" "Not your presents yet, old chap," laughed Daddy amiably, "Granny first, remember?" And Granny sighed and said she had no interest in presents, she could see nothing to celebrate – but she didn't want to spoil anyone else's fun, obviously, and so if they had presents to give her now would be as good a time to put up with them as any. Daddy had bought a few gifts, and labelled a couple from Sarah and Graham. It turned out that they'd bought Granny some perfume, "Your favourite, isn't it?" asked Daddy, "and with their very own pocket money too!" "What use have I got with perfume now that Arthur's dead?" said Granny curtly. And tilted her face forwards so that Sarah and Graham could kiss it, by way of a thank you.

Graham was delighted with his werewolf suit. "Werewolf!" he shouted, and waving the box above his head tore around the sitting room in excitement. "And if you settle down, old chap," laughed Daddy, "you can try it on for size!" They took the cellophane off the box, removed the lid, and took out the instructions for use. The recommended age was ten and above, but as Daddy said, it was just a recommendation, and besides, there were plenty of adults there to supervise. There was a furry werewolf mask, furry werewolf slippers, and an entire furry werewolf body suit. Granny looked disapproving. "In my day, little boys didn't want to be werewolves," she said. "They wanted to be soldiers and train drivers." Graham put the mask over his face, and almost immediately they could all see how the fur seemed to grow in response – not only outwards, what would be the fun in that? – but inwards too, each tiny hair follicle burying itself deep within Graham's face, so you could really believe that all this fur had naturally come out of a little boy. With a crack the jaw elongated too, into something like a snout – it wasn't a full wolf's snout, of course not, this was only a toy, and you could see that the red raw gums inside that slavering mouth were a bit too rubbery to be real, but it was still effective enough for Granny to be impressed. "Goodness," she said. But that was nothing. When Daddy fastened the buckle around the suit, straight away Graham's entire body contorted in a manner that could only be described as feral. The spine snapped and popped as Graham grew bigger, and then it twisted and curved over, as if in protest that a creature on four legs should be supporting itself on two – the now-warped spine bulged angrily under the fur. Graham gave a yelp. "Doesn't that hurt?" said Mummy, and Daddy said no, these toys were all the rage, all the kids loved them. Graham tried out his new body. He threw himself around the room, snarling in almost pantomime fashion; he got so carried away whipping his tail about he nearly knocked over the coffee table – and it didn't matter, everyone was laughing at the fun, even Sarah, even Granny. "He's a proper little beast, isn't he!" Granny said. "And you see, it's also educational," Daddy leapt in, "because Graham will learn so much more about animals this way, I bet this sends him straight to the library." Mummy said, "I wonder if he'll howl at the moon!" and Daddy said, "Well, of course he'll howl at the moon," and Granny said, "All wolves howl at the moon, even I know that," and Mummy looked crestfallen. "Silly Mummy," growled Graham.

From the first rip of the pink wrapping paper Sarah could see that she hadn't been given a vampire suit. But she hoped it wasn't a zombie, even when she could see the sickly green of the mask, the bloated liver spots, the word ZOMBIE! far too proudly emblazoned upon the box. She thought it must be a mistake. And was about to say something, but when she looked up at her parents she saw they were beaming at her, encouraging, urging her on, urging her to open the lid, urging her to become one of the walking dead. So she smiled back, and she remembered not to make a fuss, that it was Granny's day – and hoped they'd kept the receipt so she could swap it for a vampire later. Daddy asked if he could give her a hand, and Sarah said she could manage, but he was helping her already, he'd already got out the zombie mask, he was already enveloping her whole face within it. He helped her with the zombie slippers, thick slabs of feet with overgrown toenails and peeling skin. He helped her with the suit, snapped the buckle. Sarah felt cold all around her, as if she'd just been dipped into a swimming pool – but it was dry inside this pool, as dry as dust, and the cold dry dust was inside her. And the surprise of it made her want to retch, but she caught herself, she swallowed it down, though there was no saliva in that swallow. Her face slumped, and bulged out a bit, like a huge spot just ready to be burst – and she felt heavier, like a sack, sodden – but sodden with what, there was no water, was there, no wetness at all, so what could she be sodden with? "Turn around!" said Daddy, and laughed, and she heard him with dead ears, and so she turned around, she lurched, the feet wouldn't let her walk properly, the body felt weighed down in all the wrong areas. Daddy laughed again, they all laughed at that, and Sarah tried to laugh too. She stuck out her arms in comic zombie fashion. "Grr," she said. Daddy's face was shining, Mummy looked just a little afraid. Granny was staring, she couldn't take her eyes off her. "Incredible," she breathed. And then she smiled, no, it wasn't a smile, she *grinned*. "Incredible." Graham had got bored watching, and had gone back to doing whatever it was that werewolves do around Christmas trees.

"And after all that excitement, roast turkey, with all the trimmings!" said Mummy. Sarah's stomach growled, though she hadn't known she was hungry. "Come on, children, toys away." "I think Sarah should wear her suit to dinner," said Granny. "I agree," said Daddy, "she's only just put it on." "All right," said Mummy. "Have it your own way. But not you, Graham. I don't want a werewolf at the dining table. I want my little boy." "That's not fair!" screamed Graham. "But werewolves don't have good table manners, darling," said Mummy. "You'll get turkey everywhere." So Graham began to cry, and it came out as a particularly plaintive howl, and he wouldn't take his werewolf off, he *wouldn't*, he wanted to live in his werewolf forever, and Mummy gave him a slap, just a little one, and it only made him howl all the more. "For God's sake, does it matter?" said Daddy, "let him be a werewolf if he wants to." "Fine," said Mummy, "they can be monsters then, let's *all* be monsters!" And then she smiled to show everyone she was happy really, she only sounded angry, really she was happy. Mummy scraped Graham's Christmas dinner into a bowl, and set it on to the floor. "Try and be careful, darling," she said, "remember how hard we worked to get this carpet clean? You'll sit at the table, won't you, Sarah? I don't know much about zombies, do zombies eat at the table?" "Sarah's sitting next to me," said Granny, and she grinned again, and her whole face lit up, she really had quite a nice face after all. And everyone cheered up at that, and it was a happy dinner, even though Granny didn't think the turkey was the best cut, and that the vegetables had been overcooked. Sarah coated her turkey with gravy, and with cranberry sauce, she even crushed then smeared peas into it just to give the meat a bit more juice – it was light and buttery, she knew, it looked so good on the fork, but no sooner had it passed her lips than the food seemed stale and ashen. "Would you pull my cracker, Sarah?" asked Granny brightly, and Sarah didn't want to, it was hard enough to grip the cutlery with those flaking hands. "Come on, Sarah," laughed Daddy, and so Sarah put down her knife and fork, and fumbled for the end of Granny's cracker, and hoped that when she pulled nothing terrible would happen – she'd got it into her head that her arm was hanging by a thread, just one firm yank and it'd come off. But it didn't – *bang!* went the cracker, Granny had won, she liked that, and she read out the joke, and everyone said they found it funny, and she even put on her paper hat. "I feel like the belle of the ball!" she said. "Dear me, I *am* enjoying myself!"

After dinner Granny and Sarah settled down on the sofa to watch the Bond movie. Mummy said she'd do the washing up, and as she needed to clean the carpet too, she might be quite a while. And Daddy volunteered to help her, he said he'd seen this Bond already. Graham wanted to pee, so they'd let him out into the garden. So it was just Granny and Sarah sitting there, just the two of them, together. "I miss Arthur," Granny said during the title sequence. "Sonia tells me I need to get over it, but what does Sonia know about love?" Sarah had nothing to say to that. Sitting on the sofa was hard for her, she was top heavy and lolled to one side. She found though that she was able to reach for the buckle on her suit. She played with it, but her fingers were too thick, she couldn't get purchase. The first time Bond snogged a woman Granny reached for Sarah's hand. Sarah couldn't be sure whether it was Granny's hand or her own that felt so leathery. "Do you know how I met Arthur?" asked Granny. Sitting in her slumped position, Sarah could feel something metal jab into her, and realized it must be the necklace that Mummy had given her. It was buried somewhere underneath all this dead male flesh. "Arthur was already married. Did you know that? Does it shock you? But I just looked at him, and said to myself, I'm having that." And there was a funny smell too, thought Sarah, and she supposed that probably *was* her. James Bond got himself into some scrapes, and then got out of them again using quips and extreme violence. Granny hadn't let go of Sarah's hand. "You know what love is? It's being prepared to let go of who you are. To change yourself entirely. Just for someone else's pleasure." The necklace was really rather sharp, but Sarah didn't mind, it felt *real*, and she tried to shift her body so it would cut into her all the more. Perhaps it would cut through the layers of skin on top of it, perhaps it would come poking out, and show that Sarah was hiding underneath! "Before I met him, Arthur was a husband. And a father. For me, he became a nothing. A nothing." With her free hand Sarah tried at the buckle again, this time there was a panic to it, she dug in her nails but only succeeded in tearing a couple off altogether. And she knew what that smell was, Sarah had thought it had been rotting, but it wasn't, it was old cigarette smoke. Daddy came in from the kitchen. "You two lovebirds getting along?" he said. And maybe even winked. James Bond made a joke about re-entry, and at that Granny gripped Sarah's hand so tightly that she thought it'd leave an imprint for sure. "I usually get what I want," Granny breathed. Sarah stole a look out of the window. In the frosted garden Graham had clubbed down a bird, and was now playing with its body. He'd throw it up into the air and catch it between his teeth. But he looked undecided too, as if he were wondering whether eating it might be taking things too far.

Graham had tired of the werewolf suit before his bedtime. He'd undone the belt all by himself, and left the suit in a pile on the floor. "I want a vampire!" he said. "Or a zombie!" Mummy and Daddy told him that maybe he could have another monster next Christmas, or on his birthday maybe. That wasn't good enough, and it wasn't until they suggested there might be discounted monsters in the January sales that he cheered up. He could be patient, he was a big boy. After he'd gone to bed, Granny said she wanted to turn in as well – it had been such a long day. "And thank you," she said, and looked at Sarah. "It's remarkable." Daddy said that she'd now understand why he'd asked for all those photographs; to get the resemblance just right there had been lots of special modifications, it hadn't been cheap, but he hoped it was a nice present? "The best I've ever had," said Granny. "And here's a little something for both of you." And she took out a cheque, scribbled a few zeroes on to it, and handed it over. She hoped this might see them through the recession. "And merry Christmas!" she said gaily.

Granny stripped naked, and got into her nightie – but not so fast that Sarah wasn't able to take a good look at the full reality of her. She didn't think Granny's skin was very much different to the one she was wearing, the same lumps and bumps and peculiar crevasses, the same scratch marks and mottled specks. Hers was just slightly fresher. And as if Granny could read Sarah's mind, she told her to be a good boy and sit at the dressing table. "Just a little touch up," she said. "Nothing effeminate about it. Just to make you a little more you." She smeared a little rouge on to the cheeks, a dash of lipstick, mascara. "Can't do much with the eyeballs," Granny mused, "but I'll never know in the dark." And the preparations weren't just for Sarah. Granny sprayed behind both her ears from her new perfume bottle. "Just for you, darling," she said. "Your beautiful little gift." Sarah gestured towards the door, and Granny looked puzzled, then brightened. "Yes, you go and take a tinkle. I'll be waiting, my sweet." But Sarah had nothing to tinkle, had she, didn't Granny realize there was no liquid inside her, didn't she realize she was composed of dust? Sarah lurched past the toilet, and downstairs to the sitting room where her parents were watching the repeat of the Queen's speech. They started when she came in. Both looked a little guilty. Sarah tried to find the words she wanted, and then how to say them at all, her tongue lay cold in her mouth. "Why me?" she managed finally.

Daddy said, "I loved him. He was a good man, he was a kind man." Mummy looked away altogether. Daddy went on, "You do see why it couldn't have been Graham, don't you? Why it had to be you?" And had Sarah been a werewolf like her brother, she might at that moment have torn out their throats, or clubbed them down with her paws. But she was a dead man, and a dead man who'd been good and kind. So she nodded briefly, then shuffled her way slowly back upstairs.

"Hold me," said Granny. Sarah didn't know how to, didn't know where to put her arms or her legs. She tried her best, but it was all such a tangle. Granny and Sarah lay side by side for a long time in the dark. Sarah tried to feel the necklace under her skin, but she couldn't, it had gone. That little symbol of whatever femininity she'd had was gone. She wondered if Granny was asleep. But then Granny said, "If only it were real. But it's not real. You're not real." She stroked Sarah's face. "Oh, my love," she whispered. "Oh, my poor dead love."

And something between Sarah's legs twitched. Something that had long rotted came to life, and slowly, weakly, struggled to attention. "You're not real", Granny was still saying, and now she was crying, and Sarah thought of how Granny had looked that day at the funeral, her face all soggy and out of shape, and she felt a stab of pity for her – and that was *it*, the pity was the jolt it needed, there was something liquid in this body after all. "You're not real," Granny said. "I am real," he said, and he lent across, and kissed her on the lips. And the lips beneath his weren't dry, they were plump, they were moist, and now he was chewing at her face, and she was chewing right back, like they wanted to eat each other, like they were so hungry they could just eat each other alive. Sharon Weekes was wrong, it was a stray thought that flashed through his mind, Sharon Weekes didn't know the half of it. This is what it's like, this is like kissing, this is like kissing a boy.

# ROSALIE PARKER

## In the Garden

ROSALIE PARKER GREW UP on a farm in Buckinghamshire and has lived subsequently in Stockholm, Oxford, Dorset, Somerset, Sheffield, Sussex and North Yorkshire. She took degrees in English Literature and History, and a Masters in Archaeology, working as an archaeologist before returning to her first love of books.

She now co-runs the independent publishing house, Tartarus Press (winner of three World Fantasy Awards), and lives in the Yorkshire Dales with her partner, the writer and publisher R.B. Russell, and their son Tim. Her interests include writing articles for *The Book and Magazine Collector*, gardening, hill-walking and antiques.

Parker's short fiction has appeared in *The Black Veil and Other Tales of Supernatural Sleuths*, *The Fifth Black Book of Horror* and *Supernatural Tales* #15, and her first collection of stories, *The Old Knowledge*, is to be published by Swan River Press.

"'In the Garden' was written after I challenged myself to write a horror story about gardening," explains the author. "It emerged more quickly and easily than anything I've ever written. I think of it more as a prose poem than a story."

IT REALLY IS a lovely day.

I'm not used to sitting in the garden, basking in the pleasant weather and enjoying the fruits of my labour. I spend most of my time here weeding and pruning, so I'm grateful for the opportunity to laze around for a change, watching the flower heads bob gently in the soft breeze, listening to the drowsy hum of the bees as they gorge on the comfrey blossoms.

You'll have noticed that where we're sitting, beneath the high wall, is concealed from view. None of the surrounding houses overlooks us. We can lounge in perfect peace while we chat – and I'm in a chatty mood today. An afternoon of rest after all my work. Yesterday's showers mean that even the vegetable plot doesn't need watering.

It never ceases to amaze me how the garden, cold and as good as dead just a few months ago, has burgeoned into lush green life. Is it only two years since I hacked back the old lilac tree behind you there – and look at it now! Tall enough to peep over the wall, its vigour restored by the judicious elimination of unproductive wood.

You're not a gardener, are you? So perhaps you don't know that once a garden is established, much of good gardening is about removal rather than planting, honing what you have to produce a pleasing effect, sacrificing the particular for the good of the whole. Gardening is a creative pastime, but the result is always a work in progress; unlike a painting or a piece of music a garden is never fixed in time.

I couldn't see the attraction when I was a child. My mother would sometimes ask me to help weed our extensive vegetable beds, and it seemed a thankless task to me. I didn't understand or appreciate the work that went into it, just the end result, which I viewed as entirely natural and given. Perhaps that's how you see it now? As an adult I have learned to appreciate the satisfaction of managing nature, but as a child the garden was simply my world, the arena of my imagination, the setting for my elaborate games.

In those games I would order existence to suit myself. One day I'd be head of an animal capture company, exploring the rainforest in search of wildlife to sell to zoos, the next, the tamer of a wild bronco stallion, galloping on my hobby horse round and round the corral until the animal became tired and more responsive to my commands. My favourite game involved my brother as my trusted chimpanzee servant as I ruled, queen-like, over a large household. I expect many children have played similar games in gardens over the centuries, rehearsing unrealistic expectations of their adult lives. The green shoots of our imagination are soon blighted by the late frosts of adolescence.

Before we moved here I'd never owned a garden larger than a postage stamp and at first I was daunted by it. I tinkered around the edges, snipping a twig here, pulling a weed there. But gradually I've become more confident, until now, I feel I have ordered it how I want it, within the limits of the time available and the amount of money I've had to spend. I think you'll agree that it pleases the eye – is well designed, both ornamental and practical. The oriental poppies are over now and I have tidied them away but they are one of my additions, along with the ferns and hostas in the shade of the southern wall. I removed the rowan tree that overshadowed the goldfish pond and dug the vegetable beds over by the pear tree. The chairs we are sitting on I found in an architectural salvage yard. Despite the occasional attack of aphids and the despoilations of the wind that blows down this valley, I have charmed – and coerced – nature into doing my bidding.

Stephan doesn't spend much time working in the garden; he regards it as my domain, which suits me. As you know, he prefers to tinker around with car engines. Each to their own. In the summer he comes out here to eat his meals in the sun, and he feeds the goldfish every day. I think he appreciates the garden, although he's been so busy recently he's not spent much time at home. We have achieved a hard-won symbiosis, he and I, which is as satisfying to me as it is, I have always thought, to him. We rub along well together, which is more than you can say for most couples. You're probably too young to understand.

I wouldn't want you to think that I am totally obsessed by my garden. I do have other interests: reading, for one, and my voluntary work. But gardening is the way I unwind; it soothes away the cares of the day, and keeps me fit. I've never been one for the gym – by the look of you I expect you go regularly. When you get to my age you have to allow for a bit of running to seed, middle-aged spread – as you know, we don't have any children to chase around after – although I must say that Stephan somehow manages to keep himself in trim.

We did try to have children but it wasn't to be. I'm not one for test tubes and hormones and what have you. I think it's best to accept the hand you're dealt on that score. I thought about adoption or fostering, but Stephan wasn't keen. He said, "I don't want to look after someone else's kids", which is, I suppose, an entirely natural response. This would've been a good garden for children to play in, though, wouldn't it? With all its nooks and crannies. There are plenty of places to hide and you could play cricket on the lawn.

I love columbines – don't you? So willowy and delicate-looking. And so easy to grow; they sow themselves everywhere. In fact I spend quite a lot of time digging up the seedlings so that they don't completely take over. For such a fragile-looking plant it's very invasive.

Some plants are like that; you have to take them in hand. Others – that delphinium there, for instance – need nurturing and protecting from slugs and the wind otherwise they'd never flower at all. And the lilies, so showy and fragrant, so worth the wait! I have even had some success with roses, although black-spot is a perennial problem. Each flower in the garden has its season – its time and its place – and the picture changes from week to week, day to day even, so you never get bored. Well I don't, anyway. I feel I am here to nurture each plant and encourage it to perform to the best of its ability.

The blackbird is singing again I hear – such a chirpy bird and so unafraid. Of course they're a devil when it comes to fruit! I protect the currant bushes and the strawberries with netting, but they always manage to get in somehow. I have come to accept a certain amount of depredation, but how far should you allow it to go before taking more stringent measures? And just how rigorous should those measures be? Most people would think nothing of spraying aphids with insecticide or poisoning slugs and snails, even trapping a mouse. Is it the size of the predator that determines our response? To my way of thinking you should not be squeamish when protecting your own.

The shotgun belongs to my uncle: I've borrowed it to shoot the rabbits that have been eating my vegetables. Not strictly legal, I know – I don't have a firearms' licence – but it's the only way I can think of to get rid of them. My neighbours have become used to the occasional shot and they're sympathetic because the rabbits are menacing their gardens too.

I'm always on the lookout for new ways to adorn the garden – I did well at the salvage yard, not only finding these chairs and the table, but also the wrought-iron bench through the archway and the stone mermaid fountain in the fishpond. I thought as soon as I saw you that you would be an adornment to any setting, so slim and young and pretty – I could understand what Stephan sees in you – but you're a bit of a disappointment close up.

In fact you don't look too good at all now – bloated and blue around the edges, with the flies crawling into your eyes.

Like the honey fungus in my soil, the blight in my crop, I have dug you out, and now I must burn you. The neighbours are used to my bonfires and will think nothing of it. Stephan is coming home from his work trip this evening and unless I get on with it, you will still be sitting here, corrupting my garden. I thought that I had found the way to end the situation but after our chat I can see that you're going to be another work in progress. If I am not careful and clever about disposing of you, you could still spoil my design. I have to maintain constant vigilance to keep everything in the garden rosy.

# STEPHEN VOLK

## After the Ape

STEPHEN VOLK IS THE creator/writer of ITV's award-winning paranormal drama series *Afterlife* and the notorious, some say legendary, BBC-TV "Hallowe'en hoax" *Ghostwatch*.

His other credits as screenwriter include *Gothic,* directed by Ken Russell, *The Guardian,* directed by William Friedkin, and *Octane.* He also won a BAFTA Award for *The Deadness of Dad,* an acclaimed short film starring Rhys Ifans. His latest feature script, *The Awakening,* is now in production starring Rebecca Hall, Dominic West and Imelda Staunton.

Volk's first short-story collection, *Dark Corners,* featured the story "31/10", which was nominated for both a British Fantasy Award and a Bram Stoker Award, and was reprinted in *The Year's Best Fantasy and Horror: Twentieth Annual Collection.* More recently, he has been nominated for a Shirley Jackson Award for his novella *Vardøger.* He is also a regular columnist for the British horror and dark fantasy magazine *Black Static.*

"The notion of 'what happened next?' following a classic monster movie – probably the biggest and best – was an intriguing one to me," says the author, "and not only the initial considerations of public health issues.

"Somehow kicking this off and shadowing its development was reading somewhere that *King Kong* was Hitler's favourite film. Why?

"Anyway the ape is not the monster in this tale. Far from it."

IT WAS DIFFICULT for her to function with any kind of normality. Not when her lover was lying below, crisscrossed by ropes like Gulliver, people hacking out the insides of his body like whalers from Nantucket.

She'd taken to having her first cigarette while still horizontal, sucking in her already sunken cheeks, drifting into the penumbra of being fully awake. The morning newspaper was always lying outside the door but she didn't read it any more. Always full of stuff she didn't want to hear. Stuff that made her feel angry and sickened. Him. Herself. The lies. The legend. The jungle. What did they know about the jungle? They hadn't been there. None of them had.

In time the salty soreness of her tears compelled her to sit up in the cold of the hotel room, icy shoulders trembling, tiny arms frozen and white.

Doll eyes stared from the mirror. She hadn't set foot outside for how many days now? How many weeks?

She didn't care: the room was safe. She was untouchable there, alone with her menagerie of thoughts and memories. Sometimes she wondered if she left or was made to leave those thoughts and memories might remain, like ghosts, her misbegotten soul haunting the building while her physical body was wheeled away on a gurney, nothing left of her but a soft-focus studio publicity shot and an obit in *Variety*. Somehow she knew how the headline would go.

What did they know? *They knew shit.*

That was the Bowery girl talking. That's what she was, after all, down to her raggedy-ass bones. And none of the glamour and pearls and platinum curls of Hollywood could cover that up for her in the end. *Once a bum, always a bum.*

She unscrewed the cap from the bourbon.

*(Poppa's favourite)*

Prohibition. Joke. There were ways. The tumbler told her it hated to be half full.

The numb, plummeting wash of it brought up an acid reflux that hauled her monstrous hangover with it, dispelling any faint illusion her head was clear. Still, she was grateful for a taste of oblivion. Oblivion was her prime concern, of late. Any other concern – eating, sleeping, dressing – fell poor second. What could you do, when the hangover felt like it would kill you? Keep drinking. Truth is, she barely even tasted it any more.

On her wrist a gift from a producer who had a taste in watching instead of doing said eleven forty-five. Hell. Not that she'd missed anything – just that so much of the goddamn day loomed ahead of her. These days she despised being awake, because being awake meant thinking, and thinking meant remembering.

Twig fingers tweaked at the drapes. She knew sunlight was going to be painful on skeleton skin, but managed to let a gap of a few inches illuminate the scrunched-up sheets, the full ash trays, the dirty glasses, the scattered shoes, the half-hung clothes, the latest Paris fashion fur coat strewn on the floor – where it would lie forever if she had her way.

*Fur.*

Those insensitive bastards at the studio.

*Fur.*

Last time she listened to the radio it was saying they were giving tours of him now. Taking folks on tours *inside* him, now. She pictured his chest cavity lit by strings of lamps like Jewel Cave in Custer, South Dakota she remembered visiting as a frightened, inexpressive, barefoot child. She knew they'd take out *her* insides too, if they could. The birds of prey of the *Herald* and *Times*, the graveyard worms and rats in raincoats with Underwoods where their morals should be.

The Story: it was all about getting the Story.

And the Story was her.

And sometimes in the darkness of night and nicotine with the shakes and spiders (Giant! Huge!) it was oh so appealing sometimes to say "Here I am you sons of bitches, do with me what you will – here I am, chained, naked, shrieking – and then it'll be over and I'll have peace."

But this wasn't just about her. It was about the special thing that she and her lover had found and lost in a heartbeat, a great heartbeat like a jungle drum, and it was *that* they wanted to stamp all over with their dirty thoughts and bad jokes and fabrications, and she wouldn't let them. It was too precious. Too rare. Too wonderful. Too strange. Too romantic. Too scary. She wouldn't let them abuse it and she wouldn't let them have it to do with as they pleased. It belonged to *her*. It was all she had left.

That and the feeling as she slumbered that once again her lover's giant fingers were closing warmly around her body and she was safe again. It was the one thing, the giant thing they could never, ever destroy. Not with airplanes. Not with anything.

She heard the beeping of taxi cabs from the street far below. The traffic was moving. The traffic always moved.

She wanted to open the window but she daren't. The streets of Manhattan still ran sweet with blood. The oceanic stench of decay – a graveyard up-ended, said the radio – hung heavy in the air, and even as the lumberjacks and slaughter-men changed shifts day in, day out, nothing could be done to diminish it. It was a brave tourist indeed among the throng of sightseers from every state in the Union who wouldn't hold their nose or cover their lower face with a handkerchief when viewing the colossal remains. This Wonder of the World. This hairy Behemoth. This Goliath slain by David.

Goose bumps rose on her arms.

She picked up her dressing gown embossed with the hotel's elaborate crest and wrapped it around her shoulders. It gave her the warmth of a surrogate embrace. The bourbon – telling her, don't be shy – gave her another.

It didn't improve on the first. Instead made her feel sour and queasy, mingling with the disquiet she felt in her nerves and, far from acting as an anaesthetic as she prayed, made her even more anxious with the hermetic silence of the room.

Not suddenly, but with conviction, she realized the very real possibility that she'd go mad here, and be carted to the nut hatch, or end up howling at the wallpaper, or running out into Fifth Avenue, half-naked like Mrs Partigan, who lost her brain and took to going shopping on icy winter nights wearing nothing but her undies, and would be chauffeured home by Rolly Absolom, the local deputy, with admirably sanguine regularity.

That was in Marshall, Nebraska, where she grew up, cold and unhappy, raised under the jurisdiction of her Aunt Jelly after Ma's last illness. She wished she'd seen her mother before she died – but Brice was on the scene by then and Brice and her didn't get along, which was like saying the War in Europe was a difference of opinion. So doll-face, porcelain and pure, skipped off school (never did like it, got beat a lot) and hopped on a cattle train to New York like a hobo, but her Ma was already in the ground and Brice was damned if he'd pay the return fare, so she earned that singing on street corners and in various other manners, with a pair of goodish legs and a singing voice that got her by.

It was a tough climb and mostly she counted herself lucky if she made it to the soup kitchen every day. Hoofer. Chorus girl. Arm candy for a rich guy. Good-time Annie for the distracted and misunderstood. Wasn't too choosy. Couldn't afford to be. When you've slept on a doorstep in the pouring rain, you didn't ask to see a resumé. If the collar was clean, or if there *was* a collar, the feller was plenty good enough for you. For a night, anyhow: especially if he was paying for a bed. They started saying she should be in movies, and she heard that so many times it turned out to be true. She *was* good at acting. Every day of her goddamn life.

Tired of her own prehistory, she sat on the side of the bed and rang down for room service. The hotel operator's voice was chirpy and infantile, making her wonder if the girl was retarded: nobody could be *that* happy – unless maybe she was on the bourbon too.

She had a difficult time with the words so she stayed monosyllabic: ham, bread, eggs. The girl repeated back her order, making it sound much more coherent and said it would be twenty, twenty-five minutes.

"Is there anything else I can help you with, ma'am?"

The actress spooled through a list of requests in her mind: *a life, happiness* . . . but said: "No. Just that."

Hung up, thinking, did she know? Of course she *knew*. They all did. Probably snickering up her sleeve right now. Calling her boyfriend, eager with the gossip. *Guess who we've got staying? No! Guess!*

The idea of food made her think of the slabs of meat being shorn off her lover's corpse. The two-man saws at work under the same hefty spotlights the studio wheeled out for the big night at that Broadway theatre when he was shown to the public for the very first time. Before all hell broke loose. She thought of the massive steaks being packed in ice trucks and sent to the deprived, the poor, the needy. There were placards out there saying it was near as God to cannibalism, but the Hungry didn't care. The Homeless didn't debate. The Jobless didn't grumble. Her lover had died and his flesh was being used to feed the poor. There was something desperately Christian in that, but wholly blasphemous at the same time.

When it came, the knuckle-rap on the door was brisk, snapping her blank stare.

Another glass since the phone call (pointless but effortless), she tucked her breasts inside her robe and tightened the belt with a tug. By the time she opened the door her fringe had drooped over one eye, her belt had loosened and her left tit was about to poke out and say Howdy if she hadn't rescued it.

Focusing before her stood a kid with short blond hair, his ears razored islands on the side of his head, standing to attention like a marine. He wore the white jacket with the horizontal epaulettes that was the hotel staff uniform, and first impression was the whole guy seemed as starched as it was. Black slacks straight as ramrods. Black polished shoes at six thirty. The whole package making her feel even more sluttish and trashy.

"Come in."

The clockwork soldier entered with the tray. "Where would you like, please?"

She waved indiscriminately. "Anywhere."

"Very good, ma'am." Clipped. She tried to pinpoint his accent. European for sure. Hungarian? She should be able to tell. Plenty of those at the studios. Fleeing the old country. Fleeing their wives, too, mostly. Now he was running out of ideas, she could tell.

"Anywhere you can find a space."

He balanced it on a footstool at the bottom of the bed, uncertainly, and wiped his hands on his behind as he backed away.

She located her purse and spilled out some coins, picked up a few with her thumb and forefinger and dangled them towards him until he held out his palm. He nodded his thanks for the tip and, swear to God, a click of the heels went with it. In the mirror she'd seen his eyes on the bottle of ruin.

As his hand touched the door handle she said: "Can I interest you in an illicit beverage by any chance?"

The kid turned back, painfully polite and not a little nervous. "Thank you, but I do not drink." Eyes anywhere but on her.

"You mean you don't, or you won't?"

His cheeks flushed a little red, which she thought was sweet, and a curse. A display of his un-worldliness which must be a burden to carry into adulthood, poor sap. A kind of affliction.

"Come on. Live a little. You're a long time dead. You don't get any prize in the hereafter for being stone cold sober. Not according to the churches I go to."

"I'm sorry. I should explain. The hotel, yes? I will be in a lot of trouble. In USA this is against the law."

"No kidding? What law? The law of the jungle?"

"I'm sorry. These are the rules."

"Oh, get the lead pipe out of your ass and enjoy yourself, kid. What's the worst that can happen? Nobody'll *know*. I won't *tell*. Promise." She put on a Shirley Temple voice: "*Cwoss my heart and hope to die.*" She genuflected and he noticed her fingernails made little white lines in her skin as they brushed it just above the bra-line of her nightgown. Her skin seemed soft and still had the sheen of sleep. He looked away.

Turning from him she filled her glass, then turned back to him and drank from it as if demonstrating the procedure.

He looked at the coins in his hand and put them deep in the pocket of his slacks and didn't leave. She thought he was holding his breath, and maybe he was.

She sat on the unmade bed and crossed her legs, positioning the glass on her knee. The hem of her nightdress rode up her bare, shaved calf.

"You're German, aren't you?"

He made an apologetic face. "My English is not so good."

"Ditto." She smiled to put him at his ease. "You're doing fine." She wanted him to smile back and he did. "Where you from?"

"Bavaria. Munchen. Munich." He pronounced it moon-itch, like something you'd scratch. "In the south. Close to the mountains."

"Yeah. We got those too. What's your name?"

"Peter."

"Peter," she repeated. "Hi, Peter."

Aged about eighteen, she guessed, he had a good ten, twelve years on her. She liked that. She liked the young. There was something optimistic about them. They didn't know what was to come.

"I—I better go."

"No. Stay," she said. "Talk to me."

He laughed uneasily. "You are a very nice lady, but I don't want to lose my job."

"You won't lose your job. I'm a guest. You're attending to the requirements of a guest. You won't lose your job. Sit down. Relax. Oh please fucking relax, Peter."

Her language shocked him. That wasn't the way women spoke. Not what he was used to. It was another thing that surprised him about America. It made him feel a little sickened and a little excited at the same time.

"Okay. I sit."

He could see what was attractive about her. Even now, here, in this state, like some bedraggled bird with a broken wing she had some quality. Downstairs he had wondered if he would be able to tell that by meeting her, and he *could*, in an *instant*. It was true what they said, when they called them stars because they *shone*.

"What do you want to talk about?"

"Oh, surprise me." The arm that propped her up slid down the bed. "I haven't had human contact in seven days. I'm adrift. I'm shipwrecked. Do you know what *shipwrecked* means?"

"Of course. On an island. In stories."

She rested the glass on her forehead. "Not just in stories, baby."

Baby was an American expression. He told himself she didn't mean anything by it. It was a term made by a boyfriend to a girlfriend in this country. It was strange, but it was okay.

"Have you ever been to an island?" she asked.

"America is an island," he said. "A big one, but an island."

"That's not what I mean." She flicked ash on to the carpet. "I mean trees with coconuts on. Big green leaves as big as this carpet. Beaches where no white man has ever trod. You get the idea? Tribes with plumes in their hair and bones through their noses who live in fear of their god. Who sacrifice humans to him with the beating of dinosaur-skin drums." She sipped her poison, her eyes not leaving him the whole time. "That kind of island."

The kid didn't know how to answer. Instead he looked around the room – away from her – as if taking it in for the first time, or pretending to.

"You like this hotel?"

"Oh, it's peachy."

He took a step towards the door. "I can get you something, perhaps?"

"Sit down for Christ sakes, Peter. I want company, that's all. I'm not going to eat you." For some reason she laughed. For some reason this tickled her and she said it again while she was still laughing like a mule: "*I'm not going to eat you!*"

He smiled so that she didn't laugh alone, but he didn't know what was so funny. He looked at her where she lay. Her flat stomach under the silk night gown shook with mirth until she felt foolish and ceased. He was still looking down at her in silence and she let him.

The room was dark. Sirens broke the air like wild beasts in the distance. It made them both remember where they were, and why.

He coughed and moved to the curtains to open them.

"Don't do that. People can see in. I don't want them to see in. Talk to me." She bent her elbow to prop up her head. Moved the glass to rest on the pinnacle of her hip bone. "Talk to me."

"What do you want me to say?"

She cocked her head to where the light was trying to get in. "Tell me what's happening outside."

"Outside?"

She took a mouthful of liquor and swallowed: "What's happening to my lover."

She blinked her eyes once, dreamily. He wasn't sure if it was the drink. She looked very sad and alone; he couldn't remember ever seeing someone looking so sad and alone. Her eyes hid back in their sockets like his grandmother's eyes.

"Tell me the truth. I can take it."

Her breasts were tiny, like a girl's, and the space created by the fall of the night gown was too big for them.

Afraid to go closer – touch her, break her – he leaned back against the wall as if, if he pressed hard enough, he might escape – but did he *want* to escape? A pencil-line of sunlight from behind the drapes cast down his cheekbone, his throat muscle, one bicep, one golden button. The rest was in shadow.

"The traffic is flowing again," he began tentatively. "People are returning to work. President Franklin D. Roosevelt said in a speech yesterday that this great city *might be bloodied* but was *most certainly* unbowed."

He raised a fist but she didn't look at him and he wasn't sure she was listening as he spoke, but he spoke anyway, as he'd been bidden, hiding the fist again self-consciously behind his back.

"They are writing names on the walls of buildings. The relatives. Parents. Husbands. Wives. Writing the names of their loved ones. The ones who died in the slaughter." He saw her flinch a little at the word, and kept his voice low. "There were many, I think. Over seventy on the subway train alone. Many, they say in the bulletins, are missing. Still – what are the words? – *unaccounted for*. The parents and wives and sons sleep on the streets now, asking anybody passing for information. For hope, I guess. Or peace, when the bodies are found. It is a funny word – peace." For a moment he was lost for something to add. He looked at her face as if it might offer him a hint, but it didn't. "The rubble from the destroyed buildings has not all been removed. The trucks come and go through the night but they are hills that do not seem to get smaller. It is a huge job of course. The public services work like crazy around the clock to make stable the buildings they think might collapse and cause more destruction. Oh and dust. Yes. Dust still hangs in the air out there. It doesn't go away. It clings to your clothes. You go outside in a black suit and in five minutes it is white. Even funerals look like they have been sprinkled with icing sugar. Figures from a candy shop. It's not right."

He shook his head. When he looked up his jaw was set.

"Meanwhile the giant … he pays the price. The authorities, they are cutting and peeling off the skin from his arms in long strips, and rolling it up like carpet, taking it away to turn into leather – so the rumour goes – for use as upholstering in government limousines. I don't know if you should believe the rumours."

He wished that a little more light would fall on her but it didn't.

"There is a beggar," he said, filling the silence. "A bearded old Ashkenazer who sells souvenirs outside Macy's. You know the wind-up monkeys who play ... *clish! clish!*" Not knowing the word in English, he mimed clapping his hands.

"The toys?"

He nodded. "He has taken the – *clish-clish* off them, so they look like little replicas of the monster opening and closing his arms. But if you look closely you can see the little holes in the middle of their hands. I talked to him about the attack. He just shook his head and said it's biblical. 'It's *biblical*,' he kept saying."

A memory returned to him and he recounted it quickly and with enthusiasm. "Yesterday when I walked past the scene I saw gang of children bouncing a basketball to each other then tossing it high in the air, trying to get it to land in the dead beast's nostril. Younger kids, on a dare, were plucking out the monster's hair – it took quite a tug, I could see! – and flicking them at each other like bullwhips." He chuckled.

The actress said nothing and hardly moved. But she wasn't chuckling, he could tell that. His heart tightened in his chest.

"In the kitchen they said it was you. I didn't believe them."

She looked up. "Do I look like the photographs?" Aware of her appearance, she swiftly added: "Don't answer that question."

He laughed, shook his head in disbelief. "I am in the same room as the woman who was held in the hand of a damn monkey."

She lit a cigarette and left the packet sitting between her legs.

"He wasn't a damn monkey. He was a damn gorilla."

He could see the curve of her thighs so clearly it was as if she was naked. He wanted to feel the silk and feel her skin. If it was cold he wanted to warm it for her. If she was cold all over he could hold her to his body. He was not cold.

"Are *you* German? You look German."

She ran a hand through her curls and laughed.

"I've got news for you, kid. I'm not a natural blonde."

He blushed to his bootstraps.

"Greek Scottish on my father's side," she said. "Norwegian English on my mother's. Coat of many colours."

"Bella – she's a Pole who works downstairs washing dishes. She went with her sister and brother-in-law to see it. She was very excited. They all were. Hopping up and down like they were going to a Broadway show. Wrapped up in their scarves. She thought it would be somehow frightening, like a fairyground ride."

"Fairground. *Fairground* ride."

He nodded. "Like Coney Island."

*Roll up, roll up.*

"Go on."

"She said it wasn't. It wasn't at all." Eyes downcast, he looked unsure whether to continue. "When she came back she was real quiet. Just put her frozen hands in water and got to work. Later I asked her what happened and she said the head of it was as high as two tram cars on top of each other. Huge. As big as a house. You could live in it, she said."

*Don't give them ideas,* the actress thought, blowing cigarette smoke then waving it gently from her face.

"They looked up and they saw something catching the light. They couldn't work out what it was. Big. Glassy. Round. Then they realized. It was a tear. Frozen. Turned to ice on the creature's cheek. Big as a glitterball in a dance hall, they said. Like I say, they weren't laughing. They came back, like I say, real quiet." He shrugged. "Then the kitchen got busy. A hundred covers. We didn't have time to think about it after that. I don't know."

"What else don't you know?"

He looked up. "Sorry?"

"What else?"

He sighed. "Captain O'Rourke and his men, the pilots of the biplanes, had dinner at the White House." He heard her make a little snort of disdain. "Well, they are heroes, no? They risk their lives for the sake of the Motherland."

"They didn't die. He did."

"The enemy."

"Enemy of what, exactly?"

"I'm sorry . . . I don't understand."

Shivering, she picked up the fur coat from the carpet and wrapped it around her shoulders.

"Did you see his silhouette against the sunset?"

He shook his head.

"Then you *don't* understand," she said without any note of accusation, hardly louder than a whisper.

Her throat was dry and needy. She struck a match and the lit cigarette dangled from her pale, dry lips, its tip bobbing as she spoke. "Tell me about you. You have a family?"

"In Germany. I will tell them I met you."

"Uhuh. What will you tell them?"

"You are famous."

"I am now."

"You are pretty."

She laughed into a cough. "Once upon a time. This room sure is dark." (She wanted to ask him: *Was I pretty before I was famous?*) "Do you have a girl, Peter?"

"Sisters? Three."

"That's not what I mean. Sit next to me. You're a long way away. I can't see you over there in the gloom."

When he did, she patted the mattress next to her for him to move closer. Then did it again for him to move closer still. She placed her hand on his thigh and saw him shudder.

"Is my hand cold? Am I cold?"

He shook his head. She put it to his cheek.

"Will you take a drink with me? I don't like drinking alone."

He didn't say no, so she held up the bottle of bourbon and pressed it against his lips. She tilted it up like it was a baby's bottle. Without moving his body he took a mouthful and swallowed, and when the bottle was taken away, with a sucking noise, he gulped air.

"That's it, now. You'll lose your job. They'll smell it on your breath. You've broken the rules, chum."

"I don't *care*," he said, tugging the bottle from her and swigging from it a second time, longer and deeper. She was astonished, and had to take it – *snatch* it – from him before he demolished the whole bottle. *Greedy little—*

Down the hatch.

"What's it for, eh? Booze?" She stared at the label. It swam. "Just a way to get back to the animal: that's all, when you think about it. Look at us. Human fucking beings. We've got hundreds, thousands of years of fucking civilization. We've got intelligence and progress coming out of our ears. We've got motor cars and fashion and society and welfare and adding-up machines and rotivators. And what do we need? When a man and woman get together we need something to evaporate all that. To get us back to the jungle. To wipe out history, to tear up books and wisdom, shed William Shakespeare, Homer, Jesus Christ and Henry Ford, Abraham Lincoln, Greta Garbo, Thomas Edison. To be what we were. Are. *Animals*." She rose to unsteady feet in the middle of the swamp of sheets and pillows. "What's a bed if it's not an island in the room? The island where we return to the past, the scary past, the exciting past, where we live or die on our instinct, on the blood pumping in our veins; not the whim of some bank manager or casting agent. We're at the mercy of the beasts that can eat us or save us or take us or raise us up to the – shit, the heavens!" The bed undulated under her.

He laughed. "Lady, you drink too much."

"And you don't drink *enough*. You better catch up. I'm waaay ahead of you."

"You'll fall."

"I *won't*."

She did. On her back, legs up from under her. Landed flat, breathless, next to him. Her hair dancing as the bed springs whined like an orchestra tuning up. He leaned over and plucked each strand of hair from her face individually, an archaeologist carefully revealing a piece of precious treasure.

The kid said: "I am not an animal."

She smiled up at him. "I was kinda hoping you were."

Her upside-down eyes glinted.

He placed his hand on her belly and let the warmth spread out from him into her body.

She didn't move, kept staring at the ceiling. She'd had plenty of men touch her before. Boy, and how. Hock Sinnerd who took her to the creek and read to her from the Book of Genesis and told her if she held it a while it would get bigger and guess what? It did. Three guys from Winslow who told her how come babies got cooked up, and illustrated, one of them with a hoard of pimples on his neck jumping out at her like frogs. The sweat and beer-breath of a married guy named Ivan Ives: he quoted from the Bible too, as he hitched up his forty-four-inch pants, as if to convince himself of the fact. Grass stains on your summer dress, carpet burns and hickeys: such a catalogue. The infections and insertions. All kinds, all ways, pleading, threatening, all wanting it then wanting you gone just as fast. Life as a receptacle. That's the way you know it's going to be. Learn pretty fast in this world.

She thought: That wasn't *love*. Not the love *he* gave me. *How could you compare?*

He who owned all he surveyed. Who knew no other of his kind. Who stood alone, Lord of Creation, as far as the eye could see. He saved me from monsters. Took me in his hairy hand and wouldn't let go. Wouldn't let the demons get me, even when they buzzed him and stuck him with their beaks and claws and drew blood. Carried me through the vitriolic swamp like a cannonball – miasma smell making me heady and giddy as a child taking their first sip of champagne. He never let me fall. Held me up to his face, that big dark wall, carnage breath wrapping me like a gift, eyes black tunnels with a freight train coming. Swatted a pterodactyl. Picked my clothes off one by one. Peeled me like a grape. Examined me under the Hollywood chiffon naked and white to see me as I really was. Rolled me to and fro so he could look me over back and front. Blew at my hair. Gazed at me in wonder. Took me to his home in the clouds.

And it wasn't about sex for once because sex was impossible. And that made her so, so safe. And so, so happy then, in a lost world, far away, but found.

She reached down to the kid's hand and held it, to stop it moving.

She said: "I was dreaming of him when his hand came through the window of my apartment. Shards of glass rained down over my bed and he hauled me out into the night sky. I thought I was still dreaming because I was floating. I could hear the wailing traffic a million miles below and the police cars whining and the thunder of his growl getting louder in his chest as he climbed and climbed—" She stopped. ". . . Do you want to hear this?"

He didn't say anything. He didn't move, epaulettes hunched over her.

She said: "I can still smell his hand, like a big black leather couch, the smell of a hothouse, of the Bronx Zoo, of a Mississippi swamp, of alligator gumbo, of nuts and palm trees and oil and dates and the blood of unsuspecting prey. And if I close my eyes I can see my own reflection right now, frightened and amazed, pinned there in his big brown eyes."

Her own unblinking eyes became baubles of tears. Lost again. From the lost land to lost love: her perilous journey, and now ashore where the rivers were brake lights and the cliffs were Wall Street, and the toucan-calls were *Extra, Extra*.

"He was a wonderful thing. He was a god," she said. "I couldn't escape then and I can't escape now. Because he died for me. I know he did. He placed me down in a place of safety so that I wouldn't get killed when they came in that last figure of eight." She shuddered and hugged the fur tighter around her. "He knew what he was doing. He died for love. And nothing can ever be the same, because that day, when the stream of bullets from the airplanes tore into his skin, I died inside too."

Her whole body wept.

The kid touched her shoulder. She sat up briskly and unexpectedly and threw her arms around him and held him tight. At first he didn't know what to do with his hands, so he wrapped them around her. He could feel her ribs, her shoulder-bones. He could feel her heart beating, like a frightened bird's you'd pick up in your hand, a damaged thing you'd want to save.

The kid didn't want her to die, he wanted her to live.

His fingers sank into her, shocking her. He held her by the shoulders and pressed his lips on to hers, into hers, forcing her head back sharply and mouth open and his mouth over it, hard. Sucking the breath out of her he twisted her and pushed her down on to her back on the bed. She was weak and frail and it didn't take a fraction of his strength to overpower her. Was he overpowering her? No, because she wasn't resisting in the least. She simply lay there before him, her cage of a chest rising and falling quickly through the shimmering silk of the night gown to catch her breath, eyes flickering like a doe deer brought down by a predator. Startled, afraid – but the kind of fear, he thought, that meant excitement and desire and longing and lust and not Stop, not No. If she meant No she would say No.

Sirens and car horns battled in the street a million miles below.

He knelt across her, Colossus – (or so he thought. Men!) – taking her hand and putting it on his full erection coiled and pressing against the cloth of his slacks. She didn't like to take it away and hurt his feelings. Without a sound he furiously unbuttoned his jacket from the bottom to the top. In the dark the golden orbs popped and flew. She watched the vest come up off over his head and saw that his emaciated chest had hardly any hair on it. Saw the smoothness, the *pinkness* of him. All she could think was, he *shone*. Then his pants were down and her nightdress slid up in almost the same moment, as his weight dropped down on her. His back made a bridge and he wriggled his hips till the tip of his thing breached her and went deep so fast she uttered a cry and dug her fingernails into his cold, doughy flesh – not an expression of pleasure, but she'd learned that the male of the species liked this kind of thing. Her knees dropped aside. Memories tumbled on her in a barrage of the past; a wall crumbling on top of her she couldn't stop. He gripped her face and pushed it back into the sheets, smothering her with fingers and thumbs as she struggled to gulp air down her throat. She grunted and sobbed – another requirement, thinking Why? What? How? And he was stabbing into her: a noble act, a heroic act, he thought – a Redemption, a Resurrection, yes – *ja, jawohl*. It was time she entered the world of the living again, and he was the man to do it. (Do it! Do it!) She would thank him. She would worship him. He'd be a God. And she'd be renewed and whole again and perfect and pretty and famous and fucked. And just as she was thinking, Oh God, I wonder if it's possible to enjoy this, and not the pounding sweat of it, the grunting bourbon breath of it, the slow, numbing death of it, the disgust of it – it was over.

And he felt the heat of fame washing over him, like reporter's flashbulbs going off, like Valentino's smile, like a tuxedo on fire.

And she only felt the weight of him, the dead weight of him. And not that she didn't want it, but not that she did. And the Grand Canyon like someone had hollowed her out with a big spoon. And the Grand Canyon being full of trash, which was where she belonged, said Poppa, because that was what she was, and that's what she would always be – *you hear me?*

(*But you asked me to, Poppa.*)

(*I believed you, Poppa.*)

He slid his penis out of her, thinking that behind her closed eyes and smiling lips she'd rediscovered love.

(*Poppa?*)

But she was thinking of the ape's tree-trunk finger pressing against her belly atop the Empire State Building, his ebony fingernail a tarnished mirror. His caress so gentle for a big guy.

She rolled on to her side and hugged herself as the chill of the room returned.

They want the Story, she thought. Well you know what the Story is? The Story is: no man has ever come close to how I felt with him. On that mountain top, on that skyscraper, with him at my side, towering so high, roaring as they came out of the sun.

*Stand in front of it, said Poppa.*

*Look right into the camera, said Poppa.*

*Look frightened, said Poppa.*

*Beautiful, said Poppa.*

*Beautiful!*

*Beautiful!*

Would anyone scare me like Poppa?

Would anyone love me like Poppa?

Then she remembered the blood in her lover's fur, cloying, clammy, clotted. How he swayed from side to side in startled puzzlement. Ageless. A Sequoia hacked down. A century collapsing, a world destroyed, a country eradicated. How she wanted to communicate, but could not. How she wanted to forgive him, but could not. Save him, but could not. How she wanted to be scared but fear was gone. His majesty. His Highness. His – *gone*.

She turned over and saw the German boy's head against the pillow and thought of the giant's head against the pillow of the sidewalk below, at the same angle, eyes non-focused in death.

He rolled his head to her. "It is what you wanted, yes?"

She paused before deciding to nod.

He smiled and lit one of her cigarettes and sat up – you could easily count his vertebrae – and stretched over to pick up his vest and hotel staff jacket, and dressed with his bare back to her as an airplane passed overhead with the monotone murmur of a disappointed voyeur.

Oh, the *pinkness* of him.

Her insides congealed. There was something inside-out about the feeling. The nausea of stepping off a carousel, which was supposed to be an enjoyable experience but wasn't – and yet the relief of *being* off. She didn't want to think about it.

He handed her his cigarette and lit another for himself. She considered the action unbearably familiar and unbearably arrogant. She wanted to cry again.

He stood up, his shadowy cock, now shrunken and unattentive, dangling under the rim of his white jacket, and peeked behind the drapes at the afternoon sunlight. "Damn monkey." He chuckled as he buttoned up his collar. "We socked him good, huh?"

She pulled the sheets around her in a nest.

He got on to the bed on all fours and kissed her with puckered lips, which she endured. His grin was horribly self-congratulatory and she wondered how much of this had been his purpose: to screw the actress in 7205? Perhaps he had announced it to the others as he picked up her tray. Perhaps he'd brag about it tonight in a bar. He had not been violent and hadn't hurt her, even, as others had done – that was exactly it: she felt nothing. Nothing at all. There was a gaping hole inside her where he'd been and it was as if it hadn't happened at all, and she knew with great clarity that was the way it would always be from now on.

She sat up in bed with her breasts and knees covered.

"I hope you don't lose your job."

"Screw my job," he said.

He was a different person now, as they always were. And it was never a surprise to her, but it always hurt.

"You know what they call me in the kitchen? *Sauerkraut.* This was supposed to be the land of the free, the home of the brave, of democracy and opportunity. I came expecting bright, clean Americans like bright clean American automobiles, not sweaty Turks tweaking my ass and blowing me kisses and Italians barking and cursing at me, sticking my hand into boiling water for dropping a plate, a Jew begrudgingly giving me my stinking wages at the end of the week. I expected New York to be like an elevator, going up, always up, like the tall buildings, taller, higher, always higher. A place of money, a place of glamour and power and gasoline. Not foreigners and perverts."

He held his stomach in, puffing his hairless chest as he pulled on his slacks. "My father sent me here to learn the hotel trade. One year, he said; you will learn more than in any university. He owns three of the biggest hotels in Munich, one in Frankfurt, two in Berlin."

He tucked in his genitals. "I always thought the United States would be great, but it is not so great. I expected a strong country, but it is not strong. It is weak. A cripple, like your President. You have no work – no good work. Thirteen million unemployed. Almost every bank is closed. People are losing their farms, homes, businesses. You have no money, no hope . . ."

"We have movies."

He snorted. "Which is what? Nothing but a sign of decadence." Threading his belt buckle, tugging it to the right hole and poking the pin through. "I have read the history books. This is the way empires fall. Look around you from your high buildings and what do you see? The poor rewarded for doing nothing, immigrants like me given opportunities while patriotic Americans struggle. Your country is sick and your men are standing by watching it happen. They are not fighting for what they value. They are not fighting for the future. They do not have a leader powerful enough to make things change."

The actress held her cigarette vertically with her fingertips and blew on it so that the tip glowed red.

"I'm going back home. Not to Munich. To Potsdam," he said. "I have an uncle there, an industrialist. I know there is always a job there open for me." He waited for a reaction from her but all he saw was a long glowing red puff on her cigarette. The blue smoke hung flatly in the air between them. He crushed his own cigarette out on the plate of cold, untouched food.

"Come with me. A new life. A good life." he said. "America – it is a place for dreams. But for some dreams you have to return to Germany."

She said: "I think there's a Potsdam up in Saint Lawrence County."

The kid laughed through his nose at that – funny girl, crazy girl.

*Stupid girl, said Poppa.*

"I'm serious. Come. It is beautiful."

*Beautiful.*

*This way. To the camera.*

*You're frightened. You're amazed. You're terrified.*

As the jungle drums began pounding in her heart, she imagined marrying this man. She could, so very easily. After all he thought she was a star. He *knew* she was a star. You could see it in his eyes. He wanted that radiance of fame, of anecdote, of fable, to fall on him. He wanted to be larger than life too. He wanted to have her on his arm, to show her off to bosses and officers and leaders. Own her forever and have her obey his orders. She could see herself making home with him in some little cuckoo-clock house with deer buck heads on the wall, with parties hunting boar or gnawing chicken legs and swilling beer. Or a trophy wife in Los Angeles. She a star – the parts would come knocking ("No jungle pictures!") – him a screenwriter, or producer, or both. Kids, several. Nannies, English. Stern, but not too stern. He'd slap her occasionally, but only when she'd deserve it. He'd have affairs, but then so would she. He'd find some younger, prettier version. So would she. The divorce would be expensive. She'd get the children and dogs. He'd get fat, bitter and twisted, not necessarily in that order.

"You know," she said, "I'm ready for breakfast now."

He gave a broad grin exposing his white, so-perfect teeth. The parenthesis grin of a football player with a chiselled jaw. So American.

"And some good, strong, black American coffee," she said.

He picked up the tray. "You are on the mend, yes?"

"Yes."

"I love you."

*Everyone wants to love you, said Poppa, on the boat, during the voyage to the island. And you know what? Let them.*

"I know," she said.

When the kid had gone and the door was closed and she was alone again in the room she imagined her lover's gigantic skull, polished and white in the lobby of the Smithsonian, surrounded by a party of eager schoolchildren, any one of them smaller than his pointed teeth. The skeletons of dinosaurs keeping a respectful distance. The stare of aeons in the space where his beautiful eyes used to be.

She got out of bed and took a sheet of hotel notepaper from the drawer. Sitting with her reflection in front of her – who was that woman with ribs in her chest you could count? Pale, gaunt, frightening: why would anyone make love to *that*? – she changed her mind and rummaged in her purse. She spiralled out her lipstick and wrote on the mirror:

*Thank you, Peter.*

Thanking him for making it clear. Even if he wouldn't understand. Couldn't understand. Could anyone? Then she signed her name. Her autograph. Maybe it would be worth something one day.

(*See, Poppa, I'm worth something after all.*)

She had to hurry now. It would only take so long for the elevator to descend and return.

Light flooded the room like a bomb blast so bright she had to cover her eyes. When she opened them again, blinking, her surroundings took on a different aspect, washed with colour anew. It seemed she was in a different hemisphere now. A different latitude. The world up-ended, transformed, and rare. And she felt no longer weak and fragile and worthless: she felt strong and excited and loved.

The drapes fluttered like flags, horizontal into the room.

She shed the fur from her shoulders. It gathered behind her feet.

She knelt, then stood. Bare feet. Bare legs. Goosebumps. White skin. (The kid with the whitest skin in school – so poor she couldn't afford *shoes*.) Silk dressing gown (*silk* – how she'd moved up in the world) clinging, a goldy sheen over the dark nipples and black vee of her gender – invisible.

Looking down at ants the way he looked down.

Like her lover, she felt no fear.

The unnatural blonde closed her eyes.

Doll eyes.

Drums in her chest.

Took one foot from the window ledge, then the other.

As it had to be – falling like he fell. Seventy floors, sixty, fifty – then the numbers floated away, irrelevant like everything else.

Wind raked through her frizzled hair, an ice-blonde blur as she dropped, pinioned by her plummeting. All her senses peeled away to reveal a peculiar kind of freedom, a strange kind of pleasure that life would not be there to torment her very much longer, and that was fine, that was okay. A euphoric surge enraptured her: *Thank God for that*, and she prepared to enjoy her last few seconds on this earth, unencumbered by the future. And all she could think of was the smallness of it all. And the air rushing past. And that his mighty hand might catch her, even now. And his mighty roar might yet echo in the canyon of the skyscrapers with the mighty beating of his chest. And he would save her. And they would be together on the mountaintop. Because it wasn't like the papers said, oh no. It wasn't "Beauty killed the Beast." It was Romeo and Juliet. Of course it was. And that was how all great love stories ended, didn't they? . . . Like this.

*What is the ape to Man? A laughing stock or a painful embarrassment. And Man shall be just that for the Superman: a laughing stock or a painful embarrassment. Once you were apes, and even now, too, Man is more ape than any ape . . . Behold, I teach you the Superman! The Superman is the meaning of the Earth. Let your will say: the Superman shall be the meaning of the Earth!*

– Friedrich Nietzsche
*Thus Spoke Zarathustra*

# BRIAN LUMLEY

## The Nonesuch

BRIAN LUMLEY'S FIRST STORIES and books were published by the then "dean of macabre publishers", August W. Derleth, at the now-legendary Arkham House imprint. Upon leaving the British Army in December 1980 (after completing a full military career of twenty-two years), Lumley began writing full time, and four years later completed his breakthrough novel, *Necroscope®*, featuring Harry Keogh – a psychically-endowed hero who could communicate with the dead.

*Necroscope* has now grown to sixteen large volumes, published in fourteen countries and many millions of copies. In addition, there are *Necroscope* comic books, graphic novels, a role-playing game, quality figurines and a series of German audio books, while the original story has been optioned for movies for four consecutive years. Lumley is also the award-winning author of more than forty other titles, and his most recent book is *Necroscope: The Plague-Bearer*, a long novella from Subterranean Press featuring Harry Keogh. Forthcoming is a futuristic vampire novel entitled *The Fly-By-Nights*.

"Readers who attended the KeoghCons in Torquay, Devon, will immediately recognize the only slightly disguised location in which this story is set," explains the author. "Two previous tales in this sequence ('The Thin People' and 'Stilts') were narrated first-person by the protagonist, an unfortunate fellow who, where weird or unconventional collisions are concerned, appears to be accident prone – in spades! And being a recovering alcoholic hasn't much helped his case, because pink elephants just don't compare with the creatures he's wont to bump into.

"The earlier tales are alluded to, but briefly, which barely interferes with the pace of the current story. As to why I wrote this one: it's simply that I have a fondness for trilogies, let alone outré encounters . . ."

I'VE OFTEN HEARD IT SAID that lightning never strikes twice. Oh really? Then how about three times? Or perhaps, in some unknown fashion, I'm some kind of unusually prominent lightning conductor whose prime function is to absorb something of the physical and psychological shocks of these *by no means rare* events, thus shielding the rest of humanity and keeping them out of the line of fire. Something like that, anyway.

Or there again perhaps not. My being there didn't much help Barmy Bill of Barrows Hill that time in old London Town. It was more like I was an observer . . . except even now I can't be sure of what I saw, what really happened. Perhaps I was drinking too much, in which case it could have been a very bad attack of the dreaded delirium tremens. That's what I tell myself anyway, because it's a whole lot easier than recalling to mind the actual details of that morning when the police required me to identify Barmy Bill's dramatically – in fact his radically, *hideously* – altered body where it had been dumped in that skip on Barchington, just off The Larches . . .

Anyway, let's stop there, because that's another story and somewhere I really don't want to go, not in any detail. But if we're still talking lightning strikes, then Barmy Bill and the Thin People would be *numero uno*'s Numero Uno: my personal Number One, my first but by no means my last.

Or maybe we should be talking something else. There's this dictionary definition that comes to mind: "nonesuch: a *unique*, unparalleled or extraordinary thing". And if we break that down into its component parts:

"Unique". But doesn't that describe a one-off? So how many nonesuches are there supposed to be? I mean is a nonesuch, like a lightning strike, only supposed to occur once? Well not in my case, brother! No, not at all in my case. But as for "unparalleled" and "extraordinary thing(s)": Those at least are parts of the definition that I can go along with. But definitely.

Putting it simply, there are some weird things in this old world, and then there are some *really* weird things – nonesuches of a different colour, as it were – and it seems to me that indeed I am destined to attract or collide with them. Not so much a lightning conductor as a magnet, maybe? Or perhaps the weirdness itself is the magnet and I'm simply an iron filing, unable to escape its attraction.

High-flown, fanciful analogies? Well, perhaps . . .

Anyway and whichever, the nightmarish fate of Barmy Bill of Barrows Hill at the hands of the Thin People was one such occurrence – my first collision with a nonesuch or nonesuches, so to speak – which seems almost to have been instrumental in jarring the rest of these things into monstrous motion . . .

I used to keep a diary, but no longer . . . because it's not easy to forget things once you write them down. And there are things I would much prefer to forget.

So why am I writing this? Well, maybe I'm hoping it will be cathartic, that I'll purge myself of some of the after-effects, the lingering emotional baggage and psychoses – especially the nightmares and constant panic attacks – the fear, even in broad daylight, that something terrifying knows who I am, and where I live, and might be waiting for me just around the next corner.

You see, no sooner had I got – or thought I had got – Barmy Bill's weird fate out of my mind, my system, than up popped the next nonesuch: the Clown on Stilts. I had been drinking again – "under the influence of my peers", as we frequently tend to excuse ourselves – and so, once again, I can't be one hundred per cent sure of what I saw, imagined, nightmared, or whatever.

But I had moved out of London (*had* to move away from Barrows Hill and memories of Barmy Bill) to Newcastle in the north-east. There was a fairground, which I'm sure was real enough, a scruffy little girl with a yappy little dog, a troupe of really strange people from the Freak House marquee, and finally – as if emerging from nowhere, or from the darkness beyond the fairground's perimeter – there was the Clown on Stilts.

But that's enough, I won't go into it except to say that it ended quite horribly, with that little girl out in the midnight fields, running like a wild thing, and calling . . . calling—

—Calling in a panic for her suddenly vanished dog: "Woofy! Woofy!"

And I'm sure I remember thinking through my alcoholic haze, *You won't find Woofy, you snotty little girl. I don't think you're ever going to find Woofy!*

Later there was evidence of sorts – evidence of a monstrous incursion and a dreadful abduction – but no, I won't go there. As in the case of my first nonesuch, I have said enough . . .

As for this latest thing, lightning strike Number Three, as I'm inclined to call it, this time I'll try to tell it all; catharsis and what have you. But I have to admit that I was once more under the influence, this time for the last time – definitely. Oh yes, for I've been stone cold sober ever since, which is how I intend to stay despite that I feel justified in saying I have been sorely tempted. But for all that I was intoxicated at the time, still it's barely possible I *might* have been dreaming . . . no, let's make that nightmaring.

I should start at the beginning.

Just as lightning strike Number One had prompted me to move out of London, so after my experience at the fairground in Newcastle I once again felt the need to change my address: in fact, to depart *urgently* from the north-east in its entirety. I would head south again – but *not* the south-east or anywhere close to the capital.

I had been doing fairly well as a reporter with a newspaper in Newcastle and still fancied myself a journalist. Fortunately there was an opening with a small regional newspaper in Exeter. I applied for the job, got it, and moved into cheap, reasonably comfortable lodgings. All went well; inside twelve months I was settled in; I accepted the more or less menial or general work that at first I was required to perform around the office, and despite my newcomer status my co-workers accepted and appeared to like me.

Summer came around and apart from the city itself I hadn't yet found time to explore the region. In fact, in all my twenty-nine years on this planet I had never before visited the south-west; Devon and Cornwall were completely unknown territories to me. But now, settled in my new job, and having purchased a five-year-old set of wheels with the proceeds of a small win on the national lottery – a win which seemed to confirm the fact that my luck was finally changing – I decided to have a look around the local countryside, in particular the dramatic Cornish coast-line, and took a week out of my annual fortnight's allowance. I would try for the other week later in the year, probably around Christmas or possibly New Year.

The weather was disappointing; Land's End was drab, and the moors more so. Unseasonably cold and blustery winds blew in off the sea, and even a locale as legendary as Tintagel, perched on its storm-weathered cliffs, looked uninviting, with much of its antique mystery lost to a dank, swirling mist.

Feeling let down, a little depressed, I drove south across country towards Torbay, and the closer I got to the south coast the more the weather seemed to be improving. So much so that by the time I found myself on the approach road to . . . well, maybe the name of the town doesn't matter. And for a fact, I wouldn't want anyone of an enquiring mind to go exploring there, perhaps seeking the location of lightning strike Number Three. No, that might not be entirely advisable.

And so we get to it . . . and so *I* got to it.

To the small hotel on a hill looking down on the promenade; where, beyond a sturdy, red stone sea wall, the English Channel glinted azure blue in the warm summer sunlight. The tide was on its way in, sending slow-rolling wavelets that were little more than ripples to break gently on the sandy shore. Blankets, wind-breaks and parasols were plentiful above the tidemark; below it some dozens of children braved the shallow water, and a handful of adults with trousers rolled up, or skirts held high, paddled at the very rim of the sea, occasionally stooping to gather seashells.

The scene was peaceful, idyllic, irresistible: I could look at it for hours! And, since several of this small hotel's rooms had canopied balconies facing the sea, I could probably do just that. A simple sign inside the lobby's glass doors said VACANCIES: ROOMS AVAILABLE, which helped me make up my mind. It was high season; many of the hotels were full to brimming; I considered myself fortunate to have discovered this quaint old Victorian place.

Leaving the road and following a sign to the parking lot, I drove carefully down a steep driveway to the rear of this once-handsome, now slightly careworn four-storey building, and there found a small, walled rock garden and swimming pool. Below this vantage point, the tiled roofs of a handful of other establishments – hotels and cafeterias – flanked the road down the hillside to the seafront. Parking my car, I stood admiring the view for a few moments more, then used the hotel's rear entrance and climbed two flights of stairs to the reception area.

There were two people at the desk: the receptionist, a pleasant German woman in her late twenties, who I later discovered to be the hotel's general dogsbody; and a pale middle-aged woman, the proprietress, who seemed somewhat nervous and quietly preoccupied. I can't better describe this first, lasting impression she made on me – with her periods of fitful, apparently involuntary blinking, and the way her hands were wont to flutter like caged birds – except to say she appeared more than a little neurotic. I didn't notice this immediately, however, for at first it was the German girl who saw to my requirements.

I asked about a room, if possible one with a balcony facing the sea. She checked in a ledger, ran her finger down the page, paused at a certain blank space and frowned. Then with a brief, obligatory smile for me, she turned a curious, enquiring glance on the pale owner of the place. And:

"Room number, er, seven?" she said. But with the inflection or emphasis that she placed on "seven", it was almost as if she had said "thirteen".

And it was then that I noticed the other woman's agitation. Ah! *That's* the word I was looking for, missing from my previous brief description: her "agitation", yes! A sort of physical and (however suppressed) mental disquiet. She opened her mouth, and her throat bobbed as if she swallowed, but no word was uttered, just a small dry cough.

I turned back to the German girl. "Room seven? Does it look out across the Channel? Does it have a balcony? I'll be needing it for four or five days."

"It is—" the girl began to answer, at which the pale woman found her suddenly urgent voice:

"Seven is a corner room. It only looks halfway out to sea. That is, the view isn't direct. We usually leave it . . . we *keep* number seven empty, as a storeroom." And nodding – blinking and fluttering her hands – she repeated herself: "Yes, we use it as a storeroom . . . Well, usually."

Now disappointed and perhaps a little annoyed, I said, "The sign at the main entrance says you have vacancies. That's why I stopped here. So are you now telling me I'm wasting my time? Or rather that *you* are wasting it, by causing me to stop for nothing?"

"Mister, er . . . ?" She managed to control her blinking.

"Smith," I told her. "George Smith." (Actually, that isn't the name I gave her; George might be correct, but Smith definitely isn't. I think I'll keep my real name to myself if only for fear of ridicule. And anyway, what's in a name?)

"Well, I'm Mrs Anderson – Janet Anderson – and this is my hotel," she replied. "And I must apologize, but we've been very busy and I'm really not sure that room seven is ready for occupancy. It may well be full of linens and . . . and blankets?" She seemed almost to expect me to answer some unspoken question, or perhaps to accept what she'd told me.

"It *may* be?" Frowning, looking from one to the other of the pair, I shook my head. "So what's the problem? I mean, can't we simply send someone to check it out?"

By now Mrs Anderson's hands (and incidentally, that wasn't *her* name) looked ready to fly off her wrists! "A problem?" she repeated me, and then: "Send someone to . . . to check it out?"

"*Ah . . . !*" the German girl's sigh was perfectly audible, and probably deliberately so. "*Das ist mein fehler! Ich bin schuldig!*" she muttered. And then, reverting to English as she turned to the older woman: "No, no, Madame! I am sorry, but this is my fault. I did not think it was important to tell you that I have tidied and made clean number seven. The room has been empty for quite some time, yes, but is now ready for a guest . . . er, with your permission?"

Gripping the edge of the desk – in order to steady herself, I supposed – Mrs Anderson said, "Do you think so? Ready for a guest?" She sounded anxious. "Is it all right? Is it really?"

"I am sure of it." The German girl nodded. "Shall I let Mr, er, Smith see the room for himself? Perhaps he will not want it after all."

She turned and reached for a key in an open cabinet on the wall behind the desk, at which the older woman at once appeared galvanized and quickly moved to block her access. For a moment the scene was frozen, the two women staring hard at each other, until finally Mrs Anderson gave way and, however reluctantly, stepped aside. Then, blinking her eyes ever more rapidly, in a veritable torrent of words, she said, "Yes of course ... by all means ... do show him the room ... there's no problem ... none at all! Be so good as to attend to it, will you, Hannah?"

With which she hurried out from behind the desk, offered me an almost apologetic, twitching half-smile, and without further pause went off into the hotel's cool interior.

More than a little bemused, I could only shake my head as I watched her pass out of sight. It had been a very odd five minutes ...

It was as Hannah had said: room number seven was very clean and tidy. Small but spacious enough for me, with its single bed and white-tiled bathroom, it was most privately situated on a split-level landing three steps up from the main floor at that end of the hotel farthest from reception. And I could see why it might be used occasionally as a storeroom: set apart from the rest of the guest-rooms, it could well be that it was originally intended as such, only to be converted at a later date.

Following Hannah through the hotel, which seemed paradoxically empty, I had attempted to orient myself as best possible, only to find it a rambling, irregular sort of place whose design overall was higgledy-piggledy and very confusing. One thing I had noticed for sure: close to the bottom of the three steps that rose to my landing, there was one door that opened into a small bar-room – a little too close for my liking, by reason of my *once*-liking, and I could smell the beer – and another leading to the large dining-room with its panoramic window looking across the bay. To one side there was also a flight of dog-leg stairs marked PRIVATE: STAFF ONLY, that climbed to a landing before angling out of sight toward the front of the hotel. According to Hannah the rooms up there were occupied by a pair of female, casual workers from the Czech Republic – "common room-maids," as she described them, sniffing and tilting her nose – also by Mrs Anderson, by Hannah herself, and by "the chef".

So much for the interior layout . . .

As for number seven, the somewhat isolated room I was being offered: "I'll take it," I told her, after opening curtains and double-glazed, floor-to-ceiling sliding doors, and stepping out onto the canopied balcony, from which the view of the promenade and beach was sidelong, less than perfect, but acceptable.

"As you wish," Hannah answered, handing me the key. "When you return to reception you may want to check in. Mrs Anderson insists on payment in advance – by cash or card, whichever you choose, but no cheques – and, if you intend to eat in the hotel this evening, you may wish to order your meal in advance. Now, if there is nothing else, I—"

"Hannah, if you'll permit such familiarity," I cut her off, "may I ask you a rather awkward question?"

"An awkward ques—?" she began to repeat me, then paused to raise a knowing eyebrow before continuing: "Ah! About Mrs Anderson, I think. Her, er, mannerisms?"

I nodded. "You're very astute."

"No, not really." She shrugged. "Anyone could see that Mrs Anderson is of a nervous nature. Well, she always has been, but recently . . ." And there she paused.

"Recently?" I prompted her.

But Hannah shook her head. "No, it is not my place to speak of such things. Not behind her back, and not to a stranger."

"Of course not," I agreed. "It's just that I feel concerned about her. Perhaps I've upset her in some way – something I may have said or done? She didn't seem to want me here!"

Hannah bit her lip, thought it over for a moment, and said, "No, it is not you. It is this place, this area which she finds disturbing . . ." And looking around the room, and out through the balcony doors, she waved a vague, all-inclusive hand at nothing in particular. "Even this room – perhaps especially this room – or some of the things that have happened here."

"Things have happened? In this room?"

She shrugged, stepped closer to the open balcony doors, and looked out. "Out there, and . . . and up there."

I followed her gaze – out across the ribbon of the road and up a hillside clad in ivy and old man's beard – craning my neck to take in the gaunt aspect of another, rather dilapidated-looking hotel perched up there on that higher level.

"Yes," she said, nodding. "Up there,"

"But you also mentioned this room," I pressed her.

"Yes," Hannah said, moving towards the door. "Mrs Anderson does not like this room. This is the first time she has let it in the eleven months I have worked here. But we had a very poor winter, with only a few guests, and while things are now improving, I know she still needs the money. That is why . . ." But here she paused.

"Why you argued on my behalf? At the desk, I mean?"

Now she smiled and said, "Aha! But you too are very astute! Also persistent! Myself, I am not a superstitious person. There is nothing wrong with this room, Mr Smith, and I hope you enjoy your stay here."

"But—"

"Now I have work," she said. "You will excuse me?"

While I would like to have known more, what else could I do but let her go?

As she left, Hannah closed the door quietly behind her . . .

Moving my luggage, a single small suitcase, from my car to room number seven, I stopped at the desk to order dinner and pay for four nights in advance. Hannah was obviously busy elsewhere for when I rang the bell it was Mrs Anderson who came from a small office at the end of the desk to attend to me. She looked a lot more settled than the last time I had seen her, and while dealing with the business in hand she was able to talk to me.

"You're from London, Mr Smith?"

"Ah, my accent!" I said, nodding. "No mistaking London, eh? Well yes, I'm London born and bred, but not just recently. Newcastle, but I wasn't there long enough to pick up the accent – thank goodness!"

She smiled. "I hear lots of accents. I've become expert in recognizing them."

"And how about you?" I answered. "I'm no expert myself but I'd guess you're local – or West-Country at least? – or then again, maybe not. It's like I said: I'm no expert!"

"From Cornwall originally," she said. "We owned a hotel in Polperro, that is, my husband and I. But business was very bad three years in a row, so we sold up, moved here six years ago, fell in love with this place and . . . and bought it."

As she paused her smile gradually faded, then for a moment or two she began that rapid blinking again. She must have seen my reaction however – my startled expression – and as quickly took hold of herself.

"I'm sorry," she began to apologize, "but my nerves aren't up to much these days. I'm sure you've noticed, and . . ."

I held up a hand to stop her. "There's really no need."

But with her voice trembling ever so slightly, she quickly continued: ". . . *And* I think that you deserve an explanation. For it might have appeared I was being unnecessarily rude to you."

"Mrs Anderson," I began, "whatever the problem is, I don't need you to explain. I'm only a little worried that my presence here might be aggravating things . . . my presence in room number seven, that is."

Despite my apparent concern and words of sympathy, however, my mentioning the room was quite deliberate. Hannah had told me something about that room – she had even made it sound as if it was haunted or something – and I wanted to know more; it was as simple as that. Looking back on it, maybe I should have remembered what people say about cats and curiosity.

Mrs Anderson seemed to have gone three shades paler. "Room number seven," she finally said. Not a question, nothing emphasized, she had simply repeated me coldly and parrot-fashion . . . as if my words had triggered some response in her brain causing it to switch off, or at the very least to switch channels. Then the blinking started up again and her hands began fluttering on the desk's mahogany top.

Whatever this recurring condition of hers was, it was obvious that my words had brought on this latest attack. And now my concern was very real.

On impulse I reached across the desk and trapped her hands, pinning them there. She at once relaxed and in that moment, but only for the moment, I almost felt uplifted: some kind of faith healer! . . . But no, I didn't have the touch; it was little more than concerned, caring human contact.

Sensing the calm come over her, as quickly as I had reacted to her problem I now released her and took a pace back from the desk. And: "I'm . . . so *sorry*!" I said, not knowing what else to say.

"There's really no need," she answered, no longer blinking and apparently in control once again, but avoiding further eye-to-eye contact by gazing at her slender white hands. "It's not your fault, Mr Smith. It's a matter of association: that room, and the memories. You see, I loved my husband very much, and—"

She paused, and before she was able to continue – assuming she intended to – the hotel's frosted-glass outer doors beyond the small lobby swung open, and a rising babble reached us as a large party of noisy, chattering people began entering from the pavement in front of the place. Out there, a coach was just now pulling away.

Now Mrs Anderson looked up, away from me and towards these others as they claimed her attention, smiling and trading small talk with her where they passed us by. And some colour returned to her face when a pair of men carrying a wicker basket between them stopped and nodded, beamed their satisfaction and indicated their burden.

"For tonight," one of the two said with a laugh, "that's if chef will oblige?"

"Oh, I'm sure he will!" Mrs Anderson answered him. "That's if you'll pay something for his time, Mr Carson, and if you'll also cover my losses?"

"But of course we'll look after the chef!" Carson answered. "And your takings won't suffer any. These—" he tapped a finger on the basket, "—are only for those who caught 'em, who took a chance and held back from ordering an evening meal. And there's maybe a couple of pounds extra left over for your freezer."

Now she was smiling, albeit a little wanly. "You had a good day, then? You made a good catch?"

"Some nice ling," the other replied. "Wreck-fish, you know? And a few beautiful red mullet! Do you want to see?" He made as if to lift the basket's lid.

"Goodness no!" She turned her face away. "Better get off to the kitchen before you stink the whole place out!"

And laughing, the two made off after the rest of the group.

"A fishing party," I said, unnecessarily; many of them had been carrying their fishing tackle, and they'd certainly seemed overdressed for a warm summer day! Anyway, I now understood why the place had seemed so empty.

"Two coach loads of them," Mrs Anderson answered. "They've been here for a week, fishing from some boats they've hired out of Brixham. The other coach should be arriving any time now. In a few more days they'll be gone; the place will be mostly empty again and I'll miss their custom. They're no trouble and during the day they're mostly out, but they do use the bar quite a lot in the evenings."

Smiling, I replied, "Where they down a few drinks and start telling tall tales of the ones that got away, right?"

"Myself, I don't really approve of drink," she said, frowning for no apparent reason. "Though I must confess that the bar keeps the place ticking over. Which reminds me: I have stock to take care of. Please excuse me . . ."

She went off about her business, and as Hannah appeared and began making entries in books behind the desk, once again I was obliged to rein in my curiosity. Then again – as I grudgingly told myself – whatever the mystery was here it wasn't my business anyway. And some ten minutes later, finished with unpacking my few belongings, I was out on my balcony in time to watch the second coach unloading its passengers with their rods and gear. Quieter than the first batch, it appeared that their day hadn't quite matched up to expectations . . .

I had checked into the hotel (which I'll call the Seaview, once again because that wasn't its name) in the middle of the afternoon. Now, with nothing to engage me until dinner, I determined to look more closely at the hotel's exterior, fixing its design and orientation more firmly in my mind.

At the desk I collected a front door "key" – a swipe card – from Hannah, and left the hotel by the front entrance. Outside, I crossed the steeply sloping road's canyon-like cutting to the high-walled far side, where because there was no pavement I was obliged to huddle close to the old stone wall in order to avoid descending cars. And from that somewhat dubious vantage point I scanned the wedge-shaped bulk of the Seaview.

Apart from the canopied entrance, the windows of Mrs Anderson's office and those of the top floor, which were little more than a row of fanlights – and with one other exception, but an important one – the Seaview's anterior aspect was more or less a blank wall and scarcely interesting, causing me to wonder why I had found the place so attractive in the first place. In just a little while I would discover the answer to that question.

I have mentioned the hotel's wedge shape. The thick, unadorned end of this wedge was at the Seaview's higher elevation, while the narrow, lower end sported and supported, at a height of some nine feet over the pavement, a lone, canopied balcony: in fact, *my* balcony, that of room number seven. And it was because the balcony was set at a skewed angle on the "pointed" or thin end of the building that it was able to offer sidelong views of both the seafront and the hillside . . . not to mention that other, higher, rather more dilapidated or deserted hotel that loomed up there, set well back from the road in rank and neglected gardens.

Standing in the road's cutting under the massive, backward-leaning retaining wall that was literally securing the hillside, I wasn't actually able to see that place on high; yet somehow I was aware of it, had been aware of it ever since gazing upon it from my room's balcony. Indeed I could sense it – could almost *feel* it – frowning coldly down on the Seaview. Even in the glow of a late summer afternoon I could feel this oppressive weight; or perhaps it was only the fearful tonnage of the hillside that I felt, held back by the great wall . . .

There in the shade of that wall, just for a moment I felt a chill; or more properly I felt slightly uneasy. But then, as my gaze once more swept the Seaview end to end – and passed beyond the hotel, down the road to the seafront – all such weird imaginings were put aside when I was suddenly reminded what it was that had inspired me to turn off the main road into the hotel's car park in the first place. Quite simply, it was the view below and beyond the hotel: that of the promenade and inviting golden sands, and the glittering blue waters reaching right across the bay to the horizon. These were the things that had coloured my first impression of the hotel, not the building itself but that marvellous view which it commanded.

As for the intimidating chill I had felt: well, I had been standing in the shade of the great retaining wall, after all . . .

Back over the road, I walked along the pavement in front of the Seaview down to the building's "sharp" end under the balcony of room number seven, then turned right to descend the steep drive to the gardens, the pool and parking lot.

By this time the shadows were falling slantingly towards the sea as inland the sun prepared to set behind higher ground. The back of the Seaview, with its double row of canopied balconies, now stood in its own shadow, and looking up at it I finally recognized the extent of my error in perspective. For the *front* of the hotel, with its more or less blank stone wall, was the actual *rear* of the place, while this ocean-facing, far more ornate elevation with its truly wonderful view of the bay was the real front.

The beach was beginning to clear; tourists and other holiday-makers strolled the esplanade where sunlight yet struck home; with two hours yet to dinner, I spent a few minutes watching a lone swimmer performing his expert crawl, to and fro, the full length of the pool, before going in through the Seaview's rear entrance and up to my room . . .

As if to counter the unseasonal chill that I had felt earlier, the room was very warm. This was, however, in no way unnatural; despite that the hotel's central heating had been shut down for the summer, number seven's floor-to-ceiling sliding glass doors had trapped much of the day's sunlight, and I could still feel its warmth radiating from the walls and floor.

Showering, drying off and changing for the evening from my rough driving clothes into summer casuals – slacks and a light shirt – I went out on to the balcony. Along with a small table, there was a deckchair which I unfolded and set to a comfortable angle, so that I could sit facing that portion of the bay which my rather awkward sidelong view afforded me.

In a little while, however, I became aware of the strain on my neck – and sensed once again that indefinable heaviness of atmosphere: an "unparalleled, extraordinary nonesuch sensation" perhaps? Or more properly feeling that someone's unfriendly eyes were fixed upon me, I repositioned the deckchair to face the road and settled back with my eyes closed, gradually easing the cramps in my neck and shoulder. More comfortable in that position I began to nod off . . . only to start awake again as the notion that I was under observation returned in such force that I could no longer ignore it!

Not that there was any way some unknown other could have me under observation . . . nor any reason he would want to, for that matter. But still I snatched open my eyes, as if to catch someone at it.

Across the road, the retaining wall rose in its own shadow; above it, the steep weed- and ivy-festooned hillside climbed up and back through neglected, overgrown terraces to that frowning scarecrow of a place, the deserted hotel up there. Standing now in early evening shade – with its empty, higher windows behind their balconies staring lifelessly out; also its lower windows, like a row of bleary eyes, gazing over the parapet of a balustraded patio – the place looked more gaunt than ever, and even ghostly.

But that was all. No one was spying on me – except perhaps that forsaken hotel itself, if that were at all possible. Which it wasn't . . .

But in any case I narrowed my eyes and studied the place more closely. Not that there was much to study, for the hotel's front was more properly a façade: an Andalusian mask – plaster as opposed to plastic surgery – applied over bricks and mortar presumably in order to enhance the looks of the place, in which task it had failed utterly.

Craning my neck, I stared at the place top to bottom and in that order. Three storeys high, with its close to gothic aspect it reminded me of a de-sanctified church. Above the flat roof's parapet wall, the hollow, sharply-pointed triangles of ornamental gables were pierced through by shallowly slanting beams of sunlight. Then there was that frowning façade, and finally the patio behind its balustrade wall.

As to the latter: because of the steep angle I couldn't see the patio in its entirety, but even so there was something up there that I found just a little odd. While it was obvious that the place had been stripped to the bone and no longer functioned as a hotel, still it appeared that certain of its former embellishments had been left behind.

At each end of the patio and in its centre, standing there like stiff, lonely sentinels, a trio of large, folded-down sunshade parasols continued to watch over places once occupied by hotel guests at alfresco tables. In the case of the parasol on the far right, however, "standing" is probably misleading; for, in fact, it had toppled and now leaned over the parapet in that corner, where its canvas burden tended to sag a little. At the far left its opposite number remained upright but it, too, had suffered an indignity: its canopy had not been fully collapsed, resulting in bare ribs and a badly torn canvas that flapped in an evening breeze off the sea like a tattered pennant.

Only the central parasol appeared in good functional condition: its stem entirely perpendicular and its folded-down canvas canopy secured at the frill three-quarters of the way down its length. I knew that under that frill eight hardwood spokes would be clasped about the stem in a circle, like the arms of some deep-sea octopus. I understood the design of these things by virtue of the fact that my landlady in Exeter had just such a parasol in her garden, beneath which I would often sit reading a book.

As for this forlorn trio: since in their day these sunshades would have been attractive and expensive heavy-duty items of outdoor furniture, I was at first surprised that they had been left behind – especially the pair that appeared to be in good order. That was what I had found a little strange. On reflection, however, I reasoned that just like the parasol with the torn canvas, the other two might also be damaged, their defects hidden or disguised by distance, but sufficient to make salvaging them unprofitable.

Then, as the shadows deepened and my balcony cooled, I went inside, fell asleep on my bed, and woke from disturbing but unremembered dreams barely in time for dinner . . .

At dinner I discovered that the Czech girls – Hannah's "common room-maids" – had duties other than cleaning, tidying and changing the linen: they also served meals. They were pretty girls, too, very much down to earth, unlike the rather haughty Hannah.

"Haughty Hannah" . . . from Hamburg, or maybe Hanover? I had to smile at the alliterative "sound" of it: even though it only sounded in my mind, it served to bring *back* to mind the title of that novelty song, "Hard-Hearted Hannah", about a lady who "pours water on a drowning man". Also, it told me that for some reason I couldn't quite put my finger on I had taken a dislike to the German woman. Perhaps it was because she had "poured water" on my questions about Mrs Anderson.

Anyway, the Czech girls served dinner to me and a room full of amateur fishermen and women, and the chef – decked out in a white hat and apron – came out of the kitchen to enquire about his culinary offerings: were they up to expectations? And actually they had been; indeed the food had been exceptional.

I told him so in the bar later, where I was drinking Coca-Cola with a slice of lemon, and lusting after his Jack Daniel's Old No. 7 on the rocks. A burly, pigtailed Scotsman – "It keeps mah hair oot o' the grub!" – he appreciated my compliments, and he fully understood why I refrained from joining him in a glass of the hard stuff.

"Oh aye," Gavin McCann quietly announced, nodding and lifting a confidential forefinger to tap the side of his nose. "Mah old man – mah father – he found it somethin' o' a problem, too. He liked his wee dram. Truth is, he liked every wee dram in the whole damn bottle! And he paid for it, the old lad: he saw more than his fair share o' pink elephants, that yin. Until the time came when they stampeded all over him, especially on his liver! Aye, and they made a right mess o' that, too."

Pink elephants? Well, I hadn't come across any of them. But other stuff? Oh yes, I had seen other stuff.

"How about you?" I asked him – and quickly added. "But hey, ignore me if that's a bit too personal! It's just that—"

"Am I an alcoholic, d'ye mean?" He shook his head. "No, not yet. So don't be affeard o' buyin' me a drink or two! Mind you, I've seen enough o' drinkin' in this place – and in the town – not tae mention the Andersons' old place down in Polperro. Aye, and ye'd think it would put a body off; but a man gets a taste, and . . . well, let's face it: There's no too much else tae enjoy any more, now is there?" With which he tossed back the drink he was working on, stared expectantly at me, and speculatively at his empty glass.

This was rather more than a subtle hint, but with a little luck I might finally have found a means of discovering something more about the Seaview's – or Mrs Anderson's – mystery, assuming there was such a thing. And so when McCann was sipping on his next drink, a double I had bought him, and which I wished was mine: "Chef," I asked him, "Gavin, what do you make of Mrs Anderson, the Seaview's boss lady?"

"Eh?" he answered sharply, narrowing his eyes and lowering his glass. "What's that, ye say? Janet Anderson? Ye've noticed somethin' about that poor lass? Well let me tell ye: she's one very unfortunate lady, aye! But not so unlucky as some I could mention. *Hmm*! Maybe ye'd care tae hear about it?"

I said I would, of course. And as the drink went in so the story came out and the mystery began to unravel; by which time we had moved to a corner table well away from the other guests, where McCann could tell his story in relative privacy . . .

"Unlucky, aye, Janet and Kevin both," McCann reiterated, with a customary nod and confidential finger tapping his nose. "But as tae who was unluckiest . . . well, at least Janet's still here!"

"Kevin?" I raised a querying eyebrow.

"He was her husband," McCann answered. "And he had the self-same problem as mah old man and yersel' – er, no offence! But ye'll ken mah meanin'."

"No offence taken," I answered. "And I'm not convinced that I was ever a full-fledged alcoholic anyway. You see, it affects me very quickly and so badly that I've never been able to drink that much in the first place! But whether or no, I'm off it and glad to be." Which was at least half true: I was off it.

"Enough said," said he, and again his nod of understanding.

"So?" I shrugged, as if only casually interested. "This, er, Kevin is Mrs Anderson's husband? And he what? Ran off and left her or something?"

He gave me an odd look. "Aye, or somethin' . . ." But then:

"Ye ken," said McCann, "I've always believed there's only one right and proper way tae tell a story, and that's frae the beginnin'. And for that I'll need tae take ye back tae Polperro all of seven long years ago. That's where they met and wed, and began their first business venture together: a small hotel that was on the slide when they bought it and kept right on slidin'. The Andersons, aye – a *verra* odd couple from the start! Janet, so straight-laced and, well, just straight! – but naturally so, ye ken? I mean: never holier-than-thou, no, not at all. Just a steady, level-headed lass. As for Kevin, her junior by some seven or eight years: he was a wee bit immature, somethin' o' a Jack-the-lad, if ye get mah meanin'. Like chalk and cheese, the pair o' them, but they do say opposites attract. And anyway, who was I tae judge or make observations? Nobody.

"As to who I *really* was:

"I was the top chef on a cruise liner until I lost mah job tae a poncy French cook who was havin' it off with the captain! Anyway, that's a whole other story. The thing is, I was discharged frae mah duties in Plymouth in the summer, and so took time off to rethink mah life. A bit o' tourin' found me in Polperro, and that's where I met up with Kevin in a pub one night. He had a few personal problems, too, for which reason he was sinkin' a dram or two . . . or perhaps three or four. This was before Janet knew just how dependent he was becomin' – on booze, ye ken.

"But how's this for a coincidence, eh? Kevin and Janet Anderson, they'd purchased their wee place just a month ago, since when a cook they'd taken on had walked out over some petty argument or other. So there they were without a chef, and me, Gavin McCann, I was without mah cook's whites! But no for long.

"Well, I took the job, got mahsel' installed in the Lookout – a place as wee and quaint as ye could imagine, sittin' there on a hill – and cooked mah heart out for the pair; because 'A' they paid a decent wage and 'B' I really liked them. They treated me right and were like family, the Andersons. She was like a little sister, while he . . . well, I found Kevin much o' a muchness as I mahsel' had been as a young man fifteen years earlier. So I could sort o' watch over her while yet enjoyin' a wee dram with him frae time tae time. That was before his drinkin' got a lot more disruptive, which, lookin' back on it now, didn't take all that long. No, not long at all.

"Ye see, the fact is he couldn't face up tae responsibility o' any kind. Kevin wasn't a waster as such – he wasn't a complete good-for-nothin', ye understand – but simply immature. And when it came tae takin' charge, makin' decisions, well, he just couldn't. Which put a load o' weight on poor Janet's wee shoulders. And him feelin' useless, which I can only suppose he must have, that fuelled the need which only drink could satisfy. And it's a fact that many alcoholics drink because they're unhappy. Kevin was unhappy, I'm certain sure o' that . . . not with Janet, but with his own weaknesses.

"Now, I've told ye how the Lookout was goin' downhill. That was partly because it had been up for sale, empty for a year or so, and was in need o' repairs, some sprucin' up and a touch o' paint here and there. And bein' located inland a mile or so, it wasn't exactly ye're typical seafront property. Janet's plan – and ye'll note I say *her* plan, because she was the thinker, aye and the doer, too – was tae refurbish the place in the autumn and through the winter, when tourism fell off, and get it ready for the spring and summer seasons, when all the grockles – the holidaymakers – would be back in force. O' course, with bills and a mercifully small mortgage tae be paid, it was still necessary that the Lookout should tick over and stay in the black through that first winter.

"Anyway, I ken now that I was perhaps a bit insensitive tae what was happenin' with Kevin but it was Janet hersel' brought it tae mah attention. She asked me straight out but in a verra cordial manner, not tae drink so much with Kevin because it was 'interferin'' with business. And I finally saw what she meant.

"Kevin sometimes worked the bar: oh aye, servin' drinks was one of the few things he was good at. In fact he was *verra* good at it! For every drink I bought in the bar when I was done with mah work in the kitchen, there'd be another 'on the house' frae him. And for every free one Kevin served me, he'd serve another tae himsel'. The bar was scarcely makin' a penny because he was drinkin' it up as fast as he took it in!

"But though his eyes might glaze and his speech slur a wee, he was rarely anythin' other than steady as a rock on his feet. That's the kind o' drunk he was, aye. Which I suppose makes his passin' just a might more peculiar. I mean, it was unlike Kevin tae fall, no matter how much he'd put down his neck . . . But fall he did. Cracked his skull, broke his back, and even crushed his ribs, though how that *last* came about is anybody's guess . . . !"

When McCann paused to sip at his drink I took the opportunity to get a few questions in. "Kevin's passing? You mean there was as accident: he got drunk, fell and died? My God! But with all those injuries . . . that must have been some fall, and from one hell of a height!"

"Ye'd think so, would ye no?" McCann cocked his head on one side enquiringly. "But no, not really. No more than nine or ten feet, actually, or maybe thirteen, if ye include the balcony wall."

The balcony wall? And then, as certain of the Seaview's hitherto unexplained curiosities – its mysteries – began slotting themselves uneasily into place, suddenly I saw it coming. But to be absolutely certain: "And what balcony would that be?" I asked, my own voice and question distant in my ears, as if spoken by some other.

"The one on the corner there," he answered. "The balcony on room number seven, which Janet lets stand empty now, though for no good reason that I can see. A room's a room, is it no? If we were all tae shun rooms or houses where kith and kin died, why, there'd be nowhere left for us tae live! I mean, a body has tae die somewhere, does he no?"

To which, for a moment or two, I could find no answer . . .

He had obviously seen the look on my face and sensed the change in me.

"Ah hah!" he gasped. "But . . . ye came in today, did ye no? And ye found the place full tae brimmin', all except room seven. Well, well! And she actually let ye have it, did she? So then, maybe things are lookin' up after all. And no before time at that."

While I now understood something of what had happened here, there were still several vague areas. Since McCann had intimate knowledge of the Andersons, however – since he'd known them and worked for them all those years – it seemed more than likely he would be able to fill in the blank spots.

Unfortunately, before I could get anything more out of him, Janet Anderson herself came into the bar-room, smiling and nodding at myself and her chef as she crossed to the bar where one of the Czech girls was serving. The pair spoke briefly over the bar, before Mrs Anderson headed back our way and paused to have a word with us, or rather with McCann.

"Do excuse me," she spoke to me first. And then to McCann: "Gavin, I know you're off-duty and I so dislike disturbing you, but would you mind doing up some sandwiches – say nine or ten rounds – for an evening fishing party? I would have asked you earlier, but they've only just spoken to me. And of course you may keep the proceeds."

McCann was up on his feet at once. "No problem at all, mah bonny," he said. And to me, as he turned to go: "I'm obliged to ye for ye're company—" with a knowing wink and a finger to his nose, "—But now ye must excuse me." With which he was gone . . .

I too had stood up at Janet Anderson's approach. Now I offered her a seat and asked if she would like something: a soft drink, perhaps? But she shook her head, saying: "It's kind of you, but there's always work: things to be done, problems to solve." And yet, seeming uncertain of herself and of two minds, she continued to hover there, until finally I felt I had to enquire: "Is there perhaps, er, something . . . ?"

"Oh, no!" She smiled, her hand on my arm, where I sensed a tremor coming through the sleeve of my light jacket. But in another moment the smile left her face, and taking a deep breath, as if suddenly arriving at a decision, she said, "Please do sit down, Mr Smith." And as I seated myself she quickly, nervously continued: "You see, I . . . well, it's just that I've been wondering about . . . about your room. Room number seven hasn't had a paying guest for quite a while, and empty rooms often develop a sort of neglected, even unfriendly atmosphere. I mean, what I'm trying to say is: do you find the room comfortable enough? Have you any complaints? Does the room feel, well, *right* for you?"

"Why, yes!" I replied. "Everything feels just fine!" Which wasn't exactly true, and I would have preferred to answer: "Why are you asking me such odd questions, Mrs Anderson? I mean, what *else* is there about that room – other than what I already know of your troubles – that so concerns you?" But since I *did* know at least that much, and since it was obvious that she was close to the edge, I was naturally unwilling to risk pushing her over. And anyway, if anything remained to be discovered, I believed I could probably find out about it later from McCann. But for the moment, because she was still standing there, I added, "In fact you needn't be at all concerned, because I find the room private and very pleasant. As for complaints: I simply don't have any! I would have to be very fussy to call one small fault a complaint, now wouldn't I? And—"

"—A fault?" she cut me off. "Something . . . well, not quite right? Something you find just a little, er, odd, perhaps?" Her voice was beginning to shake along with her hands.

"No," I quickly answered, finding her nervousness – or perhaps more properly her anxiety – disconcerting. "Nothing at all that you might call 'odd'." Which again wasn't the entire truth. "It's just the view, Mrs Anderson! Just the view from the balcony." By which I meant the partial or sidelong view of the seafront, the beach, and the blue expanse of the bay itself.

But she obviously thought I meant something else. "The view across the road," she said with a knowing nod. "And up the hill to that awful old place." And even though she was steadier now, still her words had come out as breathless as a whisper.

"No, really—" I began, shaking my head. "I'm only talking about—"

But she had already turned and was moving a little unsteadily away, and over her shoulder, interrupting me before I could continue, she very quietly said, "Well if I were you, Mr Smith, I wouldn't look at it. Yes, it's best not to look at it, that's all . . ."

And that did it. Whatever this thing is in me – this lodestone that forever seeks to point me towards the strange and the nonesuch – I was feeling it now as an almost tangible force. And of course I knew that having begun to investigate I must follow it through and track the mystery down. Because if once again I was about to come face to face with . . . well whatever, then I damn well wanted to know everything there was to know about it!

And so I stayed there at that corner table, nursing nothing like a real drink, for at least another hour, until it was dark out and the bar had all but emptied, and still Gavin McCann had not returned. Finally, as the last few guests went off to their rooms or wherever, and the Czech girl was shuttering the bar, I went to her and enquired after the Seaview's chef.

"Gavin?" she said, smiling. "Oh, he'll have gone into town. I think there's a place where they playing the jazz musics. Gavin like a lot these musics. He going most nights."

More than a little frustrated, I said my thanks, goodnight, and went up to my room. There was always tomorrow . . . perhaps

I could find this jazz bar tomorrow night. But in any case, right now I was feeling tired. It had been a long day.

And a weird one . . .

I went out on my balcony, sat in the deckchair in the darkness, with only the street lighting, the glimmer of myriad stars in a clear sky, and the sweeping headlights of vehicles on the steep road for company. Though the flow of the traffic wasn't especially heavy, still the engine sounds of the cars seemed subdued. Which wasn't so strange really, because as I had already noted – and as McCann had pointed out in detailing Kevin Anderson's tragic fall – the balcony was some nine or ten feet above the pavement. This meant that most of the noise was muffled, contained within the road's canyon-like cutting, while the rest of it was deflected upwards by the balcony's wall.

With Anderson's demise in mind, I went to the low wall and looked over. Hard to imagine that someone toppling to the road from here could actually kill himself. Or maybe not, not if he fell on his head. But as for broken ribs: well, that was difficult to picture. Was it possible he'd slipped and fallen with his chest across the wall before he toppled over?

I shook my head, went and sat down again.

The night was refreshingly cool now. To my right, far down below, the glow of seafront illuminations fell on a straggle of couples in holiday finery, strolling arm in arm along the promenade. But I was straining my neck again, and in a little while I averted my gaze, repositioned and reclined my deckchair, and lay back more or less at ease.

Looking across the road and up at a steep angle, I saw the upper reaches of the hillside silhouetted as a solid black mass set against a faint blue nimbus: the glow from the town centre, nestled in a shallow valley lying just beyond the ridge. But as my eyes gradually adjusted, so the silhouette took on a variety of dusky shapes, the most recognizable being that of the derelict hotel.

Where before warm summer sunlight had come slanting through the flat roof's ornamental gables, now there was only the glow of the hidden town's lights . . . like huge three-cornered eyes, burning faintly in the night. And the longer I looked the more acute my night vision became, so that soon the hotel's entire façade was visible to me, if only in degrees of grey and black shade. But . . . that feeling, that sensation, of other, perhaps inimical eyes staring at me was back, and it was persistent. I gave myself a shake, told myself to wake up, laughed at my own fancies. But then, when the chuckles had died away, I strained my eyes more yet to penetrate the night, the smoky frontage of that forsaken old place. And as before I examined its façade – or what I could see of it – from top to toe.

First the flat roof and false gables with their background glow: ghostly but lifeless, inert. Next the face of the place: its window eyes – yet more eyes, yes, but glazed and blind – staring sightlessly out over their balconies. And three floors down the balustraded patio with its trio of guardian parasols.

Except now they were no longer a trio, only a pair . . .

I stared harder yet. On the far right, as before, that one leaned like a bowsprit or a slender figurehead over the corner of the parapet wall. At the far left its opposite number – the one with the partly collapsed canopy – continued to stand upright, but in the still of the night its torn canvas no longer flapped but simply hung there like a dislodged bandage.

So then, maybe the third member of the watch, the one that had seemed intact, had finally fallen over, the victim of gravity or a rotted, broken pole, or both.

But here an odd and fanciful thought. Perhaps there was a *reason* – albeit a hitherto subconscious one – why I imagined and likened these inanimate things to sentinels, guardians, or more properly yet guardian angels: simply that there was something about them. But what? At which point in my introspection, as my gaze continued its semi-automatic descent down the over-grown hillside's night dark terraces, I discovered the missing parasol.

It stood halfway down the terraces facing in my direction. Now I say "facing" because in the darkness it had taken on the looks of a basically human figure that seemed to be gazing out across the bay . . . or perhaps not. Perhaps it was staring down at me?

Let me explain, because I'm pretty sure that you will know what I mean – that you will have seen and even sheltered from the sun under any number of these eight-foot-tall umbrellas in as many hotel gardens and forecourts home and abroad – and so will recognize the following description and understand what I am trying to say.

At the apex of a parasol, its spokes are hinged on a tough wire ring threaded through a circular wooden block. Now this is a vulnerable junction of moving parts – indeed the most important part of the entire ensemble – for which reason it is protected overhead by a scalloped canvas cowl which also serves to over-lap the main canopy, keeping unseasonal rains out. When the parasol is not in use and folded down, however, this cowl often looks like a small tent atop the main body of the thing.

Now, though, with visibility limited by the dark of night, and the canvas canopy not quite fully collapsed, it looked like something else entirely and loaned the contraption this vaguely human shape. The cowl had transformed into a peaked hood, while the partly folded canopy had become a cloak or cassock, so that overall the parasol's appearance was now that of a styl-ized anthropomorph. It looked "human" but to much the same degree as a snowman looks human. It could be argued, however, that the snowman looks *more nearly* human on account of having eyes – albeit that they're made from lumps of coal.

And as for my having endowed this parasol thing with sight: I think that happened when a motorcyclist coming down the hill rounded a bend higher up, and for a split second his headlight beam lit up the figure on the terrace. Just a split second, in which the shadow under the parasol's hood was briefly dispelled and some bright item or items – in fact two of them – reflected the electric glare of the headlight.

Moreover that same headlight beam continued to sweep, until a moment later it swept me! Momentarily dazzled – as the motor-cycle and rider passed beneath my balcony on their descent – I quickly withdrew from whatever reverie or fantasy it was that I had allowed to engulf me. And as my eyes once more adjusted, so the figure halfway down the high terraces was once more a parasol. And nothing more . . .

While it should come as no surprise, there followed one of the most restless nights I have ever known. I dreamed of unfriendly eyes drilling into me, and the inexorable approach of the float-ing, pulsating owner of those eyes which I knew – despite that its actual nature remained shrouded and obscure – was nevertheless intent upon harming me. A nightmare, yes, but a persistent one that had me starting awake on more than one occasion.

The last time this happened I got out of bed and closed the balcony's sliding doors, which I had left half-open against the warmth of the night. A breeze had come up, causing the curtains to flutter and tap against the glass panes. This must have been the billowing motion I had sensed subconsciously, which my mind had translated into the approach of a fiendish alien power.

So I reasoned to myself, but still it was unsettling . . .

The next morning, following an early breakfast, with the strange events of the previous day and night quickly fading, I set out on foot to go up the hill and down into the valley, exploring the centre of the town; and I came across McCann's jazz bar haunt less than half a mile from the Seaview. It sat out of the way in a cul-de-sac housing various indifferent enterprises – a charity shop, barber-shop, hardware store, chemist's shop, etc. As I arrived it was being slopped out by a fat gentleman in a waistcoat, apron and rolled-up shirt-sleeves, who went on to sweep up and bin the somewhat more solid debris of last night's entertainment: some bottle glass and pieces of a glass ashtray, empty cigarette packs and cigarette ends, and the flimsy packaging from various fast foods.

Answering my casual enquiry, this fellow told me the place should now be considered closed for a week to ten days: it was being refurbished. Which put paid to any plan I had entertained about finding and questioning McCann here; for the time being I would have to put the mystery of Janet Anderson and room number seven aside. But then again, now that McCann's favour-ite watering-hole had dried up, as it were, perhaps he would stick more closely to home and the bar at the Seaview. I could always test out this theory tonight.

And I did, but of course that was several hours later. And meanwhile shortly after dinner, finding the bar empty, I walked downhill to the promenade and turned east along the coast road.

On rounding the point, there, hidden from sight of the Seaview beyond Jurassic cliffs of Devon's unique red rock, I found various amusement arcades, cafés, and fish-'n'-chip shops lining the road below the cliffs; and, on the opposite side towards the sea, a modern theatre and a quarter-mile of public flower gardens bordered (astonishingly) by palm trees that flourished here by virtue of Torbay's semi-temperate climate. All very pleasant fare for holidaymakers to the so-called English Riviera, making their all too brief annual escapes from often drab Midland and northern cities.

But I myself was now a holidaymaker or tourist of sorts, and for all that I should be enjoying the adventure – these new sights and pleasing surroundings, and the soft, salty wafts off the sea – still there was something on my mind. And as I retraced my steps along the seafront my thoughts returned to the parasol as I had seen it last night up on the high terraces; and finally, curiously for the first time, I found myself wondering how it had accomplished its migration from the derelict hotel's patio to its new location.

Well, of course I at once recognized at least one perfectly obvious answer to this riddle: for some reason, someone or ones had moved the thing! But as for what reason that might be . . .

It was summer, the nights were warm, and there were plenty of young lovers in the town: I had seen and envied lots of them strolling on the promenade. Local folks would certainly know of the deserted hotel, whose empty grounds must surely make an excellent trysting place; and as for the privacy of the neglected terraces and rampant shrubbery . . . perhaps the shrubbery wasn't the only thing in rampant mode up there!

I'll leave that last to your imagination.

But in any case, that seemed the best answer to the riddle: that some enterprising young lover had moved the parasol to its current location in order to invite his lady-love to a night or nights of passion beneath its sheltering canopy.

And now I know what you're thinking: that I must be a complete and utter idiot, and looking back on it I can't help thinking that perhaps you're right . . .

Back at the Seaview while I found the bar open, only a handful of the less dedicated fishermen were enjoying a drink. Most of the others were out on a boat in the bay, while a few more had invested in a show at the theatre on the promenade: the REANIMATED RAT PACK REVIEW! And according to some of the hoardings I had seen during my short walk: YOU'LL ACTUALLY BELIEVE IT'S *THEM*, DIRECT FROM 1960S LAS VEGAS, ALIVE AND KICKING!

Well "reanimated" or not – dead or alive – I hoped the audience enjoyed the show. But with all the absentees, it did make for a very quiet hotel and bar. And suddenly, out of nowhere, I felt rather alone.

Shortly after settling myself at the same corner table that McCann and I had shared previously, however, who but that self-same Scottish gentleman should appear and proceed direct to the bar. Intent on buying a drink, McCann hadn't as yet noticed me but as I caught the bar girl's eye and signalled her to put his drink on my tab, he turned and saw me. A moment later he joined me, thanked me warmly for his "wee dram", and without any prompting picked up more or less where our initial conversation had left off.

"So then," he began, "ye're lodged in number seven, are ye? And can I take it all's well with ye? No problems with that wee room? I would have asked ye when last we chanced tae speak, but the dear lady o' the house sort o' interrupted our conversation and I didnae wish tae disturb her by havin' her hear mention o' that room. Aye, and it seems we have similar sensibilities, you and me, for which I'm glad."

"Room seven, yes," I told him. "Which is a very nice room, really! The receptionist, Hannah, appears to think so but she didn't tell me much about it, didn't go into details. So Kevin Anderson got drunk and died in a fall from my balcony, did he?" I shook my head wonderingly, and continued: "I suppose there's no accounting for the way a tragedy like that – the loss of a loved one – will affect someone. And ever since his accident, Kevin's widow has shunned that room, eh?"

"Hmmm!" McCann pondered, frowning by way of reply. "Shunned it, aye. Well, that's true as far as it goes. Mahsel', I rather fancy she's affeard o' it! It's possible she dwells too much on what happened tae Kevin in that room: the part it played in his . . . well, while I'm sorry tae be sayin' this, in his frequently drunken deliriums . . ."

I stared hard at McCann's dour face with its grey, serious eyes. "You were party to the way the room seemed to affect him? As if it had some sort of bad or even evil influence on him?"

"But did I no just say so?" McCann replied sharply, raising an eyebrow. And he sipped thoughtfully at his drink before continuing. "Aye, I was privy tae all such. Oh, I worked for them, it's true, but at the same time I'd become a verra close friend tae both o' them. And I'm still close tae Janet . . ."

At which point he paused – possibly to consider his loyalty to the Andersons – and I sensed his sudden reticence. I waited, but after several long moments, while I didn't want to seem too eager for knowledge, still I felt obliged to press him, even to bribe him.

"Gavin, let me get you another drink—" I signalled the bar girl, indicating our requirements, "—to wet your whistle while you tell me the rest of it."

"The rest o' it?" he replied. "Well yes, there is a rest o' it – for what it's worth and for all that it's strange – but I must have ye'r word on it that it's strictly between the two o' us! We must have respect . . . not only for the dead but also for the livin', meanin' Janet. Kevin Anderson wasnae a madman, just an addict, a slave tae Demon Drink . . ." With which he tossed his own drink back, and without so much as a grimace.

Kevin Anderson a madman? Well it was the first I had heard of that possibility. But I nodded and repeated McCann, saying, "As you wish, between the two of us; you have my word on it." But at that very moment our drinks arrived – and both of them were the real thing: two small glasses, full to the brim with amber whisky!

As the girl turned to leave I caught her elbow, explaining, "I didn't want whisky. Whisky for the chef, yes, but I'm drinking Coke – with a slice of lemon!"

"Oh!" Her hand went to her mouth. "I make mistake! I thinking you want same for both! No problem, I take it back."

"No need for that!" said the canny Scot, reaching for both glasses. Much to my shame, however, I beat him to it!

"What?" he said, seeing me take up one of the glasses. "But ye cannae be serious! Not with ye'r problem as ye told it tae me. I'll no be party tae it. Man, with what happened tae Kevin, with what goes on with any alcoholic, I'd have tae hold mahsel' at least partly tae blame!"

"One drink," I told him as the girl moved off. "One and one only. And anyway, surely you can recall my mentioning how I was never a full-blown alcoholic in the first place?"

He nodded. "So ye did, aye. Ah well then, cheers!" And once again he threw back his drink in a single gulp, licked his lips and settled back in his chair. "But no more interruptions, now. Let me get done with it while I'm still in the mood." And after a moment's reflection.

"After we moved in here Kevin's drinkin' really took off. I think maybe he felt even more insecure. That first year, business was only middlin'; they took in enough tae keep their heads above water, but that's all. He was hittin' the stock; she told him tae stop; he began drinkin' in the town. He'd run a message for the hotel – frequently for me, stuff for mah kitchen – and come back two hours later under the influence. It was verra bad o' him, or perhaps not. I mean, it was the booze! He was like a man possessed, and what could he do about it? Oh, it had *such* a grip on him! And yet if ye didnae know him, ye wouldnae ken the state he was in. He kept it hid, drank vodka which is difficult tae smell on a man's breath, managed tae control his speech and balance both; that is, while yet he retained at least a *measure* o' control . . .

"Aye, but then he took tae sneakin' in, goin' tae room number seven – which at the time was a stock room – and sleepin' it off in there. Janet asked me tae keep an eye on him, tae try and wean him off the drink. *Hah*! Poor woman. She neither understood the insidious power o' the booze, nor the strength o' her husband's addiction.

"Well, I tried. I'd have a drink with him in town, try tae get him out o' there when I thought he'd had enough, then shake mah head and leave him tae get on with it when he'd shrug me off and order, 'just one last drink, Gavin my friend'. For that was the problem: it never was the last one. And that's how it went for three years and more, until a time two summer seasons ago.

"That was when Kevin began tae ramble: his 'hallucinations' and what have ye – which probably had their origin not only in the booze but also in the problems at the old hotel up there on the hill. Aye, that's when the worst o' it began, with all the trouble up there: the weird deaths and what all.

"And it all came taegether as spring turned tae summer . . .

"First off, a young fellow – fit, full o' life – was found dead in bed in his balcony room, one o' them rooms lookin' down on your room number seven. An autopsy said he'd been smothered, but how when the door was locked from the inside? Accidentally? That didn't seem right at all! His balcony doors were open, but those balconies up there are too far apart for someone tae jump across from one tae the next. So in the end they had tae settle for a respiratory disorder or some such – maybe a heart attack? Asthma? Hay bleddy fever? None o' which quite fitted the bill – and they left it at that. The only other thing: he'd had quite a few drinks, and maybe too many, on the night he died. Accordin' tae the autopsy, however, that hadnae contributed tae what was considered 'death from natural causes'.

"But a mystery? Damn right! And such a mystery that as I've said, I think it may have added tae Kevin's problem, his drunken hallucinations and delirious raving, for after that he got a lot worse. He was forever in that room; he no longer slept with wee Janet at all but we always knew where tae find him: in room number seven, aye. And if he wasnae sleepin' he'd be sittin' on the balcony gazin' out and up at that place on the hill. As for what he saw up there – what attracted him, other than the mystery o' that young man's inexplicable death – well, who can say? But sometimes we'd hear him chunterin' away tae himsel', ravin' on about . . . well of all things, about a nun!"

A nun? That rang a bell, but one that tolled faintly as yet in the back of my mind. An alarm bell, perhaps? But while I was still trying to locate the source of a suddenly sharpened sensation of unease, McCann was continuing with his story.

"Well, the time came when Janet asked him tae see a psychiatrist: a 'trick cyclist', as Kevin would have it. He must have seen it as a real threat, though, for it did in fact straighten him up . . . well, for a wee while. But the booze and room number seven – and I think that ghostly place up there – they all had him in their thrall, so that in a matter o' weeks his addiction had the upper hand again and he'd reverted tae his auld habits.

"But ye ken, the locals can tell ye tales about that crumbling place up there; rumour has it that it's always had a verra unfortunate, even a bad reputation. And as tae why I bring that up now: it's because o' another occurrence no more than a month or so after that young fellow pegged it in his room from no apparent cause other than a severe lack o' breath. But actually it was far more than just another incident or 'occurrence': it was the death o' another guest!

"Aye, and would ye believe, it was also another tumble from a balcony? Indeed the first such tumble, because it took place some weeks in advance o' Kevin's and from a higher balcony. And that's one o' the most irritatin', aggravatin' things about the whole tragedy – Kevin's tragedy, that is: the muchness that the local press made o' it. Ye see, some bleddy journalist ended up theorizin' that Kevin's fall was possibly – even probably – a copycat suicide, o' all unlikely things! What's more, this same so-called 'reporter' must have been doin' some serious snoopin', because he also mentioned Kevin's 'mania', his ravin' and such, which he could only have extracted from one o' the staff here.

"Well o' course Janet sacked the entire gang without delay, except mahsel and Hannah. But too late for poor Kevin, who had already achieved the posthumous reputation o' havin' been a madman . . .

"Goin' back a wee bit tae the second death up there on the hill: once again this was a young man on his own, and there may have been drink involved. But tae my way o' thinkin', while the booze will put a body tae sleep, it'll rarely find him staggerin' about on a balcony in the wee small hours o' the mornin'!

"Anyway, the experts in the case had their own ideas. Their solution tae this second 'death by misadventure' was that gettin' up tae relieve himsel', this young man had turned the wrong way and, confused by alcohol and still half asleep, had crashed over the balcony wall.

"Now I'm not sayin' that's at all unlikely, ye understand – but I really don't recall too much credence bein' given tae the couple in the room next door, who swore they'd heard him cryin' out and bangin' about before performin' his high dive.

"But anyway that was the end o' that old place on the hill. What with its history, the rumours and all, and two deaths in a row, the place would have been done for even without the people from the Ministry. Oh aye, the Health and Safety men. They came tae check out the balconies – which oddly enough were found tae be perfectly safe! – but as for the rest o' the place: a deathtrap, apparently. And a fire risk tae boot. The owners couldnae sell it so they left it and moved on . . .

"And that's about it; no more tae tell ye. Except maybe one last thing, which I'm a wee bit reluctant tae repeat because it just might tend tae reinforce that crazy-man theory. Anyway –

"Almost the whole hotel, the Seaview in its entirety, would have heard Kevin's ravin' the night he died. And his last words – words that he shrieked, apparently in some kind o' terror – were these: 'The nun! The nun! Oh Janet – it's the nun!' before the sound o' his skull breakin' and that last long silence.

"It woke me up in mah room all flooded in full golden moonlight, so that at first I thought he wasnae shoutin' about some phantom nun at all. No, he could as easily have been howlin' at the full moon. 'The moon! The moon! Oh Janet – it's the moon!' Except as I've said, that might tend tae corroborate that silly lunatic theory. Or is it really so silly after all?

"*Huh*! Who am I kiddin' if not mahsel'? And havin' hinted as much already, I might as well go whole hog and give ye one last tidbit. Aye, for the moon – that bleddy moon – was a *full* moon on all three o' those fateful, indeed fatal occasions!

"But there, all done and I'll say no more, and ye must make what ye will o' it . . ."

With which, and without so much as a goodnight, McCann got up and left. And a little while later, so did I.

But just that single shot of whisky had done its dirty work on me, and utterly incapable of resistance I first went to the bar, bought a half-bottle of the filthy stuff, and without even trying to conceal it took it with me up to room number seven . . .

I remember something of it. Such as sitting on my balcony thinking, drinking. And out there over the night dark sea, a shining silver disc – oh yes, a bright full moon – laying its shimmering pathway on the slumbering waters of the bay.

Lying back in my deckchair and looking the other way, looking up at that great grim shape silhouetted against the glow of the hidden town, my rebellious or simply lying eyes were having more than a little trouble penetrating the darkness on the high hillside terraces. It was the booze, of course, but I persisted . . . at least until I forgot what I was looking for, only remembering when finally I found it.

Previously it had stood watch up there along with a pair of damaged companion sentinels behind the derelict hotel's balustraded patio wall; then it had reappeared at a location halfway down the terraces, perhaps placed there – or so I had conjectured – by some midnight Romeo, to act as a roof over his bower or love nest. And now . . .

But, how had it made its way here? To this spot directly across the dark canyon of the road, behind the rim of the great retaining wall, where only its cowl and upper half were visible from my balcony? Perhaps a freakish gust of wind had carried it aloft, tumbling it down the terraces and landing it right-side-up, trapped against the hillside's retaining wall.

Well yes, perhaps. And perhaps not.

But there it was, for all the world like the top half of an eerily human figure – indeed of a cowled nun! – looking down on me. And as a car crested the hill and its headlights shone however briefly on that oddly religious shape behind the high wall, so the darkness under the cowl flashed alive in a pair of triangular flares, which were at once extinguished as the beam swept on.

These things I remember, and also laughing to myself in the stupid way that drunks do, as I stumbled in through the balcony doors to collapse upon my bed . . .

I felt it coming. But don't ask me how; I just knew. Perhaps it was this affinity of mine for weirdness, this magnetism working on my mind, my being. I had felt it, it had felt me. I had seen it, it had seen me. I definitely had *not* wanted to know it, and that could be why I had failed to recognize it: a natural reluctance to engage yet again with the Great and Terrible Unknown. And it very definitely did *not* want its existence revealed!

Of necessity a secretive creature, it had become, unfortunately for me, practised in the erasure of any suspect knowledge of its being. And quite simply – as an adept of this indelicate art – it now intended to erase me!

I felt it coming, its flexible mantle fully open, parachuting on the night air. But immobilized, my mind dulled by drink, I refused to believe; I denied it. It could not be . . . it was a nightmare . . . the Demon Drink had filled my mind with monsters. Ah! But what then of the Thin People of old London Town? Or the Clown on Stilts as I believed I had once seen him or it? Or had they too been impure and not so simple fantasies of the flowing bowl, mere figments of fermentation, tremens of delirium?

Yet now I could even smell it: a not-quite-taint, a waft of mushroomy fungus spores, a hybrid thing's clammy innards, contracting to engulf and smother me . . .

My God! I felt it on my face like a slither of wet leather! And knowing that it was real, *I came awake screaming!*

It was there in room number seven with me, inside the wide-open balcony doors, leaning over my bed. Its membraneous canopy was closing over my head, shutting off my air, holding me down. I lashed out with both arms, groped beyond the perimeter of the thing's web. My left hand found and grasped the bedside lamp. I automatically thumbed the switch and dragged the softly glowing lamp inside the living canopy with me.

I was stone-cold sober in a moment, as this alien – what, intelligence? – was illumined from within. And seeing it like that, *literally* from within, I remembered comparing the structure of more orthodox, man-made parasols to the physical form of the octopus. Oh, yes! And now . . . well it wasn't only the more orthodox ones!

For there beneath its mantle – where, thank God, there was no huge parrot beak but, instead, surrounding a pulsating slit-like mouth, a ring of eight short, worm-like tongues, spatulate at their tips for the delivery of whatever food sustained it – I saw that indeed the thing had tentacular limbs, all eight of them connected by webbing and lined with grasping suckers.

As for the mantle stretched between these limbs, while it was flexible and had the consistency of a bat's wing, allowing my lamp to shine through it, still it had the strength of fine leather and was redolent of the thing's alien essences: anaesthetic odours which were aiding it in my suffocation! Except I wasn't about to die like that, or by allowing it to drag me to the balcony and hurling me over!

Holding my breath, I stopped breathing the thing's poisons and thrust my glowing lamp deep into the ugly gash of its mouth. The lamp, too, had a canopy of sorts: its shade, which crumpled up and fell apart as the electric bulb penetrated the monster's pulsing, dribbling mouth. Only moments ago energized, that bulb couldn't be very warm, but still it was hot enough to alarm the thing.

Muscles inside the mouth closed on the bulb like a ray fish crushing a mollusk – and the bulb exploded with a loud popping sound. The thing's mouth was lacerated internally. It spat thin shards of glass into my face, however harmlessly, thank God; it also spat foul, stinking yellow fluid, its blood, and commenced a violent shuddering as it jerked up and away from my face and upper torso.

Then, trying to yell, I only succeeded in gasping, and when at last I could breathe properly I shouted my outrage. This was as much to hasten the creature's retreat as an expression of my horror. Vivid curses poured out of me as I reached up and tried to throttle its central column, a thin stem of a "body" and, as if these breathy obscenities had helped to inflate it, the monster's canopy bulged and began to open.

Still shuddering, now it convulsed, and chitin hooks on the ends of its flailing tentacles caught on the frame of my single bed, turning it on its side. Saying a silent prayer of thanks, I sprawled on the floor, from where I could see the thing's mushroom shape, its silhouette, against a faint night glow. In full flight now, it was desperately squeezing the bulk of its partly opened canopy out through the sliding doors on to the balcony.

Getting up from the floor I lunged after it. I didn't know what I could do, if anything, but I was more angry than afraid. It wasn't my fault that this creature, like others I had known, was attracted to me – or me to them, whichever – and I wanted it, them, to know we could fight back, that men could be deadly dangerous too.

And still shouting at the top of my voice I rushed out on to the balcony where, fully inflated, the monster was now drifting aloft. How such a thing could fly or glide – well, don't ask me – perhaps by generating gasses within its mantle? I don't know. But anyway I tried to get hold of the clawed, club-like foot at the base of its slimy stem of a body. It was a wasted effort; I couldn't get a grip and those retractable claws were sharp.

In another moment it was gone, rising into darkness, ascending by means of unknown gravity-defying abilities, assisted by the smallest of breezes off the sea.

"Damn you, you bastard thing!" I yelled after it, and suddenly realized that for some little time I'd been hearing a loud hammering at my door. And there I was, leaning across the balcony wall, when the door to the landing crashed inwards from its hinges and Gavin McCann lurched into the room. Close behind the Scotsman came a shrill Janet Anderson, both she and he in nightclothes under their dressing-gowns.

While a single dim night-light was burning on the landing, the ceiling light in my room had remained switched off since I came up from the bar. Which meant the eyes of the newcomers – my would-be rescuers – would take a moment or two to adjust to the gloom. And indeed I clearly heard McCann's gasping, urgent question: "Damn! Where's the bleddy light switch?"

That and Janet Anderson's trembling, panted answer: "Here, Gavin – I know where it is – let me do it!" But then, before she could find the switch, that smell, a faint fungus reek wafting down to me where I leaned out across the balcony wall and scanned the sky. It came from . . . from over there, yes, borne on the breeze off the sea! And as I turned my eyes toward the bay at that awkward angle, I saw something blot the moon in the instant before the monster's clawed, club-like foot swung at me like a pendulum, catching in my shirt.

I was almost but not quite dragged bodily from the balcony. I felt my shirt rip, and I fell! I fell—

—But on the *inside* of the wall. Brilliant lights flashed in my head as my skull cracked against the top of the wall. My body flopped to the floor and the very last thing I remember: Janet Anderson's arms cradling me, and her sobbing, hysterical voice fading into a painful, rushing darkness as she questioned me: "What happened, Mr Smith? What did you see? Was it . . . was it the nun?"

And then, nothing . . .

I had suffered a cut scalp and very bad concussion, which kept me out of it for four days, three of which I was semi-conscious and had my doctors fearing there could even be some brain damage. While that might seem serious enough, poor Janet Anderson had suffered rather more: a total nervous breakdown. She spent a month in what was referred to euphemistically as "a refuge", the secure mental wing of a local hospital.

As for the Seaview's chef, bless his heart: in addition to cooking and helping Hannah to run the hotel, Gavin McCann dedicated what was left of his time during that period to visiting Janet Anderson and myself in equal measure: his employer out of friendship and loyalty, and myself, oddly enough, out of guilt. And it was during one such visit after I returned to full consciousness that he asked me what it was all about: what exactly had I seen?

But I didn't tell him. For from the moment I had opened my eyes to perceive the world afresh, I had been thinking it over. And I had come to a conclusion, settled on an explanation which I might at least *attempt* to believe. For, let's face it, I still could not state with absolute conviction that there really were thin, telegraph-pole-tall people in London; I couldn't swear to them any more than to pink elephants! And likewise clowns – or at least one such – on stilts!

What, a clown with stilt legs, and wings? A clown who flew away with a small girl's smaller dog and who would, presumably, if they were available, fly off with other rather more meaningful small things? No, of course I couldn't believe in him. Not while it was even remotely possible that he had been . . . well, simply a strikingly original clown, and what I had made of him had been fevered guesswork, imagination and hallucination, but mainly nightmares spawned in a bottle of booze.

That is what I told myself to believe; I must at least *try* to believe in that. Because if I failed to do so, then I might have to accept advanced degenerative alcoholic madness. And as for the latter, well, Gavin McCann was able – in his way and mistakenly or not – to corroborate something of what I was forcing myself to accept. And seated by my bed wringing his hands, on that occasion when I had nothing to tell him: "I blame mahsel'!" he said. "Me and the bleddy booze both! I should *never* have let ye take that short, not knowin' how it was with ye! Aye, and Janet and me, we found ye're empty bleddy bottle on the balcony. Man, ye must have been drunk out o' ye're mind!"

Well yes, maybe then. But no more . . .

*       *       *

And something a little over a month later – after reading in my Exeter newspaper about a hotel fire in a certain resort: an unsolved case of arson in a disused, derelict building, according to a police report – I called McCann on the number he'd given me to find out what he knew.

"Aye, that old place on the hill," he told me, guardedly I thought. "I was in the bar and heard the sirens. Janet was out in the town doin' some late shoppin' when it went up. She came in and we watched the blaze taegether. But it was arson, definitely. Why, we could smell the petrol fumes right down there on the balcony o' room number seven! And do ye know what? That poor woman's been right as rain ever since!"

So there you go. I've told myself I can stay off the booze and avoid further imaginary confrontations, or I can take the occasional drink and suffer the consequences, whatever.

But you know, when my mind is clear and the night is dark, I lie in my bed and turn things over in my head, and then it's as if I am fully in touch with *un*natural Nature. I've heard of the octopuses that imitate coconuts to "stroll" on their dangling tentacles through dangerous shallows. I've read of insects that imitate leaves, and seahorse fishes that are indistinguishable from the seaweeds they live in. There are so many kinds of insects, plants and animals that pretend for their security or, as often as not, their fell purposes to be other than they are. And there are thousands of small species that aren't even catalogued as yet.

And that's only the *small* species . . .

As for me and my problem, if indeed I have a problem other than the alcohol, can it be coincidence, pure and simple? Or is it that I am in fact a lodestone, a lightning-rod for the weird and the wonderful? Because if the latter is true, then it seems I'm actually destined to be drawn to such things: to these thin people, these clowns-on-stilts, these nuns and nonesuches.

In which case so be it.

But if I can't avoid them, you can at least be sure I'll be looking out for them!

# MICHAEL KELLY

## Princess of the Night

FOLLOWING HIS AWARD-NOMINATED ANTHOLOGY *Apparitions*, Canadian Michael Kelly currently has a further two projects as an editor forthcoming: *Chilling Tales* is a volume featuring Canadian horror writers, while *Shadows & Tall Trees* is a literary journal of contemporary strange tales. The author's recent fiction can be found in *PostScripts*, *Space & Time* and *Supernatural Tales*.

About his second story in this volume, Kelly recalls: "The genesis of 'Princess of the Night' is a little murky. It was written for an anthology of Halloween tales. Alas, it didn't make it into the book.

"The tale then sold to a slick new professional magazine, where it promptly languished for four years until the magazine (which published four issues, I believe) folded before publication. I forgot about the story for a while. Then, one day, as I was looking through my files for possible stories to include in a new collection, I chanced upon it again."

Let's be grateful he rediscovered the story, because it rounds off this edition of *Best New Horror* with a nice short, sharp jolt in the EC comics tradition . . .

WARREN HEARD IT, quite plainly, outside his front door; a faint stirring, a sigh, a melancholy moan. He waited . . . waited . . . but no knock came. Then another sound, like shuffling feet.

Warren groaned, dropped the magazine, and lifted his tired bones from the rocker. He shuffled over to the door and pulled it open.

"Trick or treat."

Warren looked down, puzzled. The first thing he noticed about her was the scar; a livid line that zigzagged from the corner of her mouth to her earlobe. In the wan light of the full moon it pulsed, as if alive. She was a wee pale thing with fine blond hair and cool blue eyes that gazed flatly at him. Couldn't have been more than nine or ten years old, Warren thought. She was dressed in a purple robe, trimmed in gold. A tiara sat on her head. A little princess. She clutched an orange plastic pumpkin that grinned blackly.

Dead leaves skittered on the porch. The wind rushed in, carrying a touch of frost. It smelled like earth and worms and rain. It snatched at his sweater, the wind. It swirled around him, whispering secrets only he knew.

Warren breathed deeply. Burning leaves and peppermint rain. Autumn! A half-smile creased his face. Once – long, long ago – he'd been an autumn person. Once, long ago, he'd been a man who'd smiled.

"*Trick or treat.*" Her voice was an autumn voice, a voice of fog and rain and green mystery. And Warren hadn't seen her mouth move.

Warren sighed. He hadn't left the porch light on, hadn't left a Jack-O-Lantern in the window. Didn't they know he never celebrated Halloween? He hadn't celebrated Halloween in a very long time, not since . . . since . . . Why were they knocking at his door? Then he remembered that there hadn't actually been a knock. And another memory came bubbling to the surface, one that had lain hidden like a dark stone in a cool riverbed: wet and foggy night; a sudden blur of blond hair; hiss of tyres; a faint *thump*; and Warren – before driving away – watching through the rain-blurred window as a plastic pumpkin bumped and rolled down the dark, almost empty street.

"*Trick or treat.*" Her voice was an autumn voice – dead leaves, rich earth and green menace.

Warren shuddered, took a step back. Though her mouth didn't move, Warren heard a sigh, a miserable moan. And as the little princess took a slow step forward, one dim thought entered Warren's head:

It wasn't Halloween.

# STEPHEN JONES and KIM NEWMAN

---

# Necrology: 2009

ONCE AGAIN, WE ACKNOWLEDGE the passing of writers, artists, performers and technicians who, during their lifetimes, made significant contributions to the horror, science fiction and fantasy genres (or left their mark on popular culture and music in other, often fascinating, ways) . . .

## AUTHORS/ARTISTS/COMPOSERS

American fan artist **Randy Bathurst** died of a heart attack on January 10. He contributed cartoons to many 1970s fanzines, including the first issue of *File 770*, and also designed the first FAAn Award.

British science fiction fan and artist **Harry** (Henry) **Turner** died on January 11, aged eighty-eight. The son of a music hall escapologist and illusionist, Turner developed a life-long interest in space travel and science fiction at an early age. He first became involved in fandom in the 1930s as a member of the Manchester Interplanetary Society, editing the group's journal *The Astronaut*. He began publishing his own fanzine, *Zenith*, in the early 1940s, and the following decade published (with Eric Needham) *Now & Then*. Turner continued to contribute his illustrations of "impossible objects" to numerous fan publications until a stroke wiped out many of his fan memories a few years before his death.

American writer **Hortense Calisher** died on January 13, aged ninety-seven. She began her career writing for *The New Yorker*, and her works include the alternate history novel *Journey from Ellipsia* and the 1951 horror story "Heartburn".

British-born Emmy Award-winning composer **Angela Morely**, who before a sex change operation in 1972 was credited as Wally Stott, died of complications from a fall and subsequent heart attack in Arizona on January 14. She was eighty-four. A former conductor of the BBC Radio Orchestra, her credits include *Captain Nemo and the Underwater City* (as "Stott"), *The Slipper and the Rose*, *Watership Down* and episodes of TV's *Wonder Woman*. She also worked as an uncredited musical arranger on *Peeping Tom*, *The Private Life of Sherlock Holmes*, *The Little Prince*, *Star Wars*, *Superman* (1978), *The Empire Strikes Back*, *Deathtrap* (1982), *E.T. The Extraterrestrial*, *Fire and Ice*, *The Day After* and *Hook*.

British novelist, playwright and barrister **Sir John** [Clifford] **Mortimer** died following a long illness on January 16, aged eighty-five. Best known for creating *Rumpole of the Bailey*, he also worked on the scripts for *The Innocents* (based on Henry James' "Turn of the Screw"), *Bunny Lake is Missing*, and Ray Bradbury's *Something Wicked This Way Comes* (uncredited). In 1971 he successfully defended *Oz* magazine against charges of obscenity.

American TV writer and jazz musician **Gordon** "Whitey" **Mitchell** died of cancer on January 16, aged seventy-six. He was a story editor and staff writer on CBS-TV's *Get Smart* (1969–70) and his other credits include episodes of *My Mother the Car*, *Mork and Mindy* and a 1986 *Twilight Zone*.

Screenwriter, celebrity journalist and a publicist for Warner Bros., **Mickell Novack** died of heart failure on January 22, aged ninety-one. The wife of film producer Walter Seltzer, she co-scripted *One Million B.C.* starring Lon Chaney, Jr (remade by Hammer as *One Million Years B.C.*) and the film version of Thorne Smith's body-swap novel *Turnabout*.

Seventy-six-year-old **John** [Hoyer] **Updike**, widely recognized as one of the "greatest generation" of American authors, died of lung cancer on January 27. Best known for his 1984 novel *The Witches of Eastwick* and its belated sequel, *The Widows* *of Eastwick*, the Pulitzer Prize-winning writer, critic and poet's 1997 novel, *Toward the End of Time*, was science fiction.

Influential Italian SF writer **Lino Aldani** died of lung disease on January 31, aged eighty-two. He began publishing SF stories in 1960, and his novels include *Quando le radici, Eclissi 2000* and *Nel segno della luna bianca*. In 1963 he founded his own short-lived SF magazine, *Futuro*, which was revived many years later as *Futuro Europa*.

Scottish-born author and English teacher **Stuart Gordon** (Richard Alexander Steuart Gordon, aka Richard A. Gordon and Alex R. Stuart) died of a heart attack in Shanghai, China, on February 7, aged sixty-one. He began his career contributing to *New Worlds* in the mid-1960s, and he also sold stories to Philip Harbottle's *Vision of Tomorrow* magazine. His SF novels include *Time Story, Slaine and the Crow God, Smile on the Void, Fire in the Abyss*, and the "Eye" and "Watchers" trilogies. Gordon also wrote a number of non-fiction works, including *The Paranormal: An Illustrated Encyclopedia, The Encyclopedia of Myths and Legends* and *The Book or Curses*.

**Edward** (Falaise) **Upward**, considered to be the oldest living author in the UK, died on February 13 at the age of 105. While at Cambridge in the 1920s, he created the surreal "Mortmere" series of stories with Christopher Isherwood.

American publisher **Alfred A. Knopf, Jr** died of complications following a fall on February 14. He was ninety. After working at the eponymous publishing company his father founded, he left in 1959 to co-found independent imprint Atheneum. Following a series of takeovers, Knopf eventually became senior vice-president at Macmillan until his retirement in 1988.

American fan and convention runner **Chuck** (Charles Albert) **Crayne** died of cardiac problems on February 16, his seventy-first birthday. He had been disgnosed with spinal cancer a few days earlier. During the 1960s he edited the Los Angeles Science Fiction Society newszine *De Profundis* and co-chaired the 1972 Worldcon – the largest SF convention held at that time. Crayne also helped found the mystery convention Bouchercon in 1970, and in 1976 he was involved in creating the first NASFiC.

Legendary SF and fantasy author **Philip José Farmer** died in his sleep on February 25, aged ninety-one. His transgressive alien sex story "The Lovers" was rejected by twenty-six publishers before it appeared in *Startling Stories* in 1952. The author's more than seventy-five books include the "Riverworld", "The World of Tiers", "Herald Childe", "Dayworld" and the pulp-influenced "Doc Caliban and Lord Grandrith" series. He also published fictional biographies of Tarzan and Doc Savage, plus such literary pastiches as *The Wind Whales of Ishmael, The Other Log of Phileas Fogg, The Adventure of the Peerless Peer by John H. Watson M.D., Hadon of Ancient Opar* and *Flight to Opar, A Barnstormer in Oz, Escape from Loki: Doc Savage's First Adventure* and the Tarzan novel *The Dark Heart of Time. Venus on the Half-Shell* was published under the byline of Kurt Vonnegut's hack SF writer "Kilgore Trout" (reputedly partly inspired by Farmer), his numerous short stories were collected in *The Book of Philip José Farmer, Riders of the Purple Wage* and *The Best of Philip José Farmer*, amongst many other titles, and he edited the anthology *Mother Was a Lovely Beast*. He was a winner of the Hugo Award, a SFWA Grand Master Award and a World Fantasy Life Achievement Award.

Oscar-nominated Italian screenwriter, **Tullio Pinelli**, died in Rome on March 7, aged 100. Best known for his collaborations with Federico Fellini, Pinelli's credits include the director's *8½* and *Juliet of the Spirits*.

Prolific French horror and SF author **André Caroff** (André Carpouzis), who produced the eighteen-volume "Madame Atomos" horror series, died on March 13, aged eighty-four.

Spanish comic-strip artist, **"Pepe" Gonzalez** (José González Navarro), best known for drawing *Vampirella* for Warren Publishing throughout the 1970s and early 1980s, died on March 13, aged sixty-nine. He had fallen into a coma following a long illness. While still a teenager in the late 1950s, Gonzalez began working for such British publications as *TV Heroes* and *Young Marvelman Annual*. As well as contributing to various UK romance titles, in the mid-1960s he also illustrated a syndicated strip based on TV's *The Avengers*.

Another Spanish comics artist, **José (María) Casanovas, Sr**, died on March 14, aged seventy-four. He began drawing from Spanish comics in 1957, and later worked extensively outside his native country, with strips appearing in Germany, Italy, Holland, Finland and America. During the 1970s and 1980s he contributed to such UK titles as *2000AD*, *Starlord*, *Starblazer*, *Scream!!*, *Eagle* and *Judge Dredd Annual*.

Oscar-nominated American screenwriter **Millard Kaufman** died from complications from open-heart surgery the same day, aged ninety-two. Best known for co-creating the near-sighted cartoon character *Mr Magoo* in 1949 with animator John Hubley, Kaufman also wrote *Unknown World*, *Aladdin and His Lamp*, *Bad Day at Black Rock* and *The War Lord* before becoming MGM's leading script doctor, working on countless films uncredited. He also "fronted" the script of Joseph H. Lewis' cult classic *Gun Crazy* (aka *Deadly is the Female*, 1950) for blacklisted writer Dalton Trumbo. Kaufman's first novel was published in 2007 when he was eighty-six.

American songwriter **Jack Lawrence** [Schwartz] died of complications from a fall on March 15, aged ninety-six. Best known for the songs "Beyond the Sea" and "Tenderly", he also wrote the songs for Disney's *Sleeping Beauty* (1959).

Hollywood comedy scriptwriter and TV director **Mort** (Morton) **Lachman**, who was the head writer for Bob Hope's "joke factory" for twenty-seven years, died of a heart attack on March 17, aged eighty-nine. He had been suffering from diabetes.

American writer **John Kennedy**, who had some SF stories published in *Galaxy* and elsewhere, died on March 18, aged sixty-three. His short fiction was collected in the chapbook *Nova in a Bottle* (2003).

Canadian writer and collector **Chester D. Cuthbert**, a member of First Fandom, died on March 20, aged ninety-six. He had two stories published in Hugo Gernsback's pulp magazine *Wonder Stories* in 1934, and in 2007 he donated 60,000 SF books and magazines to the University of Alberta.

Triple Oscar-winning film composer and conductor **Maurice**(-Alexis) **Jarre** died of cancer in Malibu, California, on March 29, aged eighty-four. The French-born Jarre composed the music for more than 150 movies, including Georges Franju's *Les yeux sans visage* (aka *Eyes Without a Face/The Horror Chamber of Dr Faustus*), *Judex*, *The Collector*, *The Night of the Generals*,

Disney's *The Island at the Top of the World*, *Mr Sycamore*, *The Man Who Would Be King*, *Ressurection*, *Firefox*, *Dreamscape*, *Mad Max Beyond Thunderdome*, *The Bride*, *Enemy Mine*, *Solarbabies*, *Fatal Attraction*, *Julia and Julia*, *Ghost*, *Solar Crisis* and *Jacob's Ladder*.

British author, anthologist and biographer **Michael** (Andrew) **Cox** died on March 31, aged sixty. He had been suffering for some years from a rare and aggressive form of cancer that gradually causes blindness. A former singer-songwriter (he recorded two albums under the name "Matthew Ellis" and another as "Obie Clayton"), in 1977 he joined Thorsons Publishing Group, and in 1989 he became a senior commissioning editor at Oxford University Press, where he edited *The Oxford Book of English Ghost Stories* and *The Oxford Book of Victorian Ghost Stories* (both with R.A. Gilbert), *The Oxford Book of Twentieth-Century Ghost Stories*, *Twelve Tales of the Supernatural* and *Twelve Victorian Ghost Stories*, as well as several other anthologies. Cox also wrote the acclaimed biography *M.R. James: An Informal Portrait* (1983), and he received a record-breaking advance of £430,000 for his debut novel, the Victorian mystery *The Meaning of Night* (2005). It was followed three years later by a sequel, *The Glass of Time*, and he was working on a third novel at the time of his death.

British writer, playwright and poet **John** (Alfred) **Atkins** died on March 31, aged ninety-two. When he was called up for war service in 1943 (often going AWOL), his job as Literary Editor at the left-wing newspaper *Tribune* was taken by George Orwell. He published literary biographies of Walter de la Mare, J.B. Priestley and Orwell, amongst others, and his 1955 study, *Tomorrow Revealed*, drew on prophetic and utopian writings.

Comics artist **Frank Springer** died of prostate cancer on April 2, aged seventy-nine. He began his career in the early 1950s, working on newspaper strips such as *Terry and the Pirates*, *Rex Morgan M.D.* and, later, *The Incredible Hulk*. During the 1960s and 1970s he worked for Dell Comics, DC Comics and Marvel Comics, most notably on *Nick Fury Agent of S.H.I.E.L.D.* and *Conan the Barbarian*. Springer also contributed to *National Lampoon* and worked on the animated TV show *Space Ghost*. He retired from comics in 1992 and took up oil painting.

The sixty-one-year-old Dungeons and Dragons co-creator Dave (Lance) **Arneson** died of cancer on April 7, just over a year after the death of the game's other creator, Gary Gygax.

American author **Jack Owen Jardine**, who wrote SF and fantasy under a number of pseudonyms, died on April 14 after a long illness. He was seventy-seven and had suffered a stroke in 2005, from which he never fully recovered. As "Larry Maddock" he wrote four *Agent of T.E.R.R.A.* time-travel novels: *The Flying Saucer Gambit*, *The Golden Goddess Gambit*, *The Emerald Elephant Gambit* and *The Time Trap Gambit*; as "Howard L. Cory" he collaborated with his wife at the time, Julie Ann Jardine, on *The Mind Monsters* and *The Sword of Lankor*, and as "Arthur Farmer" he produced several erotic novels, including *The Nymph and the Satyr*. During the 1960s Jardine published a number of stories in *Alfred Hitchcock's Mystery Magazine* and *Ellery Queen's Mystery Magazine*, and *Unaccustomed As I Am to Public Dying* was a collection of his mystery stories published in 2005.

German-born broadcaster, writer, celebrity chef and former British politician **Sir Clement Freud** (Clemens Raphael Freud) died in London on April 15, aged eighty-four. The grandson of Sigmund Freud and brother of artist Lucian Freud, his 1968 best-selling children's book, *Grimble*, has 150,000 members in its fan club and is a favourite of J.K. Rowling and Neil Gaiman. For almost sixty years, Freud was married to June Flewett, who was the inspiration for the character of "Lucy Pevensie" in C.S. Lewis' "Chronicles of Narnia" books.

Acclaimed and often controversial British "New Wave" SF author **J.** (James) **G.** (Graham) **Ballard** died of complications from prostate cancer on April 19, aged seventy-eight. Born in the International Settlement in Shanghai, China, his family was imprisoned by the Japanese during World War II, and Ballard moved to the UK in 1946. His first short stories appeared in *New Worlds* and *Science Fantasy* in December 1956, and he went on to write a number of dystopian or fantastic novels, including *The Wind from Nowhere*, *The Drowned World*, *The Burning World*, *The Crystal World*, *Crash* (filmed by David Cronenberg), *Concrete Island*, *High-Rise*, *The Unlimited Dream Company* and *Hello America*. His short fiction is collected in *Billenium*,

*The Four-Dimensional Nightmare*, *Passport to Eternity*, *The Terminal Beach*, *The Impossible Man*, *The Day of Forever*, *The Disaster Area*, *The Overloaded Man*, *The Atrocity Exhibition*, *Vermillion Sands*, *Chronopolis*, *The Venus Hunters* and *The Voices of Time*, amongst other titles. Steven Spielberg filmed his semi-autobiographical childhood memoir *Empire of the Sun* in 1987. Ballard's archive of papers and manuscripts was subsequently donated by his family to the British Library.

American author and journalist **Ken Rand** died of complications from a rare abdominal cancer on April 21. He was sixty-two. Rand's work was published widely in the small presses, and his novels include *Phoenix*, *The Golems of Laramie County*, *Fairy BrewHaHa at the Lucky Nickel Saloon* and *A Cold Day in Hell*. His prolific short fiction is collected in *Tales of the Lucky Nickel Saloon*, *Bad News from Orbit*, *Soul Taster*, *Through Wyoming Eyes*, *Where Angels Fear: The Collected Short Fiction Volume One* and *The Gods Perspire: The Collected Short Fiction Volume Two*. Rand also published a number of non-fiction titles, including *The Human Visions: The Talebones Interviews*.

New Zealand-born British TV writer and Western and thriller novelist **John Gillies** (aka Jacques Gillies, John Gill and Jake Gillies) died in April. He wrote the original TV play that Hammer's *Cash on Demand* (starring Peter Cushing) was based on, along with episodes of *Danger Man*, *Armchair Thriller*, *Menace* and *Shadows of Fear*.

Austrian-born parapsychologist and novelist **Hans Holzer** died in Manhattan after a long illness on April 26, aged eighty-nine. He travelled the world investigating reportedly haunted houses and wrote more than 140 books, starting with *Ghost Hunter* in 1963 and including *Where the Ghosts Are*, *Haunted House Album* and *Hans Holzer's The Supernatural*. With medium Ethel Johnson-Meyers he visited the house in Long Island in which Ronald DeFeo, Jr killed six family members in 1974. As a result, Holzer's 1979 non-fiction book *Murder in Amityville* became the basis of the 1982 movie *Amityville II: The Possession*. He also published two related novels, *The Amityville Curse* (filmed in 1990) and *The Secret of Amityville*. In 1971 Holzer was a technical advisor on the movie *Night of Dark Shadows*, and he also wrote the "Randy Knowles: Psychic

Detective" trilogy in the 1970s. His other novels include *The Psychic World of Bishop Pike*, *The Clairvoyant*, *Star of Destiny* and *The Entry*.

Fifty-seven-year-old American fantasy author **Tom** (Thomas Franklin) **Deitz** died on April 27 of complications following a serious heart attack in January. His fifteen novels include *Windmaster's Bane* (1986) and nine further volumes in the "David Sullivan" series, the "Soulsmith" series, the "Thunderbird O'Conner" duology and the "Tale of Eron" quartet.

Sometimes controversial writer and movie collector **Richard** "Bojack" **Bojarski** died in April while visiting a friend in New York. Known for his "Hugo Headstone" comics in *Castle of Frankenstein* magazine and *The Monster Times*, he also wrote the early reference books *The Films of Boris Karloff* and *The Films of Bela Lugosi*.

British fanzine and feminist writer **Abigail Frost** was found dead in her London apartment on May 1, aged fifty-seven. She had been battling cancer and apparently died the day before from an undiagnosed heart problem. Frost contributed articles and convention reports (sometimes in collaboration with Roz Kaveney) to a number of fan publications and, for a couple of years in the early 1980s, she was the designer for *Interzone*. Frost won the 1993 Trans Atlantic Fan Fund (TAFF) to attend the World SF Convention in San Francisco, but created controversy three years later when, as European administrator, she used the funds to pay her own debts.

Cuban-born American comics artist and animator **Ric Estrada** died of prostate cancer on May 1, aged eighty-one. He moved to New York in the late 1940s to study art and began working on EC's *Two-Fisted Tales* and *Frontline Combat* in the early 1950s. Although the penciller also worked for Dell Comics and Warren Publishing's *Eerie*, he is best remembered for his work with DC Comics, which included *Wonder Woman*, *Legion of Super-Heroes*, and many war titles. Estrada also occasionally contributed to the syndicated *Flash Gordon* newspaper strip and, during the 1980s, he worked on such cartoon TV series as *He-Man and the Masters of the Universe*, *Jonny Quest* and *Bionic Six*.

Court clerk and political journalist **Herbert A. Goldstone**, whose much-anthologized story "Virtuoso" appeared in *The Magazine of Fantasy & Science Fiction* in 1953, died on May 6, aged eighty-eight.

American fanzine editor and SF bibliographer **A.** (Arthur) **Langley Searles** died of prostate cancer on May 7, also aged eighty-eight. From 1943 to 1953 he published *Fantasy Commentator*, and revived the title in the late 1970s, first as an annual and later semi-annual until 2004. Searles received a First Fandom Hall of Fame Award in 1999.

Hollywood scriptwriter and producer **John Furia, Jr**, whose credits include episodes of TV's *The Twilight Zone* and *Kung Fu*, died the same day, aged seventy-nine. He was a former president of the Writers Guild of America, West.

French book editor and translator **Robert Louitt**, who translated J.G. Ballard's *Crash*, died of cancer on May 13, aged sixty-four. From 1973 to 1984 he edited the Dimensions SF imprint, then founded the Double Star line for Denoël, which combined two novels in each volume.

British scriptwriter **Alan** (Charles Langley) **Hackney**, best known for co-writing the Peter Sellers comedy *I'm All Right Jack* (based on his own novel), died on May 15, aged eighty-four. Among his other credits are Hammer's TV spin-off *Sword of Sherwood Forest* (starring Peter Cushing) and the 1972 comedy *Go For a Take* (which featured Dennis Price as a movie Dracula).

British playwright and scriptwriter, **Kenneth Jupp**, died of lung cancer on May 18, aged eighty. In the early 1970s, he wrote three episodes of TV's *Orson Welles' Great Mysteries*.

British author and playwright **Barry England** died on May 21, aged seventy-seven. Best known for his 1968 novel *Figures in a Landscape* (filmed in 1970), he also wrote the post-holocaust novel *No Man's Land*.

Fifty-two-year-old British movie fan **Alan Keeley** who, as "Mister Damage", co-edited the spoof fanzine *Horrorshow* (1992–93) with Steve Green (aka Eddie Trenchcoat), died on May 22.

American screenwriter **Jack Lewis** died of lung cancer in Hawaii on May 24, aged eighty-four. A decorated Korean War veteran who, as a stuntman, had small uncredited roles in a few "B" Westerns in the 1950s, he scripted *The Amazing*

*Transparent Man.* Lewis also wrote the cult classic *Billy the Kid vs. Dracula* (starring John Carradine), but sold all rights to credited screenwriter Carl K. Hittleman for a reported $250. He later became a novelist (as C. Jack Lewis) and founded *Gun World Magazine.* His autobiography, *White Horse, Black Hat: A Quarter-Century on Hollywood's Poverty Row*, was published in 2002.

Japanese author **Kaoru Kurimoto** (Sumiyo Imaoka, aka Azusa Nakajima), who wrote more than 400 books, including the 127-volume "Guin Saga" heroic fantasy series, died of pancreatic cancer on May 26, aged fifty-six. Her books were adapted into manga, animation, musical albums, games and a play.

Best-selling American fantasy writer **David** (Carroll) **Eddings** died on June 2, aged seventy-seven. Beginning in 1982 with *Pawn of Prophecy*, the first volume in "The Belgariad" sequence, former grocery store manager Eddings and his wife Leigh (who died in 2007) turned out a string of popular post-Tolkien fantasies that also included "The Mallorean", "The Elenium", "The Tamuli" and "Dreamers" series. They also wrote the stand-alone fantasy *The Redemption of Althalus*. Leigh Eddings was only credited on the books from the mid-1990s onwards.

The 1983 John W. Campbell Award-winning SF author, poet and academic **Paul O.** (Osborne) **Williams** died of an aortic dissection the same day, aged seventy-four. He published seven novels in the "Pelbar Cycle" (1981–85), set in a post-apocalyptic Illinois, along with two other books in the "Gorboduc" series.

American artist **Ilene Meyer**, whose work appeared on book covers by Harlan Ellison, Jack Vance and Philip K. Dick, amongst others, died on June 3, aged sixty-nine. She also contributed to *Omni* and *The Magazine of Fantasy & Science Fiction*, and her work was collected in *Ilene Meyer: Paintings, Drawings, Perceptions* (2004).

American comic book artist **Dave Simons** died after a long battle with cancer on June 9, aged fifty-four. For Marvel he worked on *Ghost Rider*, *King Conan*, *Red Sonja*, *Kull the Conqueror*, *Savage Sword of Conan* and *The Spectacular Spider-Man*, amongst many other titles. Simons moved to DC Comics in the 1990s, where his credits include *The Terminator*,

*Dragonlance* and *Forgotten Realms*. In later years, he created storyboards for the TV cartoon series *Captain Planet*, *Exo-Squad* and *Masters of the Universe*, and his last comic work was on *Army of Darkness*.

Eighty-six-year-old **Bette Farmer** (Bette Virginia Andre) died on June 10, exactly fifteen weeks after the death of her husband, author Philip José Farmer. The couple married in 1941.

American children's author **H.** (Harriet) **B. Gilmore**, who is best known for the ten-book "T*witches" series (2001–04) with Randi Reisfield, died on June 21, aged sixty-nine. She worked for such publishing houses as E.P. Dutton, Bantam and Scholastic, before becoming a full-time writer in 1995. Her more than fifty other books include the film novelizations *Saturday Night Fever*, *Eyes of Laura Mars*, *All That Jazz*, *Fatal Attraction*, *Pretty in Pink* and *Godzilla: A Junior Novelization*. The "T*witches" books were turned into two popular TV movies by Disney.

Underground film-maker, musician and shock artist **Joe Christ** (Joe Linhart) died in his sleep of a heart attack on June 21, three days after turning fifty-two. For a number of years he was married to horror writer Nancy A. Collins.

American fan magazine and video game artist **G. Scott Heckenlively** died on June 26, aged forty-five. He had a history of heart problems.

**Robert A.** (Arnold) **Collins** who, as a professor of English at Florida Atlantic University founded the annual International Conference on the Fantastic in the Arts, died of lung cancer on June 27, aged eighty. From 1981 to 1988 he took over the magazine *Fantasy Newsletter*, changing the name to *Fantasy Review*. He also edited a number of hardcover volumes of the *Science Fiction and Fantasy Book Review Annual* with Rob Latham.

Nashville fan, collector and convention-runner **Ken Moore** (Kenneth Alan Moore, aka Khen) died after a long illness on June 30, aged sixty-six. A founding member and former president of the Nashville Science Fiction Club, he co-chaired DeepSouthCon in 1986, chaired it in 1995 and was Guest of Honour in 1991. He also founded and chaired the Kubla Khan convention and ran the art shows at the 1978 World Fantasy Convention and the 1979 NASFiC.

American UFOlogist and journalist **John A.** (Alva) **Keel**

(Alva John Kiehle) died on July 3, aged seventy-nine. He had undergone surgery the previous October after suffering a heart attack. His many non-fiction books include *UFOs: Operation Trojan Horse*, *Strange Creatures from Time and Space* (aka *The Complete Guide to Mysterious Beings*), *Our Haunted Planet*, *The Flying Saucer Subculture*, *The Mothman Prophecies* (filmed in 2002 with Richard Gere) and *Disneyland of the Gods*.

**Charles N.** (Nikki) **Brown**, co-founder, editor-in-chief and publisher of *Locus*, "The Magazine of the Science Fiction and Fantasy Field", died in his sleep of ventricular fibrillation on July 12 on his flight back to California from Readercon in Massachusetts. He was seventy-two. He started the magazine in 1968 with Ed Meskys and Dave Vanderwerf as a one-sheet news fanzine. The magazine grew from there to become the premier information source in the genre, winning the first of its twenty-nine Hugo Awards in 1971. Brown also edited the SF anthologies *Alien Worlds*, *Far Travellers* and *The Locus Awards*, along with a series of annual bibliographical indexes on CD-ROM with William G. Contento. He was the first book reviewer for *Asimov's*, wrote the "Best of the Year" summary for Terry Carr's annual SF anthologies and attended numerous conventions.

British television scriptwriter **Vince** (Vincent) **Powell** died on July 13, aged eighty. Although best known for a string of sitcoms through the 1960s, '70s and '80s (often in collaboration with Harry Driver, who died in 1973), the pair also wrote five episodes of *Adam Adamant Lives!* (1966–67). Powell also co-devised the celebrity game show *Give Us a Clue* (1979–97).

Eighty-three-year-old Canadian SF writer, poet and playright **Phyllis Gotlieb** (Phyllis Fay Bloom) died of complications from a burst appendix on July 14. Her first story appeared in *Fantastic* in 1959, and her novels include *Sunburst*, *O Master Caliban!*, *A Judgment of Dragons*, *Emperor Swords Pentacles*, *Kingdom of the Cats*, *Heart of Red Iron*, *Flesh and Gold*, *Violet Stars*, *Mindworlds* and *Birthstones*, while her short fiction has been collected in *Son of the Morning and Other Stories* and *Blue Apes*. She also co-edited *Tesseracts 2* with Douglas Barbour. Often called "The Founder of Canadian Science Fiction", that country's SF prize, the Sunburst Award, is named in her honour and in 1982 she received Canada's Aurora Award for Life Achievement.

**Eleanor** "Ellie" **Frazetta** (Eleanor Kelly), the wife of famed fantasy artist Frank Frazetta, died of cancer on July 17, aged seventy-four. The couple married in 1956 and, as her husband's business partner, she was credited with establishing the record prices paid for his work.

Academic **Arthur O.** (Orcutt) **Lewis, Jr.,** who was president of the Science Fiction Research Association from 1977 to 1978, died on July 18, aged eighty-eight. The author of the reference works *Of Men and Machines*, *American Utopias: Selected Short Fiction* and *A Directory of Utopian Scholars*, the latter title led to the creation of the national Society for Utopian Studies, which in 1984 named an award in his honour. In 2003 the Special Collections Library at the Pennsylvania State University Libraries also named its collection of utopian literature in his honour.

Czechoslovakian-born graphic designer and illustrator **Heinz Edelmann**, who created the psychedelic landscapes of Pepperland for the 1968 animated Beatles film *Yellow Submarine*, died from heart and kidney disease in Stuttgart, Germany, on July 21. He was seventy-five. Edelmann also illustrated the first German edition of J.R.R. Tolkien's *Lord of the Rings*.

Scottish author, illustrator and animator **John** (Gerald Christopher) **Ryan**, who created children's cartoon character "Captain Horatio Pugwash", died on July 22, aged eighty-eight. Pugwash made his debut in the first issue of *Eagle* comic in April 1950, before the bumbling buccaneer and his shipmates moved to *Radio Times* and eventually became a long-running animated series on BBC television. Eighty-six episodes of *The Adventures of Captain Pugwash* were filmed between 1957 and 1975 in "real-time", using cardboard cut-outs. Ryan also created inept special agent "Harris Tweed" for *Eagle*, *Mary, Mungo and Midge* (1969) and *The Adventures of Sir Prancelot* (1972) for the BBC, and wrote and illustrated more than fifty books.

Italian screenwriter and occasional actor **Renato Izzo** died on July 30, aged eighty. Best known for his Spaghetti Westerns in the late 1960s and early 1970s, he also scripted the thrillers *The Killer Wore Gloves* and *Night Train Murders*. As a voice actor, Izzo dubbed more than 1,000 films and was the voice of Paul Newman and Gregory Peck, amongst many others.

Journalist, novelist and screenwriter **Budd** (Wilson) **Schulberg**, who won an Academy Award for scripting *On the Waterfront*, died on August 4, aged ninety-nine. Although his novels include the controversial *What Makes Sammy Run?* and *The Harder They Fall*, Schulberg is best remembered for naming names – including two of the "Hollywood 10" – before the 1951 House Un-American Activities Committee.

American pop culture collector **Lester Glassner** died of pancreatic cancer on August 9, aged seventy. For almost fifty years the former picture editor, designer and art librarian for CBS Records accumulated a massive and diverse collection of vintage movie material, books, magazines, records, mechanical toys, antique postcards and other kitsch items numbering into the hundreds of thousands. In 1981 he published *Dime-Store Days* with photographer Brownie Harris, which featured choice items from his various collections.

Rhode Island specialty press publisher and bookseller **Donald M.** (Metcalf) **Grant**, best known for his influential Donald M. Grant publishing imprint, died on August 19, aged eighty-two. He had been in declining health for many years. Grant's first book was *Rhode Island on Lovecraft* (1945), and he went on to publish books by Robert E. Howard, A. Merritt, H. Warner Munn, C.L. Moore, William Hope Hodgson, Fritz Leiber, Talbot Mundy and many others, including Stephen King's *Dark Tower* sequence. Grant was also involved, in various capacities, with Grant-Hadley Enterprises, the Buffalo Book Company, Grandon Publishers, Centaur Press, Shroud, Fantasy Press, Phantagraph Press and Macabre House. A founding member of the World Fantasy Convention, he won three World Fantasy Awards for publishing and was given the Life Achievement Award in 2003.

American SF fan and occasional writer **Anne J.** (Janet) **Braude** died of complications from advanced intestinal infection on August 25, aged sixty-seven. She had undergone abdominal surgery two months earlier. A contributor to the 1960s fanzines as *Yandro* and *Niekas* (she was a co-editor with Ed Meskys and Mike Bastraw), her fiction appeared in such anthologies as *Catfantastic IV* and *Olympus*, and she edited *Andre Norton: Fables and Futures*.

American songwriter, singer and producer **Ellie Greenwich**

(Eleanor Louise Greenwich) died of a heart attack the same day, aged sixty-eight. She had been suffering from pneumonia. With her husband Jeff Barry she wrote such early 1960s hits as "Da Doo Ron Ron", "Then He Kissed Me", "Be My Baby", "Baby I Love You", "Chapel of Love", "Leader of the Pack", "Do Wah Diddy Diddy", "I Can Hear Music" and "River Deep, Mountain High", often working closely with producer Phil Spector. Greenwich suffered a nervous breakdown after she and Barry divorced in 1965, but she made a comeback in the 1980s with *Leader of the Pack*, a stage musical about her life.

Acclaimed British novelist, journalist, playwright and screen-writer **Keith** (Spencer) **Waterhouse** died after a long illness on September 4, aged eighty. Best known for his satirical novel *Billy Liar*, Waterhouse was also the co-creator (with Willis Hall) of the children's TV fantasy series *Worzel Gummidge* (1979–81), star-ring Jon Pertwee as the bumbling scarecrow who came to life.

American artist **Ed** (Edward I.) **Valigursky** (aka "William Rembach") died of heart failure on September 7, aged eighty-two. Best known for his depictions of robots and other mechanical devices, he became a staff artist at the Ziff-Davis Publishing Company in the early 1950s, working as a cover artist on *Amazing* and *Fantastic Adventures*. He later contributed to *Galaxy*, *Argosy* and *If* (where he was briefly art director). In a career spanning more than sixty years as a commercial illustra-tor, Valigursky also produced countless paperback covers for Ace Doubles, Bantam, Ballantine, Lancer, Pyramid and other publishers.

Emmy and Tony Award-winning American comedy writer and producer **Larry** [Simon] **Gelbert** died of cancer on September 11, aged eighty-one. Best known for developing the long-running TV series *M\*A\*S\*H*, he also wrote the movie *Oh God!* and contrib-uted to the script for the 2000 remake of *Bedazzled* (which he unsuccessfully tried to have his name removed from).

Scottish-born scriptwriter **Troy Kennedy Martin**, best known for writing the 1969 crime caper *The Italian Job*, died of liver cancer on September 15, aged seventy-seven. His other credits include the acclaimed BBC mini-series *Edge of Darkness* and an episode of *Out of the Unknown* ("The Midas Plague", based on the story by Frederik Pohl).

Irish-born scriptwriter and TV producer **Frank Deasy** died of liver cancer in Edinburgh, Scotland, on September 17, aged forty-nine. The Emmy Award-winning writer scripted the 2002 TV movie *The Rats* (which had nothing to do with James Herbert's novel of the same title).

Literary agent **Barbara Bova**, the wife of SF author Ben Bova, died of cancer on September 23, aged seventy-four.

American writer **Mary H.** (Hunter) **Schaub** died of cancer on September 25, aged sixty-six. She collaborated with Andre Norton on the 1996 novel *The Magestone* and published a number of stories, as well as the solo novel *Exile*, set in Norton's "Witch World".

American SF fan, critic and author **Ben P. Indick** (Benjamin Philip Indick) died after a long illness on September 28, aged eighty-six. From 1983 onwards he published more than ninety issues of *Ben's Beat* and contributed to numerous other fanzines, anthologies and reference books (including studies of Stephen King and Robert E. Howard). Indick's non-fiction books include *Ray Bradbury: Dramatist, A Gentleman from Providence Pens a Letter* and *George Alec Effinger: From Entropy to Budayeen*. He was inducted into the First Fandom Hall of Fame in 2009.

American-born SF writer and journalist **Jennifer Swift** died of breast cancer in Oxford on September 30. She was 54. A British resident since the mid-1980s, her work appeared in *Amazing*, *Asimov's*, *The Magazine of Fantasy & Science Fiction* and *Interzone*.

Edgar Award-winning mystery writer **Stuart M.** (Melvin) **Kaminsky**, best known for his 1940s movie-inspired "Toby Peters" series, died of complications from hepatitis and a recent stroke on October 9, aged seventy-five. He also wrote a number of fantasy stories, two graphic novels and a graphic story about *Kolchak: The Night Stalker*. Kaminsky's other books include non-fiction works about John Huston, Don Siegel, Ingmar Bergman and novelizations of *The Rockford Files* and *CSI*, and he contributed dialogue to Sergio Leone's film *Once Upon a Time in America*. He received the Grand Master Award from the Mystery Writers of America in 2006.

American scriptwriter **Al C.** (Altie) **Ward**, who scripted the American-shot sequences for *Godzilla, King of the Monsters!*

(1956), died the same day, aged ninety. He mostly wrote for TV and co-created the 1969–76 CBS series *Medical Center*.

American artist **Dean Ellis** died on October 12, aged 88. During the 1960s and 1970s he painted covers for many publishers and magazines, most notably for several Ray Bradbury novels. He also designed stamps for the US Postal Service.

British composer and arranger **Albert** (George) **Elms** died on October 14, aged eighty-nine. Best known for his work as musical director for ITV's *The Prisoner* (1967–68), his other credits include *Devil Girl from Mars*, *Alias John Preston* (featuring Christopher Lee), *Manfish* (featuring Lon Chaney, Jr), *Satellite in the Sky*, *The Man Without a Body*, *Bluebeard's Ten Honeymoons* and *The Omegans*, along with episodes of *The Champions* and *Randall and Hopkirk (Deceased)*.

Veteran American comics artist **George Tuska** died on October 15, aged ninety-three. He began his career in 1939 and worked on *Captain Marvel Adventures*, *The Spirit*, *Uncle Sam*, *Adventure Into Weird Worlds*, *Adventures Into Terror*, *Mystic*, *Menace* and *Strange Tales* before moving to Marvel Comics in the 1960s where his credits include *Sub-Mariner*, *The X-Men*, *Planet of the Apes* and ten years on *Iron Man*. From 1959 to 1967 he was the final artist on the *Buck Rogers* comic strip, and between 1978 and 1993 he illustrated the DC Comics newspaper strip *The World's Greatest Superheroes*.

**Vic Mizzy**, who composed and sang the memorable finger-snapping theme for the 1960s and 1990s *The Addams Family* TV series, died of heart failure on October 17, aged ninety-three. His other credits include William Castle's *The Night Walker* (scripted by Robert Bloch), *The Busy Body* and *The Spirit is Willing*, *The Ghost and Mr Chicken* and *The Reluctant Astronaut* (both starring Don Knotts), *The Perils of Pauline* (1967), *Halloween with the New Addams Family*, *The Munsters' Revenge*, and episodes of *Shirley Temple's Storybook* (including "The House of the Seven Gables") and *Captain Nice*.

Prolific British fantasy author **Louise Cooper** (Louise Antell) died of a brain aneurysm on October 21, aged fifty-seven. She worked in publishing before becoming a full-time writer in 1977, and her more than eighty books for both adults and children included her debut, *The Book of Paradox* (1973), plus the "Time Master" trilogy (*The Initiate*, *The Outcast* and *The Master*), the "Indigo" sequence (*Nemesis*, *Inferno*, *Infanta*, *Nocturne*, *Troika*, *Avatar*, *Revenant* and *The Aisling*), the "Daughter of Storms" trilogy (*Daughter of Storms*, *The Dark Caller* and *Keepers of the Light*), the "Mirror, Mirror" trilogy (*Breaking Through*, *Running Free* and *Testing Limits*), *Storm Ghost*, *The Summer Witch*, *Hunter's Moon*, *The Bad Seed* and *Doctor Who: Rip Tide*.

American writer and editor **Janet** [Kaye] **Fox** died the same day after a long struggle against cancer. She was sixty-eight. A former high school teacher, she was best known as the editor of the monthly writers' market report *Scavenger's Newsletter* from 1984 to 2003. Fox's short stories and poems appeared in *Twilight Zone Magazine*, *Weird Tales*, *Cemetery Dance*, *Weirdbook*, *Whispers*, *Fantasy Tales* and elsewhere, and some of her fiction was collected in *Witch's Dozen* (2003). Between 1990 and 1993 she also wrote five of the six novels in Ace Books' "Scorpio" SF series under the house name "Alex McDonough" (*Scorpio Rising*, *Scorpio Descending*, *Dragon's Blood*, *Dragon's Eye* and *Dragon's Claw*).

**Maureen Doyle**, the wife of agent/editor/publisher Philip Harbottle, died of a massive pulmonary embolism on October 21. Together they worked on the short-lived 1970s British SF magazine *Vision of Tomorrow*, which Harbottle edited.

Seventy-three-year-old American artist **Don Ivan Punchatz**, who studied with Burne Hogarth and designed the first *Star Wars* poster, died on October 22. He had suffered a heart attack eleven days earlier and never regained consciousness. From 1970 onwards, the artist used a team of multiple assistants, known as "the elves", to help him meet tight deadlines. His work appeared in numerous magazines, including *Playboy*, *Esquire*, *Rolling Stone*, *Time*, *National Lampoon* and *National Geographic*, and he also produced book covers for Isaac Asimov's "Foundation" trilogy, Philip José Farmer's "Riverworld" series, Harlan Ellison's *Dangerous Visions* anthology and various Ray Bradbury titles, along with the packaging art for the original *Doom* video game. During his career, Punchatz worked for publishers Ace, Dell, Avon, Warner and New American Library.

Comic-book collector **Sheldon Dorf**, the freelance artist and letterer who founded the hugely successful and influential San Diego Comic-Con in 1970, died of kidney failure on November 3, aged seventy-six. He had been hospitalized for more than a year, suffering from complications of diabetes. Dorf was hired to letter Milton Caniff's *Steve Canyon* strip during its final fourteen years and he was also a consultant on the 1990 film *Dick Tracy*. Characters based on him appeared in Caniff's *Steve Canyon* and Jack Kirby's *Mister Miracle*. The first San Diego event attracted 300 people, which was enough to keep it going, and by 2009 attendance had risen to more than 125,000.

Ninety-one-year-old British SF bibliographer **I.** (Ignatius) **F.** (Frederic) "Ian" **Clarke** died on November 5, following complications from a leg amputation three months earlier. An expert on future-war fiction, he wrote *The Tale of the Future*, *Voices Prophesying War*, *The Pattern of Expectation* and eight volumes of the "British Future Fiction" series. In 1974 he received the Pilgrim Award from the Science Fiction Research Association for distinguished contribution to science fiction studies.

British editor, publisher and literary agent **William Miller** died in Japan the same day, aged seventy-five. After working at the Four Square paperback imprint, he joined John Boothe in the early 1960s as joint managing editor of Panther Books, which published H.P. Lovecraft and others. Panther was bought by Granada Publishing in 1965, and seven years later Miller and Boothe resigned from Granada to launch Quartet Books along with Ken Banerji and Brian Thompson. The new imprint included Michael Moorcock and Angela Carter. Miller moved to Tokyo in 1979, where he co-founded the English Agency to sell translation rights to Japanese publishers.

**Ron Sproat**, who was the head writer (1966–69) for TV's *Dark Shadows* and created that series' vampire character, Barnabas Collins, died of a heart attack on November 6, aged seventy-seven.

American H.G. Wells scholar **David C. Smith**, who was vice-president of The H.G. Wells Society and wrote the respected 1988 Wells biography *Desperately Mortal*, died on November 7.

American academic and scholar **Karl Kroeber**, the brother of Ursula K. Le Guin, died after a long battle with cancer on November 8, aged eighty-three. He wrote the 1988 non-fiction study *Romantic Fantasy and Science Fiction*.

British author **Robert** (Paul) **Holdstock** died of a severe *E. coli* infection on November 29, aged sixty-one. He had been admitted to a London hospital after collapsing two weeks earlier and moved to intensive care after slipping into a coma with complete organ failure. Holdstock's first story appeared in *New Worlds* in 1968, and during the 1970s and 1980s he published a number of novels in various genres under a wide variety of pseudonyms, including "Robert Faulcon" (the "Night Hunter" series), "Chris Carlsen" (the "Beserker" series) and "Richard Kirk" (the "Raven" series). He also wrote the film novelizations of *Legend of the Werewolf* (as "Robert Black") and *The Emerald Forest*. But the author is best-known for his World Fantasy Award-winning novel *Mythago Wood* (1984) and its various sequels: *Lavondyss: Journey to an Unknown Region*, *The Hollowing*, *Merlin's Wood*, *Gate of Ivory Gate of Horn* and *Avilion*. His other novels include *Eye Among the Blind*, *Earthwind*, *Necromancer*, *Stars of Albion*, *Where the Time Winds Blow*, *The Fetch*, *Ancient Echoes*, *Unknown Regions* and the "Merlin Codex" (*Celtika*, *The Iron Grail* and *The Broken Kings*). He co-edited the anthologies *Stars of Albion* with Christopher Priest and three volumes of *Other Edens* with Christopher Evans, and he co-wrote a number of art books with Malcolm Edwards, including *Alien Landscapes*, *Tour of the Universe*, *Magician*, *Realms of Fantasy* and *Lost Realms*.

American writer and publisher [Marcelo] **"Buddy" Martinez** committed suicide by hanging himself on November 30. He had apparently been depressed about money problems. In 1990, Martinez, Jesus (J.F.) Gonzalez and Bill Furtado founded the horror magazine *Iniquities* (later *Phantasm*). He then took over *Afraid* after the magazine's founder, Mike Baker, died, and went on to publish a short-lived spin-off title, *Skull*. Martinez also handled layout and design for a number of Gauntlet Press titles, and he wrote several short stories (which appeared in *Mondo Zombie* and elsewhere). An eBay auction was organized to help pay for his funeral costs.

American literary agent **Don** (Donald) [Keith] **Congdon**, who was Ray Bradbury's agent for more than fifty years (*Fahrenheit 451* is dedicated to him), died the same day, aged ninety-one. Congdon's other clients included Jack Finney, C.L. Moore and

Henry Kuttner, and he edited the anthologies *Alone by Night* (with Michael Congdon), *Tales of Love and Horror* and *Stories for the Dead of Night*.

**Harry C. Crosby, Jr**, who wrote science fiction under his own name and that of "Christopher Anvil", also died on November 30, aged eighty-four. His first story appeared in *Imagination* in 1952, and over the next couple of decades he appeared in *Astounding/Analog* more than any other author. His novels include *The Day the Machines Stopped*, *Strangers in Paradise*, *Warlord's World*, *The Steel the Mist and the Blazing Sun* and *Pandora's Legions* (2002). A recent reissue series edited by Eric Flint, "The Complete Christopher Anvil" (2002–10), collected all his SF work in eight volumes.

**Kennedy "Kippy" Poyser**, the former husband of Hugo Award-winning artist Victoria Poyser, died of a heart attack the same day in San Miguel de Allende, Mexico. He worked on various Norwescons, ran the Connecticut Hatcon in the 1980s and was Fan Guest of Honor at the 1981 Orycon. Poyser also designed and edited the 1982 World Fantasy Convention programme book and owned bookstores at various times in Connecticut and Texas.

Eighty-three-year-old American songwriter, publisher and record producer **Aaron [Harold] Schroeder** died of complications from dementia on December 2. He is credited with writing more than 2,000 songs, recorded by Frank Sinatra, Tony Bennett, Roy Orbison, Nat King Cole, the Beatles and many others. Seventeen of his songs were recorded by Elvis Presley, including "It's Now or Never", the King's biggest hit. Schroeder also reportedly wrote the theme song for *Scooby Doo, Where Are You!*

American writer and academic **Jeffrey M. Elliot** died of cancer on December 12, aged sixty-two. His numerous interviews with SF and fantasy writers were published widely, and he worked on biographies of Raymond Z. Gallum, Stanton A. Coblentz, George Zebrowski, Pamela Sargent and Jack Dann. Elliot's books include the children's fantasy *Olgethorpe the Hip Hippopotamus*, the SF novel *If J.F.K. Had Lived* (with Robert Reginald), and the SF anthology *Kindred Spirits*.

American bibliographer and small press publisher **Mark [Samuel] Owings** died of pancreatic cancer on December 13. He was sixty-four. He worked with Jack Chalker on *The Index to the Science-Fantasy Publishers* and *The Revised H.P. Lovecraft Bibliography*, and was a publisher at Croatan House. A founder of the Baltimore Science Fiction Society, he chaired various Balticons and the Compton Crook Award committee.

Screenwriter and director **Dan O'Bannon** (Daniel Thomas O'Bannon), best known for co-scripting *Alien* (1979) with Ronald Shusett, died of Crohn's disease on December 17, aged sixty-three. O'Bannon got his start collaborating with fellow USC student John Carpenter on the script of the low budget SF comedy *Dark Star* (in which he played Sgt Pinback). After working on the special effects for *Star Wars*, his other film writing credits include the underrated *Dead & Buried* (again with Shusett), *Heavy Metal, Blue Thunder, Lifeforce, Invaders from Mars* (1986), *Total Recall, Screamers, Bleeders* (aka *Hemoglobin*, an uncredited adaptation of H.P. Lovecraft's "The Lurking Fear" with Shusett) and *AVP: Alien vs. Predator*. O'Bannon also wrote and directed *The Return of the Living Dead*, and directed another Lovecraft adaptation, *The Resurrected*, based on "The Case of Charles Dexter Ward".

American film writer/critic **Chas** (Charlie) **Balun** died after a long battle with cancer on December 18, aged sixty-one. A regular contributor to *Fangoria* and *GoreZone* (with his opinionated "Piece of Mind" column from 1988 to 1991), he created his own self-published magazine, *Deep Red*, and wrote the novel *Ninth and Hell Street*. Balun's non-fiction books include *The Connoisseur's Guide to Contemporary Horror Film, The Gore Score, More Gore Score, Horror Holocaust* and *Beyond Horror Holocaust*. An underground cartoonist and graphic designer, he also designed the monster for Fred Olen Ray's 1991 horror comedy *Evil Toons* and he appeared in the 2001 documentary *In the Belly of the Beast*.

British film teacher and critic **Robin** (Robert Paul) **Wood** died in Toronto, Canada, the same day, aged seventy-eight. His essay "The American Nightmare" was one of the first to take 1970s horror movies seriously. Wood's influential 1965 volume *Hitchcock's Films* was amongst the earliest critical studies of a movie director in the English language, and he went on to write books about directors Howard Hawks, Michaelangelo Antonioni, Arthur Penn and Claude Chabrol.

American scriptwriter and producer **Michael Fisher** died on December 31, aged sixty-nine. A story editor on *Starsky and Hutch* (including "The Vampire" episode) and producer of the TV movie *Return to Fantasy Island*, Fisher scripted episodes of *The Evil Touch*, *Matt Helm* and *Fantasy Island*, plus the 1981 SF movie *Earthbound*.

## PERFORMERS/PERSONALITIES

British-born actor **Edmund** [Anthony Cutlar] **Purdom** died in Rome, Italy, on January 1, aged eighty-four. He began his film career in the early 1950s and quickly moved to Hollywood before settling in Europe after gaining a reputation as a "difficult" actor. His credits include *The Night They Killed Rasputin* (as Rasputin), *Queen of the Nile* (with Vincent Price), *The Man Who Laughs* (1966), *Evil Fingers* (aka *The Fifth Cord*), *The Devil's Lover*, *Jungle Master* (aka *Karzan, Jungle Lord*), Jesus Franco's *Los ojos siniestros del doctor Orloff*, *Frankenstein's Castle of Freaks*, *The Cursed Medallion*, *Nightmare City* (aka *City of the Walking Dead*), *Anthropophagus 2*, *Pieces*, *Ator the Fighting Eagle*, *Invaders of the Lost Gold*, *2019: After the Fall of New York*, *Fracchia contro Dracula* (as the Count) and *The Rift*. In the 1960s Purdom narrated a number of "educational" sex documentaries (including the infamous *Sweden: Heaven and Hell*), along with *Witchcraft '70*-(aka *The Satanists*). He also directed and starred in the 1980s British slasher film *Don't Open 'Til Christmas* (which even had its own "making of" documentary). Married four times, Purdom left his first wife to marry Mexican actress Linda Christian.

Veteran character actor **Steven Gilborn** died of cancer on January 2, aged seventy-two. A former humanities professor at MIT, he appeared in such TV shows as *Beauty and the Beast*, *The Dreamer of Oz*, *Lois and Clark: The New Adventures of Superman*, *Touched by an Angel*, *The Tick* and *Buffy the Vampire Slayer*. He also appeared in the movies *Timescape* (based on a novel by Henry Kuttner and C.L. Moore), *Doctor Dolittle* (1998) and *Evolution*, and his voice was heard in *Alien: Resurrection*.

Busy American character actor **Pat Hingle** (Martin Patterson

Hingle), best known for playing Commissioner James Gordon in Tim Burton's *Batman* (1989) and its three sequels, died of blood cancer on January 3, aged eighty-four. Often cast as judges or police detectives, Hingle also appeared in the movies *Sweet Sweet Rachel*, *Nightmare Honeymoon*, *Tarantulas: The Deadly Cargo*, Stephen King's *Maximum Overdrive*, *Not of This World* (1991), *The Shining* (1997) and *Muppets from Space*, along with episodes of TV's *Suspense* ("Dr Jekyll and Mr Hyde"), *Alfred Hitchcock Presents*, *The Twilight Zone*, *The Invaders*, *Kung Fu*, *The Six Million Dollar Man*, *Amazing Stories*, *American Gothic* and *Touched by an Angel*.

British character actor **John Scott Martin**, who died of Parkinson's disease on January 6, aged eighty-two, is probably best known for being the chief Dalek operator in more than seventy episodes of the BBC's *Doctor Who* between 1964 and 1980. He also appeared in supporting roles in TV's *Quatermass and the Pit* (1959), *A for Andromeda*, *Adam Adamant Lives!*, *Out of the Unknown*, *The Tripods* and such movies as *The Blood Beast Terror* (aka *The Vampire-Beast Craves Blood*, with Peter Cushing), *Pink Floyd The Wall*, *The Meaning of Life*, *Young Sherlock Holmes* and the 1986 musical remake of *Little Shop of Horrors*.

The original horror host of San Francisco's KTVU *Creature Features* show (1970–79), **Bob Wilkins** (Robert Gene Wilkins), who sat in a rocking chair to introduce movies, died of complications from Alzheimer's disease on January 7, aged seventy-six. From 1977 to 1979 he hosted the afternoon TV show *Captain Cosmic and 2T2* with the titular robot sidekick. Wilkins also appeared in the 1975 movie *The Milpitas Monster* and the 2006 documentary *American Scary*.

**Billy Powell**, the long-time keyboard artist with Southern rock band Lynyrd Skynyrd, died of a suspected heart attack the same day, aged fifty-six. Powell joined the group around 1972 and survived the plane crash five years later that killed three band members. Lynyrd Skynyrd's hits include "Free Bird" and "Sweet Home Alabama".

British actress **Leigh Madison** (Pamela Williams), who starred in *Behemoth the Sea Monster* (aka *The Giant Behemoth*), died of complications from a degenerative neurological condition on

January 8, aged eighty-three. She also appeared in a couple of early *Carry On* films and an episode of TV's *The Invisible Man* (1959).

Three-foot, six-inch **Steve Luncinski,** who played Stefan, the Castle Prankster in Pittsburgh TV horror host Chilly Billy's (Bill Cardille) *Chiller Theatre* show from 1976 to 1983, died the same day, aged fifty-two.

American actor **Don Galloway** (Donald Poe Galloway), best remembered for playing Sgt Ed Brown in NBC-TV's *Ironside* (1967–75) and a pioneering 1972 cross-over episode of *The Bold Ones: The New Doctors,* died of complications from a stroke on January 8, aged seven. He also appeared in episodes of *Gemini Man, Mork and Mindy, Automan, Fantasy Island, Knight Rider, MacGyver* and the movie *Satan's Mistress* (with John Carradine). Galloway portrayed director John Frankenheimer in a 1990 TV biopic of actor Rock Hudson.

1960s British pop star **Dave Dee** (David Herman), the lead singer with Dave Dee, Dozy, Beaky, Mick and Tich, died following a three-year battle with cancer on January 9, aged sixty-five. Between 1965 and 1969 the group spent more weeks in the UK singles charts than any other band with hits that included "Hold Tight", "Bend It" and the whip-cracking "The Legend of Xanadu". A former police officer who attended the 1960 car crash that killed Eddie Cochran and injured Gene Vincent, he was later head of A&R at WEA Records, signing new bands (including AC/DC, Boney M and Gary Numan) and continued to tour with his original group.

Canadian-born actor **Russ Conway** (Russell Zink) died in California on January 12, aged ninety-six. Often appearing (uncredited) in films like *A Double Life, One Touch of Venus, Abbott and Costello Meet the Invisible Man, Abbott and Costello Go to Mars* and *War of the Worlds,* he was billed in *Flight to Mars, Bomba and the Killer Leopard, The Screaming Skull, What Ever Happened to Baby Jane?, Our Man Flint* and the TV movie *The Space-Watch Murders* (with Barbara Steele), along with episodes of *Science Fiction Theatre, The Hardy Boys* (playing Fenton Hardy), *Men Into Space, Thriller, The Alfred Hitchcock Hour, The Munsters, The Time Tunnel, The Green Hornet, The Invaders* and *Get Smart.*

American-born Irish actor **Patrick** [Joseph] **McGoohan** died after a short illness on January 13, aged eighty. The Emmy Award-winning actor starred as John Drake in TV's *Danger Man* (aka *Secret Agent*), and in 1967 he co-created, produced, directed and scripted (often pseudonymously) and starred as the rebellious Number Six in the controversial 1967–68 series *The Prisoner*. He recreated the character for a 2000 episode of *The Simpsons*. McGoohan's other credits include Disney's *The Scarecrow of Romney Marsh*, *The Three Lives of Thomasina*, *Baby: Secret of the Lost Legend* and *Treasure Planet*, David Cronenberg's *Scanners*, *The Phantom* (1996) and *Hysteria* (1998). During his career he reportedly turned down the roles of TV's *The Saint* (it went to Roger Moore), James Bond (it went to Moore again for *Live and Let Die*), Gandalf in *The Lord of the Rings* trilogy (it went to Ian McKellan) and Dumbledore in the *Harry Potter* series (it went to Richard Harris).

Russian-born actress **Evelyn Kraft** died of a heart attack the same day, aged fifty-seven. She appeared in *The French Sex Murders*, *Goliathon* (aka *Mighty Peking Man*) and in the title role of *Lady Dracula*, before she apparently retired from the screen in the early 1980s.

Mexican-born leading man **Ricardo Montalban** (Ricardo Gonzalo Pedro Montalbán y Merino) died of congestive heart failure in Los Angeles on January 14, aged eighty-eight. Best known for his role as Mr Roarke, the mysterious white-suited host of CBS-TV's *Fantasy Island* (1977–84), he made more than a dozen films in Mexico before MGM brought him to Hollywood in 1947. His many credits include *Alice Through the Looking Glass* (1966), *Escape from the Planet of the Apes*, *Conquest of the Planet of the Apes*, *Wonder Woman* (1974), the two *Spy Kids* sequels *Island of Lost Dreams* and *Game Over*, and *The Ant Bully*, plus episodes of *Alfred Hitchcock Presents*, *The Man from U.N.C.L.E.*, *The Wild Wild West*, *Switch*, *Freakazoid!* and *Buzz Lightyear of Star Command*. In the 1967 *Star Trek* episode "Space Seed" he portrayed genetically-created villain "Khan Noonien Singh", and recreated the role for the popular 1982 movie *Star Trek: The Wrath of Khan*.

American leading lady **Susanna Foster** (Suzanne DeLee Flanders Larson) died of heart failure on January 17, aged eighty-four. Brought to Hollywood at the age of twelve by MGM, she was schooled (alongside Mickey Rooney and Judy Garland) for a singing and acting career. After the studio let her go when she turned down the lead role in *National Velvet* (it went to a young Elizabeth Taylor instead), and a brief stint at Paramount, Universal signed her in 1941 as leverage against Deanna Durbin. Her most famous role – as Christine Dubois in the 1943 remake of *The Phantom of the Opera* – was reportedly turned down by Durbin. Foster's other credits include *The Climax*, which starred Boris Karloff. She retired from the screen in 1945, and was reportedly found homeless and living in a car in 1982.

British stage and screen actress **Kathleen Byron** (Kathleen Elizabeth Fell) died on January 18, a week after her eighty-eighth birthday. She had been suffering from Alzheimer's disease for the past five years. Best remembered for her role as the psychologically disturbed nun Sister Ruth in Powell and Pressburger's *Black Narcissus* (1947), her other credits include *A Matter of Life and Death* (aka *Stairway to Heaven*, as an angel), *The House in the Square* (aka *I'll Never Forget You*), *Night of the Eagle* (aka *Burn, Witch, Burn!* based on the book by Fritz Leiber), Hammer's *Twins of Evil*, *Nothing But the Night* (with Christopher Lee and Peter Cushing), *Craze* (with Jack Palance), Disney's *One of Our Dinosaurs is Missing*, and *The Elephant Man*, along with episodes of *The Avengers*, *The Rivals of Sherlock Holmes*, *Supernatural* ("Night of the Marionettes"), *Blake's 7*, *The Memoirs of Sherlock Holmes* and *Frighteners*.

Actor and stuntman **Bob** (Robert M.) **May**, who was under the suit of the Robot in Irwin Allen's TV series *Lost in Space* (1965–68), died of congestive heart disease the same day, aged 69. Announcer Dick Tufeld supplied the Robot's voice ("Danger, Will Robinson!"). The grandson of vaudeville comedian Chic Johnson (of Olsen and Johnson fame), May began acting at the age of two in the duo's *Hellzappopin'* comedy stage review. He also appeared in *The Nutty Professor* (uncredited stunts) and an episode of Allen's *The Time Tunnel* (as Adolf Hitler).

British stunt co-ordinator and actor **Gerry Crampton** (Robert Gerald Crampton) died on January 24, aged seventy-eight. As an actor he appeared (often uncredited) in small roles in

Hammer's *Captain Clegg* (aka *Night Creatures*), *Death Line* (aka *Raw Meat*), *The Bride*, *Willow*, *The Jungle Book* (1994), and episodes of *The Avengers*, *The Prisoner* and *Tales from the Crypt*. He performed stunts for six James Bond films, *Tarazan Goes to India*, *Psychomania* (aka *The Death Wheelers*), *Raiders of the Lost Ark*, *The Bride*, *Biggles*, *Willow*, *Batman* (1989), *A Connecticut in King Arthur's Court* (1989), *The Jungle Book*, *Mary Reilly*, *Dragonheart*, *The Odyssey*, *Merlin*, *The Infinite Worlds of H.G. Wells* and *Revelation*. He was one of the first British stuntmen to be inducted into the Hollywood Stuntmen's Hall of Fame.

Seventy-eight-year-old American actor **Darrell Sandeen** died on January 26 after suffering a brain haemorrhage following a serious fall. His credits include the low-budget *The Education of a Vampire* (2001).

British singer-songwriter **John Martyn** OBE (Iain David McGeachy) died of double pneumonia on January 29, aged sixty. The respected folk, jazz and blues guitarist and singer had suffered from drug and alcohol problems for many years, and he had a leg amputated in 2003, although he continued to perform. Martyn's best-known albums include *Solid Air* and *Grace and Danger*, and he worked with Eric Clapton, David Gilmour and Phil Collins, amongst many others.

American TV character actor and real-life cowboy **Clint Ritchie** died of a blood clot on January 31 following surgery to implant a pacemaker. He was seventy. Best known for playing Clint Buchanan on ABC-TV's daily soap opera *One Life to Live*, he also appeared in episodes of *The Wild Wild West*, *Batman*, *Land of the Giants*, *Ghost Story* and *Fantasy Island*.

**Lux Interior** (Erick Lee Purkhiser), co-founder and lead singer of the pioneering punk-horror band The Cramps, died of a pre-existing heart condition on February 4, aged sixty. The band's 1979 debut EP was entitled *Gravest Hits*, and their songs include "I Was a Teenage Werewolf" and "Bikini Girls with Machine Guns".

Veteran Hollywood actor **James Whitmore** died of lung cancer on February 6, aged eighty-eight. Best remembered as the heroic police sergeant battling mutated giant ants in *Them!* (1954), his many other film credits include *The Next Voice You*

*Hear ...*, *Angels in the Outfield*, *Face of Fire*, *The Canterville Ghost* (1974), *The Shawshank Redemption* and *The Relic*, plus episodes of TV's *The Twilight Zone*, *The Invaders*, *Tarzan*, *Planet of the Apes* and *The Ray Bradbury Theater*.

Dependable American leading man **Philip Carey** (Eugene Joseph Carey) died of lung cancer the same day, aged eighty-three. After making his movie debut in the early 1950s, his films include *Screaming Mimi* (based on the novel by Fredric Brown), *Dead Ringer* (aka *Dead Image*), *The Time Travelers*, *Scream of the Wolf* (scripted by Richard Matheson and based on the story by David Case) and *Monster* (with John Carradine). He also appeared in episodes of *Thriller*, *Kolchak the Night Stalker* and *The Bionic Woman*, and over three decades he played Texas tycoon Asa Buchanan on ABC's daytime soap opera *One Life to Live*.

**Shirley Jean Rickert**, who was one of the child actors in Hal Roach's "Our Gang"/"The Little Rascals" shorts in the 1930s, died of cardiovascular disease on February 6, aged eighty-two. After appearing in more than 100 movies (often uncredited), in the 1950s she became a burlesque dancer who performed under the name "Gilda and Her Crowning Glory" because of her striking long blonde hair.

**Estelle Bennett**, a singer with Phil Spector's 1960s girl group the Ronettes, was found dead in her home on February 11, aged sixty-seven. The singing trio's hits included "Be My Baby" (described by Brian Wilson as the best pop record of all time), "Frosty the Snowman", "Baby I Love You", "(The Best Part of) Breakin' Up", "Walking in the Rain" and "I Can Hear Music" before they disbanded in 1966. The Ronettes were inducted into the Rock and Roll Hall of Fame in 2007.

Greek-born comedian, character actor and mimic **Oreste Lionello** died in Rome after a long illness on February 12, aged eighty-one. One of Italy's most prolific dubbing artists, he voiced most of Woody Allen and Jerry Lewis' performances in Italian. He also lent his voice to Mickey Mouse, Bugs Bunny, Peter Sellers in *Dr Strangelove*, Dick Van Dyke in *Mary Poppins*, Federico Boido in Fellini's "Toby Dammit" episode of *Spirits of the Dead*, Gene Wilder in *Young Frankenstein*, and Robin Williams in TV's *Mork and Mindy*. Lionello made his acting debut in the 1956 children's SF TV series *Il Marziano Filippo*, and he went on to appear in *The Beast of Babylon Against the Son of Hercules*, *Four Flies on Grey Velvet* and *The Case of the Bloody Iris*.

American actor **Robert** [Walter] **Quarry**, best known for his portrayal of vampire Count Yorga in *Count Yorga, Vampire* (1970) and its even better sequel, *The Return of Count Yorga* (1971), died of a heart condition at the Motion Picture and Television Fund Hospital in Woodland Hills, California, on February 20. He was eighty-three. Quarry began his career as a juvenile actor (he had a small uncredited role in Alfred Hitchcock's *Shadow of a Doubt* and was in *A Kiss Before Dying*), but after getting the role of Count Yorga, American International Pictures groomed him for a few years as the studio's Next Big Horror Star, until the genre fizzled out in the mid-1970s. His credits include *Agent for H.A.R.M.*, *Deathmaster* (as another vampire), *Sugar Hill*, and *Dr Phibes Rises Again* and *Madhouse* (both with Vincent Price and Peter Cushing), but, following a serious car accident in the 1970s, he ended up in such direct-to-video dross (sometimes hiding behind the pseudonym "Robert Connell") as *Moon in Scorpio*, *Cyclone*, *Warlords*, *The Phantom Empire*, *Beverly Hills Vamp*, *Evil Spirits*, *Alienator*, *Spirits*, *Haunting Fear*, *Teenage Exorcist*, *Inner Sanctum II*, *Cyberzone*, *Secret Santa*, *Jungle Boy*, *Fugitive Mind* and *Invisible Mom II*. Quarry also appeared in episodes of the children's TV shows *Far Out Space Nuts* and *The Lost Saucer*, plus *Buck Rogers in the 25th Century*. At the time of his death, the actor was set to appear in a new version of *The Tell-Tale Heart*.

British leading man and crime novelist **Laurence** [Stanley] **Payne**, who portrayed Sexton Blake in the long-running children's TV series from 1967 to 1971, died on February 23, aged eighty-nine. He also starred in *The Trollenberg Terror* (both TV series and movie, aka *The Crawling Eye*), *The Tell-Tale Heart* (aka *The Hidden Room of 1,000 Horrors*) and Hammer's *Vampire Circus*, as well as appearing in episodes of *Colonel March of Scotland Yard* (with Boris Karloff), *The Saint* ("The Convenient Monster"), *The Rivals of Sherlock Holmes*, *Thriller* (1974), *Tales of the Unexpected* and *Doctor Who*.

Born in Shanghai, China, British leading man **Edward Judd** died of bronchial pneumonia on February 24, aged seventy-six. He made his film debut in the late 1940s and his credits include Hammer's *X The Unknown* and *The Vengeance of She*, *The Day the Earth Caught Fire*, *First Men in the Moon*, *Invasion*, *Island of Terror* (with Peter Cushing), *The Vault of Horror*, *O Lucky Man!*, *The Hound of the Baskervilles* (1983) and *Jack the Ripper* (1988), along with episodes of *Invisible Man* (1959), *Out of the Unknown*, *Thriller* (1974) and *The New Avengers*. He retired in the early 1990s and was reportedly in frail health due to his heavy drinking.

[August] **Clarence Swensen**, who had an uncredited role as one of twenty-five marching Munchkin soldiers in *The Wizard of Oz* (1939), died on February 25, aged ninety-one. He also played seven uncredited roles in the midget Western *The Terror of Tiny Town* and donned an ape suit to appear as a chimpanzee riding an elephant in *Tarzan Finds a Son*.

*Carry On* actress **Wendy Richard** MBE (Wendy Emerton) died of breast cancer on February 26, aged sixty-seven. She contributed her distinctive Cockney vocals to Mike Sarne's #1 novelty pop hit "Come Inside" and appeared in an episode of TV's *Danger Man* and the dystopian SF movie *No Blade of Grass*. Richards' scenes in the 1965 Beatles' film *Help!* were cut, but she is probably best remembered for her roles as Miss Shirley Brahms in the long-running BBC-TV sitcom *Are You Being Served?* and as matriarch Pauline Fowler in the dour soap opera *Eastenders*. She recreated the latter character in 1993 for the rarely-seen charity 3-D short *Doctor Who: Dimensions in Time*.

Veteran American actor **John Alvin** [Hoffstadt] died on February 27 from complications from a fall. He was ninety-one. Alvin appeared in such films as *The Horn Blows at Midnight* (as an uncredited angel), *The Beast with Five Fingers*, *The Couch*, *The Legend of Lizzie Borden* and *Somewhere in Time*, along with episodes of TV's *Climax!* ("The Thirteenth Chair"), *Rocky Jones Space Ranger*, *Science Fiction Theatre*, *Sheena Queen of the Jungle*, *Thriller*, *One Step Beyond*, *The Munsters*, *My Favorite Martian*, *The Man from U.N.C.L.E.* ("The Very Important Zombie Affair"), *Get Smart*, *Kolchak: The Night Stalker*, *The Incredible Hulk* and *Amazing Stories*.

**Sydney** [Earle] **Chaplin**, the eldest living child of legendary comedian Charlie Chaplin, died on March 3 of complications from a stroke, aged eighty-two. He appeared in his father's films *Limelight* and *A Countess from Hong Kong*, and his other credits include *Land of the Pharaohs*, *So Evil My Sister* and *Satan's Cheerleaders*, along with an episode of TV's *The Bionic Woman*.

British magician **Ali Bongo** (William Wallace), who became president of the Magic Circle in 2008, died of pneumonia on March 8, aged seventy-nine. An advisor to other stage magicians, he was a consultant for such TV series as *Doctor Who*, *Ace of Wands* and *Jonathan Creek*. He also appeared in a two-part episode of *The Tomorrow People* in 1975.

American actor **Jack Grimes**, who voiced Superman's best friend Jimmy Olsen in various TV cartoon series during the 1960s, died on March 10, aged eighty-two. He also appeared in episodes of *Inner Sanctum* and *Tom Corbett Space Detective* (playing T.J. Thistle).

British character actor and playwright **Derek Benfield** died the same date, a day before his eighty-third birthday. Best known for his role as the long-suffering Robert Wainthropp in BBC-TV's *Hetty Wainthropp Investigates* (1996–98), his many other credits include episodes of TV's *Return to the Lost Planet* (1955), *Timeslip*, *Out of the Unknown*, *Doomwatch*, *Hammer House of Mystery and Suspense* ("The Late Nancy Irving"), *Worlds Beyond* and *Frightners*, along with the movies *I Don't Want to Be Born* (aka *The Devil Within Her*) and *Lifeforce* (based on the novel by Colin Wilson).

Welsh-born television newscaster **Huw** [Gruffyd Edwards] **Thomas** died on March 12, aged eighty-one. He reported the news from 1956 to 1964 for ITN, and also appeared as an uncredited announcer in *First Men in the Moon* (1964) and turned up as a newscaster in *The Ghost Goes Gear* (1966).

Oscar-nominated American actress **Betsy Blair** (Elizabeth Winifred Boger) died of cancer in London on March 13, aged eighty-five. She made her screen debut in 1947, but moved to Britain a decade later after being blacklisted for her leftwing sympathies by Senator Joe McCarthy's House of Un-American Activities Committee. Her credits include *A Double Life*, *The Snake Pit*, and an episode of *Tales of the Unexpected*. She was married to Gene Kelly from 1940 to 1957, and her second husband was film director Karl Reisz (from 1963 until his death in 2002).

Silent film child actor **Coy Watson, Jr** (James Caughey Watson Jr) died of stomach cancer on March 14, aged ninety-six. The eldest of nine sibling actors, he earned the name The Keystone Kid after appearing in Mack Sennett's "Keystone Cops" comedies from the age of nine months until he was twenty-two. Among his numerous credits are *The Hunchback of Notre Dame* (1923) with Lon Chaney, Sr Watson retired soon after the advent of sound pictures and later became a news photographer and TV cameraman on the West Coast. He was also featured on a 1958 episode of NBC-TV's *This is Your Life*. His father, Coy Watson, Sr, created the flying carpet sequence in *The Thief of Bagdad* (1924), starring Douglas Fairbanks.

Hollywood actor and political activist **Ron Silver** (Ronald Arthur Silver) died on March 15 after a two-year battle with oesophageal cancer. He was sixty-two. Silver began his acting career in the 1970s, and his credits include *The Return of the World's Greatest Detective*, *The Entity*, *Silent Rage*, *Oh God! You Devil*, *Eat and Run*, *Blue Steel*, *Lifepod* (which he also directed), *Timecop*, *The Arrival*, *Shadow Zone: The Undead Express* (as a vampire), *Skeletons*, *Ratz*, *The Wisher* and *Xenophobia*. The actor turned from being a staunch Democrat to an outspoken supporter of US President George W. Bush's Republican administration following the 9/11 attacks on New York and Washington.

Canadian-born singer **Edmund** [James Arthur] **Hockridge** died the same day, aged eighty-nine. The baritone moved to Britain in the 1950s, where he starred in a number of West End musicals, including *Carousel* (1951). Hockridge had a number of hit records in the mid-1950s, including "Young and Foolish" and "No Other Love", and he made fleeting appearances in a few films.

Tony Award-winning British-born actress **Natasha** [Jane] **Richardson**, a member of the legendary Richardson acting dynasty, died in a New York hospital on March 18, three days after sustaining a head injury on a beginners' ski slope in Canada. Although she originally refused treatment after the fall, she later complained that she did not feel well. Her life support was switched off after her family had said their goodbyes. The daughter of actress Vanessa Redgrave and wife of actor Liam

Neeson, the forty-five-year-old actress played Mary Shelley in Ken Russell's *Gothic* (1986), and she also appeared in *The Handmaid's Tale* (based on the novel by Margaret Atwood), a BBC-TV remake of *Suddenly Last Summer* (1993), and the 2005 version of Patrick McGrath's *Asylum*, plus episodes of TV's *The Adventures of Sherlock Holmes*, *Worlds Beyond* and *Tales from the Crypt*. Theatres on Broadway and in London's West End dimmed their lights in tribute to the actress.

Dependable British character actor **John** [Edward] **Cater** died of liver cancer on March 21, aged seventy-seven. His numerous credits include *The Abominable Dr Phibes*, *Dr Phibes Rises Again*, Hammer's *Captain Kronos – Vampire Hunter* (as Professor Hieronymous Grost), *The Woman in Black*, *Rasputin* (1996) and *Alien Autopsy*. Cater was also in episodes of *Out of This World* (hosted by Boris Karloff), *Doctor Who*, *The Avengers*, *Department S*, *Orson Welles' Great Mysteries*, *Thriller* (1975), *The 10th Kingdom* and *Bonekickers*.

British character actor **John Franklyn-Robbins**, one of only a small number of actors to have speaking roles in both the *Doctor Who* and *Star Trek* franchises, died on March 21, aged eighty-four. His many films include Hammer's *Dracula A.D. 1972*, *Asylum* (1972), *Miss Morison's Ghosts*, *The Plague Dogs*, *The Woman in Black*, *The Dream Stone*, *Dr Jekyll and Ms Hyde*, *A Christmas Carol* (1999), *C.S. Lewis: Beyond Narnia*, *Hogfather* and *The Golden Compass*, and he appeared in episodes of TV's *The Avengers* ("The Cybernauts"), *Mystery and Imagination* (J. Sheridan Le Fanu's "The Flying Dragon"), *The Champions*, *Doctor Who* ("Genesis of the Daleks"), *The Storyteller* and *Star Trek: The Next Generation*.

**Danny Wayland Seals**, one half of American pop rock duo England Dan & John Ford Coley, died of complications from cancer on March 25, aged sixty-one. The pair were best known for their 1976 debut single "I'd Really Love to See You Tonight".

American actor and singer **Andy Hallett** (Andrew Alcott Hallett), who portrayed the laconic green-skinned demon Lorne in the final four seasons of Warner Bros.' *Angel* (2000–04), died of heart failure on March 29. The thirty-three-year-old had battled congestive heart disease for five years. He also appeared as an uncredited student in the classic "Hush" episode of the companion series, *Buffy the Vampire Slayer*, and voiced the character of the Cricket in the animated fantasy *Geppetto's Secret*.

The 1940s "singing cowboy" **Monte Hale** (Samuel Buren Ely) died the same day, aged eighty-nine. He made nearly three dozen "B" Westerns for Republic Pictures and had a small role as Rock Hudson's lawyer in *Giant*. Hale also appeared in the 1945 serial *The Purple Monster Strikes* and an episode of TV's *Honey West*. The actor also had his own popular comic book series, which were translated into twenty-seven languages. He later became the original owner of the Los Angeles Angels baseball team, and helped establish the Autry National Center of the American West.

Canadian-born actor and country music disc jockey **Murray Kash**, who voiced the character Colonel Raeburn in the 1960s puppet TV series *Space Patrol*, died in London on March 30, aged eighty-five. He had small roles in episodes of *Tales of Adventure* ("20,000 Leagues Under the Sea"), *The New Adventures of Charlie Chan*, *Invisible Man* (1959), *Out of the Unknown* and *Whoops Apocalypse*, plus the movies *Mouse on the Moon*, *Devils of Darkness* and *Thunderball*. His scenes were cut from *The Pink Panther Strikes Again*. Kash was married to singer and comedienne Libby Morris.

Texan character actor **Lou Perryman** (Louis Byron Perryman, aka Lou Perry) was shot to death on April 1 by a mentally ill convict who was out on parole. He was sixty-seven. After working as an assistant cameraman on *The Texas Chain Saw Massacre*, Perryman had small roles in *The Blues Brothers*, *Poltergeist*, *The Texas Chainsaw Massacre 2*, *The Cellar* and *The Monster Hunter* (aka *Natural Selection*).

Veteran Hispanic character actor **Victor Millán** (Joseph Brown), who portrayed Zahir in the 1950s TV series *Ramar of the Jungle*, died on April 3, aged eighty-nine. He also appeared in such movies as Orson Welles' *Touch of Evil*, *Doc Savage The Man of Bronze*, and episodes of *Bewitched*, *The Flying Nun*, *Kung Fu*, *The Six Million Dollar Man* and *Knight Rider*.

**Jody McCrea** (Joel Dee McCrea), the eldest son of actors Joel McCrea and Frances Dee, died of cardiac arrest on April 4, aged seventy-four. The six-foot, three-inch actor was best known for his role as the dimwitted surfer Deadhead/Bonehead in AIP's

*Beach Party*, *Muscle Beach Party*, *Bikini Beach*, *Pajama Party*, *Beach Blanket Bingo* and *How to Stuff a Wild Bikini*. He also appeared in a number of Westerns (four with his father), along with *The Monster That Challenged the World* and *The Glory Stompers*. He all-but-retired from acting in 1970 and became a cattle and elk rancher in Hondo, New Mexico.

American character actress and political activist **Maxine Cooper**, who memorably made her film debut as Ralph Meeker's sexy secretary Velda in Robert Aldrich's classic *film noir*, *Kiss Me Deadly* (1955), died the same day, aged eighty-four. She married Oscar-nominated screenwriter Sy Gomberg in 1957, but was "grey-listed" by the Hollywood establishment for her outspoken political views. Subsequently only featured in supporting roles, her later credits include Aldritch's *What Ever Happened to Baby Jane?* and episodes of *Alfred Hitchcock Presents* and *The Twilight Zone*.

Philippine actress **Tita Muñoz** (Maria Theresa Sanchez Muñoz) died on April 11, aged eighty. She appeared in *Mad Doctor of Blood Island*.

Former advertising model and actress **Marilyn Chambers** (Marilyn Ann Briggs), who had a career in both adult films and mainstream movies, died in her mobile home of a cerebral haemorrhage following an aortic aneurysm on April 12. She was fifty-seven. As well as appearing in such movies as *Behind the Green Door*, *Resurrection of Eve*, *Beyond De Sade* and *Insatiable* and *Insatiable II*, she also starred in David Cronenberg's *Rabid* and the sci-spy spoof *Angel of H.E.A.T.* More recently she appeared such direct-to-video fare as *Bedtime Fantasies*, *Lusty Busty Fantasies*, *Dark Chambers*, *Little Shop of Erotica* and *Naked Fairy Tales*.

Former actress and community activist **Lesley Gilb** [Taplin], who played the seductive title role in the 1973 vampire film *Lemora: A Child's Tale of the Supernatural*, was killed on April 13 in a six-car pile-up on Los Angeles' Highway 101. She was sixty-two.

British actor, musician and writer **Bob Hewis** (Robert John Hewis) died of an aneurysm the same day, aged fifty-six. He appeared on stage (as The Actor) in *The Woman in Black* and scripted a radio and stage adaptation of Edgar Allan Poe's *The Tell-Tale Heart*.

Thin-faced Spanish character actor **Fernando** [Jose] **Hilbeck** [Gavalda] died on April 25, aged seventy-five. His many movies include *Pyro*, *It Happened at Nightmare Inn*, *Voodoo Black Exorcist*, *Clockwork Terror*, *Creation of the Damned*, *The Living Dead at the Manchester Morgue*, *The Possessed*, *Flesh + Blood*, *Howl of the Devil* (with Paul Naschy) and *Mi nombre es sombra*, a 1996 version of *Dr Jekyll and Mr Hyde*.

Tony and Emmy Award-winning actress-comedienne **Bea Arthur** (Bernice Frankel), best known for her role as Dorothy Zbornak on the NBC sitcom *The Golden Girls* (1985–92), died of cancer the same day, aged eighty-six. In 1958 she played an ugly witch in an episode of the 1950s *Omnibus* TV series, was an alien bartender in the infamous *The Star Wars Holiday Special* (1978), and contributed her voice to an episode of *Futurama*.

Overweight comedian **Dom DeLuise** (Dominick DeLuise) died of kidney failure and respiratory complications from cancer on May 4, aged seventy-five. His many film credits include *Fail-Safe* (1964), *The Glass Bottom Boat*, *The Busy Body*, *The Adventure of Sherlock Holmes' Smarter Brother*, *The Muppet Movie*, *Wholly Moses!*, *The Secret of NIMH* and its sequel, *Haunted Honeymoon*, *An American Tail* and *All Dogs Go to Heaven*, along with their sequels and spin-off TV series, *Spaceballs*, the uncompleted *The Princess and the Dwarf*, *The Magic Voyage*, *Munchie*, *The Silence of the Hams*, *A Troll in Central Park* and *Lion of Oz*, plus episodes of *The Munsters*, *The Girl from U.N.C.L.E.*, *The Ghost & Mrs Muir*, *Amazing Stories*, *SeaQuest DSV*, *3rd Rock from the Son*, *Hercules*, *Sabrina the Teenage Witch*, *Stargate SG-1* and *Duck Dodgers*.

Hollywood leading lady **Jane Randolph** (Jane Roemer), who starred in Val Lewton's *Cat People* and its sequel, *Curse of the Cat People*, died the same day in Gstaad, Switzerland, of complications from hip surgery. She was ninety-three. Her other films include *The Falcon's Brother*, *The Falcon Strikes Back*, the Universal serial *The Mysterious Mr M*, and (Abbott and Costello) *Meet Frankenstein*. She retired in the late 1940s and moved to Spain with her husband, property developer Jaime del Amo, and became a Madrid socialite. Disney reportedly used Randolph as a model for one of the humans in the ice-skating sequence in the 1942 cartoon *Bambi*.

Lynyrd Skynyrd bass player **Donald "Ean" Evans** died of cancer on May 6, aged forty-eight. Evans joined the tragedy-hit band in 2001, after the death of Leon Wilkeson.

Four-foot, seven-inch **Mickey Carroll** (Michael Finocchiaro), another of the last surviving Munchkins from *The Wizard of Oz* (1939), died of a heart ailment and complications from Alzheimer's disease on May 7, aged eighty-nine. He played the candy-striped Fiddler Munchkin, for which he claimed he was paid just $125 a week. He also reportedly appeared in the *Spanky and Our Gang* film series and his godfather was mobster Al Capone. Carroll later worked for his family's gravestone-making business and replaced the worn headstone for L. Frank Baum's niece, Dorothy Gage, when her grave was rediscovered. Carroll's family subsequently sued his caregiver, who he had signed control of his assets over to four months prior to his death.

The sixty-seven-year-old actress and dancer **Linda Dangcil** lost a seven-year battle with tonsilar cancer the same day. In 1954, at the age of twelve, she made her Broadway debut as a Native American dancer in *Peter Pan*, starring Mary Martin. She recreated the role in the 1960 TV version, and her other credits include playing Sister Ana in ABC's *The Flying Nun* (1967–70), portraying a singing trucker in an episode of *3rd Rock from the Sun*, and contributing voice work to the cartoon series *A Pup Named Scooby-Doo* and *Batman*.

American character actor **Frank Aletter** died of lung cancer on May 13, aged eighty-three. Best known for his roles in sitcoms, he also appeared in Disney's *Now You See Him Now You Don't*, and episodes of *The Twilight Zone*, *My Favorite Martian*, *Planet of the Apes*, *The Six Million Dollar Man*, *Kolchak: The Night Stalker*, *The Invisible Man* (1975), *Holmes and Yo-Yo*, *The Bionic Woman*, *Project U.F.O.*, *Fantasy Island* and *Automan*. From 1958 to 1974 Aletter was married to actress and former Miss America Lee Meriweather.

Australian actor and director **Charles "Bud" [William] Tingwell** died of complications from prostate cancer on May 15, aged eighty-six. He flew Spitfires for the Royal Australian Air Force during World War II, and throughout the 1960s became a familiar face on British television in such shows as *Adam*

*Adamant Lives!*, *The Avengers* ("Return of the Cybernauts"), *Sherlock Holmes*, *Out of the Unknown*, *Catweazle* and *U.F.O.*, as well as voicing Captain Brown on *Captain Scarlet and the Mysterons*. He returned to his native Australia in 1973, where he starred in 126 episodes of the popular police series *Homicide* (1973–77) and guested on an episode of the children's superhero series *Legacy of the Silver Shadow*. Tingwell's film credits include *Tarzan the Magnificent*, Hammer's *The Secret of Blood Island* and *Dracula Prince of Darkness*, *Thunderbirds Are GO!*, *On the Beach* (2000), *WillFull* and *Antigravity*. He was given a state funeral at St Paul's Cathedral, Melbourne.

Busy Norwegian-born German actor, stunt co-ordinator, assistant director and special effects expert **Freddy** (Goffredo) **Unger** died in Italy in mid-May, aged around seventy-six. He had suffered a stroke some years earlier and was confined to an electric wheelchair. Unger appeared in such films as Mario Bava's *Blood and Black Lace* and *Knives of the Avenger*, *Hercules Against the Moon Men*, *Wild Wild Planet*, *The War of the Planets*, *War Between the Planets*, *Snow Demons*, *Cannibal Apocalypse*, *Absurd*, *Panic*, *Exterminators in the Year 3000*, *Devil Fish*, Lamberto Bava's *Demons*, *Wax Mask* and numerous Spaghetti Westerns. Behind the camera, he worked on *The Humanoid*, *Treasure of the Four Crowns*, *Hercules* (1983), *Yor the Hunter from the Future* and *Demons 5: The Devil's Veil*.

Former sound-effects editor **Wayne** [Anthony] **Allwine**, the voice of Disney's Mickey Mouse for thirty-two years, died of complications from diabetes on May 18, aged sixty-two. His wife, Russi Taylor, who was the voice of Minnie Mouse, was at his side. Allwine started his career as a Disney post room assistant before becoming the voice of Mickey in 1977 for *The New Mickey Mouse Club*. His many credits include *Mickey's Christmas Carol*, *The Black Cauldron*, *The Great Mouse Detective*, *Who Framed Roger Rabbit*, *Runaway Brain*, *How to Haunt a House*, *Mickey's Once Upon a Christmas*, *Fantasia 2000* and *Mickey's House of Villains*, plus *Splash* and *Star Trek V: The Final Frontier*. In 1986 he won an Emmy Award for his sound editing on Steven Spielberg's NBC-TV series *Amazing Stories*.

British leading man **Simon Oates** (Arthur Charles Oates),

who portrayed the rebellious and flamboyant Dr John Ridge in the BBC-TV series *Doomwatch* (1970–72) and the spin-off movie from Tigon British, died of prostate cancer on May 20, aged seventy-seven. His other credits include episodes of *The Avengers*, Nigel Kneale's *Beasts*, *The New Avengers* and the Polish-made *Sherlock Holmes and Doctor Watson*. He portrayed John Steed in a 1971 London stage version of *The Avengers*, and also co-starred with Zena Marshall (who died in July) in the low-budget Amicus SF movie *The Terrornauts*, scripted by John Brunner and based on Murray Leinster's novel *The Wailing Asteroid*.

British actress and former model **Lucy Gordon** hanged herself the same day in the Paris apartment she shared with her cinematographer boyfriend. The twenty-eight-year-old was reportedly despondent over the recent suicide of a friend. She appeared in small roles in the films *Perfume*, *Serial* and *Spider-Man 3*.

Voice actress **Joan Alexander** (Louise Abras, aka Joan A. Stanton), who made a career of portraying *Daily Planet* reporter Lois Lane, died of an intestinal ailment on May 21, aged ninety-four. She played the Man of Steel's girlfriend on Mutual Radio's *The Adventures of Superman* (1940–51), Max Fleischer's *Superman* cartoon shorts of the early 1940s, and episodes of the 1960s animated shows *The New Adventures of Superman*, *The Superman/Aquaman Hour of Adventure* and *The Batman/ Superman Hour*. The actress was also a regular on the *Philo Vance* and *Perry Mason* radio series, and appeared in TV's *Captain Video and his Video Rangers*.

Veteran British character actor and amateur numerologist **Terence** [Joseph] **Alexander** died of Parkinson's disease on May 28, aged eighty-six. A regular on the BBC's detective drama *Bergerac* (1981–91) as Charlie Hungerford, he also appeared in episodes of *The New Adventures of Charlie Chan*, *The Avengers*, *The Champions*, *Star Maidens*, *The New Avengers*, *Doctor Who*, *Hammer House of Mystery and Suspense* ("The Corvini Inheritance") and *Worlds Beyond*. Alexander's movies included *Carry On Regardless*, *The Mind Benders*, *The Magic Christian*, *The Vault of Horror* and the 1984 TV movie *Frankenstein*. He retired from acting in 1999.

**Millvina Dean**, the last survivor of the *Titanic*, died at a nursing home in Hampshire on May 31, aged ninety-seven. At just nine weeks old, Dean was the youngest person on the liner when, during its maiden voyage, it struck an iceberg on April 14, 1912 and sank. A month before Dean's death, Leonardo DiCaprio, Kate Winslet and James Cameron, the stars and director of the 1997 movie *Titanic*, collectively donated $30,000 to a fund to pay her nursing home fees.

On June 3, the body of seventy-two-year-old American actor and singer **David Carradine** (John Arthur Carradine), the eldest son of veteran actor John Carradine, was found hanging naked in a closet in a hotel room in Bangkok, Thailand. He had been shooting a movie in the country, and the cause of death was allegedly an attempt at auto-erotic asphyxiation that went wrong, although an autopsy failed to confirm an exact cause of death. Best known for his role as Kwai Chang Caine in the popular ABC series *Kung Fu* (1972–75) and the syndicated *Kung Fu: The Legend Continues* (1993–97), Carradine appeared in more than 200 movies and TV shows, including *Death Race 2000*, *Deathsport*, *Circle of Iron* (aka *The Silent Flute*, with Christopher Lee), *Trick or Treats*, *The Warrior and the Sorceress*, *The Bad Seed* (1985), *Warlords*, *I Saw What You Did*, *Wizards of the Lost Kingdom II*, *Future Force*, *Sundown The Vampire in Retreat* (as Count Dracula), *Dune Warriors*, *Future Zone*, *Evil Toons*, *Waxwork II Lost in Time*, *Light Speed*, *Children of the Corn V: Fields of Terror*, *Knocking on Death's Door*, *The Shepherd*, *The Monster Hunter*, *Nightfall*, *Dead & Breakfast*, *The Last Sect* (as Van Helsing), *Fall Down Dead*, *The Rain*, *Detention*, *Dinocroc vs. Supergator*, *Night of the Templar*, *Eldorado*, *The Alfred Hitchcock Hour*, *Night Gallery* ("The Phantom Farmhouse"), *Darkroom*, *The Fall Guy* ("October 31st"), *Hammer House of Mystery and Suspense* ("A Distant Scream"), *Amazing Stories*, *The Ray Bradbury Theater*, *Charmed* and *Medium*. He also hosted a video version of the silent classic *Nosferatu: The First Vampire* that featured a soundtrack by Goth-metal band Type-O Negative. Carradine's acting career received a much-needed boost when he starred in the titular role in Quentin Tarantino's two-part over-the-top action movie *Kill Bill*, and he voiced his original character of Frankenstein in the 2008 remake of *Death Race*.

Veteran Chinese kung fu actor **Kien Shih** (Wing-Cheung Shek) died of kidney failure the same day, aged ninety-six. He began his career in 1939 as a make-up man in Hong Kong and is probably best known for his role in *Enter the Dragon* (1973) opposite Bruce Lee. From the 1940s onwards Shih appeared in more than 300 films, including *A Ghostly Tale*, *The Ten Brothers vs. the Sea Monster*, *Ali Baba and the 40 Robbers*, *The Blonde Hair Monster*, *The Magic Whip*, *The Horrors of the Evil Shadow*, *Magic Snowflake Sword*, *Blood Reincarnation*, *A Friend from Inner Space* and *The Magic Crystal*. Because he could not speak English, many of Shih's performances were dubbed by Keye Luke.

Hollywood leading man **Ward Costello** died of complications due to a stroke on June 4, aged eighty-nine. His many credits include AIP's *Terror from the Year 5000* (aka *Cage of Doom*), Disney's *Return from Witch Mountain*, *Bloody Birthday*, *Firefox* and *Project X*, plus episodes of *Alfred Hitchcock Presents* and *Star Trek: The Next Generation*.

American character actor **Del**(bert) **Monroe**, who appeared in the 1961 movie *Voyage to the Bottom of the Sea* and played Kowalski in all four seasons of the ABC-TV spin-off series, died of leukaemia on June 5, aged seventy-three. He also appeared in episodes of *The Time Tunnel*, *Mission Impossible*, *Ark II*, *The Amazing Spider-Man*, *Wonder Woman*, *Time Express*, *The Incredible Hulk* and *Medium*.

Kenyan-born British actor and Church of England minister [Walter] **Tenniel Evans** died of emphysema on June 10, aged eighty-three. Descended from Mary Anne Evans (aka "George Eliot") and *Alice in Wonderland* illustrator John Tenniel, he was the son-in-law of actor Leslie Banks. Evans appeared in episodes of *The Avengers*, *Out of the Unknown*, *Journey to the Unknown*, *Randall and Hopkirk (Deceased)*, *Menace*, *The Ghosts of Motley Hall*, *Ripping Yarns* ("The Curse of the Claw"), *The Adventures of Sherlock Holmes* and *Worlds Beyond*. He encouraged his friend Jon Pertwee to audition for *Doctor Who* and Evans appeared with the actor in the show's four-part "Carnival of Monsters" serial.

American TV announcer **Ed McMahon** (Edward Peter Leo McMahon, Jr) died on June 23, aged eighty-six. For thirty years he worked as Johnny Carson's straight man on NBC's *The*

*Tonight Show*. McMahon also narrated the 1955 horror film *Dementia* (aka *Daughter of Horror*) and was in *Slaughter's Big Rip-Off*, *Legends of the Superheroes* and *Full Moon High*. He guested as himself in *Elvira's Movie Macabre*, *Bewitched* (2005), and episodes of *Amazing Stories*, *ALF*, *Pinky and the Brain*, *The Simpsons* ("Treehouse of Horror IX"), *Sabrina the Teenage Witch* and *Duck Dodgers*.

Welsh-born character actress **Irene Richmond** died on June 24, aged ninety-seven. She had roles in *The Brain*, *Dr Terror's House of Horrors* and Hammer's *Nightmare* and *Hysteria*.

Singer, dancer and songwriter **Michael** [Joseph] **Jackson**, who sold an estimated 200 million albums while he was alive, died from apparent cardiac arrest on June 25, aged fifty. A much-publicized autopsy revealed that his body contained lethal doses of a powerful medical anaesthetic – propofol – and at least two sedatives. A former child singer with his brothers in the 1970s Motown group The Jackson 5, he later became a solo artist with a string of mega-hits culminating in 1982 with the biggest-selling record album of all time, *Thriller*. In later years Jackson became a reclusive and controversial figure due to his bizarre behaviour and odd physical appearance. John Landis directed a thirteen-minute promotional video for the title song from *Thriller* (featuring a "rap" by Vincent Price), in which the King of Pop played both a zombie and a werewolf. Jackson also appeared in *The Wiz* (as the Scarecrow), Disney's 3-D attraction *Captain EO*, *Michael Jackson's Ghosts* and *Men in Black II*, and he sang the title song for the 1972 killer rat movie *Ben*. Jackson's plans to produce and star in a 2002 biopic, *The Nightmares of Edgar Allan Poe*, came to nothing.

The sixty-two-year-old Hollywood actress **Farrah Fawcett** (Ferrah Leni Fawcett) died after a long and very public battle against cancer the same day. After appearing on an iconic 1970s poster, the Texas-born actress was cast as Jill Munroe in the first season of ABC-TV's *Charlie's Angels* (1976–77) before she abruptly quit the show. She also appeared in *I Dream of Jeannie*, *The Flying Nun* and four episodes of *The Six Million Dollar Man* (opposite her husband [1973–82] Lee Majors), while her movie credits include *Myra Breckinridge* (with John Carradine), *Logan's Run*, *Saturn 3* and Disney's *The Brave Little Toaster*

*Goes to Mars*. The month before her death, NBC aired a documentary in which the actress allowed cameras to chronicle her fight against cancer. From 1980 to 1997 Fawcett dated Ryan O'Neal, and the actor was at her bedside when she died.

Perky Hollywood "B" movie actress and singer **Gale Storm** (Josephine Owaissa Cottle) died on June 27, aged eighty-seven. She appeared in the Monogram mysteries *Cosmo Jones Crime Smasher* (based on the radio series) and *Revenge of the Zombies* (with John Carradine), along with an episode of TV's *The Unexpected*. She had her own eponymous TV series from 1956 to 1960 (Boris Karloff appeared as himself in a 1959 episode) and recorded a number of chart hits, including "I Hear You Knocking" and "Dark Moon", which reached #4 on the *Billboard* chart.

Comedian, impersonator and voice artist **Fred Travalena** (Frederick Albert Travalena III) died of non-Hodgkin's lymphoma on June 28, aged sixty-six. He appeared on TV in episodes of *Fantasy Island* and *Black Scorpion*, and contributed voice-work to *The Jetsons*, *The ABC Comedy Hour*, *Scooby-Doo and Scrappy-Doo*, *Smurfs*, *Dinosaurs* and *King Fu Magoo*.

Czechoslovakian-born actor **Jan Rubes** died of complications from a stroke in Toronto, Canada, on June 29. He was eighty-nine. A former opera singer, Rubes emigrated to Canada in 1948. He appeared in such films as *Deadly Harvest*, *Murder in Space*, *Dead of Winter*, *Blood Relations*, *The Kiss*, *The Amityville Curse*, *Lamb Chop and the Haunted Studio* (as the Phantom) and *The Birds II: Land's End*, along with episodes of *The New Avengers*, *War of the Worlds*, the unsold 1992 TV pilot for *The Witches of Eastwick*, *The X Files*, *The Outer Limits* (1999), *Stargate SG-1* and *Mentors*.

Brothers **Alberto Jiménez** and **Alejandro Pérez Jiménez**, two masked Mexican midget wrestlers ("Lucha Mini") who fought professionally under the names "La Parkita" ("Little Death") and "Espectrito II", were found dead by cleaners in a low-rent Mexico City hotel the same day. They were both thirty-six. Police believe that following a TV appearance, the pair picked up two women posing as prostitutes who gave them a cocktail of alcohol and drugs so that they could rob them. Although not usually lethal, the dose may have been too strong for the sibling *luchadors*. Their masks were placed on their coffins at the funeral. Police later arrested a sixty-five-year-old woman in connection with the deaths.

American singer and actor **Harve Presnell** (George Harvey Presnell), who portrayed Little Orphan Annie's millionaire benefactor Daddy Warbucks on stage more than 2,000 times, died of pancreatic cancer on June 30, aged seventy-five. On TV he was best known in the recurring roles of Dr Sam Lane in *Lois and Clark: The New Adventures of Superman* (1995–97) and Mr Parker in *The Pretender* (1997–2000) and the show's spin-off movies *The Pretender 2001* and *The Pretender: Island of the Haunted*. Presnell also appeared in episodes of *Alfred Hitchcock Presents* (uncredited), *Star Trek: Voyager*, *The Guardian*, *The Outer Limits* (1998) and *Charmed*, along with the movies *Blood Bath* (1976), *The Whole Wide World* (as Robert E. Howard's father), *Tidal Wave: No Escape*, *Escanaba in da Moonlight*, *Face/Off* and *Evan Almighty*.

Veteran Oscar-winning American actor **Karl Malden** (Malden George Sekulovich), who starred as Detective Lt Mike Stone in ABC-TV's popular police series *The Streets of San Francisco* (1972–77) and the 1992 spin-off movie, died in his sleep on July 1, aged ninety-seven. Malden also starred in the 1954 3-D movie *Phantom of the Rue Morgue* (based on Edgar Allan Poe's "The Murders in the Rue Morgue"), and his other film credits include *Dead Ringer* (aka *Dead Image*), *Murderer's Row*, *Billion Dollar Brain*, Dario Argento's *The Cat o'Nine Tales*, *Beyond the Poseidon Adventure*, *Meteor*, and as the Walrus in the musical *Alice in Wonderland* (1985).

American actress and former model **Anna Karen** [Morrow], who was married to actor Jeff Morrow from 1947 until his death in 1993, died the same day, aged ninety-four. She had roles in episodes of TV's *Lights Out*, *One Step Beyond*, *Star Trek* ("All Our Yesterdays") and *Project U.F.O.*

**Bob** (Robert Bostwick) **Mitchell**, one of the last silent film organists in Hollywood, also died on July 1, aged ninety-six. Although the arrival of sound put an end to his career at the age of sixteen, in the early 1990s he became the resident organist at the Silent Movie Theatre on Fairfax Avenue. He also appeared (usually uncredited as a choir conductor) in a few films, including *The Big Broadcast of 1938*.

Hollywood leading lady **Brenda Joyce** (Betty "Graftina" Leabo), who played Jane to both Johnny Weissmuller's and Lex Barker's Tarzans, died of pneumonia on July 4, aged ninety-seven. She had been battling dementia for a decade. The former model made her screen debut in the Oscar-winning *The Rains Came* (1939) before being relegated to such "B" movies as *Whispering Ghosts* (with John Carradine), the "Inner Sanctum" mysteries *Strange Confession* (aka *The Missing Head*) and *Pillow of Death* (both with Lon Chaney, Jr) and *The Spider Woman Strikes Back* (with Gale Sondergaard). Succeeding Maureen O'Sullivan in the role, she portrayed the jungle man's mate in *Tarzan and the Amazons*, *Tarzan and the Leopard Woman* (with Acquenetta), *Tarzan and the Huntress*, *Tarzan and the Mermaids* (with George Zucco) and *Tarzan's Magic Fountain*. Leaving movies in the late 1940s, she worked incognito for a decade in Washington for the Department of Immigration, and she also kept her past secret from staff at the nursing home in Santa Monica, where she spent her final years.

British singer, sailor, cook, property developer, sometime-actor and general *bon vivant* **Hugh** [Geoffroy] **Millais**, the great-grandson of the Pre-Raphaelite painter Sir John Everett Millais, died the same day, aged seventy-nine. A friend to the rich and famous, including Salvador Dali, Orson Welles and Ernest Hemingway, he appeared in a few films, including Robert Altman's psychological mystery *Images*.

British actress **Zena Marshall**, who was born in Nairobi, Kenya, died in London of cancer on July 10, aged eighty-three. A member of Rank's famous "Charm School" (alongside Christopher Lee and Diana Dors), she played seductive villain Miss Taro in the first James Bond movie, *Dr No* (1962). Her other film credits include *Miranda*, *Helter Skelter* (1949), *So Long at the Fair*, *Three Cases of Murder* (the "Lord Mountdrago" episode with Orson Welles) and the Amicus SF movie *The Terrornauts*, plus episodes of TV's *Colonel March of Scotland Yard* (with Boris Karloff) and *Invisible Man* (1959).

British character actor **John** [Patrick] **Breslin**, best known for his role as Alan-a-Dale in the 1953 TV series *Robin Hood*, died on July 11, aged eighty. He apparently turned up in a couple of uncredited roles in *The 3 Worlds of Gulliver* and *Gorgo*, and appeared in the *Doctor Who* series "Spearhead from Space" and an episode of *U.F.O.* During the 1960s, Breslin reportedly dubbed Steve Reeves in a number of Italian muscleman films.

Hollywood leading lady **Beverly** [Louise] **Roberts**, who co-starred with Boris Karloff in Warner Bros.' *West of Shanghai*, died on July 13, aged ninety-five.

Albanian-born Italian actress **Romana Francesca Coluzzi** died of lung cancer on July 15, aged sixty-six. Best remembered for her sex comedies of the 1970s, she made her uncredited screen debut in Lucio Fulci's SF comedy *002 operazione Luna* (1965), and her other film credits include *Themroc, Il cav. Costante Nicosia demoniaco, ovvero: Dracula in Brianza, Bollenti spiriti* and *Red Sonja*.

Respected TV broadcaster and commentator ("The Most Trusted Man in America") **Walter Cronkite** (Walter Leland Cronkite, Jr), died of cerebrovascular disease on July 17, aged ninety-two. While a news anchor for CBS, he covered the Apollo XI Moon landing in 1969 for twenty-seven out of the thirty hours of the flight. He also hosted the 2000 TV movie *Fail Safe* and contributed his voice to the animated movie *We're Back! A Dinosaur's Story*.

Musician **Gordon Waller**, one half of the 1960s British pop duo Peter & Gordon (with Jane Asher's brother, Peter), died of cardiac arrest in Norwich, Connecticut, the same day, aged sixty-four. The duo's biggest hit was "A World Without Love" in 1964, written by Paul McCartney.

British stage, screen and radio actress **Jill** [Angela Henriette] **Balcon**, the daughter of Ealing Studios boss Sir Michael Balcon, died on July 18, aged eighty-four. She married future poet laureate C. Day-Lewis after a very public scandal in 1951, and the couple remained together until his early death from cancer in 1972. The second of their two children is Oscar-winning actor Daniel Day-Lewis.

Hollywood actress and former department store model **Virginia** [Elizabeth] **Carroll**, who appeared (uncredited) with her first husband, actor Ralph Byrd, in the 1938 Republic serial *Dick Tracy Returns*, died on July 23, aged ninety-five. She was also in the serials *Mysterious Doctor Satan, G-Men vs. the Black Dragon* (aka *Black Dragons of Manzanar*), *The Crimson Ghost* (aka *Cyclotrode 'X'*), *The Black Widow* (aka *Sombra, the Spider Woman*) and *Superman* (1948, as Martha Kent). Her many other credits include episodes of TV's *Adventures of Superman* and *The Adventures of Dr Fu Manchu*.

Irish-born character actor **Harry Towb** died of cancer in London on July 24, aged eighty-three. He was in *Digby the Biggest Dog in the World*, and appeared on TV in a 1958 adaptation of *Arsenic and Old Lace* for ITV *Play of the Week* and episodes of the 1950s *Sherlock Holmes*, *Suspense*, *The Avengers*, *The Champions* and *Doctor Who*.

Character actor **Clayton D.** (David) **Hill**, who played a lead zombie in George A. Romero's *Dawn of the Dead*, died of complications from pneumonia on July 27, aged eighty-eight. A former singer who also worked as a location casting director, weapons co-ordinator and second unit director, Hill appeared in *Knightriders*, *Hellraiser III: Hell on Earth* (as The Priest) and was about to start filming *River of Darkness* when he died.

Sixty-six-year-old Italian-born singer **Renato Pagliari** who, as one half of the duo Renée (Hilary Lester) and Renato, topped the UK charts for four weeks in 1982 with "Save Your Love", died following surgery for a brain tumour on July 29. He also sang the jingle "Just One More Cornetto" in the memorable Wall's ice-cream commercial.

The same day saw the deaths of twenty-eight-year-old **Michelle Partlow** (aka Amber Harris) and fifty-nine-year-old **Wanda Faye** [Mabrey] in an automobile accident in Beebe, Arkansas. Both actresses appeared in the direct-to-video movies *Evil on Queen Street*, *Evil on Queen Street: Ascension*, *StoryLine* and *Pray for the Hunters*.

Influential American folk musician and folklorist **Mike** (Michael) **Seeger**, half-brother of Pete Seeger and brother of Peggy Seeger, died on August 7, aged seventy-five. A founding member in the late 1950s of the music group The New Lost City Ramblers, his own record albums include *Tipple Loom and Rail* and *Music from True Vine*.

Film and TV character actor **John Quade** (John William Saunders III), who made a career out of playing "heavies" and sheriffs, died in his sleep on August 9, aged seventy-one. A former worker in the missile and aerospace industry before he became an actor, Quade appeared in the pilot for *Planet Earth*, *The Swinging Cheerleaders*, *The Ghost of Flight 401*, *The Highwayman*, *And You Thought Your Parents Were Weird*, plus episodes of *The Wild Wild West*, *The Bionic Woman*, *Buck Rogers in the 25th Century*, *Galactica 1980*, *Manimal* and *Werewolf*.

Romanian-born character actor **Henry Ramer** died in Toronto, Canada, the same day. He was thought to be in his eighties. Ramer's credits include *Change of Mind*, *Welcome to Blood City*, *Starship Invasions* (with Christopher Lee) and *Virus*, plus voice work on the 1960s *Spider-Man* cartoon series, *Friday the 13th The Series*, *Screamers* and *Mythic Warriors: Guardians of the Legend*. The actor was also the voice of "the mysterious Luther Kranst", who introduced 100 episodes of the Canadian late-night radio series *Nightfall* (1980–83), which included adaptations of "The Tell-Tale Heart" and "The Monkey's Paw".

Former fashion model/Hollywood actress **Ruth Ford** died on August 12, aged ninety-eight. A member of Orson Welles' Mercury Theatre group, during the 1940s she appeared in such "B" movies as *Secrets of the Lone Wolf*, *The Hidden Hand* (with Milton Parsons), *The Woman Who Came Back* and *Dragonwyck* (uncredited), before making a belated comeback in *Too Scared to Scream* (1985). She was married to actors Peter van Eyck and Zachary Scott.

Actor and comedian **Sammy Petrillo** (Sam Patrello, aka Samuel Petrillo), who made a career out of looking and sounding like Jerry Lewis, died of cancer on August 15, aged seventy-four. Best known for playing himself in the not-quite-dreadful 1952 horror comedy *Bela Lugosi Meets a Brooklyn Gorilla* (aka *The Boys from Brooklyn*), he also appeared in *The Brain That Wouldn't Die* (uncredited), the nudie comedies *Shangri-La* and Doris Wishman's *Keyholes Are For Peeping*, along with the 1997 documentary *Lugosi: Hollywood's Dracula*. As the owner of a Pittsburgh comedy nightclub, he gave Richard Pryor and Dennis Miller their first big breaks.

Ninety-year-old **Virginia Davis** who, as a four-year-old, was the curly-haired star of Walt Disney's pioneering *Alice* films (1923–25), combining animation with live-action, died the same day. She also had an uncredited role in the old dark house mystery *Murder at the Vanities* (1934) and provided some background voices for Disney's *Pinocchio*. Davis later became an interior designer, magazine editor and a real estate agent.

Mexican character actor **Héctor Gómez** [Sotomayor] died of cancer on August 15, aged seventy-four. He appeared in *Invisible Man in Mexico*, *Blue Demon destructor de espías*, *Pasaporte a la muerte* and the 1962 TV series *Las momias de Guanajuato*.

**Johnny Carter**, lead tenor of the 1960s group The Dells ("Oh, What a Night") and the last surviving member of the 1950s group The Flamingos ("I Only Have Eyes for You"), died of lung cancer on August 21, aged seventy-five.

Diminutive British variety actress **Sadie Corré** died of complications from a stroke on August 26, aged ninety-one. Her first film role was as the ventriloquist dummy Hugo in the 1964 *Devil Doll*, and she also had small roles in *Chitty Chitty Bang Bang*, *The Rocky Horror Picture Show*, *Wombling Free*, *The Dark Crystal*, *Star Wars Episode VI: Return of the Jedi* (as an Ewok), *Brazil*, *Willow* and *Who Framed Roger Rabbit*. The four-foot, two-inch Corré also played various pantomime cats on stage.

American actor **Wayne Tippit** died on August 28, aged seventy-six. Tippit, who underwent a lung transplant in 2000, died of complications from emphysema. In 1964 he was assistant director and played the drunk killed by a monster in *The Horror of Party Beach*. His other credits include episodes of *Tales from the Darkside*, *Quantum Leap*, *Dark Shadows* (1990–91), *The X Files* and *Dark Skies* (as J. Edgar Hoover).

German actress and dancer **Mady Rahl** (Edith Gertrud Meta Raschke), reportedly the last surviving star of the UFA studio, died of cancer the same day, aged ninety-four. She made her film debut in 1934, and her numerous credits include *The Inn on Dartmoor*, *The Horror of Blackwood Castle*, *Venus in Furs* and the TV comedy *Faust auf eigene Faust*.

Mexican actress **Yolanda Varela** (Carmen Yolanda Sainz Reyes) died of a cerebral embolism on August 29, aged seventy-nine. She began her film career while a teenager, and her credits include *La casa del terror* (aka *Face of the Screaming Werewolf*, with Lon Chaney, Jr).

Dependable Scottish actor **Iain Cuthbertson** died on September 4, aged seventy-nine. Although he appeared in a number of films, he is better known for his TV work in Nigel Kneale's *The Stone Tape* and episodes of *Adam Adamant Lives!*, *The Avengers*, *The Ghosts of Motley Hall*, *Children of the Stones*, *Survivors*, *Doctor Who* ("The Ribos Operation") and *The Ray Bradbury Theater*.

Former child actor **Frank** [Francis Edward] **Coghlan, Jr** (aka Junior Coghlan) who, as Billy Batson, shouted "Shazam!" and turned into the adult superhero (Tom Tyler) of the 1941 serial *The Adventures of Captain Marvel*, died on September 7, aged ninety-three. His many other films (often uncredited) include *Charlie Chan at the Race Track*, *It's a Wonderful Life*, *Murder Over New York* and *Valley of the Dolls*. In 1974 he had a cameo role in the CBS-TV series *Shazam!*

Australian-born actor **Ray Barrett** (Raymond Charles Barrett), who voiced both John Tracy and the villainous Hood in *Thunderbirds* (1965–66) and *Thunderbirds Are GO!*, died on September 8 of a brain haemorrhage on Australia's Gold Coast. He was eighty-two. Barrett worked in Britain during the 1960s and 1970s, appearing in such movies as *The Reptile* for Hammer and *Revenge*, while his TV credits include *Out of This World*, *The Avengers*, *Doctor Who* and *Stingray* (as the voice of Commander Sam Shore who announced "Stand by for action!").

South African-born actor **Zakes Mokae** died in Las Vegas of complications from a stroke on September 11, aged seventy-five. He had suffered from Parkinson's disease for a number of years. Mokae moved to London in the early 1960s when his acting career was blocked in his own country, and he eventually relocated to America in the mid-1970s. He appeared in the films *The Island*, *The Serpent and the Rainbow*, *Body Parts*, *Dust Devil*, *Vampire in Brooklyn*, *Outbreak* and *Waterworld*, along with episodes of *Knight Rider* and *The X Files*.

American actor **Paul Burke** died of leukaemia and non-Hodgkin's lymphoma on September 13, aged eighty-three. Although he made his film debut in the early 1950s and appeared in such movies as *Francis Goes to West Point*, *Francis in the Navy*, *The Disembodied*, *Daddy's Gone A-Hunting*, *Crowhaven Farm* (with John Carradine) and *Psychic Killer*, he was better known as a TV star with appearances in such shows as *Adventures of Superman*, *Men Into Space*, *Thriller* (1974) and *Fantasy Island* to his credit.

Hollywood leading man **Patrick** [Wayne] **Swayze** died on September 14 after losing his two-year battle against pancreatic cancer. He was fifty-seven. A trained dancer, Swayze starred in *Red Dawn*, *Steel Dawn*, *Dirty Dancing*, *Ghost*, *Tall Tale*, *Three Wishes*, *Donnie Darko*, *George and the Dragon*, *King Solomon's Mines* (2004), Disney's *The Fox and the Hound 2* and an episode of TV's *Amazing Stories*.

American character actor **Henry Gibson** (James Bateman), best known as a regular cast member on NBC-TV's *Rowan and Martin's Laugh-In* from 1967 to 1971, died of cancer the same day, aged seventy-three. Gibson made his movie debut in *The Nutty Professor* (1963), and his other credits include *Charlotte's Web* (1973), *Halloween is Grinch Night*, *The Halloween That Almost Wasn't* (as Igor), *The Incredible Shrinking Woman*, *Monster in the Closet* (with John Carradine), *Innerspace*, *The 'burbs*, *Around the World in 80 Days* (1989), *Night Visitor*, *Brenda Starr*, *Gremlins 2: The New Batch* (with Christopher Lee), *Escape to Witch Mountain* (1995), *Asylum* (1997) and *The Luck of the Irish*. Gibson was also in episodes of TV's *My Favorite Martian*, *Bewitched*, *Wonder Woman*, *Fantasy Island*, *The Twilight Zone* (1986), *Knight Rider*, *Eerie Indiana*, *Tales from the Crypt*, *Star Trek: Deep Space Nine*, *Total Recall 2070*, *Sabrina the Teenage Witch*, *Early Edition*, *Stagate: SG-1* and *Charmed*, and he was a regular voice on *Galaxy High School*.

British actor **John** [Patrick] **Joyce**, who worked with Ken Campbell's Science Fiction Theatre of Liverpool on such stage productions as the nine-hour *Illuminatus!* (1977) and the twenty-two hour *The Warp* (1979), died from oesophageal cancer on September 15, aged seventy. His film and TV appearances include *Morons from Outer Space* and *Doctor Who* ("The Daemons"), and for the last ten years of his life he worked as a dummy patient for doctors training in London hospitals.

Busy character actor **Timothy** [Dingwall] **Bateson** died the same day, aged eighty-three. He appeared in the first British stage production of Samuel Beckett's *Waiting for Godot* in 1955, and his numerous film and TV credits include *Vice Versa* (1948), *What a Carve Up!* (aka *No Place Like Homicide!*), *The Day the Earth Caught Fire*, Hammer's *Nightmare*, *The Evil of Frankenstein* and *The Anniversary*, *Torture Garden*, *Twisted*

*Nerve*, *A Christmas Carol* (1984), *Labyrinth*, *Merlin* (1998), *The 10th Kingdom*, *Terry Pratchett's Hogfather* and *Harry Potter and the Order of the Phoenix* (as the voice of Kreacher), along with episodes of *Out of the Unknown*, *The Avengers*, *The Rivals of Sherlock Holmes*, *Doctor Who*, Neil Gaiman's *Neverwhere*, *Polterguests* and *Relic Hunter*.

**Mary Travers**, who sang with the 1960s American folk group Peter, Paul and Mary, died of leukaemia on September 16, aged seventy-two. The trio's hits include "Puff the Magic Dragon", Bob Dylan's "Blowin' in the Wind" and their only #1 hit, "Leaving on a Jet Plane".

Six-foot, five-inch tall American stuntman and actor **Dick Durock**, who portrayed the heroic monster in Wes Craven's *Swamp Thing*, *The Return of Swamp Thing* and the 1990s cable TV series, died after a long battle with pancreatic cancer on September 17, aged seventy-two. He began his career as a stunt double for Guy Williams on the final season of *Lost in Space*, and his other credits include *Conquest of the Planet of the Apes*, *The Thing with Two Heads*, *Battle for the Planet of the Apes*, *The Dark Secret of Harvest Home*, *Doc Savage Man of Bronze*, *The Nude Bomb*, *More Wild Wild West*, *The Return of the Man from U.N.C.L.E.: The Fifteen Years Later Affair*, *The Sword and the Sorcerer*, *Stand By Me*, *Ewocks: The Battle for Endor*, *Howard the Duck*, *The Monster Squad* and *Remote Control*, plus episodes of *Star Trek*, *The Six Million Dollar Man*, *Battlestar Galactica* (as the Imperious Leader), *Quark*, *Buck Rogers in the 25th Century*, *The Incredible Hulk*, *The Powers of Matthew Star*, *Knight Rider* and *Hard Time on Planet Earth*.

Prolific Spanish character actor **Víctor Israel** (Josep Maria Soler Vilanova) died on September 19, aged eighty. His many credits include *The Sweet Sound of Death*, *The House That Screamed*, *Exorcism's Daughter*, *The Light at the Edge of the World* (based on the novel by Jules Verne), *Murders in the Rue Morgue* (1971), *Necrophagus*, *The Witches' Mountain*, *Horror Express* (with Christopher Lee and Peter Cushing), *The Mysterious Island* (1973), *Devil's Kiss*, *Night of the Howling Beast* and *Crimson* (both with Paul Naschy), *El jovencito Drácula*, *Zombie Creeping Flesh* (aka *Night of the Zombies*), *The Sea Serpent* (with Ray Milland), *Más allá de la muerte* and

*El anticristo 2*, along with numerous Spaghetti Westerns and comedies.

American actor **John Hart**, who took over from Clayton Moore as TV's *The Lone Ranger* in 1952–53, died on September 20. He was ninety-one and had been suffering from dementia for some years. Hart appeared (often uncredited) in the serials *Jack Armstrong*, *Brick Bradford*, *Batman and Robin*, *Atom Man vs. Superman* and *Adventures of Captain Africa*, plus the movies *Fury of the Congo*, *Aladdin and His Lamp*, *Jungle Jim in the Forbidden Land*, *Thief of Damascus* (with Lon Chaney, Jr), *The Ten Commandments* (1956), Disney's *The Shaggy Dog* (1959), *Atlantis the Lost Continent*, *Simon King of the Witches*, *Blackenstein*, *Welcome to Arrow Beach*, *Blood Voyage* (aka *Nightmare Voyage*), *The Astral Factor* (aka *Invisible Strangler*) and *Cheerleaders Beach Party*. He co-starred with Chaney, Jr again in the TV series *Hawkeye and the Last of the Mohicans*, and was also in episodes of *World of Giants* and *The Addams Family*. Hart reprised the role of the Lone Ranger in *The Phynx* (1970), plus episodes of *The Greatest American Hero* and *Happy Days*. He had a cameo role in *The Legend of the Lone Ranger* (1981). In later years he became a dubbing supervisor on cartoon shows.

Former musician-turned-painter and actor **Robert** [Winthrop] **Ginty** died of cancer on September 21, aged sixty. Following *The Exterminator* (1980), Ginty became a direct-to-video action/horror star in such films as *Warrior of the Lost World*, *The Alchemist*, *Scarab*, *Exterminator 2*, *Maniac Killer* and *Programmed to Kill*. He appeared in episodes of *Project U.F.O.*, *Knight Rider*, *Baywatch Nights* and the TV movie *The Big One: The Great Los Angeles Earthquake* before becoming a successful director on such shows as *Lois and Clark: The New Adventures of Superman*, *Early Edition*, *Honey I Shrunk the Kids: The TV Show*, *Xena: Warrior Princess*, *Charmed*, *Tracker* and the 1995 TV movie *Here Come the Munsters*. In 2004 he directed a rap/hip-hop musical stage version of Anthony Burgess' *A Clockwork Orange*.

Argentinian actress **Inés** [Escariz] **Fernández**, who starred in *El fantasma de la opera* (1955), died on September 22, aged seventy-seven.

**Lucy O'Donnell** (Lucy Vodden) died of complications from lupus the same day, aged forty-seven. It was a drawing of her by nursery school friend Julian Lennon that inspired his father, John, to write the song "Lucy in the Sky with Diamonds" for The Beatles in 1967.

American character actor **Vincent Russo**, who appeared in *Screamtime* and *Maniac Cop 2*, died on September 26, aged fifty-eight.

British actress **Margo Johns** (Jessie Margaret Johns), who co-starred with Michael Gough and a giant gorilla in *Konga* (1961), died on September 29, aged ninety. She also appeared in *Meet Sexton Blake* and *Murder at the Windmill* (aka *Murder at the Burlesque*), and was married to actor William Franklyn from 1952 to 1962.

American actor and singer **Byron Palmer**, who portrayed a Scotland Yard inspector in the 1953 Jack the Ripper thriller *Man in the Attic*, died on September 30, aged eighty-nine.

"B" movie heroine **Pamela Blake** (Adele Pearce) died on October 6, aged ninety-four. A former teenage beauty queen, she appeared in *The Unknown Guest* and such serials as *Chick Carter Detective*, *The Mysterious Mr M* and *Ghost of Zorro*. Blake retired from the screen in 1953 and moved with her family to Las Vegas.

Irish actor **Sean Lawlor**, who portrayed a modern-day Captain Nemo in the direct-to-video *30,000 Leagues Under the Sea* (2007), died on October 10, aged fifty-five. He also appeared in *Space Truckers*, *Mega Shark vs. Giant Octopus*, *The Black Waters of Echo's Pond*, the fantasy short *Scarecrow Joe* and an episode of TV's *Night Man*.

**Cynthia Ann Thompson** (aka Cindy Ann Thompson), who starred in the 1985 comedy *Cavegirl*, died of cancer the same day, aged fifty. She was also in a handful of other films during the decade, including Ruggero Deodato's *Body Count* (aka *The Eleventh Commandment*) and the 1988 remake of *Not of This Earth*.

Thirty-three-year-old Irish boyband singer **Stephen** [Patrick David] **Gately** was found dead in his £1 million apartment in Majorca, Spain, on October 10. A post-mortem examination revealed that he had died of a pulmonary oedema – an accumulation of fluid on the lungs. During the 1990s he was one of five members of Boyzone, who had six #1 singles in the UK. He played the lead in *Joseph and the Amazing Technicolor Dreamcoat* in London's West End and, in 2008, Gately had an acting role the independent British horror film *Credo* (aka *The Devil's Curse*).

Italian-American crooner **Al Martino** (Alfred Cini), who appeared as Johnny Fontane in *The Godfather*, died on October 13, aged eighty-two. Martino was the first singer to top the UK charts when they began in November 1952 with "Here In My Heart", which remained there for nine weeks (only six records have had a longer continuous run). During a fifty-year career, his other hits included "Spanish Eyes" and "The Man from Laramie", and he also sang the theme song for Robert Aldrich's *Hush . . . Hush, Sweet Charlotte* (1964).

American actress **Collin Wilcox** (aka Collin Wilcox-Horne and Collin Wilcox Paxton) died on October 14, aged seventy-four. Best remembered for her debut film role as the teenage girl in the 1962 version of *To Kill a Mockingbird*, she also appeared in *The Name of the Game is Kill*, *Catch-22*, *Jaws 2*, *Fluke* (based on the novel by James Herbert) and *The Crying Child*, plus episodes of TV's *Alfred Hitchcock Presents*, *Great Ghost Tales*, *The Twilight Zone*, *The Alfred Hitchcock Hour* (Ray Bradbury's "The Jar"), *The Immortal*, *Ghost Story* and *American Gothic*. When diagnosed with brain cancer, the actress arranged and attended her own memorial service.

WWE pro-wrestler "Captain" **Lou Albano** (Louis Vincent Albano), who appeared in his manager Cyndi Lauper's music videos "Girls Just Want to Have Fun" and "Time After Time", died the same day, aged seventy-six. In 1989 he voiced Mario "Jumpman" Mario for TV's *The Super Mario Bros. Super Show!* and had a cameo in the movie *Stay Tuned*.

Irish-born actor **Denys** [Vernon] **Hawthorne** died on October 16, aged seventy-seven. He had suffered a debilitating stroke some years earlier. Hawthorne appeared in episodes of *Play for Tomorrow* ("Easter 2016"), *The Adventures of Sherlock Holmes* and *Doctor Who* ("The Trial of a Time Lord"), plus the 1988 TV movie *Jack the Ripper*.

Canadian-born character actor **Joseph Wiseman** died in New

York on October 19, aged ninety-one. Best remembered for playing the eponymous super-villain in the first James Bond film, *Dr No* (1962), he also appeared in a TV version of *The Suicide Club* (1974), plus episodes of *Lights Out*, *Tales of Tomorrow*, *Suspense*, *Inner Sanctum*, *Kraft Television Theatre* ("Death Takes a Holiday"), *Shirley Temple's Storybook*, *The Twilight Zone*, *Night Gallery*, *Buck Rogers in the 25th Century* and *The Greatest American Hero*.

Pie-throwing American comedian **Soupy Sales** (Milton Supman), who had his own children's TV series in the 1950s and 1960s, died on October 22, following a fall at a local Emmy Awards show in New York. He was eighty-three. Towards the end of his career he appeared in the movies *The Innocent and the Damned* and *Angels with Angles*, was in an episode of the syndicated TV show *Monsters*, and appeared in a few episodes of Roger Corman's *Black Scorpion* as Sonny Dey aka Professor Prophet.

Moustachioed Canadian-born character actor and comic **Lou Jacobi** (Louis Harold Jacobovitch) died in New York City on October 23, aged ninety-five. He appeared in *Little Murders*, *Everything You Always Wanted to Know About Sex\* \*But Were Afraid to Ask*, and *Amazon Women on the Moon*, along with episodes of *The Alfred Hitchcock Hour*, *The Man from U.N.C.L.E.*, *Tales of the Unexpected* and *Tales from the Darkside*.

American character actor and comedy magician **Carl Ballantine** (Meyer Kessler, aka The Amazing Mr Ballantine), best known for playing crew-member Lester Gruber in the 1962–66 TV series *McHale's Navy* and the 1964 spin-off movie, died on November 3, aged ninety-two. He also appeared in episodes of *Shirley Temple's Storybook* ("Babes in Toyland"), *The Monkees*, *I Dream of Jeannie*, *The Ghost Busters* and *Fantasy Island*, as well as the John Landis movie *Susan's Plan*, and he contributed voices to the *Freakazoid!* and *Spider-Man* cartoon series. Ballantine was presented with a Lifetime Achievement Fellowship from the Magic Castle in Hollywood in 2007.

British stage and screen actor **David Tree** (David Parsons) died on November 4, aged ninety-four. After making a number of films in the 1930s and early 1940s, he lost a hand during a training exercise in World War II and retired from acting to become a farmer. He was convinced by his friend Nicolas Roeg to return to the screen one final time in *Don't Look Now*.

British actor **Edward** [Albert Arthur] **Woodward**, OBE, died of complications from pneumonia on November 16, aged seventy-nine. Best remembered for starring in such TV series as *Callan* (1967–72) and *The Equalizer* (1985–89), he also portrayed the doomed Sergeant Howie in *The Wicker Man* (1973). Woodward's other credits include *Incense for the Damned* (aka *Bloodsuckers*), *10 Rillington Place*, *A Christmas Carol* (1984), *Merlin and the Sword*, *Hands of a Murderer* (as Sherlock Holmes), *Gulliver's Travels* (1996) and *Hot Fuzz*, plus episodes of TV's *Mystery and Imagination*, *Sherlock Holmes* (1968), *Alfred Hitchcock Presents* (1988) and *Dark Realm*. He was married to actress Michele Dotrice.

Welsh-born painter, scientist and film extra **Richard** [Henry Louen] **Jones** died of complications from a genetic disorder on November 18, aged sixty-four. The four-foot-tall Jones was inside R2D2 as well as playing an Ewok in *Star Wars: Return of the Jedi*. He also appeared in *Flash Gordon* (1980) and *Labyrinth*.

Hollywood "B" movie actress **Beatrice** [Kimbrough] **Gray**, the mother of child actor Billy Gray (*The Day the Earth Stood Still*), died on November 25, aged ninety-eight. She had uncredited roles in *Laura*, *A Double Life* and *Abbott and Costello Meet the Killer Boris Karloff*.

Italian leading man **Tony Kendall** (Luciano Stella) died of cancer on November 28, aged seventy-three. His credits include Mario Bava's *What* (aka *The Whip and the Body*, with Christopher Lee), *The Three Fantastic Supermen*, *The Return of the Evil Dead*, *When the Screaming Stops*, *The People Who Own the Dark*, *Giant of the 20th Century* and the popular *Kommissar X* series of 1960s spy movies.

Spain's great horror star **Paul Naschy** (Jacinto Molina Álvarez) died in Madrid of cancer on November 30, aged seventy-five. A former weightlifting champion and stunt player-turned-writer, producer, director and actor, he is best known for playing the doomed werewolf Waldemar Daninsky in a series of unconnected films that included *Hell's Creatures* (aka *Frankenstein's Bloody*

Terror), *Nights of the Werewolf*, *Dracula vs. Frankenstein* (aka *Assignment Terror*), *The Fury of the Wolfman*, *The Werewolf versus the Vampire Woman*, *Dr Jekyll and the Werewolf* (in both roles!), *Curse of the Devil*, *Night of the Howling Beast*, *The Craving* (aka *Night of the Werewolf*), *The Beast and the Magic Sword*, *Howl of the Devil* and *Lycantropus: The Moonlight Murders*. Naschy's other genre films included *Jack the Ripper* (1971), *Dracula's Great Love* (as the Count), *House of Psychotic Women*, *The Mummy's Revenge*, *Horror Rises from the Tomb*, *Vengeance of the Zombies*, *Hunchback of the Morgue*, *The Hanging Woman* (aka *Terror of the Living Dead*), *Exorcism*, *Inquisition*, *Crimson*, *The People Who Own the Dark*, *Mystery on Monster Island* (with Peter Cushing), *Good Night Mr Monster*, *Panic Beats*, *The Beasts' Carnival* and *La hija de Fu Manchú* (as Fu Manchu). He also appeared (uncredited) in the *I Spy* TV episode "Mainly on the Plains", which guest-starred Boris Karloff. The actor suffered a major heart attack in 1991 but made a full recovery, publishing his autobiography *Memoirs of a Wolfman* in 1997. More recently he appeared in a couple of low-budget American productions that did nothing for his career: *Tomb of the Werewolf* (as Daninsky again) and *Countess Dracula's Orgy of Blood*, and he continued to work up to his death on such productions as *Rottweiler*, *A Werewolf in the Amazon* (as Dr Moreau), *La herencia Valdemar* and the short film *La duodécima hora*.

American actress **Carolyn de Fonseca**, who worked in Rome voice-dubbing the English-language versions of many Italian movies from the early 1960s onwards, died towards the end of 2009. Among the numerous films she worked on (usually uncredited) are *Mole Men Against the Son of Hercules*, Mario Bava's *What* (aka *The Whip and the Body*, dubbing Daliah Lavi), *Hercules vs. the Moon Men*, *The Last Man on Earth*, *Terror-Creatures from the Grave* (dubbing Barbara Steele), *Blade of the Ripper*, *Seven Blood-Stained Orchids*, *Torso*, *Spasmo*, *Deep Red*, *Suspiria*, *Buried Alive* (1979), *Antropophagus*, *Night of the Zombies*, *Burial Ground*, *The House by the Cemetery*, *Inferno*, *Macabre*, *Absurd*, *Murder in an Etruscan Cemetery*, *Piranha II: The Spawning*, *Ator the Fighting Eagle*, *The New York Ripper*, *Pieces*, *Monster Dog*, *Miami Golem*, *Phenomena*, *Ratman*, *Alien degli abissi*, *Bronx Executioner* and *Killer Crocodile II*.

From *The Loves of Hercules* (1960) onwards she was also Jayne Mansfield's official dubbing voice in European productions, even recreating the late actress' voice for the mondo documentary *The Wild Wild World of Jayne Mansfield* (1968). De Fonseca also appeared in a number of small roles in films and was married to actor/director Ted Rusoff (the nephew of AIP producer Samuel Z. Arkoff).

**Olivier Rollin**, the half-brother of French director Jean Rollin, died of cancer in Paris on December 2. He appeared in Rollin's *La vampire nue* (aka *The Nude Vampire*) and *Les Raisins de la mort*, also working as a production assistant on the latter film.

British character actress **Maggie Jones**, who played Blanche Hunt in the long-running soap opera *Coronation Street* since 1974, died after a long illness the same day, aged seventy-five. She also appeared in the movie *Every Home Should Have One* (aka *Think Dirty*) and episodes of *The Adventures of Sherlock Holmes* and *Goodnight Sweetheart*.

Stiff upper-lipped leading man **Richard Todd**, OBE (Richard Andrew Palethorpe-Todd), best known for his roles in classic war films, died of cancer on December 3, aged ninety. The Irish-born Todd also appeared in *Dorian Gray* (1970), *Asylum* (1972), *House of Long Shadows* (with Vincent Price, Christopher Lee, Peter Cushing and John Carradine) and *Incident at Victoria Falls* (with Lee as Sherlock Holmes), along with episodes of TV's *Thriller* (1974), *Doctor Who* ("Kinda"), *Virtual Murder* and the revival of *Randall and Hopkirk (Deceased)*. The actor's youngest son shot himself in 1977 at the age of twenty, and eight years later his eldest son also committed suicide after suffering from depression. Todd was named a Disney Legend in 2002 for his roles in *The Story of Robin Hood and His Merrie Men*, *The Sword and the Rose* and *Rob Roy the Highland Rogue*.

Dependable British character actor **Garfield Morgan** died of cancer on December 5, aged seventy-eight. He appeared in the movies *Digby the Biggest Dog in the World* and *28 Weeks Later*, plus episodes of *Out of This World*, three episodes of *The Avengers*, *Out of the Unknown*, *Randall and Hopkirk (Deceased)* and *The Tripods*. Morgan also narrated four Rick Wakeman albums between the late 1980s and mid-1990s.

Rugged and debonair American leading man **Gene Barry**

(Eugene Klass) died of congestive heart disease on December 9, aged ninety. He had been suffering from Alzheimer's disease for the past five years. The star of such popular TV series as *Bat Masterson* (1958–61), *Burke's Law* (1963–66 and 1994–95), *The Name of the Game* (1968–71) and *The Adventurer* (1972–73), Barry also appeared in *War of the Worlds* (both the 1953 and 2005 versions), *The 27th Day*, *The Devil and Miss Sarah*, *The Girl, the Gold Watch and Dynamite* and episodes of *Science Fiction Theatre*, *Alfred Hitchcock Presents*, *The Alfred Hitchcock Hour*, *Fantasy Island* and *The Twilight Zone* (1987).

Irish-born character actor **Charles** [Jessee] **Davis** died in California of a heart attack on December 12, aged eighty-four. He travelled to America in the 1940s to play Og the Leprechaun in the Broadway musical production of *Finian's Rainbow*, making more than 1,000 appearances in the role. He went on to appear in the movies *The Man from Planet X* and *Moonfleet*, along with episodes of TV's *Rocky Jones Space Ranger*, *Shirley Temple's Storybook*, *Alfred Hitchcock Presents*, *The Wild Wild West* (in a recurring role), *Rod Serling's Night Gallery*, *Man from Atlantis*, *Knight Rider* and *Starman*.

Tough guy character actor **Val Avery** (Sebouh Der Abrahamian) died the same day, aged eighty-five. The son of a revolutionary who founded the Republic of Armenia, Avery appeared in *The Legend of Hillbilly John* (based on Manly Wade Wellman's "John the Balladeer" stories), *The Amityville Horror* (1979) and *Too Scared to Scream*, plus episodes of *The Twilight Zone*, *The Munsters*, *Get Smart*, *The Wild Wild West*, *The Invaders*, *Man from Atlantis* and *Friday the 13th The Series*.

The seventy-six-year-old American actor **Conard Fowkes** (aka "Conrad Fowkes") died of pancreatic cancer on December 14. From 1966 to 1967 he was a regular on *Dark Shadows* as Frank Garner, and his other credits include an episode of *Way Out* before he was elected to American Equity's Council in the early 1970s.

Oscar-winning actress **Jennifer Jones** (Phylis Lee Isley), who starred in the 1948 version of Robert Nathan's romantic fantasy *Portrait of Jennie*, died on December 17, aged ninety. She also appeared in the serial *Dick Tracy's G-Men* (under the name "Phyllis Isley"), *Angel Angel Down We Go* and *The Towering*

*Inferno*. Her first marriage, to actor Robert Walker, ended when she began an affair with film producer David O. Selznick, who she eventually married in 1949.

American TV actress **Connie Hines**, who co-starred with Alan Young in CBS' talking horse comedy series *Mister Ed* (1961–66), died of complications from heart problems on December 18, aged seventy-eight. She retired from the screen in the early 1970s.

British character actor **Donald** [Ellis] **Pickering**, who played Dr Watson to Geoffrey Whitehead's consulting detective in the rarely-seen Polish-shot series *Sherlock Holmes and Doctor Watson* (1980), died on December 19, aged seventy-six. Pickering appeared in *Doctor Who* opposite three different Doctors (William Hartnell, Patrick Troughton and Sylvester McCoy), and his numerous other appearances include the films *Fahrenheit 451* (uncredited) and *Scarab*, a 1964 TV adaptation of John Buchan's novel *Witch Wood*, and episodes of *Out of the Unknown*, *The Champions*, *The Avengers*, *The Rivals of Sherlock Holmes* and *Tales of the Unexpected*.

American actress and singer **Brittany** [Anne] **Murphy** (Brittany Bertolotti) died of cardiac arrest in her Hollywood Hills home on December 20, aged thirty-two. The cause of death was later revealed to be pneumonia complicated by anaemia and an overdose of prescription drugs. The Los Angeles Coroner found that the actress had "elevated levels" of Vicodin and other over-the-counter cold medicine in her system. A former child actress whose TV credits include an episode of *SeaQuest DSV*, she appeared in such movies as *Freeway*, *Drive*, *The Prophecy II*, *Cherry Falls*, *Sin City*, *Neverwas*, *Deadline*, *MegaFault*, *Abandoned* and *Something Wicked*, and she voiced an animated penguin in *Happy Feet*. Her single "Faster Kill Pussycat" (with DJ Paul Oakenfold) reached #7 in the UK music charts in May 2006. Murphy was married to British screenwriter/producer Simon Monjack.

American comedy actor and voice artist **Arnold Stang**, best known as the voice of Herman the mouse in a series of 1950s Paramount cartoons and the feline star of Hanna-Barbera's TV show *Top Cat* (1961–62), died of pneumonia the same day, aged ninety-one. He appeared in *The Wonderful World of the*

*Brothers Grimm*, *It's a Mad Mad Mad Mad World*, *Skidoo*, *Hercules in New York* and *Ghost Dad*, along with episodes of *Captain Video and His Video Rangers*, *Batman* and *Tales from the Dark Side*. Stang also contributed voice characterizations to *Pinocchio in Outer Space*, *Marco Polo Junior versus The Red Dragon* and *Pogo for President: "I Go Pogo"*.

**James Gurley**, who was a guitarist with the 1960s rock band Big Brother and the Holding Company, died of a heart attack on December 20, aged seventy. The group was one of a number that appeared at the influential Monterey Pop Festival in 1967.

Incredibly prolific British character actress **Marianne Stone** (aka "Mary Stone"), who was the second wife of film critic/historian Peter Noble (who died in 1997), died on December 21, aged eighty-seven. She appeared, often uncredited, in *Brighton Rock*, *Seven Days to Noon*, *Horrors of the Black Museum*, *Jack the Ripper* (1959), *The Day the Earth Caught Fire*, *Witchcraft* (with Lon Chaney, Jr), *A Hard Day's Night*, *Devils of Darkness*, *The Night Caller* (aka *Blood Beast from Outer Space*), *Berserk*, *Twisted Nerve*, *Scrooge* (1970), *Incense for the Damned* (aka *Bloodsuckers*), *Whoever Slew Auntie Roo?*, *Assault* (aka *Tower of Terror*), *Tower of Evil* (aka *Horror on Snape Island*), *The Creeping Flesh* (with Christopher Lee and Peter Cushing), *The Vault of Horror* and *Craze* (aka *The Infernal Idol*). Stone also had small roles in Hammer's *Spaceways*, *The Quatermass Experiment* (aka *The Creeping Unknown*), *Quatermass 2* (aka *Enemy from Space*), *Paranoiac*, *The Curse of the Mummy's Tomb*, *Hysteria* and *Countess Dracula*, plus nine *Carry On* films (including *Carry On Screaming*). Her scenes were cut from the mermaid comedy *Mad About Men*, and her credits also include episodes of TV's *Dead of Night* and *Hammer House of Mystery and Suspense*.

American character actor **Michael Currie** (Herman Christian Schwenk, Jr), who portrayed Sheriff Jonas Carter in five 1966 episodes of the daytime soap opera *Dark Shadows*, died on December 22, aged eighty-one. His other credits include four films with Clint Eastwood, plus *Dead and Buried*, *Halloween III: Season of the Witch*, *Starflight: The Plane That Couldn't Land* (aka *Starflight One*), *The Philadelphia Experiment*, and episodes of TV's *Voyagers!* and *Wizards and Warriors*.

NWA and WCW professional wrestler **Steve Williams** (aka Dr Death) died of throat cancer on December 29, aged forty-nine.

Italian actor **Glauco Onorato** died of cancer on December 31, aged seventy-three. Best known as the Italian dubbing voice of actor Bud Spencer, he appeared in Mario Bava's *Black Sabbath* (in "The Wurdalak" segment with Boris Karloff), *Deep Red* and an episode of *Dario Argento's Door Into Darkness* TV series.

Adult film actress **Erica Boyer** (Amanda Margaret Jensen) was killed instantly while crossing the road the same day when she was struck by a car being driven by an off-duty Florida Highway Patrol officer. She was fifty-three. Known as "The Ultimate Goddess of Erotica", Boyer began her porn career in the late 1970s and appeared under a number of pseudonyms, including "Carol Christy" and "Joanne McRay". Her more than 180 credits include *The Night of the Headhunter*, *Wet Science*, *The Devil in Miss Jones 4: The Final Outrage*, *Black to the Future*, *Backside to the Future*, *Robofox*, *Barbara the Barbarian*, *Amazing Tails 4* and *Snatched to the Future*. Having retired from the adult film industry in 1994, she made one further film in 2000.

## FILM/TV TECHNICIANS AND PRODUCERS

American TV director **Alvin Ganzer** died in Hawaii on January 3, aged ninety-seven. He joined Paramount in 1932 casting extras and went on to work as an assistant director on a number of movies during the 1940s and 1950s (including *Road to Utopia*). Ganzer also directed episodes of *Science Fiction Theatre*, *The Twilight Zone*, *Men Into Space*, *Lost in Space*, *The Wild Wild West*, *The Man from U.N.C.L.E.* and *The Hardy Boys/Nancy Drew Mysteries*.

Former Universal Pictures and Paramount president **Ned** [Stone] **Tanen**, the son-in-law of director Howard Hawks, died on January 5, aged seventy-seven. Among the box-office hits he presided over were *E.T. The Extra-Terrestrial* and *Ghost*. A former talent agent who worked with Elton John, Neil Diamond and Olivia Newton-John, Tanen also produced *Mary Reilly*, based on Valerie Martin's novel about Dr Jekyll and Mr Hyde. The character Biff Tannen in *Back to the Future* (1985) was reportedly named after him.

Low-budget film-maker **Ray Dennis Steckler** died of a heart attack in Las Vegas (where he ran a video business) on January 7, aged seventy. His films as a director include the infamous *The Incredibly Strange Creatures Who Stopped Living and Became Mixed-Up Zombies!!?*, *The Thrill Killers*, *Lemon Grove Kids Meet the Monsters*, *Rat Pfink a Boo Boo*, *Sinthia the Devil's Doll*, *The Mad Love Life of a Hot Vampire*, *The Horny Vampire*, *Blood Shack*, *Sexorcist Devil*, *The Hollywood Strangler Meets the Skidrow Slasher* and *Las Vegas Serial Killer*, many of them starring his first wife, Carolyn Brandt (he produced a documentary about the actress in 1994). Steckler directed many of his softcore adult films under pseudonyms, including "Sven Christian" and "Sven Hellstrom". He often also worked as editor, cinematographer, writer and producer, and he acted under the name "Cash Flagg". One of his early jobs was as assistant cameraman on *Eegah* (1962), in which he also appeared.

**Gary Goch** (aka Gary Grotch), who worked in the film business in various capacities, often in collaboration with Bob Clark and Alan Ormsby, died on January 8. He was a camera assistant on *The Female Bunch* (featuring Lon Chaney, Jr), musical director on *Pink Narcissus*, edited and produced *Children Shouldn't Play with Dead Things*, did sound on *Dead of Night* (aka *Deathdream*), was a production assistant on *Black Christmas* (1974) and produced *Popcorn*.

American theatrical director **Tom O'Horgan** died of complications from Alzheimer's disease on January 11, aged eighty-four. Best remembered as the man who brought *Hair* to Broadway in 1968, he also composed the music for *Alex in Wonderland*, directed the 1974 movie version of Eugene Ionesco's *Rhinoceros*, and conceived the original stage production of The Beatles' *Sgt. Pepper's Lonely Hearts Club Band* (filmed in 1978).

French film producer **Jacques Bar** (Jean Louis Alfred Bar) died on January 19, aged eighty-seven. His many films include the 1966 remake of *The Man Who Laughs* and *The Mysterious Island* (1973), based on the novel by Jules Verne.

American camera effects expert **Bob** (Robert C.) **Broughton** died of pneumonia the same day, aged ninety-one. He reportedly worked on almost every Walt Disney film from *Snow White and* *the Seven Dwarfs* (1937) to *Tron* (1982). He also created the visual effects for Alfred Hitchcock's *The Birds*.

Hollywood movie producer **Charles H.** (Hirsh) **Schneer** died in Florida after a long illness on January 21, aged eighty-eight. He was best known for his many collaborations with stop-motion animator Ray Harryhausen – *It Came from Beneath the Sea, Earth vs. the Flying Saucers, 20 Million Miles to Earth, The 7th Voyage of Sinbad, The 3 Worlds of Gulliver, Mysterious Island* (1961), *Jason and the Argonauts, First Men in the Moon, The Valley of Gwangi, The Golden Voyage of Sinbad, Sinbad and the Eye of the Tiger* and *Clash of the Titans*.

American film and TV producer **Arthur A. Jacobs** died of congestive heart failure on January 25, aged eighty-six. In 1958 he teamed up with his friend and business partner Richard E. Cunha for the low-budget movies *Giant from the Unknown* and *She Demons*. As "Art Jacobs" he also produced the 1974 horror nudie *The Beauties and the Beast* featuring Uschi Digard.

Television producer and director **Kim Manners** died of lung cancer the same day, aged fifty-nine. He produced and executive produced *The X Files* and *Supernatural*, and directed episodes of both those shows, along with *Automan, Star Trek: The Next Generation, The Adventures of Brisco County Jr, M.A.N.T.I.S.* and *Harsh Realm*.

Actor turned television producer/director **Peter Duguid** (George Duguid) died of Parkinson's disease on March 3, aged eighty-six. He directed the BBC's 1982 version of *The Hound of the Baskervilles*, starring Tom Baker as Sherlock Holmes, and three episodes of *Chocky's Children* (1985), based on the novel by John Wyndham. He was reportedly nearly cast as the first Doctor Who in 1963, but had already enrolled in a BBC training programme to become a director.

Sound-effects editor turned Emmy Award-winning TV director **Harry Harris** died of complications from myelodysplasia on March 19, aged eighty-six. His prolific credits include episodes of *Lost in Space, The Time Tunnel, Voyage to the Bottom of the Sea, Land of the Giants, Kung Fu, Man from Atlantis, MacGyver* and the 1985 TV movie *Alice in Wonderland*.

Former United Artists (UA) executive **Steven Bach**, who was fired over the *Heaven's Gate* debacle in 1980, died of lung cancer on March 25, aged seventy. While senior VP of worldwide production at UA, Bach presided over the making of Michael Cimino's epic Western, which was budgeted at $7.5 million, cost anywhere from $36–44 million to make, and grossed just $2 million at the time. As a result, the film became synonymous with Hollywood excess. He later wrote a book about the experience, *Final Cut: Dreams and Disaster in the Making of Heaven's Gate*.

American theatre designer and director **John** [Edward] **Blankenchip**, who since 1972 was resident designer for Ray Bradbury's Pandemonium Theatre Company, died following a brief illness on April 1, aged eighty-nine. Among the productions he designed based on Bradbury's work were *Something Wicked This Way Comes* and *The Incredible Ice Cream Suit*, and he was working on a stage adaptation of *The Martian Chronicles* at the time of his death.

British TV director and animator **David Wheatley** died after a long illness on April 5, aged fifty-nine. He directed the BBC *Omnibus* documentaries "The Illustrated Man" (about Ray Bradbury) and "The Brothers Grimm", and the *Arena* documentary "Borges and I", with Argentinian writer Jorge Luis Borges. His other credits include the award-winning docudrama *The Road to 1984* with James Fox as George Orwell, the 1987 adaptation of Angela Carter's *The Magic Toyshop*, the apocalyptic *The March*, and episodes of the Canadian TV series *Starhunter 2300*.

Controversial Scottish pop group manager **"Tam" Paton** (Thomas Dougal Paton) died on April 8, aged seventy-one. The former manager of 1970s band The Bay City Rollers, Paton was accused of swindling the group out of their royalties, and in 1982 he went to prison for committing indecent acts with males under the age of consent. In 2004 he was fined £200,000 for dealing in cannabis. At the same time that he managed the Rollers, Paton also looked after another Scottish band, the J.R.R. Tolkien-inspired Bilbo Baggins. They had one hit as Bilbo in 1978, "She's Gonna Win", before splitting with their management.

American screenwriter and director **Lee Madden** died of complications from pneumonia on April 9, aged eighty-two. His credits include AIP's *Hell's Angels '69*, *Angel Unchained*,

*The Night God Screamed*, *Night Creature* (starring Donald Pleasence) and *Ghost Fever* (as Alan Smithee).

Japanese film producer **Fumio Tanaka** died of a brain haemorrhage on April 12, aged sixty-seven. He produced Toho's vampire trilogy *Bloodsucking Doll*, *Lake of Dracula* and *Evil of Dracula*, plus *Yog: Monster from Space*, *Esupai*, *Battle in Out Space 2*, *Murders in the Doll House*, *Bye Bye Jupiter* and *Godzilla 1985*.

British producer **Peter Rogers**, best known for the series of thirty-one *Carry On* films from 1958 onwards, including *Carry on Spying* and *Carry on Screaming*, died on April 13, aged ninety-five. A former journalist, his other credits include *The Cat Girl* (starring Barbara Shelley), *Revenge* (aka *Inn of the Frightened People*) and *Quest for Love* (based on John Wyndham's story "Random Quest"). His wife Betty Box OBE, who produced the rival *Doctor* film series, died in 1999.

Veteran British cinematographer and director, **Jack Cardiff** OBE, who was awarded an honorary Oscar in 2001, died on April 22, aged ninety-four. He worked in various capacities (usually uncredited) on *The Ghost Train* (1931), *The Ghost Goes West*, *Things to Come* (1936), *The Man Who Could Work Miracles* and *The Last Days of Pompeii*, before becoming one of the screen's most acclaimed cinematographers with such films as *A Matter of Life and Death* (aka *Stairway to Heaven*), *Black Narcissus*, *The Red Shoes*, *Pandora and the Flying Dutchman*, *The Awakening*, *Ghost Story*, *Conan the Destroyer*, *Cat's Eye*, the Showscan short *Call from Space* and a 2004 adaptation of Edgar Allan Poe's *The Tell-Tale Heart*. Cardiff also directed the first (and only) film in "Smell-o-Vision", *Scent of Mystery* (aka *Holiday in Spain*) featuring Peter Lorre and scripted by Gerald Kersh, and the 1974 horror film *The Mutations* (aka *The Freakmaker*).

British-born film director, **Ken Annakin** OBE (Kenneth Cooper Annakin), died at his Beverly Hills home the same day, aged ninety-four. He had been in failing health since suffering a heart attack and a stroke two months earlier. Annakin's credits include the 1948 mermaid comedy *Miranda* and Disney's *Swiss Family Robinson*.

British record producer **Ron Richards** (Ronald Richard Pratley), who produced The Beatles, Gerry and the Pacemakers, The Hollies and P.J. Proby during the 1960s, died on April 30, aged eighty. Among the memorable songs he worked on were "Love Me Do", "You'll Never Walk Alone", "He Ain't Heavy He's My Brother" and "The Air That I Breathe". Along with fellow Parlephone producer George Martin, he was responsible for the decision to replace Beatles' drummer Pete Best with Ringo Starr. Richards also did much of the administrative work on the soundtrack of *Yellow Submarine*.

American cinematographer **Irv** (Irving/Irvin) **Goodnoff** died of a heart attack on May 3, aged sixty-one. He photographed the short *The Tell-Tale Heart* (1971) starring Sam Jaffe, *Rattlers*, *Jennifer*, *Evilspeak*, Dan O'Bannon's *The Resurrected* (based on H.P. Lovecraft's *The Case of Charles Dexter Ward*), *The Dark Mist* (aka *Lord Protector*), *Jennifer is Dead*, *Planet Ibsen*, *The Cursed* and *Legend of the Red Reaper*, along with two unsold TV pilots (1989 and 2002) for shows based on *The Witches of Eastwick*.

Show business agent **Sam Cohen** (Samuel Charles Cohn), who represented Robert Altman, Sidney Lumet, Woody Allen, Paul Newman, Meryl Streep and Arthur Miller, amongst many others, died on May 6, aged seventy-nine. For three decades he worked at International Creative Management (ICM) and was regarded by his clients as an "auteur agent", helping to creatively shape their careers. He also reportedly liked to eat paper.

Prop-maker **Jenny Heap**, who created the Triffids for the 1962 movie *The Day of the Triffids*, died in May of cancer, aged seventy-one. During a varied career she taught prop and mask-making at RADA and managed the prop department at the Royal National Theatre. She later became a touring production manager.

Film and TV producer **Mort Abrahams** died after a long illness on May 28, aged ninety-three. He began his career with the 1950 series *Tom Corbett Space Cadet*, and he went on to produce or executive produce such TV series as *Tales of Tomorrow*, *Route 66* (including "Lizard's Leg and Owlet's Wing" with Boris Karloff, Peter Lorre and Lon Chaney, Jr) and *The Man from U.N.C.L.E.* His movie credits include *Doctor Dolittle* (1967), *Planet of the Apes* (1967), the sequel *Beneath the Planet of the Apes*, and *Rhinoceros*.

Producer and director **Don Edmonds** died of liver cancer on May 30, aged seventy-two. Best known for directing the cult softcore

"Nazisploitation" movies *Ilsa, She Wolf of the SS* (1975) and *Ilsa, Harem Keeper of the Oil Sheiks* (1976), his other directing credits include the 1980 horror film *Terror on Tour* and he worked in various production capacities on *Home Sweet Home*, *The Night Stalker*, *Skeeter* and *Last Gasp*. In the 1980s he was vice-president of production at Producers Sales Organization (PSO), where he was responsible for such movies as *Short Circuit* and *Clan of the Cave Bear*. As an actor, Edmonds appeared in *Gidget Goes Hawaiian*, Disney's *Son of Flubber*, *Home Sweet Home*, *Last Gasp*, and episodes of TV's *Men Into Space* and *The Munsters*.

British art director **Bob** (Robert) **Bell**, who worked on such Gerry Anderson TV shows as *Fireball XL5*, *Stingray*, *Thunderbirds*, *Captain Scarlet and the Mysterons* and *U.F.O.*, died on June 6. Bell's other credits include *Thunderbird 6*, *Doppelgänger* (aka *Journey to the Far Side of the Sun*) and *The New Avengers*; he was assistant art director on the 1980 series *Hammer House of Horror*, and he created the matte paintings for Clive Barker's *Nightbreed*.

Canadian TV director and producer **Allan** [Winton] **King** died of brain cancer on June 15, aged seventy-nine. He directed episodes of *Friday the 13th: The Series*, the new *Twilight Zone* and *Alfred Hitchcock Presents*, *Dracula: The Series*, *The Odyssey* and *Kung Fu: The Legend Continues*.

British producer and cinematographer **Peter** [Austin Harely] **Newbrook**, best known for his only directing credit on the underrated 1973 horror film *The Asphyx*, died of a heart attack on June 19, aged eighty-eight. Newbrook produced and contributed the original story to the legendary 1965 SF musical *Gonks Go Beat*, and his other credits as a producer include *Corruption* and *Incense for the Damned* (both with Peter Cushing), and *Crucible of Terror* (with Mike Raven). He photographed *The Black Torment*, *Corruption* and *Crucible of Terror*, and worked as a camera operator on Hammer's *Dick Barton Strikes Back*.

American music manager, recording executive and film producer **Allen Klein** died of complications from Alzheimer's disease on July 4, aged seventy-seven. During an often controversial career, the former New Jersey accountant managed the affairs of such recording artists and groups as Donovan, Connie Francis, The Animals, The Rolling Stones and three out of four of The Beatles (his involvement reportedly contributed to the break-up of the Fab Four). He also produced a number of movies, including Alejandro Jodorowsky's religious fantasy *The Holy Mountain*.

Eighty-six-year-old **George** [William] **Fullerton**, who partnered electric guitar pioneer Leo Fender in the manufacturing of the Telecaster and Stratocaster guitars, died of congestive heart failure the same day in Fullerton, California.

Film and TV producer **Ted** [Adams] **Swanson**, whose credits include *Island Claws* (co-scripted by Ricou Browning), *The Presence* (aka *Danger Island*) and *The Tale of Sweeney Todd*, died on July 23, aged seventy-two. Swanson also worked in various production capacities (often uncredited) on *The Omega Man*, *Don't Be Afraid of the Dark*, *Harry and the Hendersons* and *Jaws The Revenge*.

Italian-born first assistant director **Tony** (Antonio) **Brandt** died on July 25, aged seventy-nine. He worked as an additional assistant director on *Apocalypse Now*, and his other credits include *She* (1982), *Warrior of the Lost World*, Roger Corman's *Frankenstein Unbound*, *F/X 2* and *The Eighteenth Angel*.

Emmy Award-winning American TV producer **Harvey Frand** died of respiratory failure on July 28, aged sixty-eight. His many credits include the 1980s revival of *The Twilight Zone*, *The Pretender*, *Strange World*, and the new series of *Battlestar Galactica* and *The Bionic Woman*, along with the TV movies *New Eden* and *Painkiller Jane*.

Legendary British film producer **Harry Alan Towers** died of pneumonia and heart failure in Toronto, Canada, on August 2. He was eighty-eight. A genius for putting together co-production deals, Towers made more than 100 films around the world, from Austria to Zimbabwe (many scripted under his pseudonym "Peter Welbeck" and starring his wife, actress Maria Rohm). Among his numerous credits are *The Anatomist*, *The Face of Fu Manchu* and its four sequels (all starring Christopher Lee), *Circus of Fear* (aka *Psycho-Circus*), *Sumuru* (aka *The Million Eyes of Sumuru*), *Rocket to the Moon*, *House of 1,000 Dolls* (with Vincent Price), *The Girl from Rio* (aka *Future Women*), *Deadly Sanctuary*, Jesus Franco's *Night of the Blood Monster* and *Count Dracula* (1970), *Dorian Gray* (1970), *King Solomon's Treasure*, *The Shape of Things* to Come, Gor and Outlaw of Gor, Howling IV: The Original Nightmare, Edge of Sanity, The House of Usher (1989), The Phantom of the Opera (1989), Masque of the Red Death (1990), Buried Alive (with John Carradine), The Lost World (1992) and Return to the Lost World, Sherlock Holmes and the Leading Lady and Incident at Victoria Falls (both starring Lee as Holmes), Dance Macabre, The Mummy Lives (with Tony Curtis!), Night Terrors, The Mangler (based on the story by Stephen King), Pact with the Devil, She (2001) and Sumuru (2003). Always happy to recycle properties he had the rights to, Towers made three not-quite-star-studded versions of Agatha Christie's Ten Little Indians (aka And Then There Were None) in 1965, 1974 and 1989, and he was developing a new version of Fu Manchu at the time of his death.

Reclusive director, producer and screenwriter **John Hughes** [Jr] (aka Edmond Dantès), who was responsible for such iconic 1980s comedies as The Breakfast Club and Ferris Bueller's Day Off, died of a heart attack while walking in Manhattan on August 6. He was fifty-nine. Hughes' credits also include Weird Science and the remakes of Miracle on 34th Street (1994), 101 Dalmations (1996), Flubber (1997) and Just Visiting (2001).

British film producer [Anthony Simon] **Clive Parsons** died of pancreatic cancer on August 12, aged sixty-six. His credits (with business partner Davina Belling) ranged from the soft-core comedy Rosie Dixon – Night Nurse, through Lindsay Anderson's Britannia Hospital, to the low-budget horror films Half Light and Splintered.

Widely regarded as revolutionizing the music industry as a pioneer of electric guitar design and recording technology, **Les Paul** (Lester William Polsfuss) died of complications from pneumonia on August 13, aged ninety-four. A former performer in the early 1950s with a string of hits, including "Mockin' Bird Hill", "Vaya Con Dios" and "How High the Moon" with his then-wife Mary Ford, Paul created the Gibson Les Paul, one of the most iconic electric guitars ever made, as well as inventing tape echo, sound-on-sound recording and multitrack technology.

British TV director/producer **John** [Steven Rule] **Stroud** died of a brain tumour on August 15, aged fifty-four. His credits include the 1980s children's anthology series Spooky, So Haunt Me, Bugs and the superhero comedy My Hero.

American cinematographer **Richard Moore**, whose single directing credit was *Circle of Iron* (aka *The Silent Flute*) starring David Carradine and Christopher Lee, died on August 16, aged eighty-three. The co-creator (with Robert Gottschalk) of the anamorphic wide-screen Panavision format, he worked uncredited as an underwater camera operator on *Thunderball*, and his other credits include *The Wild Angels*, *Devil's Angels*, *Wild in the Streets* and *Myra Breckinridge*.

American make-up artist **Michael R. Thomas** (aka Mike Thomas) died following a minor hospital procedure on August 24, three days before his sixtieth birthday. He had suffered from a heart condition for a few years. During the mid-1960s he made himself up as a dancing Frankenstein Monster for the live TV show *Disc-O-Teen*, and Thomas was a regular at horror movie fan conventions made up as Bela Lugosi's Dracula or Ygor. As a make-up artist he worked on such movies as *The Wonderful Land of Oz* (1969), *The Sentinel*, *The Wiz*, *Wolfen*, *Ghostbusters*, *Fear City*, *My Demon Lover*, *Fatal Attraction*, *Ghostbusters II*, *Play-Mate of the Apes*, *The Lord of the G-Strings: The Femaleship of the Ring*, *Dr Horror's Erotic House of Idiots*, *The Stepford Wives* (2004), *Bite Me!*, *An Erotic Werewolf in London*, Disney's *Enchanted* and the 2007 version of *I Am Legend*. As an actor he appeared in many of these films, and also turned up in *Fanny Hill Meets Dr Erotico* (as The Monster), *Titanic 2000*, *Erotic Witch 2: Book of Seduction*, *Mistress Frankenstein* (in various roles, including The Monster again), *Witchbabe: The Erotic Witch Project 3*, *Vampire Vixens*, *Spiderbabe*, *Rectuma*, *The Ghosts of Angela Webb*, *Shock-O-Rama*, *Skin Crawl*, *Sculpture* and *House of the Wolf Man* (as Dracula).

**Dick** (Richard J.) **Berg**, a pioneer of 1970s made-for-TV movies, died on September 1 of complications from a fall, aged eighty-seven. A former scriptwriter, he executive produced such TV films and mini-series as *The Spell*, *Night Cries*, *Are You in the House Alone?* and Ray Bradbury's *The Martian Chronicles*.

American film and TV director/producer/screenwriter **Arnold Laven** died of pneumonia on September 13, aged eighty-seven. A former script supervisor and co-founder of the independent Levy-Gardner-Laven production company, he directed *The Monster That Challenged the World* and produced *The Vampire* (both 1957). His TV credits include episodes of *Alfred Hitchcock Presents*, *The Alfred Hitchcock Hour*, *Ghost Story*, *Shazam!*, *Planet of the Apes*, *Isis*, *The Six Million Dollar Man*, *Fantasy Island* (including the "Vampire" episode), *Turnabout*, *Time Express* (starring Vincent Price) and *The Greatest American Hero*.

American film producer **Melvin Simon** died of pancreatic cancer on September 16, aged eighty-three. While an executive at Columbia Pictures, he founded AVCO Embassy Pictures in 1967 and produced a number of films during the 1970s and 1980s, including *Dominique* (aka *Dominique is Dead*), *The Manitou*, *Love at First Bite*, *When a Stranger Calls* (1979), *UFOria* and the *Porky's* series. With his younger brother Herbert, Simon developed shopping mall sites, including the Mall of America near Minneapolis, which opened in 1992.

Romanian-born British film editor **Teddy Darvas** died on September 27, aged eighty-four. His credits include *Gonks Go Beat*, *The Man Who Haunted Himself*, *Tales from the Crypt* (1972), *The Amazing Mr Blunden* and *Dark Places*.

Veteran British film producer, cinematographer, screenwriter and director **Robert S.** (Sidney) **Baker** who, with his business partner Monty Berman, was a low-budget rival to Hammer Films in the late 1950s and early 1960s, died on September 30, aged ninety-three. Among the many "B" movies produced by Baker and Berman were *Blood of the Vampire*, *The Trollenberg Terror* (aka *The Crawling Eye*), *The Flesh and the Fiends* (aka *Mania/ The Fiendish Ghouls*) and *What a Carve Up!* (aka *No Place Like Homicide*), and the pair also co-directed *Jack the Ripper* (1959) and *The Hellfire Club* (both of which Baker photographed). He later went on to co-produce the TV series *The Saint* and *The Persuaders*, both with star Roger Moore.

French-born Hollywood agent and film producer **Alain Bernheim** died of complications during kidney dialysis in Paris on October 2, three days before his eighty-seventh birthday. As a talent agent he represented such writers as Gore Vidal, Pierre Boulle and Jean-Paul Sartre, along with film directors Jules Dassin, Louis Malle, Nicholas Ray, John Frankenheimer and Joseph Losey. During the communist witch-hunts in America, Bernheim represented a number of blacklisted talents.

Italian exploitation writer, producer and director **Rino Di**

**Silvestro** died of cancer on October 3, aged seventy-seven. His credits include the prison sexploitation films *Women in Cell Block 7* and *SS Special Section Women*, plus the 1976 horror movie *Werewolf Woman* (*La lupa mannara*).

American make-up artist **Bob** (Robert A.) **Westmoreland** died of a heart attack in Hawaii on October 6, aged seventy-four. He was the make-up supervisor on *Close Encounters of the Third Kind* (which he also had a cameo in), and his other credits include *Love Me Deadly*, the TV movie *Satan's Triangle*, *Invasion of the Body Snatchers* (1978), *Ravagers*, *1941*, *The Island* and *Twilight Zone The Movie*.

**Barry** [Leopold] **Letts**, a former actor-turned-TV producer/director/writer, died of cancer on October 9, aged eighty-four. He appeared in such series as *The Moonstone* (1959), *Invisible Man* (1959), *City Beneath the Sea* and *The Avengers* before moving to the other side of the camera. Letts produced the 1973 BBC series *Moonbase 3*, *Sexton Blake and the Demon God*, *The Hound of the Baskervilles* (1982) *The Invisible Man* (1984) and nearly 130 episodes of *Doctor Who* between 1967 and 1981, many of which he also directed. In the 1990s he scripted a couple of BBC Radio 2 serials for Jon Pertwee's Doctor, *The Paradise of Death* and *Doctor Who and the Ghosts of N-Space*, which he subsequently novelized. The 2009 *Doctor Who* special, *The Waters of Mars*, was dedicated to Letts' memory.

Italian cinematographer **Franco Villa** (aka "Frank Town") died on October 12. After working as a camera assistant during the 1950s on such films as *My Friend Dr Jekyll*, his exploitation credits include *Asylum Erotica* (aka *Slaughter Hotel*), *Jungle Master*, *The Return of the Exorcist*, *Giallo a Venezia*, *Patrick Still Lives*, *A Girl for Satan* and a number of Spaghetti Westerns.

**Daniel Melnick**, film producer and the former head of production at MGM and Columbia studios, died of lung cancer on October 13, aged seventy-seven. Credited as the creative force behind the comedy sci-spy TV series *Get Smart* (1965–70), his film credits include *Straw Dogs*, *All That Jazz*, *Altered States*, *Get Smart Again!* and *Universal Soldier The Return*.

American film and TV director [Abraham] **Paul Wendkos** died of a lung infection on November 12, aged eighty-four. He had earlier suffered a stroke. Wendkos' many credits include *Gidget* and its two sequels, *Fear No Evil*, *The Brotherhood of the Bell*, *The Mephisto Waltz*, *Haunts of the Very Rich*, *The Legend of Lizzie Borden*, *Good Against Evil*, *The Bad Seed* (1985), *From the Dead of Night* and episodes of *The Wild Wild West* and *The Invaders*.

Hollywood costume designer **Robert Turturice**, who was president of the Costume Designers Guild from 1992 to 1996, died of a heart attack on December 15. He was sixty. Turturice began his career designing the costumes for the 1975–76 Filmation TV series *The Ghost Busters*, and his other credits include *The Star Wars Holiday Special*, *Big-Top Pee-Wee*, *Solar Crisis*, *Fade to Black*, Joel Schumacher's infamous *Batman and Robin* and *The Flintstones in Viva Rock Vegas*.

**Roy E.** [Edward] **Disney**, the nephew of Walt Disney who led two successful shareholder revolts at the family's company, died of stomach cancer on December 16, aged seventy-nine. The son of Roy O. Disney, who co-founded the company with his brother Walt, Roy E. Disney was elected to the Board of Directors in 1967. In 1984, having led a campaign to replace Walt Disney's son-in-law, Ron Miller, because he felt that he was guiding the company in the wrong direction, he returned as vice chairman of the Board and head of the Animation Department. Almost twenty years later he helped remove Disney chairman and CEO Michael Eisner, the man he had brought in after the previous shareholder revolt. Among the films he presided over were *Beauty and the Beast*, *Aladdin* and *Fantasia 2000*.

British production designer **Peter Murton** died just before Christmas. He began his career in the art department in the mid-1940s, working his way up to art director on such films as *Tarzan's Greatest Adventure*, *Dr Strangelove or: How I Learned to Stop Worrying and Love the Bomb*, *Goldfinger*, *Thunderball*, *Night Watch* and *Stargate*. As a production designer, his credits include *The Ruling Class*, *The Possession of Joel Delaney*, *The Man with the Golden Gun*, *Dracula* (1979), *Superman II*, *Superman III*, *Sheena*, *King Kong Lives*, *Popcorn* and the Disney theme park attraction *From Time to Time* (featuring Jeremy Irons as H.G. Wells). In later years Murton was a guest speaker at a number of James Bond-themed events.

# USEFUL ADDRESSES

THE FOLLOWING LISTING OF organizations, publications, dealers and individuals is designed to present readers and authors with further avenues to explore. Although I can personally recommend most of those listed on the following pages, neither the publisher nor myself can take any responsibility for the services they offer. Please also note that the information below is only a guide and is subject to change without notice.

—Editor

## ORGANIZATIONS

**The Australian Horror Writers Association** (*www.australianhorror.com*) is a non-profit organization that formed as a way of providing a unified voice and a sense of community for Australian (and New Zealand) writers of horror/dark fiction, while furthering the development and evolution of this genre within Australia. AHWA aims to become the focal point and first point of reference for Australian writers and fans of the dark side of literature, and to improve the acceptance and understanding of what horror is to a wider audience. For more information mail to: Australian Horror Writers Association, Post Office, Elphinstone, Victoria 3448, Australia. E-mail: *ahwa@australianhorror.com*

**The British Fantasy Society** (*www.britishfantasysociety.org*) was founded in 1971 and publishes the newsletter *Prism* and the magazines *Dark Horizons* and *New Horizons*, featuring articles, interviews and fiction, along with occasional special booklets. The BFS also enjoys a lively online community – there is an e-mail news-feed, a discussion board with numerous links, and a CyberStore selling various publications. FantasyCon is one of the UK's friendliest conventions and there are social gatherings and meet-the-author events organized around Britain. For yearly membership details, e-mail: *secretary@britishfantasysociety.org. uk*. You can also join online through the CyberStore.

**The Friends of Arthur Machen** (*www.machensoc.demon. co.uk*) is a literary society whose objectives include encouraging a wider recognition of Machen's work and providing a focus for critical debate. Members get a hardcover journal, *Faunus*, twice a year, and also the informative newsletter *Machenalia*. For membership details, contact Jeremy Cantwell, FOAM Treasurer, Apt. 5, 26 Hervey Road, Blackheath, London SE3 8BS, UK.

**The Friends of the Merril Collection** (*www.friendsofmerril. org*) is a volunteer organization that provides support and assistance to the largest public collection of science fiction, fantasy and horror books in North America. Details about annual membership and donations are available from the website or by contacting The Friends of the Merril Collection, c/o Lillian H. Smith Branch, Toronto Public Library, 239 College Street, 3rd Floor, Toronto, Ontario M5T 1R5, Canada. E-mail: *ltoolis@tpl. toronto.on.ca*

**The Horror Writers Association** (*www.horror.org*) is a worldwide organization of writers and publishing professionals dedicated to promoting the interests of writers of horror and dark fantasy. It was formed in the early 1980s. Interested individuals may apply for active, affiliate or associate membership. Active membership is limited to professional writers. HWA publishes a monthly online newsletter, and sponsors the annual Bram Stoker Awards. Apply online or write to HWA Membership, PO Box 50577, Palo Alto, CA 94303, USA.

**World Fantasy Convention** (*www.worldfantasy.org*) is an annual convention held in a different (usually American) city each year, oriented particularly towards serious readers and genre professionals.

**World Horror Convention** (*www.worldhorrorsociety.org*) is a smaller, more relaxed, event. It is aimed specifically at horror fans and professionals, and is held in a different city (usually American) each year.

## SELECTED SMALL PRESS PUBLISHERS

**Apex Publications LLC** (*www.apexbookcompany.com*), PO Box 24323, Lexington, KY 40524, USA. E-mail: *jason@apexdigest.com*

**Ash-Tree Press** (*www.ash-tree.bc.ca*), PO Box 1360, Ashcroft, British Columbia V0K 1A0, Canada. E-mail: *ashtree@ash-tree.bc.ca*

**Bad Moon Books/Eclipse** (*www.badmoonbooks.com*), 1854 W. Chateau Avenue, Anaheim, CA 92804, USA.

**BearManor Media** (*www.bearmanormedia.com*), PO Box 71426, Albany, GA 31708, USA.

**Brimstone Press** (*www.brimstonepress.com.au*), PO Box 4, Woodvale, WA 6026, Australia. E-mail: *mail@brimstonepress.com.au*

**Burning Effigy Press** (*www.burningeffigy.com*).

**Centipede Press** (*www.centipedepress.com*), 2565 Teller Court, Lakewood, CO 80214, USA.

**Cemetery Dance Publications** (*www.cemeterydance.com*), 132-B Industry Lane, Unit #7, Forest Hill, MD 21050, USA. E-mail: *info@cemeterydance.com*

**Counterpoint Press** (*www.counterpointpress.com*), 2117 Fourth Street, Suite D, Berkley, CA 94710, USA.

**DarkArts Books** (*www.darkartsbooks.com*).

**Darkhouse Publishing** (*www.darkhousepublishing.com*).

**Dark Regions Press/Ghost House** (*www.darkregions.com*), PO Box 1264, Colusa, CA 95932, USA.

**Dark Scribe Press** (*www.darkscribepress.com*), 10 Deer Path, Smith Point, NY 11967, USA.

**DemonicClown Books** (*www.khpindustries.com*).

**Earthling Publications** (*www.earthlingpub.com*), PO Box 413, Northborough, MA 01532, USA. E-mail: *earthlingpub@yahoo.com*

**Edge Science Fiction and Fantasy Publishing** (*www.edgewebsite.com*), PO Box 1714, Calgary, Alberta T2P 2L7, Canada.

**Eternal Press** (*www.eternalpress.ca*), 206-58059 Pandora Street, Burnaby, British Columbia V5B 1M4, Canada.

**The Exaggerated Press.** E-mail: *terrygrimwood@msn.com*

**Ex Occidente Press** (*www.exoccidente.com*). E-mail: *exoccidente@gmail.com*

**Fantagraphics Books** (*www.fantagraphics.com*), 7563 Lake City Way N.E., Seattle, WA 98115, USA.

**Gauntlet Publications** (*www.gauntletpress.com*), 5307 Arroyo Street, Colorado Springs, CO 80922, USA. E-mail: *info@gauntletpress.com*

**Gray Friar Press** (*www.grayfriarpress.com*), 9 Abbey Terrace, Whitby, North Yorkshire Y021 3HQ, UK. E-mail: *gary.fry@virgin.net*

**Hippocampus Press** (*www.hippocampuspress.com*), PO Box 641, New York, NY 10156, USA. E-mail: *info@hippocampuspress.com*

**Horror Reanimated** (*www.horrorreanimated.com*).

**Immediate Direction Publications** (*www.midnightstreet.co.uk*), 7 Mount View, Church Lane West, Aldershot, Hampshire GU11 3LN, UK. E-mail: *tdenyer@ntlworld.com*

**McFarland & Company, Inc., Publishers** (*www.mcfarlandpub.com*), Box 611, Jefferson, NC 28640, USA.

**Morrigan Books** (*www.morriganbooks.com*), Östra Promenaden 43, 602 29 Norrköping, Sweden.

**Mythos Books, LLC** (*www.mythosbooks.com*), 351 Lake Ridge Road, Poplar Buff, MO 63901, USA.

**Necropolitan Press** (*www.necropolitan-press.com*), PO Box 1217, New Paltz, NY 12561-1217, USA.

**Newmedia Publishing** (*www.newmediapublishing.com*), PO Box 546, Montvale, NJ 07645, USA.

**Nightjar Press** (*http://nightjarpress.wordpress.com*), 38 Belfield Road, Manchester M20 6BH, UK.

**Night Shade Books** (*www.nightshadebooks.com*), 1661 Tennessee Street, #3H, San Francisco, CA 94107, USA. E-mail: *night@nightshadebooks.com*

**Norilana Press** (*www.norilana.com*), PO Box 2188, Winnetka, CA 91396, USA.

**PS Publishing Ltd** (*www.pspublishing.co.uk*), Grosvenor House, 1 New Road, Hornsea HU18 1PG, UK. E-mail: *editor@pspublishing.co.uk*

**Raw Dog Screaming Press** (*www.rawdogscreaming.com*), 5103 72nd Place, Hyattsville, MD 20784, USA. E-mail: *books@ rawdogscreaming.com*

**Screaming Dreams** (*www.screamingdreams.com*), 25 Heol Evan Wynne, Pontlottyn, Bargoed, Mid Glamorgan CF81 9PQ, UK. E-mail: *steve@screamingdreams.com*

**Shroud Publishing LLC** (*www.shroudmagazine.com*), 121 Mason Road, Milton, NH 03851, USA.

**Stygian Publications** (*www.necrotictissue.com*), PO Box 787, Forest Lake, MN 55025, USA. E-mail: *anthology@ nectrotictissue.com*

**Subterranean Press** (*www.subterraneanpress.com*), PO Box 190106, Burton, MI 48519, USA. E-mail: *subpress@earthlink. net*

**Tachyon Publications** (*www.tachyonpublications.com*), 1459 18th Street #139, San Francisco, CA 94107, USA.

**Tartarus Press** (http://*tartaruspress.com*), Coverley House, Carlton-in-Coverdale, Leyburn, North Yorkshire DL8 4AY, UK. E-mail: *tartarus@pavilion.co.uk*

**Telos Publishing Ltd** (*www.telos.co.uk*), Beech House, Chapel Lane, Moulton, Cheshire CW9 8PQ, UK. E-mail: *feedback@ telos.co.uk*

**Undertow Publications** (*www.undertowbooks.com*), Pickering, ON Canada. E-mail: *undertowbooks@gmail.com*

## SELECTED MAGAZINES

**Albedo One** (*www.albedo1.com*) is a speculative fiction magazine from Ireland. The editorial address is Albedo One, 2 Post Road, Lusk, Co. Dublin, Ireland. E-mail: *bobn@yellowbrickroad.ie*

**Ansible** is a highly entertaining monthly SF and fantasy newsletter/gossip column edited by David Langford. It is available free electronically by sending an e-mail to: *ansible-request@dcs.gla.ac.uk* with a subject line reading "subscribe", or you can receive the print version by sending a stamped and self-addressed envelope to Ansible, 94 London Road, Reading, Berks RG1 5AU, UK. Back issues, links and book lists are also available online.

**Apex Magazine** (*www.apexbookcompany/apex-online*).

**Black Gate: Adventures in Fantasy Literature** (*www. blackgate.com*) is an attractive pulp-style publication that includes heroic fantasy and horror fiction. Subscriptions are available from: New Epoch Press, 815 Oak Street, St. Charles, IL 60174, USA. E-mail: *john@blackgate.com*

**Black Static** (*www.ttapress.com*) is the UK's premier horror fiction magazine. Published bi-monthly, six- and twelve-issue subscriptions are available from TTA Press, 5 Martins Lane, Witcham, Ely, Cambs CB6 2LB, UK, or from the secure TTA website. E-mail: *blackstatic@ttapress.com*

**Cemetery Dance Magazine** (*www.cemeterydance.com*) is edited by Richard Chizmar and includes fiction up to 5,000 words, interviews, articles and columns by many of the biggest names in horror. For subscription information contact: Cemetery Dance Publications, PO Box 623, Forest Hill, MD 21050, USA. E-mail: *info@cemeterydance.com*

**Dark Discoveries** (*www.darkdiscoveries.com*) is a nicely produced quarterly magazine devoted to horror fiction and those who create it. For submission queries and subscription orders, contact: Dark Discoveries Publications, 142 Woodside Drive, Longview, WA 98632, USA. E-mail: *info@darkdiscoveries.com*

**Locus** (*www.locusmag.com*) is the monthly newspaper of the SF/fantasy/horror field. Contact: Locus Publications, PO Box 13305, Oakland, CA 94661, USA. Subscription information with other rates and order forms are also available on the website. E-mail: *locus@locusmag.com*

**Locus Online** (*www.locusmag.com/news*) is an excellent online source for the latest news and reviews.

**The Magazine of Fantasy & Science Fiction** (*www.fandsf. com*) has been publishing some of the best imaginative fiction for more than sixty years. Edited by Gordon Van Gelder, and now published bi-monthly, single copies or an annual subscription (which includes the bumper October/November anniversary issue) are available by US cheques or credit card from: Fantasy & Science Fiction, PO Box 3447, Hoboken, NJ 07030, USA, or you can subscribe via the new website.

**Midnight Street: Journeys Into Darkness** (*www.midnightstreet. co.uk*).

**Morpheus Tales** (*www.morpheustales.com*).

**New Genre**, PO Box 270092, West Hartford, CT 06127, USA. E-mail: *info@new-genre.com*

**One Eye Grey** (*www.fandmpublications.co.uk*) is described as "a penny dreadful for the twenty-first century" and contains stories (up to 3,000 words) from another London based on old folktales or ghost stories. F&M Publications, PO Box 51243, London SE17 3WP, UK. E-mail: *penny@fandmpublications. co.uk*

**The Paperback Fanatic** (*www.thepaperbackfanatic.com*) is a fascinating magazine dedicated to old paperbacks and the people who produced and published them. With numerous interviews and many cover reproductions. E-mail: *justin@justincultprint. free-online.co.uk*

**Rabbit Hole** is a semi-regular newsletter about Harlan Ellison®. A subscription is available from The Harlan Ellison® Recording Collection, PO Box 55548, Sherman Oaks, CA 91413-0548, USA.

**Rue Morgue** (*www.rue-morgue.com*), is a glossy bi-monthly magazine edited by Dave Alexander and subtitled "Horror in Culture and Entertainment". Each issue is packed with full-colour features and reviews of new films, books, comics, music and game releases. Subscriptions are available from: Marrs Media Inc., 2926 Dundas Street West, Toronto, ON M6P 1Y8, Canada, or by credit card on the website. E-mail: *info@rue-morgue.com*. Rue Morgue also runs the Festival of Fear: Canadian National Horror Expo in Toronto. Every Friday you can log on to a new show at Rue Morgue Radio at *www.ruemorgueradio.com* and your horror shopping online source, The Rue Morgue Marketplace, is at *www. ruemorguemarketplace.com*

**Space and Time: The Magazine of Fantasy, Horror, and Science Fiction** (*www.spaceandtimemagazine.com*) is published quarterly. Single issues and subscriptions are available from the website or Space and Time Magazine, 1308 Centennial Avenue Ste. 101, Piscataway, NJ 08854, USA. In the UK and Europe, copies can be ordered from BBR Distributing, PO Box 625, Sheffield S1 3GY, UK.

**Subterranean Press Magazine** (*www.supterraneanpress.com/ magazine*)

**Supernatural Tales** (*suptales.blogspot.com*) is a twice-yearly fiction magazine edited by David Longhorn. Three-issue subscriptions are available via post (UK cheques or PayPal only) to: Supernatural Tales, 291 Eastbourne Avenue, Gateshead NE8 4NN, UK. E-mail: *davidlonghorn@hotmail.com*

**Tales of the Talisman** (*www.talesofthetalisman.com*) is a speculative fiction and poetry magazine published quarterly by Hadrosaur Publications, PO Box 2194, Mesilla Park, NM 88047-2194, USA.

**Weird Tales** (*www.weirdtalesmagazine.com*) continues to seek out that which is most weird and unsettling for the reader's own edification and alarm. Single copies or a six-issue subscription are available from: Wildside Press, 9710 Traville Gateway Drive #234, Rockville, MD 20850-7408, USA. E-mail: *info@weirdtales.net*. For subscriptions in the UK contact: Cold Tonnage Books, 22 Kings Lane, Windlesham, Surrey, GU20 6JQ, UK E-mail: *andy@coldtonnage.co.uk*

**Writing Magazine** (*www.writingmagazine.co.uk*) is the UK's best-selling magazine aimed at writers and poets and those who want to be. It is published by Warners Group Publications plc, 5th Floor, 31–32 Park Row, Leeds LS1 5JD, UK. E-mail: *writingmagazine@warnersgroup.co.uk*

## DEALERS

**Ted Ball**, who co-owned the late and lamented Fantasy Centre bookstore, has set up a new mail-order business, with catalogues issued by e-mail (with a few print copies for those who do not have Internet access). Orders by post (E.W. Ball, 3 Barmouth Avenue, Andover Road, London N7 7HT, UK). Tel: +44 (0)20 7272-3046. E-mail: *tedball@btinternet.com*. Payment by PayPal or a cheque in UK pounds drawn on a UK bank.

**Bookfellows/Mystery and Imagination Books** (*www.mysteryandimagination.com*) is owned and operated by Malcolm and Christine Bell, who have been selling fine and rare books since 1975. This clean and neatly organized store includes SF/fantasy/horror/mystery, along with all other areas of popular literature. Many editions are signed, and catalogues are issued regularly. Credit cards accepted. Open seven days a week at 238

N. Brand Blvd, Glendale, CA 91203, USA. Tel: (818) 545-0206. Fax: (818) 545-0094. E-mail: *bookfellows@gowebway.com*

**Borderlands Books** (*www.borderlands-books.com*) is a nicely designed store with friendly staff and an impressive stock of new and used books from both sides of the Atlantic. 866 Valencia Street (at 19th), San Francisco, CA 94110, USA. Tel: (415) 824-8203 or (888) 893-4008 (toll-free in the US). Credit cards accepted. Worldwide shipping. E-mail: *office@borderlands-books.com*

**Cold Tonnage Books** (*www.coldtonnage.com*) offers excellent mail-order new and used SF/fantasy/horror, art, reference, limited editions etc. Write to: Andy and Angela Richards, Cold Tonnage Books, 22 Kings Lane, Windlesham, Surrey GU20 6JQ, UK. Credit cards accepted. Tel: +44 (0)1276-475388. E-mail: *andy@coldtonnage.com*

**Dark Delicacies** (*www.darkdel.com*) is a friendly Burbank, California, store specializing in horror books, toys, vampire merchandise and signings. They also do mail order and run money-saving book club and membership discount deals. Note the new address: 3512 W. Magnolia Blvd, Burbank, CA 91505, USA. Tel: (818) 556-6660. Credit cards accepted. E-mail: *darkdel@darkdel.com*

**DreamHaven Books and Comics** (*www.dreamhavenbooks.com*) store and mail-order offers new and used SF/fantasy/horror/art and illustrated etc. with regular catalogues (both print and e-mail). Write to: 2301 E. 38th Street, Minneapolis, MN 55406, USA. Credit cards accepted. Tel: (612) 823-6070. E-mail: *dream@dreamhavenbooks.com*

**Fantastic Literature** (*www.fantasticliterature.com*) mail-order offers the UK's biggest online out-of-print SF/fantasy/horror genre bookshop. Fanzines, pulps and vintage paperbacks as well. Write to: Simon and Laraine Gosden, Fantastic Literature, 35 The Ramparts, Rayleigh, Essex SS6 8PY, UK. Credit cards and PayPal accepted. Tel/Fax: +44 (0)1268-747564. E-mail: *sgosden @netcomuk.co.uk*

**Ghost Stories** run by Richard Dalby issues semi-regular mail-order lists of used ghost and supernatural volumes at very reasonable prices. Write to: 4 Westbourne Park, Scarborough, North Yorkshire YO12 4AT, UK.

**Horrorbles** (*www.horribles.com*), 6731 West Roosevelt Road, Berwyn, IL 60402, USA. Small, friendly Chicago store selling horror and sci-fi toys, memorabilia and magazines and has monthly specials and in-store signings. Specializes in exclusive "Basil Gogos" and "Svengoolie" items. Tel: (708) 484-7370. E-mail: *store@horrorbles.com*

**Kayo Books** (*www.kayobooks.com*) is a bright, clean treasure-trove of used SF/fantasy/horror/mystery/pulps spread over two floors. Titles are stacked alphabetically by subject, and there are many bargains to be had. Credit cards accepted. Visit the store (Wednesday–Saturday, 11.00 a.m. to 6.00 p.m.) at 814 Post Street, San Francisco, CA 94109, USA or order off their website. Tel: (415) 749-0554. E-mail: *kayo@kayobooks.com*

**Iliad Bookshop** (*www.iliadbooks.com*), 5400 Cahuenga Blvd, North Hollywood, CA 91601, USA. General used bookstore that has a very impressive genre section, reasonable prices and knowledgeable staff. They have recently expanded their fiction section into an adjacent building. Tel: (818) 509-2665.

**Porcupine Books** offers regular catalogues and extensive mail-order lists of used fantasy/horror/SF titles via e-mail: *brian@porcupine.demon.co.uk* or write to: 37 Coventry Road, Ilford, Essex IG1 4QR, UK. Tel: +44 (0)20 8554-3799.

**Kirk Ruebotham** (*www.ukbookworld.com/members/kirk*) is a mail-order only dealer, who sells out-of-print and used horror/SF/fantasy/crime and related non-fiction at very good prices, with regular catalogues. Write to: 16 Beaconsfield Road, Runcorn, Cheshire WA7 4BX, UK. Tel: +44 (0)1928-560540. E-mail: *kirk.ruebotham@ntlworld.com*

**The Talking Dead** is run by Bob and Julie Wardzinski and offers reasonably priced paperbacks, rare pulps and hardcovers, with catalogues issued occasionally. They accept wants lists and are also the exclusive supplier of back issues of *Interzone*. Credit cards accepted. Contact them at: 12 Rosamund Avenue, Merley, Wimborne, Dorset BH21 1TE, UK. Tel: +44 (0)1202-849212 (9.00 a.m. to 9.00 p.m.). E-mail: *books@thetalkingdead.fsnet.co.uk*

**Ygor's Books** specializes in out-of-print science fiction, fantasy and horror titles, including British, signed, speciality press and limited editions. They also buy books, letters and original art in these fields. E-mail: *ygorsbooks@earthlink.net*

## ONLINE

**All Things Horror** (*www.allthingshorror.co.uk*) is a genre interview site run by Johnny Mains that mainly focuses on authors, editors, artists and movie stars of the 1960s, 1970s and 1980s. It also caters to reviews of both films and books, and features a short fiction section that is open to submissions.

**Fantastic Fiction** (*www.fantasticfiction.co.uk*) features more than 2,000 best-selling author biographies with all their latest books, covers and descriptions.

**Hellnotes** (*www.hellnotes.com*) is now in its fourteenth year of publication, offering news and reviews of novels, collections, magazines, anthologies, non-fiction works and chapbooks. Materials for review should be sent to editor and publisher David B. Silva, Hellnotes, 5135 Chapel View Court, North Las Vegas, NV 89031, USA. E-mail: *news@hellnotes.com* or *dbsilva13@ gmail.com*

**Pan Book of Horror Stories** (*www.panbookofhorrorstories. co.uk*) is a tribute site dedicated to the best-known horror anthology series ever published in the UK. Comprehensive listings of all stories and authors can be found here, along with rare contractual and promotional material that has been gathered together for the first time, giving a unique insight into the series' publishing history.

**SF Site** (*www.sfsite.com*) has been posted twice each month since 1997. Presently, it publishes around thirty to fifty reviews of SF, fantasy and horror from mass-market publishers and some small press. They also maintain link pages for author and fan tribute sites and other facets including pages for interviews, fiction, science fact, bookstores, small press, publishers, e-zines and magazines, artists, audio, art galleries, newsgroups and writers' resources. Periodically, they add features such as author and publisher reading lists.

**Vault of Evil** (*www.vaultofevil.wordpress.com*) is a site dedicated to celebrating the best in British horror with special emphasis on UK anthologies. There is also a lively forum devoted to many different themes at *www.vaultofevil.proboards.com*

# The Mammoth Book of Wolf Men

Edited by Stephen Jones

ISBN: 978-1-84901-031-3
Price: £7.99

**Twenty-four thrilling short stories of werewolf horror**

Entrenched in an ancient curse, and inspired by the classic werewolf movies and legends that launched a legacy of horror, these are twenty-four of the finest werewolf stories ever collected in a single volume.

These stories reflect centuries of terrifying tales of men who change into savage and bloodthirsty creatures at the full moon, destroying those around them.

They include classic novellas such as 'The Hairy Ones Shall Dance' by Manly Wade Wellman, 'The Whisperers' by Hugh B. Cave and 'The Cell' by David Case, as well as such modern masterpieces as Clive Barker's 'Twilight at the Towers', Suzy McKee Charnas' award-winning 'Boobs' and Neil Gaiman's tale of lycanthropic adjustor Lawrence Talbot, 'Only the End of the World Again'.

'A quality assortment of lycanthropic yarns.'

*Time Out*

'Thoughtfully put together, and excellent value for money.'

*The Dark Side*

# The Mammoth Book of Monsters

Edited by Stephen Jones

ISBN: 978-1-84529-594-3
Price: £7.99

### A world of monsters . . .

Everybody knows the most memorable monsters – vampires, were-wolves, zombies, mad scientists' creations – and you will find all of those classic creatures suitably featured in this monsterrific new anthology from multiple award-winning editor Stephen Jones.

But other monstrosities are also ably represented within these pages . . . An academic goes in search of a mythological creature in Thomas Ligotti's 'The Medusa', a stone gargoyle is brought to life in 'Downmarket' by Sydney J. Bounds, and a reclusive islander shares his world with shape-changing selkies in Robert Holdstock's haunting tale 'The Silvering'.

Late-night office workers are menaced by hungry horrors in Ramsey Campbell's claustrophobic 'Down There', while the monsters of both Brian Lumley's 'The Thin People' and Basil Copper's 'The Flabby Men' share only a semblance of humanity. The King of Monsters himself turns up in 'Godzilla's Twelve Step Program' by Joe R. Lansdale. R. Chetwynd-Hayes' 'The Shadmock' and Clive Barker's 'Rawhead Rex' are genuinely new monsters, and the last monster-fighter and the last classic monster confront each other in Kim Newman's 'The Chill Clutch of the Unseen'.

**If you like monsters, then there are plenty to choose from in this creature-filled collection boasting some of the biggest names in horror, fantasy and science fiction.**